Verner's Pride by Mrs Henry Wood

Ellen Price was born on 17th January 1814 in Worcester.

In 1836 she married Henry Wood, whose career in banking and shipping meant living in Dauphiné, in the South of France, for two decades. During their time there they had four children.

Henry's business collapsed and he and Ellen together with their four children returned to England and settled in Upper Norwood near London.

Ellen now turned to writing and with her second book 'East Lynne' enjoyed remarkable popularity. This enabled her to support her family and to maintain a literary career.

It was a career in which she would write over 30 novels including 'Danesbury House', 'Oswald Cray', 'Mrs. Halliburton's Troubles', 'The Channings' and 'The Shadow of Ashlydyat'.

Sadly, her husband, Henry died in 1866.

Ellen though continued to strive on. In 1867, she purchased the magazine 'Argosy', founded two years previously by Alexander Strahan. She was a prolific writer and wrote much of the magazine herself although she had some very respected contributors, amongst them Hesba Stretton and Christina Rossetti. Although she would gradually pare down writing for the magazine she continued to write novel after novel. Such was her talent that for a time she was, in Australia, more popular than Charles Dickens.

Apart from novels she was an excellent translator and a writer of short stories. 'Reality or Delusion?' is a staple of supernatural anthologies to this day.

Ellen Wood died of bronchitis on 10th February 1887. He estate was valued at a very considerable £36,000.

She is buried in Highgate Cemetery, London.

A monument to her in Worcester Cathedral was unveiled in 1916.

Index of Contents

CHAPTER I

RACHEL FROST

The slanting rays of the afternoon sun, drawing towards the horizon, fell on a fair scene of country life; flickering through the young foliage of the oak and lime trees, touching the budding hedges, resting on the growing grass, all so lovely in their early green, and lighting up with flashes of yellow fire the windows of the fine mansion, that, rising on a gentle eminence, looked down on that fair scene as if it were its master, and could boast the ownership of those broad lands, of those gleaming trees.

Not that the house possessed much attraction for those whose taste savoured of the antique. No time-worn turrets were there, or angular gables, or crooked eaves, or mullioned Gothic casements, so chary of glass that modern eyes can scarcely see in or out; neither was the edifice constructed of gray stone, or of bricks gone black and green with age. It was a handsome, well-built white mansion, giving the promise of desirable rooms inside, whose chimneys did not smoke or their windows rattle, and where there was sufficient space to turn in. The lower windows opened on a gravelled terrace, which ran along the front of the house, a flight of steps descending from it in its midst. Gently sloping lawns extended from the terrace, on either side the steps and the broad walks which branched from them; on which lawns shone gay parterres of flowers already scenting the air, and giving promise of the advancing summer. Beyond, were covered walks, affording a shelter from the sultry noontide sun; shrubberies and labyrinths of many turnings and windings, so suggestive of secret meetings, were secret meetings desirable; groves of scented shrubs exhaling their perfume; cascades and rippling fountains; mossy dells, concealing the sweet primrose, the sweeter violet; and verdant, sunny spots open to the country round, to the charming distant scenery. These open spots had their benches, where you might sit and feast the eyes through the live-long summer day.

It was not summer yet—scarcely spring—and the sun, I say, was drawing to its setting, lighting up the large clear panes of the windows as with burnished gold. The house, the ornamental grounds, the estate around, all belonged to Mr. Verner. It had come to him by bequest, not by entailed inheritance. Busybodies were fond of saying that it never ought to have been his; that, if the strict law of right and justice had been observed, it would have gone to his elder brother; or, rather, to that elder brother's son. Old Mr. Verner, the father of these two brothers, had been a modest country gentleman, until one morning when he awoke to the news that valuable mines had been discovered on his land. The mines brought him in gold, and in his later years he purchased this estate, pulled down the house that was upon it—a high, narrow, old thing, looking like a crazy tower or a capacious belfry—and had erected this one, calling it "Verner's Pride."

An appropriate name. For if ever poor human man was proud of a house he has built, old Mr. Verner was proud of that—proud to folly. He laid out money on it in plenty; he made the grounds belonging to it beautiful and seductive as a fabled scene from fairyland; and he wound up by leaving it to the younger of his two sons.

These two sons constituted all his family. The elder of them had gone into the army early, and left for India; the younger had remained always with his father, the helper of his money-making, the sharer of the planning out and building of Verner's Pride, the joint resident there after it was built. The elder son—Captain Verner then—paid one visit only to England, during which visit he married, and took his wife out with him when he went back. These long-continued separations, however much we may feel inclined to gloss over the fact, do play strange havoc with home affections, wearing them away inch by inch.

The years went on and on. Captain Verner became Colonel Sir Lionel Verner, and a boy of his had been sent home in due course, and was at Eton. Old Mr. Verner grew near to death. News went out to India that his days were numbered, and Sir Lionel Verner was instructed to get leave of absence, if possible, and start for home without a day's loss, if he would see his father alive. "If possible," you observe, they put to the request; for the Sikhs were at that time giving trouble in our Indian possessions, and Colonel Verner was one of the experienced officers least likely to be spared.

But there is a mandate that must be obeyed whenever it comes—grim, imperative death. At the very hour when Mr. Verner was summoning his son to his death-bed, at the precise time that military authority in India would have said, if asked, that Colonel Sir Lionel Verner could not be spared, death had marked out that brave officer for his own especial prey. He fell in one of the skirmishes that took place near Moultan, and the two letters—one going to Europe with tidings of his death, the other going to India with news of his father's illness—crossed each other on the route.

"Steevy," said old Mr. Verner to his younger son, after giving a passing lament to Sir Lionel, "I shall leave Verner's Pride to you."

"Ought it not to go to the lad at Eton, father?" was the reply of Stephen Verner.

"What's the lad at Eton to me?" cried the old man. "I'd not have left it away from Lionel, as he stood first, but it has always seemed to me that you had the most right to it; that to leave it away from you savoured of injustice. You were at its building, Steevy; it has been your home as much as it has been mine; and I'll never turn you from it for a stranger, let him be whose child he may. No, no! Verner's Pride shall be yours. But, look you, Stephen! you have no children; bring up young Lionel as your heir, and let it descend to him after you."

And that is how Stephen Verner had inherited Verner's Pride. Neighbouring gossipers, ever fonder of laying down the law for other people's business than of minding their own, protested against it among themselves as a piece of injustice. Had they cause? Many very just-minded persons would consider that Stephen Verner possessed more fair claim to it than the boy at Eton.

I will tell you of one who did not consider so. And that was the widow of Sir Lionel Verner. When she arrived from India with her other two children, a son and daughter, she found old Mr. Verner dead, and Stephen the inheritor. Deeply annoyed and disappointed, Lady Verner deemed that a crying wrong had been perpetrated upon her and hers. But she had no power to undo it.

Stephen Verner had strictly fulfilled his father's injunctions touching young Lionel. He brought up the boy as his heir. During his educational days at Eton and at college, Verner's Pride was his holiday home, and he subsequently took up his permanent residence at it. Stephen Verner, though long married, had no children. One daughter had been born to him years ago, but had died at three or four years old. His wife had died a very short while subsequent to the death of his father. He afterwards married again, a widow lady of the name of Massingbird, who had two nearly grown-up sons. She had brought her sons home with her to Verner's Pride, and they had made it their home since.

Mr. Verner kept it no secret that his nephew Lionel was to be his heir; and, as such, Lionel was universally regarded on the estate. "Always provided that you merit it," Mr. Verner would say to Lionel in private; and so he had said to him from the very first. "Be what you ought to be—what I fondly believe my brother Lionel was: a man of goodness, of honour, of Christian integrity; a gentleman in the highest acceptation of the term—and Verner's Pride shall undoubtedly be yours. But if I find you forget your fair conduct, and forfeit the esteem of good men, so surely will I leave it away from you."

And that is the introduction. And now we must go back to the golden light of that spring evening.

Ascending the broad flight of steps and crossing the terrace, the house door is entered. A spacious hall, paved with delicately-grained marble, its windows mellowed by the soft tints of stained glass, whose pervading hues are of rose and violet, gives entrance to reception rooms on either side. Those on the right hand are mostly reserved for state occasions; those on the left are dedicated to common use. All these rooms are just now empty of living occupants, save one. That one is a small room on the right, behind the two grand drawing-rooms, and it looks out on the side of the house towards the south. It is called "Mr. Verner's study." And there sits Mr. Verner himself in it, leaning back in his chair and reading. A large fire burns in the grate, and he is close to it: he is always chilly.

Ay, always chilly. For Mr. Verner's last illness—at least, what will in all probability prove his last, his ending—has already laid hold of him. One generation passes away after another. It seems but the other day that a last illness seized upon his father, and now it is his turn: but several years have elapsed since then. Mr. Verner is not sixty, and he thinks that age is young for the disorder that has fastened on him. It is no hurried disorder; he may live for years yet; but the end, when it does come, will be tolerably sudden: and that he knows. It is water on the chest. He is a little man with light eyes; very much like what his father was before him: but not in the least like his late brother Sir Lionel, who was a very fine and handsome man. He has a mild, pleasing countenance: but there arises a slight scowl to his brow as he turns hastily round at a noisy interruption.

Some one had burst into the room—forgetting, probably, that it was the quiet room of an invalid. A tall, dark young man, with broad shoulders and a somewhat peculiar stoop in them. His hair was black, his complexion sallow; but his features were good. He might have been called a handsome man, but for a strange, ugly mark upon his cheek. A very strange-looking mark indeed, quite as large as a pigeon's egg, with what looked like radii shooting from it on all sides. Some of the villagers, talking familiarly among themselves, would call it a hedgehog, some would call it a "porkypine"; but it resembled a star as much as anything. That is, if you can imagine a black star. The mark was black as jet; and his pale cheek, and the fact of his possessing no whiskers, made it all the more conspicuous. He was born with the mark; and his mother used to say—But that is of no consequence to us. It was Frederick Massingbird, the present Mrs. Verner's younger son.

"Roy has come up, sir," said he, addressing Mr. Verner. "He says the Dawsons have turned obstinate and won't go out. They have barricaded the door, and protest that they'll stay, in spite of him. He wishes to know if he shall use force."

"No," said Mr. Verner. "I don't like harsh measures, and I will not have such attempted. Roy knows that."

"Well, sir, he waits your orders. He says there's half the village collected round Dawson's door. The place is in a regular commotion."

Mr. Verner looked vexed. Of late years he had declined active management on his estate; and, since he grew ill, he particularly disliked being disturbed with details.

"Where's Lionel?" he asked in a peevish tone.

"I saw Lionel ride out an hour ago. I don't know where he is gone."

"Tell Roy to let the affair rest until to-morrow, when Lionel will see about it. And, Frederick, I wish you would remember that a little noise shakes me: try to come in more quietly. You burst in as if my nerves were as strong as your own."

Mr. Verner turned to his fire again with an air of relief, glad to have got rid of the trouble in some way, and Frederick Massingbird proceeded to what was called the steward's room, where Roy waited. This Roy, a hard-looking man with a face very much seamed with the smallpox, was working bailiff to Mr. Verner. Until within a few years he had been but a labourer on the estate. He was not liked among the poor tenants, and was generally honoured with the appellation "Old Grips," or "Grip Roy."

"Roy," said Frederick Massingbird, "Mr. Verner says it is to be left until to-morrow morning. Mr. Lionel will see about it then. He is out at present."

"And let the mob have it all their own way for to-night?" returned Roy angrily. "They be in a state of mutiny, they be; a-saying everything as they can lay their tongues to."

"Let them say it," responded Frederick Massingbird. "Leave them alone, and they'll disperse quietly enough. I shall not go in to Mr. Verner again, Roy. I caught it now for disturbing him. You must let it rest until you can see Mr. Lionel."

The bailiff went off, growling. He would have liked to receive carte-blanche for dealing with the mob—as he was pleased to term them—between whom and himself there was no love lost. As he was crossing a paved yard at the back of the house, some one came hastily out of the laundry in the detached premises to the side, and crossed his path.

A very beautiful girl. Her features were delicate, her complexion was fair as alabaster, and a bright colour mantled in her cheeks. But for the modest cap upon her head, a stranger might have been puzzled to guess at her condition in life. She looked gentle and refined as any lady, and her manners and speech would not have destroyed the illusion. She may be called a protégée of the house, as will be explained presently; but she acted as maid to Mrs. Verner. The bright colour deepened to a glowing one when she saw the bailiff.

He put out his hand and stopped her. "Well, Rachel, how are you?"

"Quite well, thank you," she answered, endeavouring to pass on. But he would not suffer it.

"I say, I want to come to the bottom of this business between you and Luke," he said, lowering his voice. "What's the rights of it?"

"Between me and Luke?" she repeated, turning upon the bailiff an eye that had some scorn in it, and stopping now of her own accord. "There is no business whatever between me and Luke. There never has been. What do you mean?"

"Chut!" cried the bailiff. "Don't I know that he has followed your steps everywhere like a shadder; that he has been ready to kiss the very ground you trod on? And right mad I have been with him for it. You can't deny that he has been after you, wanting you to be his wife."

"I do not wish to deny it," she replied. "You and the whole world are quite welcome to know all that has passed between me and Luke. He asked to be allowed to come here to see me—to 'court' me, he phrased it—which I distinctly declined. Then he took to following me about. He did not molest me, he was not rude—I do not wish to make it out worse than it was—but it is not pleasant, Mr. Roy, to be followed whenever you may take a walk. Especially by one you dislike."

"What is there to dislike in Luke?" demanded the bailiff.

"Perhaps I ought to have said by one you do not like," she resumed. "To like Luke, in the way he wished, was impossible for me, and I told him so from the first. When I found that he dodged my steps, I spoke to him again, and threatened that I should acquaint Mr. Verner. I told him, once for all, that I could not like him, that I never would have him; and since then he has kept his distance. That is all that has ever passed between me and Luke."

"Well, your hard-heartedness has done for him, Rachel Frost. It has drove him away from his native home, and sent him, a exile, to rough it in foreign lands. You may fix upon one as won't do for you and be your slave as Luke would. He could have kept you well."

"I heard he had gone to London," she remarked.

"London!" returned the bailiff slightingly. "That's only the first halt on the journey. And you have drove him to it!"

"I can't help it," she replied, turning to the house. "I had no natural liking for him, and I could not force it. I don't believe he has gone away for that trifling reason, Mr. Roy. If he has, he must be very foolish."

"Yes, he is foolish," muttered the bailiff to himself, as he strode away. "He's a idiot, that's what he is! and so be all men that loses their wits a-sighing after a girl. Vain, deceitful, fickle creatures, the girls be when they're young; but once let them get a hold on you, your ring on their finger, and they turn into vixenish, snarling women! Luke's a sight best off without her."

Rachel Frost proceeded indoors. The door of the steward's room stood open, and she turned into it, fancying it was empty. Down on a chair sat she, a marked change coming over her air and manner. Her bright colour had faded, her hands hung down listless; and there was an expression on her face of care, of perplexity. Suddenly she lifted her hands and struck her temples, with a gesture that looked very like despair.

"What ails you, Rachel?"

The question came from Frederick Massingbird, who had been standing at the window behind the high desk, unobserved by Rachel. Violently startled, she sprang up from her seat, her face a glowing crimson, muttering some disjointed words, to the effect that she did not know anybody was there.

"What were you and Roy discussing so eagerly in the yard?" continued Frederick Massingbird. But the words had scarcely escaped his lips, when the housekeeper, Mrs. Tynn, entered the room. She had a mottled face and mottled arms, her sleeves just now being turned up to the elbow.

"It was nothing particular, Mr. Frederick," replied Rachel.

"Roy is gone, is he not?" he continued to Rachel.

"Yes, sir."

"Rachel," interposed the housekeeper, "are those things not ready yet, in the laundry?"

"Not quite. In a quarter of an hour, they say."

The housekeeper, with a word of impatience at the laundry's delay, went out and crossed the yard towards it. Frederick Massingbird turned again to Rachel.

"Roy seemed to be grumbling at you."

"He accused me of being the cause of his son's going away. He thinks I ought to have noticed him."

Frederick Massingbird made no reply. He raised his finger and gently rubbed it round and round the mark upon his cheek: a habit he had acquired when a child, and they could not entirely break him of it. He was seven-and-twenty years of age now, but he was sure to begin rubbing that mark unconsciously, if in deep thought. Rachel resumed, her tone a covert one, as if the subject on which she was about to speak might not be breathed, even to the walls.

"Roy hinted that his son was going to foreign lands. I did not choose to let him see that I knew anything, so remarked that I had heard he was gone to London. 'London!' he answered; 'that was only the first halting-place on the journey!'"

"Did he give any hint about John?"

"Not a word," replied Rachel. "He would not be likely to do that."

"No. Roy can keep counsel, whatever other virtues he may run short of. Suppose you had joined your fortunes to sighing Luke's, Rachel, and gone out with him to grow rich together?" added Frederick Massingbird, in a tone which could be taken for either jest or earnest.

She evidently took it as the latter, and it appeared to call up an angry spirit. She was vexed almost to tears. Frederick Massingbird detected it.

"Silly Rachel!" he said, with a smile. "Do you suppose I should really counsel your throwing yourself away upon Luke Roy?—Rachel," he continued, as the housekeeper again made her appearance, "you must bring up the things as soon as they are ready. My brother is waiting for them."

"I'll bring them up, sir," replied Rachel.

Frederick Massingbird passed through the passages to the hall, and then proceeded upstairs to the bedroom occupied by his brother. A sufficiently spacious room for any ordinary purpose, but it did not look half large enough now for the litter that was in it. Wardrobes and drawers were standing open, their contents half out, half in; chairs, tables, bed, were strewed; and boxes and portmanteaus were gaping open on the floor. John Massingbird, the elder brother, was stowing away some of this litter into the boxes; not all sixes and sevens, as it looked lying there, but compactly and artistically. John Massingbird possessed a ready hand at packing and arranging; and therefore he preferred doing it himself to deputing it to others. He was one year older than his brother, and there was a great likeness between them in figure and in feature. Not in expression: in that, they were widely different. They were about the same height, and there was the same stoop observable in the shoulders; the features also were similar in cast, and sallow in hue; the same the black eyes and hair. John had large whiskers, otherwise the likeness would have been more striking; and his face was not disfigured by the strange black mark. He was the better looking of the two; his face wore an easy, good-natured, free expression; while Frederick's was cold and reserved. Many people called John Massingbird a handsome man. In character they were quite opposite. John was a harum-scarum chap, up to every scrape; Fred was cautious and steady as Old Time.

Seated in the only free chair in the room—free from litter—was a tall, stout lady. But that she had so much crimson about her, she would have borne a remarkable resemblance to those two young men, her sons. She wore a silk dress, gold in one light, green in another, with broad crimson stripes running across it; her cap was of white lace garnished with crimson ribbons, and her cheeks and nose were crimson to match. As if this were not enough, she wore crimson streamers at her wrists, and a crimson bow on the front of her gown. Had you been outside, you might have seen that the burnished gold on the window-panes had turned to crimson, for the setting sun had changed its hue: but the panes could not look more brightly, deeply crimson, than did Mrs. Verner. It seemed as if you might light a match at her face. In that particular, there was a contrast between her and the perfectly pale, sallow faces of her sons; otherwise the resemblance was great.

"Fred," said Mrs. Verner, "I wish you would see what they are at with the shirts and things. I sent Rachel after them, but she does not come back, and then I sent Mary Tynn, and she does not come. Here's John as impatient as he can be."

She spoke in a slow, somewhat indifferent tone, as if she did not care to put herself out of the way about it. Indeed it was not Mrs. Verner's custom to put herself out of the way for anything. She liked to eat, drink, and sleep in undisturbed peace; and she generally did so.

"John's impatient because he wants to get it over," spoke up that gentleman himself in a merry voice. "Fifty thousand things I have to do, between now and to-morrow night. If they don't bring the clothes soon, I shall close the boxes without them, and leave them a legacy for Fred."

"You have only yourself to thank, John," said his mother. "You never gave the things out until after breakfast this morning, and then required them to be done by the afternoon. Such nonsense, to say they had grown yellow in the drawers! They'll be yellower by the time you get there. It is just like you! driving off everything till the last moment. You have known you were going for some days past."

John was stamping upon a box to get down the lid, and did not attend to the reproach. "See if it will lock, Fred, will you?" said he.

Frederick Massingbird stooped and essayed to turn the key. And just then Mrs. Tynn entered with a tray of clean linen, which she set down. Rachel followed, having a contrivance in her hand, made of silk, for the holding of needles, threads, and pins, all in one.

She looked positively beautiful as she held it out before Mrs. Verner. The evening rays fell upon her exquisite face, with its soft, dark eyes and its changing colour; they fell upon her silk dress, a relic of Mrs. Verner's—but it had no crimson stripes across it; upon her lace collar, upon the little edge of lace at her wrists. Nature had certainly intended Rachel for a lady, with her graceful form, her charming manners, and her delicate hands.

"Will this do, ma'am?" she inquired. "Is it the sort of thing you meant?"

"Ay, that will do, Rachel," replied Mrs. Verner. "John, here's a huswife for you!"

"A what?" asked John Massingbird, arresting his stamping.

"A needle-book to hold your needles and thread. Rachel has made it nicely. Sha'n't you want a thimble?"

"Goodness knows," replied John. "That's it, Fred! that's it! Give it a turn."

Frederick Massingbird locked the box, and then left the room. His mother followed him, telling John she had a large steel thimble somewhere, and would try to find it for him. Rachel began filling the huswife with needles, and John went on with his packing.

"Hollo!" he presently exclaimed. And Rachel looked up.

"What's the matter, sir?"

"I have pulled one of the strings off this green case. You must sew it on again, Rachel."

He brought a piece of green baize to her and a broken string. It looked something like the cover of a pocket-book or of a small case of instruments.

Rachel's nimble fingers soon repaired the damage. John stood before her, looking on.

Looking not only at the progress of the work, but at her. Mr. John Massingbird was one who had an eye for beauty; he had not seen much in his life that could match with that before him. As Rachel held the case up to him, the damage repaired, he suddenly bent his head to steal a kiss.

But Rachel was too quick for him. She flung his face away with her hand; she flushed vividly; she was grievously indignant. That she considered it in the light of an insult was only too apparent; her voice was pained—her words were severe.

"Be quiet, stupid! I was not going to eat you," laughed John Massingbird. "I won't tell Luke."

"Insult upon insult!" she exclaimed, strangely excited. "You know that Luke Roy is nothing to me, Mr. Massingbird; you know that I have never in my life vouchsafed to give him an encouraging word. But, much as I despise him—much as he is beneath me—I would rather submit to have my face touched by him than by you."

What more she would have said was interrupted by the reappearance of Mrs. Verner. That lady's ears had caught the sound of the contest; of the harsh words; and she felt inexpressibly surprised.

"What has happened?" she asked. "What is it, Rachel?"

"She pricked herself with one of the needles," said John, taking the explanation upon himself; "and then said I did it."

Mrs. Verner looked from one to the other. Rachel had turned quite pale. John laughed; he knew his mother did not believe him.

"The truth is, mother, I began teasing Rachel about her admirer, Luke. It made her angry."

"What absurdity!" exclaimed Mrs. Verner testily, to Rachel. "My opinion is, you would have done well to encourage Luke. He was steady and respectable; and old Roy must have saved plenty of money."

Rachel burst into tears.

"What now!" cried Mrs. Verner. "Not a word can anybody say to you lately, Rachel, but you must begin to cry as if you were heart-broken. What has come to you, child? Is anything the matter with you?"

The tears deepened into long sobs of agony, as though her heart were indeed broken. She held her handkerchief up to her face, and went sobbing from the room.

Mrs. Verner gazed after her in very astonishment. "What has taken her? What can it possibly be?" she uttered. "John, you must know."

"I, mother! I declare to you that I know no more about it than Adam. Rachel must be going a little crazed."

CHAPTER II

THE WILLOW POND

Before the sun had well set, the family at Verner's Pride were assembling for dinner. Mr. and Mrs. Verner, and John Massingbird: neither Lionel Verner nor Frederick Massingbird was present. The usual custom appeared somewhat reversed on this evening: while roving John would be just as likely to absent himself from dinner as not, his brother and Lionel Verner nearly always appeared at it. Mr. Verner looked surprised.

"Where are they?" he cried, as he waited to say grace.

"Mr. Lionel has not come in, sir," replied the butler, Tynn, who was husband to the housekeeper.

"And Fred has gone out to keep some engagement with Sibylla West," spoke up Mrs. Verner. "She is going to spend the evening at the Bitterworths, and Fred promised, I believe, to see her safely thither. He will take his dinner when he comes in."

Mr. Verner bent his head, said the grace, and the dinner began.

Later—but not much later, for it was scarcely dark yet—Rachel Frost was leaving the house to pay a visit in the adjoining village, Deerham. Her position may be at once explained. It was mentioned in the last chapter that Mr. Verner had had one daughter, who died young. The mother of Rachel Frost had been this child's nurse, Rachel being an infant at the same time, so that the child, Rachel Verner, and Rachel Frost—named after her—had been what is called foster-sisters. It had caused Mr. Verner, and his wife also while she lived, to take an interest in Rachel Frost; it is very probable that their own child's death only made this interest greater. They were sufficiently wise not to lift the girl palpably out of her proper sphere; but they paid for a decent education for her at a day-school, and were personally kind to her. Rachel—I was going to say fortunately, but it may be as just to say unfortunately—was one of those who seem to make the best of every trifling advantage: she had grown, without much effort of her own, into what might be termed a lady, in appearance, in manners, and in speech. The second Mrs. Verner also took an interest in her; and nearly a year before this period, on Rachel's eighteenth birthday, she took her to Verner's Pride as her own attendant.

A fascinating, lovable child had Rachel Frost ever been: she was a fascinating, lovable girl. Modest, affectionate, generous, everybody liked Rachel; she had not an enemy, so far as was known, in all Deerham. Her father was nothing but a labourer on the Verner estate; but in mind and conduct he was superior to his station; an upright, conscientious, and, in some degree, a proud man: her mother had been dead several years. Rachel was proud too, in her way; proud and sensitive.

Rachel, dressed in her bonnet and shawl, passed out of the house by the front entrance. She would not have presumed to do so by daylight; but it was dusk now, the family not about, and it cut off a few yards of the road to the village. The terrace—which you have heard of as running along the front of the house—sloped gradually down at either end to the level ground, so as to admit the approach of carriages.

Riding up swiftly to the door, as Rachel appeared at it, was a gentleman of some five or six and twenty years. Horse and man both looked thoroughbred. Tall, strong, and slender, with a keen, dark blue eye, and regular features of a clear, healthy paleness, he—the man—would draw a second glance to himself wherever he might be met. His face was not inordinately handsome; nothing of the sort; but it wore an air of candour, of noble truth. A somewhat impassive face in repose, somewhat cold; but, in speaking, it grew expressive to animation, and the frank smile that would light it up made its greatest charm. The smile stole over it now, as he checked his horse and bent towards Rachel.

"Have they thought me lost? I suppose dinner is begun?"

"Dinner has been in this half-hour, sir."

"All right. I feared they might wait. What's the matter, Rachel? You've been making your eyes red."

"The matter! There's nothing the matter with me, Mr. Lionel," was Rachel's reply, her tone betraying a touch of annoyance. And she turned and walked swiftly along the terrace, beyond reach of the glare of the gas-lamp.

Up stole a man at this moment, who must have been hidden amid the pillars of the portico, watching the transient meeting, watching for an opportunity to speak. It was Roy, the bailiff; and he accosted the gentleman with the same complaint, touching the ill-doings of the Dawsons and the village in general, that had previously been carried to Mr. Verner by Frederick Massingbird.

"I was told to wait and take my orders from you, sir," he wound up with. "The master don't like to be troubled, and he wouldn't give none."

"Neither shall I give any," was the answer, "until I know more about it."

"They ought to be got out to-night, Mr. Lionel!" exclaimed the man, striking his hand fiercely against the air. "They sow all manner of incendiarisms in the place, with their bad example."

"Roy," said Lionel Verner, in a quiet tone, "I have not, as you know, interfered actively in the management of things. I have not opposed my opinion against my uncle's, or much against yours; I have not come between you and him. When I have given orders, they have been his orders, not mine. But many things go on that I disapprove of; and I tell you very candidly that, were I to become master to-morrow, my first act would be to displace you, unless you could undertake to give up these nasty acts of petty oppression."

"Unless some of 'em was oppressed and kept under, they'd be for riding roughshod over the whole of us," retorted Roy.

"Nonsense!" said Lionel. "Nothing breeds rebellion like oppression. You are too fond of oppression, Roy, and Mr. Verner knows it."

"They be a idle, poaching, good-for-nothing lot, them Dawsons," pursued Roy. "And now that they be behind-hand with their rent, it is a glorious opportunity to get rid of 'em. I'd turn 'em into the road, without a bed to lie on, this very night!"

"How would you like to be turned into the road, without a bed to lie on?" demanded Lionel.

"Me!" returned Roy, in deep dudgeon. "Do you compare me to that Dawson lot? When I give cause to be turned out, then I hope I may be turned out, sir, that's all. Mr. Lionel," he added, in a more conciliating tone, "I know better about out-door things than you, and I say it's necessary to be shut of the Dawsons. Give me power to act in this."

"I will not," said Lionel. "I forbid you to act in it at all, until the circumstances shall have been inquired into."

He sprung from his horse, flung the bridle to the groom, who was at that moment coming forward, and strode into the house with the air of a young chieftain. Certainly Lionel Verner appeared fitted by nature to be the heir of Verner's Pride.

Rachel Frost, meanwhile, gained the road and took the path to the left hand; which would lead her to the village. Her thoughts were bent on many sources, not altogether pleasant, one of which was the annoyance she had experienced at finding her name coupled with that of the bailiff's son, Luke Roy. There was no foundation for it. She had disliked Luke, rather than liked him, her repugnance to him no doubt arising from the very favour he felt disposed to show to her; and her account of past matters to the bailiff was in accordance with the facts. As she walked along, pondering, she became aware that two people were advancing towards her in the dark twilight. She knew them instantly, almost by intuition, but they were too much occupied with each other yet to have noticed her. One was Frederick Massingbird, and the young lady on his arm was his cousin, Sibylla West, a girl young and fascinating as was Rachel. Mr. Frederick Massingbird had been suspected of a liking, more than ordinary, for this young lady; but he had protested in Rachel's hearing, as in that of others, that his was only cousin's love. Some impulse prompted Rachel to glide in at a field-gate which she was then passing, and stand behind the hedge until they should have gone by. Possibly she did not care to be seen.

It was a still night, and their voices were borne distinctly to Rachel as they slowly advanced. The first words to reach her came from the young lady.

"You will be going out after him, Frederick. That will be the next thing I expect."

"Sibylla," was the answer, and his accents bore that earnest, tender, confidential tone which of itself alone betrays love, "be you very sure of one thing: that I go neither there nor elsewhere without taking you."

"Oh, Frederick, is not John enough to go?"

"If I saw a better prospect there than here, I should follow him. After he has arrived and is settled, he will write and report. My darling, I am ever thinking of the future for your sake."

"But is it not a dreadful country? There are wolves and bears in it that eat people up."

Frederick Massingbird slightly laughed at the remark. "Do you think I would take my wife into the claws of wolves and bears?" he asked, in a tone of the deepest tenderness. "She will be too precious to me for that, Sibylla."

The voices and the footsteps died away in the distance, and Rachel came out of her hiding-place, and went quickly on towards the village. Her father's cottage was soon gained. He did not live alone. His only son, Robert—who had a wife and family—lived with him. Robert was the son of his youth; Rachel the daughter of his age; the children of two wives. Matthew Frost's wife had died in giving birth to Robert, and twenty years elapsed ere he married a second. He was seventy years of age now, but still upright as a dart, with a fine fresh complexion, a clear bright eye, and snow-white hair that fell in curls behind, on the collar of his white smock-frock.

He was sitting at a small table apart when Rachel entered, a candle and a large open Bible on it. A flock of grandchildren crowded round him, two of them on his knees. He was showing them the pictures. To gaze wonderingly on those pictures, and never tire of asking explanations of their mysteries, was the chief business of the little Frosts' lives. Robert's wife—but he was hardly ever called anything but Robin—was preparing something over the fire for the evening meal. Rachel went up and kissed her father. He scattered the children from him to make room for her. He loved her dearly. Robin loved her dearly. When Robin was a grown-up young man the pretty baby had come to be his plaything. Robin seemed to love her still better than he loved his own children.

"Thee'st been crying, child!" cried old Matthew Frost. "What has ailed thee?"

Had Rachel known that the signs of her past tears were so palpable as to call forth remark from everybody she met, as it appeared they were doing, she might have remained at home. Putting on a gay face, she laughed off the matter. Matthew pressed it.

"Something went wrong at home, and I got a scolding," said Rachel at length. "It was not worth crying over, though."

Mrs. Frost turned round from her saucepan.

"A scolding from the missis, Rachel?"

"There's nobody else at Verner's Pride should scold me," responded Rachel, with a charming little air of self-consequence. "Mrs. Verner said a cross word or two, and I was so stupid as to burst out crying. I have had a headache all day, and that's sure to put me out of sorts."

"There's always things to worry one in service, let it be ever so good on the whole," philosophically observed Mrs. Frost, bestowing her attention again upon the saucepan. "Better be one's own missus on a crust, say I, than at the beck and call of others."

"Rachel," interrupted old Matthew, "when I let you go to Verner's Pride, I thought it was for your good. But I'd not keep you there a day, child, if you be unhappy."

"Dear father, don't take up that notion," she quickly rejoined. "I am happier at Verner's Pride than I should be anywhere else. I would not leave it. Where is Robin this evening?"

"Robin—"

The answer was interrupted by the entrance of Robin himself. A short man with a red face, somewhat obstinate-looking. His eye lighted up when he saw Rachel; Mrs. Frost poured out the contents of her saucepan, which appeared to be a compound of Scotch oatmeal and treacle. Rachel was invited to take some, but declined. She lifted one of the children on her knee—a pretty little girl named after herself. The child did not seem well, and Rachel hushed it to her, bringing down her own sweet face caressingly upon the little one's.

"So I hear as Mr. John Massingbird's a-going to London on a visit?" cried Robin to his sister, holding out his basin for a second supply of the porridge.

The question had to be repeated three times, and then Rachel seemed to awake to it with a start. She had been gazing at vacancy, as if buried in a dream.

"Mr. John? A visit to London? Oh, yes, yes; he is going to London."

"Do he make much of a stay?"

"I can't tell," said Rachel slightingly. A certain confidence had been reposed in her at Verner's Pride; but it was not her business to make it known, even in her father's home. Rachel was not a good hand at deception, and she changed the subject. "Has there not been some disturbance with the Dawsons to-day? Old Roy was at Verner's Pride this afternoon, and the servants have been saying he came up about the Dawsons."

"He wanted to turn 'em out," replied Robin.

"He's Grip Roy all over," said Mrs. Frost.

Old Matthew Frost shook his head. "There has been ill-feeling smouldering between Roy and old Dawson this long while," said he. "Now that it's come to open war, I misdoubt me but there'll be violence."

"There's ill-feeling between Roy and a many more, father, besides the Dawsons," observed Robin.

"Ay! Rachel, child"—turning his head to the hearth, where his daughter sat apart—"folks have said that young Luke wants to make up to you. But I'd not like it. Luke's a good-meaning, kind-hearted lad himself, but I'd not like you to be daughter-in-law to old Roy."

"Be easy, father dear. I'd not have Luke Roy if he were made of gold. I never yet had anything to say to him, and I never will have. We can't help our likes and dislikes."

"Pshaw!" said Robin, with pardonable pride. "Pretty Rachel is not for a daft chap like Luke Roy, that's a head and ears shorter nor other men. Be you, my dear one?"

Rachel laughed. Her conscience told her that she enjoyed a joke at Luke's undersize. She took a shower of kisses from the little girl, put her down, and rose.

"I must go," she said. "Mrs. Verner may be calling for me."

"Don't she know you be come out?" asked old Matthew.

"No. But do not fear that I came clandestinely—or, as our servants would say, on the sly," added Rachel, with a smile. "Mrs. Verner has told me to run down to see you whenever I like, after she has gone in to dinner. Good-night, dear father."

The old man pressed her to his heart: "Don't thee get fretting again my blessing. I don't care to see thee with red eyes."

For answer, Rachel burst into tears then—a sudden, violent burst. She dashed them away again with a defiant, reckless sort of air, broke, into a laugh, and laid the blame on her headache. Robin said he would walk home with her.

"No, Robin, I would rather you did not to-night," she replied. "I have two or three things to get at Mother Duff's, and I shall stop there a bit, gossiping. After that, I shall be home in a trice. It's not dark; and, if it were, who'd harm me?"

They laughed. To imagine harm of any sort occurring, through walking a mile or so alone at night, would never enter the head of honest country people. Rachel departed; and Robin, who was a domesticated man upon the whole, helped his wife to put the children to bed.

Scarcely an hour later, a strange commotion arose in the village. People ran about wildly, whispering dread words to one another. A woman had just been drowned in the Willow Pond.

The whole place flocked down to the Willow Pond. On its banks, the centre of an awe-struck crowd, which had been quickly gathering, lay a body, recently taken out of the water. It was all that remained of poor Rachel Frost—cold, and white, and DEAD!

CHAPTER III

THE NEWS BROUGHT HOME

Seated in the dining-room at Verner's Pride, comfortably asleep in an arm-chair, her face turned to the fire and her feet on a footstool, was Mrs. Verner. The dessert remained on the table, but nobody was there to partake of it. Mr. Verner had retired to his study upon the withdrawal of the cloth, according to his usual custom. Always a man of spare habits, shunning the pleasures of the table, he had scarcely taken sufficient to support nature since his health failed. Mrs. Verner would remonstrate; but his medical attendant, Dr. West, said it was better for him that it should be so. Lionel Verner (who had come in for the tail of the dinner) and John Massingbird had likewise left the room and the house, but not together. Mrs. Verner sat on alone. She liked to take her share of dessert, if the others did not, and she generally remained in the dining-room for the evening, rarely caring to move. Truth to say, Mrs. Verner was rather addicted to dropping asleep with her last glass of wine and waking up with the tea-tray, and she did so this evening.

Of course work goes on downstairs (or is supposed to go on) whether the mistress of a house be asleep or awake. It really was going on that evening in the laundry at Verner's Pride, whatever it may have been doing in the other various branches and departments. The laundry-maids had had heavy labour on their hands that day, and they were hard at work still, while Mrs. Verner slept.

"Here's Mother Duff's Dan a-coming in!" exclaimed one of the women, glancing over her ironing-board to the yard. "What do he want, I wonder?"

"Who?" cried Nancy, the under-housemaid, a tart sort of girl, whose business it was to assist in the laundry on busy days.

"Dan Duff. Just see what he wants, Nancy. He's got a parcel."

The gentleman familiarly called Dan Duff was an urchin of ten years old. He was the son of Mrs. Duff, linen-draper-in-ordinary to Deerham—a lady popularly spoken of as "Mother Duff," both behind her back and before her face. Nancy darted out at the laundry-door and waylaid the intruder in the yard.

"Now, Dan Duff!" cried she, "what do you want?"

"Please, here's this," was Dan Duff's reply, handing over the parcel. "And, please, I want to see Rachel Frost."

"Who's it for? What's inside it?" sharply asked Nancy, regarding the parcel on all sides.

"It's things as Rachel Frost have been a-buying," he replied. "Please, I want to see her."

"Then want must be your master," retorted Nancy. "Rachel Frost's not at home."

"Ain't she?" returned Dan Duff, with surprised emphasis. "Why, she left our shop a long sight afore I did! Mother says, please, would she mind having some o' the dark lavender print instead o' the light, 'cause Susan Peckaby's come in, and she wants the whole o' the light lavender for a gownd, and there's only just enough of it. And, please, I be to take word back."

"How are you to take word back if she's not in?" asked Nancy, whose temper never was improved by extra work. "Get along, Dan Duff! You must come along again to-morrow if you want her."

Dan Duff turned to depart, in meek obedience, and Nancy carried the parcel into the laundry and flung it down on the ironing-board.

"It's fine to be Rachel Frost," she sarcastically cried. "Going shopping like any lady, and having her things sent home for her! And messages about her gownds coming up—which will she have, if you please, and which won't she have! I'll borror one of the horses to-morrow, and go shopping myself on a side-saddle!"

"Has Rachel gone shopping to-night?" cried one of the women, pausing in her ironing. "I did not know she was out."

"She has been out all the evening," was Nancy's answer. "I met her coming down the stairs, dressed. And she could tell a story over it, too, for she said she was going to see her old father."

But Master Dan Duff is not done with yet. If that gentleman stood in awe of one earthly thing more than another, it was of the anger of his revered mother. Mrs. Duff, in her maternal capacity, was rather free both with her hands and tongue. Being sole head of her flock, for she was a widow, she deemed it best to rule with firmness, not to say severity; and her son Dan, awed by his own timid nature, tried hard to steer his course so as to avoid shoals and quicksands. He crossed the yard, after the rebuff administered by Nancy, and passed out at the gate, where he stood still to revolve affairs. His mother had imperatively ordered him to bring back the answer touching the intricate question of the light and the dark lavender prints; and Susan Peckaby—one of the greatest idlers in all Deerham—said she would wait in the shop until he came with it. He stood softly whistling, his hands in his pockets, and balancing himself on his heels.

"I'll get a basting, for sure," soliloquised he. "Mother'll lose the sale of the gownd, and then she'll say it's my fault, and baste me for it. What's of her? Why couldn't she ha' come home, as she said?"

He set his wits to work to divine what could have "gone of her"—alluding, of course, to Rachel. And a bright thought occurred to him—really not an unnatural one—that she had probably taken the other road home. It was a longer round, through the fields, and there were stiles to climb, and gates to mount; which might account for the delay. He arrived at the conclusion, though somewhat slow of drawing conclusions in general, that if he returned home that way, he should meet Rachel; and could then ask the question.

If he turned to his left hand—standing as he did at the gate with his back to the back of the house—he would regain the high road, whence he came. Did he turn to the right, he would plunge into fields and lanes, and covered ways, and emerge at length, by a round, in the midst of the village, almost close to his own house. It was a lonely way at night, and longer than the other, but Master Dan Duff regarded those as pleasant evils, in comparison with a "basting." He took his hands out of his pockets, brought down his feet to a level, and turned to it, whistling still.

It was a tolerably light night. The moon was up, though not very high, and a few stars might be seen here and there in the blue canopy above. Mr. Dan Duff proceeded on his way, not very quickly. Some dim idea was penetrating his brain that the slower he walked, the better chance there might be of his meeting Rachel.

"She's just a cat, is that Susan Peckaby!" decided he, with acrimony, in the intervals of his whistling. "It was her as put mother up to the thought o' sending me to-night: Rachel Frost said the things 'ud do in the morning. 'Let Dan carry 'em up now,' says Dame Peckaby, 'and ask her about the print, and then I'll take it home along o' me.' And if I go in without the answer, she'll be the first to help mother to baste me! Hi! ho! hur! hur-r-r-r!"

This last exclamation was caused by his catching sight of some small animal scudding along. He was at that moment traversing a narrow, winding lane; and, in the field to the right, as he looked in at the open gate, he saw the movement. It might be a cat, it might be a hare, it might be a rabbit, it might be some other animal; it was all one to Mr. Dan Duff; and he had not been a boy had he resisted the propensity to pursue it. Catching up a handful of earth from the lane, he shied it in the proper direction, and tore in at the gate after it.

Nothing came of the pursuit. The trespasser had earthed itself, and Mr. Dan came slowly back again. He had nearly approached the gate, when somebody passed it, walking up the lane with a very quick step, from the direction in which he, Dan, was bound. Dan saw enough to know that it was not Rachel, for it was the figure of a man; but Dan set off to run, and emerged from the gate just in time to catch another glimpse of the person, as he disappeared beyond the windings of the lane.

"'Twarn't Rachel, at all events," was his comment. And he turned and pursued his way again.

It was somewhere about this time that Tynn made his appearance in the dining-room at Verner's Pride, to put away the dessert, and set the tea. The stir woke up Mrs. Verner.

"Send Rachel to me," said she, winking and blinking at the tea-cups.

"Yes, ma'am," replied Tynn.

He left the room when he had placed the cups and things to his satisfaction. He called for Rachel high and low, up and down. All to no purpose. The servants did not appear to know anything of her. One of them went to the door and shouted out to the laundry to know whether Rachel was there, and the answering shout "No" came back. The footman at length remembered that he had seen her go out at the hall door while the dinner was in. Tynn carried this item of information to Mrs. Verner. It did not please her.

"Of course!" she grumbled. "Let me want any one of you particularly, and you are sure to be away! If she did go out, she ought not to stay as long as this. Who's this coming in?"

It was Frederick Massingbird. He entered, singing a scrap of a song; which was cut suddenly short when his eye fell on the servant.

"Tynn," said he, "you must bring me something to eat. I have had no dinner."

"You cannot be very hungry, or you'd have come in before," remarked Mrs. Verner to him. "It is tea-time now."

"I'll take tea and dinner together," was his answer.

"But you ought to have been in before," she persisted; for, though an easy mistress and mother, Mrs. Verner did not like the order of meals to be displaced. "Where have you stayed, Fred? You have not been all this while taking Sibylla West to Bitterworth's."

"You must talk to Sibylla West about that," answered Fred. "When young ladies keep you a good hour waiting, while they make themselves ready to start, you can't get back precisely to your own time."

"What did she keep you waiting for?" questioned Mrs. Verner.

"Some mystery of the toilette, I conclude. When I got there, Amilly said Sibylla was dressing; and a pretty prolonged dressing it appeared to be! Since I left her at Bitterworth's, I have been to Poynton's about my mare. She was as lame as ever to-day."

"And there's Rachel out now, just as I am wanting her!" went on Mrs. Verner, who, when she did lapse into a grumbling mood, was fond of calling up a catalogue of grievances.

"At any rate, that's not my fault, mother," observed Frederick. "I dare say she will soon be in. Rachel is not given to stay out, I fancy, if there's a chance of her being wanted."

Tynn came in with his tray, and Frederick Massingbird sat down to it. Tynn then waited for Mr. Verner's tea, which he carried into the study. He carried a cup in every evening, but Mr. Verner scarcely ever touched it. Then Tynn returned to the room where the upper servants took their meals and otherwise congregated, and sat down to read a newspaper. He was a little man, very stout, his plain clothes always scrupulously neat.

A few minutes, and Nancy came in, the parcel left by Dan Duff in her hand. The housekeeper asked her what it was. She explained in her crusty way, and said something to the same effect that she had said in the laundry—that it was fine to be Rachel Frost. "She's long enough making her way up here!" Nancy wound up with. "Dan Duff says she left their shop to come home before he did. If Luke Roy was in Deerham one would know what to think!"

"Bah!" cried the housekeeper. "Rachel Frost has nothing to say to Luke Roy."

Tynn laid down his paper, and rose. "I'll just tell the mistress that Rachel's on her way home," said he. "She's put up like anything at her being out—wants her for something particular, she says."

Barely had he departed on his errand, when a loud commotion was heard in the passage. Mr. Dan Duff had burst in at the back door, uttering sounds of distress—of fright—his eyes starting, his hair standing on end, his words nearly unintelligible.

"Rachel Frost is in the Willow Pond—drownded!"

The women shrieked when they gathered in the sense. It was enough to make them shriek. Dan Duff howled in concert. The passages took up the sounds and echoed them; and Mrs. Verner, Frederick Massingbird, and Tynn came hastening forth. Mr. Verner followed, feeble, and leaning on his stick. Frederick Massingbird seized upon the boy, questioning sharply.

"Rachel Frost's a-drowned in the Willow Pond," he reiterated. "I see'd her."

A moment of pause, of startled suspense, and then they flew off, men and women, as with one accord, Frederick Massingbird leading the van. Social obligations were forgotten in the overwhelming excitement, and Mr. and Mrs. Verner were left to keep house for themselves. Tynn, indeed, recollected himself, and turned back.

"No," said Mr. Verner. "Go with the rest, Tynn, and see what it is, and whether anything can be done."

He might have crept thither himself in his feeble strength, but he had not stirred out of the house for two years.

CHAPTER IV

THE CROWD IN THE MOONLIGHT

The Willow Pond, so called from its being surrounded with weeping willows, was situated at the corner of a field, in a retired part of the road, about midway between Verner's Pride and Deerham. There was a great deal of timber about that part; it was altogether as lonely as could be desired. When the runners from Verner's Pride reached it, assistance had already arrived, and Rachel, rescued from the pond, was being laid upon the grass. All signs of life were gone.

Who had done it?—what had caused it?—was it an accident?—was it a self-committed act?—or was it a deed of violence? What brought her there at all? No young girl would be likely to take that way home (with all due deference to the opinion of Master Dan Duff) alone at night.

What was to be done? The crowd propounded these various questions in so many marvels of wonder, and hustled each other, and talked incessantly; but to be of use, to direct, nobody appeared capable. Frederick Massingbird stepped forward with authority.

"Carry her at once to Verner's Pride—with all speed. And some of you"—turning to the servants of the house—"hasten on, and get water heated and blankets hot. Get hot bricks—get anything and everything likely to be required. How did she get in?"

He appeared to speak the words more in the light of a wailing regret, than as a question. It was a question that none present appeared able to answer. The crowd was increasing rapidly. One of them suggested that Broom the gamekeeper's cottage was nearer than Verner's Pride.

"But there will be neither hot water nor blankets there," returned Frederick Massingbird.

"The house is the best. Make haste! don't let grass grow under your feet."

"A moment," interposed a gentleman who now came hastily up, as they were raising the body. "Lay her down again."

They obeyed him eagerly, and fell a little back that he might have space to bend over her. It was the doctor of the neighbourhood, resident at Deerham. He was a fine man in figure, dark and florid in face, but a more impassive countenance could not well be seen, and he had the peculiarity of rarely looking a person in the face. If a patient's eyes were mixed on Dr. West's, Dr. West's were invariably fixed upon something else. A clever man in his profession, holding an Edinburgh degree, and practising as a general practitioner. He was brother to the present Mrs. Verner; consequently, uncle to the two young Massingbirds.

"Has anybody got a match?" he asked.

One of the Verner's Pride servants had a whole boxful, and two or three were lighted at a time, and held so that the doctor could see the drowned face better than he could in the uncertain moonlight. It was a strange scene. The lonely, weird character of the place; the dark trees scattered about; the dull pond with its bending willows; the swaying, murmuring crowd collected round the doctor and what he was bending over; the bright flickering flame of the match-light; with the pale moon overhead, getting higher and higher as the night went on, and struggling her way through passing clouds.

"How did it happen?" asked Dr. West.

Before any answer could be given, a man came tearing up at the top of his speed; several men, indeed, it may be said. The first was Roy, the bailiff. Upon Roy's leaving Verner's Pride, after the rebuke bestowed upon him by its heir, he had gone straight down to the George and Dragon, a roadside inn, situated on the outskirts of the village, on the road from Verner's Pride. Here he had remained, consorting with droppers-in from Deerham, and soothing his mortification with a pipe and sundry cans of ale. When the news was brought in that Rachel Frost was drowned in the Willow-pond, Roy, the landlord, and the company collectively, started off to see.

"Why, it is her!" uttered Roy, taking a hasty view of poor Rachel. "I said it wasn't possible. I saw her and talked to her up at the house but two or three hours ago. How did she get in?"

The same question always; from all alike: how did she get in? Dr. West rose.

"You can move her," he said.

"Is she dead, sir?"

"Yes."

Frederick Massingbird—who had been the one to hold the matches—caught the doctor's arm.

"Not dead!" he uttered. "Not dead beyond hope of restoration?"

"She will never be restored in this world," was the reply of Dr. West. "She is quite dead."

"Measures should be tried, at any rate," said Frederick Massingbird warmly.

"By all means," acquiesced Dr. West. "It will afford satisfaction, though it should do nothing else."

They raised her once more, her clothes dripping, and turned with quiet, measured steps towards Verner's Pride. Of course the whole assemblage attended. They were eagerly curious, boiling over with excitement; but, to give them their due, they were earnestly anxious to afford any aid in their power, and contended who should take turn at bearing that wet burden. Not one but felt sorely grieved for Rachel. Even Nancy was subdued to meekness, as she sped on to be one of the busiest in preparing remedies; and old Roy, though somewhat inclined to regard it in the light of a judgment upon proud Rachel for slighting his son, felt some twinges of pitying regret.

"I have knowed cases where people, dead from drownding, have been restored to life," said Roy, as they walked along.

"That you never have," replied Dr. West. "The apparently dead have been restored; the dead, never."

Panting, breathless, there came up one as they reached Verner's Pride. He parted the crowd, and threw himself almost upon Rachel with a wild cry. He caught up her cold, wet face, and passing his hands over it, bent down his warm cheek upon it.

"Who has done it?" he sobbed. "What has done it? She couldn't have fell in alone."

It was Robin Frost. Frederick Massingbird drew him away by the arm. "Don't hinder, Robin. Every minute may be worth a life."

And Robin, struck with the argument, obeyed docilely like a little child.

Mr. Verner, leaning on his stick, trembling with weakness and emotion, stood just without the door of the laundry, which had been hastily prepared, as the bearers tramped in.

"It is an awful tragedy!" he murmured. "Is it true"—addressing Dr. West—"that you think there is no hope?"

"I am sure there is none," was the answer. "But every means shall be tried."

The laundry was cleared of the crowd, and their work began. One of the next to come up was old Matthew Frost. Mr. Verner took his hand.

"Come in to my own room, Matthew," he said. "I feel for you deeply."

"Nay, sir; I must look upon her."

Mr. Verner pointed with his stick in the direction of the laundry.

"They are shut in there—the doctor and those whom he requires round him," he said. "Let them be undisturbed; it is the only chance."

All things likely to be wanted had been conveyed to the laundry; and they were shut in there, as Mr. Verner expressed it, with their fires and their heat. On dragged the time. Anxious watchers were in the house, in the yard, gathered round the back gate. The news had spread, and gentlepeople, friends of the Verners, came hasting from their homes, and pressed into Verner's Pride, and asked question upon question of Mr. and Mrs. Verner, of everybody likely to afford an answer. Old Matthew Frost stood outwardly calm and collected, full of inward trust, as a good man should be. He had learned where to look for support in the darkest trial. Mr. Verner in that night of sorrow seemed to treat him as a brother.

One hour! Two hours! and still they plied their remedies, under the able direction of Dr. West. All was of no avail, as the experienced physician had told them. Life was extinct. Poor Rachel Frost was really dead!

CHAPTER V

THE TALL GENTLEMAN IN THE LANE

Apart from the horror of the affair, it was altogether attended with so much mystery that that of itself would have kept the excitement alive. What could have taken Rachel Frost near the pond at all? Allowing that she had chosen that lonely road for her way home—which appeared unlikely in the extreme—she must still have gone out of it to approach the pond, must have walked partly across a field to gain it. Had her path led close by it, it would have been a different matter: it might have been supposed (unlikely still, though) that she had missed her footing and fallen in. But unpleasant rumours were beginning to circulate in the crowd. It was whispered that sounds of a contest, the voices being those of a man and a woman, had been heard in that direction at the time of the accident, or about the time; and these rumours reached the ear of Mr. Verner.

For the family to think of bed, in the present state of affairs, or the crowd to think of dispersing, would have been in the highest degree improbable. Mr. Verner set himself to get some sort of solution first. One told one tale; one, another: one asserted something else; another, the exact opposite. Mr. Verner—and in saying Mr. Verner, we must include all—was fairly puzzled. A notion had sprung up that Dinah Roy, the bailiffs wife, could tell something about it if she would. Certain it was, that she had stood amid the crowd, cowering and trembling, shrinking from observation as much as possible, and recoiling visibly if addressed.

A word of this suspicion at last reached her husband. It angered him. He was accustomed to keep his wife in due submission. She was a little body, with a pinched face and a sharp red nose, given to weeping upon every possible occasion, and as indulgently fond of her son Luke as she was afraid of her husband. Since Luke's departure she had passed the better part of her time in tears.

"Now," said Roy, going up to her with authority, and drawing her apart, "what's this as is up with you?"

She looked round her, and shuddered.

"Oh, law!" cried she, with a moan. "Don't you begin to ask, Giles, or I shall be fit to die."

"Do you know anything about this matter, or don't you?" cried he savagely. "Did you see anything?"

"What should I be likely to see of it?" quaked Mrs. Roy.

"Did you see Rachel fall into the pond? Or see her a-nigh the pond?"

"No, I didn't," moaned Mrs. Roy. "I never set eyes on Rachel this blessed night at all. I'd take a text o' scripture to it."

"Then what is the matter with you?" he demanded, giving her a slight shake.

"Hush, Giles!" responded she, in a tone of unmistakable terror. "I saw a ghost!"

"Saw a—what?" thundered Giles Roy.

"A ghost!" she repeated. "And it have made me shiver ever since."

Giles Roy knew that his wife was rather prone to flights of fancy. He was in the habit of administering one sovereign remedy, which he believed to be an infallible panacea for wives' ailments whenever it was applied—a hearty good shaking. He gave her a slight instalment as he turned away.

"Wait till I get ye home," said he significantly. "I'll drive the ghosts out of ye!"

Mr. Verner had seated himself in his study, with a view of investigating systematically the circumstances attending the affair, so far as they were known. At present all seemed involved in a Babel of confusion, even the open details.

"Those able to tell anything of it shall come before me, one by one," he observed; "we may get at something then."

The only stranger present was Mr. Bitterworth, an old and intimate friend of Mr. Verner. He was a man of good property, and resided a little beyond Verner's Pride. Others—plenty of them—had been eager to assist in what they called the investigation, but Mr. Verner had declined. The public investigation would come soon enough, he observed, and that must satisfy them. Mrs. Verner saw no reason why she should be absent, and she took her seat. Her sons were there. The news had reached John out-of-doors, and he had hastened home full of consternation. Dr. West also remained by request, and the Frosts, father and son, had pressed in. Mr. Verner could not deny them.

"To begin at the beginning," observed Mr. Verner, "it appears that Rachel left this house between six and seven. Did she mention to anybody where she was going?"

"I believe she did to Nancy, sir," replied Mrs. Tynn, who had been allowed to remain.

"Then call Nancy in," said Mr. Verner.

Nancy came, but she could not say much: only that, in going up the front stairs to carry some linen into Mrs. Verner's room, she had met Rachel, dressed to go out. Rachel had said, in passing her, that she was about to visit her father.

"And she came?" observed Mr. Verner, turning to Matthew Frost, as Nancy was dismissed.

"She came, sir," replied the old man, who was having an incessant battle with himself for calmness; for it was not there, in the presence of others, that he would willingly indulge his grief. "I saw that she had been fretting. Her eyes were as red as ferrets'; and I taxed her with it. She was for turning it off at first, but I pressed for the cause, and she then said she had been scolded by her mistress."

"By me!" exclaimed Mrs. Verner, lifting her head in surprise. "I had not scolded her."

But as she spoke she caught the eye of her son John, and she remembered the little scene of the afternoon.

"I recollect now," she resumed. "I spoke a word of reproof to Rachel, and she burst into a violent flood of tears, and ran away from me. It surprised me much. What I said was not sufficient to call forth one tear, let alone a passionate burst of them."

"What was it about?" asked Mr. Verner.

"I expect John can give a better explanation of it than I," replied Mrs. Verner, after a pause. "I went out of the room for a minute or two, and when I returned, Rachel was talking angrily at John. I could not make out distinctly about what. John had begun to tease her about Luke Roy, I believe, and she did not like it."

Mr. John Massingbird's conscience called up the little episode of the coveted kiss. But it might not be altogether prudent to confess it in full conclave.

"It is true that I did joke Rachel about Luke," he said. "It seemed to anger her very much, and she paid me out with some hard words. My mother returned at the same moment. She asked what was the matter; I said I had joked Rachel about Luke, and that Rachel did not like it."

"Yes, that was it," acquiesced Mrs. Verner. "I then told Rachel that in my opinion she would have done well to encourage Luke, who was a steady young man, and would no doubt have a little money. Upon which she began weeping. I felt rather vexed; not a word have I been able to say to her lately, but tears have been the answer; and I asked what had come to her that she should cry for every trifle as if she were heart-broken. With that, she fell into a burst of sobs, terrifying to see, and ran from the room. I was thunderstruck. I asked John what could be the matter with her, and he said he could only think she was going crazed."

John Massingbird nodded his head, as if in confirmation. Old Matthew Frost spoke up, his voice trembling with the emotion that he was striving to keep under—

"Did she say what it was that had come to her, ma'am?"

"She did not make any reply at all," rejoined Mrs. Verner. "But it is quite nonsense to suppose she could have fallen into that wild burst of grief simply at being joked about Luke. I could not make her out."

"And she has fallen into fretting, you say, ma'am, lately?" pursued Matthew Frost, leaning his venerable white head forward.

"Often and often," replied Mrs. Verner. "She has seemed quite an altered girl in the last few weeks!"

"My son's wife has said the same," cried old Matthew. "She has said that Rachel was changed. But I took it to mean in her looks—that she had got thinner. You mind the wife saying it, Robin?"

"Yes, I mind it," shortly replied Robin, who had propped himself against the wall, his arms folded and his head bent. "I'm a-minding all."

"She wouldn't eat a bit o' supper," went on old Matthew. "But that was nothing," he added; "she used to say she had plenty of food here, without eating ours. She sat apart by the fire with one o' the little uns in her lap. She didn't stay over long; she said the missus might be wanting her, and she left; and when she was kissing my poor old face, she began sobbing. Robin offered to see her home—"

"And she wouldn't have it," interrupted Robin, looking up for the first time with a wild expression of despair. "She said she had things to get at Mother Duff's, and should stop a bit there, a-gossiping. It'll be on my mind by day and by night, that if I'd went with her, harm couldn't have come."

"And that was how she left you," pursued Mr. Verner. "You did not see her after that? You know nothing further of her movements?"

"Nothing further," assented Robin. "I watched her down the lane as far as the turning, and that was the last."

"Did she go to Mrs. Duff's, I wonder?" asked Mr. Verner.

Oh, yes; several of those present could answer that. There was the parcel brought up by Dan Duff, as testimony; and, if more had been needed, Mrs. Duff herself had afforded it, for she made one of the crowd outside.

"We must have Mrs. Duff in," said Mr. Verner.

Accordingly, Mrs. Duff was brought in—a voluble lady with red hair. Mr. Verner politely asked her to be seated, but she replied that she'd prefer to stand, if 'twas all the same. She was used to standing in her shop, and she couldn't never sit for a minute together when she was upset.

"Did Rachel Frost purchase things of you this evening, Mrs. Duff?"

"Well, she did, and she didn't," responded Mrs. Duff. "I never calls it purchasing of things, sir, when a customer comes in and says, 'Just cut me off so and so, and send it up.' They be sold, of course, if you look at it in that light; but I'm best pleased when buyers examines the goods, and chats a bit over their merits. Susan Peckaby, now, she—"

"What did Rachel Frost buy?" interrupted Mr. Verner, who knew what Mrs. Duff's tongue was, when it was once set going.

"She looked in at the shop, sir, while I was a-serving little Green with some bone buttons, that her mother had sent her for. 'I want some Irish for aprons, Mrs. Duff,' says she. 'Cut off the proper quantity for a couple, and send it me up some time to-morrow. I'd not give the trouble,' says she, 'but I can't wait to take it now, for I'm in a hurry to get home, and I shall be wanting the aprons.' 'What quality—pretty good?' said I. 'Oh, you know,' says she; 'about the same that I bought last time. And put in the tape for strings, and a reel of white cotton, No. 30. And I don't mind if you put in a piece of that German ribbon, middling width,' she went on. 'It's nicer than tape for nightcaps, and them sort o' things.' And with that, sir, she was turning out again, when her eyes was caught by some lavender prints, as was a-hanging just in the doorway. Two shades of it, there was, dark and light. 'That's pretty,' says she. 'It's beautiful,' said I; 'they be the sweetest things I have had in, this many a day; and they be the wide width. Won't you take some of it for a gownd?' 'No,' says she, 'I'm set up for cotton gownds.' 'Why not buy a bit of it for a apron or two?' I said. 'Nothing's cleaner than them lavender prints for morning aprons, and they saves the white.' So she looked at it for a minute, and then she said I might cut her off a couple o' yards of the light, and send it up with the other things. Well, sir, Sally Green went away with her buttons, and I took down the light print, thinking I'd cut off the two yards at once. Just then, Susan Peckaby comes in for some gray worsted, and she falls right in love with the print. 'I'll have a gownd of that,' says she, 'and I'll take it now.' In course, sir, I was only too glad to sell it to her, for, like Rachel, she's good pay; but when I come to measure it, there was barely nine yards left, which is what Susan Peckaby takes for a gownd, being as tall as a maypole. So I was in a mess; for I couldn't take and sell it all, over Rachel's head, having offered it to her. 'Perhaps she wouldn't mind having her aprons off the dark,' says Susan Peckaby; 'it don't matter what colour aprons is of—they're not like gownds.' And then we agreed that I should send Dan up here at once to ask her, and Susan Peckaby—who seemed mighty eager to have the print—said she'd wait till he come back. And I cut off the white Irish, and wrapped it up with the tape and things, and sent him."

"Rachel Frost had left your shop, then?"

"She left it, sir, when she told me she'd have some of the lavender print. She didn't stay another minute."

Robin Frost lifted his head again. "She said she was going to stop at your place for a bit of a gossip, Mother Duff."

"Then she didn't stop," responded that lady. "She never spoke a single word o' gossip, or looked inclined to speak it. She just spoke out short, as if she was in a hurry, and she turned clean out o' the shop afore the words about the lavender print had well left her. Ask Sally Green, if you don't believe me."

"You did not see which way she took?" observed Mr. Verner.

"No, sir, I didn't; I was behind my counter. But, for the matter o' that, there was two or three as saw her go out of my shop and take the turning by the pound—which is a good proof she meant to come home here by the field way, for that turning, as you know, sir, leads to nowhere else."

Mr. Verner did know it. He also knew—for witnesses had been speaking of it outside—that Rachel had been seen to take that turning after she left Mrs. Duff's shop, and that she was walking with a quick step.

The next person called in was Master Dan Duff—in a state of extreme consternation at being called in at all. He was planted down in front of Mr. Verner, his legs restless. An idea crossed his brain that they might be going to accuse him of putting Rachel into the pond, and he began to cry. With a good deal of trouble on Mr. Verner's part, owing to the young gentleman's timidity, and some circumlocution on his own, the facts, so far as Dan was cognisant of them, were drawn forth. It appeared that after he had emerged from the field when he made that slight diversion in pursuit of the running animal, he continued his road, and had gained the lonely part near where the pond was situated, when young Broom, the son of Mr. Verner's gamekeeper, ran up and asked him what was the matter, and whether anybody was in the pond. Broom did not wait for an answer, but went on to the pond, and Dan Duff followed him. Sure enough, Rachel Frost was in it. They knew her by her clothes, as she rose to the surface. Dan Duff, in his terror, went back shrieking to Verner's Pride, and young Broom, more sensibly, ran for help to get her out.

"How did young Broom know, or suspect, there was anybody in the pond?" questioned Mr. Verner.

"I dun know, please, sir," sobbed Dan Duff; "that was what he said as he runned off to it. He asked me if I had seen any folks about, and I said I'd only seen that un in the lane."

"Whom did you see in the lane?"

"I dun know who it was, please, sir," returned Dan, sniffing greatly. "I wasn't a-nigh him."

"But you must have been nigh him if you met him in the lane."

"Please, sir, I wasn't in the lane then. I had runned into the field after a cat."

"After a cat?"

"Please, sir, 'twere a cat, I think. But it got away, and I didn't find it. I saw somebody a-passing of the gate up the lane, but I warn't quick enough to see who."

"Going which way?"

"Please, sir, up towards here. If I hadn't turned into the field, I should ha' met him face to face. I dun know who it was."

"Did you hear any noise near the pond, or see any movement in its direction, before you were accosted by Broom?"

"Please, sir, no."

It appeared to be of little use to detain Mr. Duff. In his stead young Broom was called in. A fine-grown young fellow of nineteen, whose temperament may be indicated by two words—cool and lazy. He was desired to give his own explanation.

"I was going home for the night, sir," he began, in answer, "when I heard the sound of voices in dispute. They seemed to come from the direction of the grove of trees near the Willow Pond, and I stayed to listen. I thought perhaps some of the Dawsons and Roy had come to an encounter out there; but I soon found that one of the voices was that of a woman. Quite a young voice it sounded, and it was broke by sobs and tears. The other voice was a man's."

"Only two! Did you recognise them?"

"No, sir, I did not recognise them; I was too far off, maybe. I only made out that it was two—a man's and a woman's. I stopped a few minutes, listening, and they seemed to quiet down, and then, as I was going on again, I came up to Mrs. Roy. She was kneeling down, and—"

"Kneeling down?" interrupted Mr. Verner.

"She was kneeling down, sir, with her hands clasped round the trunk of a tree, like one in mortal fright. She laid hold of me then, and I asked what was the matter with her, and she answered that she had been a'most frightened to death. I asked whether it was at the quarrel, but she only said, 'Hush! listen!' and at last she set on to cry. Just then we heard an awful shriek, and a plunge into the water. 'There goes something into the Willow Pond,' said I, and I was turning to run to it, when Mrs. Roy shrieked out louder than the other shriek had been, and fell flat down on the earth. I never hardly see such a face afore for ghastliness. The moon was shining out full then, and it daunted me to look at her. I thought she was dead—that the fright had killed her. There wasn't a bit o' breath in her body, and I raised her head up, not knowing what to do with her. Presently she heaved a sort of sigh, and opened her eyes; and with that she seemed to recollect herself, and asked what was in the pond. I left her and went off to it, meeting Dan Duff—and we found it was Rachel Frost. Dan, he set on to howl, and wouldn't stay, and I went for the nearest help, and got her out. That's all, sir."

"Was she already dead?"

"Well, sir, when you first get a person out of the water it's hard to say whether they be dead or not. She seemed dead, but perhaps if there had been means right at hand, she might have been brought-to again."

A moan of pain from old Matthew. Mr. Verner continued as it died out—

"Rachel Frost's voice must have been one of those you heard in dispute?"

"Not a doubt of that, sir," replied young Broom. "Any more than that there must have been foul play at work to get her into the pond, or that the other disputing voice must have belonged to the man who did it."

"Softly, softly," said Mr. Verner. "Did you see any man about?"

"I saw nobody at all, sir, saving Dan Duff and Mrs. Roy; and Rachel's quarrel could not have been with either of them. Whoever the other was, he had made himself scarce."

Robin Frost took a step forward respectfully.

"Did you mind, sir, that Mother Duffs Dan spoke to seeing some person in the lane?"

"I do," replied Mr. Verner. "I should like to ask the boy another question or two upon that point. Call him in, one of you."

John Massingbird went out and brought back the boy.

"Mind you have your wits sharp about you this time, Mr. Duff," he remarked. Which piece of advice had the effect of scaring Mr. Duff's wits more completely away than they had been scared before.

"You tell us that you saw a man pass up the lane when you were in the field after the cat," began Mr. Verner. "Was the man walking fast?"

"Please, sir, yes. Afore I could get out o' the gate he was near out o' sight. He went a'most as fast as the cat did."

"How long was it, after you saw him, before you met young Broom, and heard that somebody was in the pond?"

"Please, sir, 'twas a'most directly. I was running then, I was."

As the boy's answer fell upon the room, a conviction stole over most of those collected in it that this man must have been the one who had been heard in dispute with Rachel Frost.

"Were there no signs about him by which you could recognise him?" pursued Mr. Verner. "What did he look like? Was he tall or short?"

"Please, sir, he were very tall."

"Could you see his dress? Was it like a gentleman's or a labourer's?"

"Please, sir, I think it looked like a gentleman's—like one o' the gentlemen's at Verner's Pride."

"Whose? Like which of the gentlemen's?" rang out Mr. Verner's voice, sharply and sternly, after a moment's pause of surprise, for he evidently had not expected the answer.

"Please, sir, I dun know which. The clothes looked dark, and the man were as tall as the gentlemen, or as Calves."

"Calves?" echoed Mr. Verner, puzzled.

John Massingbird broke into an involuntary smile. He knew that their tall footman, Bennet, was universally styled "Calves" in the village. Dan Duff probably believed it to be his registered name.

But Frederick Massingbird was looking dark and threatening. The suspicion hinted at—if you can call it a suspicion—angered him. The villagers were wont to say that Mr. Frederick had ten times more pride than Mr. John. They were not far wrong—Mr. John had none at all.

"Boy!" Frederick sternly said, "what grounds have you for saying it was like one of the gentlemen?"

Dan Duff began to sob. "I dun know who it were," he said; "indeed I don't. But he were tall, and his clothes looked dark. Please, sir, if you basted me, I couldn't tell no more."

It was believed that he could not. Mr. Verner dismissed him, and John Massingbird, according to order, went to bring in Mrs. Roy.

He was some little time before he found her. She was discovered at last in a corner of the steward's room, seated on a low stool, her head bent down on her knees.

"Now, ma'am," said John, with unwonted politeness, "you are being waited for."

She looked up, startled. She rose from her low seat, and began to tremble, her lips moving, her teeth chattering. But no sound came forth.

"You are not going to your hanging, Dinah Roy," said John Massingbird, by way of consolation. "Mr. Verner is gathering the evidence about this unfortunate business, and it is your turn to go in and state what you know, or saw."

She staggered back a step or two, and fell against the wall, her face changing to one of livid terror.

"I—I—saw nothing!" she gasped.

"Oh, yes, you did! Come along!"

She put up her hands in a supplicating attitude; she was on the point of sinking on her knees in her abject fear, when at that moment the stern face of her husband was pushed in at the door. She sprang up as if electrified, and meekly followed John Massingbird.

CHAPTER VI

DINAH ROY'S "GHOST"

The moon, high in the heavens, shone down brightly, lighting up the fair domain of Verner's Pride, lighting up the broad terrace, and one who was hasting along it; all looking as peaceful as if a deed of dark mystery had not that night been committed.

He, skimming the terrace with a fleet foot, was that domain's recognised heir, Lionel Verner. Tynn and others were standing in the hall, talking in groups, as is the custom with dependents when something unusual and exciting is going on. Lionel appeared full of emotion when he burst in upon them.

"Is it true?" he demanded, speaking impulsively. "Is Rachel really dead?"

"She is dead, sir."

"Drowned?"

"Yes, sir, drowned."

He stood like one confounded. He had heard the news in the village, but this decided confirmation of it was as startling as if he now heard it for the first time. A hasty word of feeling, and then he looked again at Tynn.

"Was it the result of accident?"

Tynn shook his head.

"It's to be feared it was not, sir. There was a dreadful quarrel heard, it seems, near to the pond, just before it happened. My master is inquiring into it now, sir, in his study. Mr. Bitterworth and some more are there."

Giving his hat to the butler, Lionel Verner opened the study door, and entered. It was at that precise moment when John Massingbird had gone out for Mrs. Roy; so that, as may be said, there was a lull in the proceedings.

Mr. Verner looked glad when Lionel appeared. The ageing man, enfeebled with sickness, had grown to lean on the strong young intellect. As much as it was in Mr. Verner's nature to love anything, he loved Lionel. He beckoned him to a chair beside himself.

"Yes, sir, in an instant," nodded Lionel. "Matthew," he whispered, laying his hand kindly on the old man's shoulder as he passed, and bending down to him with his sympathising eyes, his pleasant voice, "I am grieved for this as if it had been my own sister. Believe me."

"I know it; I know you, Mr. Lionel," was the faint answer. "Don't unman me, sir, afore 'em here; leave me to myself."

With a pressure of his hand on the shoulder ere he quitted it, Lionel turned to Frederick Massingbird, asking of him particulars in an undertone.

"I don't know them myself," replied Frederick, his accent a haughty one. "There seems to be nothing but uncertainty and mystery. Mr. Verner ought not to have inquired into it in this semi-public way. Very disagreeable things have been said, I assure you. There was not the least necessity for allowing such absurdities to go forth, as suspicions, to the public. You have not been running from the Willow Pond at a strapping pace, I suppose, to-night?".

"That I certainly have not," replied Lionel.

"Neither has John, I am sure," returned Frederick resentfully. "It is not likely. And yet that boy of Mother Duff's—"

The words were interrupted. The door had opened, and John Massingbird appeared, marshalling in Dinah Roy. Dinah looked fit to die, with her ashy face and her trembling frame.

"Why, what is the matter?" exclaimed Mr. Verner.

The woman burst into tears.

"Oh, sir, I don't know nothing of it; I protest I don't," she uttered. "I declare that I never set eyes on Rachel Frost this blessed night."

"But you were near the spot at the time?"

"Oh, bad luck to me, I was!" she answered, wringing her hands. "But I know no more how she got into the water nor a child unborn."

"Where's the necessity for being put out about it, my good woman?" spoke up Mr. Bitterworth. "If you know nothing, you can't tell it. But you must state what you do know—why you were there, what startled you, and such like. Perhaps—if she were to have a chair?" he suggested to Mr. Verner in a whisper. "She looks too shaky to stand."

"Ay," acquiesced Mr. Verner. "Somebody bring forward a chair. Sit down, Mrs. Roy."

Mrs. Roy obeyed. One of those harmless, well-meaning, timid women, who seem not to possess ten ideas of their own, and are content to submit to others, she had often been seen in a shaky state from very trifling causes. But she had never been seen like this. The perspiration was pouring off her pinched face, and her blue check apron was incessantly raised to wipe it.

"What errand had you near the Willow Pond this evening?" asked Mr. Verner.

"I didn't see anything," she gasped, "I don't know anything. As true as I sit here, sir, I never saw Rachel Frost this blessed evening."

"I am not asking you about Rachel Frost. Were you near the spot?"

"Yes. But—"

"Then you can say what errand you had there; what business took you to it," continued Mr. Verner.

"It was no harm took me, sir. I went to get a dish o' tea with Martha Broom. Many's the time she have asked me since Christmas; and my husband, he was out with the Dawsons and all that bother; and Luke, he's gone, and there was nothing to keep me at home. I changed my gownd and I went."

"What time was that?"

"'Twas the middle o' the afternoon, sir. The clock had gone three."

"Did you stay tea there?"

"In course, sir, I did. Broom, he was out, and she was at home by herself a-rinsing out some things. But she soon put 'em away, and we sat down and had our teas together. We was a-talking about—"

"Never mind that," said Mr. Verner. "It was in coming home, I conclude, that you were met by young Broom."

Mrs. Roy raised her apron again, and passed it over her face but not a word spoke she in answer.

"What time did you leave Broom's cottage to return home?"

"I can't be sure, sir, what time it was. Broom's haven't got no clock; they tells the time by the sun."

"Was it dark?"

"Oh, yes, it was dark, sir, except for the moon. That had been up a good bit, for I hadn't hurried myself."

"And what did you see or hear, when you got near the Willow Pond?"

The question sent Mrs. Roy into fresh tears; into fresh tremor.

"I never saw nothing," she reiterated. "The last time I set eyes on Rachel Frost was at church on Sunday."

"What is the matter with you?" cried Mr. Verner, with asperity. "Do you mean to deny that anything had occurred to put you in a state of agitation, when you were met by young Broom?"

Mrs. Roy only moaned.

"Did you hear people quarrelling?" he persisted.

"I heard people quarrelling," she sobbed. "I did. But I never saw, no more than the dead, who it was."

"Whose voices were they?"

"How can I tell, sir? I wasn't near enough. There were two voices, a man's and a woman's; but I couldn't catch a single word, and it did not last long. I declare, if it were the last word I had to speak, that I heard no more of the quarrel than that, and I wasn't no nearer to it."

She really did seem to speak the truth, in spite of her shrinking fear, which was evident to all. Mr. Verner inquired, with incredulity equally evident, whether that was sufficient to put her into the state of tremor spoken of by young Broom.

Mrs. Roy hung her head.

"I'm timid at quarrels, 'specially if it's at night," she faintly answered.

"And was it just the hearing of that quarrel that made you sink down on your knees, and clasp hold of a tree?" continued Mr. Verner. Upon which Mrs. Roy let fall her head on her hands, and sobbed piteously.

Robin Frost interrupted, sarcasm in his tone—"There's a tale going on, outside, that you saw a ghost, and it was that as frighted you," he said to her. "Perhaps, sir"—turning to Mr. Verner—"you'll ask her whose ghost it was."

This appeared to put the finishing touch to Mrs. Roy's discomfiture. Nothing could be made of her for a few minutes. Presently, her agitation somewhat subsided; she lifted her head, and spoke as with a desperate effort.

"It's true," she said. "I'll make a clean breast of it. I did see a ghost, and it was that as upset me so. It wasn't the quarrelling frighted me: I thought nothing of that."

"What do you mean by saying you saw a ghost?" sharply reproved Mr. Verner.

"It was a ghost, sir," she answered, apparently picking up a little courage, now the subject was fairly entered upon.

A pause ensued. Mr. Verner may have been at a loss what to say next. When deliberately assured by any timorous spirit that they have "seen a ghost," it is waste of time to enter an opposing argument.

"Where did you see the ghost?" he asked.

"I had stopped still, listening to the quarrelling, sir. But that soon came to an end, for I heard no more, and I went on a few steps, and then I stopped to listen again. Just as I turned my head towards the grove, where the quarrelling had seemed to be, I saw something a few paces from me that made my flesh creep. A tall, white thing it looked, whiter than the moonlight. I knew it could be nothing but a ghost, and my knees sunk down from under me, and I laid hold o' the trunk o' the tree."

"Perhaps it was a death's head and bones?" cried John Massingbird.

"Maybe, sir," she answered. "That, or something worse. It glided through the trees with its great eyes staring at me; and I felt ready to die."

"Was it a man's or a woman's ghost?" asked Mr. Bitterworth, a broad smile upon his face.

"Couldn't have been a woman's, sir; 'twas too tall," was the sobbing answer. "A great tall thing it looked, like a white shadder. I wonder I be alive!"

"So do I," irascibly cried Mr. Verner. "Which way was it going? Towards the village, or in this direction?"

"Not in either of 'em, sir. It glided right off at a angle amid the trees."

"And it was that—that folly, that put you into the state of tremor in which Broom found you?" said Mr. Verner. "It was nothing else?"

"I declare, before Heaven, that it was what I saw as put me into the fright young Broom found me in," she repeated earnestly.

"But if you were so silly as to be alarmed for the moment, why do you continue to show alarm still?"

"Because my husband says he'll shake me," she whimpered, after a long pause. "He never has no patience with ghosts."

"Serve you right," was the half-audible comment of Mr. Verner. "Is this all you know of the affair?" he continued, after a pause.

"It's all, sir," she sobbed. "And enough too. There's only one thing as I shall be for ever thankful for."

"What's that?" asked Mr. Verner.

"That my poor Luke was away afore this happened. He was fond of hankering after Rachel, and folks might have been for laying it on his shoulders; though, goodness knows, he'd not have hurt a hair of her head."

"At any rate, he is out of it," observed John Massingbird.

"Ay," she replied, in a sort of self-soliloquy, as she turned to leave the room, for Mr. Verner told her she was dismissed, "it'll be a corn o' comfort amid my peck o' troubles. I have fretted myself incessant since Luke left, a-thinking as I could never know comfort again; but perhaps it's all for the best now, as he should ha' went."

She curtsied, and the door was closed upon her. Her evidence left an unsatisfactory feeling behind it.

An impression had gone forth that Mrs. Roy could throw some light upon the obscurity; and, as it turned out, she had thrown none. The greater part of those present gave credence to what she said. All believed the "ghost" to have been pure imagination; knowing the woman's proneness to the marvellous, and her timid temperament. But, upon one or two there remained a strong conviction that Mrs. Roy had not told the whole truth; that she could have said a great deal more about the night's work, had she chosen to do so.

No other testimony was forthcoming. The cries and shouts of young Broom, when he saw the body in the water, had succeeded in arousing some men who slept at the distant brick-kilns; and the tidings soon spread, and crowds flocked up. These people were eager to pour into Mr. Verner's room now, and state all they knew, which was precisely the evidence not required; but of further testimony to the facts there was none.

"More may come out prior to the inquest; there's no knowing," observed Mr. Bitterworth, as the gentlemen stood in a group, before separating. "It is a very dreadful thing, demanding the most searching investigation. It is not likely she would throw herself in."

"A well-conducted girl like Rachel Frost throw herself wilfully into a pond to be drowned!" indignantly repeated Mr. Verner. "She would be one of the last to do it."

"And equally one of the last to be thrown in," said Dr. West. "Young women are not thrown into ponds without some cause; and I should think few ever gave less cause for maltreatment of any kind than she. It appears most strange to me with whom she could have been quarrelling—if indeed it was Rachel that was quarrelling."

"It is all strange together," cried Lionel Verner. "What took Rachel that way at all, by night time?"

"What indeed!" echoed Mr. Bitterworth. "Unless—"

"Unless what?" asked Mr. Verner; for Mr. Bitterworth had brought his words to a sudden standstill.

"Well, I was going to say, unless she had an appointment there. But that does not appear probable for Rachel Frost."

"It is barely possible, let alone probable," was the retort of Mr. Verner.

"But still, in a case like this, every circumstance must be looked at, every trifle weighed," resumed Mr. Bitterworth. "Does Rachel's own conduct appear to you to have been perfectly open? She has been indulging, it would seem, in some secret grief latterly; has been 'strange,' as one or two have expressed it. Then, again, she stated to her brother that she was going to stay at Duffs for a gossip, whereas the woman says she had evidently no intention of gossiping, and barely gave herself time to order the articles spoken of. Other witnesses observed her leave Duff's, and walk with a hasty step direct to the field road, and turn down it. All this does not sound quite clear to me."

"There was one thing that did not sound clear to me," broke in Lionel abruptly, "and that was Dinah Roy's evidence. The woman's half a fool; otherwise I should think she was purposely deceiving us."

"A pity but she could see a real ghost!" cried John Massingbird, looking inclined to laugh, "It might cure her for fancy ones. She's right in one thing, however; poor Luke might have got this clapped on his shoulders had he been here."

"Scarcely," dissented Dr. West. "Luke Roy is too inoffensive to harm any one, least of all a woman, and Rachel; and that the whole parish knows."

"There's no need to discuss Luke's name in the business," said Mr. Verner; "he is far enough away. Whoever the man may have been, it was not Luke," he emphatically added. "Luke would have been the one to succour Rachel, not to hurt her."

Not a soul present but felt that Mr. Verner spoke in strict accordance with the facts, known and presumptive. They must look in another quarter than Luke for Rachel's assailant.

Mr. Verner glanced at Mr. Bitterworth and Dr. West, then at the three young men before him.

"We are amongst friends," he observed, addressing the latter. "I would ask you, individually, whether it was one of you that the boy, Duff, spoke of as being in the lane?"

They positively disclaimed it, each one for himself. Each one mentioned that he had been elsewhere at the time, and where he had been.

"You see," said Mr. Verner, "the lane leads only to Verner's Pride."

"But by leaping a fence anywhere, or a gate, or breaking through a hedge, it may lead all over the country," observed Frederick Massingbird. "You forget that, sir."

"No, Frederick, I do not forget it. But unless a man had business at Verner's Pride, what should he go into the lane for? On emerging from the field on this side the Willow Pond, any one, not bound for Verner's Pride, would take the common path to the right hand, open to all; only in case of wanting to come here would he take the lane. You cannot suppose for a moment that I suspect any one of you has had a hand in this unhappy event; but it was right that I should be assured, from your own lips, that you were not the person spoken of by young Duff."

"It may have been a stranger to the neighbourhood, sir. In that case he would not know that the lane led only to Verner's Pride."

"True—so far. But what stranger would be likely to quarrel with Rachel?"

"Egad, if you come to that, sir, a stranger's more likely to pick a quarrel with her than one of us," rejoined John Massingbird.

"It was no stranger," said Mr. Verner, shaking his head. "We do not quarrel with strangers. Had any stranger accosted Rachel at night, in that lonely spot, with rude words, she would naturally have called out for help; which it is certain she did not do, or young Broom and Mrs. Roy must have heard her. Rely upon it, that man in the lane is the one we must look for."

"But where to look?" debated Frederick Massingbird.

"There it is! The inference would be that he was coming to Verner's Pride; being on its direct way and nearly close upon it. But, the only tall men (as the boy describes) at Verner's Pride, are you three and Bennet. Bennet was at home, therefore he is exempt; and you were scattered in different directions—Lionel at Mr. Bitterworth's, John at the Royal Oak—I wonder you like to make yourself familiar with those tap-rooms, John!—and Frederick coming in from Poynton's to his dinner."

"I don't think I had been in ten minutes when the alarm came," remarked Frederick.

"Well, it is involved in mystery at present," cried Mr. Bitterworth, shaking hands with them. "Let us hope that to-morrow will open more light upon it. Are you on the wing too, doctor? Then we'll go out together."

CHAPTER VII

THE REVELATION AT THE INQUEST

To say that Deerham was rudely disturbed from its equanimity; that petty animosities, whether concerning Mr. Roy and the Dawsons or other contending spirits, were lost sight of, hushed to rest in the absorbing calamity which had overtaken Rachel; to say that occupations were partially suspended, that there ensued a glorious interim of idleness, for the female portion of it—of conferences in gutters and collectings in houses; to say that Rachel was sincerely mourned, old Frost sympathised with, and the supposed assailant vigorously sought after, would be sufficient to indicate that public curiosity was excited to a high pitch; but all this was as nothing compared to the excitement that was to ensue upon the evidence given at the coroner's inquest.

In the absence of any certain data to go upon, Deerham had been content to take uncertain data, and to come to its own conclusions. Deerham assumed that Rachel, from some reasons which they could not fathom, had taken the lonely road home that night, had met with somebody or other with whom had ensued a quarrel and scuffle, and that, accidentally or by intent, she had been pushed into the pond, the coward decamping.

"Villainy enough! even if 'twas but an accident!" cried wrathful Deerham.

Villainy enough, beyond all doubt, had this been the extent. But, Deerham had to learn that the villainy had had a beginning previous to that.

The inquest had been summoned in due course. It sat two days after the accident. No evidence, tending to further elucidate the matter, was given, than had been elicited that first night before Mr. Verner; except the medical evidence. Dr. West and a surgeon from a neighbouring town, who had jointly made the post-mortem examination, testified that there was a cause for Rachel Frost's unevenness of spirits, spoken to by her father and by Mrs. Verner. She might possibly, they now thought, have thrown herself into the pool; induced to it by self-condemnation.

It electrified Deerham. It electrified Mr. Verner. It worse than electrified Matthew Frost and Robin. In the first impulse of the news, Mr. Verner declared that it could not be. But the medical men, with their impassive faces, calmly said that it was.

But, so far as the inquiry went, the medical testimony did not carry the matter any further. For, if the evidence tended to induce a suspicion that Rachel might have found life a burden, and so wished to end it, it only rendered stronger the suspicion against another. This supplied the very motive for that other's conduct which had been wanting, supposing he had indeed got rid of her by violence. It gave the clue to much which had before been dark. People could understand now why Rachel should hasten to keep a stealthy appointment; why quarrelling should be heard; in short, why poor Rachel should have been found in the pond. The jury returned an open verdict—"Found drowned; but how she got into the water, there is no precise evidence to show."

Robin Frost struggled out of the room as the crowd was dispersing. His eye was blazing, his cheek burning. Could Robin have laid his hand at that moment upon the right man, there would speedily have ensued another coroner's inquest. The earth was not wide enough for the two to live on it. Fortunately, Robin could not fix on any one, and say, Thou art the man! The knowledge was hidden from him. And yet, the very man may have been at the inquest, side by side with himself. Nay, he probably was.

Robin Frost cleared himself from the crowd. He gave vent to a groan of despair; he lifted his strong arms in impotency. Then he turned and sought Mr. Verner.

Mr. Verner was ill; could not be seen. Lionel came forward.

"Robin, I am truly sorry—truly grieved. We all are. But I know you will not care to-day to hear me say it."

"Sir, I wanted to see Mr. Verner," replied Robin. "I want to know if that inquest can be squashed." Don't laugh at him now, poor fellow. He meant quashed.

"The inquest quashed!" repeated Lionel. "Of course it cannot be. I don't know what you mean, Robin. It has been held, and it cannot be unheld."

"I should ha' said the verdict," explained Robin. "I'm beside myself to-day, Mr. Lionel. Can't Mr. Verner get it squashed? He knows the crowner."

"Neither Mr. Verner nor anybody else could do it, Robin. Why should you wish it done?"

"Because it as good as sets forth a lie," vehemently answered Robin Frost. "She never put herself into the water. Bad as things had turned out with her, poor dear, she never did that. Mr. Lionel, I ask you, sir, was she likely to do it?"

"I should have deemed it very unlikely," replied Lionel. "Until to-day," he added to his own thoughts.

"No, she never did! Was it the work of one to go and buy herself aprons, and tape, and cotton for sewing, who was on her way to fling herself into a pond, I'd ask the crowner?" he continued, his voice rising almost to a shriek in his emotion. "Them aprons be a proof that she didn't take her own life. Why didn't they bring it in Wilful Murder, and have the place scoured out to find him?"

"The verdict will make no difference to the finding him, Robin," returned Lionel Verner.

"I dun know that, sir. When a charge of wilful murder's out in a place, again' some one of the folks in it, the rest be all on the edge to find him; but 'Found drownded' is another thing. Have you any suspicion again' anybody, sir?"

He put the question sharply and abruptly, and Lionel Verner looked full in his face as he answered, "No, Robin."

"Well, good-afternoon, sir."

He turned away without another word. Lionel gazed after him with true sympathy. "He will never recover this blow," was Lionel Verner's mental comment.

But for this unfortunate occurrence, John Massingbird would have already departed from Verner's Pride. The great bane of the two Massingbirds was, that they had been brought up to be idle men. A sum of money had become theirs when Frederick came of age—which sum you will call large or small, as it may please you. It would be as a drop of water to the millionaire; it would be as a countless fortune to one in the depths of poverty: we estimate things by comparison. The sum was five thousand pounds each—Mrs. Massingbird, by her second marriage with Mr. Verner, having forfeited all right in it. With this sum the young Massingbirds appeared to think that they could live as gentlemen, and need not seek to add to it.

Thrown into the luxurious home of Verner's Pride—again we must speak by comparison: Verner's Pride was luxurious compared to the moderate home they had been reared in—John and Frederick Massingbird suffered that worst complaint of all complaints, indolence, to overtake them and become their master. John, careless, free, unsteady in many ways, set on to spend his portion as fast as he could; Frederick, more cold, more cautious, did not squander as his brother did, but he had managed to get rid of a considerable amount of his own share in unfortunate speculations. While losses do not affect our personal convenience they are scarcely felt. And so it was with the Massingbirds. Mr. Verner was an easy man in regard to money matters; he was also a man who was particularly sensitive to the feelings of other people, and he had never breathed a word to his wife about the inexpediency of her keeping her sons at home in idleness. He feared his motives might be misconstrued—that it might be thought he grudged the expense. He had spoken once or twice of the desirability of his step-sons pursuing some calling in life, and intimated that he should be ready to further their views by pecuniary help; but the advice was not taken. He offered to purchase a commission for one or both of them; he hinted that the bar afforded a stepping-stone to fame. No; John and Frederick Massingbird were conveniently deaf; they had grown addicted to field-sports, to a life of leisure, and they did not feel inclined to quit it for one of obligation or of labour. So they had stayed on at Verner's Pride in the enjoyment of their comfortable quarters, of the well-spread table, of their horses, their dogs. All these sources of expense were provided without any cost or concern of theirs, their own private expenditure alone coming out of their private purses. How it was with their clothes, they and Mrs. Verner best knew; Mr. Verner did not. Whether these were furnished at their own cost, or whether their mother allowed them to draw for such on her, or, indeed, whether they were scoring up long bills on account, Mr. Verner made it no concern of his to inquire.

John—who was naturally of a roving nature, and who, but for the desirable home he was allowed to call his, would probably have been all over the world before he was his present age, working in his shirt sleeves for bread one day, exalted to some transient luck the next—had latterly taken a fancy in his head to emigrate to Australia. Certain friends of his had gone out there a year or two previously, and were sending home flaming accounts of their success at the gold-fields. It excited in John Massingbird a strong wish to join them. Possibly other circumstances urged him to the step; for it was certain that his finances were not in so desirable a state as they might be. With John Massingbird to wish a thing was to do it; and almost before the plan was spoken of, even in his own family, he was ready to start. Frederick was in his confidence, Lionel partly so, and a hint to his mother was sufficient to induce her to preserve reticence on the subject. John Massingbird had his reasons for this. It was announced in the household that Mr. Massingbird was departing on a visit to town, the only one who was told the truth being Rachel Frost. Rachel was looked upon almost as one of themselves. Frederick Massingbird had also confided it to Sibylla West—but Frederick and Sibylla were on more confidential terms than was suspected by the world. John had made a confident on his own part, and that was of Luke Roy. Luke, despised by Rachel, whom he truly loved, clearly seeing there was no hope whatever that she would ever favour him, was eager to get away from Deerham—anywhere, so that he might forget her. John Massingbird knew this; he liked Luke, and he thought Luke might prove useful to him in the land to which he was emigrating, so he proposed to him to join in the scheme. Luke warmly embraced it. Old Roy, whom they were obliged to take into confidence, was won over to it. He furnished Luke with the needful funds, believing he should be repaid four-fold; for John Massingbird had contrived to imbue him with the firm conviction that gold was to be picked up for the stooping.

Only three days before the tragic event occurred to Rachel, Luke had been despatched to London by John Massingbird to put things in a train of preparation for the voyage. Luke said nothing abroad of his going, and the village only knew he was away by missing him.

"What's gone of Luke?" many asked of his father.

"Oh, he's off to London on some spree; he can tell ye about it when he gets back," was Roy's answer.

When he got back! John's departure was intended for the day following that one when you saw him packing his clothes, but the untimely end of Rachel had induced him to postpone it. Or, rather, the command of Mr. Verner—a command which John could not conveniently disobey had he wished. He had won over Mr. Verner to promise him a substantial sum, to "set him up," as he phrased it, in Australia; and that sum was not yet handed to him.

CHAPTER VIII

ROBIN'S VOW

The revelation at the inquest had affected Mr. Verner in no measured degree, greatly increasing, for the time, his bodily ailments. He gave orders to be denied to all callers; he could not bear the comments that would be made. An angry, feverish desire to find out who had played the traitor grew strong within him. Innocent, pretty, child-like Rachel! who was it that had set himself, in his wickedness, deliberately to destroy her? Mr. Verner now deemed it more than likely that she had been the author of her own death. It was of course impossible to tell: but he dwelt on that part of the tragedy less than on the other. The one injury was uncertain; the other was a fact.

What rendered it all the more obscure was the absence of any previous grounds of suspicion. Rachel had never been observed to be on terms of intimacy with any one. Luke Roy had been anxious to court her, as Verner's Pride knew; but Rachel had utterly repudiated the wish. Luke it was not. And who else was there?

The suspicions of Mr. Verner veered, almost against his will, towards those of his own household. Not to Lionel; he honestly believed Lionel to be too high-principled: but towards his step-sons. He had no particular cause to suspect either of them, unless the testimony of Mrs. Duff's son about the tall gentleman could furnish it; and it may be said that his suspicion strayed to them only from the total absence of any other quarter to fix it upon. Of the two, he could rather fix upon John, than Frederick. No scandal, touching Frederick, had ever reached his ears: plenty of it touching John. In fact, Mr. Verner was rather glad to help in shipping John off to some faraway place, for he considered him no credit to Verner's Pride, or benefit to the neighbourhood. Venial sins sat lightly on the conscience of John Massingbird.

But this was no venial sin, no case of passing scandal; and Mr. Verner declared to that gentleman that if he found him guilty, he would discard him from Verner's Pride without a shilling of help. John Massingbird protested, in the strongest terms, that he was innocent as Mr. Verner himself.

A trifling addition was destined to be brought to the suspicion already directed by Mr. Verner towards Verner's Pride. On the night of the inquest Mr. Verner had his dinner served in his study—the wing of a fowl, of which he ate about a fourth part. Mrs. Tynn attended on him: he liked her to do so when he was worse than usual. He was used to her, and he would talk to her when he would not to others. He spoke about what had happened, saying that he felt as if it would shorten his life. He would give anything, he added, half in self-soliloquy, to have the point cleared up of who it was young Duff had seen in the lane. Mrs. Tynn answered this, lowering her voice.

"It was one of our young gentlemen, sir; there's, no doubt of it. Dolly saw one of them come in."

"Dolly did!" echoed Mr. Verner.

Mrs. Tynn proceeded to explain. Dolly, the dairymaid at Verner's Pride, was ill-conducted enough (as Mrs. Tynn would tell her, for the fact did not give that ruling matron pleasure) to have a sweetheart. Worse still, Dolly was in the habit of stealing out to meet him when he left work, which was at eight o'clock. On the evening of the accident, Dolly, abandoning her dairy, and braving the wrath of Mrs. Tynn, should she be discovered, stole out to a sheltered spot in the rear of the house, the usual meeting-place. Scarcely was she ensconced here when the swain arrived; who, it may be remarked, en passant, filled the important post of waggoner to Mr. Bitterworth. The spot was close to the small green gate which led to the lane already spoken of; it led to that only; and, while he and Dolly were talking and making love, after their own rustic fashion, they saw Dan Duff come from the direction of the house, and pass through the gate, whistling. A short while subsequently the gate was heard to open again. Dolly looked out, and saw what she took to be one of the gentlemen come in, from the lane, walking very fast. Dolly looked but casually, the moonlight was obscured there, and she did not particularly notice which of them it was; whether Mr. Lionel, or either of Mrs. Verner's sons. But the impression received into her mind was that it was one of the three; and Dolly could not be persuaded out of that to this very day.

"Hush—sh—sh!" cried she to her sweetheart, "it's one o' the young masters."

The quick steps passed on: but whether they turned into the yard, or took the side path which would conduct round to the front entrance, or bore right across, and so went out into the public road, Dolly did not notice. Very shortly after this—time passes swiftly when people are courting, of which fact the Italians have a proverb—Dan Duff came bursting back again, calling, and crying, and telling the tidings of Rachel Frost. This was the substance of what Mrs. Tynn told Mr. Verner.

"Dolly said nothing of this before!" he exclaimed.

"Not she, sir. She didn't dare confess that she'd been off all that while from her dairy. She let drop a word, and I have got it out of her piecemeal. I have threatened her, sir, that if ever she mentions it again, I'll get her turned off."

"Why did you threaten her?" he hastily asked.

Mrs. Tynn dropped her voice. "I thought it might not be pleasant to have it talked of, sir. She thinks I'm only afraid of the neglect of work getting to the ears of Mrs. Verner."

This was the trifling addition. Not very much in itself, but it served to bear out the doubts Mr. Verner already entertained. Was it John or was it Frederick who had come in? Or was it—Lionel? There appeared to be no more certainty that it was one than another. Mr. Verner had minutely inquired into the proceedings of John and Frederick Massingbird that night, and he had come to the conclusion that both could have been in the lane at that particular hour. Frederick, previously to entering the house for his dinner, after he had left the veterinary surgeon's, Poynton; John, before he paid his visit to the Royal Oak. John appeared to have called in at several places, and his account was not particularly clear. Lionel, Mr. Verner had not thought it necessary to question. He sent for him as soon as his dinner-tray was cleared away: it was as well to be indisputably sure of him before fastening the charge on either of the others.

"Sit down, Lionel," said Mr. Verner. "I want to talk to you. Had you finished your dinner?"

"Quite, thank you. You look very ill to-night," Lionel added, as he drew a chair to the fire; and his tone insensibly became gentle, as he gazed on his uncle's pale face.

"How can I look otherwise? This trouble is worrying me to death. Lionel, I have discovered, beyond doubt, that it was one of you young men who was in the lane that night."

Lionel, who was then leaning over the fire, turned his head with a quick, surprised gesture towards Mr. Verner. The latter proceeded to tell Lionel the substance of the communication made to him by Mrs. Tynn. Lionel sat, bending forward, his elbow on his knee, and his fingers unconsciously running amidst the curls of his dark chestnut hair, as he listened to it. He did not interrupt the narrative, or speak at its conclusion.

"You see, Lionel, it appears certain to have been some one belonging to this house."

"Yes, sir. Unless Dolly was mistaken."

"Mistaken as to what?" sharply asked Mr. Verner, who, when he made up his own mind that a thing was so-and-so, could not bear to be opposed. "Mistaken that some one came in at the gate?"

"I do not see how she could be mistaken in that," replied Lionel. "I meant mistaken as to its being any one belonging to the house."

"Is it likely that any one would come in at that gate at night, unless they belonged to the house, or were coming to the house?" retorted Mr. Verner. "Would a stranger drop from the clouds to come in at it? Or was it Di Roy's 'ghost,' think you?" he sarcastically added.

Lionel did not answer. He vacantly ran his fingers through his hair, apparently in deep thought.

"I have abstained from asking you the explicit details of your movements on that evening," continued Mr. Verner, "but I must demand them of you now."

Lionel started up, his cheek on fire. "Sir," he uttered, with emotion, "you cannot suspect me of having had act or part in it! I declare, before Heaven, that Rachel was as sacred for me—"

"Softly, Lionel," interrupted Mr. Verner, "there's no cause for you to break your head against a wheel. It is not you whom I suspect—thank God! But I wish to be sure of your movements—to be able to speak of them as sure, you understand—before I accuse another."

"I will willingly tell you every movement of mine that evening, so far as I remember," said Lionel, resuming his calmness. "I came home when dinner was half over. I had been detained—but you know all that," he broke off. "When you left the dining-room, I went on to the terrace, and sat there smoking a cigar. I should think I stayed there an hour, or more; and then I went upstairs, changed my coat, and proceeded to Mr. Bitterworth's."

"What took you to Mr. Bitterworth's that evening, Lionel?"

Lionel hesitated. He did not choose to say, "Because I knew Sibylla West was to be there;" but that would have been the true answer. "I had nothing particular to do with my evening, so I went up," he said aloud. "Mr. Bitterworth was out. Mrs. Bitterworth thought he had gone into Deerham."

"Yes. He was at Deerham when the alarm was given, and hastened on here. Sibylla West was there, was she not?"

"She was there," said Lionel. "She had promised to be home early; and, as no one came for her, I saw her home. It was after I left her that I heard what had occurred."

"About what time did you get there—I mean to Bitterworth's?" questioned Mr. Verner, who appeared to have his thoughts filled with other things at that moment than with Sibylla West.

"I cannot be sure," replied Lionel. "I think it must have been nine o'clock. I went into Deerham to the post-office, and then came back to Bitterworth's."

Mr. Verner mused.

"Lionel," he observed, "it is a curious thing, but there's not one of you but might have been the party to the quarrel that night; so, far as that your time cannot be positively accounted for by minutes and by hours. I mean, were the accusation brought publicly against you, you would, none of you, be able to prove a distinct alibi, as it seems to me. For instance, who is to prove that you did not, when you were sitting on the terrace, steal across to a rendezvous at the Willow Pond, or cut across to it when you were at the post-office at Deerham?"

"I certainly did not," said Lionel quietly, taking the remarks only as they were meant—for an illustration. "It might, sir, as you observe, be difficult to prove a decided alibi. But"—he rose and bent to Mr. Verner, with a bright smile, a clear, truthful eye—"I do not think you need one to believe me."

"No, Lionel, I do not. Is John Massingbird in the dining-room?"

"He was when I left it."

"Then go and send him to me."

John Massingbird was found and despatched to Mr. Verner, without any reluctance on his own part. He had been bestowing hard words upon Lionel for "taking up the time of the old man" just on the evening when he wanted to take it up himself. The truth was, John Massingbird was intending to depart the following morning, the Fates and Mr. Verner permitting him.

Their interview was a long one. Two hours, full, had they been closeted together when Robin Frost made his appearance again at Verner's Pride, and craved once more an interview with Mr. Verner. "If it was only for a minute—only for a minute!" he implored.

Remembering the overwhelming sorrow which had fallen on the man, Lionel did not like again to deny him without first asking Mr. Verner. He went himself to the study.

"Come in," called out Mr. Verner, in answer to the knock.

He was sitting in his chair as usual; John Massingbird was standing up, his elbow on the mantle-piece. That their conversation must have been of an exciting nature was evident, and Lionel could not help noticing the signs. John Massingbird had a scarlet streak on his sallow cheek, never seen there above once or twice in his life, and then caused by deep emotion. Mr. Verner, on his part, looked livid. Robin Frost might come in.

Lionel called him, and he came in with Frederick Massingbird.

The man could hardly speak for agitation. He believed the verdict could not be set aside, he said; others had told him so besides Mr. Lionel. He had come to ask if Mr. Verner would offer a reward.

"A reward!" repeated Mr. Verner mechanically, with the air of a man whose mind is far away.

"If you'd please to offer it, sir, I'd work the flesh off my bones to pay it back again," he urged. "I'll live upon a crust myself, and I'll keep my home upon a crust, but what I'll get it up. If there's a reward pasted up, sir, we might come upon the villain."

Mr. Verner appeared, then, to awake to the question before him, and to awake to it in terrible excitement.

"He'll never be found, Robin—the villain will never be found, so long as you and I and the world shall last!"

They looked at him in consternation—Lionel, Frederick Massingbird, and Robin Frost. Mr. Verner recollected himself, and calmed his spirit down.

"I mean, Robin," he more quietly said, "that a reward will be useless. The villain has been too cunning, rely upon it, to—to—leave his traces behind him."

"It might be tried, sir," respectfully urged Robin. "I'd work—"

"You can come up to-morrow, Robin, and I'll talk with you," interrupted Mr. Verner. "I am too ill—too much upset to-night. Come at any hour you please, after twelve, and I will see you."

"I'll come, sir. I've registered a vow afore my old father," went on Robin, lifting his right arm, "and I register it again afore you, sir—afore our future master, Mr. Lionel—that I'll never leave a stone unturned by night nor by day, that I'll make it my first and foremost business in life to find that man. And when I've found him—let him be who he will—either him or me shall die. So help me—"

"Be still, Robin!" passionately interposed Mr. Verner, in a voice that startled the man. "Vows are bad things. I have found them so."

"It was registered afore, sir," significantly answered Robin, as he turned away. "I'll be up here to-morrow."

The morrow brought forth two departures from Verner's Pride. John Massingbird started for London in pursuit of his journey, Mr. Verner having behaved to him liberally. And Lionel Verner was summoned in hot haste to Paris, where his brother had just met with an accident, and was supposed to be lying between life and death.

CHAPTER IX

MR VERNER'S ESTRANGEMENT

The former chapters may be looked upon somewhat in the light of an introduction to what is to follow. It was necessary to relate the events recorded in them, but we must take a leap of not far short of two years from the date of their occurrence.

John Massingbird and his attendant, Luke Roy, had arrived safely at Melbourne in due course. Luke had written home one letter to his mother, and there his correspondence ended; but John Massingbird wrote frequently, both to Mrs. Verner and to his brother Frederick. John, according to his own account, appeared to be getting on all one way. The money he took out had served him well. He had made good use of it, and was accumulating a fortune rapidly. Such was his statement; but whether implicit reliance might be placed upon it was a question. Gay John was apt to deceive himself; was given to look on the bright side, and to imbue things with a tinge of couleur de rose; when, for less sanguine eyes, the tinge would have shone out decidedly yellow. The time went on, and his last account told of a "glorious nugget" he had picked up at the diggings. "Almost as big as his head," a "fortune in itself," ran some of the phrases in his letters; and his intention was to go down himself to Melbourne and "realise the thousands" for it. His letter to Frederick was especially full of this; and he strongly recommended his brother to come out and pick up nuggets on his own score. Frederick Massingbird appeared very much inclined to take the hint.

"Were I only sure it was all gospel, I'd go to-morrow," observed Frederick Massingbird to Lionel Verner, one day that the discussion of the contents of John's letter had been renewed, a month or two subsequent to its arrival. "A year's luck, such as this, and a man might come home a millionaire. I wish I knew whether to put entire faith in it."

"Why should John deceive you?" asked Lionel.

"He'd not deceive me wilfully. He has no cause to deceive me. The question is, is he deceived himself? Remember what grand schemes he would now and then become wild upon here, saying and thinking he had found the philosopher's stone. And how would they turn out? This may be one of the same calibre. I wonder we did not hear again by the last month's mail."

"There's a mail due now."

"I know there is," said Frederick. "Should it bring news to confirm this, I shall go out to him."

"The worst is, those diggings appear to be all a lottery," remarked Lionel. "Where one gets his pockets lined, another starves. Nay, ten—fifty—more, for all we know, starve for the one lucky one. I should not, myself, feel inclined to risk the journey to them."

"You! It's not likely you would," was the reply of Frederick Massingbird. "Everybody was not born heir to Verner's Pride."

Lionel laughed pleasantly. They were pacing the terrace in the sunshine of a winter's afternoon, a crisp, cold, bright day in January. At that moment Tynn came out of the house and approached them.

"My master is up, sir, and would like the paper read to him," said he, addressing Frederick Massingbird.

"Oh, bother, I can't stop now," broke from that gentleman involuntarily. "Tynn, you need not say that you found me here. I have an appointment, and I must hasten to keep it."

Lionel Verner looked at his watch.

"I can spare half an hour," he observed to himself; and he proceeded to Mr. Verner's room.

The old study that you have seen before. And there sat Mr. Verner in the same arm-chair, cushioned and padded more than it had used to be. What a change there was in him! Shrunken, wasted, drawn: surely there would be no place very long in this world for Mr. Verner.

He was leaning forward in his chair, his back bowed, his hands resting on his stick, which was stretched out before him. He lifted his head when Lionel entered, and an expression, partly of displeasure, partly of pain, passed over his countenance.

"Where's Frederick?"

"Frederick has an appointment out, sir. I will read to you."

"I thought you were going down to your mother's," rejoined Mr. Verner, his accent not softening in the least.

"I need not go for this half hour yet," replied Lionel, taking up the Times, which lay on a table near Mr. Verner. "Have you looked at the headings of the news, sir; or shall I go over them for you, and then you can tell me what you wish read?"

"I don't want anything read by you," said Mr. Verner. "Put the paper down."

Lionel did not immediately obey. A shade of mortification had crossed his face.

"Do you hear me, Lionel? Put the paper down. You know how it fidgets me to hear those papers ruffled, when I am not in a mood for reading."

Lionel rose, and stood before Mr. Verner. "Uncle, I wish you would let me do something for you. Better send me out of the house altogether, than treat me with this estrangement. Will it be of any use my asking you, for the hundredth time, what I did to displease you?"

"I tell you I don't want the paper read," said Mr. Verner. "And if you'd leave me alone I should be glad. Perhaps I shall get a wink of sleep. All night, all night, and my eyes were never closed! It's time I was gone."

The concluding sentences were spoken as in soliloquy; not to Lionel. Lionel, who knew his uncle's every mood, quitted the room. As he closed the door, a heavy groan, born of displeasure mingled with pain, as the greeting look had been, was sent after him by Mr. Verner. Very emphatically did it express his state of feeling with regard to Lionel; and Lionel felt it keenly.

Lionel Verner had remained in Paris six months, when summoned thither by the accident to his brother. The accident need not have detained him half that period of time; but the seductions of the gay French capital had charms for Lionel. From the very hour that he set foot in Verner's Pride on his return, he found that Mr. Verner's behaviour had altered to him. He showed bitter, angry estrangement, and Lionel could only conceive one cause for it—his long sojourn abroad. Fifteen or sixteen months had now elapsed since his return, and the estrangement had not lessened. In vain Lionel sought an explanation. Mr. Verner would not enter upon it. In fact, so far as direct words went, Mr. Verner had not expressed much of his displeasure; he left it to his manner. That said enough. He had never dropped the slightest allusion as to its cause. When Lionel asked an explanation, he neither accorded nor denied it, but would put him off evasively; as he might have put off a child who asked a troublesome question. You have now seen him do so once again.

After the rebuff, Lionel was crossing the hall when he suddenly halted, as if a thought struck him, and he turned back to the study. If ever a man's attitude bespoke utter grief and prostration, Mr. Verner's did, as Lionel opened the door. His head and hands had fallen, and his stick had dropped upon the carpet. He started out of his reverie at the appearance of Lionel, and made an effort to recover his stick. Lionel hastened to pick it up for him.

"I have been thinking, sir, that it might be well for Decima to go in the carriage to the station, to receive Miss Tempest. Shall I order it?"

"Order anything you like; order all Verner's Pride—what does it matter? Better for some of us, perhaps, that it had never existed."

Hastily, abruptly, carelessly was the answer given. There was no mistaking that Mr. Verner was nearly beside himself with mental pain.

Lionel went round to the stables, to give the order he had suggested. One great feature in the character of Lionel Verner was its complete absence of assumption. Courteously refined in mind and feelings, he could not have presumed. Others, in his position, might have deemed they were but exercising a right. Though the presumptive heir to Verner's Pride, living in it, brought up as such, he would not, you see, even send out its master's unused carriage, without that master's sanction. In little things as in great, Lionel Verner could but be a thorough gentleman: to be otherwise he must have changed his nature.

"Wigham, will you take the close carriage to Deerham Court. It is wanted for Miss Verner."

"Very well, sir." But Wigham, who had been coachman in the family nearly as many years as Lionel had been in the world, wondered much, for all his prompt reply. He scarcely ever remembered a Verner's Pride carriage to have been ordered for Miss Verner.

Lionel passed into the high road from Verner's Pride, and, turning to the left, commenced his walk to Deerham. There were no roadside houses for a little way, but they soon began, by ones, by twos, until at last they grew into a consecutive street. These houses were mostly very poor; small shops, beer-houses, labourers' cottages; but a turning to the right in the midst of the village led to a part where the houses were of a superior character, several gentlemen living there. It was a new road, called Belvedere Road; the first house in it being inhabited by Dr. West.

Lionel cast a glance across at that house as he passed down the long street. At least, as much as he could see of it, looking obliquely. His glance was not rewarded. Very frequently pretty Sibylla would be at the windows, or her vain sister Amilly. Though, if vanity is to be brought in, I don't know where it would be found in an equal degree, as it was in Sibylla West. The windows appeared to be untenanted, and Lionel withdrew his eyes and passed straightly on his way. On his left hand was situated the shop of Mrs. Duff; its prints, its silk neckerchiefs, and its ribbons displayed in three parts of its bow-window. The fourth part was devoted to more ignominious articles, huddled indiscriminately into a corner. Children's Dutch dolls and black-lead, penny tale-books and square pink packets of cocoa, bottles of ink and india-rubber balls, side combs and papers of stationery, scented soap and Circassian cream (home made), tape, needles, pins, starch, bandoline, lavender-water, baking-powder, iron skewers, and a host of other articles too numerous to notice. Nothing came amiss to Mrs. Duff. She patronised everything she thought she could turn a penny by.

"Your servant, sir," said she, dropping a curtsy as Lionel came up; for Mrs. Duff was standing at the door.

He merely nodded to her, and went on. Whether it was the sight of the woman or of some lavender prints hanging in her window, certain it was, that the image of poor Rachel Frost came vividly into the mind of Lionel. Nothing had been heard, nothing found, to clear up the mystery of that past night.

CHAPTER X

LADY VERNER

At the extremity of the village, lying a little back from it, was a moderate-sized, red brick house, standing in the midst of lands, and called Deerham Court. It had once been an extensive farm; but the present tenant, Lionel's mother, rented the house, but only very little of the land. The land was let to a neighbouring farmer. Nearly a mile beyond—you could see its towers and its chimneys from the Court—rose the stately old mansion, called Deerham Hall, Deerham Court, and a great deal of the land and property on that side of the village, belonged to Sir Rufus Hautley, a proud, unsociable man. He lived at the Hall; and his only son, between whom and himself it was conjectured there existed some estrangement, had purchased into an Indian regiment, where he was now serving.

Lionel Verner passed the village, branched off to the right, and entered the great iron gates which enclosed the courtyard of Deerham Court. A very unpretending entrance admitted him into a spacious hall, the hall being the largest and best part of the house. Those great iron gates and the hall would have done honour to a large mansion; and they gave an appearance of pretension to Deerham Court which it did not deserve.

Lionel opened a door on the left, and entered a small ante-room. This led him into the only really good room the house contained. It was elegantly furnished and fitted up, and its two large windows looked towards the open country, and to Deerham Hall. Seated by the fire, in a rich violet dress, a costly white lace cap shading her delicate face, that must have been so beautiful, indeed, that was beautiful still, was a lady of middle age. Her seat was low—one of those chairs we are pleased to call, commonly and irreverently, a prie-dieu. Its back was carved in arabesque foliage, and its seat was of rich violet velvet. On a small inlaid table, whose carvings were as beautiful, and its top inlaid with mosaic-work, lay a dainty handkerchief of lace, a bottle of smelling-salts, and a book turned with its face downwards, all close at the lady's elbow. She was sitting in idleness just then—she always did sit in idleness—her face bent on the fire, her small hands, cased in white gloves, lying motionless on her lap—ay, a beautiful face once, though it had grown habitually peevish and discontented now. She turned her head when the door opened, and a flush of bloom rose to her cheeks when she saw Lionel.

He went up and kissed her. He loved her much. She loved him, too, better than she loved anything in life; and she drew a chair close to her, and he sat down, bending towards her. There was not much likeness between them, the mother and the son; both were very good-looking, but not alike.

"You see, mother mine, I am not late, as you prophesied I should be," said he, with one of his sweetest smiles.

"You would have been, Lionel, but for my warning. I'm sure I wish—I wish she was not coming! She must remember the old days in India, and will perceive the difference."

"She will scarcely remember India, when you were there. She is only a child yet, isn't she?"

"You know nothing about it, Lionel," was the querulous answer. "Whether she remembers or not, will she expect to see me in such a house, in such a position as this? It is at these seasons, when people are coming here, who know what I have been and ought to be, that I feel all the humiliation of my poverty. Lucy Tempest is nineteen."

Lionel Verner knew that it was of no use to argue with his mother, when she began upon that most unsatisfactory topic, her position; which included what she called her "poverty" and her "wrongs." Though, in truth, not a day passed but she broke out upon it.

"Lionel," she suddenly said.

He had been glancing over the pages of the book—a new work on India. He laid it down as he had found it, and turned to her.

"What shall you allow me when you come into Verner's Pride?"

"Whatever you shall wish, mother. You shall name the sum, not I. And if you name too modest a one," he added laughingly, "I shall double it. But Verner's Pride must be your home then, as well as mine."

"Never!" was the emphatic answer. "What! to be turned out of it again by the advent of a young wife? No, never, Lionel."

Lionel laughed—constrainedly this time.

"I may not be bringing home a young wife for this many and many a year to come."

"If you never brought one, I would not make my home at Verner's Pride," she resumed, in the same impulsive voice. "Live in the house by favour, that ought to have been mine by right? You would not be my true son to ask me, Lionel. Catherine, is that you?" she called out, as the movements of some one were heard in the ante-room.

A woman-servant put in her head.

"My lady?"

"Tell Miss Verner that Mr. Lionel is here?"

"Miss Verner knows it, my lady," was the woman's reply. "She bade me ask you, sir," addressing Lionel, "if you'd please to step out to her."

"Is she getting ready, Catherine?" asked Lady Verner.

"I think not, my lady."

"Go to her, Lionel, and ask her if she knows the time. A pretty thing if you arrive at the station after the train is in!"

Lionel quitted the room. Outside in the hall stood Catherine, waiting for him.

"Miss Verner has met with a little accident and hurt her foot, sir," she whispered. "She can't walk."

"Not walk!" exclaimed Lionel. "Where is she?"

"She is in the store-room, sir; where it happened."

Lionel went to the store-room, a small boarded room at the back of the hall. A young lady sat there; a very pretty white foot in a wash-hand basin of warm water, and a shoe and stocking lying; near, as if hastily thrown off.

"Why, Decima! what is this?"

"Why, Decima! what is this?"

She lifted her face. A face whose features were of the highest order of beauty, regular as if chiselled from marble, and little less colourless. But for the large, earnest, dark-blue eyes, so full of expression, it might have been accused of coldness. In sleep, or in perfect repose, when the eyelids were bent, it looked strangely cold and pure. Her dark hair was braided; and she wore a dress something the same in colour as Lady Verner's.

"Lionel, what shall I do? And to-day of all days! I shall be obliged to tell mamma; I cannot walk a step."

"What is the injury? How did you meet with it?"

"I got on a chair. I was looking for some old Indian ornaments that I know are in that high cupboard, wishing to put them in Miss Tempest's room, and somehow the chair tilted with me, and I fell upon my foot. It is only a sprain; but I cannot walk."

"How do you know it is only a sprain, Decima? I shall send West to you."

"Thank you all the same, Lionel, but, if you please, I don't like Dr. West well enough to have him," was Miss Verner's answer. "See! I don't think I can walk."

She took her foot out of the basin, and attempted to try. But for Lionel she would have fallen; and her naturally pale face became paler from the pain.

"And you say you will not have Dr. West!" he cried, gently putting her into the chair again. "You must allow me to judge for you, Decima."

"Then, Lionel, I'll have Jan—if I must have any one. I have more faith in him," she added, lifting her large blue eyes, "than in Dr. West."

"Let it be Jan, then, Decima. Send one of the servants for him at once. What is to be done about Miss Tempest?"

"You must go alone. Unless you can persuade mamma out. Lionel, you will tell mamma about this. She must be told."

As Lionel crossed the hall on his return, the door was being opened; the Verner's Pride carriage had just driven up. Lady Verner had seen it from the window of the ante-room, and her eyes spoke her displeasure.

"Lionel, what brings that here?"

"I told them to bring it for Decima. I thought you would prefer that Miss Tempest should be met with that rather than with a hired one."

"Miss Tempest will know soon enough that I am too poor to keep a carriage," said Lady Verner. "Decima may use it if she pleases. I would not."

"My dear mother, Decima will not be able to use it. She cannot go to the station. She has hurt her foot."

"How did she do that?"

"She was on a chair in the store-room, looking in the cupboard. She—"

"Of course; that's just like Decima!" crossly responded Lady Verner. "She is everlastingly at something or other, doing half the work of a servant about the house."

Lionel made no reply. He knew that, but for Decima, the house would be less comfortable than it was for Lady Verner; and that what Decima did, she did in love.

"Will you go to the station?" he inquired.

"I! In this cold wind! How can you ask me, Lionel? I should get my face chapped irretrievably. If Decima cannot go, you must go alone."

"But how shall I know Miss Tempest?"

"You must find her out," said Lady Verner. "Her mother was as tall as a giantess; perhaps she is the same. Is Decima much hurt?"

"She thinks it is only a sprain. We have sent for Jan."

"For Jan! Much good he will do!" returned Lady Verner, in so contemptuous a tone as to prove she had no very exalted opinion of Mr. "Jan's" abilities.

Lionel went out to the carriage, and stepped in. The footman did not shut the door. "And Miss Verner, sir?"

"Miss Verner is not coming. The railway station. Tell Wigham to drive fast, or I shall be late."

"My lady wouldn't let Miss Decima come out in it," thought Wigham to himself, as he drove on.

CHAPTER XI

LUCY TEMPEST

The words of my lady, "as tall as a giantess," unconsciously influenced the imagination of Lionel Verner. The train was steaming into the station at one end as his carriage stopped at the other. Lionel leaped from it, and mingled with the bustle of the platform.

Not very much bustle, either; and it would have been less, but that Deerham Station was the nearest approach, as yet, by rail, to Heartburg, a town of some note about four miles distant. Not a single tall lady got out of the train. Not a lady at all that Lionel could see. There were two fat women, tearing about after their luggage, both habited in men's drab greatcoats, or what looked like them; and there was one very young lady, who stood back in apparent perplexity, gazing at the scene of confusion around her.

"She cannot be Miss Tempest," deliberated Lionel. "If she is, my mother must have mistaken her age; she looks but a child. No harm in asking her, at any rate."

He went up to the young lady. A very pleasant-looking girl, fair, with a peach bloom upon her cheeks, dark brown hair and eyes, soft and brown and luminous. Those eyes were wandering to all parts of the platform, some anxiety in their expression.

Lionel raised his hat.

"I beg your pardon. Have I the honour of addressing Miss Tempest?"

"Oh, yes, that is my name," she answered, looking up at him, the peach bloom deepening to a glow of satisfaction, and the soft eyes lighting with a glad smile. "Have you come to meet me?"

"I have. I come from my mother, Lady Verner."

"I am so glad," she rejoined, with a frank sincerity of manner perfectly refreshing in these modern days of artificial young ladyism. "I was beginning to think nobody had come; and then what could I have done?"

"My sister would have come with me to receive you, but for an accident which occurred to her just before it was time to start. Have you any luggage?"

"There's the great box I brought from India, and a hair-trunk, and my school-box. It is all in the van."

"Allow me to take you out of this crowd, and it shall be seen to," said Lionel, bending to offer his arm.

She took it, and turned with him; but stopped ere more than a step or two had been taken.

"We are going wrong. The luggage is up that way."

"I am taking you to the carriage. The luggage will be all right."

He was placing her in it, when she suddenly drew back and surveyed it.

"What a pretty carriage!" she exclaimed.

Many said the same of the Verner's Pride equipages. The colour of the panels was of that rich shade of blue called ultra-marine, with white linings and hammer-cloths, while a good deal of silver shone on the harness of the horses. The servants' livery was white and silver, their small-clothes blue.

Lionel handed her in.

"Have we far to go?" she asked.

"Not five minutes' drive."

He closed the door, gave the footman directions about the luggage, took his own seat by the coachman, and the carriage started. Lady Verner came to the door of the Court to receive Miss Tempest.

In the old Indian days of Lady Verner, she and Sir Lionel had been close and intimate friends of Colonel and Mrs. Tempest. Subsequently Mrs. Tempest had died, and their only daughter had been sent to a clergyman's family in England for her education—a very superior place, where six pupils only were taken. But she was of an age to leave it now, and Colonel Tempest, who contemplated soon being home, had craved of Lady Verner to receive her in the interim.

"Lionel," said his mother to him, "you must stop here for the rest of the day, and help to entertain her."

"Why, what can I do towards it?" responded Lionel.

"You can do something. You can talk. They have got Decima into her room, and I must be up and down with her. I don't like leaving Lucy alone the first day she is in the house; she will take a prejudice against it. One blessed thing, she seams quite simple—not exacting."

"Anything but exacting, I should say," replied Lionel. "I will stay for an hour or two, if you like, mother, but I must be home to dinner."

Lady Verner need not have troubled herself about "entertaining" Lucy Tempest. She was accustomed to entertain herself; and as to any ceremony or homage being paid to her, she would not have understood it, and might have felt embarrassed had it been tendered. She had not been used to anything of the sort. Could Lady Verner have seen her then, at the very moment she was talking to Lionel, her fears might have been relieved. Lucy Tempest had found her way to Decima's room, and had taken up her position in a very undignified fashion at that young lady's feet, her soft, candid brown eyes fixed upwards on Decima's face, and her tongue busy with reminiscences of India. After some time spent in this manner, she was scared away by the entrance of a gentleman whom Decima called "Jan." Upon which she proceeded to the chamber she had been shown to as hers, to dress; a process which did not appear to be very elaborate by the time it took, and then she went downstairs to find Lady Verner.

Lady Verner had not quitted Lionel. She had been grumbling and complaining all that time. It was half the pastime of Lady Verner's life to grumble in the ears of Lionel and Decima. Bitterly mortified had Lady Verner been when she found, upon her arrival from India, that Stephen Verner, her late husband's younger brother, had succeeded to Verner's Pride, to the exclusion of herself and of Lionel; and bitterly mortified she remained. Whether it had been by some strange oversight on the part of old Mr. Verner, or whether it had been intentional, no provision whatever had been left by him to Lady Verner and to her children. Stephen Verner would have remedied this. On the arrival of Lady Verner, he had proposed to pay over to her yearly a certain sum out of the estate; but Lady Verner, smarting under disappointment, under the sense of injustice, had flung his proposal back to him. Never, so long as he lived, she told Stephen Verner, passionately, would she be obliged to him for the worth of a sixpence in money or in kind. And she had kept her word.

Her income was sadly limited. It was very little besides her pay as a colonel's widow; and to Lady Verner it seemed less than it really was, for her habits were somewhat expensive. She took this house, Deerham Court, then to be let without the land, had it embellished inside and out—which cost her more than she could afford, and had since resided in it. She would not have rented under Mr. Verner had he paid her to do it. She declined all intercourse with Verner's Pride; had never put her foot over its threshold. Decima went once in a way; but she, never. If she and Stephen Verner met abroad, she was coldly civil to him; she was indifferently haughty to Mrs. Verner, whom she despised in her heart for not being a lady. With all her deficiencies, Lady Verner was essentially a gentlewoman—not to be one amounted in her eyes to little less than a sin. No wonder that she, with her delicate beauty of person, her quiet refinements of dress, shrank within herself as she swept past poor Mrs. Verner, with her great person, her crimson face, and her flaunting colours! No wonder that Lady Verner, smarting under her wrongs, passed half her time giving utterance to them; or that her smooth face was acquiring premature wrinkles of discontent. Lionel had a somewhat difficult course to steer between Verner's Pride and Deerham Court, so as to keep friends with both.

Lucy Tempest appeared at the door. She stood there hesitating, after the manner of a timid school-girl. They turned round and saw her.

"If you please, may I come in?"

Lady Verner could have sighed over the deficiency of "style," or confidence, whichever you may like to term it. Lionel laughed, as he crossed the room to throw the door wider by way of welcome.

She wore a light shot pink dress of peculiar material, a sort of cashmere, very fine and soft. Looking at it one way it was pink, the other, mauve; the general shade of it was beautiful. Lady Verner could have sighed again: if the wearer was deficient in style, so also was the dress. A low body and short sleeves, perfectly simple, a narrow bit of white lace alone edging them: nothing on her neck, nothing on her arms, no gloves. A child of seven might have been so dressed. Lady Verner looked at her, her brow knit, and various thoughts running through her brain. She began to fear that Miss Tempest would require so much training as would give her trouble.

Lucy saw the look, and deemed that her attire was wrong.

"Ought I to have put on my best things—my new silk?" she asked.

My new silk! My best things! Lady Verner was almost at a loss for an answer. "You have not an extensive wardrobe, possibly, my dear?"

"Not very," replied Lucy. "This was my best dress, until I had my new silk. Mrs. Cust told me to put this one on for dinner to-day, and she said if Lady—if you and Miss Verner dressed very much, I could change it for the silk to-morrow. It is a beautiful dress," Lucy added, looking ingenuously at Lady Verner, "a pearl gray. Then I have my morning dresses, and then my white for dancing. Mrs. Cust said that anything you found deficient in my wardrobe it would be better for you to supply, than for her, as you would be the best judge of what I should require."

"Mrs. Cust does not pay much attention to dress, probably," observed Lady Verner coldly. "She is a clergyman's wife. It is sad taste when people neglect themselves, whatever may be the duties of their station."

"But Mrs. Cust does not neglect herself," spoke up Lucy, a surprised look upon her face. "She is always dressed nicely—not fine, you know. Mrs. Cust says that the lower classes have become so fine nowadays, that nearly the only way you may know a lady, until she speaks, is by her quiet simplicity."

"My dear, Mrs. Cust should say elegant simplicity," corrected Lady Verner. "She ought to know. She is of good family."

Lucy humbly acquiesced. She feared she herself must be too "quiet" to satisfy Lady Verner. "Will you be so kind, then, as to get me what you please?" she asked.

"My daughter will see to all these things, Lucy," replied Lady Verner. "She is not young like you, and she is remarkably steady, and experienced."

"She does not look old," said Lucy, in her open candour. "She is very pretty."

"She is turned five-and-twenty. Have you seen her?"

"I have been with her ever so long. We were talking about India. She remembers my dear mamma; and, do you know"—her bright expression fading to sadness—"I can scarcely remember her! I should have stayed with Decima—may I call her Decima?" broke off Lucy, with a faltering tongue, as if she had done wrong.

"Certainly you may."

"I should have stayed with Decima until now, talking about mamma, but a gentleman came in."

"A gentleman?" echoed Lady Verner.

"Yes. Some one tall and very thin. Decima called him Jan. After that, I went to my room again. I could not find it at first," she added, with a pleasant little laugh. "I looked into two; but neither was mine, for I could not see the boxes. Then I changed my dress, and came down."

"I hope you had my maid to assist you," quickly remarked Lady Verner.

"Some one assisted me. When I had my dress on, ready to be fastened, I looked out to see if I could find any one to do it, and I did. A servant was at the end of the corridor, by the window."

"But, my dear Miss Tempest, you should have rung," exclaimed Lady Verner, half petrified at the young lady's unformed manners, and privately speculating upon the sins Mrs. Cust must have to answer for. "Was it Thérèse?"

"I don't know," replied Lucy. "She was rather old, and had a broom in her hand."

"Old Catherine, I declare! Sweeping and dusting as usual! She might have soiled your dress."

"She wiped her hands on her apron," said Lucy simply. "She had a nice face: I liked it."

"I beg, my dear, that in future you will ring for Thérèse," emphatically returned Lady Verner, in her discomposure. "She understands that she is to wait upon you. Thérèse is my maid, and her time is not half occupied. Decima exacts very little of her. But take care that you do not allow her to lapse into English when with you. It is what she is apt to do unless checked. You speak French, of course?" added Lady Verner, the thought crossing her that Mrs. Cust's educational training might have been as deficient on that point, as she deemed it had been on that of "style."

"I speak it quite well," replied Lucy; "as well, or nearly as well, as a French girl. But I do not require anybody to wait on me," she continued. "There is never anything to do for me, but just to fasten these evening dresses that close behind. I am much obliged to you, all the same, for thinking of it, Lady Verner."

Lady Verner turned from the subject: it seemed to grow more and more unprofitable. "I shall go and hear what Jan says, if he is there," she remarked to Lionel.

"I wonder we did not see or hear him come in," was Lionel's answer.

"As if Jan could come into the house like a gentleman!" returned Lady Verner, with intense acrimony. "The back way is a step or two nearer, and therefore he patronises it."

She quitted the room as she spoke, and Lionel turned to Miss Tempest. He had been exceedingly amused and edified at the conversation between her and his mother; but while Lady Verner had been inclined to groan over it, he had rejoiced. That Lucy Tempest was thoroughly and genuinely unsophisticated; that she was of a nature too sincere and honest for her manners to be otherwise than of truthful simplicity, he was certain. A delightful child, he thought; one he could have taken to his heart and loved as a sister. Not with any other love: that was already given elsewhere by Lionel Verner.

The winter evening was drawing on, and little light was in the room, save that cast by the blaze of the fire. It flickered upon Lucy's face, as she stood near it. Lionel drew a chair towards her. "Will you not sit down, Miss Tempest?"

A formidable-looking chair, large and stately, as Lucy turned to look at it. Her eyes fell upon the low one which, earlier in the afternoon, had been occupied by Lady Verner. "May I sit in this one instead? I like it best."

"You 'may' sit in any chair that the room contains, or on an ottoman, or anywhere that you like," answered Lionel, considerably amused. "Perhaps you would prefer this?"

"This" was a very low seat indeed—in point of fact, Lady Verner's footstool. He had spoke in jest, but she waited for no second permission, drew it close to the fire, and sat down upon it. Lionel looked at her, his lips and eyes dancing.

"Possibly you would have preferred the rug?"

"Yes, I should," answered she frankly, "It is what we did at the rectory. Between the lights, on a winter's evening, we were allowed to do what we pleased for twenty minutes, and we used to sit down on the rug before the fire, and talk."

"Mrs. Cust, also?" asked Lionel.

"Not Mrs. Cust; you are laughing at me. If she came in, and saw us, she would say we were too old to sit there, and should be better on chairs. But we liked the rug best."

"What had you used to talk of?"

"Of everything, I think. About the poor; Mr. Cust's poor, you know; and the village, and our studies, and—But I don't think I must tell you that," broke off Lucy, laughing merrily at her own thoughts.

"Yes, you may," said Lionel.

"It was about that poor old German teacher of ours. We used to play her such tricks, and it was round the fire that we planned them. But she is very good," added Lucy, becoming serious, and lifting her eyes to Lionel, as if to bespeak his sympathy for the German teacher.

"Is she?"

"She was always patient and kind. The first time Lady Verner lets me go to a shop, I mean to buy her a warm winter cloak. Hers is so thin. Do you think I could get her one for two pounds?"

"I don't know at all," smiled Lionel. "A greatcoat for me would cost more than two pounds."

"I have two sovereigns left of my pocket-money, besides some silver. I hope it will buy a cloak. It is Lady Verner who will have the management of my money, is it not, now that I have left Mrs. Cust's?"

"I believe so."

"I wonder how much she will allow me for myself?" continued Lucy, gazing up at Lionel with a serious expression of inquiry, as if the question were a momentous one.

"I think cloaks for old teachers ought to be apart," cried Lionel. "They should not come out of your pocket-money."

"Oh, but I like them to do so. I wish I had a home of my own!—as I shall have when papa returns to Europe. I should invite her to me for the holidays, and give her nice dinners always, and buy her some nice clothes, and send her back with her poor old heart happy."

"Invite whom?"

"Fraulein Müller. Her father was a gentleman of good position, and he somehow lost his inheritance. When he died she found it out—there was not a shilling for her, instead of a fortune, as she had always thought. She was over forty then, and she had to come to England and begin teaching for a living. She is fifty now, and nearly all she gets she sends to Heidelberg to her poor sick sister. I wonder how much good warm cloaks do cost?"

Lucy Tempest spoke the last sentence dreamily. She was evidently debating the question in her own mind. Her small white hands rested inertly upon her pink dress, her clear face with its delicate bloom was still, her eyes were bent on the fire. But that Lionel's heart was elsewhere, it might have gone out, there and then, to that young girl and her attractive simplicity.

"What a pretty child you are!" involuntarily broke from him.

Up came those eyes to him, soft and luminous, their only expression being surprise, not a shade of vanity.

"I am not a child; why do you call me one? But Mrs. Cust said you would all be taking me for a child, until you knew me."

"How old are you?" asked Lionel.

"I was eighteen last September."

"Eighteen!" involuntarily repeated Lionel.

"Yes; eighteen. We had a party on my birthday. Mr. Cust gave me a most beautifully bound copy of Thomas à Kempis; he had had it bound on purpose. I will show it to you when my books are unpacked. You would like Mr. Cust, if you knew him. He is an old man now, and he has white hair. He is twenty years older than Mrs. Cust; but he is so good!"

"How is it," almost vehemently broke forth Lionel, "that you are so different from others?"

"I don't know. Am I different?"

"So different—so different—that—that—"

"What is the matter with me?" she asked timidly, almost humbly, the delicate colour in her cheeks deepening to crimson.

"There is nothing the matter with you," he answered, smiling; "a good thing if there were as little the matter with everybody else. Do you know that I never saw any one whom I liked so much at first sight as I like you, although you appear to me only as a child? If I call here often I shall grow to love you almost as much as I love my sister Decima."

"Is not this your home?"

"No. My home is at Verner's Pride."

CHAPTER XII

DR WEST'S HOME

The house of Dr. West was already lighted up. Gas at its front door, gas at its surgery door, gas inside its windows: no habitation in the place was ever so extensively lighted as Dr. West's. The house was inclosed with iron railings, and on its side—detached—was the surgery. A very low place, this surgery; you had to go down a step or two, and then plunge into a low door. In the time of the last tenant it had been used as a garden tool-house. It was a tolerably large room, and had a tolerably small window, which was in front, the door being on the side, opposite the side entrance of the house. A counter ran along the room at the back, and a table, covered with miscellaneous articles, stood on the right. Shelves were ranged completely round the room aloft, and a pair of steps, used for getting down the jars and bottles, rested in a corner. There was another room behind it, used exclusively by Dr. West.

Seated on the counter, pounding desperately away at something in a mortar, as if his life depended on it, was a peculiar-looking gentleman in shirt-sleeves. Very tall, very thin, with legs and arms that bore the appearance of being too long even for his tall body, great hands and feet, a thin face dark and red, a thin aquiline nose, black hair, and black prominent eyes that seemed to be always on the stare—there sat he, his legs dangling and his fingers working. A straightforward, honest, simple fellow looked he, all utility and practicalness—if there is such a word. One, plain in all ways.

It was Janus Verner—never, in the memory of anybody, called anything but "Jan"—second and youngest son of Lady Verner, brother to Lionel. He brother to courtly Lionel, to stately Decima, son to refined Lady Verner? He certainly was; though Lady Verner in her cross moods would declare that Jan must have been changed at nurse—an assertion without foundation, since he had been nursed at home under her own eye. Never in his life had he been called anything but Jan; address him as Janus, or as Mr. Verner, and it may be questioned if Jan would have answered to it. People called him "droll," and, if to be of plain, unvarnished manners and speech is to be droll, Jan decidedly was so. Some said Jan was a fool, some said he was a bear. Lady Verner did not accord him any great amount of favour herself. She had tried to make Jan what she called a gentleman, to beat into him suavity, gracefulness, tact, gloss of speech and bearing, something between a Lord Chesterfield and a Sir Roger de Coverley; and she had been obliged lo give it up as a hopeless job. Jan was utterly irreclaimable: Nature had made him plain and straightforward, and so he remained. But there was many a one that the world would bow down to as a model, whose intrinsic worth was poor compared to unoffending Jan's. Lady Verner would tell Jan he was undutiful. Jan tried to be as dutiful to her as ever he could; but he could not change his ungainly person, his awkward manner. As well try to wash a negro white.

Lady Verner had proposed that Jan should go into the army, Jan (plain spoken as a boy, as he was still) had responded that he'd rather not go out to be shot at. What was she to do with him? Lady Verner peevishly asked. She had no money, she lamented, and she would take care Jan was not helped by Mr. Verner. To make him a barrister, or a clergyman, or a Member of Parliament (it was what Lady Verner said), would cost vast sums of money; a commission could be obtained for him gratis, in consideration of his father's services.

"Make me an apothecary," said Jan.

"An apothecary!" echoed Lady Verner, aghast. "That's not a gentleman's calling."

Jan opened his great eyes. Had he taken a liking for carpentering, he would have deemed it gentlemanly enough for him.

"What has put an apothecary's business into your head?" cried Lady Verner.

"I should like the pounding," replied Jan.

"The pounding!" reiterated Lady Verner, in astonishment.

"I should like it altogether," concluded Jan, "I wish you'd let me go apprentice to Dr. West."

Jan held to his liking. In due course of time he was apprenticed to Dr. West, and pounded away to his heart's content. Thence he went to London to walk the hospitals, afterwards completing his studies in

Paris. It was at the latter period that the accident happened to Jan that called Lionel to Paris. Jan was knocked down by a carriage in the street, his leg broken, and he was otherwise injured. Time and skill cured him. Time and perseverance completed his studies, and Jan became a licensed surgeon of no mean skill. He returned to Deerham, and was engaged as assistant to Dr. West. No very ambitious position, but "it's good enough for Jan," slightingly said Lady Verner. Jan probably thought the same, or he would have sought a better. He was four-and-twenty now. Dr. West was a general practitioner, holding an Edinburgh degree only. There was plenty to do in Deerham and its neighbourhood, what with the rich and what with the poor. Dr. West chiefly attended the rich himself and left Jan to take care of the poor. It was all one to Jan.

Jan sat on the counter in the surgery, pounding and pounding. He had just come in from his visit to Deerham Court, summoned thither by the slight accident to his sister Decima. Leaning his two elbows on the counter, his pale, puffy cheeks on his hands, and intently watching Jan with his light eyes, was a young gentleman rising fifteen, with an apron tied round his waist. This was Master Cheese; an apprentice, as Jan once had been. In point of fact, the pounding now was Master Cheese's proper work, but he was fat and lazy, and as sure as Jan came into the surgery, so sure would young Cheese begin to grunt and groan, and vow that his arms were "knocked off" with the work. Jan, in his indolent manner—and in motion and manner Jan appeared intensely indolent, as if there was no hurry in him; he would bring his words, too, out indolently—would lift the pounding machine aloft, sit himself down on the counter, and complete the work.

"I say," said young Cheese, watching the progress of the pestle with satisfaction, "Dame Dawson has been here."

"What did she want?" asked Jan.

"Bad in her inside, she says. I gave her three good doses of jalap."

"Jalap!" echoed Jan. "Well, it won't do her much harm. She won't take 'em; she'll throw 'em away."

"Law, Jan!" For, in the private familiarity of the surgery, young Cheese was thus accustomed unceremoniously to address his master—as Jan was. And Jan allowed it with composure.

"She'll throw 'em away," repeated Jan. "There's not a worse lot for physic in all the parish than Dame Dawson. I know her of old. She thought she'd get peppermint and cordials ordered for her—an excuse for running up a score at the public-house. Where's the doctor?"

"He's off somewhere. I saw one of the Bitterworth grooms come to the house this afternoon, so perhaps something's wrong there. I say, Jan, there'll be a stunning pie for supper!"

"Have you seen it?"

"Haven't I! I went into the kitchen when she was making it. It has got a hare inside it, and forcemeat balls."

"Who?" asked Jan—alluding to the maker.

"Miss Deb," replied young Cheese. "It's sure to be something extra good, for her to go and make it. If she doesn't help me to a rare good serving, sha'n't I look black at her!"

"It mayn't be for supper," debated Jan.

"Cook said it was. I asked her. She thought somebody was coming. I say, Jan, if you miss any of the castor oil, don't go and say I drank it."

Jan lifted his eyes to a shelf opposite, where various glass bottles stood. Among them was the one containing the castor oil. "Who has been at it?" he asked.

"Miss Amilly. She came and filled that great fat glass pot of hers, with her own hands; and she made me drop in some essence of cloves to scent it. Won't her hair smell of it to-night!"

"They'll make castor oil scarce, if they go at it like that," said Jan indifferently.

"They use about a quart a month; I know they do; the three of 'em together," exclaimed young Cheese, as vehemently as if the loss of the castor oil was personal. "How their nightcaps must be greased!"

"Sibylla doesn't use it," said Jan.

"Doesn't she, though!" retorted young Cheese, with acrimony. "She uses many things on the sly that she pretends not to use. She's as vain as a peacock. Did you hear about—"

Master Cheese cut his question short. Coming in at the surgery door was Lionel Verner.

"Well, Jan! What about Decima? After waiting ages at the Court for you to come downstairs and report, I found you were gone."

"It's a twist," said Jan. "It will be all right in a few days. How's Uncle Stephen to-day?"

"Just the same. Are the young ladies in?"

"Go and see," said Jan. "I know nothing about 'em."

"Yes, they are in, sir," interrupted Master Cheese. "They have not been out all the afternoon, for a wonder."

Lionel left the surgery, stepped round to the front door, and entered the house.

In a square, moderate-sized drawing-room, with tasty things scattered about it to catch the eye, stood a young lady, figuring off before the chimney-glass. Had you looked critically into the substantial furniture you might have found it old and poor; of a different class from the valuable furniture at Verner's Pride; widely different from the light, elegant furniture at Lady Verner's. But, what with white antimacassars, many coloured mats on which reposed pretty ornaments, glasses and vases of flowers, and other trifles, the room looked well enough for anything. In like manner, had you, with the same critical eye, scanned the young lady, you would have found that of real beauty she possessed little. A small, pretty doll's face with blue eyes and gold-coloured ringlets; a round face, betraying nothing very great, or good, or intellectual; only something fascinating and pretty. Her chief beauty lay in her complexion; by candle-light it was radiantly lovely, a pure red and white, looking like wax-work. A pretty, graceful girl she looked; and, what with her fascinations of person, of dress, and of manner, all of which she perfectly well knew how to display, she had contrived to lead more than one heart captive, and to hold it in fast chains.

The light of the gas chandelier shone on her now; on her blue gauzy dress, set off with ribbons, on her sleepy, blue eyes, on her rose-coloured cheeks. She was figuring off before the glass, I say, twisting her ringlets round her fingers, and putting them in various positions to try the effect; her employment, her look, her manner, all indicating the very essence of vanity. The opening of the door caused her to turn her head, and she shook her ringlets into their proper place, and dropped her hands by her side, at the entrance of Lionel Verner.

"Oh, Lionel! is it you?" said she, with as much composure as if she had not been caught gazing at herself. "I was looking at this," pointing to an inverted tumbler on the mantel-piece. "Is it not strange that we should see a moth at this cold season? Amilly found it this afternoon on the geraniums."

Lionel Verner advanced and bent his head to look at the pretty speckled moth reposing so still on its green leaf. Did he see through the artifice? Did he suspect that the young lady had been admiring her own pretty face, and not the moth? Not he. Lionel's whole heart had long ago been given to that vain butterfly, Sibylla West, who was gay and fluttering, and really of little more use in life than the moth. How was it that he had suffered himself to love her? Suffered! Love plays strange tricks, and it has fooled many a man as it was fooling Lionel Verner.

And what of Sibylla? Sibylla did not love him. The two ruling passions of her heart were vanity and ambition. To be sometime the mistress of Verner's Pride was a very vista of desire, and therefore she encouraged Lionel. She did not encourage him very much; she was rather in the habit of playing fast and loose with him; but that only served to rivet tighter the links of his chain. All the love—such as it was!—that Sibylla West was capable of giving, was in possession of Frederick Massingbird. Strange tricks again! It was scarcely credible that one should fall in love with him by the side of attractive Lionel; but so it had been. Sibylla loved Frederick Massingbird for himself, she liked Lionel because he was the heir to Verner's Pride, and she had managed to keep both her slaves.

Lionel had never spoken of his love. He knew that his marriage with Sibylla West would be so utterly distasteful to Mr. Verner, that he was content to wait. He knew that Sibylla could not mistake him—could not mistake what his feelings were; and he believed that she also was content to wait until he should be his own master and at liberty to ask for her. When that time should come, what did she intend to do with Frederick Massingbird, who made no secret to her that he loved her and expected to make her his wife? Sibylla did not know; she did not much care; she was of a careless nature, and allowed the future to take its chance.

The only person who had penetrated to the secret of her love for Frederick Massingbird was her father, Dr. West.

"Don't be a simpleton, child, and bind yourself with your eyes bandaged," he abruptly and laconically said to her one day. "When Verner's Pride falls in, then marry whoever is its master."

"Lionel will be its master for certain, will he not?" she answered, startled out of the words.

"We don't know who will be its master," was Dr. West's rejoinder. "Don't play the simpleton, I say, Sibylla, by entangling yourself with your cousin Fred."

Dr. West was one who possessed an eye to the main chance; and, had Lionel Verner been, beyond contingency, "certain" of Verner's Pride, there is little doubt but he would have brought him to book at once, by demanding his intentions with regard to Sibylla. There were very few persons in Deerham but deemed Lionel as indisputably certain of Verner's Pride as though he were already in possession of it. Dr. West was probably an unusually cautious man.

"It is singular," observed Lionel, looking at the moth. "The day has been sunshiny, but far too cold to call these moths into life. At least, according to my belief; but I am not learned in entomology."

"Ento—, what a hard word!" cried Sibylla, in her prettily affected manner. "I should never find out how to spell it."

Lionel smiled. His deep love was shining out of his eyes as he looked down upon her. He loved her powerfully, deeply, passionately; to him she was as a very angel, and he believed her to be as pure-souled, honest-hearted, and single-minded.

"Where did my aunt go to-day?" inquired Sibylla, alluding to Mrs. Verner.

"She did not go anywhere that I am aware of," he answered.

"I saw the carriage out this afternoon."

"It was going to the station for Miss Tempest."

"Oh! she's come, then? Have you seen her? What sort of a demoiselle does she seem?"

"The sweetest child!—she looks little more than a child!" cried Lionel impulsively.

"A child, is she? I had an idea she was grown up. Have any of you at Verner's Pride heard from John?"

"No."

"But the mail's in, is it not? How strange that he does not write!"

"He may be coming home with his gold," said Lionel.

They were interrupted. First of all came in the tea-things—for at Dr. West's the dinner-hour was early—and, next, two young ladies, bearing a great resemblance to each other. It would give them dire offence not to call them young. They were really not very much past thirty, but they were of that class of women who age rapidly; their hair was sadly thin, some of their teeth had gone, and they had thin, flushed faces and large twisted noses; but their blue eyes had a good-natured look in them. Little in person, rather bending forward as they walked, and dressing youthfully, they yet looked older than they really were. Their light brown hair was worn in short, straggling ringlets in front, and twisted up with a comb behind. Once upon a time that hair was long and tolerably thick, but it had gradually and spitefully worn down to what it was now. The Misses West were proud of it still, however; as may be inferred by the disappearance of the castor oil. A short while back, somebody had recommended to them castor oil as the best specific for bringing on departed hair. They were inoffensive in mind and manners, rather simple, somewhat affected and very vain, quarrelling with no person under the sun, except Sibylla. Sibylla was the plague of their lives. So many years younger than they, they had petted her and indulged her as a child, until at length the child became their mistress. Sibylla was rude and ungrateful, would cast scornful words at them and call them "old maids," with other reproachful terms. There was open warfare between them; but in their hearts they loved Sibylla still. They had been named respectively Deborah and Amilly. The latter name had been intended for Amélie; but by some mistake of the parents or of the clergyman, none of them French scholars, Amilly, the child was christened and registered. It remained a joke against Amilly to this day.

"Sibylla!" exclaimed Deborah, somewhat in surprise, as she shook hands with Lionel, "I thought you had gone to Verner's Pride."

"Nobody came for me. It got dusk, and I did not care to go alone," replied Sibylla.

"Did you think of going to Verner's Pride this evening, Sibylla?" asked Lionel. "Let me take you now. We shall be just in time for dinner. I'll bring you back this evening."

"I don't know," hesitated Sibylla. The truth was, she had expected Frederick Massingbird to come for her. "I—think—I'll—go," she slowly said, apparently balancing some point in her mind.

"If you do go, you should make haste and put your things on," suggested Miss Amilly. And Sibylla acquiesced, and left the room.

"Has Mr. Jan been told that the tea's ready, I wonder?" cried Miss Deborah.

Mr. Jan apparently had been told, for he entered as she was speaking: and Master Cheese—his apron off and his hair brushed—with him. Master Cheese cast an inquisitive look at the tea-table, hoping he should see something tempting upon it; eating good things forming the pleasantest portion of that young gentleman's life.

"Take this seat, Mr. Jan," said Miss Amilly, drawing a chair forward next her own. "Master Cheese, have the kindness to move a little round: Mr. Jan can't see the fire if you sit there."

"I don't want to see it," said literal Jan. "I'm not cold." And Master Cheese took the opportunity which the words gave to remain where he was. He liked to sit in warmth with his back to the fire.

"I cannot think where papa is," said Miss Deborah. "Mr. Lionel, is it of any use asking you to take a cup of tea?"

"Thank you, I am going home to dinner," replied Lionel. "Dr. West is coming in now," he added, perceiving that gentleman's approach from the window.

"Miss Amilly," asked Jan, "have you been at the castor oil?"

Poor Miss Amilly turned all the colours of the rainbow; if she had one weakness, it was upon the subject of her diminishing locks. While Cheese, going red also, administered to Jan sundry kicks under the table, as an intimation that he should have kept counsel. "I—took—just a little drop, Mr. Jan," said she. "What's the dose, if you please? Is it one tea-spoonful or two?"

"It depends upon the age," said Jan, "if you mean taken inwardly. For you it would be—I say, Cheese, what are you kicking at?"

Cheese began to stammer something about the leg of the table; but the subject was interrupted by the entrance of Sibylla. Lionel wished them good-evening, and went out with her. Outside the room door they encountered Dr. West.

"Where are you going, Sybilla?" he asked, almost sharply, as his glance fell upon his daughter and Lionel.

"To Verner's Pride."

"Go and take your things off. You cannot go to Verner's Pride this evening."

"But, papa, why?" inquired Sibylla, feeling that she should like to turn restive.

"I have my reasons for it. You will know them later. Now go and take your things off without another word."

Sibylla dared not openly dispute the will of her father, neither would she essay to do it before Lionel Verner. She turned somewhat unwillingly towards the staircase, and Dr. West opened the drawing-room door, signing to Lionel to wait.

"Deborah, I am going out. Don't keep the tea. Mr. Jan, should I be summoned anywhere, you'll attend for me, I don't know when I shall be home."

"All right," called out Jan. And Dr. West went out with Lionel Verner.

"I am going to Verner's Pride," he said, taking Lionel's arm as soon as they were in the street. "There's news come from Australia. John Massingbird's dead."

The announcement was made so abruptly, with so little circumlocution or preparation, that Lionel Verner failed at the first moment to take in the full meaning of the words. "John Massingbird dead?" he mechanically asked.

"He is dead. It's a sad tale. He had the gold about him, a great quantity of it, bringing it down to Melbourne, and he was killed on the road; murdered for the sake of the gold."

"How have you heard it?" demanded Lionel.

"I met Roy just now," replied Dr. West. "He stopped me, saying he had heard from his son by this afternoon's post; that there was bad news in the letter, and he supposed he must go to Verner's Pride, and break it to them. He gave me the letter, and I undertook to carry the tidings to Mrs. Verner."

"It is awfully sudden," said Lionel, "By the mail, two months ago, he wrote himself to us, in the highest spirits. And now—dead!"

"Life, over there, is not worth a month's purchase just now," remarked Dr. West; and Lionel could but note that had he been discussing the death of a total stranger, instead of a nephew, he could only have spoken in the same indifferent, matter-of-fact tone. "By all accounts, society is in a strange state there," he continued; "ruffians lying in wait ever for prey. The men have been taken, and the gold found upon them, Luke writes."

"That's good, so far," said Lionel.

When they reached Verner's Pride, they found that a letter was waiting for Frederick Massingbird, who had not been home since he left the house early in the afternoon. The superscription was in the same handwriting as the letter Dr. West had brought—Luke Roy's. There could be no doubt that it was only a confirmation of the tidings.

Mrs. Verner was in the drawing-room alone, Tynn said, ready to go in to dinner, and rather cross that Mr. Lionel should keep her waiting for it.

"Who will break it to her—you or I?" asked Dr. West of Lionel.

"I think it should be you. You are her brother."

Broken to her it was, in the best mode they were able. It proved a severe shock. Mrs. Verner had loved John, her eldest born, above every earthly thing. He was wild, random, improvident, had given her incessant trouble as a child and as a man; and so, mother fashion, she loved him best.

CHAPTER XIII

A CONTEMPLATED VOYAGE

Frederick Massingbird sat perched on the gate of a ploughed field, softly whistling. His brain was busy, and he was holding counsel with himself, under the gray February skies. Three weeks had gone by since the tidings arrived of the death of his brother, and Frederick was deliberating whether he should, or should not, go out. His own letter from Luke Roy had been in substance the same as that which Luke had written to his father. It was neither more explanatory, nor less so. Luke Roy was not a first-hand at epistolary correspondence. John had been attacked and killed for the sake of his gold, and the attackers and the gold had been taken hold of by the law; so far it said, and no further. That the notion should occur to Frederick to go out to Melbourne, and lay claim to the gold and any other property left by John, was only natural. He had been making up his mind to do so for the last three weeks; and perhaps the vision of essaying a little business in the gold-fields on his own account, urged him on. But he had not fully made up his mind yet. The journey was a long and hazardous one; and—he did not care to leave Sibylla.

"To be, or not to be?" soliloquised he, from his seat on the gate, as he plucked thin branches off from the bare winter hedge, and scattered them. "Old stepfather's wiry yet, he may last an age, and this is getting a horrid, humdrum life. I wonder what he'll leave me, when he does go off? Mother said one day she thought it wouldn't be more than five hundred pounds. She doesn't know; he does not tell her about his private affairs—never has told her. Five hundred pounds! If he left me a paltry sum such as that, I'd fling it in the heir's face—Master Lionel's."

He put a piece of the thorn into his mouth, bit it up, spat it out again, and went on with his soliloquy.

"I had better go. Why, if nothing to speak of does come to me from old Verner, this money of John's would be a perfect windfall. I must not lose the chance of it—and lose it I should, unless I go out and see after it. No, it would never do. I'll go. It's hard to say how much he has left, poor fellow. Thousands—if one may judge by his letters—besides this great nugget that they killed him for, the villains! Yes, I'll go—that's settled. And now, to try to get Sibylla. She'll accompany me fast enough. At least, I fancy she would. But there's that old West! I may have a battle over it with him."

He flung away what remained in his hand of the sticks, leaped off the gate, and bent his steps hastily in the direction of Deerham. Could he be going, there and then, to Dr. West's, to try his fate with Sibylla? Very probably. Frederick Massingbird liked to deliberate well when making up his mind to a step; but, that once done, he was wont to lose no time in carrying it out.

On this same afternoon, and just about the same hour, Lionel Verner was strolling through Deerham on his way to pay a visit to his mother. Close at the door he encountered Decima—well, now—and Miss Tempest, who were going out. None would have believed Lionel and Decima to be brother and sister, judging by their attire—he wore deep mourning, she had not a shred of mourning about her. Lady Verner, in her prejudice against Verner's Pride, had neither put on mourning herself for John Massingbird, nor allowed Decima to put it on. Lionel was turning with them; but Lady Verner, who had seen him from the window, sent a servant to desire him to come to her.

"Is it anything particular, mother?" he hastily inquired. "I am going with Decima and Lucy."

"It is so far particular, Lionel, that I wish you to stay with me, instead of going with them," answered Lady Verner. "I fancy you are getting rather fond of being with Lucy, and—and—in short, it won't do."

Lionel, in his excessive astonishment, could only stare at his mother.

"What do you mean?" he asked. "Lucy Tempest! What won't do?"

"You are beginning to pay Lucy Tempest particular attention," said Lady Verner, unscrewing the silver stopper of her essence-bottle, and applying some to her forehead. "I will not permit it, Lionel."

Lionel could not avoid laughing.

"What can have put such a thing in your head, mother, I am at a loss to conceive. Certainly nothing in my conduct has induced it. I have talked to Lucy as a child, more than as anything else; I have scarcely thought of her but as one—"

"Lucy is not a child," interrupted Lady Verner.

"In years I find she is not. When I first saw her at the railway-station, I thought she was a child, and the impression somehow remains upon my mind. Too often I talk to her as one. As to anything else—were I to marry to-morrow, it is not Lucy Tempest I should make my wife."

The first glad look that Lionel had seen on Lady Verner's face for many a day came over it then. In her own mind she had been weaving a pretty little romance for Lionel; and it was her dread, lest that romance should be interfered with, which had called up her fears, touching Lucy Tempest.

"My darling Lionel, you know where you might go and choose a wife," she said. "I have long wished that you would do it. Beauty, rank, wealth—you may win them for the asking."

A slightly self-conscious smile crossed the lips of Lionel.

"You are surely not going to introduce again that nonsense about Mary Elmsley!" he exclaimed. "I should never like her, never marry her, therefore—"

"Did you not allude to her when you spoke but now—that it was not Lucy Tempest you should make your wife?"

"No."

"To whom, then? Lionel, I must know it."

Lionel's cheek flushed scarlet. "I am not going to marry yet—I have no intention of it. Why should this conversation have arisen?"

The words seemed to arouse a sudden dread on the part of Lady Verner. "Lionel," she gasped in a low tone, "there is a dreadful fear coming over me. Not Lady Mary! Some one else! I remember Decima said one day that you appeared to care more for Sibylla West than for her, your sister. I have never thought of it from that hour to this. I paid no more attention to it than though she had said you cared for my maid Thérèse. You cannot care for Sibylla West!"

Lionel had high notions of duty as well as of honour, and he would not equivocate to his mother. "I do care very much for Sibylla West," he said in a low tone; "and, please God, I hope she will sometime be my wife. But, mother, this confidence is entirely between ourselves. I beg you not to speak of it; it must not be suffered to get abroad."

The one short sentence of avowal over, Lionel might as well have talked to the moon. Lady Verner heard him not. She was horrified. The Wests in her eyes were utterly despicable. Dr. West was tolerated as her doctor; but as nothing else. Her brave Lionel—standing there before her in all the pride of his strength and his beauty—he sacrifice himself to Sibylla West! Of the two, Thérèse might have been the less dreadful to the mind of Lady Verner.

A quarrel ensued. Stay—that is a wrong word. It was not a quarrel, for Lady Verner had all the talking, and Lionel would not respond angrily; he kept his lips pressed together lest he should. Never had Lady Verner been moved to make a like scene. She reproached, she sobbed, she entreated. And, in the midst of it, in walked Decima and Lucy Tempest.

Lady Verner for once forgot herself. She forgot that Lucy was a stranger; she forgot the request of Lionel for silence; and, upon Decima's asking what was amiss, she told all—that Lionel loved Sibylla West, and meant to marry her.

Decima was too shocked to speak. Lucy turned and looked at Lionel, a pleasant smile shining in her eyes. "She is very pretty; very, very pretty; I never saw any one prettier."

"Thank you, Lucy," he cordially said; and it was the first time he had called her Lucy.

Decima went up to her brother. "Lionel, must it be? I do not like her."

"Decima, I fear that you and my mother are both prejudiced," he somewhat haughtily answered. And there he stopped. In turning his eyes towards his mother as he spoke of her, he saw that she had fainted away.

Jan was sent for, in all haste. Dr. West was Lady Verner's medical adviser; but a feeling in Decima's heart at the moment prevented her summoning him. Jan arrived, on the run; the servant had told him she was not sure but her lady was dying.

Lady Verner had revived then; was better; and was re-entering upon the grievance which had so affected her. "What could it have been?" wondered Jan, who knew his mother was not subject to fainting fits.

"Ask your brother, there, what it was," resentfully spoke Lady Verner. "He told me he was going to marry Sibylla West."

"Law!" uttered Jan.

Lionel stood; haughty, impassive; his lips curling, his figure drawn to its full height. He would not reproach his mother by so much as a word, but the course she was taking, in thus proclaiming his affairs to the world, hurt him in no measured degree.

"I don't like her," said Jan. "Deborah and Amilly are not much, but I'd rather have the two, than Sibylla."

"Jan," said Lionel, suppressing his temper, "your opinion was not asked."

Jan sat down on the arm of the sofa, his great legs dangling. "Sibylla can't marry two," said he.

"Will you be quiet, Jan?" said Lionel. "You have no right to interfere. You shall not interfere."

"Gracious, Lionel, I don't want to interfere," returned Jan simply. "Sibylla's going to marry Fred Massingbird."

"Will you be quiet?" reiterated Lionel, his brow flushing scarlet.

"I'll be quiet," said Jan, with composure. "You can go and ask her for yourself. It has all been settled this afternoon; not ten minutes ago. Fred's going out to Australia, and Sibylla's going with him, and Deborah and Amilly are crying their eyes out, at the thought of parting with her."

Lady Verner looked up at Jan, an expression of eager hope on her face. She could have kissed him a thousand times. Lionel—Lionel took his hat and walked out.

Believing it? No. The temptation to chastise Jan was growing great, and he deemed it well to remove himself out of it. Jan was right, however.

Much to the surprise of Frederick Massingbird, very much to the surprise of Sibylla, Dr. West not only gave his consent to the marriage as soon as asked, but urged it on. If Fred must depart in a week, why, they could be married in a week, he said. Sibylla was thunderstruck: Miss Deborah and Miss Amilly gave vent to a few hysterical shrieks, and hinted about the wedding clothes and the outfit. That could be got together in a day, was the reply of Dr. West, and they were too much astonished to venture to say it could not.

"You told me to wait for Lionel Verner," whispered Sibylla, when she and her father were alone, as she stood before him, trembling. In her mind's eye she saw Verner's Pride slipping from her; and it gave her chagrin, in spite of her love for Fred Massingbird.

Dr. West leaned forward and whispered a few words in her ear. She started violently, she coloured crimson. "Papa!"

"It is true," nodded the doctor.

As Lionel passed the house on his way from Deerham Court to Verner's Pride, he turned into it, led by a powerful impulse. He did not believe Jan, but the words had made him feel twitchings of uneasiness. Fred Massingbird had gone then, and the doctor was out. Lionel looked into the drawing-room, and there found the two elder Misses West, each dissolved in a copious shower of tears. So far, Jan's words were borne out. A sharp spasm shot across his heart.

"You are in grief," he said, advancing to them. "What is the cause?"

"The most dreadful voyage for her!" ejaculated Miss Deborah. "The ship may go to the bottom before it gets there."

"And not so much as time to think of proper things for her, let alone getting them!" sobbed Miss Amilly. "It's all a confused mass in my mind together—bonnets, and gowns, and veils, and wreaths, and trunks, and petticoats, and calico things for the voyage!"

Lionel felt his lips grow pale. They were too much engrossed to notice him; nevertheless, he covered his face with his hand as he stood by the mantel-piece. "Where is she going?" he quietly asked.

"To Melbourne, with Fred," said Miss Deborah. "Fred's going out to see about the money and gold that John left, and to realise it. They are not to stay: it will only be the voyage out and home. But if she should be taken ill out there, and die! Her sisters died, Mr. Lionel. Fred is her cousin, too. Better have married one not of kin."

They talked on. Lionel heard them not. After the revelation, that she was about to marry, all else seemed a chaos. But he was one who could control his feelings.

"I must be going," said he quietly, moving from his standing-place with calmness. "Good-day to you."

He shook hands with them both, amidst a great accession of sobs, and quitted the room. Running down the stairs at that moment, singing gaily a scrap of a merry song, came Sibylla, unconscious of his vicinity; indeed, of his presence in the house. She started when she saw him, and stopped in hesitation.

Lionel threw open the door of the empty dining-room, caught her arm and drew her into it—his bearing haughty, his gestures imperative. There they stood before each other, neither speaking for some moments. Lionel's very lips were livid; and her rich wax-work colour went and came, and her clear blue eyes fell under the stern gaze of his.

"Is this true, which I have been obliged to hear?" was his first question.

She knew that she had acted ill. She knew that Lionel Verner deserved to have a better part played by him. She had always looked up to him—all the Wests had—as one superior in birth, rank, and station to herself. Altogether, the moment brought to her a great amount of shame and confusion.

"Answer me one question; I demand it of you," exclaimed Lionel. "Have you ever mistaken my sentiments towards you in the least degree?"

"Have—I—I don't know," she faltered.

"No equivocation," burst Lionel. "Have you not known that I loved you? that I was only waiting my uncle's death to make you my wife?—Heaven forgive me that I should thus speak as though I had built upon it!"

Sibylla let fall some tears.

"Which have you loved?—all this while! Me?—or him?"

"Oh! don't speak to me like that," sobbed Sibylla. "He asked me to marry him, and—and—papa said yes."

"I ask you," said Lionel in a low voice, "which is it that you love?"

She did not answer. She stood before him the prettiest picture of distress imaginable; her hands clasped, her large blue eyes filled with tears, her shower of golden hair shading her burning cheeks.

"If you have been surprised or terrified into this engagement, loving him not, will you give him up for me?" tenderly whispered Lionel. "Not—you understand—if your love be his. In that case, I would not ask it. But, without reference to myself at all, I doubt—and I have my reasons for it—if Frederick Massingbird be worthy of you."

Was she wavering in her own mind? She stole a glance upward—at his tall, fine form, his attractive face, its lineaments showing out in that moment, all the pride of the Verners. A pride that mingled with love.

Lionel bent to her—

"Sibylla, if you love him I have no more to say; if you love me, avow it, as I will then avow my love, my intentions, in the face of day. Reflect before you speak. It is a solemn moment—a moment which holds alike my destiny and yours in its hands."

A rush of blood to her heart, a rush of moisture to her forehead; for Sibylla West was not wholly without feeling, and she knew, as Lionel said, that it was a decision fraught with grave destiny. But Frederick Massingbird was more to her than he was.

"I have given my promise. I cannot go from it," was her scarcely breathed answer.

"May your falsity never come home to you!" broke from Lionel, in the bitterness of his anguish. And he strode from the room without another word or look, and quitted the house.

CHAPTER XIV

THE NIGHT BEFORE THE WEDDING

Deerham could not believe the news. Verner's Pride could not believe it. Nobody believed it, save Lady Verner, and she was only too thankful to believe it and hug it. There was nothing surprising in Sibylla's marrying her cousin Fred, for many had shrewdly suspected that the favour between them was not altogether cousinly favour; but the surprise was given to the hasty marriage. Dr. West vouchsafed an explanation. Two of his daughters, aged respectively one year and two years younger than Amilly, had each died of consumption, as all Deerham knew. On attaining her twenty-fifth year, each one had shown rapid symptoms of the disease, and had lingered but a few weeks. Sibylla was only one-and-twenty yet; but Dr. West fancied he saw, or said he saw, grounds for fear. It was known of what value a sea-voyage was in these constitutions; hence his consent to the departure of Sibylla. Such was the explanation of Dr. West.

"I wonder whether the stated 'fear of consumption' has been called up by himself for the occasion?" was the thought that crossed the mind of Decima Verner. Decima did not believe in Dr. West.

Verner's Pride, like the rest, had been taken by surprise. Mrs. Verner received the news with equanimity. She had never given Fred a tithe of the love that John had had, and she did not seem much to care whether he married Sibylla, or whether he did not—whether he went out to Australia, or whether he stayed at home. Frederick told her of it in a very off-hand manner; but he took pains to bespeak the approbation of Mr. Verner.

"I hope my choice is pleasant to you, sir. That you will cordially sanction it."

"Whether it is pleasant to me or not, I have no right to say it shall not be," was the reply of Mr. Verner. "I have never interfered with you, or with your brother, since you became inmates of my house."

"Do you not like Sibylla, sir?"

"She is a pretty girl. I know nothing against her. I think you might have chosen worse."

Coldly, very coldly were the words delivered, and there was a strangely keen expression of anguish on Mr. Verner's face; but that was nothing unusual now. Frederick Massingbird was content to accept the words as a sanction of approval.

A few words—I don't mean angry ones—passed between him and Lionel on the night before the wedding. Lionel had not condescended to speak to Frederick Massingbird upon the subject at all; Sibylla had refused him for the other of her own free will; and there he let it rest. But the evening previous to the marriage day, Lionel appeared strangely troubled; indecisive, anxious, as if he were debating some question with himself. Suddenly he went straight up to Frederick Massingbird's chamber, who was deep in the business of packing, as his unfortunate brother John had been, not two short years before.

"I wish to speak to you," he began. "I have thought of doing so these several days past, but have hesitated, for you may dream that it is no business of mine. However, I cannot get it off my mind that it may be my duty; and I have come to do it."

Frederick Massingbird was half buried amid piles of things, but he turned round at this strange address and looked at Lionel.

"Is there nothing on your conscience that should prevent your marrying that girl?" gravely asked Lionel.

"Do you want her left for yourself?" was Fred's answer, after a prolonged stare.

Lionel flushed to his very temples. He controlled the hasty retort that rose to his tongue. "I came here not to speak in any one's interest but hers. Were she free as air this moment—were she to come to my feet and say, 'Let me be your wife,' I should tell her that the whole world was before her to choose from, save myself. She can never again be anything to me. No. I speak for her alone. She is marrying you in all confidence. Are you worthy of her?"

"What on earth do you mean?" cried Frederick Massingbird.

"If there be any sin upon your conscience that ought to prevent your taking her, or any confiding girl, to your heart, as wife, reflect whether you should ignore it. The consequences may come home later; and then what would be her position?"

"I have no sin upon my conscience, Poor John, perhaps, had plenty of it. I do not understand you, Lionel Verner."

"On your sacred word?"

"On my word, and honour, too."

"Then forgive me," was the ready reply of Lionel. And he held out his hand with frankness to Frederick Massingbird.

CHAPTER XV

A TROUBLED MIND

Just one fortnight from the very day that witnessed the sailing of Frederick Massingbird and his wife, Mr. Verner was taken alarmingly ill. Fred, in his soliloquy that afternoon, when you saw him upon the gate of the ploughed field,—"Old stepfather's wiry yet, and may last an age,"—had certainly not been assisted with the gift of prevision, for there was no doubt that Mr. Verner's time to die had now come.

Lionel had thrown his sorrow bravely from him, in outward appearance at any rate. What it might be doing for him inwardly, he alone could tell. These apparently calm, undemonstrative natures, that show a quiet exterior to the world, may have a fire consuming their heartstrings. He did not go near the wedding; but neither did he shut himself up indoors, as one indulging lamentation and grief. He pursued his occupations just as usual. He read to Mr. Verner, who allowed him to do so that day; he rode out; he saw people, friends and others whom it was necessary to see. He had the magnanimity to shake hands with the bride, and wish her joy.

It occurred in this way. Mrs. Verner declined to attend the ceremony. Since the news of John's death she had been ailing both in body and mind. But she desired Frederick to take Verner's Pride in his road when driving away with his bride, that she might say her last farewell to him and Sibylla, neither of whom she might ever see again. Oh, she'd see them again fast enough, was Fred's response; they should not be away more than a year. But he complied with her request, and brought Sibylla. About three o'clock in the afternoon, the ceremony and the breakfast over, the carriage, with its four horses, clattered on to the terrace, and Fred handed Sibylla out of it. Lionel was crossing the hall at the moment of their entrance; his horse had just been brought round for him. To say he was surprised at seeing them there would not be saying enough; he had known nothing of the intended call. They met face to face. Sibylla wore a sweeping dress of silk; a fine Indian shawl, the gift of Mrs. Verner, was folded round her, and her golden hair fell beneath her bonnet. Her eyes fell, also, before the gaze of Lionel.

Never had she looked more beautiful, more attractive; and Lionel felt it. But, had she been one for whom he had never cared, he could not have shown more courtly indifference. A moment given to the choking down of his emotion, to the stilling of his beating pulses, and he stood before her calmly self-possessed; holding out his hand, speaking in a low, clear tone.

"Allow me to offer you my good wishes for your welfare, Mrs. Massingbird."

"Thank you; thank you very much," replied Sibylla, dropping his hand, avoiding his eye, and going on to find Mrs. Verner.

"Good-bye, Lionel," said Frederick Massingbird. "You are going out, I see."

Lionel shook his hand cordially. Rival though he had proved to him, he did not blame Frederick Massingbird; he was too just to cast blame where it was not due.

"Fare you well, Frederick. I sincerely hope you will have a prosperous voyage; that you will come safely home again."

All this was over, and they had sailed; Dr. West having exacted a solemn promise from his son-in-law that they should leave for home again the very instant that John's property had been realised. And now, a fortnight after it, Mr. Verner was taken—as was believed—for death. He himself believed so. He knew what his own disorder was; he knew that the moment the water began to mount, and had attained a certain height, his life would be gone.

"How many hours have I to live?" he inquired of Dr. West.

"Probably for some days," was the answer.

What could it have been that was troubling the mind of Mr. Verner? That it was worldly trouble was certain. That other trouble, which has been known to distract the minds of the dying, to fill them with agony, was absent from his. On that score he was in perfect peace. But that some very great anxiety was racking him might be seen by the most casual observer. It had been racking him for a long time past, and it was growing worse now. And it appeared to be what he could not, or would not, speak of.

The news of the dangerous change in the master of Verner's Pride circulated through the vicinity, and it brought forth, amidst other of his friends, Mr. Bitterworth. This was on the second day of the change. Tynn received Mr. Bitterworth in the hall.

"There's no hope, sir, I'm afraid," was Tynn's answer to his inquiries. "He's not in much pain of body, but he is dreadfully anxious and uneasy."

"What about?" asked Mr. Bitterworth, who was a little man with a pimpled face.

"Nobody knows, sir; he doesn't say. For myself, I can only think it must be about something connected with the estate. What else can it be?"

"I suppose I can see him, Tynn?"

"I'll ask, sir. He refuses visitors in his room, but I dare say he'll admit you."

Lionel came to Mr. Bitterworth in the drawing-room. "My uncle will see you," he said, after greetings had passed.

"Tynn informs me that he appears to be uneasy in his mind," observed Mr. Bitterworth.

"A man so changed, as he has been in the last two years, I have never seen," replied Lionel. "None can have failed to remark it. From entire calmness of mind, he has exhibited anxious restlessness; I may say irritability. Mrs. Verner is ill," Lionel added, as they were ascending the stairs. "She has not been out of bed for two days."

Not in his study now; he had done with the lower part of the house for ever; but in his bed-chamber, never to come out of it alive, was Mr. Verner. They had got him up, and he sat in an easy-chair by the bedside, partially dressed, and wrapped in his dressing-gown. On his pale, worn face there were the unmistakable signs of death. He and Mr. Bitterworth were left alone.

"So you have come to see the last of me, Bitterworth!" was the remark of Mr. Verner.

"Not the last yet, I hope," heartily responded Mr. Bitterworth, who was an older man than Mr. Verner, but hale and active. "You may rally from this attack and get about again. Remember how many serious attacks you have had."

"None like this. The end must come; and it has come now. Hush, Bitterworth! To speak of recovery to me is worse than child's play. I know my time has come. And I am glad to meet it, for it releases me from a world of care."

"Were there any in this world who might be supposed to be exempt from care, it is you," said Mr. Bitterworth, leaning towards the invalid, his hale old face expressing the concern he felt. "I should have judged you to be perfectly free from earthly care. You have no children; what can be troubling you?"

"Would to Heaven I had children!" exclaimed Mr. Verner; and the remark appeared to break from him involuntarily, in the bitterness of his heart.

"You have your brother's son, your heir, Lionel."

"He is no heir of mine," returned Mr. Verner, with, if possible, double bitterness.

"No heir of yours!" repeated Mr. Bitterworth, gazing at his friend, and wondering whether he had lost his senses.

Mr. Verner, on his part, gazed on vacancy, his thoughts evidently cast inwards. He sat in his old favourite attitude; his hands clasped on the head of his stick, and his face bent down upon it. "Bitterworth," said he presently "when I made my will years ago, after my father's death, I appointed you one of the executors."

"I know it," replied Mr. Bitterworth. "I was associated—as you gave me to understand—with Sir Rufus Hautley."

"Ay. After the boy came of age,"—and Mr. Bitterworth knew that he alluded to Lionel—"I added his name to those of Sir Rufus and yourself. Legacies apart, the estate was all left to him."

"Of course it was," assented Mr. Bitterworth.

"Since then, I have seen fit to make an alteration," continued Mr. Verner. "I mention it to you, Bitterworth, that you may not be surprised when you hear the will read. Also I would tell you that I made the change of my own free act and judgment, unbiassed by any one, and that I did not make it without ample cause. The estate is not left to Lionel Verner, but to Frederick Massingbird."

Mr. Bitterworth had small round eyes, but they opened now to their utmost width. "What did you say?" he repeated, after a pause, like a man out of breath.

"Strictly speaking, the estate is not bequeathed to Frederick Massingbird; he will inherit it in consequence of John's death," quietly went on Mr. Verner. "It is left to John Massingbird, and to Frederick after him, should he be the survivor. Failing them both—"

"And I am still executor?" interrupted Mr. Bitterworth, in a tone raised rather above the orthodox key for a sick-room.

"You and Sir Rufus. That, so far, is not altered."

"Then I will not act. No, Stephen Verner, long and close as our friendship has been, I will not countenance an act of injustice. I will not be your executor, unless Verner's Pride goes, as it ought, to Lionel Verner."

"Lionel has forfeited it."

"Forfeited it!—how can he have forfeited it? Is this"—Mr. Bitterworth was given to speak in plain terms when excited—"is this the underhand work of Mrs. Verner?"

"Peace, Bitterworth! Mrs. Verner knows nothing of the change. Her surviving son knows nothing of it; John knew nothing of it. They have no idea but that Lionel is still the heir. You should not jump to unjust conclusions. Not one of them has ever asked me how my property was left; or has attempted, by the smallest word, to influence me in its disposal."

"Then, what has influenced you? Why have you done it?" demanded Mr. Bitterworth, his voice becoming more subdued.

To this question Mr. Verner did not immediately reply. He appeared not to have done with the defence of his wife and her sons.

"Mrs. Verner is not of a covetous nature; she is not unjust, and I believe that she would wish the estate willed to Lionel, rather than to her sons. She knows no good reason why it should not be willed to him. And for those sons—do you suppose either of them would have gone out to Australia, had he been cognisant that he was heir to Verner's Pride?"

"Why have you willed it away from Lionel?"

"I cannot tell you," replied Mr. Verner, in a tone of sharp pain. It betrayed to Mr. Bitterworth what sharper pain the step itself must have cost.

"It is this which has been on your mind, Verner—disturbing your closing years?"

"Ay, it is that; nothing else!" wailed Mr. Verner, "nothing else, nothing else! Has it not been enough to disturb me?" he added, putting the question in a loud, quick accent. "Setting aside my love for Lionel, which was great, setting aside my finding him unworthy, it has been a bitter trial to me to leave Verner's Pride to a Massingbird. I have never loved the Massingbirds," he continued, dropping his voice to a whisper.

"If Lionel were unworthy,"—with a stress upon the "were,"—"you might have left it to Jan," spoke Mr. Bitterworth.

"Lady Verner has thrown too much estrangement between Jan and me. No. I would rather even a Massingbird had it than Jan."

"If Lionel were unworthy, I said," resumed Mr. Bitterworth. "I cannot believe he is. How has he proved himself so? What has he done?"

Mr. Verner put up his hands as if to ward off some imaginary phantom, and his pale face turned of a leaden hue.

"Never ask me," he whispered. "I cannot tell you. I have had to bear it about with me," he continued, with an irrepressible burst of anguish; "to bear it here, within me, in silence; never breathing a word of my knowledge to him, or to any one."

"Some folly must have come to your cognisance," observed Mr. Bitterworth; "though I had deemed Lionel Verner to be more free from the sins of hot-blooded youth than are most men. I have believed him to be a true gentleman in the best sense of the word—a good and honourable man."

"A silent stream runs deep," remarked Mr. Verner.

Mr. Bitterworth drew his chair nearer to his friend, and, bending towards him, resumed solemnly—

"Verner's Pride of right (speaking in accordance with our national notions) belonged to your brother, Sir Lionel. It would have been his, as you know, had he lived but a month or two longer; your father would not have willed it away from him. After him it would have been Lionel's. Sir Lionel died too soon, and it was left to you; but what injunction from your father accompanied it? Forgive my asking you the question, Stephen."

"Do you think I have forgotten it?" wailed Mr. Verner. "It has cost me my peace—my happiness, to will it away from Lionel. To see Verner's Pride in possession of any but a Verner will trouble me so—if, indeed, we are permitted in the next world still to mark what goes on in this—that I shall scarcely rest quiet in my grave."

"You have no more—I must speak plainly, Stephen—I believe that you have no more right in equity to will away the estate from Lionel, than you would have were he the heir-at-law. Many have said—I am sure you must be aware that they have—that you have kept him out of it; that you have enjoyed what ought to have been his, ever since his grandfather's death."

"Have you said it?" angrily asked Mr. Verner.

"I have neither said it nor thought it. When your father informed me that he had willed the estate to you, Sir Lionel being dead, I answered him that I thought he had done well and wisely; that you had far more right to it, for your life, than the boy Lionel. But, Stephen, I should never sanction your leaving it away from him after you. Had you possessed children of your own, they should never have been allowed to shut out Lionel. He is your elder brother's son, remember."

Mr. Verner sat like one in dire perplexity. It would appear that there was a struggle going on in his own mind.

"I know, I know," he presently said, in answer. "The worry, the uncertainty, as to what I ought to do, has destroyed the peace of my later days. I altered my will when smarting under the discovery of his unworthiness; but, even then a doubt as to whether I was doing right caused me to name him as inheritor, should the Massingbirds die."

"Why, that must have been a paradox!" exclaimed Mr. Bitterworth. "Lionel Verner should inherit before all, or not inherit at all. What your ground of complaint against him is, I know not; but whatever it may be, it can be no excuse for your willing away from him Verner's Pride. Some youthful folly of his came to your knowledge, I conclude."

"Not folly. Call it sin—call it crime," vehemently replied Mr. Verner.

"As you please; you know its proper term better than I. For one solitary instance of—what you please to name it—you should not blight his whole prospects for life. Lionel's general conduct is so irreproachable (unless he be the craftiest hypocrite under the sun) that you may well pardon one defalcation. Are you sure you were not mistaken?"

"I am sure. I hold proof positive."

"Well, I leave that. I say that you might forgive him, whatever it may be, remembering how few his offences are. He would make a faithful master of Verner's Pride. Compare him to Fred Massingbird! Pshaw!"

Mr. Verner did not answer. His face had an aching look upon it, as it leaned out over the top of his stick. Mr. Bitterworth laid his hand upon his friend's knee persuasively.

"Do not go out of the world committing an act of injustice; an act, too, that is irreparable, and of which the injustice must last for ever. Stephen, I will not leave you until you consent to repair what you have done."

"It has been upon my mind to do it since I was taken worse yesterday," murmured Stephen Verner. "Our Saviour taught us to forgive. Had it been against me only that he sinned, I would have forgiven him long ago."

"You will forgive him now?"

"Forgiveness does not lie with me. It was not against me, I say, that he sinned. Let him ask forgiveness of God and of his own conscience. But he shall have Verner's Pride."

"Better that you should see it in its proper light at the eleventh hour, than not at all, Stephen," said Mr. Bitterworth. "By every law of right and justice, Verner's Pride, after you, belongs to Lionel."

"You speak well, Bitterworth, when you call it the eleventh hour," observed Mr. Verner. "If I am to make this change you must get Matiss here without an instant's delay. See him yourself, and bring him back. Tell him what the necessity is. He will make more haste for you than he might for one of my servants."

"Does he know of the bequest to the Massingbirds?"

"Of course he knows of it. He made the will. I have never employed anybody but Matiss since I came into the estate."

Mr. Bitterworth, feeling there was little time to be lost, quitted the room without more delay. He was anxious that Lionel should have his own. Not so much because he liked and esteemed Lionel, as that he possessed a strong sense of justice within himself. Lionel heard him leaving the sick-room, and came to him, but Mr. Bitterworth would not stop.

"I cannot wait," he said. "I am bound on an errand for your uncle."

CHAPTER XVI

AN ALTERED WILL

Mr. Bitterworth was bound to the house of the lawyer, Mr. Matiss, who lived and had his office in the new part of Deerham, down by Dr. West's. People wondered that he managed to make a living in so small a place; but he evidently did make one. Most of the gentry in the vicinity employed him for trifling things, and he held one or two good agencies. He kept no clerk. He was at home when Mr. Bitterworth entered, writing at a desk in his small office, which had maps hung round it. A quick-speaking man, with dark hair and a good-natured face.

"Are you busy, Matiss?" began Mr. Bitterworth, when he entered; and the lawyer looked at him through the railings of his desk.

"Not particularly, Mr. Bitterworth. Do you want me?"

"Mr. Verner wants you. He has sent me to bring you to him without delay. You have heard that there's a change in him?"

"Oh, yes, I have heard it," replied the lawyer. "I am at his service, Mr. Bitterworth."

"He wants his last will altered. Remedied, I should say," continued Mr. Bitterworth, looking the lawyer full in the face, and nodding confidentially.

"Altered to what it was before?" eagerly cried the lawyer.

Mr. Bitterworth nodded again. "I called in upon him this morning, and in the course of conversation it came out what he had done about Verner's Pride. And now he wants it undone."

"I am glad of it—I am glad of it, Mr. Bitterworth. Between ourselves—though I mean no disrespect to them—the young Massingbirds were not fit heirs for Verner's Pride. Mr. Lionel Verner is."

"He is the rightful heir as well as the fit one, Matiss," added Mr. Bitterworth, leaning over the railings of the desk, while the lawyer was hastily putting his papers in order, preparatory to leaving them, placing some aside on the desk, and locking up others. "What was the cause of his willing it away from Lionel Verner?"

"It's more than I can tell. He gave no clue whatever to his motive. Many and many a time have I thought it over since, but I never came near fathoming it. I told Mr. Verner that it was not a just thing, when I took his instructions for the fresh will. That is, I intimated as much; it was not my place, of course, to speak out my mind offensively to Mr. Verner. Dr. West said a great deal more to him than I did; but he could make no impression."

"Was Dr. West consulted, then, by Mr. Verner?"

"Not at all. When I called at Verner's Pride with the fresh will for Mr. Verner to execute, it happened that Tynn was out. He and one of the other servants were to have witnessed the signature. Dr. West came in at the time, and Mr. Verner said he would do for a witness in Tynn's place. Dr. West remonstrated most strongly when he found what it was; for Mr. Verner told him in confidence what had been done. He, the doctor, at first refused to put his hand to anything so unjust. He protested that the public would cry shame, would say John Massingbird had no human right to Verner's Pride, would suspect he had obtained it by fraud, or by some sort of underhand work. Mr. Verner replied that I— Matiss—could contradict that. At last the doctor signed."

"When was this?"

"It was the very week after John started for Australia. I wondered why Mr. Verner should have allowed him to go, if he meant to make him his heir. Dr. West wondered also, and said so to Mr. Verner, but Mr. Verner made no reply."

"Mr. Verner has just told me that neither the Massingbirds nor Mrs. Verner knew anything of the fresh will. I understood him to imply that no person whatever was cognisant of it but himself and you."

"And Dr. West. Nobody else."

"And he gave no reason for the alteration—either to you or to Dr. West?"

"None at all. Beyond the assertion that Lionel had displeased him. Dr. West would have pressed him upon the point, but Mr. Verner repulsed him with coldness. He insisted upon our secrecy as to the new will; which we promised, and I dare say have never violated. I know I can answer for myself."

They hastened back to Verner's Pride. And the lawyer, in the presence of Mr. Bitterworth, received instructions for a codicil, revoking the bequest of the estate to the Massingbirds, and bestowing it absolutely upon Lionel Verner. The bequests to others, legacies, instructions in the former will, were all to stand. It was a somewhat elaborate will; hence Mr. Verner suggested that that will, so far, could still stand, and the necessary alteration be made by a codicil.

"You can have it ready by this evening?" Mr. Verner remarked to the lawyer.

"Before then, if you like, sir. It won't take me long to draw that up. One's pen goes glibly when one's heart is in the work. I am glad you are willing it back to Mr. Lionel."

"Draw it up then, and bring it here as soon as it's ready. You won't find me gone out," Mr. Verner added, with a faint attempt at jocularity.

The lawyer did as he was bid, and returned to Verner's Pride about five o'clock in the afternoon. He found Dr. West there. It was somewhat singular that the doctor should again be present, as he had been at the previous signing. And yet not singular, for he was now in frequent attendance on the patient.

"How do you feel yourself this afternoon, sir?" asked Mr. Matiss, when he entered, his greatcoat buttoned up, his hat in his hand, his gloves on; showing no signs that he had any professional document about him, or that he had called in for any earthly reason, save to inquire in politeness after the state of the chief of Verner's Pride.

"Pretty well, Matiss. Are you ready?"

"Yes, sir."

"We'll do it at once, then. Dr. West," Mr. Verner added, turning to the doctor, "I have been making an alteration in my will. You were one of the former witnesses; will you be so again?"

"With pleasure. An alteration consequent upon the death of John Massingbird, I presume?"

"No. I should have made it, had he been still alive. Verner's Pride must go to Lionel. I cannot die easy unless it does."

"But—I thought you said Lionel had done—had done something to forfeit it?" interrupted Dr. West, whom the words appeared to have taken by surprise.

"To forfeit my esteem and good opinion. Those he can never enjoy again. But I doubt whether I have a right to deprive him of Verner's Pride. I begin to think I have not. I believe that the world generally will think I have not. It may be that a Higher Power, to whom alone I am responsible, will judge I have not. There's no denying that he will make a more fitting master of it than would Frederick Massingbird; and for myself I shall die the easier knowing that a Verner will succeed me. Mr. Matiss, be so kind as read over the deed."

The lawyer produced a parchment from one of his ample pockets, unfolded, and proceeded to read it aloud. It was the codicil, drawn up with all due form, bequeathing Verner's Pride to Lionel Verner. It was short, and he read it in a clear, distinct voice.

"Will you like to sign it, sir?" he asked, as he laid it down.

"When I have read it for myself," replied Mr. Verner.

The lawyer smiled as he handed it to him. All his clients were not so cautious. Some might have said, "so mistrustful."

Mr. Verner found the codicil all right, and the bell was rung for Tynn. Mrs. Tynn happened to come in at the same moment. She was retreating when she saw business a-gate, but her master spoke to her.

"You need not go, Mrs. Tynn. Bring a pen and ink here."

So the housekeeper remained present while the deed was executed. Mr. Verner signed it, proclaiming it his last will and testament, and Dr. West and Tynn affixed their signatures. The lawyer and Mrs. Tynn stood looking on.

Mr. Verner folded it up with his own hands, and sealed it.

"Bring me my desk," he said, looking at Mrs. Tynn.

The desk was kept in a closet in the room, and she brought it forth. Mr. Verner locked the parchment within it.

"You will remember where it is," he said, touching the desk, and looking at the lawyer. "The will is also here."

Mrs. Tynn carried the desk back again; and Dr. West and the lawyer left the house together.

Later, when Mr. Verner was in bed, he spoke to Lionel, who was sitting with him.

"You will give heed to carry out my directions, Lionel, so far as I have left directions, after you come into power."

"I will, sir," replied Lionel, never having had the faintest suspicion that he had been near losing his inheritance.

"And be more active abroad than I have been. I have left too much to Roy and others. You are young and strong; don't you leave it to them. Look into things with your own eyes."

"Indeed I will. My dear uncle," he added, bending over the bed, and speaking in an earnest tone, "I will endeavour to act in all things as though in your sight, accountable to God and my own conscience. Verner's Pride shall have no unworthy master."

"Try to live so as to redeem the past."

"Yes," said Lionel. He did not see what precise part of it he had to redeem, but he was earnestly anxious to defer to the words of a dying man. "Uncle, may I dare to say that I hope you will live yet?" he gently said.

"It is of no use, Lionel. The world is closing for me."

It was closing for him even then, as he spoke—closing rapidly. Before another afternoon had come round, the master of Verner's Pride had quitted that, and all other pride, for ever.

CHAPTER XVII

DISAPPEARED

Sweeping down from Verner's Pride towards the church at Deerham came the long funeral train—mutes with their plumes and batons, relays of bearers, the bier. It had been Mr. Verner's express desire that he should be carried to the grave, that no hearse or coaches should be used.

"Bury me quietly; bury me without show," had been his charge. And yet a show it was, that procession, if only from its length. Close to the coffin walked the heir, Lionel; Jan and Dr. West came next; Mr. Bitterworth and Sir Rufus Hautley. Other gentlemen were there, followers or pall-bearers; the tenants followed; the servants came last. A long, long line, slow and black; and spectators gathered on the side of the road, underneath the hedges, and in the upper windows at Deerham, to see it pass. The under windows were closed.

A brave heir, a brave master of Verner's Pride! was the universal thought, as eyes were turned on Lionel, on his tall, noble form, his pale face stilled to calmness, his dark hair. He chose to walk bare-headed, his hat, with its sweeping streamers, borne in his hand. When handed to him in the hall he had not put it on, but went out as he was, carrying it. The rest, those behind him, did not follow his example; they assumed their hats; but Lionel was probably unconscious of it, probably he never gave it a thought.

At the churchyard entrance they were met by the Vicar of Deerham, the Reverend James Bourne. All hats came off then, as his voice rose, commencing the service. Nearly one of the last walked old Matthew Frost. He had not gone to Verner's Pride, the walk so far was beyond him now, but fell in at the churchyard gate. The fine, upright, hale man whom you saw at the commencement of this history had changed into a bowed, broken mourner. Rachel's fate had done that. On the right as they moved up the churchyard, was the mound which covered the remains of Rachel. Old Matthew did not look towards it; as he passed it he only bent his head the lower. But many others turned their heads; they remembered her that day.

In the middle of the church, open now, dark and staring, was the vault of the Verners. There lay already within it Stephen Verner's father, his first wife, and the little child Rachel, Rachel Frost's foster-sister. A grand grave this, compared to that lowly mound outside; there was a grand descriptive tablet on the walls to the Verners; while the mound was nameless. By the side of the large tablet was a smaller one, placed there to the memory of the brave Sir Lionel Verner, who had fallen near Moultan. Lionel involuntarily glanced up at it, as he stood now over the vault, and a wish came across him that his father's remains were here, amidst them, instead of in that far-off grave.

The service was soon over, and Stephen Verner was left in his resting-place. Then the procession, shorn of its chief and prominent features, went back to Verner's Pride. Lionel wore his hat this time.

In the large drawing-room of state, in her mourning robes and widow's cap, sat Mrs. Verner. She had not been out of her chamber, until within the last ten minutes, since before Mr. Verner's death; scarcely out of her bed. As they passed into the room—the lawyer, Dr. West, Jan, Mr. Bitterworth, and Sir Rufus Hautley—they thought how Mrs. Verner had changed, and how ill she looked; not that her florid complexion was any paler. She had, indeed, changed since the news of John Massingbird's death; and some of them believed that she would not be very long after Mr. Verner.

They had assembled there for the purpose of hearing the will read. The desk of Mr. Verner was brought forward and laid upon the table. Lionel, taking his late uncle's keys from his pocket, unlocked it, and delivered a parchment which it contained to Mr. Matiss. The lawyer saw at a glance that it was the old will, not the codicil, and he waited for Lionel to hand him also the latter.

"Be so kind as read it, Mr. Matiss," said Lionel, pointing to the will.

It had to be read; and it was of no consequence whether the codicil was taken from the desk before reading the original will, or afterwards, so Mr. Matiss unfolded it, and began.

It was a somewhat elaborate will—which has been previously hinted. Verner's Pride, with its rich lands, its fine income, was left to John Massingbird; in the event of John's death, childless, it went to Frederick; in the event of Frederick's death, childless, it passed to Lionel Verner. There the conditions ended; so that, if it did lapse to Lionel, it lapsed to him absolutely. But it would appear that the contingency of both the Massingbirds dying had been only barely glanced at by Mr. Verner. Five hundred pounds were left to Lionel: five hundred to Jan; five hundred to Decima; nothing to Lady Verner. Mrs. Verner was suitably provided for, and there were bequests to servants. Twenty-five pounds for "a mourning ring" were bequeathed to each of the two executors, Sir Rufus Hautley, and Mr. Bitterworth; and old Matthew Frost had forty pounds a year for his life. Such were the chief features of the will; and the utter astonishment it produced on the minds and countenances of some of the listeners was a sight to witness. Lionel, Mrs. Verner, Jan, and Sir Rufus Hautley were petrified.

Sir Rufus rose. He was a thin, stately man, always dressed in hessian boots and the old-fashioned shirt-frill. A proud, impassive countenance was his, but it darkened now. "I will not act," he began. "I beg to state my opinion that the will is an unfair one—"

"I beg your pardon, Sir Rufus," interrupted the lawyer. "Allow me a word. This is not the final will of Mr. Verner; much of it has been revoked by a recent codicil. Verner's Pride comes to Mr. Lionel. You will find the codicil in the desk, sir," he added to Lionel.

Lionel, his pale face haughty, and quite as impassive as that of Sir Rufus, for anything like injustice angered him, opened the desk again. "I was not aware," he observed. "My uncle told me on the day of his death that the will would be found in his desk; I supposed that to be it."

"It is the will," said Mr. Matiss. "But he caused me to draw up a later codicil, which revoked the bequest of Verner's Pride. It is left to you absolutely."

Lionel was searching in the desk. The few papers in it appeared to be arranged with the most methodical neatness: but they were small, chiefly old letters. "I don't see anything like a codicil," he observed. "You had better look yourself, Mr. Matiss; you will probably recognise it."

Mr. Matiss advanced to the desk and looked in it. "It is not here!" he exclaimed.

Not there! They gazed at him, at the desk, at Lionel, half puzzled. The lawyer, with rapid fingers, began taking out the papers one by one.

"No, it is not here, in either compartment. I saw it was not, the moment I looked in; but it was well to be sure. Where has it been put?"

"I really do not know anything about it," answered Lionel, to whom he looked as he spoke. "My uncle told me the will would be found in his desk. And the desk has not been opened since his death."

"Could Mr. Verner himself have changed its place to somewhere else?" asked the lawyer, speaking with more than usual quickness, and turning over the papers with great rapidity.

"Not after he told me where the will was. He did not touch the desk after that. It was but just before his death. So far as I know, he had not had his desk brought out of the closet for days."

"Yes, he had," said the lawyer. "After he had executed the codicil on the evening previous to his death, he called for his desk, and put the parchment into it. It lay on the top of the will—this one. I saw that much."

"I can testify that the codicil was locked in the desk, and the desk was then returned to the closet, for I happened to be present," spoke up Dr. West. "I was one of the witnesses to the codicil, as I had been to the will. Mr. Verner must have moved it himself to some safer place."

"What place could be safer than the desk in his own bedroom?" cried the lawyer. "And why move the codicil and not the will?"

"True," assented Dr. West. "But—I don't see—it could not go out of the desk without being moved out. And who would presume to meddle with it but himself? Who took possession of his keys when he died?" added the doctor, looking round at Mrs. Verner.

"I did," said Lionel. "And they have not been out of my possession since. Nothing whatever has been touched; desk, drawers, every place belonging to him are as they were left when he died."

Of course the only thing to do was to look for the codicil. Great interest was excited; and it appeared to be altogether so mysterious an affair that one and all flocked upstairs to the room; the room where he had died! whence the coffin had but just been borne. Mrs. Tynn was summoned; and when she found what was amiss, she grew excited; fearing, possibly, that the blame might in some way fall upon her. Saving Lionel himself, she was the only one who had been alone with Mr. Verner; of course, the only one who could have had an opportunity of tampering with the desk. And that, only when the patient slept.

"I protest that the desk was never touched, after I returned it to the closet by my master's desire, when the parchment was put into it!" she cried. "My master never asked for his desk again, and I never so much as opened the closet. It was only the afternoon before he died, gentlemen, that the deed was signed."

"Where did he keep his keys?" asked Mr. Bitterworth.

"In the little table-drawer at his elbow, sir. The first day he took to his bed, he wanted his keys, and I got them out of his dressing-gown pocket for him. 'You needn't put them back,' he says to me; 'let them stop inside this little drawer.' And there they stayed till he died, when I gave them up to Mr. Lionel."

"You must have allowed somebody to get into the room, Mrs. Tynn," said Dr. West.

"I never was away from the room above two minutes at a time, sir," was the woman's reply, "and then either Mr. Lionel or Tynn would be with him. But, if any of 'em did come in, it's not possible they'd get picking at the master's desk to take out a paper. What good would the paper do any of the servants?"

Mrs. Tynn's question was a pertinent one. The servants were neither the better nor the worse for the codicil; whether it were forthcoming, or not, it made no difference to them. Sir Rufus Hautley inquired upon this point, and the lawyer satisfied him.

"The codicil was to this effect alone," he explained. "It changed the positions of Mr. Lionel and Mr. John Massingbird, the one for the other, as they had stood in the will. Mr. Lionel came into the inheritance, and Mr. Frederick Massingbird to five hundred pounds only. Mr. John was gone—as everybody knows."

"These two, Mr. Lionel and Frederick Massingbird, were the only parties interested in the codicil, then?"

"The only two. John Massingbird's name was mentioned, but only to revoke all former bequests to him."

"Then—were John Massingbird alive, he could not now succeed to the estate!" cried Sir Rufus.

"He could not, Sir Rufus," replied the lawyer. "He would be debarred from all benefit under Mr. Verner's will. That is, provided we can come across the codicil. Failing that, he would succeed were he in life, to Verner's Pride."

"The codicil must be found," cried Mr. Bitterworth, getting heated. "Don't say, 'if we can come across it,' Matiss."

"Very good, Mr. Bitterworth. I'm sure I should be glad to see it found. Where else are we to look?"

Where else, indeed! That Mr. Verner could not get out of the room to hide the codicil was an indisputable fact; and nobody else seemed to know anything whatever about it. The only one personally interested in the suppression of the codicil was Frederick Massingbird; and he, hundreds of miles away, could neither have secured it nor sent his ghost to secure it. In a less degree, Mrs. Verner and Dr. West were interested; the one in her son, the other in that son's wife. But the doctor was not an inmate of Verner's Pride; and Mrs. Tynn could have testified that she had been present in the room and never left it during each of the doctor's professional visits, subsequent to the drawing out of the codicil. As for Mrs. Verner, she had not been out of her bed. Mr. Verner, at the last, had gone off suddenly, without pain, and there had been no time to call his wife. Mrs. Tynn excused the negligence by saying she did not think her master had been quite so near his end; and it was a true excuse. But no one dreamed of attaching suspicion to Mrs. Verner, or to Dr. West. "I'd rather it had been Lionel to succeed than Frederick," spoke the former, honestly, some faint idea that people might think she was pleased suggesting the avowal to her. "Lionel has more right than Fred to Verner's Pride."

"More right!" ejaculated Dr. West warmly. "Frederick Massingbird has no right, by the side of Lionel Verner. Why Mr. Verner ever willed it away from Lionel we could not understand."

"Fred needn't take it—even if the codicil can't be found—he can give it back to Lionel by deed of gift," said practical Jan. "I should."

"That my master meant Mr. Lionel to succeed, is certain," interposed Tynn, the butler. "Nearly the last word he said to me, before the breath went out of his body, was an injunction to serve Mr. Lionel faithfully at Verner's Pride, as I had served him. There can be no difficulty in Mr. Lionel's succeeding, when my master's intentions were made so plain."

"Be quiet, Tynn," said Lionel. "I succeed by means of legal right to Verner's Pride, or I will not succeed at all."

"That's true," acquiesced the lawyer. "A will is a will, and must be acted upon. How on earth has that codicil got spirited away?"

How indeed! But for the plain fact, so positive and palpable before them, of the codicil's absence, they would have declared the loss to be an impossibility. Upstairs and down, the house was vainly searched for it; and the conclusion was at length unwillingly come to that Mr. Verner had repented of his bequest, had taken the codicil out of the desk, and burned it. The suggestion came from Mr. Bitterworth; and Mrs. Tynn acknowledged that it was just possible Mr. Verner's strength would allow him to accomplish so much, while her back was turned. And yet, how reconcile this with his dying charges to Lionel, touching the management of the estate?

The broad fact that there was the will, and that alone to act upon, untempered by a codicil, shone out all too clearly. Lionel Verner was displaced, and Frederick Massingbird was the heir.

Oh, if some impossible electric telegraph could but have carried the news over the waves of the sea, to the ship ploughing along the mid-path of the ocean; if the two fugitives in her could but have been spirited back again, as the codicil seemed to have been spirited away, how triumphantly would they have entered upon their sway at Verner's Pride.

CHAPTER XVIII

PERPLEXITY

It was a terrible blow; there was no doubt of that; very terrible to Lionel Verner, so proud and sensitive. Do not take the word proud in its wrong meaning. He did not set himself up for being better than others, or think everybody else dirt beneath his feet; but he was proud of his independence, of his unstained name—he was proud to own that fine place, Verner's Pride. And now Verner's Pride was dashed from him, and his independence seemed to have gone out with the blow, and a slight seemed to have fallen upon him, if not upon his name.

He had surely counted upon Verner's Pride. He had believed himself as indisputably its heir, as though he had been Stephen Verner's eldest son, and the estate entailed. Never for a moment had a doubt that he would succeed entered his own mind, or been imparted to it from any quarter. In the week that intervened between Mr. Verner's death and burial, he had acted as entire master. It was he who issued orders—from himself now, not from any other—it was he who was appealed to. People, of their own accord, began to call him Mr. Verner. Very peremptory indeed had been a certain interview of his with Roy the bailiff. Not, as formerly, had he said, "Roy, my uncle desires me to say so and so;" or, "Roy, you must not act in that way, it would displease Mr. Verner;" but he issued his own clear and unmistakable orders, as the sole master of Verner's Pride. He and Roy all but came to loggerheads that day; and they would have come quite to it, but that Roy remembered in time that he, before whom he stood, was his head and master—his master to keep him on, or to discharge him at pleasure, and who would brook no more insubordination to his will. So Roy bowed, and ate humble pie, and hated Lionel all the while.

Lionel had seen this; he had seen how the man longed to rebel, had he dared: and now a flush of pain rose to his brow as he remembered that in that interview he had not been the master; that he was less master now than he had ever been. Roy would likewise remember it.

Mr. Bitterworth took Lionel aside. Sir Rufus Hautley had gone out after the blow had fallen, when the codicil had been searched for in vain, had gone out in anger, shaking the dust from his feet, declining to act as executor, to accept the mourning-ring, to have to do with anything so palpably unjust. The rest lingered yet. It seemed that they could not talk enough of it, could not tire of bringing forth new conjectures, could not give vent to all the phases of their astonishment.

"What could have been your offence, that your uncle should alter his will, two years ago, and leave the estate from you?" Mr. Bitterworth inquired of Lionel, drawing him aside.

"I am unable to conjecture," replied Lionel. "I find by the date of this will that it was made the week subsequent to my departure for Paris, when Jan met with the accident. He was not displeased with me then, so far as I knew—"

"Did you go to Paris in opposition to his wish?" interrupted Mr. Bitterworth.

"On the contrary, he hurried me off. When the news of Jan's accident arrived, and I went to my uncle with the message, he said to me—I remember his very words—'Go off at once; don't lose an instant,' and he handed me money for the journey and for my stay; for Jan, also, should any great expense be needed for him; and in an hour I was away on my route. I stayed six months in Paris, as you may remember—the latter portion of the time for my own pleasure. When I did return home, I was perfectly thunderstruck at the change in my uncle's appearance, and at the change in his manners to me. He was a bowed, broken man, with—as it seemed to me—some care upon his mind; and that I had offended him in some very unfortunate way, and to a great extent, was palpable. I never could get any solution to it, though I asked him repeatedly. I do not know, to this hour, what I had done. Sometimes I thought he was angry at my remaining so long away; but, if so, he might have given me a hint to return, or have suffered some one else to give it, for he never wrote to me."

"Never wrote to you?" repeated Mr. Bitterworth.

"Not once, the whole of the time I was away. I wrote to him often; but if he had occasion to send me a message, Mrs. Verner or Fred Massingbird would write it. Of course, this will, disinheriting me, proves that my staying away could not have been the cause of displeasure—it is dated only the week after I went."

"Whatever may have been the cause, it is a grievous wrong inflicted on you. He was my dear friend, and we have but now returned from laying him in his grave, but still I must speak out my sentiments—that he had no right to deprive you of Verner's Pride."

Lionel knit his brow. That he thought the same; that he was feeling the injustice as a crying and unmerited wrong, was but too evident. Mr. Bitterworth had bent his head in a reverie, stealing a glance at Lionel now and then.

"Is there nothing that you can charge your conscience with; no sin, which may have come to the knowledge of your uncle, and been deemed by him a just cause for disinheritance?" questioned Mr. Bitterworth, in a meaning tone.

"There is nothing, so help me Heaven!" replied Lionel, with emotion. "No sin, no shame; nothing that could be a cause, or the shade of a cause—I will not say for depriving me of Verner's Pride, but even for my uncle's displeasure."

"It struck me—you will not be offended with me, Lionel, if I mention something that struck me a week back," resumed Mr. Bitterworth. "I am a foolish old man, given to ponder much over cause and effect— to put two and two together, as we call it; and the day I first heard from your uncle that he had had good cause—it was what he said—for depriving you of Verner's Pride, I went home, and set myself to think. The will had been made just after John Massingbird's departure for Australia. I brought before me all the events which had occurred about that same time, and there rose up naturally, towering above every other reminiscence, the unhappy business touching Rachel Frost. Lionel"—laying his hand on the young man's shoulder and dropping his voice to a whisper—"did you lead the girl astray?"

Lionel drew himself up to his full height, his lip curling with displeasure.

"Mr. Bitterworth!"

"To suspect you never would have occurred to me. I do not suspect you now. Were you to tell me that you were guilty of it, I should have difficulty in believing you. But it did occur to me that possibly your uncle may have cast that blame on you. I saw no other solution of the riddle. It could have been no light cause to induce Mr. Verner to deprive you of Verner's Pride. He was not a capricious man.'

"It is impossible that my uncle could have cast a shade of suspicion on me, in regard to that affair," said Lionel. "He knew me better. At the moment of its occurrence, when nobody could tell whom to suspect, I remember a word or two were dropped which caused me to assure him I was not the guilty party, and he stopped me. He would not allow me even to speak of defence; he said he cast no suspicion on me."

"Well, it is a great mystery," said Mr. Bitterworth. "You must excuse me, Lionel. I thought Mr. Verner might in some way have taken up the notion. Evil tales, which have no human foundation, are sometimes palmed upon credulous ears for fact, and do their work."

"Were it as you suggest, my uncle would have spoken to me, had it been only to reproach," said Lionel. "It is a mystery, certainly, as you observe; but that is nothing to this mystery of the disappearance of the codicil—"

"I am going, Lionel," interrupted Jan, putting his head round the room door.

"I must go, too," said Lionel, starting from the sideboard against which he had been leaning. "My mother must hear of this business from no one but me."

Verner's Pride emptied itself of its mourners, who betook themselves their respective ways. Lionel, taking the long crape from his hat, and leaving on its deep mourning band alone, walked with a quick step through the village. He would not have chosen to be abroad that day, walking the very route where he had just figured chief in the procession, but to go without delay to Lady Verner was a duty. And a duty was never willingly omitted by Lionel Verner.

CHAPTER XIX

THE REVELATION TO LADY VERNER

In the drawing-room at Deerham Court, in their new black dresses, sat Lady Verner and Decima; Lucy Tempest with them. Lady Verner held out her hand to Lionel when he entered, and lifted her face, a strange eagerness visible in its refinement.

"I thought you would come to me, Lionel!" she uttered. "I want to know a hundred things.—Decima, have the goodness to direct your reproachful looks elsewhere; not to me. Why should I be a hypocrite, and feign a sorrow for Stephen Verner which I do not feel? I know it is his burial-day as well as you know it; but I will not make that a reason for abstaining from questions on family topics, although they do relate to money and means that were once his. I say it would be hypocritical affectation to do so. Lionel," she deliberately continued, "has Jan an interest in Verner's Pride after you, or is it left to you unconditionally? And what residence is appointed for Mrs. Verner?"

Lionel leaned over the table, apparently to reach something that was lying on it, contriving to bring his lips close to Decima. "Go out of the room, and take Lucy," he whispered.

Decima received the hint promptly. She rose as of her own accord. "Lucy, let us leave mamma and Lionel alone. We will come back when your secrets are over," she added, turning round with a smile as she left the room, drawing Lucy with her.

"You don't speak, Lionel," impatiently cried Lady Verner. In truth he did not; he did not know how to begin. He rose, and approached her.

"Mother, can you bear disappointment?" he asked, taking her hand, and speaking gently, in spite of his agitation.

"Hush!" interrupted Lady Verner. "If you speak of 'disappointment' to me, you are no true son of mine. You are going to tell me that Stephen Verner has left nothing to me. Let me tell you, Lionel, that I would not have accepted it—and this I made known to him. Accept money from him! No. But I will accept it from my dear son,"—looking at him with a smile—"now that he enjoys the revenues of Verner's Pride."

"It was not with money left, or not left, to you, that I was connecting disappointment," answered Lionel. "There is a worse disappointment in store for us than that, mother."

"A worse disappointment!" repeated Lady Verner, looking puzzled. "You are never to be saddled with the presence of Mrs. Verner at Verner's Pride, until her death!" she hastily added. A great disappointment, that would have been; a grievous wrong, in the estimation of Lady Verner.

"Mother, dear, Verner's Pride is not mine."

"Not yours!" she slowly said. "He surely has not done as his father did before him?—left it to the younger brother, over the head of the elder? He has never left it to Jan!"

"Neither to Jan nor to me. It is left to Frederick Massingbird. John would have had it, had he been alive."

Lady Verner's delicate features became crimson; before she could speak, they had assumed a leaden colour. "Don't play with me, Lionel," she gasped, an awful fear thumping at her heart that he was not playing with her. "It cannot be left to the Massingbirds!"

He sat down by her side, and gave her the history of the matter in detail. Lady Verner caught at the codicil, as a drowning man catches at a straw.

"How could you terrify me?" she asked. "Verner's Pride is yours, Lionel. The codicil must be found."

"The conviction upon my mind is that it never will be found," he resolutely answered. "Whoever took that codicil from the desk where it was placed, could have had but one motive in doing it—the depriving me of Verner's Pride. Rely upon it, it is effectually removed ere this, by burning, or otherwise. No. I already look upon the codicil as a thing that never existed. Verner's Pride is gone from us."

"But, Lionel, whom do you suspect? Who can have taken it? It is pretty nearly a hanging matter to steal a will!"

"I do not suspect any one," he emphatically answered. "Mrs. Tynn protests that no one could have approached the desk unseen by her. It is very unlikely that any one could have burnt it. They must, first of all, have chosen a moment when my uncle was asleep; they must have got Mrs. Tynn from the room; they must have searched for and found the keys; they must have unlocked the desk, taken the codicil, relocked the desk, and replaced the keys. All this could not be done without time, and familiarity with facts. Not a servant in the house—save the Tynns—knew the codicil was there, and they did not know its purport. But the Tynns are thoroughly trustworthy."

"It must have been Mrs. Verner—"

"Hush, mother! I cannot listen to that, even from you. Mrs. Verner was in her bed—never out of it; she knew nothing whatever of the codicil. And, if she had, you will, I hope, do her the justice to believe that she would be incapable of meddling with it."

"She benefits by its loss, at any rate," bitterly rejoined Lady Verner.

"Her son does. But that he does was entirely unknown to her. She never knew that Mr. Verner had willed the estate away from me; she never dreamed but that I, and no other, would be his successor. The accession of Frederick Massingbird is unwelcome to her, rather than the contrary; he has no right to it, and she feels that he has not. In the impulse of the surprise, she said aloud that she wished it had been left to me; and I am sure these were her true sentiments."

Lady Verner sat in silence, her white hands crossed on her black dress, her head bent down. Presently she lifted it—

"I do not fully understand you, Lionel. You appear to imply that—according to your belief—no one has touched the codicil. How, then, can it have got out of the desk?"

"There is only one solution. It was suggested by Mr. Bitterworth; and, though I refused credence to it when he spoke, it has since been gaining upon my mind. He thinks my uncle must have repented of the codicil after it was made, and himself destroyed it. I should give full belief to this were it not that at the very last he spoke to me as the successor to Verner's Pride."

"Why did he will it from you at all?" asked Lady Verner.

"I know not. I have told you how estranged his manner has been to me for the last year or two; but wherefore, or what I had done to displease him, I cannot think or imagine."

"He had no right to will away the estate from you," vehemently rejoined Lady Verner. "Was it not enough that he usurped your father's birth-right, as Jacob usurped Esau's, keeping you out of it for years and years, but he must now deprive you of it for ever? Had you been dead—had there been any urgent reason why you should not succeed—Jan should have come in. Jan is the lawful heir, failing you. Mark me, Lionel, it will bring no good to Frederick Massingbird. Rights, violently diverted out of their course, can bring only wrong and confusion."

"It would be scarcely fair were it to bring him ill," spoke Lionel, in his strict justice. "Frederick has had nothing to do with my uncle's bequeathing the estate to him."

"Nonsense, Lionel! you cannot make me believe that no cajolery has been at work from some quarter or other," peevishly answered Lady Verner. "Tell the facts to an impartial person—a stranger. They were always about him—his wife and those Massingbirds—and at the last moment it is discovered that he has left all to them, and disinherited you."

"Mother, you are mistaken. What my uncle has done, he has done of his own will alone, unbiassed by others; nay, unknown to others. He distinctly stated this to Matiss, when the change was made. No, although I am a sufferer, and they benefit, I cannot throw a shade of the wrong upon Mrs. Verner and the Massingbirds."

"I will tell you what I cannot do—and that is to accept your view of the disappearance of the codicil," said Lady Verner. "It does not stand to reason that your uncle would cause a codicil to be made, with all the haste and parade you speak of, only to destroy it afterwards. Depend upon it, you are wrong. He never took it."

"It does appear unlikely," acquiesced Lionel, after some moments of deliberation. "It was not likely, either, that he would destroy it in secret; he would have done it openly. And still less likely, that he would have addressed me as his successor in dying, and given me charges as to the management of the estate, had he left it away from me."

"No, no; no, no!" emphatically returned Lady Verner. "That codicil has been stolen, Lionel."

"But, by whom?" he debated. "There's not a servant in the house would do it; and there was no other inmate of it, save myself. This is my chief difficulty. Were it not for the total absence of all other suspicion, I should not for a moment entertain the thought that it could have been my uncle. Let us leave the subject, mother. It seems to be an unprofitable one, and my head is weary."

"Are you going to give the codicil tamely up for a bad job, without further search?" asked Lady Verner. "That I should live—that I should live to see Sibylla West's children inherit Verner's Pride!" she passionately added.

Sibylla West's children! Lionel had enough pain at his heart, just then, without that shaft. A piercing shaft truly, and it dyed his brow fiery red.

"We have searched already in every likely or possible place that we can think of; to-morrow morning, places unlikely and impossible will be searched," he said, in answer to his mother's question. "I shall be aided by the police; our searching is nothing compared with what they can do. They go about it artistically, perfected by practice."

"And—if the result should be a failure?"

"It will be a failure," spoke Lionel, in his firm conviction. "In which case I bid adieu to Verner's Pride."

"And come home here; will you not, Lionel?"

"For the present. And now, mother, that I have told you the ill news, and spoiled your rest, I must go back again."

Spoiled her rest! Ay, for many a day and night to come. Lionel disinherited! Verner's Pride gone from them for ever! A cry went forth from Lady Verner's heart. It had been the moment of hope which she had looked forward to for years; and, now that it was come, what had it brought?

"My own troubles make me selfish," said Lionel, turning back when he was half out at the door. "I forgot to tell you that Jan and Decima inherit five hundred pounds each."

"Five hundred pounds!" slightingly returned Lady Verner. "It is but of a piece with the rest."

He did not add that he had five hundred also, failing the estate. It would have seemed worse mockery still.

Looking out at the door, opposite to the ante-room, on the other side of the hall, was Decima. She had heard his step, and came to beckon him in. It was the dining-parlour, but a pretty room still; for Lady Verner would have nothing about her inelegant or ugly, if she could help it. Lucy Tempest, in her favourite school attitude, was half-kneeling, half-sitting on the rug before the fire; but she rose when Lionel came in.

Decima entwined her arm within his, and led him up to the fire-place. "Did you bring mamma bad news?" she asked. "I thought I read it in your countenance."

"Very bad, Decima. Or I should not have sent you away while I told it."

"I suppose there's nothing left for mamma, or for Jan?"

"Mamma did not expect anything left for her, Decima. Don't go away, Lucy," he added, arresting Lucy Tempest, who, with good taste, was leaving them alone. "Stay and hear how poor I am; all Deerham knows it by this time."

Lucy remained. Decima, her beautiful features a shade paler than usual, turned her serene eyes on Lionel. She little thought what was coming.

"Verner's Pride is left away from me, Decima."

"Left away from you! From you?"

"Frederick Massingbird inherits. I am passed over."

"Oh, Lionel!" The words were not uttered angrily, passionately, as Lady Verner's had been; but in a low, quiet voice, wrung from her, seemingly, by intense inward pain.

"And so there will be some additional trouble for you in the housekeeping line," went on Lionel, speaking gaily, and ignoring all the pain at his heart. "Turned out of Verner's Pride, I must come to you here—at least, for a time. What shall you say to that, Miss Lucy?"

Lucy was looking up at him gravely, not smiling in the least. "Is it true that you have lost Verner's Pride?" she asked.

"Quite true."

"But I thought it was yours—after Mr. Verner."

"I thought so too, until to-day," replied Lionel. "It ought to have been mine."

"What shall you do without it?"

"What, indeed!" he answered. "From being a landed country gentleman—as people have imagined me—I go down to a poor fellow who must work for his bread and cheese before he eats it. Your eyes are laughing, Miss Lucy, but it is true."

"Bread and cheese costs nothing," said she.

"No? And the plate you put it on, and the knife you eat it with, and the glass of beer to help it go down, and the coat you wear during the repast, and the room it's served in?—they cost something, Miss Lucy."

Lucy laughed. "I think you will always have enough bread and cheese," said she. "You look as though you would."

Decima turned to them. She had stood buried in a reverie, until the light tone of Lionel aroused her from it. "Which is real, Lionel? This joking, or that you have lost Verner's Pride?"

"Both," he answered. "I am disinherited from Verner's Pride; better perhaps that I should joke over it, than cry."

"What will mamma do? What will mamma do?" breathed Decima. "She has so counted upon it. And what will you do, Lionel?"

"Decima!" came forth at this moment from the opposite room, in the imperative voice of Lady Verner.

Decima turned in obedience to it, her step less light than usual. Lucy addressed Lionel.

"One day at the rectory there came a gipsy woman, wanting to tell our fortunes; she accosted us in the garden. Mr. Cust sent her away, and she was angry, and told him his star was not in the ascendant. I think it must be the case at present with your star, Mr. Verner."

Lionel smiled. "Yes, indeed."

"It is not only one thing that you are losing; it is more. First, that pretty girl whom you loved; then, Mr. Verner; and now, Verner's Pride. I wish I knew how to comfort you."

Lucy Tempest spoke with the most open simplicity, exactly as a sister might have done. But the one allusion grated on Lionel's heart.

"You are very kind, Lucy. Good-bye. Tell Decima I shall see her some time to-morrow."

Lucy Tempest looked after him from the window as he paced the inclosed courtyard. "I cannot think how people can be unjust!" was her thought. "If Verner's Pride was rightly his, why have they taken it from him?"

CHAPTER XX

DRY WORK

Certainly Lionel Verner's star was not in the ascendant—though Lucy Tempest had used the words in jest. His love gone from him; his fortune and position wrested from him; all become the adjuncts of one man, Frederick Massingbird. Serenely, to outward appearance, as Lionel had met the one blow, so did he now meet the other; and none, looking on his calm bearing, could suspect what the loss was to him. But it is the silent sorrow that eats into the heart; the loud grief does not tell upon it.

An official search had been made; but no trace could be found of the missing codicil. Lionel had not expected that it would be found. He regarded it as a deed which had never had existence, and took up his abode with his mother. The village could not believe it; the neighbourhood resented it. People stood in groups to talk it over. It did certainly appear to be a most singular and almost incredible thing, that, in the enlightened days of the latter half of the nineteenth century, an official deed should disappear out of a gentleman's desk, in his own well-guarded residence, in his habited chamber. Conjectures and thoughts were freely bandied about; while Dr. West and Jan grew nearly tired of the particulars demanded of them in their professional visits, for their patients would talk of nothing else.

The first visible effect that the disappointment had, was to stretch Lady Verner on a sick-bed. She fell into a low, nervous state of prostration, and her irritability—it must be confessed—was great. But for this illness, Lionel would have been away. Thrown now upon his own resources, he looked steadily into the future, and strove to chalk out a career for himself; one by which—as he had said to Lucy Tempest—he might earn bread and cheese. Of course, at Lionel Verner's age, and reared to no profession, unfamiliar with habits of business, that was easier thought of than done. He had no particular talent for literature; he believed that, if he tried his hand at that, the bread might come, but the cheese would be doubtful—although he saw men, with even less aptitude for it than he, turning to it and embracing it with all the confidence in the world, as if it were an ever-open resource for all, when other trades failed. There were the three professions; but were they available? Lionel felt no inclination to become a working drudge like poor Jan; and the Church, for which he had not any liking, he was by far too conscientious to embrace only as a means of living. There remained the Bar; and to that he turned his attention, and resolved to qualify himself for it. That there would be grinding, and drudgery, and hard work, and no pay for years, he knew; but, so there might be, go to what he would. The Bar did hold out a chance of success, and there was nothing in it derogatory to the notions in which he had been reared—those of a gentleman.

Jan came to him one day about the time of the decision, and Lionel told him that he should soon be away; that he intended to enter himself at the Middle Temple, and take chambers.

"Law!" said Jan. "Why, you'll be forty, maybe, before you ever get a brief. You should have entered earlier."

"Yes. But how was I to know that things would turn out like this?"

"Look here," said Jan, tilting himself in a very uncomfortable fashion on the high back of an arm-chair, "there's that five hundred pounds. You can have that."

"What five hundred pounds?" asked Lionel.

"The five hundred that Uncle Stephen left me. I don't want it. Old West gives me as much as keeps me in clothes and that, which is all I care about. You take the money and use it."

"No, Jan. Thank you warmly, old boy, all the same; but I'd not take your poor little bit of money if I were starving."

"What's the good of it to me?" persisted Jan, swaying his legs about. "I can't use it: I have got nothing to use it in. I have put it in the bank at Heartburg, but the bank may go smash, you know, and then who'd be the better for the money? You take it and make sure of it, Lionel."

Lionel smiled at him. Jan was as simple and single-hearted in his way as Lucy Tempest was in hers. But Lionel must want money very grievously indeed, before he would have consented to take honest Jan's.

"I have five hundred of my own, you know, Jan," he said. "More than I can use yet awhile."

So he fixed upon the Bar, and would have hastened to London but for Lady Verner's illness. In the weak, low state to which disappointment and irritability had reduced her, she could not bear to lose sight of

Lionel, or permit him to depart. "It will be time enough when I am dead; and that won't be long first," was the constant burden of her song to him.

He believed his mother to be little more likely to die than he was, but he was too dutiful a son to cross her in her present state. He gathered certain ponderous tomes about him, and began studying law on his own account, shutting himself up in his room all day to do it. Awfully dry work he found it; not in the least congenial; and many a time did he long to pitch the whole lot into the pleasant rippling stream, running through the grounds of Sir Rufus Hautley, which danced and glittered in the sun in view of Lionel's window.

He could not remain at his daily study without interruptions. They were pretty frequent. People—tenants, workmen, and others—would persist in coming for orders to Mr. Lionel. In vain Lionel told them that he could not give orders, could not interfere; that he had no longer anything to do with Verner's Pride. They could not be brought to understand why he was not their master as usual—at any rate, why he could not act as one, and interpose between them and the tyrant, Roy. In point of fact, Mr. Roy was head and master of the estate just now, and a nice head and master he made! Mrs. Verner, shut up in Verner's Pride with her ill health, had no conception what games were being played. "Let be, let be," the people would say. "When Mr. Fred Massingbird comes home, Roy'll get called to account, and receive his deserts;" a fond belief in which all did not join. Many entertained a shrewd suspicion that Mr. Fred Massingbird was too much inclined to be a tyrant on his own account, to disapprove of the acts of Roy. Lionel's blood often boiled at what he saw and heard, and he wished he could put miles between himself and Deerham.

CHAPTER XXI

A WHISPERED SUSPICION

Dr. West was crossing the courtyard one day, after paying his morning visit to Lady Verner, when he was waylaid by Lionel.

"How long will my mother remain in this weak state?" he inquired.

Dr. West lifted his arched eyebrows. "It is impossible to say, Mr. Lionel. These cases of low nervous fever are sometimes very much protracted."

"Lady Verner's is not nervous fever," dissented Lionel.

"It approaches near to it."

"The fact is, I want to be away," said Lionel.

"There is no reason why you should not be away, if you wish it," rejoined the physician. "Lady Verner is not in any danger; she is sure to recover eventually."

"I know that. At least, I hope it is sure," returned Lionel. "But, in the state she is, I cannot reason with her, or talk to her of the necessity of my being away. Any approach to the topic irritates her."

"I should go, and say nothing to her beforehand," observed Dr. West. "When she found you were really off, and that there was no remedy for it, she must perforce reconcile herself to it."

Every fond feeling within Lionel revolted at the suggestion. "We are speaking of my mother, doctor," was his courteously-uttered rebuke.

"Well, if you would not like to do that, there's nothing for it but patience," the doctor rejoined, as he drew open one of the iron gates. "Lady Verner may be no better than she is now for weeks to come. Good-day, Mr. Lionel."

Lionel paced into the house with a slow step, and went up to his mother's chamber. She was lying on a couch by the fire, her eyes closed, her pale features contracted as if with pain. Her maid Thérèse appeared to be busy with her, and Lionel called out Decima.

"There's no improvement, I hear, Decima."

"No. But, on the other hand, there is no danger. There's nothing even very serious, if Dr. West may be believed. Do you know, Lionel, what I fancy he thinks?"

"What?" asked Lionel.

"That if mamma were obliged to exert and rouse herself—were like any poor person, for instance, who cannot lie by and be nursed—she would be well directly. And—unkind, unlike a daughter as it may seem in me to acknowledge it—I do very much incline to the same opinion."

Lionel made no reply.

"Only Dr. West has not the candour to say so," went on Decima. "So long as he can keep her lying here, he will do it; she is a good patient for him. Poor mamma gives way, and he helps her to do it. I wish she would discard him, and trust to Jan."

"You don't like Dr. West, Decima?"

"I never did," said Decima. "And I believe that, in skill, Jan is quite equal to him. There's this much to be said of Jan, that he is sincere and open as if he were made of glass. Jan will never keep a patient in bed unnecessarily, or give the smallest dose more than is absolutely requisite. Did you hear of Sir Rufus Hautley sending for Jan?"

"No."

"He is ill, it seems. And when he sent to Dr. West's, he expressly desired that it might be Mr. Jan Verner to answer the summons. Dr. West will not forgive that in a hurry."

"That comes of prejudice," said Lionel; "prejudice not really deserved by Dr. West. Since the reading of the will, Sir Rufus has been bitter against the Massingbirds; and Dr. West, as connected with them, comes in for his share of the feeling."

"I hope he may not deserve it in any worse way than as connected with them," returned Decima, with more acrimony than she, in her calm gentleness, was accustomed to speak.

The significant tone struck Lionel. "What do you mean, Decima?"

Decima glanced round. They were standing at the far end of the corridor at the window which overlooked the domains of Sir Rufus Hautley. The doors of the several rooms were closed, and no one was about. Decima spoke in a whisper—

"Lionel, I cannot divest myself of the opinion that—that—"

"That what?" he asked, looking at her in wonder, for she was hesitating strangely, her manner shrinking, her voice awe-struck.

"That it was Dr. West who took the codicil."

Lionel's face flushed—partially with pain; he did not like to hear it said, even by Decima.

"You have never suspected so much yourself?" she asked.

"Never, never. I hope I never shall suspect it. Decima, you perhaps cannot help the thought, but you can help speaking of it."

"I did not mean to vex you. Somehow, Lionel, it is for your sake that I seem to have taken a dislike to the Wests—"

"To take a dislike to people is no just cause for accusing them of crime," he interrupted. "Decima, you are not like yourself to-day."

"Do you suppose that it is my dislike which caused me to suspect him. No, Lionel. I seem to see people and their motives very clearly; and I do honestly believe"—she dropped her voice still lower—"that Dr. West is a man capable of almost anything. At the time when the codicil was being searched for, I used to think and think it over, how it could be—how it could have disappeared. All its points, all its bearings, I deliberated upon again and again. One certain thing was, the codicil could not have disappeared from the desk without its having been taken out. Another point, almost equally certain to my mind, was that my Uncle Stephen did not take it out, but died in the belief that it was in, and that it would give you your inheritance. A third point was, that whoever took it must have had some strong motive for the act. Who (with possible access to the desk) could have had this motive, even in a remote degree? There were but two—Dr. West and Mrs. Verner. Mrs. Verner I judge to be incapable of anything so wrong; Dr. West I believe to be capable of even worse than that. Hence I drew my deductions."

"Deductions which I shall never accept, and which I would advise you to get rid of, Decima," was his answer. "My dear, never let such an accusation cross your lips again."

"I never shall. I have told you; and that is enough. I have longed to tell you for some time past. I did not think you would believe me."

"Believe it, you should say, Decima. Dr. West take the codicil! Were I to bring myself to that belief, I think all my faith in man would go out. You are sadly prejudiced against the Wests."

"And you in their favour," she could not help saying. "But I shall ever be thankful for one thing—that you have escaped Sibylla."

Was he thankful for it? Scarcely, while that pained heart of his, those coursing pulses, could beat on in this tumultuous manner at the bare sound of her name.

In the silence that ensued—for neither felt inclined to break it—they heard a voice in the hall below, inquiring whether Mr. Verner was within. Lionel recognised it as Tynn's.

"For all I know he is," answered old Catherine. "I saw him a few minutes agone in the court out there, a-talking to the doctor."

"Will you please ask if I can speak to him."

Lionel did not wait further, but descended to the hall. The butler, in his deep mourning, had taken his seat on the bench. He rose as Lionel approached.

"Well, Tynn, how are you? What is it?"

"My mistress has sent me to ask if you'd be so kind as come to Verner's Pride, sir?" said Tynn, standing with his hat in his hand. "She bade me say that she did not feel well enough, or she'd have written you a note with the request, but she wishes particularly to see you."

"Does she wish to see me to-day?"

"As soon as ever you could get there, sir, I fancy. I am sure she meant to-day."

"Very well, Tynn. I'll come over. How is your mistress?"

"She's very well, sir, now; but she gets worried on all sides about things out-of-doors."

"Who worries her with those tales?" asked Lionel.

"Everybody almost does, sir, as comes a-nigh her. First it's one complaint that's brought to the house, of things going wrong, and then it's another complaint—and the women servants, they have not the sense to keep it from her. My wife can't keep her tongue still upon it, and can't see that the rest do. Might I ask how her ladyship is to-day, sir?"

"Not any better, Tynn. Tell Mrs. Verner I will be with her almost immediately."

Lionel lost little time in going to Vender's Pride. Turned from it as he had been, smarting under the injustice and the pain, many a one would have haughtily refused to re-enter it, whatever might have been the emergency. Not so Lionel. He had chosen to quit Verner's Pride as his residence, but he had remained entirely good friends with Mrs. Verner, calling on her at times. Not upon her would Lionel visit his displeasure.

It was somewhat curious that she had taken to sit in the old study of Stephen Verner; a room which she had rarely entered during his lifetime. Perhaps some vague impression that she was now a woman of business, or ought to be one, that she herself was in sole charge for the absent heir, had induced her to take up her daily sitting amidst the drawers, bureaux, and other places which had contained Mr. Verner's papers—which contained them still. She had, however, never yet looked at one. If anything came up to the house, leases, deeds, other papers, she would say: "Tynn, see to it," or "Tynn, take it over to Mr. Lionel Verner, and ask what's to be done." Lionel never refused to say.

She was sitting back in Mr. Verner's old chair, now, filling it a great deal better than he used to do. Lionel took her hand cordially. Every time he saw her he thought her looking bigger and bigger. However much she may have grieved at the time for her son John's death, it had not taken away either her flesh or her high colour. Nothing would have troubled Mrs. Verner permanently, unless it had been the depriving her of her meals. Now John was gone, she cared for nothing else in life.

"It's kind of you to come, Lionel," said she. "I want to talk to you. What will you have?—some wine?"

"Not anything," replied Lionel. "Tynn said you wished to see me for something particular."

"And so I do. You must take the management of the estate until Fred's at home."

The words grated on his ear, and his brow knit itself into lines. But he answered calmly—

"I cannot do that, Mrs. Verner."

"Then what can I do?" she asked. "Here's all this great estate, nobody to see after it, nobody to take it in charge! I'm sure I have no more right to be teased over it than you have, Lionel."

"It is your son's."

"I asked you not to leave Verner's Pride. I asked you to take the management of out-door things! You did so, between your uncle's death and his burial."

"Believing that I was taking the management of what was mine," replied Lionel.

"Why do you visit upon me the blame of all that has happened?" pursued Mrs. Verner. "I declare that I knew nothing of what was done; I could not believe my own ears when I heard Matiss read out the will. You should not blame me."

"I never have blamed you for it, Mrs. Verner. I believe you to be as innocent of blame in the matter as I am."

"Then you ought not to turn haughty and cold, and refuse to help me. They are going to have me up before the Justice Courts at Heartburg!"

"Have you up before the Justice Courts at Heartburg!" repeated Lionel, in great astonishment.

"It's all through Roy; I know it is. There's some stupid dispute about a lease, and I am to be had up in evidence. Did you hear of the threat?"

"What threat?" asked he.

"Some of the men are saying they'll burn down Verner's Pride. Roy turned them off the brick-yard, and they threaten they'll do it out of revenge. If you would just look to things and keep Roy quiet, nothing of this would happen."

Lionel knew that.

"Mrs. Verner," he said, "were you the owner of Verner's Pride, I would spare no pains to help you. But I cannot act for Frederick Massingbird."

"What has Fred done to you?" she asked quickly.

"That is not the question—he has done nothing," answered Lionel, speaking more rapidly still. "My management would—if I know anything of him—be essentially different from your son's; different from what he would approve. Neither would I take authority upon myself only to have it displaced upon his return. Have Roy before you, Mrs. Verner, and caution him."

"It does no good. I have already had him. He smoothes things over to me, so that black looks white. Lionel, I must say that you are unkind and obstinate."

"I do not think I am naturally either one or the other," he answered, smiling. "Perhaps it might answer your purpose to put things into the hands of Matiss, until your son's return."

"He won't take it," she answered. "I sent for him—what with this court business and the threat of incendiarism, I am like one upon thorns—and he said he would not undertake it. He seemed to fear contact with Roy."

"Were I to take the management, Mrs. Verner, my first act would be to discharge Roy."

Mrs. Verner tried again to shake his resolution. But he was quite firm. And, wishing her good-day, he left Verner's Pride, and bent his steps towards the village.

CHAPTER XXII

PECKABY'S SHOP

On passing through Deerham from Verner's Pride, a little below the shop of Mrs. Duff, you come upon an opening on the left hand, which led to quite a swarm of cottages. Many of the labourers congregated here. If you took this turning, which was called Clay Lane, and continued your way past the cottages in a straight line over the fields, you would arrive at the residence of the gamekeeper, Broom, leaving some brick-fields to the right, and the Willow Pool, which had been the end of poor Rachel Frost, on the left. But, unless you climbed hedges, you could not get to the pool from this quarter without going round, near the gamekeeper's. The path which led to Verner's Pride past the pool, and which Rachel had taken that unfortunate night, had its commencement higher up in the village, above Mrs. Duff's. A few cottages were scattered again beyond the gamekeeper's, and one or two on this side it; but we have nothing to do with them at present.

A great part of the ill-feeling rife on the estate was connected with these brick-fields. It had been a great mistake on Mr. Verner's part ever to put Roy into power; had Mr. Verner been in the habit of going out of doors himself, he would have seen this, and not kept the man on a week. The former bailiff had died suddenly. He, the bailiff, had given some little power to Roy during his lifetime; had taken him on as a sort of inferior helper; and Mr. Verner, put to shifts by the bailiffs death, had allowed Roy so to continue. Bit by bit, step by step, gradually, covertly, the man made good his footing: no other was put over his head, and in time he came to be called Roy the bailiff, without having ever been formally appointed as bailiff. He drew his two pounds per week—his stipulated wages—and he made, it is hard to say what, besides. Avarice and tyranny were the predominant passions of Roy's mind; bad qualities, and likely to bring forth bad fruits when joined to petty power.

About three years previous to Mr. Verner's death, a stranger had appeared in Clay Lane, and set up a shop there. Nearly every conceivable thing in the shape of eatables was sold in it; that is, such eatables as are in request among the poor. Bread, flour, meat, potatoes, butter, tea, sugar, red herrings, and the like. Soap and candles were also sold; and afterwards the man added green vegetables and coals, the latter doled out by the measure, so much a "kipe." The man's name was Peckaby; he and his wife were without family, and they managed the shop between them. A tall, strong, brawny man was he; his wife was a remarkably tall woman, fond of gossip and of smart caps. She would go gadding out for hours at a stretch, leaving him to get through all the work at home, the preparing meals, the serving customers.

Folks fly to new things; to do so is a propensity inherent in human nature; and Mr. Peckaby's shop flourished. Not that he was much honoured with the complimentary "Mr."; his customers brought it out short—"Peckaby's shop." Much intimacy had appeared to exist from the first between him and Roy, so that it was surmised they had been previously acquainted. The prices were low, the shop was close at hand, and Clay Lane flocked to it.

New things, however, like new faces, are apt to turn out no better than the old; sometimes not as good. And thus it proved with Peckaby's shop. From rather underselling the shops of the village, Peckaby's shop grew to increase its charges until they were higher than those of anybody else; the wares also deteriorated in value. Clay Lane awoke to this by degrees, and would have taken its custom away; but that was more easily contemplated than done. A good many of its families had been allowed to get on Peckaby's books, and they also found that Roy set his face against their leaving the shop. For Roy to set his face against a measure was a formidable affair, not readily contended with: the labourers did not dare to fly in his face, lest he should make an excuse to take their work from them. He had already discharged several. So Clay Lane, for the most part, found itself tied to Peckaby's shop, and to paying some thirty per cent. beyond what they would have paid at the old shops; added to which was the grievance of being compelled to put up with very inferior articles. Dissatisfaction at this state of things had long been smouldering. It grew and grew, threatening to break out into open rebellion, perhaps to bloodshed. The neighbourhood cried shame upon Roy, and felt inclined to echo the cry upon Mrs. Verner; while Clay Lane openly avowed their belief that Peckaby's shop was Roy's shop, and that the Peckaby's were only put in to manage it.

One fearfully hot Monday morning, in the beginning of July, Lionel Verner was passing down Clay Lane. In another week he would be away from Deerham. Lady Verner's illness had commenced near the latter end of April, and it was growing towards the end of June before she began to get better, or would give Lionel leave to depart. Jan, plain-speaking, truth-telling Jan, had at length quietly told his mother that there was nothing the matter with her but "vexing and temper." Lady Verner went into hysterics at Jan's unfilial conduct; but, certain it was, from that very time she began to amend. July came in, and Lionel was permitted to fix the day for his departure.

Lionel was walking down Clay Lane. It was a short cut to Lord Elmsley's house over the hills, a mile or two distant. Not a very suitable day for a walk. Had Lionel been training for a light jockey, without any superfluous weight, he might have dispensed with extra covering in his exercise, and done as effectually without it. A hotter day never was known in our climate; a more intensely burning sun never rode in the heavens. It blazed down with a force that was almost unbearable, scorching and withering all within its radius. Lionel looked up at it; it seemed to blister his face and dazzle his eyes; and his resolution wavered as he thought of the walk before him. "I have a great mind not to go," said he mentally. "They can set up their targets without me. I shall be half dead by the time I get there." Nevertheless, in the indecision, he still walked on. He thought he'd see how affairs looked when he came to the green fields. Green! brown, rather.

But Lionel found other affairs to look at before he reached the fields. On turning a sharp angle of Clay Lane, he was surprised to see a crowd collected, stretching from one side of it to the other. Not a peaceable crowd evidently, although it was composed for the most part of the gentler sex; but a crowd of threatening arms and inflamed faces, and swaying white caps and noisy tongues. The female population of Clay Lane had collected there.

Smash! went the breaking of glass in Lionel's ears as he came in view; smash! went another crash. Were Peckaby's shop windows suffering? A misgiving that it must be so, crossed the mind of Lionel, and he made few steps to the scene of warfare.

Sure enough it was nothing less. Three great holes were staring in so many panes, the splinters of glass lying inside the shop-window, amidst butter and flour, and other suchlike articles. The flour looked brown, and the butter was running away in an oily stream; but that was no reason why a shower of broken glass should be added to improve their excellences. Mr. Peckaby, with white gills and hair raised up on end, stood, the picture of fear, gazing at the damage, but too much afraid to start out and prevent it. Those big men are sometimes physical cowards. Another pane smashed! the weapon used being a hard piece of flint coal, which just escaped short of Mr. Peckaby's head, and Lionel thought it time to interfere. He pushed into the midst of them.

They drew aside when they saw who it was. In their hot passions—hot and angry then—perhaps no one, friend or enemy, would have stood a chance of being deferred to but Lionel Verner. They had so long looked upon him as the future lord of Verner's Pride that they forgot to look upon him as anything less now. And they all liked Lionel. His appearance was as oil poured upon troubled waters.

"What is the meaning of this? What is the matter?" demanded Lionel.

"Oh, sir, why don't you interfere to protect us, now things is come to this pass? You be a Verner!" was the prayer of remonstrance from all sides that met his words.

"Give me an explanation," reiterated Lionel. "What is the grievance?"

The particular grievance of this morning, however easy to explain, was somewhat difficult to comprehend, when twenty tongues were speaking at once—and those, shrill and excited ones. In vain Lionel assured them that if one, instead of all, would tell it, he should understand it sooner; that if their tone were subdued, instead of loud enough to be heard yonder at the brick-fields, it might be more desirable. Excited women, suffering under what they deem a wrong, cannot be made quiet; you may as well try to put down a rising flood. Lionel resigned himself to his fate, and listened; and at this stage of the affair a new feature of it struck his eye and surprised him. Scarcely one of the women but bore in her hand some uncooked meat. Such meat! Lionel drew himself and his coat from too close proximity to it. It was of varied hues, and walking away alive. Upon plates, whole or broken, upon half-saucers, upon dust-pans, upon fire-shovels, held at the end of tongs, hooked on to a fork, spread out in a coal-box; anyhow so as to avoid contact with fingers, these dainty pieces were exhibited for inspection.

By what Lionel could gather, it appeared that this meat had been purchased on Saturday night at Peckaby's shop. The women had said then, one and all, that it was not good; and Mr. Peckaby had been regaled with various open conjectures, more plain than polite, as to the state of the animal from which it had been supplied. Independent of the quality of the meat, it was none the better, even then, for having been kept. The women scented this; but Peckaby, and Peckaby's wife, who was always in the shop with her husband on a Saturday night, protested and vowed that their customers' noses were mistaken; that the meat would be perfectly good and fresh on the Sunday, and on the Monday too, if they liked to keep it so long. The women, somewhat doubtfully giving ear to the assurance, knowing that the alternative was that or none, bought the meat and took it home. On Sunday morning they found the meat was—anything you may imagine. It was neither cookable nor eatable; and their anger against Peckaby was not diminished by a certain fact which oozed out to them; namely, that Peckaby himself did not cut his Sunday's dinner off the meat in his shop, but sent to buy it of one of the Deerham butchers. The general indignation was great; the men, deprived of their Sunday's meat, joined in it; but nothing could be done until Monday morning. Peckaby's shop was always hermetically sealed on a Sunday. Mr. Verner had been stringent in allowing no Sunday traffic on the estate.

Monday came. The men went to their work as usual, leaving their wives to deal with the matter. Behold them assembled with their meat, kept for the occasion in spite of its state, before the shop of Peckaby. But of redress they could get none; Peckaby was deaf; and Lionel arrived to find hostilities commenced. Such was the summary of the story.

"You are acting very wrongly," were Lionel's first words to them in answer. "You should blame the meat, not Peckaby. Is this weather for keeping meat?"

"The weather didn't get to this heat till yesterday in the afternoon," said they—and Lionel could not deny the fact. Mrs. Dawson took up the word.

"Our meat warn't bought at Peckaby's; our meat were got at Clark's, and it were sweet as a nut. 'Twere veal, too, and that's the worst meat for keeping. Roy 'ud kill us if he could; but he can't force us on to Peckaby's rubbish. We defy him to't."

In point of defying Roy, the Dawsons had done that long ago. There was open warfare between them, and skirmishes took place occasionally. The first act of Roy, after it was known that Lionel was disinherited, had been to discharge old Dawson and his sons from work. How they had managed to live since was a mystery; funds did not seem to run low with them; tales of their night-poaching went about, and the sons got an odd job at legitimate work now and then.

"It's an awful shame," cried a civil, quiet woman, Sarah Grind, one of a very numerous family, commonly called "Grind's lot," "that we should be beat down to have our victuals and other things at such a place as Peckaby's! Sometimes, sir, I'm almost inclined to ask, is it Christians as rules over us?"

Lionel felt the shaft levelled at his family, though not personally at himself.

"You are not beaten down to it," he said. "Why do you deal at Peckaby's? Stay a bit! I know what you would urge: that by going elsewhere you would displease Roy. It seems to me that if you would all go elsewhere, Roy could not prevent it. Should one of you attempt to go, he might; but he could not prevent it if you all go with one accord. If Peckaby's things are bad—as I believe they are—why do you buy them?"

"There ain't a single thing as is good in his place," spoke up a woman, half-crying. "Sir, it's truth. His flour is half bone-dust, and his 'taturs is watery. His sugar is sand, and his tea is leaves dried over again, while his eggs is rotten, and his coals is flint."

"Allowing that, it is no good reason for your smashing his windows," said Lionel. "It is utterly impossible that that can be tolerated."

"Why do he palm his bad things off upon us, then?" retorted the crowd. "He makes us pay half as much again as we do in the other shops; and when we gets them home, we can't eat 'em. Sir, you be Mr. Verner now; you ought to see as we be protected."

"I am Mr. Verner; but I have no power. My power has been taken from me, as you know. Mrs. Verner is—"

"A murrain light upon her!" scowled a man from the outskirts of the crowd. "Why do she call herself Mrs. Verner, and stick herself up for missis at Verner's Pride, if she is to take no notice on us? Why do she leave us in the hands of Roy, to be—"

Lionel had turned upon the man like lightning.

"Davies, how dare you presume so to speak of Mrs. Verner in my presence? Mrs. Verner is not the source of your ills; you must look nearer to you, for that. Mrs. Verner is aged and ailing; she cannot get out of doors to see into your grievances."

At the moment of Lionel's turning to the man, he, Davies, had commenced to push his way towards Lionel. This caused the crowd to sway, and Lionel's hat, which he held carelessly in his hand, having taken it off to wipe his heated brow, got knocked down. Before he could stoop for its rescue, it was trampled out of shape; not intentionally—they would have protected Lionel and his things with their lives—but inadvertently. A woman picked it up with a comical look of despair. To put on that again was impossible.

"Never mind," said Lionel good-naturedly. "It was my own fault; I should have held it better."

"Put your handkercher over your head, sir," was the woman's advice. "It'll keep the sun off."

Lionel smiled, but did not take it. Davies was claiming his attention; while some of the women seemed inclined to go in for a fight, which should secure the hat.

"Could Mr. Verner get out o' doors and look into our grievances, the last years of his life, any more, sir, nor she can?" he was asking, in continuation of the subject.

"No, sir; he couldn't, and he didn't; but things wasn't then brought to the pitch as they be now."

"No," acquiesced Lionel, "I was at hand then, to interpose between Roy and Mr. Verner."

"And don't you think, sir, as you might be able to do the same thing still?"

"No, Davies. I have been displaced from Verner's Pride, and from all power connected with it. I have no more right to interfere with the working of the estate than you have. You must make the best of things until Mr. Massingbird's return."

"There'll be some dark deed done, then, afore many weeks is gone over; that's what there'll be!" was Davies's sullen reply. "It ain't to be stood, sir, as a man and his family is to clam, 'cause Peckaby—"

"Davies, I will hear no more on that score," interrupted Lionel. "You men should be men, and make common cause in that one point for yourselves against Roy. You have your wages in your hand on a Saturday night, and can deal at any shop you please."

The man—he wore a battered old straw hat on his head, which looked as dirty as his face—raised his eyes with an air of surprise at Lionel.

"What wages, sir? We don't get ours."

"Not get your wages?" repeated Lionel.

"No, sir; not on a Saturday night. That's just it—it's where the new shoe's a-pinching. Roy don't pay now on a Saturday night. He gives us all a sort o' note, good for six shilling, and we has, us or our wives, to take that to Peckaby's, and get what we can for it. On the Monday, at twelve o'clock, which is his new time for paying the wages, he docks us of six shilling. That's his plan now; and no wonder as some of us has kicked at it, and then he have turned us off. I be one."

Lionel's brow burned; not with the blazing sun, but with indignation. That this should happen on the lands of the Verner's! Hot words rose to his lips—to the effect that Roy, as he believed, was acting against the law—but he swallowed them down ere spoken. It might not be expedient to proclaim so much to the men.

"Since when has Roy done this?" he asked. "I am surprised not to have heard of it."

"This six weeks he have done it, sir, and longer nor that. It's get our things from Peckaby's or it's not get any at all. Folks won't trust the likes of us, without us goes with the money in our hands. We might have knowed there was some evil in the wind when Peckaby's took to give us trust. Mr. Verner wasn't the best of masters to us, after he let Roy get on our backs—saving your presence for saying it, sir; but you must know as it's truth—but there's things a-going on now as 'ud make him, if he knowed 'em, rise up out of his grave. Let Roy take care of hisself, that he don't get burned up some night in his bed!" significantly added the man.

"Be silent, Davies! You—"

Lionel was interrupted by a commotion. Upon turning to ascertain its cause, he found an excited crowd hastening towards the spot from the brick-fields. The news of the affray had been carried thither, and Roy, with much intemperate language and loud wrath, had set off at full speed to quell it. The labourers set off after him, probably to protect their wives. Shouting, hooting, swearing—at which pastime Roy was the loudest—on they came, in a state of fury.

But for the presence of Lionel Verner, things might have come to a crisis—if a fight could have brought a crisis on. He interposed his authority, which even Roy did not yet dispute to his face, and he succeeded in restoring peace for the time. He became responsible—I don't know whether it was quite wise of him to do so—for the cost of the broken windows, and the women were allowed to go home unmolested. The men returned to their work, and Mr. Peckaby's face regained its colour. Roy was turning away, muttering to himself, when Lionel beckoned him aside with an authoritative hand.

"Roy, this must not go on. Do you understand me? It must not go on."

"What's not to go on, sir?" retorted Roy sullenly.

"You know what I mean. This disgraceful system of affairs altogether. I believe that you would be amenable to the law in thus paying the men, or in part paying them, with an order for goods; instead of in open, honest coin. Unless I am mistaken, it borders very closely upon the truck system."

"I can take care of myself and of the law, too, sir," was the answer of Roy.

"Very good. I shall take care that this sort of oppression is lifted off the shoulders of the men. Had I known it was being pursued, I should have stopped it before."

"You have no right to interfere between me and anything now, sir."

"Roy," said Lionel calmly, "you are perfectly well aware that the right, not only to interfere between you and the estate, but to invest me with full power over it and you, was sought to be given me by Mrs. Verner at my uncle's death. For reasons of my own I chose to decline it, and have continued to decline it. Do you remember what I once told you—that one of my first acts of power would be to displace you? After what I have seen and heard to-day, I shall deliberate whether it be not my duty to reconsider my determination, and assume this, and all other power."

Roy's face turned green. He answered defiantly, not in tone, but in spirit—

"It wouldn't be for long, at any rate, sir; and Mr. Massingbird, I know, 'll put me into my place again on his return."

Lionel did not reply immediately. The sun was coming down upon his uncovered head like a burning furnace, and he was casting a glance round to see if any friendly shade might be at hand. In his absorption over the moment's business he had not observed that he had halted with Roy right underneath its beams. No, there was no shade just in that spot. A public pump stood behind him, but the sun was nearly vertical, and the pump got as much of it as he did. A thought glanced through Lionel's mind of resorting to the advice of the women, to double his handkerchief cornerwise over his head. But he did not purpose staying above another minute with Roy, to whom he again turned.

"Don't deceive yourself, Roy. Mr. Massingbird is not likely to countenance such doings as these. That Mrs. Verner will not, I know; and, I tell you plainly, I will not. You shall pay the men's wages at the proper and usual time; you shall pay them in full, to the last halfpenny that they earn. Do you hear? I order you now to do so. We will have no underhanded truck system introduced on the Verner estate."

"You'd like to ruin poor Peckaby, I suppose, sir!"

"I have nothing to do with Peckaby. If public rumour is to be credited, the business is not Peckaby's, but yours—"

"Them that says it is a pack of liars!" burst forth Roy.

"Possibly. I say I have nothing to do with that. Peckaby—"

Lionel's voice faltered. An awful pain—a pain, the like of which, for acute violence, he had never felt—had struck him in the head. He put his hand up to it, and fell against the pump.

"Are you ill, sir?" asked Roy.

"What can it be?" murmured Lionel. "A sudden pain has attacked me here, Roy," touching his head; "an awful pain. I'll get into Frost's, and sit down."

Frost's cottage was but a minute's walk, but Lionel staggered as he went to it. Roy attended him. The man humbly asked if Mr. Lionel would be pleased to lean upon him, but Lionel waved him off. Matthew Frost was sitting indoors alone; his grandchildren were at school, his son's wife was busy elsewhere. Matthew no longer went out to labour. He had been almost incapable of it before Mr. Verner's annuity fell to him. Robin was away at work: but Robin was a sadly altered man since the death of Rachel. His very nature appeared to have changed.

"My head! my head!" broke from Lionel, as he entered, in the intensity of his pain. "Matthew, I think I must have got a sun-stroke."

Old Matthew pulled off his straw hat, and lifted himself slowly out of his chair. All his movements were slow now. Lionel had sat himself down on the settle, his head clasped by both hands, and his pale face turned to fiery red—as deep a crimson as Mrs. Verner's was habitually.

"A sun-stroke?" echoed old Matthew, leaning on his stick, as he stood before him, attentively regarding Lionel. "Ay, sir, for sure it looks like it. Have you been standing still in the sun, this blazing day?"

"I have been standing in it without my hat," replied Lionel. "Not for long, however."

"It don't take a minute, sir, to do the mischief. I had one myself, years before you were born, Mr. Lionel. On a day as hot as this, I was out in my garden, here, at the back of this cottage. I had gone out without my hat, and was standing over my pig, watching him eat his wash, when I felt something take my head— such a pain, sir, that I had never felt before, and never wish to feel again. I went indoors, and Robin, who might be a boy of five, or so, looked frightened at me, my face was so red. I couldn't hold my head up, sir; and when the doctor came, he said it was a sun-stroke. I think there must be particular moments and days when the sun has this power to harm us, though we don't know which they are nor how to avoid them," added old Matthew, as much in self-soliloquy as to Lionel. "I had often been out before, without my hat, in as great heat; for longer, too; and it had never harmed me. Since then, sir, I have put a white handkerchief inside the crown of my hat in hot weather. The doctor told me to do so."

"How long did the pain last?" asked Lionel, feeling his pain growing worse with every moment. "Many hours?"

"Hours?" repeated old Matthew, with a strong emphasis on the word. "Mr. Lionel, it lasted for days and weeks. Before the next morning came, sir, I was in a raging fever; for three weeks, good, I was in my bed, above here, and never out of it; hardly the clothes smoothed a-top of me. Sun-strokes are not frequent in this climate, sir, but when they do come, they can't be trifled with."

Perhaps Lionel felt the same conviction. Perhaps he felt that with this pain, increasing as it was in intensity, he must make the best of his way home, if he would get home at all. "Good-day, Matthew," he said, rising from the bench. "I'll go home at once!"

"And send for Dr. West, sir, or for Mr. Jan, if you are no better when you get there," was the parting salutation of the old man.

He stood at the door, leaning on his stick, and watched Lionel down Clay Lane. "A sun-stroke, for sure," repeated he, slowly turning in, as the angle of the lane hid Lionel from his view.

CHAPTER XXIII

DAYS AND NIGHTS OF PAIN

In his darkened chamber at Deerham Court lay Lionel Verner. Whether it was a sun-stroke, or whether it was but the commencement of a fever, which had suddenly struck him down that day, certain it was, that a violent sickness attacked him, and he lay for many, many days—days and weeks as old Frost had called it—between life and death. Fever and delirium struggled with life, which should get the mastery.

Very little doubt was there, that his state of mind increased the danger of his state of body. How bravely Lionel had struggled to do battle with his great anguish, he might scarcely have known himself, in all its full intensity, save for this illness. He had loved Sibylla with the pure fervour of feelings young and fresh. He could have loved her to the end of life; he could have died for her. No leaven was mixed with his love, no base dross; it was refined as the purest silver. It is only these exalted, ideal passions, which partake more of heaven's nature than of earth's, that tell upon the heart when their end comes. Terribly had it told upon Lionel Verner's. In one hour he had learned that Sibylla was false to him, was about to become the wife of another. In his sensitive reticence, in his shrinking pride, he had put a smiling face upon it before the world. He had watched her marry Frederick Massingbird, and had "made no sign." Deep, deep in his heart, fifty fathom deep, had he pressed down his misery, passing his days in what may be called a false atmosphere—showing a false side to his friends. It seemed false to Lionel, the appearing what he was not. He was his true self at night only, when he could turn, and toss, and groan out his trouble at will. But, when illness attacked him, and he had no strength of body to throw off his pain of mind, then he found how completely the blow had shattered him. It seemed to Lionel, in his sane moments, in the intervals of his delirium, that it would be far happier to die, than to wake up again to renewed life, to bear about within him that ever-present sorrow. Whether the fever—it was not brain fever, though bordering closely upon it—was the result of this state of mind, more than of the sun-stroke, might be a question. Nobody knew anything of that inward state, and the sun-stroke got all the blame—save, perhaps, from Lionel himself. He may have doubted.

One day Jan called in to see him. It was in August. Several weeks had elapsed since the commencement of his illness, and he was so far recovered as to be removed by day to a sitting-room on a level with his chamber—a wondrously pretty sitting-room over Lady Verner's drawing-room, but not so large as that, and called "Miss Decima's room." The walls were panelled in medallions, white and delicate blue, the curtains were of blue satin and lace, the furniture blue. In each medallion hung an exquisite painting in water colours, framed—Decima's doing. Lady Verner was one who liked at times to be alone, and then Decima would sit in this room, and feel more at home than in any room in the house. When Lionel began to recover, the room was given over to him. Here he lay on the sofa; or lounged on an easy-chair; or stood at the window, his hands clasping hold of some support, and his legs as tottering as were poor old Matthew Frost's. Sometimes Lady Verner would be his companion, sometimes he would be consigned to Decima and Lucy Tempest. Lucy was pleased to take her share of helping the time to pass; would read to him, or talk to him; or sit down on her low stool on the hearth-rug and only look at him, waiting until he should want something done. Dangerous moments, Miss Lucy! Unless your heart is cased in adamant, you can scarcely be with that attractive man—ten times more attractive now, in his sickness—and not get your wings singed.

Jan came in one day when Lionel was sitting on the sofa, having propped the cushion up at the back of his head. Decima was winding some silk, and Lucy was holding the skein for her. Lucy wore a summer dress of white muslin, a blue sprig raised upon it in tambour-stitch, with blue and white ribbons at its waist and neck. Very pretty, very simple it looked, but wonderfully according with Lucy Tempest. Jan looked round, saw a tolerably strong table, and took up his seat upon it.

"How d'ye get on, Lionel?" asked he.

It was Dr. West who attended Lionel, and Jan was chary of interfering with the doctor's proper patients—or, rather, the doctor was chary of his doing so—therefore Jan's visits were entirely unprofessional.

"I don't get on at all—as it seems to me," replied Lionel. "I'm sure I am weaker than I was a week ago."

"I dare say," said Jan.

"You dare say!" echoed Lionel. "When a man has turned the point of an illness, he expects to get stronger, instead of weaker."

"That depends," said Jan. "I beg your pardon, Miss Lucy; that's my foot caught in your dress, isn't it?"

Lucy turned to disentangle her dress from Jan's great feet. "You should not sway your feet about so, Jan," said she pleasantly.

"It hasn't hurt it, has it?" asked Jan.

"Oh, no. Is there another skein to hold, Decima?"

Decima replied in the negative. She rose, put the paper of silk upon the table, and then turned to Jan.

"Mamma and I had quite a contention yesterday," she said to him. "I say that Lionel is not being treated properly."

"That's just my opinion," laconically replied Jan. "Only West flares up so, if his treatment is called in question. I'd get him well in half the time."

Lionel wearily changed his position on the sofa. The getting well, or the keeping ill, did not appear to interest him greatly.

"Let's look at his medicine, Decima," continued Jan. "I have not seen what has come round lately."

Decima left the room and brought back a bottle with some medicine in it.

"There's only one dose left," she remarked to Jan.

Jan took the cork out and smelt it; then he tasted it, apparently with great gusto, as anybody else might taste port wine; while Lucy watched him, drawing her lips away from her pretty teeth in distaste at the proceeding.

"Psha!" cried Jan.

"Is it not proper medicine for him?" asked Decima.

"It's as innocent as water," said Jan. "It'll do him neither good nor harm."

And finally Jan poured the lot down his own throat.

Lucy shuddered.

"Oh, Jan, how could you take it?"

"It won't hurt me," said literal Jan.

"But it must be so nasty! I never could have believed any one would willingly drink medicine. It is bad enough to do it when compelled by sickness."

"Law!" returned Jan. "If you call this nasty, Miss Lucy, you should taste some of our physic. The smell would about knock you down."

"I think nothing is worse than the smell of drugs," resumed Lucy. "The other day, when Lady Verner called in at your surgery to speak to you, and took me with her, I was glad to get into the open air again."

"Don't you ever marry a doctor, then, Miss Lucy."

"I am not going to marry one," returned Lucy.

"Well, you need not look so fierce," cried Jan. "I didn't ask you."

Lucy laughed. "Did I look fierce, Jan? I suppose I was thinking of the drugs. I'd never, never be a surgeon, of all things in the world."

"If everybody was of your mind, Miss Lucy, how would people get doctored?"

"Very true," answered Lucy. "But I don't envy them."

"The doctors or the people?" asked Jan.

"I meant the doctors. But I envy the patients less," glancing involuntarily towards Lionel as she spoke.

Jan glanced at him too. "Lionel, I'll bring you round some better stuff than this," said he. "What are you eating?"

"Nothing," put in Decima. "Dr. West keeps him upon arrowroot and beef-tea, and such things."

"Slops," said Jan contemptuously. "Have a fowl cooked every day, Lionel, and eat it all, if you like, bones and all; or a mutton—chop or two; or some good eels. And have the window open and sit at it; don't lounge on that sofa, fancying you can't leave it; and to-morrow or the next day, borrow Mrs. Verner's carriage—"

"No, thank you," interposed Lionel.

"Have a fly, then," composedly went on Jan. "Rouse yourself, and eat and drink, and go into the air, and you'll soon be as well as I am. It's the stewing and fretting indoors, fancying themselves ill, that keeps folks back."

Something like a sickly smile crossed Lionel's wan lips. "Do you remember how you offended your mother, Jan, by telling her she only wanted to rouse herself?"

"Well," said Jan, "it was the truth. West keeps his patients dilly-dallying on, when he might have them well in no time. If he says anything about them to me, I always tell him so; otherwise I don't interfere; it's no business of mine. But you are my brother, you know."

"Don't quarrel with West on my account, Jan. Only settle it amicably between you, what I am to do, and what I am to take. I don't care."

"Quarrel!" said Jan. "You never knew me to quarrel in your life. West can come and see you as usual, and charge you, if you please; and you can just pour his physic down the sink. I'll send you some bark: but it's not of much consequence whether you take it or not; it's good kitchen physic you want now. Is there anything on your mind that's keeping you back?" added plain Jan.

A streak of scarlet rose to Lionel's white cheek.

"Anything on my mind, Jan! I do not understand you."

"Look here," said Jan, "if there is nothing, you ought to be better than this by now, in spite of old West. What you have got to do is to rouse yourself, and believe you are well, instead of lying by, here. My mother was angry with me for telling her that, but didn't she get well all one way after it? And look at the poor! They have their illnesses that bring 'em down to skeletons; but when did you ever find them lie by, after they got better? They can't; they are obliged to go out and turn to at work again; and the consequence is they are well in no time. You have your fowl to-day," continued Jan, taking himself off the table to depart; "or a duck, if you fancy it's more savoury; and if West comes in while you are eating it, tell him I ordered it. He can't grumble at me for doctoring you."

Decima left the room with Jan. Lucy Tempest went to the window, threw it open, drew an easy-chair, with its cushions, near to it, and then returned to the sofa.

"Will you come to the window?" said she to Lionel. "Jan said you were to sit there, and I have put your chair ready."

Lionel unclosed his eyelids. "I am better here, child, thank you."

"But you heard what Jan said—that you were not going the right way to get well."

"It does not much matter, Lucy, whether I get well, or whether I don't," he answered wearily.

Lucy sat down; not on her favourite stool, but on a low chair, and fixed her eyes upon him gravely.

"Do you know what Mr. Cust would say to that?" she asked. "He would tell you that you were ungrateful to God. You are already half-way towards getting well."

"I know I am, Lucy. But I am nearly tired of life."

"It is only the very old who say that, or ought to say it. I am not sure that they ought—even if they were a hundred. But you are young. Stay! I will find it for you."

He was searching about for his handkerchief. Lucy found it, fallen on the floor at the back of the sofa. She brought it round to him, and he gently laid hold of her hand as he took it.

"He gently laid hold of her hand."

"My little friend, you have yet to learn that things, not years, tire us of life."

Lucy shook her head.

"No; I have not to learn it. I know it must be so. Will you please to come to the window?"

Lionel, partly because his tormentor (may the word be used? he was sick, bodily and mentally, and would have lain still for ever) was a young lady, partly to avoid the trouble of persisting in "No," rose, and took his seat in the arm-chair.

"What an obstinate nurse you would make, Lucy! Is there anything else, pray, that you wish me to do?"

She did not smile in response to his smile; she looked very grave and serious.

"I would do all that Jan says, were I you," was her answer. "I believe in Jan. He will get you well sooner than Dr. West."

"Believe in Jan?" repeated Lionel, willing to be gay if he could. "Do you mean that Jan is Jan?"

"I mean that I have faith in Jan. I have none in Dr. West."

"In his medical skill? Let me tell you, Lucy, he is a very clever man, in spite of what Jan may say."

"I can't tell anything about his skill. Until Jan spoke now I did not know but he was treating you rightly. But I have no faith in himself. I think a good, true, faithful-natured man should be depended on for cure, more certainly than one who is false-natured."

"False-natured!" echoed Lionel. "Lucy, you should not so speak of Dr. West. You know nothing wrong of Dr. West. He is much esteemed among us at Deerham."

"Of course I know nothing wrong of him," returned Lucy, with some slight surprise. "But when I look at people I always seem to know what they are. I am sorry to have said so much. I—I think I forgot it was to you I spoke."

"Forgot!" exclaimed Lionel. "Forgot what?"

She hesitated at the last sentence, and she now blushed vividly.

"I forgot for the moment that he was Sibylla's father," she simply said.

Again the scarlet rose in the face of Lionel. Lucy leaned against the window-frame but a few paces from him, her large soft eyes, in their earnest sympathy, lifted to his. He positively shrank from them.

"What's Sibylla to me?" he asked. "She is Mrs. Frederick Massingbird."

Lucy stood in penitence. "Do not be angry with me," she timidly cried. "I ought not to have said it to you, perhaps. I see it always."

"See what, Lucy?" he continued, speaking gently, not in anger.

"I see now much you think of her, and how ill it makes you. When Jan asked just now if you had anything on your mind to keep you back, I knew what it was."

Lionel grew hot and cold with a sudden fear. "Did I say anything in my delirium?"

"Nothing at all—that I heard of. I was not with you. I do not think anybody suspects that you are ill because—because of her."

"Ill because of her!" he sharply repeated, the words breaking from him in his agony, in his shrinking dread at finding so much suspected. "I am ill from fever. What else should I be ill from?"

Lucy went close to his chair and stood before him meekly.

"I am so sorry," she whispered. "I cannot help seeing things, but I did not mean to make you angry."

He rose, steadying himself by the table, and laid his hand upon her head, with the same fond motion that a father might have used.

"Lucy, I am not angry—only vexed at being watched so closely," he concluded, his lips parting with a faint smile.

In her earnest, truthful, serious face of concern, as it was turned up to him, he read how futile it would be to persist in his denial.

"I did not watch you for the purpose of watching. I saw how it was, without being able to help myself."

Lionel bent his head.

"Let the secret remain between us, Lucy. Never suffer a hint of it to escape your lips."

Nothing answered him save the glad expression that beamed out from her countenance, telling him how implicitly he might trust to her.

CHAPTER XXIV

DANGEROUS COMPANIONSHIP

Lionel Verner grew better. His naturally good constitution triumphed over the disease, and his sick soreness of mind lost somewhat of its sharpness. So long as he brooded in silence over his pain and his wrongs, there was little chance of the sting becoming much lighter; it was like the vulture preying upon its own vitals; but that season of silence was past. When once a deep grief can be spoken of, its great agony is gone. I think there is an old saying, or a proverb—"Griefs lose themselves in telling," and a greater truism was never uttered. The ice once broken, touching his feelings with regard to Sibylla, Lionel found comfort in making it his theme of conversation, of complaint, although his hearer and confidant was only Lucy Tempest. A strange comfort, but yet a natural one, as those who have suffered as Lionel did may be able to testify. At the time of the blow, when Sibylla deserted him with coolness so great, Lionel could have died rather than give utterance to a syllable betraying his own pain; but several months had elapsed since, and the turning-point was come. He did not, unfortunately, love Sibylla one shade less; love such as his cannot be overcome so lightly; but the keenness of the disappointment, the blow to his self-esteem—to his vanity, it may be said—was growing less intense. In a case like this, of faithlessness, let it happen to man or to woman, the wounding of the self-esteem is not the least evil that must be borne. Lucy Tempest was, in Lionel's estimation, little more than a child, yet it was singular how he grew to love to talk with her. Not for love of her—do not fancy that—but for the opportunity it gave him of talking of Sibylla. You may deem this an anomaly; I know that it was natural; and, like oil poured upon a wound, so did it bring balm to Lionel's troubled spirit.

He never spoke of her save at the dusk hour. During the broad, garish light of day, his lips were sealed. In the soft twilight of the evening, if it happened that Lucy was alone with him, then he would pour out his heart—would tell of his past tribulation. As past he spoke of it; had he not regarded it as past, he never would have spoken. Lucy listened, mostly in silence, returning him her earnest sympathy. Had Lucy Tempest been a little older in ideas, or had she been by nature and rearing less entirely single-minded, she might not have sat unrestrainedly with him, going into the room at any moment, and stopping there, as she would had he been her brother. Lucy was getting to covet the companionship of Lionel very much—too much, taking all things into consideration. It never occurred to her that, for that very reason, she might do well to keep away. She was not sufficiently experienced to define her own sensations; and she did not surmise that there was anything inexpedient or not perfectly orthodox in her being so much with Lionel. She liked to be with him, and she freely indulged the liking upon any occasion that offered.

"Oh, Lucy, I loved her! I did love her!" he would say, having repeated the same words perhaps fifty times before in other interviews; and he would lean back in his easy-chair, and cover his eyes with his hand, as if willing to shut out all sight save that of the past. "Heaven knows what she was to me! Heaven only knows what her faithlessness has cost!"

"Did you dream of her last night, Lionel?" answered Lucy, from her low seat where she generally sat, near to Lionel, but with her face mostly turned from him.

And it may as well be mentioned that Miss Lucy never thought of such a thing as discouraging Lionel's love and remembrance of Sibylla. Her whole business in the matter seemed to be to listen to him, and help him to remember her.

"Ay," said Lionel, in answer to the question. "Do you suppose I should dream of anything else?"

Whatever Lucy may or may not have supposed, it was a positive fact, known well to Lionel—known to him, and remembered by him to this hour—that he constantly dreamed of Sibylla. Night after night, since the unhappy time when he learned that she had left him for Frederick Massingbird, had she formed the prominent subject of his dreams. It is the strict truth; and it will prove to you how powerful a hold she must have possessed over his imagination. This he had not failed to make an item in his revelations to Lucy.

"What was your dream last night, Lionel?"

"It was only a confused one; or seemed to be when I awoke. It was full of trouble. Sibylla appeared to have done something wrong, and I was defending her, and she was angry with me for it. Unusually confused it was. Generally my dreams are too clear and vivid."

"I wonder how long you will dream of her, Lionel? For a year, do you think?"

"I hope not," heartily responded Lionel. "Lucy, I wish I could forget her?"

"I wish you could—if you do wish to do it," simply replied Lucy.

"Wish! I wish I could have swallowed a draught of old Lethe's stream last February, and never recalled her again!"

He spoke vehemently, and yet there was a little undercurrent of suppressed consciousness deep down in his heart, whispering that his greatest solace was to remember her, and to talk of her as he was doing now. To talk of her as he would to his own soul: and that he had now learned to do with Lucy Tempest. Not to any one else in the whole world could Lionel have breathed the name of Sibylla.

"Do you suppose she will soon be coming home?" asked Lucy, after a silence.

"Of course she will. The news of his inheritance went out shortly after they started, and must have got to Melbourne nearly as soon as they did. There's little doubt they are on their road home now. Massingbird would not care to stop to look after what was left by John, when he knows himself to be the owner of Verner's Pride."

"I wish Verner's Pride had not been left to Frederick Massingbird!" exclaimed Lucy.

"Frankly speaking, so do I," confessed Lionel. "It ought to be mine by all good right. And, putting myself entirely out of consideration, I judge Frederick Massingbird unworthy to be its master. That's between ourselves, mind, Lucy."

"It is all between ourselves," returned Lucy.

"Ay. What should I have done without you, my dear little friend?"

"I am glad you have not had to do without me," simply answered Lucy. "I hope you will let me be your friend always!"

"That I will. Now Sibylla's gone, there's nobody in the whole world I care for, but you."

He spoke it without any double meaning: he might have used the same words, been actuated by precisely the same feelings, to his mother or his sister. His all-absorbing love for Sibylla barred even the idea of any other love to his mind, yet awhile.

"Lionel!" cried Lucy, turning her face full upon him in her earnestness, "how could she choose Frederick Massingbird, when she might have chosen you?"

"Tastes differ," said Lionel, speaking lightly, a thing he rarely did when with Lucy. "There's no accounting for them. Some time or other, Lucy, you may be marrying an ugly fellow with a wooden leg and red beard; and people will say, 'How could Lucy Tempest have chosen him?'"

Lucy coloured. "I do not like you to speak in that joking way, if you please," she gravely said.

"Heigh ho, Lucy!" sighed he. "Sometimes I fancy a joke may cheat me out of a minute's care. I wish I was well, and away from this place. In London I shall have my hands full, and can rub off the rust of old grievances with hard work."

"You will not like London better than Deerham."

"I shall like it ten thousand times better," impulsively answered Lionel. "I have no longer a place in Deerham, Lucy. That is gone."

"You allude to Verner's Pride?"

"Everything's gone that I valued in Deerham," cried Lionel, with the same impulse—"Verner's Pride amongst the rest. I would never stop here to see the rule of Fred Massingbird. Better that John had lived to take it, than that it should have come to him."

"Was John better than his brother?"

"He would have made a better master. He was, I believe, a better man. Not but that John had his faults, as we all have."

"All!" echoed Lucy. "What are your faults?"

Lionel could not help laughing. She asked the question, as she did all her questions, in the most genuine, earnest manner, really seeking the information. "I think for some time back, Lucy, my chief fault has been grumbling. I am sure you must find it so. Better days may be in store for us both."

Lucy rose. "I think it must be time for me to go and make Lady Verner's tea. Decima will not be home for it."

"Where is Decima this evening?"

"She is gone her round to the cottages. She does not find time for it in the day, since you were ill. Is there anything I can do for you before I go down?"

"Yes," he answered, taking her hand. "You can let me thank you for your patience and kindness. You have borne with me bravely, Lucy. God bless you, my dear child."

She neither went away, nor drew her hand away. She stood there—as he had phrased it—patiently, until he should release it. He soon did so, with a weary movement: all he did was wearisome to him then, save the thinking and talking of the theme which ought to have been a barred one—Sibylla.

"Will you please to come down to tea this evening?" asked Lucy.

"I don't care for tea; I'd rather be alone."

"Then I will bring you some up."

"No, no; you shall not be at the trouble. I'll come down, then, presently."

Lucy Tempest disappeared. Lionel leaned against the window, looking out on the night landscape, and lost himself in thoughts of his faithless love. He aroused himself from them with a stamp of impatience.

"I must shake it off," he cried to himself; "I will shake it off. None, save myself or a fool, but would have done it months ago. And yet, Heaven alone knows how I have tried and battled, and how vain the battle has been!"

CHAPTER XXV

HOME TRUTHS FOR LIONEL

The cottages down Clay Lane were ill-drained. It might be nearer the truth to say they were not drained at all. As is the case with many another fine estate besides Verner's Pride, while the agricultural land was well drained, no expense spared upon it, the poor dwellings had been neglected. Not only in the matter of draining, but in other respects, were these habitations deficient: but that strong terms are apt to grate unpleasantly upon the ear, one might say shamefully deficient. The consequence was that no autumn ever went over, scarcely any spring, but somebody would be down with ague, with low fever; and it was reckoned a fortunate season if a good many were not prostrate.

The first time that Lionel Verner took a walk down Clay Lane after his illness was a fine day in October. He had been out before in other directions, but not in that of Clay Lane. He had not yet recovered his full strength; he looked ill and emaciated. Had he been strong, as he used to be, he would not have found himself nearly losing his equilibrium at being run violently against by a woman, who turned swiftly out of her own door.

"Take care, Mrs. Grind! Is your house on fire?"

"It's begging a thousand pardons, sir! I hadn't no idea you was there," returned Mrs. Grind, in lamentable confusion, when she saw whom she had all but knocked down. "Grind, he catches sight o' one o' the brick men going by, and he tells me to run and fetch him in; but I had got my hands in the soap-suds, and couldn't take 'em convenient out of it at the minute, and I was hasting lest he'd gone too far to be caught up. He have now."

"Is Grind better?"

"He ain't no worse, sir. There he is," she added, flinging the door open.

On the side of the kitchen, opposite to the door, was a pallet-bed stretched against the wall, and on it lay the woman's husband, Grind, dressed. It was a small room, and it appeared literally full of children, of encumbrances of all sorts. A string extended from one side of the fire-place to the other, and on this hung some wet coloured pinafores, the steam ascending from them in clouds, drawn out by the heat of the fire. The children were in various stages of un-dress, these coloured pinafores doubtless constituting their sole outer garment. But that Grind's eye had caught his, Lionel might have hesitated to enter so uncomfortable a place. His natural kindness of heart—nay, his innate regard for the feelings of others, let them be ever so inferior in station—prevented his turning back when the man had seen him.

"Grind, don't move, don't get off the bed," Lionel said hastily. But Grind was already up. The ague fit was upon him then, and he shook the bed as he sat down upon it. His face wore that blue, pallid appearance, which you may have seen in aguish patients.

"You don't seem much better, Grind."

"Thank ye, sir, I be baddish just now again, but I ain't worse on the whole," was the man's reply. A civil, quiet, hard-working man as any on the estate; nothing against him but his large flock of children, and his difficulty of getting along any way. The mouths to feed were many—ravenous young mouths, too; and the wife, though anxious and well-meaning, was not the most thrifty in the world. She liked gossiping better than thrift; but gossip was the most prevalent complaint of Clay Lane, so far as its female population was concerned.

"How long is it that you have been ill?" asked Lionel, leaning his elbow on the mantel-piece, and looking down on Grind, Mrs. Grind having whisked away the pinafores.

"It's going along of four weeks, sir, now. It's a illness, sir, I takes it, as must have its course."

"All illnesses must have that, as I believe," said Lionel. "Mine has taken its own time pretty well, has it not?"

Grind shook his head.

"You don't look none the better for your bout, sir. And it's a long time you must have been a-getting strong. Mr. Jan, he said, just a month ago, when he first come to see me, as you was well, so to say, then. Ah! it's only them as have tried it knows what the pulling through up to strength again is, when the illness itself seems gone."

Lionel's conscience was rather suggestive at that moment. He might have been stronger than he was, by this time, had he "pulled through" with a better will, and given way less. "I am sorry not to see you better, Grind," he kindly said.

"You see me at the worst, sir, to-day," said the man, in a tone of apology, as if seeking to excuse his own sickness. "I be getting better, and that's a thing to be thankful for. I only gets the fever once in three days now. Yesterday, sir, I got down to the field, and earned what'll come to eighteen pence. I did indeed, sir, though you'd not think it, looking at me to-day."

"I should not," said Lionel. "Do you mean to say you went to work in your present state?"

"I didn't seem a bit ill yesterday, sir, except for the weakness. The fever, it keeps me down all one day, as may be to-day; then the morrow I be quite prostrate with the weakness it leaves; and the third day I be, so to speak, well. But I can't do a full day's work, sir; no, nor hardly half of a one, and by evening I be so done over I can scarce crawl to my place here. It ain't much, sir, part of a day's work in three; but I be thankful for that improvement. A week ago, I couldn't do as much as that."

More suggestive thoughts for Lionel.

"He'd a got better quicker, sir, if he could do his work regular," put in the woman. "What's one day's work out o' three—even if 'twas a full day's—to find us all victuals? In course he can't fare better nor we; and Peckaby's, they don't give much trust to us. He gets a pot o' gruel, or a saucer o' porridge, or a hunch o' bread with a mite o' cheese."

Lionel looked at the man. "You cannot eat plain bread now, can you, Grind?"

"All this day, sir, I shan't eat nothing; I couldn't swallow it," he answered. "After the fever and the shaking's gone, then I could eat, but not bread; it seems too dry for the throat, and it sticks in it. I get a dish o' tea, or something in that way. The next day—my well day, as I calls it—I can eat all afore me."

"You ought to have more strengthening food."

"It's not for us to say, sir, as we ought to have this here food, or that there food, unless we earns it," replied Grind, in a meek spirit of contented resignation that many a rich man might have taken a pattern from. "Mr. Jan he says, 'Grind,' says he, 'you should have some meat to eat, and some good beef-tea, and a drop o' wine wouldn't do you no harm,' says he. And it makes me smile, sir, to think where the like o' poor folks is to get such things. Lucky to be able to get a bit o' bread and a drain o' tea without sugar, them as is off their work, just to rub on and keep theirselves out o' the workhouse. I know I'm thankful to do it. Jim, he have got a place, sir."

"Jim,—which is Jim?" asked Lionel, turning his eyes on the group of children, supposing one must be meant.

"He ain't here, sir," cried the woman. "It's the one with the black hair, and he was six year old yesterday. He's gone to Farmer Johnson's to take care o' the pigs in the field. He's to get a shilling a week."

Lionel moved from his position. "Grind," he said, "don't you think it would be better if you gave yourself complete rest, not attempting to go out to work until you are stronger?"

"I couldn't afford it, sir. And as to its being better for me, I don't see that. If I can work, sir, I'm better at work. I know it tires me, but I believe I get stronger the sooner for it. Mr. Jan, he says to me, says he, 'Don't lie by never, Grind, unless you be obliged to it; it only rusts the limbs.' And he ain't far out, sir. Folks gets more harm from idleness nor they do from work."

"Well, good-day, Grind," said Lionel, "and I heartily hope you'll soon be on your legs again. Lady Verner shall send you something more nourishing than bread, while you are still suffering."

"Thank ye kindly, sir," replied Grind. "My humble duty to my lady."

Lionel went out. "What a lesson for me!" he involuntarily exclaimed. "This poor half-starved man struggling patiently onward through his sickness; while I, who had every luxury about me, spent my time in repining. What a lesson! Heaven help me to take it to my heart!"

He lifted his hat as he spoke, his feeling at the moment full of reverence; and went on to Frost's. "Where's Robin?" he asked of the wife.

"He's in the back room, sir," was the answer. "He's getting better fast. The old father, he have gone out a bit, a-warming of himself in the sun."

She opened the door of a small back room as she spoke; but it proved to be empty. Robin was discerned in the garden, sitting on a bench; possibly to give himself a warming in the sun—as Mrs. Frost expressed it. He sat in a still attitude, his arms folded, his head bowed. Since the miserable occurrence touching Rachel, Robin Frost was a fearfully changed man; never, from the hour that the coroner's inquest was held and certain evidence had come out, had he been seen to smile. He had now been ill with ague, in the same way as Grind. Hearing the approach of footsteps, he turned his head, and rose when he saw it was Lionel.

"Well, Robin, how fares it? You are better, I hear. Sit yourself down; you are not strong enough to stand. What an enemy this low fever is! I wish we could root it out!"

"Many might be all the healthier for it, sir, if it could be done," was Robin's answer, spoken indifferently—as he nearly always spoke now. "As for me, I'm not far off being well again."

"They said in the village you were going to die, Robin, did they not?" continued Lionel. "You have cheated them, you see."

"They said it, some of 'em, sir, and thought it, too. Old father thought it. I'm not sure but Mr. Jan thought it. I didn't, bad as I was," continued Robin, in a significant tone. "I had my oath to keep."

"Robin!"

"Sir, I have sworn—and you know I have sworn it—to have my revenge upon him that worked ill to Rachel. I can't die till that oath has been kept."

"There's a certain sentence, Robin, given us for our guidance, amid many other such sentences, which runs somewhat after this fashion: 'Vengeance is mine,'" quietly spoke Lionel. "Have you forgotten who it is says that?"

"Why did he—the villain—forget them sentences? Why did he forget 'em and harm her?" retorted Robin. "Sir, it's of no good for you to look at me in that way. I'll never be baulked in this matter. Old father, now and again, he'll talk about forgiveness; and when I say, 'weren't you her father?' 'Ay,' he'll answer, 'but I've got one foot in the grave, Robin, and anger will not bring her back to life.' No, it won't," doggedly went on Robin. "It won't undo what was done, neither: but I'll keep my oath—so far as it is in my power to keep it. Dead though he is, he shall be exposed to the world."

The words "dead though he is" aroused the attention of Lionel. "To whom do you allude, Robin?" he asked. "Have you obtained any fresh clue?"

"Not much of a fresh one," answered the man, with a stress upon the word "fresh." "I have had it this six or seven months. When they heard he was dead, then they could speak out and tell me their suspicions of him."

"Who could? What mystery are you talking?" reiterated Lionel.

"Never mind who, sir. It was one that kept the mouth shut, as long as there was any good in opening it. 'Not to make ill-blood,' was the excuse gave to me after. If I had but knowed at the time!" added the man, clenching his fist, "I'd have went out and killed him, if he had been double as far off!"

"Robin, what have you heard?"

"Well, sir, I'll tell you—but I have not opened my lips to a living soul,-not even to old father—The villain that did the harm to Rachel was John Massingbird!"

Lionel remained silent from surprise.

"I don't believe it," he presently said, speaking emphatically. "Who has accused him?"

"Sir, I have said that I can't tell you. I passed my word not to do it. It was one that had cause to suspect him at the time. And it was never told me—never told me—until John Massingbird was dead!"

Robin's voice rose to a sound of wailing pain, and he raised his hands with a gesture of despair.

"Did your informant know that it was John Massingbird?" Lionel gravely asked.

"They had not got what is called positive proof, such as might avail in a Court of Justice; but they was morally certain," replied Robin; "and so am I. I am only waiting for one thing, sir, to tell it out to all the world."

"And what's that?"

"The returning home of Luke Roy. There's not much doubt that he knows all about it; I have my reasons for saying so, and I'd like to be quite sure before I tell out the tale. Old Roy says Luke may be expected home by any ship as comes; he don't think he'll stop there, now John Massingbird's dead."

"Then, Robin, listen to me," returned Lionel. "I have no positive proof, any more than it appears your informant has; but I am perfectly convinced in my own mind that the guilty man was not John Massingbird, but another. Understand me," he emphatically continued, "I have good and sufficient reason for saying this. Rely upon it, whoever it may have been, John Massingbird it was not."

Robin lifted his eyes to the face of Lionel.

"You say you don't know this, sir?"

"Not of actual proof. But so sure am I that it was not he, that I could stake all I possess upon it."

"Then, sir, you'd lose it," doggedly answered Robin. "When the time comes that I choose to speak out—"

"What are you doing there?" burst forth Lionel, in a severely haughty tone.

It caused Robin to start from his seat.

In a gap of the hedge behind them, Lionel had caught sight of a human face, its stealthy ears complacently taking in every word. It was that of Roy the bailiff.

CHAPTER XXVI

THE PACKET IN THE SHIRT-DRAWER

Mrs. Tynn, the housekeeper at Verner's Pride, was holding one of those periodical visitations that she was pleased to call, when in familiar colloquy with her female assistants, a "rout out." It appeared to consist of turning a room and its contents topsy-turvy, and then putting them straight again. The chamber this time subjected to the ordeal was that of her late master, Mr. Verner. His drawers, closets, and other places consecrated to clothes, had not been meddled with since his death. Mrs. Verner, in some moment unusually (for her) given to sentiment, had told Tynn she should like to "go over his dear clothes" herself. Therefore Tynn left them alone for that purpose. Mrs. Verner, however, who loved her personal ease better than any earthly thing, and was more given to dropping off to sleep in her chair than ever, not only after dinner but all day long, never yet had ventured upon the task. Tynn suggested that she had better do it herself, after all; and Mrs. Verner replied, perhaps she had. So Tynn set about it.

Look at Mrs. Tynn over that deep, open drawer full of shirts. She calls it "Master's shirt-drawer." Have the shirts scared away her senses? She has sat herself down on the floor—almost fallen back as it seems—in some shock of alarm, and her mottled face has turned as white as her master's was, when she last saw him lying on that bed at her elbow.

"Go downstairs, Nancy, and stop there till I call you up again," she suddenly cried out to her helpmate.

And the girl left the room, grumbling to herself; for Nancy at Verner's Pride did not improve in temper.

Between two of the shirts, in the very middle of the stack, Mrs. Tynn had come upon a parcel, or letter. Not a small letter—if it was a letter—but one of very large size, thick, looking not unlike a government despatch. It was sealed with Mr. Verner's own seal, and addressed in his own handwriting—"For my nephew, Lionel Verner. To be opened after my death."

Mrs. Tynn entertained not the slightest doubt that she had come upon the lost codicil. That the parcel must have been lying quietly in the drawer since her master's death, was certain. The key of the drawer had remained in her own possession. When the search after the codicil took place, this drawer was opened—as a matter of form more than anything else—and Mrs. Tynn herself had lifted out the stack of shirts. She had assured those who were searching that there was no need to do so, for the drawer had been locked up at the time the codicil was made, and the deed could not have been put into it. They accepted her assurance, and did not look between the shirts. It puzzled Mrs. Tynn, now, to think how it could have got in.

"I'll not tell Tynn," she soliloquised—she and Tynn being somewhat inclined to take opposite sides of a question, in social intercourse—"and I'll not say a word to my mistress. I'll go straight off now and give it into the hands of Mr. Lionel. What a blessed thing!—If he should be come into his own!"

The inclosed paved court before Lady Verner's residence had a broad flower-bed round it. It was private from the outer world, save for the iron gates, and here Decima and Lucy Tempest were fond of lingering on a fine day. On this afternoon of Mary Tynn's discovery, they were there with Lionel. Decima went indoors for some string to tie up a fuchsia plant, just as Tynn appeared at the iron gates. She stopped on seeing Lionel.

"I was going round to the other entrance, sir, to ask to speak to you," she said. "Something very strange has happened."

"Come in," answered Lionel. "Will you speak here, or go indoors? What is it?"

Too excitedly eager to wait to go indoors, or to care for the presence of Lucy Tempest, Mrs. Tynn told her tale, and handed the paper to Lionel. "It's the missing codicil, as sure as that we are here, sir."

He saw the official-looking nature of the document, its great seal, and the superscription in his uncle's handwriting. Lionel did not doubt that it was the codicil, and a streak of scarlet emotion arose to his pale cheek.

"You don't open it, sir!" said the woman, as feverishly impatient as if the good fortune were her own.

No. Lionel did not open it. In his high honour, he deemed that, before opening, it should be laid before Mrs. Verner. It had been found in her house; it concerned her son. "I think it will be better that Mrs. Verner should open this, Tynn," he quietly said.

"You won't get me into a mess, sir, for bringing it out to you first?"

Lionel turned his honest eyes upon her, smiling then. "Can't you trust me better than that? You have known me long enough."

"So I have, Mr. Lionel. The mystery is, how it could ever have got into that shirt-drawer!" she continued. "I can declare that for a good week before my master died, up to the very day that the codicil was looked for, the shirt-drawer was never unlocked, nor the key of it out of my pocket."

She turned to go back to Verner's Pride, Lionel intending to follow her at once. He was going out at the gate when he caught the pleased eyes of Lucy Tempest fixed on him.

"I am so glad," she simply said. "Do you remember my telling you that you did not look like one who would have to starve on bread-and-cheese."

Lionel laughed in the joy of his heart. "I am glad also, Lucy. The place is mine by right, and it is just that I should have it."

"I have thought it very unfair, all along, that Verner's Pride should belong to her husband, and not to you, after—after what she did to you," continued Lucy, dropping her voice to a whisper.

"Things don't go by fairness, Lucy, in this world," said he, as he went through the gate. "Stay," he said, turning back from it, a thought crossing his mind. "Lucy, oblige me by not mentioning this to my mother or Decima. It may be as well to be sure that we are right, before exciting their hopes."

Lucy's countenance fell. "I will not speak of it. But, is it not sure to be the codicil?"

"I hope it is," cordially answered Lionel.

Mrs. Tynn had got back before him. She came forward and encountered him in the hall, her bonnet still on.

"I have told my mistress, sir, that I had found what I believed to be the codicil, and had took it off straight to you. She was not a bit angry; she says she hopes it is it."

Lionel entered. Mrs. Verner, who was in a semi-sleepy state, having been roused up by Mary Tynn from a long nap after a plentiful luncheon, received Lionel graciously—first of all asking him what he would take—it was generally her chief question—and then inquiring what the codicil said.

"I have not opened it," replied Lionel.

"No!" said she, in surprise. "Why did you wait?"

He laid it on the table beside her. "Have I your cordial approval to open it, Mrs. Verner?"

"You are ceremonious, Lionel. Open it at once; Verner's Pride belongs to you, more than to Fred; and you know I have always said so."

Lionel took up the deed. His finger was upon the seal when a thought crossed him; ought he to open it without further witnesses? He spoke his doubt aloud to Mrs. Verner.

"Ring the bell and have in Tynn," said she; "his wife also; she found it."

Lionel rang. Tynn and his wife both came in, in obedience to the request. Tynn looked at it curiously; and began rehearsing mentally a private lecture for his wife, for acting upon her own responsibility.

The seal was broken. The stiff writing-paper of the outer cover revealed a second cover of stiff writing-paper precisely similar to the first; but on this last there was no superscription. It was tied round with fine white twine. Lionel cut it, Tynn and Mrs. Tynn waited with the utmost eagerness; even Mrs. Verner's eyes were open wider than usual.

Alas! for the hopes of Lionel. The parcel contained nothing but a glove, and a small piece of writing-paper, folded once. Lionel unfolded it, and read the following lines:—

"This glove has come into my possession. When I tell you that I know where it was found and how you lost it, you will not wonder at the shock the discovery has been to me. I hush it up, Lionel, for your late father's sake, as much as for that of the name of Verner. I am about to seal it up that it may be given to you after my death; and you will then know why I disinherit you. S.V."

Lionel gazed on the lines like one in a dream. They were in the handwriting of his uncle. Understand them, he could not. He took up the glove—a thick, fawn-coloured riding-glove—and remembered it for one of his own. When he had lost it, or where he had lost it, he knew no more than did the table he was standing by. He had worn dozens of these gloves in the years gone by, up to the period when he had gone in mourning for John Massingbird, and, subsequently, for his uncle.

"What is it, Lionel?"

Lionel put the lines in his pocket, and pushed the glove toward Mrs. Verner. "I do not understand it in the least," he said. "My uncle appears to have found the glove somewhere, and he writes to say that he returns it to me. The chief matter that concerns us is"—turning his eyes on the servants—"that it is not the codicil!"

Mrs. Tynn lifted her hands. "How one may be deceived!" she uttered. "Mr. Lionel, I'd freely have laid my life upon it."

"It was not exactly my place to speak, sir: to give my opinion beforehand," interposed Tynn; "but I was sure that was not the lost codicil, by the very look of it. The codicil might have been about that size, and it had a big seal like that; but it was different in appearance."

"All that puzzled me was, how it could have got into the shirt-drawer," cried Mrs. Tynn. "As it has turned out not to be the codicil, of course there's no mystery about that. It may have been lying there weeks and weeks before the master died."

Lionel signed to them to leave the room: there was nothing to call for their remaining in it. Mrs. Verner asked him what the glove meant.

"I assure you I do not know," was his reply. And he took it up, and examined it well again. One of his riding gloves, scarcely worn, with a tear near the thumb; but there was nothing upon it, not so much as a trace, a spot, to afford any information. He rolled it up mechanically in the two papers, and placed them in his pocket, lost in thought.

"Do you know that I have heard from Australia?" asked Mrs. Verner.

The words aroused him thoroughly. "Have you? I did not know it."

"I wonder Mary Tynn did not tell you. The letters came this morning. If you look about"—turning her eyes on the tables and places—"you will find them somewhere."

Lionel knew that Mary Tynn had been too much absorbed in his business to find room in her thoughts for letters from Australia. "Are these the letters?" he asked, taking up two from a side-table.

"You'll know them by the post-marks. Do sit down and read them to me, Lionel. My sight is not good for letters now, and I couldn't read half that was in them. The ink's as pale as water. If it was the ink Fred took out, the sea must have washed into it. Yes, yes, you must I read both to me, and I shall not let you go away before dinner."

He did not like, in his good nature, to refuse her. And he sat there and read the long letters. Read Sibylla's. Before the last one was fully accomplished, Lionel's cheeks wore their hectic flush.

They had made a very quick and excellent passage. But Sibylla found Melbourne hateful. And Fred was ill; ill with fever. A fever was raging in a part of the crowded town, and he had caught it. She did not think it was a catching fever, either, she added; people said it arose from the over-population. They could not as yet hear of John, or his money, or anything about him; but Fred would see into it when he got better. They were at a part of Melbourne called Canvas Town, and she, Sibylla, was sick of it, and Fred drank heaps of brandy. If it were all land between her and home, she should set off at once on foot, and toil her way back again. She wished she had never come! Everything she cared for, except Fred, seemed to be left behind in England.

Such was her letter. Fred's was gloomy also, in a different way. He said nothing about any fever; he mentioned, casually, as it appeared, that he was not well, but that was all. He had not learned tidings of John, but had not had time yet to make inquiries. The worst piece of news he mentioned was the loss of his desk, which had contained the chief portion of his money. It had disappeared in a mysterious manner immediately after being taken off the ship—he concluded by the light fingers of some crimp, or thief, shoals of whom crowded on the quay. He was in hopes yet to find it, and had not told Sibylla. That was all he had to say at present, but would write again by the next packet.

"It is not very cheering news on the whole, is it?" said Mrs. Verner, as Lionel folded the letters.

"No. They had evidently not received the tidings of my uncle's death, or we should have heard that they were already coming back again."

"I don't know that," replied Mrs. Verner. "Fred worships money, and he would not suffer what was left by poor John to slip through his fingers. He will stay till he has realised it. I hope they will think to bring me back some memento of my lost boy! If it were only the handkerchief he used last, I should value it."

The tears filled her eyes. Lionel respected her grief, and remained silent. Presently she resumed, in a musing tone—

"I knew Sibylla would only prove an encumbrance to Fred, out there; and I told him so. If Fred thought he was taking out a wife who would make shift, and put up pleasantly with annoyances, he was mistaken. Sibylla in Canvas Town! Poor girl! I wonder she married him. Don't you?"

"Rather so," answered Lionel, his scarlet blush deepening.

"I do; especially to go to that place. Sibylla's a pretty flower, made to sport in the sunshine; but she never was constituted for a rough life, or to get pricked by thorns."

Lionel's heart beat. It echoed to every word. Would that she could have been sheltered from the thorns, the rough usages of life, as he would have sheltered her.

Lionel dined with Mrs. Verner, but quitted her soon afterwards. When he got back to Deerham Court, the stars were peeping out in the clear summer sky. Lucy Tempest was lingering in the courtyard, no doubt waiting for him, and she ran to meet him as soon as he appeared at the gate.

"How long you have been!" was her greeting, her glad eyes shining forth hopefully. "And is it all yours?"

Lionel drew her arm within his own in silence, and walked with her in silence until they reached the pillared entrance of the house. Then he spoke—

"You have not mentioned it, Lucy?"

"Of course I have not."

"Thank you. Let us both forget it. It was not the codicil. And Verner's Pride is not mine."

CHAPTER XXVII

DR WEST'S SANCTUM

For some little time past, certain rumours had arisen in Deerham somewhat to the prejudice of Dr. West. Rumours of the same nature had circulated once or twice before during the progress of the last half dozen years; but they had died away again, or had been hushed up, never coming to anything. For one thing, their reputed scene had not lain at the immediate spot, but at Heartburg; and distance is a great discouragement to ill-natured tattle. This fresh scandal, however, was nearer. It touched the very heart of Deerham, and people made themselves remarkably busy over it—none the less busy because the accusations were vague. Tales never lose anything in carrying, and the most outrageous things were whispered of Dr. West.

A year or two previous to this, a widow lady named Baynton, with her two daughters, no longer very young, had come to live at a pretty cottage in Deerham. Nothing was known of who they were, or where they came from. They appeared to be very reserved, and made no acquaintance whatever. Under these circumstances, of course, their history was supplied for them. If you or I went and established ourselves in a fresh place to-morrow, saying nothing of who we were, or what we were, it would only be the signal for some busybody in that place to coin a story for us, and all the rest of the busybodies would immediately circulate it. It was said of Mrs. Baynton that she had been left in reduced circumstances; had fallen from some high pedestal of wealth, through the death of her husband; that she lived in a perpetual state of mortification in consequence of her present poverty, and would not admit a single inhabitant of Deerham within her doors to witness it. There may have been as little truth in it as in the greatest canard that ever flew; but Deerham promulgated it, Deerham believed in it, and the Bayntons never contradicted it. The best of all reasons for this may have been that they never heard of it. They lived quietly on alone, interfering with nobody, and going out rarely. In appearance and manners they were gentlewomen, and rather haughty gentlewomen, too; but they kept no servant. How their work was done, Deerham could not conceive: it was next to impossible to fancy one of those ladies scrubbing a floor or making a bed. The butcher called for orders, and took in the meat, which was nearly always mutton-chops; the baker left his bread at the door, and the laundress was admitted inside the passage once a week.

The only other person admitted inside was Dr. West. He had been called in, on their first arrival, to the invalid daughter—a delicate-looking lady, who, when she did walk out, leaned on her sister's arm. Dr. West's visits became frequent; they had continued frequent up to within a short period of the present time. Once or twice a week he called in professionally; he would also occasionally drop in for an hour in the evening. Some people passing Chalk Cottage (that was what it was named) had contrived to stretch their necks over the high privet hedge which hid the lower part of the dwelling from the road, and were immensely gratified by the fact of seeing Dr. West in the parlour, seated at tea with the family. How the doctor was questioned, especially in the earlier period of their residence, he alone could tell. Who were they? Were they well connected, or ill connected, or not connected at all? Were they known to fashion? How much was really their income? What was the matter with the one whom he attended, the sickly daughter, and what was her name? The questions would have gone on until now, but that the doctor stopped them. He had not made impertinent inquiries himself, he said, and had nothing at all to tell. The younger lady's complaint arose from disordered liver; he had no objection to tell them that; she had been so long a sufferer from it that the malady had become chronic; and her name was Kitty.

Now, it was touching this very family that the scandal had arisen. How it arose was the puzzle; since the ladies themselves never spoke to anybody, and Dr. West would not be likely to invent or to spread stories affecting himself. Its precise nature was buried in uncertainty, also its precise object. Some said one thing, some another. The scandal, on the whole, tended to the point that Dr. West had misbehaved himself. In what way? What had he done? Had he personally ill-treated them—sworn at them—done anything else unbecoming a gentleman? And which had been the sufferer? The old lady in her widow's cap? or the sickly daughter? or the other one? Could he have carelessly supplied wrong medicine; sent to them some arsenic instead of Epsom Salts, and so thrown them into fright, and danger, and anger? Had he scaled the privet hedge in the night, and robbed the garden of its cabbages? What, in short, was it that he had done? Deerham spoke out pretty broadly, as to the main facts, although the rumoured details were varied and obscure. It declared that some of Dr. West's doings at Chalk Cottage had not been orthodox, and that discovery had followed.

There are two classes of professional men upon whom not a taint should rest; who ought, in familiar phrase, to keep their hands clean—the parson of the parish, and the family doctor. Other people may dye themselves in Warren's jet if they like; but let as much as a spot get on him who stands in the pulpit to preach to us, or on him who is admitted to familiar intercourse with our wives and children, and the spot grows into a dark thundercloud. What's the old saying? "One man may walk in at the gate, while another must not look over the hedge." It runs something after that fashion. Had Dr. West not been a family doctor, the scandal might have been allowed to die out: as it was, Deerham kept up the ball, and rolled it. The chief motive for this, the one that influenced Deerham above all others, was unsatisfied curiosity. Could Deerham have gratified this to the full, it would have been content to subside into quietness.

Whether it was true, or whether it was false, there was no denying that it had happened at an unfortunate moment for Dr. West. A man always in debt—and what he did with his money Deerham could not make out, for his practice was a lucrative one—he had latterly become actually embarrassed. Deerham was good-natured enough to say that a handsome sum had found its way to Chalk Cottage, in the shape of silence-money, or something of the sort; but Deerham did not know. Dr. West was at his wits' end where to turn to for a shilling—had been so, for some weeks past; so that he had no particular need of anything worse coming down upon him. Perhaps what gave a greater colour to the scandal than anything else was the fact that, simultaneously with its rise, Dr. West's visits to Chalk Cottage had suddenly ceased.

Only one had been bold enough to speak upon the subject personally to Dr. West, and that was the proud old baronet, Sir Rufus Hautley. He rode down to the doctor's house one day; and, leaving his horse with his groom, had a private interview with the doctor. That Dr. West must have contrived to satisfy him in some way, was undoubted. Rigidly severe and honourable, Sir Rufus would no more have countenanced wrongdoing, than he would have admitted Dr. West again to his house, whether as doctor or anything else, had he been guilty of it. But when Sir Rufus went away, Dr. West attended him to the door, and they parted cordially, Sir Rufus saying something to the effect that he was glad his visit had dispelled the doubt arising from these unpleasing rumours, and he would recommend Dr. West to inquire into their source, with a view of bringing their authors to punishment. Dr. West replied that he should make it his business to do so. Dr. West, however, did nothing of the sort; or if he did do it, it was in strict privacy.

Jan sat one day astride on the counter in his frequent abiding-place, the surgery. Jan had got a brass vessel before him, and was mixing certain powders in it, preparatory to some experiment in chemistry, Master Cheese performing the part of looker-on, his elbows, as usual, on the counter.

"I say, we had such a start here this morning," began young Cheese, as if the recollection had suddenly occurred to him. "It was while you had gone your round."

"What start was that?"

"Some fellow came here, and—I say, Jan," broke off young Cheese, "did you ever know that room had got a second entrance to it?"

He pointed to the door of the back room—a room which was used exclusively by Dr. West. He had been known to see patients there on rare occasions, but neither Jan nor young Cheese was ever admitted into it. It opened with a latch-key only.

"There is another door leading into it from the garden," replied Jan. "It's never opened. It has got all those lean-to boards piled against it."

"Is it never opened, then?" retorted Master Cheese. "You just hear. A fellow came poking his nose into the premises this morning, staring up at the house, staring round about him, and at last he walks in here. A queer-looking fellow he was, with a beard, and appeared as if he had come a thousand miles or two, on foot. 'Is Dr. West at home?' he asked. I told him the doctor was not at home; for, you see, Jan, it wasn't ten minutes since the doctor had gone out. So he said he'd wait. And he went peering about and handling the bottles; and once he took the scales up, as if he'd like to test their weight. I kept my eye on him. I thought a queer fellow like that might be going to walk off with some physic, like Miss Amilly walks off the castor oil. Presently he comes to that door. 'Where does this lead to?' said he. 'A private room,' said I, 'and please to keep your hands off it.' Not he. He lays hold of the false knob, and shakes it, and turns it, and pushes the door, trying to open it. It was fast. Old West had come out of there before going out, and catch him ever leaving that door open! I say, Jan, one would think he kept skeletons there."

"Is that all?" asked Jan, alluding to the story.

"Wait a bit. The fellow put his big fist upon the latch-key-hole—I think he must have been a feller of trees, I do—and his knee to the door, and he burst it open. Burst it open, Jan! you never saw such strength."

"I could burst any door open that I had a mind to," was the response of Jan.

"He burst it open," continued young Cheese, "and burst it against old West. You should have seen 'em stare! They both stared. I stared. I think the chap did not mean to do it; that he was only trying his strength for pastime. But now, Jan, the odd part of the business is, how did West get in? If there's not another door, he must have got down the chimney."

Jan went on with his compounding, and made no response.

"And if there is a door, he must have been mortal sly over it," resumed the young gentleman. "He must have gone right out from here, and in at the side gate of the garden, and got in that way. I wonder what he did it for?"

"It isn't any business of ours," said Jan.

"Then I think it is," retorted Master Cheese. "I'd like to know how many times he has been in there, listening to us, when we thought him a mile off. It's a shame!"

"It's nothing to me who listens," said Jan equably. "I don't say things behind people's backs, that I'd not say before their faces."

"I do," acknowledged young Cheese. "Wasn't there a row! Didn't he and the man go on at each other! They shut themselves up in that room, and had it out."

"What did the man want?" asked Jan.

"I'd like to know. He and old West had it out together, I say, but they didn't admit me to the conference. Goodness knows where he had come from. West seemed to know him. Jan, I heard something about him and the Chalk Cottage folks yesterday."

"You had better take yourself to a safe distance," advised Jan. "If this goes off with a bang, your face will come in for the benefit."

"I say, though, it's you that must take care and not let it go off," returned Master Cheese, edging, nevertheless, a little away. "But about that room? If old West—"

The words were interrupted. The door of the room in question was pushed open, and Dr. West came out of it. Had Master Cheese witnessed the arrival of an inhabitant from the other world, introduced by the most privileged medium extant, he could not have experienced more intense astonishment. He had truly believed, as he had just expressed it, that Dr. West was at that moment a good mile away.

"Put your hat on, Cheese," said Dr. West.

Cheese put it on, going into a perspiration at the same time. He thought nothing less than that he was about to be dismissed.

"Take this note up to Sir Rufus Hautley's."

It was a great relief; and Master Cheese received the note in his hand, and went off whistling.

"Step in here, Mr. Jan," said the doctor.

Jan took one of his long legs over the counter, jumped off, and stepped in—into the doctor's sanctum. Had Jan been given to speculation, he might have wondered what was coming; but it was Jan's method to take things cool and easy, as they came, and not to anticipate them.

"My health has been bad of late," began the doctor.

"Law!" cried Jan. "What has been the matter?"

"A general disarrangement of the system altogether, I fancy," returned Dr. West. "I believe that the best thing to restore me will be change of scene—travelling; and an opportunity to embrace it has presented itself. I am solicited by an old friend of mine, in practice in London, to take charge of a nobleman's son for some months—to go abroad with him."

"Is he ill?" asked literal Jan, to whom it never occurred to ask whether Dr. West had first of all applied to his old friend to seek after such a post for him.

"His health is delicate, both mentally and bodily," replied Dr. West. "I should like to undertake it: the chief difficulty is leaving you here alone."

"I dare say I can do it all," said Jan. "My legs get over the ground quick. I can take to your horse."

"If you find you cannot do it, you might engage an assistant," suggested Dr. West.

"So I might," said Jan.

"I should see no difficulty at all in the matter if you were my partner. It would be the same as leaving myself, and the patients could not grumble. But it is not altogether the thing to leave only an assistant, as you are, Mr. Jan."

"Make me your partner, if you like," said cool Jan. "I don't mind. What'll it cost?"

"Ah, Mr. Jan, it will cost more than you possess. At least, it ought."

"I have got five hundred pounds," said Jan. "I wanted Lionel to have it, but he won't. Is that of any use?"

Dr. West coughed. "Well, under the circumstances—But it is very little! I am sure you must know that it is. Perhaps, Mr. Jan, we can come to some arrangement by which I take the larger share for the present. Say that, for this year, you forward me—"

"Why, how long do you mean to be away?" interrupted Jan.

"I can't say. One year, two years, three years—it may be even more than that. I expect this will be a long and a lucrative engagement. Suppose, I say, that for the first year you transmit to me the one-half of the net profits, and, beyond that, hand over to Deborah a certain sum, as shall be agreed upon, towards housekeeping."

"I don't mind how it is," said easy Jan. "They'll stop here, then?"

"Of course they will. My dear Mr. Jan, everything, I hope, will go on just as it goes on now, save that I shall be absent. You and Cheese—whom I hope you'll keep in order—and the errand boy: it will all be just as it has been. As to the assistant, that will be a future consideration."

"I'd rather be without one, if I can do it," cried Jan; "and Cheese will be coming on. Am I to live with 'em?"

"With Deb and Amilly? Why not? Poor, unprotected old things, what would they do without you? And now, Mr. Jan, as that is settled so far, we will sit down, and go further into details. I know I can depend upon your not mentioning this abroad."

"If you don't want me to mention it, you can. But where's the harm?"

"It is always well to keep these little arrangements private," said the doctor. "Matiss will draw up the deed, and I will take you round and introduce you as my partner. But there need not be anything said beforehand. Neither need there be anything said at all about my going away, until I actually go. You will oblige me in this, Mr. Jan."

"It's all the same to me," said accommodating Jan. "Whose will be this room, then?"

"Yours, to do as you please with, of course, so long as I am away."

"I'll have a turn-up bedstead put in it and sleep here, then," quoth Jan. "When folks come in the night, and ring me up, I shall be handy. It'll be better than disturbing the house, as is the case now."

The doctor appeared struck with the proposition.

"I think it would be a very good plan, indeed," he said. "I don't fancy the room's damp."

"Not it," said Jan. "If it were damp, it wouldn't hurt me. I have no time to be ill, I haven't. Damp—Who's that?"

It was a visitor to the surgery—a patient of Dr. West's—and, for the time, the conference was broken up, not to be renewed until evening.

Dr. West and Jan were both fully occupied all the afternoon. When business was over—as much so as a doctor's business ever can be over—Jan knocked at the door of this room, where Dr. West again was.

It was opened about an inch, and the face of the doctor appeared in the aperture, peering out to ascertain who might be disturbing him. The same aperture which enabled him to see out, enabled Jan to see in.

"Why! what's up?" cried unceremonious Jan.

Jan might well ask it. The room contained a table, a desk or two, some sets of drawers, and other receptacles for the custody of papers. All these were turned out, desks and drawers alike stood open, and their contents, a mass of papers, were scattered everywhere.

The doctor could not, in good manners, shut the door right in his proposed new partner's face. He opened it an inch or two more. His own face was purple: it wore a startled, perplexed look, and the drops of moisture had gathered on his forehead. That he was not in the most easy frame of mind was evident. Jan put one foot into the room: he could not put two, unless he had stepped upon the papers.

"What's the matter?" asked Jan, perceiving the signs of perturbation on the doctor's countenance.

"I have had a loss," said the doctor. "It's the most extraordinary thing, but a—a paper, which was here this morning, I cannot find anywhere. I must find it!" he added, in ill-suppressed agitation. "I'd rather lose everything I possess, than lose that."

"Where did you put it? When did you have it?" cried Jan, casting his eyes around.

"I kept it in a certain drawer," replied Dr. West, too much disturbed to be anything but straightforward. "I have not had it in my hand for—oh, I cannot tell how long—months and months, until this morning. I wanted to refer to it then, and got it out. I was looking it over when a rough, ill-bred fellow burst the door open—"

"I heard of that," interrupted Jan. "Cheese told me."

"He burst the door open, and I put the paper back in its place before I spoke to him," continued Dr. West. "Half an hour ago I went to take it out again, and I found it had disappeared."

"The fellow must have walked it off," cried Jan, a conclusion not unnatural.

"He could not," said Dr. West; "it is quite an impossibility. I went back there"—pointing to a bureau of drawers behind him—"and put the paper hastily in, and locked it in, returning the keys to my pocket. The man had not stepped over the threshold of the door then; he was a little taken to, I fancy, at his having burst the door, and he stood there staring."

"Could he have got at it afterwards?" asked Jan.

"It is, I say, an impossibility. He never was within a yard or two of the bureau; and, if he had been, the place was firmly locked. That man it certainly was not. Nobody has been in the room since, save myself, and you for a few minutes to-day when I called you in. And yet the paper is gone!"

"Could anybody have come into the room by the other door?" asked Jan.

"No. It opens with a latch-key only, as this does, and the key was safe in my pocket."

"Well, this beats everything," cried Jan. "It's like the codicil at Verner's Pride."

"The very thing it put me in mind of," said Dr. West. "I'd rather—I'd rather have lost that codicil, had it been mine, than lose this, Mr. Jan."

Jan opened his eyes. Jan had a knack of opening his eyes when anything surprised him—tolerably wide, too, "What paper was it, then?" he cried.

"It was a prescription, Mr. Jan."

"A prescription!" returned Jan, the answer not lessening his wonder. "That's not much. Isn't it in the book?"

"No, it is not in the book," said Dr. West. "It was too valuable to be in the book. You may look, Mr. Jan, but I mean what I say. This was a private prescription of inestimable value—a secret prescription, I may say. I would not have lost it for the whole world."

The doctor wiped the dew from his perplexed forehead, and strove, though unsuccessfully, to control his agitated voice to calmness. Jan could only stare. All this fuss about a prescription!

"Did it contain the secret for compounding Life's Elixir?" asked he.

"It contained what was more to me than that," said Dr. West. "But you can't help me, Mr. Jan. I would rather be left to the search alone."

"I hope you'll find it yet," returned Jan, taking the hint and retreating to the surgery. "You must have overlooked it amongst some of these papers."

"I hope I shall," replied the doctor.

And he shut himself up to the search, and turned over the papers. But he never found what he had lost, although he was still turning and turning them at morning light.

CHAPTER XXVIII

MISS DEBORAH'S ASTONISHMENT

One dark morning, near the beginning of November—in fact, it was the first morning of that gloomy month—Jan was busy in the surgery. Jan was arranging things there according to his own pleasure; for Dr. West had departed that morning early, and Jan was master of the field.

Jan had risen betimes. Never a sluggard, he had been up now for some hours, and had effected so great a metamorphosis in the surgery that the doctor himself would hardly have known it again: things in it previously never having been arranged to Jan's satisfaction. And now he was looking at his watch to see whether breakfast time was coming on, Jan's hunger reminding him that it might be acceptable. He had not yet been into the house; his bedroom now being the room you have heard of, the scene of Dr. West's lost prescription. The doctor had gone by the six o'clock train, after a cordial farewell to Jan; he had gone—as it was soon to turn out—without having previously informed his daughters. But of this Jan knew nothing.

"Twenty minutes past eight," quoth Jan, consulting his watch, a silver one, the size of a turnip. Jan had bought it when he was poor: had given about two pounds for it, second-hand. It never occurred to Jan to buy a better one while that legacy of his was lying idle. Why should he? Jan's turnip kept time to a moment, and Jan did not understand buying things for show. "Ten minutes yet! I shall eat a double share of bacon this morning.—Good-morning, Miss Deb."

Miss Deb was stealing into the surgery with a scared look and a white face. Miss Deb wore her usual winter morning costume, a huge brown cape. She was of a shivery nature at the best of times, but she shivered palpably now.

"Mr. Jan, have you got a drop of ether?" asked she, her poor teeth chattering together. Jan was too good-natured to tell Deerham those teeth were false, though Dr. West had betrayed the secret to Jan.

"Who's it for?" asked Jan. "For you? Aren't you well, Miss Deb? Eat some breakfast; that's the best thing."

"I have had a dreadful shock, Mr. Jan. I have had bad news. That is—what has been done to the surgery?" she broke off, casting her eyes around it in wonder.

"Not much," said Jan. "I have been making some odds and ends of alteration. Is the news from Australia?" he continued, the open letter in her hand helping him to the suggestion. "A mail's due."

Miss Deborah shook her head. "It is from my father, Mr. Jan. The first thing I saw, upon going into the breakfast parlour, was this note for me, propped against the vase on the mantel-piece. Mr. Jan"— dropping her voice to confidence—"it says he is gone! That he is gone away for an indefinite period."

"You don't mean to say he never told you of it before!" exclaimed Jan.

"I never heard a syllable from him," cried poor Deborah. "He says you'll explain to us as much as is necessary. You can read the note. Mr. Jan, where's he gone?"

Jan ran his eyes over the note; feeling himself probably in somewhat of a dilemma as to how much or how little it might be expedient to explain.

"He thought some travelling might be beneficial to his health," said Jan. "He has got a rare good post as travelling doctor to some young chap of quality."

Miss Deborah was looking very hard at Jan. Something seemed to be on her mind; some great fear. "He says he may not be back for ever so long to come, Mr. Jan."

"So he told me," said Jan.

"And is that the reason he took you into partnership, Mr. Jan?"

"Yes," said Jan. "Couldn't leave an assistant for an indefinite period."

"You will never be able to do it all yourself. I little thought, when all this bustle and changing of bedrooms was going on, what was up. You might have told me, Mr. Jan," she added, in a reproachful tone.

"It wasn't my place to tell you," returned Jan. "It was the doctor's."

Miss Deborah looked timidly round, and then sunk her voice to a lower whisper. "Mr. Jan, why has he gone away?"

"For his health," persisted Jan.

"They are saying—they are saying—Mr. Jan, what is it that they are saying about papa and those ladies at Chalk Cottage?"

Jan laid hold of the pestle and mortar, popped in a big lump of some hard-looking white substance, and began pounding away at it. "How should I know anything about the ladies at Chalk Cottage?" asked he. "I never was inside their door; I never spoke to any one of 'em."

"But you know that things are being said," urged Miss Deborah, with almost feverish eagerness. "Don't you?"

"Who told you anything was being said?" asked Jan.

"It was Master Cheese. Mr. Jan, folks have seemed queer lately. The servants have whispered together, and then have glanced at me and Amilly, and I knew there was something wrong, but I could not get at it. This morning, when I picked up this note—it's not five minutes ago, Mr. Jan—in my fright and perplexity I shrieked out; and Master Cheese, he said something about Chalk Cottage."

"What did he say?" asked Jan.

Miss Deborah's pale face turned to crimson. "I can't tell," she said. "I did not hear the words rightly. Master Cheese caught them up again. Mr. Jan, I have come to you to tell me."

Jan answered nothing. He was pounding very fiercely.

"Mr. Jan, I ought to know it," she went on. "I am not a child. If you please I must request you to tell me."

"What are you shivering for?" asked Jan.

"I can't help it. Is—is it anything that—that he can be taken up for?"

"Taken up!" replied Jan, ceasing from his pounding, and fixing his wide-open eyes on Miss Deborah. "Can I be taken up for doing this?"—and he brought down the pestle with such force as to threaten the destruction of the mortar.

"You'll tell me, please," she shivered.

"Well," said Jan, "if you must know it, the doctor had a misfortune."

"A misfortune! He! What misfortune! A misfortune at Chalk Cottage?"

Jan gravely nodded. "And they were in an awful rage with him, and said he should pay expenses, and all that. And he wouldn't pay expenses—the chimney-glass alone was twelve pound fifteen; and there was a regular quarrel, and they turned him out."

"But what was the nature of the misfortune?"

"He set the parlour chimney on fire."

Miss Deborah's lips parted with amazement; she appeared to find some difficulty in closing them again.

"Set the parlour chimney on fire, Mr. Jan!"

"Very careless of him," continued Jan, with composure. "He had no business to carry gunpowder about with him. Of course they won't believe but he flung it in purposely."

Miss Deborah could not gather her senses. "Who won't?—the ladies at Chalk Cottage?"

"The ladies at Chalk Cottage," assented Jan. "If I saw all these bottles go to smithereens, through Cheese stowing gunpowder in his trousers' pockets, I might go into a passion too, Miss Deb."

"But, Mr. Jan—this is not what's being said in Deerham?"

"Law, if you go by all that's said in Deerham, you'll have enough to do," cried Jan. "One says one thing and one says another. No two are ever in the same tale. When that codicil was lost at Verner's Pride, ten different people were accused by Deerham of stealing it."

"Were they?" responded Miss Deborah abstractedly.

"Did you never hear it! You just ask Deerham about the row between the doctor and Chalk Cottage, and you'll hear ten versions, all different. What else could be expected? As if he'd take the trouble to explain the rights of it to them! Not that I should advise you to ask," concluded Jan pointedly. "Miss Deborah, do you know the time?"

"It must be half-past eight," she repeated mechanically, her thoughts buried in a reverie.

"And turned," said Jan. "I'd be glad of breakfast. I shall have the gratis patients here."

"It shall be ready in two minutes," said Miss Deborah meekly. And she went out of the surgery.

Presently young Cheese came leaping into it. "The breakfast's ready," cried he.

Jan stretched out his long arm, and pinned Master Cheese.

"What have you been saying to Miss Deb?" he asked. "Look here; who is your master now?"

"You are, I suppose," said the young gentleman.

"Very well. You just bear that in mind; and don't go carrying tales indoors of what Deerham says. Attend to your own business and leave Dr. West's alone."

Master Cheese was considerably astonished. He had never heard such a speech from easy Jan.

"I say, though, are you going to turn out a bashaw with three tails?" asked he.

"Yes," replied Jan. "I have promised Dr. West to keep you in order, and I shall do it."

CHAPTER XXIX

AN INTERCEPTED JOURNEY

Dr. West's was not the only departure from Deerham that was projected for that day. The other was that of Lionel Verner. Fully recovered, he had deemed it well to waste no more time. Lady Verner suggested that he should remain in Deerham until the completion of the year; Lionel replied that he had remained in it rather too long already, that he must be up and doing. He was eager to be "up and doing," and his first step towards it was the proceeding to London and engaging chambers. He fixed upon the first day of November for his departure, unconscious that that day had also been fixed upon by Dr. West for his. However, the doctor was off long before Lionel was out of bed.

Lionel rose all excitement—all impulse to begin his journey, to be away from Deerham. Somebody else rose with feelings less pleasurable; and that was Lucy Tempest. Now that the real time of separation had come, Lucy awoke to the state of her own feelings; to the fact, that the whole world contained but one beloved face for her—that of Lionel Verner.

She awoke with no start, she saw nothing wrong in it, she did not ask herself how it was to end, what the future was to be; any vision of marrying Lionel, which might have flashed across the active brain of a more sophisticated young lady, never occurred to Lucy. All she knew was that she had somehow glided into a state of existence different from anything she had ever experienced before; that her days were all brightness, the world an Eden, and that it was the presence of Lionel that made the sunshine.

She stood before the glass, twisting her soft brown hair, her cheeks crimson with excitement, her eyes bright. The morrow morning would be listless enough; but this, the last on which she would see him, was gay with rose hues of love. Stay! not gay; that is a wrong expression. It would have been gay but for that undercurrent of feeling which was whispering that, in a short hour or two, all would change to the darkest shade.

"He says it may be a twelvemonth before he shall come home again," she said to herself, her white fingers trembling as she fastened her pretty morning-dress. "How lonely it will be! What shall we do all that while without him? Oh, dear, what's the matter with me this morning?"

In her perturbed haste, she had fastened her dress all awry, and had to undo it again. The thought that she might be keeping them waiting breakfast—which was to be taken that morning a quarter of an hour earlier than usual—did not tend to expedite her. Lucy thought of the old proverb: "The more haste, the less speed."

"How I wish I dare ask him to come sooner than that to see us! But he might think it strange. I wonder he should not come! there's Christmas, there's Easter, and he must have holiday then. A whole year, perhaps more; and not to see him!"

She passed out of the room and descended, her soft skirts of pink-shaded cashmere sweeping the staircase. You saw her in it the evening she first came to Lady Verner's. It had lain by almost ever since, and was now converted into a morning dress. The breakfast-room was empty. Instead of being behind her time, Lucy found she was before it. Lady Verner had not risen; she rarely did rise to breakfast; and Decima was in Lionel's room, busy over some of his things.

Lionel himself was the next to enter. His features broke into a glad smile when he saw Lucy. A fairer picture, she, Mr. Lionel Verner, than even that other vision of loveliness which your mind has been pleased to make its ideal—Sibylla!

"Down first, Lucy!" he cried, shaking hands with her. "You wish me somewhere, I dare say, getting you up before your time."

"By how much—a few minutes?" she answered, laughing. "It wants twenty minutes to nine. What would they have said to me at the rectory, had I come down so late as that?"

"Ah, well, you won't have me here to torment you to-morrow. I have been a trouble to you, Lucy, take it altogether. You will be glad to see my back turned."

Lucy shook her head. She looked shyly up at him in her timidity; but she answered truthfully still.

"I shall be sorry; not glad."

"Sorry! Why should you be sorry, Lucy?" and his voice insensibly assumed a tone of gentleness. "You cannot have cared for me; for the companionship of a half-dead fellow, like myself!"

Lucy rallied her courage. "Perhaps it was because you were half dead that I cared for you," she answered.

"I suppose it was," mused Lionel, aloud, his thoughts cast back to the past. "I will bid you good-bye now, Lucy, while we are alone. Believe me that I part from you with regret; that I do heartily thank you for all you have been to me."

Lucy looked up at him, a yearning, regretful sort of look, and her eyelashes grew wet. Lionel had her hand in his, and was looking down at her.

"Lucy, I do think you are sorry to part with me!" he exclaimed.

"Just a little," she answered.

If you, good, grave sir, had been stoical enough to resist the upturned face, Lionel was not. He bent his lips and left a kiss upon it.

"Keep it until we meet again," he whispered.

Jan came in while they were at breakfast.

"I can't stop a minute," were his words when Decima asked him why he did not sit down. "I thought I'd run up and say good-bye to Lionel, but I am wanted in all directions. Mrs. Verner has sent for me, and there are the regular patients."

"Dr. West attends Mrs. Verner, Jan," said Decima.

"He did," replied Jan. "It is to be myself, now. West is gone."

"Gone!" was the universal echo. And Jan gave an explanation.

It was received in silence. The rumours affecting Dr. West had reached Deerham Court.

"What is the matter with Mrs. Verner?" asked Lionel. "She appeared as well as usual when I quitted her last night."

"I don't know that there's anything more the matter with her than usual," returned Jan, sitting down on a side-table. "She has been going in some time for apoplexy."

"Oh, Jan!" uttered Lucy.

"So she has, Miss Lucy—as Dr. West has said. I have not attended her."

"Has she been told it, Jan?"

"Where's the good of telling her?" asked Jan. "She knows it fast enough. She'd not forego a meal, if she saw the fit coming on before night. Tynn came round to me, just now, and said his mistress felt poorly. The Australian mail is in," continued Jan, passing to another subject.

"Is it?" cried Decima.

Jan nodded.

"I met the postman as I was coming out, and he told me. I suppose there'll be news from Fred and Sibylla."

After this little item of information, which called the colour into Lucy's cheek—she best knew why—but which Lionel appeared to listen to impassively, Jan got off the table—

"Good-bye, Lionel," said he, holding out his hand.

"What's your hurry, Jan?" asked Lionel.

"Ask my patients," responded Jan, "I am off the first thing to Mrs. Verner, and then shall take my round. I wish you luck, Lionel."

"Thank you, Jan," said Lionel. "Nothing less than the woolsack, of course."

"My gracious!" said literal Jan. "I say, Lionel, I'd not count upon that. If only one in a thousand gets to the woolsack, and all the lot expect it, what an amount of heart-burning must be wasted."

"Right, Jan. Only let me lead my circuit and I shall deem myself lucky."

"How long will it take you before you can accomplish that?" asked Jan. "Twenty years?"

A shade crossed Lionel's countenance. That he was beginning late in life, none knew better than he. Jan bade him farewell, and departed for Verner's Pride.

Lady Verner was down before Lionel went. He intended to take the quarter-past ten o'clock train.

"When are we to meet again?" she asked, holding her hand in his.

"I will come home to see you soon, mother."

"Soon! I don't like the vague word," returned Lady Verner. "Why cannot you come for Christmas?"

"Christmas! I shall scarcely have gone."

"You will come, Lionel?"

"Very well, mother. As you wish it, I will."

A crimson flush—a flush of joy—rose to Lucy's countenance. Lionel happened to have glanced at her. I wonder what he thought of it!

His luggage had gone on, and he walked with a hasty step to the station. The train came in two minutes after he reached it. Lionel took his ticket, and stepped into a first-class carriage.

All was ready. The whistle sounded, and the guard had one foot on his van-step, when a shouting and commotion was heard. "Stop! Stop!" Lionel, like others, looked out, and beheld the long legs of his brother Jan come flying along the platform. Before Lionel had well known what was the matter, or had gathered in the hasty news, Jan had pulled him out of the carriage, and the train went shrieking on without him.

"There goes my luggage, and here am I and my ticket!" cried Lionel. "You have done a pretty thing, Jan. What do you say?"

"It's all true, Lionel. She was crying over the letters when I got there. And pretty well I have raced back to stop your journey. Of course you will not go away now. He's dead."

"I don't understand yet," gasped Lionel, feeling, however, that he did understand.

"Not understand," repeated Jan. "It's easy enough. Fred Massingbird's dead, poor fellow; he died of fever three weeks after they landed; and you are master of Verner's Pride."

CHAPTER XXX

NEWS FROM AUSTRALIA

Lionel Verner could scarcely believe in his own identity. The train, which was to have contained him, was whirling towards London; he, a poor aspirant for future fortune, ought to have been in it; he had counted most certainly to be in it; but here was he, while the steam of that train yet snorted in his ears, walking out of the station, a wealthy man, come into a proud inheritance, the inheritance of his fathers. In the first moment of tumultuous thought, Lionel almost felt as if some fairy must have been at work with a magic wand.

It was all true. He linked his arm within Jan's, and listened to the recital in detail. Jan had found Mrs. Verner, on his arrival at Verner's Pride, weeping over letters from Australia; one from a Captain Cannonby, one from Sibylla. They contained the tidings that Frederick Massingbird had died of fever, and that Sibylla was anxious to come home again.

"Who is Captain Cannonby?" asked Lionel of Jan.

"Have you forgotten the name?" returned Jan. "That friend of Fred Massingbird's who sold out, and was knocking about London; Fred went up once or twice to see him. He went to the diggings last autumn, and it seems Fred and Sibylla lighted on him at Melbourne. He had laid poor Fred in the grave the day before he wrote, he says."

"I can scarcely believe it all now, Jan," said Lionel. "What a change!"

"Ay. You won't believe it for a day or two. I say, Lionel, Uncle Stephen need not have left Verner's Pride to the Massingbirds; they have not lived to enjoy it. Neither need there have been all that bother about the codicil. I know what."

"What?" asked Lionel, looking at him; for Jan spoke significantly.

"That Madam Sibylla would give her two ears now to have married you, instead of Fred Massingbird."

Lionel's face flushed, and he replied coldly, hauteur in his tone, "Nonsense, Jan! you are speaking most unwarrantably. When Sibylla chose Fred Massingbird, I was the heir to Verner's Pride."

"I know," said Jan. "Verner's Pride would be a great temptation to Sibylla; and I can but think she knew it was left to Fred when she married him."

Lionel did not condescend to retort. He would as soon believe himself capable of bowing down before the god of gold, in a mean spirit, as believe Sibylla capable of it. Indeed, though he was wont to charm himself with the flattering notion that his love for Sibylla had died out, or near upon it, he was very far off the point when he could think any ill of Sibylla.

"My patients will be foaming," remarked Jan, who continued his way to Verner's Pride with Lionel. "They will conclude I have gone off with Dr. West; and I have his list on my hands now, as well as my own. I say, Lionel, when I told you the letters from Australia were in, how little we guessed they would contain this news."

"Little, indeed!" said Lionel.

"I suppose you won't go to London now?"

"I suppose not," was the reply of Lionel; and a rush of gladness illumined his heart as he spoke it. No more toil over those dry old law books! The study had never been to his taste.

The servants were gathered in the hall when Lionel and Jan entered it. Decorously sorry, of course, for the tidings which had arrived, but unable to conceal the inward satisfaction which peeped out—not satisfaction at the death of Fred, but at the accession of Lionel. It is curious to observe how jealous the old retainers of a family are, upon all points which touch the honour or the well-being of the house. Fred Massingbird was an alien; Lionel was a Verner; and now, as Lionel entered, they formed into a double line that he might pass between them, their master from henceforth.

Mrs. Verner was in the old place, the study. Jan had seen her in bed that morning; but, since then, she had risen. Early as the hour yet was, recent as the sad news had been, Mrs. Verner had dropped asleep. She sat nodding in her chair, snoring heavily, breathing painfully, her neck and face all one colour—carmine red. That she looked—as Jan had observed—a very apoplectic subject, struck Lionel most particularly on this morning.

"Why don't you bleed her, Jan?" he whispered.

"She won't be bled," responded Jan. "She won't take physic. She won't do anything that she ought to do. You may as well talk to a post. She'll do nothing but eat and drink, and fall asleep afterwards, and then wake up to eat and drink and fall asleep again. Mrs. Verner"—exalting his voice—"here's Lionel."

Mrs. Verner partially woke up. Her eyes opened sufficiently to observe Jan; and her mind apparently grew awake to a confused remembrance of facts. "He's gone to London," said she to Jan. "You won't catch him:" and then she nodded again.

"I did catch him," shouted Jan. "Lionel's here."

Lionel sat down by her, and she woke up pretty fully.

"I am grieved at this news for your sake, Mrs. Verner," he said in a kind tone, as he took her hand. "I am sorry for Frederick."

"Both my boys gone before me, Lionel!" she cried, melting into tears—"John first; Fred next. Why did they go out there to die?"

"It is indeed sad for you," replied Lionel. "Jan says Fred died of fever."

"He has died of fever. Don't you remember when Sibylla wrote, she said he was ill with fever? He never got well. He never got well! I take it that it must have been a sort of intermittent fever—pretty well one day, down ill the next—for he had started for the place where John died—I forget its name, but you'll find it written there. Only a few hours after quitting Melbourne, he grew worse and died."

"Was he alone?" asked Lionel.

"Captain Cannonby was with him. They were going together up to—I forget, I say, the name of the place—where John died, you know. It was nine or ten days' distance from Melbourne, and they had travelled but a day of it. And I suppose," added Mrs. Verner, with tears in her eyes, "that he'd be put into the ground like a dog!"

Lionel, on this score, could give no consolation. He knew not whether the fact might be so, or not. Jan hoisted himself on to the top of a high bureau, and sat in comfort.

"He'd be buried like a dog," repeated Mrs. Verner. "What do they know about parsons and consecrated ground out there? Cannonby buried him, he says, and then he went back to Melbourne to carry the tidings to Sibylla."

"Sibylla? Was Sibylla not with him when he died?" exclaimed Lionel.

"It seems not. It's sure not, in fact, by the letters. You can read them, Lionel. There's one from her and one from Captain Cannonby."

"It's not likely they'd drag Sibylla up to the diggings," interposed Jan.

"And yet almost as unlikely that her husband would leave her alone in such a place as Melbourne appears to be," dissented Lionel.

"She was not left alone," said Mrs. Verner. "If you'd read the letters, Lionel, you would see. She stayed in Melbourne with a family: friends, I think she says, of Captain Cannonby's. She has written for money to be sent out to her by the first ship, that she may pay her passage home again."

This item of intelligence astonished Lionel more than any other.

"Written for money to be sent out for her passage home!" he reiterated. "Has she no money?"

Mrs. Verner looked at him. "They accuse me of forgetting things in my sleep, Lionel; but I think you must be growing worse than I am. Poor Fred told us in his last letter that he had been robbed of his desk, and that it had got his money in it."

"But I did not suppose it contained all—that they were reduced so low as for his wife to have no money left for a passage. What will she do there until some can be got out?"

"If she is with comfortable folks, they'd not turn her out," cried Jan.

Lionel took up the letters, and ran his eyes over them. They told him little else of the facts; though more of the details. It appeared to have taken place pretty much as Mrs. Verner said. The closing part of Sibylla's letter ran as follows:—

"After we wrote to you, Fred met Captain Cannonby. You must remember, dear aunt, how often Fred would speak of him. Captain Cannonby has relatives out here, people in very good position—if people can be said to be in a position at all in such a horrid place. We knew Captain Cannonby had come over, but thought he was at the Bendigo diggings. However, Fred met him; and he was very civil and obliging. He got us apartments in the best hotel—one of the very places that had refused us, saying they were crowded. Fred seemed to grow a trifle better, and it was decided that they should go to the place where John died, and try to get particulars about his money, etc., which in Melbourne we could hear nothing of. Indeed, nobody seemed to know even John's name. Captain Cannonby (who has really made money here in some way—trading, he says—and expects to make a good deal more) agreed to go with Fred. Then Fred told me of the loss of his desk and money, his bills of credit, and that; whatever the term may be. It was stolen from the quay, the day we arrived, and he had never been able to hear of it; but, while there seemed a chance of finding it, he would not let me know the ill news. Of course, with this loss upon us, there was all the more necessity for our getting John's money as speedily as might be. Captain Cannonby introduced me to his relatives, the Eyres, told them my husband wanted to go up the country for a short while, and they invited me to stay with them. And here I am, and very kind they are to me in this dreadful trouble.

"Aunt Verner, I thought I should have died when, a day or two after they started, I saw Captain Cannonby come back alone, with a long, sorrowful face. I seemed to know in a moment what had happened; I had thought at the time they started that Fred was too ill to go. I said to him, 'My husband is dead!' and he confessed that it was so. He had been taken ill at the end of the first day, and did not live many hours.

"I can't tell you any more, dear Aunt Verner; I am too sick and ill, and if I filled ten sheets with the particulars, it would not alter the dreadful facts. I want to come home to you; I know you will receive me, and let me live with you always. I have not any money. Please send me out sufficient to bring me home by the first ship that sails. I don't care for any of the things we brought out; they may stop here or be lost in the sea, for all the difference it will make to me: I only want to come home. Captain Cannonby says he will take upon himself now to look after John's money, and transmit it to us, if he can get it.

"Mrs. Eyre has just come in. She desires me to say that they are taking every care of me, and are all happy to have me with them: she says I am to tell you that her own daughters are about my age. It is all true, dear aunt, and they are exceedingly kind to me. They seem to have plenty of money, are intimate with the governor's family, and with what they call the good society of the colony. When I think what my position would have been now had I not met with them, I grow quite frightened.

"I have to write to papa, and must close this. I have requested Captain Cannonby to write to you himself, and give you particulars about the last moments of Frederick. Send me the money without delay, dear aunt. The place is hateful to me now he is gone, and I'd rather be dead than stop in it.

"Your affectionate and afflicted niece,

"SIBYLLA MASSINGBIRD."

Lionel folded the letter musingly. "It would almost appear that they had not heard of your son's accession to Verner's Pride," he remarked to Mrs. Verner. "It is not alluded to in any way."

"I think it is sure they had not heard of it," she answered "I remarked so to Mary Tynn. The letters must have been delayed in their passage. Lionel, you will see to the sending out of the money for me."

"Immediately," replied Lionel.

"And when do you come home?"

"Do you mean—do you mean when do I come here?" returned Lionel.

"To be sure I mean it. It is your home. Verner's Pride is your home, Lionel, now; not mine. It has been yours this three or four months past, only we did not know it. You must come home to it at once, Lionel."

"I suppose it will be right that I should do so," he answered.

"And I shall be thankful," said Mrs. Verner. "There will be a master once more, and no need to bother me. I have been bothered, Lionel. Mr. Jan,"—turning to the bureau—"it's that which has made me feel ill. One comes to me with some worry or other, and another comes to me: they will come to me. The complaints and tales of that Roy fidget my life out."

"I shall discharge Roy at once, Mrs. Verner."

Mrs. Verner made a deprecatory movement of the hands, as much as to say that it was no business of hers. "Lionel, I have only one request to make of you: never speak of the estate to me again, or of anything connected with its management. You are its sole master, and can do as you please. Shall you turn me out?"

Lionel's face flushed. "No, Mrs. Verner," he almost passionately answered. "You could not think so."

"You have the right. Had Fred come home, he would have had the right. But I'd hardly reconcile myself to any other house how."

"It is a right which I should never exercise," said Lionel.

"I shall mostly keep my room," resumed Mrs. Verner; "perhaps wholly keep it: and Mary Tynn will wait upon me. The servants will be yours, Lionel. In fact, they are yours; not mine. What a blessing! to know that I may be at peace from henceforth: that the care will be upon another's shoulders! My poor Fred! My dear sons! I little thought I was taking leave of them both for the last time!"

Jan jumped off his bureau. Now that the brunt of the surprise was over, and plans began to be discussed, Jan bethought himself of his impatient sick list, who were doubtlessly wondering at the non-appearance of their doctor. Lionel rose to depart with him.

"But, you should not go," said Mrs. Verner. "In five minutes I vacate this study; resign it to you. This change will give you plenty to do, Lionel."

"I know it will, dear Mrs. Verner. I shall be back soon, but I must hasten to acquaint my mother."

"You will promise not to go away again, Lionel. It is your lawful home, remember."

"I shall not go away again," was Lionel's answer; and Mrs. Verner breathed freely. To be emancipated from what she had regarded as the great worry of life, was felt to be a relief. Now she could eat and sleep all day, and never need be asked a single question, or hear whether the outside world had stopped, or was going on still.

"You will just pen a few words for me to Sibylla, Lionel," she called out. "I am past much writing now."

"If it be necessary that I should," he coldly replied.

"And send them with the remittance," concluded Mrs. Verner. "You will know how much to send. Tell Sibylla that Verner's Pride is no longer mine, and I cannot invite her to it. It would hardly be the—the thing for a young girl, and she's little better, to be living here with you all day long, and I always shut up in my room. Would it?"

Lionel somewhat haughtily shrugged his shoulders. "Scarcely," he answered.

"She must go to her sisters, of course. Poor girl! what a thing it seems to have to return to her old house again!"

Jan put in his head. "I thought you said you were coming, Lionel?"

"So I am—this instant." And they departed together: encountering Mr. Bitterworth in the road.

He grasped hold of Lionel in much excitement.

"Is it true—what people are saying? That you have come into Verner's Pride?"

"Quite true," replied Lionel. And he gave Mr. Bitterworth a summary of the facts.

"Now look there!" cried Mr. Bitterworth, who was evidently deeply impressed; "it's of no use to try to go against honest right: sooner or later it will triumph. In your case, it has come wonderfully soon. I told my old friend that the Massingbirds had no claim to Verner's Pride; that if they were exalted to it, over your head, it would not prosper them—not, poor fellows, that I thought of their death. May you remain in undisturbed possession of it, Lionel! May your children succeed to it after you!"

Lionel and Jan continued their road. But they soon parted company, for Jan turned off to his patients. Lionel made the best of his way to Deerham Court. In the room he entered, steadily practising, was Lucy Tempest, alone. She turned her head to see who it was, and at the sight of Lionel started up in alarm.

"What is it? Why are you back?" she exclaimed. "Has the train broken down?"

Lionel smiled at her vehemence; at her crimsoned countenance; at her unbounded astonishment altogether.

"The train has not broken down, I trust, Lucy. I did not go with it. Do you know where my mother is?"

"She is gone out with Decima."

He felt a temporary disappointment; the news, he was aware, would be so deeply welcome to Lady Verner. Lucy stood regarding him, waiting the solution of the mystery.

"What should you say, Lucy, if I tell you Deerham is not going to get rid of me at all?"

"I do not understand you," replied Lucy, colouring with surprise and emotion. "Do you mean that you are going to remain here?"

"Not here—in this house. That would be a calamity for you."

Lucy looked as if it would be anything but a calamity.

"You are as bad as our French mistress at the rectory," she said. "She would never tell us anything; she used to make us guess."

Her words were interrupted by the breaking out of the church bells: a loud peal, telling of joy. A misgiving crossed Lionel that the news had got wind, and that some officious person had been setting on the bells to ring for him, in honour of his succession. The exceeding bad taste of the proceeding— should it prove so—called a flush of anger to his brow. His inheritance had cost Mrs. Verner her son.

The suspicion was confirmed. One of the servants, who had been to the village, came running in at this juncture with open mouth, calling out that Mr. Lionel had come into his own, and that the bells were ringing for it. Lucy Tempest heard the words, and turned to Lionel.

"It is so, Lucy," he said, answering the look. "Verner's Pride is at last mine. But—"

She grew strangely excited. Lionel could see her heart beat—could see the tears of emotion gather in her eyes.

"I am so glad!" she said in a low, heartfelt tone. "I thought it would be so, sometime. Have you found the codicil?"

"Hush, Lucy! Before you express your gladness, you must learn that sad circumstances are mixed with it. The codicil has not been found; but Frederick Massingbird has died."

Lucy shook her head. "He had no right to Verner's Pride, and I did not like him. I am sorry, though, for himself, that he is dead. And—Lionel—you will never go away now?"

"I suppose not: to live."

"I am so glad! I may tell you that I am glad, may I not?"

She half timidly held out her hand as she spoke. Lionel took it between both of his, toying with it as tenderly as he had ever toyed with Sibylla's. And his low voice took a tone which was certainly not that of hatred, as he bent towards her.

"I am glad also, Lucy. The least pleasant part of my recent projected departure was the constantly remembered fact that I was about to put a distance of many miles between myself and you. It grew all too palpable towards the last."

Lucy laughed and drew away her hand, her radiant countenance falling before the gaze of Lionel.

"So you will be troubled with me yet, you see, Miss Lucy," he added, in a lighter tone, as he left her and strode off with a step that might have matched Jan's, on his way to ask the bells whether they were not ashamed of themselves.

CHAPTER XXXI

ROY EATING HUMBLE PIE

And so the laws of right and justice had eventually triumphed, and Lionel Verner took possession of his own. Mrs. Verner took possession of her own—her chamber; all she was ever again likely to take possession of at Verner's Pride. She had no particular ailment, unless heaviness could be called an ailment, and steadily refused any suggestion of Jan's.

"You'll go off in a fit," said plain Jan to her.

"Then I must go," replied Mrs. Verner. "I can't submit to be made wretched with your medical and surgical remedies, Mr. Jan. Old people should be let alone, to doze away their days in peace."

"As good give some old people poison outright, as let them always doze," remonstrated Jan.

"You'd like me to live sparingly—to starve myself, in short—and you'd like me to take exercise!" returned Mrs. Verner. "Wouldn't you, now?"

"It would add ten years to your life," said Jan.

"I dare say! It's of no use your coming preaching to me, Mr. Jan. Go and try your eloquence upon others. I always have had enough to eat, and I hope I always shall. And as to my getting about, or walking, I can't. When folks come to be my size, it's cruel to want them to do it."

Mrs. Verner was nodding before she had well spoken the last words, and Jan said no more. You may have met with some such case in your own experience.

When the news of Lionel Verner's succession fell upon Roy, the bailiff, he could have gnashed his teeth in very vexation. Had he foreseen what was to happen he would have played his cards so differently. It had not entered into the head-piece of Roy to reflect that Frederick Massingbird might die. Scarcely had it that he could die. A man, young and strong, what was likely to take him off? John had died, it was true; but John's death had been a violent one. Had Roy argued the point at all—which he did not, for it had never occurred to his mind—he might have assumed that because John had died, Fred was the more likely to live. It is a somewhat rare case for two brothers to be cut down in their youth and prime, one closely following upon the other.

Roy lived in a cottage standing by itself, a little beyond Clay Lane, but not so far off as the gamekeeper's. On the morning when the bells had rung out—to the surprise and vexation of Lionel—Roy happened to be at home. Roy never grudged himself holiday when it could be devoted to the benefit of his wife. A negative benefit she may have thought it, since it invariably consisted in what Roy called a "blowing of her up."

Mrs. Roy had heard that the Australian mail was in. But the postman had not been to their door, therefore no letter could have arrived for them from Luke. A great many mails, as it appeared to Mrs. Roy, had come in with the like result. That Luke had been murdered, as his master, John Massingbird, had been before him, was the least she feared. Her fears and troubles touching Luke were great; they were never at rest; and her tears fell frequently. All of which excited the ire of Roy.

She sat in a rocking-chair in the kitchen—a chair which had been new when the absent Luke was a baby, and which was sure to be the seat chosen by Mrs. Roy when she was in a mood to indulge any passing tribulation. The kitchen opened to the road, as the kitchens of many of the dwellings did open to it; a parlour was on the right, which was used only on the grand occasion of receiving visitors; and the stairs, leading to two rooms above, ascended from the kitchen. Here she sat, silently wiping away her dropping tears with a red cotton pocket-handkerchief. Roy was not in the sweetest possible temper himself that morning, so, of course, he turned it upon her.

"There you be, a-snivelling as usual! I'd have a bucket always at my feet, if I was you. It might save the trouble of catching rain-water."

"If the letter-man had got anything for us, he'd have been round here an hour ago," responded Mrs. Roy, bursting into unrestrained sobs.

Now, this happened to be the very grievance that was affecting the gentleman's temper—the postman's not having gone there. They had heard that the Australian mail was in. Not that he was actuated by any strong paternal feelings—such sentiments did not prey upon Mr. Roy. The hearing or the not hearing from his son would not thus have disturbed his equanimity. He took it for granted that Luke was alive somewhere—probably getting on—and was content to wait until himself or a letter should turn up. The one whom he had been expecting to hear from was his new master, Mr. Massingbird. He had fondly indulged the hope that credential letters would arrive for him, confirming him in his place of manager; he believed that this mail would inevitably bring them, as the last mails had not. Hence he had stayed at home to receive the postman. But the postman had not come, and it gave Roy a pain in his temper.

"They be a-coming back, that's what it is," was the conclusion he arrived at, when his disappointment had a little subsided. "Perhaps they might have come by this very ship! I wonder if it brings folks as well as letters?"

"I know he must be dead!" sobbed Mrs. Roy.

"He's dead as much as you be," retorted Roy. "He's a-making his fortune, and he'll come home after it—that's what Luke's a-doing. For all you know he may be come too."

The words appeared to startle Mrs. Roy; she looked up, and he saw that her face had gone white with terror.

"Why! what does ail you?" cried he, in wonder. "Be you took crazy?"

"I don't want him to come home," she replied in an awe-struck whisper. "Roy, I don't want him to."

"You don't want to be anything but a idiot," returned Roy, with supreme contempt.

"But I'd like to hear from him," she wailed, swaying herself to and fro. "I'm always a-dreaming of it."

"You'll just dream a bit about getting the dinner ready," commanded Roy morosely; "that's what you'll dream about now. I said I'd have biled pork and turnips, and nicely you be a-getting on with it. Hark ye! I'm a-going now, but I shall be in at twelve, and if it ain't ready, mind your skin!"

He swung open the kitchen door just in time to hear the church bells burst out with a loud and joyous peal. It surprised Roy. In quiet Deerham, such sounds were not very frequent.

"What's up now?" cried Roy savagely. Not that the abstract fact of the bells ringing was of any moment to him, but he was in a mood to be angry with everything. "Here, you!" continued he, seizing hold of a boy who was running by, "what be them bells a-clattering for?"

Brought to thus summarily, the boy had no resource but to stop. It was a young gentleman whom you have had the pleasure of meeting before—Master Dan Duff. So fast had he been flying, that a moment or two elapsed ere he could get breath to speak.

The delay did not tend to soothe his capturer; and he administered a slight shake. "Can't you speak, Dan Duff? Don't you see who it is that's a-asking of you? What be them bells a-working for?"

"Please, sir, it's for Mr. Lionel Verner."

The answer took Roy somewhat aback. He knew—as everybody else knew—that Mr. Lionel Verner's departure from Deerham was fixed for that day; but to believe that the bells would ring out a peal of joy on that account was a staggerer even to Roy's ears. Dan Duff found himself treated to another shake, together with a sharp reprimand.

"So they be a-ringing for him!" panted he. "There ain't no call to shake my inside out of me for saying so. Mr. Lionel have got Verner's Pride at last, and he ain't a-going away at all, and the bells be a-ringing for it. Mother have sent me to tell the gamekeeper. She said he'd sure to give me a penny, if I was the first to tell him."

Roy let go the boy. His arms and his mouth alike dropped. "Is that—that there codicil found?" gasped he.

Dan Duff shook his head. "I dun know nothink about codinals," said he. "Mr. Fred Massingbird's dead. He can't keep Mr. Lionel out of his own any longer, and the bells is a-ringing for it."

Unrestrained now, he sped away. Roy was not altogether in a state to stop him. He had turned of a glowing heat, and was asking himself whether the news could be true. Mrs. Roy stepped forward, her tears arrested.

"Law, Roy, whatever shall you do?" spoke she deprecatingly. "I said as you should have kept in with Mr. Lionel. You'll have to eat humble pie, for certain."

The humble pie would taste none the more palatable for his being reminded of it by his wife, and Roy drove her back with a shower of harsh words. He shut the door with a bang, and went out, a forlorn hope lighting him that the news might be false.

But the news, he found, was too true. Frederick Massingbird was really dead, and the true heir had come into his own.

Roy stood in much inward perturbation. The eating of humble pie—as Mrs. Roy had been kind enough to suggest—would not cost much to a man of his cringing nature; but he entertained a shrewd suspicion that no amount of humble pie would avail him with Mr. Verner; that, in short, he should be discarded entirely. While thus standing, the centre of a knot of gossipers, for the news had caused Deerham to collect in groups, the bells ceased as suddenly as they had begun, and Lionel Verner himself was observed coming from the direction of the church. Roy stood out from the rest, and, as a preliminary slice of the humble pie, took off his hat, and stood bare-headed while Lionel passed by.

It did not avail him. On the following day Roy found himself summoned to Verner's Pride. He went up, and was shown to the old business room—the study.

Ah! things were changed now—changed from what they had been; and Roy was feeling it to his heart's core. It was no longer the feeble invalid, Stephen Verner, who sat there, to whom all business was unwelcome, and who shunned as much of it as he could shun, leaving it to Roy; it was no longer the ignorant and easy Mrs. Verner to whom (as she herself had once expressed it) Roy could represent white as black, and black as white: but he who reigned now was essentially master—master of himself and of all who were dependent on him.

Roy felt it the moment he entered; felt it keenly. Lionel stood before a table covered with papers. He appeared to have risen from his chair and to be searching for something. He lifted his head when Roy appeared, quitted the table and stood looking at the man, his figure drawn to its full height. The exceeding nobility of the face and form struck even Roy.

But Lionel greeted him in a quiet, courteous tone; to meet any one, the poorest person on his estate, otherwise than courteously was next to an impossibility for Lionel Verner. "Sit down, Roy," he said. "You are at no loss, I imagine, to guess what my business is with you."

Roy did not accept the offered seat. He stood in discomfiture, saying something to the effect that he'd change his mode of dealing with the men, would do all he could to give satisfaction to his master, Mr. Verner, if the latter would consent to continue him on.

"You must know, yourself, that I am not likely to do it," returned Lionel briefly. "But I do not wish to be harsh, Roy—I trust I never shall be harsh with any one—and if you choose to accept of work on the estate, you can do so."

"You'll not continue me in my post over the brick-yard, sir—over the men generally?"

"No," replied Lionel, "Perhaps the less we go into those past matters the better. I have no objection to speak of them, Roy; but, if I do, you will hear some home truths that may not be palatable. You can have work if you wish for it; and good pay."

"As one of the men, sir?" asked Roy, a shade of grumbling in his tone.

"As one of the superior men!"

Roy hesitated. The blow had fallen; but it was only what he feared. "Might I ask as you'd give me a day to consider it over, sir?" he presently said.

"A dozen days if you choose. The work is always to be had; it will not run away; if you prefer to spend time deliberating upon the point, it is your affair, not mine."

"Thank ye, sir. Then I'll think it over. It'll be hard lines, coming down to be a workman, where I've been, as may be said, a sort of master."

"Roy."

Roy turned back. He had been moving away. "Yes, sir."

"I shall expect you to pay rent for your cottage now, if you remain in it. Mr. Verner, I believe, threw it into your post; made it part of your perquisites. Mrs. Verner has, no doubt, done the same. But that is at an end. I can show no more favour to you than I do to others."

"I'll think it over, sir," concluded Roy, his tone as sullen a one as he dared let appear. And he departed.

Before the week was out, he came again to Verner's Pride, and said he would accept the work, and pay rent for the cottage; but he hoped Mr. Verner would name a fair rent.

"I should not name an unfair one, Roy," was the reply of Lionel. "You will pay the same that others pay, whose dwellings are the same size as yours. Mr Verner's scale of rents is not high, but low, as you know; I shall not alter it."

And so Roy continued on the estate.

CHAPTER XXXII

"IT'S APPLEPLEXY"

A short period elapsed. One night Jan Verner, upon getting into bed, found he need not have taken the trouble, for the night-bell rang, and Jan had to get up again. He opened his window and called out to know who was there. A boy came round from the surgery door into view, and Jan recognised him for the youngest son of his brother's gamekeeper, a youth of twelve. He said his mother was ill.

"What's the matter with her?" asked Jan.

"Please, sir, she's took bad in the stomach. She's a-groaning awful. Father thinks she'll die."

Jan dressed himself and started off, carrying with him a dose of tincture of opium. When he arrived, however, he found the woman so violently sick and ill, that he suspected it did not arise simply from natural causes. "What has she been eating?" inquired Jan.

"Some late mushrooms out of the fields."

"Ah, that's just it," said Jan. And he knew the woman had been poisoned. He took a leaf from his pocket-book, wrote a rapid word on it, and ordered the boy to carry it to the house, and give it to Mr. Cheese.

"Now, look you, Jack," said he, "if you want your mother to get well, you'll go there and back as fast as your legs can carry you. I can do little till you bring me what I have sent for. Go past the Willow Pool, and straight across to my house."

The boy looked aghast at the injunction. "Past the Willow Pool!" echoed he. "I'd not go past there, sir, at night, for all the world."

"Why not?" questioned Jan.

"I'd see Rachel Frost's ghost, may be," returned Jack, his round eyes open with perplexity.

The conceit of seeing a ghost amused Jan beyond everything. He sat down on a high press that was in the kitchen, and grinned at the boy. "What would the ghost do to you?" cried he.

Jack Broom could not say. All he knew was that neither he, nor a good many more, had gone near that pond at night since the report had arisen (which, of course, it had, simultaneously with the death) that Rachel's ghost was to be seen there.

"Wouldn't you go to save your mother?" cried Jan.

"I'd—I'd not go to be made winner of the leg of mutton atop of a greased pole," responded the boy, in a mortal fright lest Jan should send him.

"You are a nice son, Mr. Jack! A brave young man, truly!"

"Jim Hook, he was a-going by the pond one night, and he see'd it," cried the boy earnestly. "It don't take two minutes longer to cut down Clay Lane, please, sir."

"Be off, then," said Jan, "and see how quick you can be. What has put such a thing into his head?" he presently asked of the gamekeeper, who was hard at work preparing hot water.

"Little fools!" ejaculated the man. "I think the report first took its rise, sir, through Robin Frost's going to the pond of a moonlight night, and walking about on its brink."

"Robert Frost did!" cried Jan. "What did he do that for?"

"What indeed, sir! It did no good, as I told him more than once, when I came upon him there. He has not been lately, I think. Folks get up a talk that Robin went there to meet his sister's spirit, and it put the youngsters into a fright."

Back came Mr. Jack in an incredibly short time. He could not have come much quicker, had he dashed right through the pool. Jan set himself to his work, and did not leave the woman until she was better. That was the best of Jan Verner. He paid every atom as much attention to the poor as he did to the rich. Jan never considered who or what his patients were: all his object was, to get them well.

His nearest way home lay past the pool, and he took it: he did not fear poor Rachel's ghost. It was a sharpish night, bright, somewhat of a frost. As Jan neared the pool, he turned his head towards it and half stopped, gazing on its still waters. He had been away when the catastrophe happened; but the circumstances had been detailed to him. "How it would startle Jack and a few of those timid ones," said he aloud, "if some night—"

"Is that you, sir?"

Some persons, with nerves less serene than Jan's, might have started at the sudden interruption there and then. Not so Jan. He turned round with composure, and saw Bennet, the footman from Verner's Pride. The man had come up hastily from behind the hedge.

"I have been to your house, sir, and they told me you were at the gamekeeper's, so I was hastening there. My mistress is taken ill, sir."

"Is it a fit?" cried Jan, remembering his fears and prognostications, with regard to Mrs. Verner.

"It's worse than that, sir; it's appleplexy. Leastways, sir, my master and Mrs. Tynn's afraid that it is. She looks like dead, sir, and there's froth on her mouth."

Jan waited for no more. He turned short round, and flew by the nearest path to Verner's Pride.

The evil had come. Apoplexy it indeed was, and Jan feared that all his efforts to remedy it would be of no avail.

"It was by the merest chance that I found it out, sir," Mrs. Tynn said to him. "I happened to wake up, and I thought how quiet my mistress was lying; mostly she might be heard ever so far off when she was asleep. I got up, sir, and took the rushlight out of the shade, and looked at her. And then I saw what had happened, and went and called Mr. Lionel."

"Can you restore her, Jan?" whispered Lionel.

Jan made no reply. He had his own private opinion; but, whatever that may have been, he set himself to the task in right earnest.

She never rallied. She lived only until the dawn of morning. Scarcely had the clock told eight, when the death-bell went booming over the village; the bell of that very church which had recently been so merry for the succession of Lionel. And when people came running from far and near to inquire for whom the passing-bell was ringing out, they hushed their voices and their footsteps when informed that it was for Mrs. Verner.

Verily, within the last year, Death had made himself at home at Verner's Pride!

CHAPTER XXXIII

JAN'S REMEDY FOR A COLD

A cold bright day in mid-winter. Luncheon was just over at Deerham Court, and Lady Verner, Decima, and Lucy Tempest had gathered round the fire in the dining-room. Lucy had a cold. She laughed at it; said she was used to colds; but Lady Verner had insisted upon her wrapping herself in a shawl, and not stirring out of the dining-room—which was the warmest room in the house—for the day. So there reclined Lucy in state, in an arm-chair with cushions; half laughing at being made into an invalid, half rebelling at it.

Lady Verner sat opposite to her. She wore a rich black silk dress—the mourning for Mrs. Verner—and a white lace cap of the finest guipure. The white gloves on her hands were without a wrinkle, and her curiously fine handkerchief lay on her lap. Lady Verner could indulge her taste for snowy gloves and for delicate handkerchiefs now, untroubled by the thought of the money they cost. The addition to her income, which she had spurned from Stephen Verner, she accepted willingly from Lionel. Lionel was liberal as a man and as a son. He would have given the half of his fortune to his mother, and not said, "It is a gift." Deerham Court had its carriage and horses now, and Deerham Court had its additional servants. Lady Verner visited and received company, and the look of care had gone from her face, and the querulousness from her tone.

But it was in Lady Verner's nature to make a trouble of things; and if she could not do it in a large way, she must do it in a small. To-day, occurred this cold of Lucy's, and that afforded scope for Lady Verner. She sent for Jan as soon as breakfast was over, in defiance of the laughing protestations of Lucy. But Jan had not made his appearance yet, and Lady Verner waxed wroth.

He was coming in now—now, as the servant was carrying out the luncheon-tray, entering by his usual mode—the back-door, and nearly knocking over the servant and tray in his haste, as his long legs strode to the dining-room. Lady Verner had left off reproaching Jan for using the servants' entrance, finding it waste of breath: Jan would have come down the chimney with the sweeps, had it saved him a minute's time. "Who's ill?" asked he.

Lady Verner answered the question by a sharp reprimand, touching Jan's tardiness.

"I can't be in two places at once," good-humouredly replied Jan. "I have been with one patient since four o'clock this morning, until five minutes ago. Who is it that's ill?"

Lucy explained her ailments, giving Jan her own view of them, that there was nothing the matter with her but a bit of a cold.

"Law!" contemptuously returned Jan. "If I didn't think somebody must be dying! Cheese said they'd been after me about six times!"

"If you don't like to attend Miss Tempest, you can let it alone," said Lady Verner. "I can send elsewhere."

"I'll attend anybody that I'm wanted to attend," said Jan. "Where d'ye feel the symptoms of the cold?" asked he of Lucy. "In the head or chest?"

"I am beginning to feel them a little here," replied Lucy, touching her chest.

"Only beginning to feel them, Miss Lucy?"

"Only beginning, Jan."

"Well, then, you just wring out a long strip of rag in cold water, and put it round your neck, letting the ends rest on the chest," said Jan. "A double piece, from two to three inches broad. It must be covered outside with thin waterproof skin to keep the wet in; you know what I mean; Decima's got some; oil-skin's too thick. And get a lot of toast and water, or lemonade; any liquid you like; and sip a drop of it every minute, letting it go down your throat slowly. You'll soon get rid of your sore chest if you do this; and you'll have no cough."

Lady Verner listened to these directions of Jan's in unqualified amazement. She had been accustomed to the very professional remedies of Dr. West. Decima laughed. "Jan," said she, "I could fancy an old woman prescribing this, but not a doctor."

"It'll cure," returned Jan. "It will prevent the cough coming on; and prevention's better than cure. You try it at once, Miss Lucy; and you'll soon see. You will know then what to do if you catch cold in future."

"Jan," interposed Lady Verner, "I consider the very mention of such remedies beneath the dignity of a medical man."

Jan opened his eyes. "But if they are the best remedies, mother?"

"At any rate, Jan, if this is your fashion of prescribing, you will not fill your pockets," said Decima.

"I don't want to fill my pockets by robbing people," returned plain Jan. "If I know a remedy that costs nothing, why shouldn't I let my patients have the benefit of it, instead of charging them for drugs that won't do half the good?"

"Jan," said Lucy, "if it cost gold I should try it. I have great faith in what you say."

"All right," replied Jan. "But it must be done at once, mind. If you let the cold get ahead first, it will not be so efficacious. And now good-day to you all, for I must be off to my patients. Good-bye, mother."

Away went Jan. And, amidst much laughter from Lucy, the wet "rag," Jan's elegant phrase for it, was put round her neck, and covered up. Lionel came in, and they amused him by reciting Jan's prescription.

"It is this house which has given her the cold," grumbled Lady Verner, who invariably laid faults and misfortunes upon something or somebody. "The servants are for ever opening that side-door, and then there comes a current of air throughout the passage. Lionel, I am not sure but I shall leave Deerham Court."

Lionel leaned against the mantel-piece, a smile upon his face. He had completely recovered his good looks, scared away though they had been for a time by his illness. He was in deep mourning for Mrs. Verner. Decima looked up, surprised at Lady Verner's last sentence.

"Leave Deerham Court, mamma! When you are so much attached to it!"

"I don't dislike it," acknowledged Lady Verner. "But it suited me better when we were living quietly, than it does now. If I could find a larger house with the same conveniences, and in an agreeable situation, I might leave this."

Decima did not reply. She felt sure that her mother was attached to the house, and would never quit it. Her eyes said as much as they encountered Lionel's.

"I wish my mother would leave Deerham Court!" he said aloud.

Lady Verner turned to him. "Why should you wish it, Lionel?"

"I wish you would leave it to come to me, mother. Verner's Pride wants a mistress."

"It will not find one in me," said Lady Verner. "Were you an old man, Lionel, I might then come. Not as it is."

"What difference can my age make?" asked he.

"Every difference," said Lady Verner. "Were you an old man, you might not be thinking of getting married; as it is, you will be. Your wife will reign at Verner's Pride, Lionel."

Lionel made no answer.

"You will be marrying sometime, I suppose?" reiterated Lady Verner, with emphasis.

"I suppose I shall be," replied Lionel; and his eyes, as he spoke, involuntarily strayed to Lucy. She caught the look, and blushed vividly.

"How much of that do you intend to drink, Miss Lucy?" asked Lionel, as she sipped the tumbler of lemonade, at her elbow.

"Ever so many tumblers of it," she answered. "Jan said I was to keep sipping it all day long. The water, going down slowly, heals the chest."

"I believe if Jan told you to drink boiling water, you'd do it, Lucy," cried Lady Verner. "You seem to fall in with all he says."

"Because I like him, Lady Verner. Because I have faith in him; and if Jan prescribes a thing, I know that he has faith in it."

"It is not displaying a refined taste to like Jan," observed Lady Verner, intending the words as a covert reprimand to Lucy.

But Lucy stood up for Jan. Even at the dread of openly disagreeing with Lady Verner, Lucy would not be unjust to one whom she deemed of sterling worth.

"I like Jan very much," said she resolutely, in her championship. "There's nobody I like so well as Jan, Lady Verner."

Lady Verner made a slight movement with her shoulders. It was almost as much as to say that Lucy was growing as hopelessly incorrigible as Jan. Lionel turned to Lucy.

"Nobody you like so well as Jan, did you say?"

Poor Lucy! If the look of Lionel, just before, had brought the hot blush to her cheek, that blush was nothing compared to the glowing crimson which mantled there now. She had not been thinking of one sort of liking when she so spoke of Jan: the words had come forth in the honest simplicity of her heart.

Did Lionel read the signs aright, as her eyes fell before his? Very probably. A smile stole over his lips.

"I do like Jan very much," stammered Lucy, essaying to mend the matter. "I may like him, I suppose? There's no harm in it."

"Oh! no harm, certainly," spoke Lady Verner, with a spice of irony. "I never thought Jan could be a favourite before. Not being fastidiously polished yourself, Lucy—forgive my saying it—you entertain, I conclude, a fellow feeling for Jan."

Lucy—for Jan's sake—would not be beaten.

"Don't you think it is better to be like Jan, Lady Verner, than—than—like Dr. West, for instance?"

"In what way?" returned Lady Verner.

"Jan is so true," debated Lucy, ignoring the question.

"And Dr. West was not, I suppose," retorted Lady Verner. "He wrote false prescriptions, perhaps? Gave false advice?"

Lucy looked a little foolish. "I will tell you the difference, as it seems to me, between Jan and other people," she said. "Jan is like a rough diamond—real within, unpolished without—but a genuine diamond withal. Many others are but the imitation stone—glittering outside, false within."

Lionel was amused.

"Am I one of the false ones, Miss Lucy?"

She took the question literally.

"No; you are true," she answered, shaking her head, and speaking with grave earnestness.

"Lucy, my dear, I would not espouse Jan's cause so warmly, were I you," advised Lady Verner. "It might be misconstrued."

"How so?" simply asked Lucy.

"It might be thought that you—pray excuse the common vulgarity of the suggestion—were in love with Jan."

"In love with Jan!" Lucy paused for a moment after the words, and then burst into a merry fit of laughter. "Oh, Lady Verner! I cannot fancy anybody falling in love with Jan. I don't think he would know what to do."

"I don't think he would," quietly replied Lady Verner.

A peal at the courtyard bell, and the letting down the steps of a carriage. Visitors for Lady Verner. They were shown to the drawing-room, and the servant came in.

"The Countess of Elmsley and Lady Mary, my lady."

Lady Verner rose with alacrity. They were favourite friends of hers—nearly the only close friends she had made in her retirement.

"Lucy, you must not venture into the drawing-room," she stayed to say. "The room is colder than this. Come."

The last "come" was addressed conjointly to her son and daughter. Decima responded to it, and followed; Lionel remained where he was.

"The cold room would not hurt me, but I am glad not to go," began Lucy, subsiding into a more easy tone, a more social manner, than she ventured on in the presence of Lady Verner. "I think morning visiting the greatest waste of time! I wonder who invented it?"

"Somebody who wanted to kill time," answered Lionel.

"It is not as though friends, who really cared for each other, met and talked. The calls are made just for form's sake, and for nothing else, I will never fall into it when I am my own mistress."

"When is that to be?" asked Lionel, smiling.

"Oh! I don't know," she answered, looking up at him in all confiding simplicity. "When papa comes home, I suppose."

Lionel crossed over to where she was sitting.

"Lucy, I thank you for your partisanship of Jan," he said, in a low, earnest tone. "I do not believe anybody living knows his worth."

"Yes; for I do," she replied, her eyes sparkling.

"Only, don't you get to like him too much—as Lady Verner hinted," continued Lionel, his eyes dancing with merriment at his own words.

Lucy's eyelashes fell on her hot cheek. "Please not to be so foolish," she answered, in a pleading tone.

"Or a certain place—that has been mentioned this morning—might have to go without a mistress for good," he whispered.

What made him say it? It is true he spoke in a light, joking tone; but the words were not justifiable, unless he meant to follow them up seriously in future. He did mean to do so when he spoke them.

Decima came in, sent by Lady Verner to demand Lionel's attendance.

"I am coming directly," replied Lionel. And Decima went back again.

"You ought to take Jan to live at Verner's Pride," said Lucy to him, the words unconsciously proving that she had understood Lionel's allusion to it. "If he were my brother, I would not let him be always slaving himself at his profession."

"If he were your brother, Lucy, you would find that Jan would slave just as he does now, in spite of you. Were Jan to come into Verner's Pride to-morrow, through my death, I really believe he would let it, and live on where he does, and doctor the parish to the end of time."

"Will Verner's Pride go to Jan after you?"

"That depends. It would, were I to die as I am now, a single man. But I may have a wife and children some time, Lucy."

"So you may," said Lucy, filling up her tumbler from the jug of lemonade. "Please to go into the drawing-room now, or Lady Verner will be angry. Mary Elmsley's there, you know."

She gave him a saucy glance from her soft bright eyes. Lionel laughed.

"Who made you so wise about Mary Elmsley, young lady?"

"Lady Verner," was Lucy's answer, her voice subsiding into a confidential tone. "She tells us all about it, me and Decima, when we are sitting by the fire of an evening. She is to be the mistress of Verner's Pride."

"Oh, indeed," said Lionel. "She is, is she! Shall I tell you something, Lucy?"

"Well?"

"If that mistress-ship—is there such a word?—ever comes to pass, I shall not be the master of it."

Lucy looked pleased. "That is just what Decima says. She says it to Lady Verner. I wish you would go to them."

"So I will. Good-bye. I shall not come in again. I have a hundred and one things to do this afternoon."

He took her hand and held it. She, ever courteous of manner, simple though she was, rose and stood before him to say her adieu, her eyes raised to his, her pretty face upturned.

Lionel gazed down upon it, and, as he had forgotten himself once before, so he now forgot himself again. He clasped it to him with a sudden movement of affection, and left on it some fervent kisses, whispering tenderly—

"Take care of yourself, my darling Lucy!"

Leaving her to make the best of the business, Mr. Lionel proceeded to the drawing-room. A few minutes' stay in it, and then he pleaded an engagement, and departed.

CHAPTER XXXIV

IMPROVEMENTS

Things were changed now out of doors. There was no dissatisfaction, no complaining. Roy was deposed from his petty authority, and all men were at peace, with the exception, possibly, of Mr. Peckaby. Mr. Peckaby did not, find his shop flourish. Indeed, far from flourishing, so completely was it deserted, that he was fain to give up the trade, and accept work at Chuff the blacksmith's forge, to which employment, it appeared, he had been brought up. A few stale articles remained in the shop, and the counters remained; chiefly for show. Mrs. Peckaby made a pretence of attending to customers; but she did not get two in a week. And if those two entered, they could not be served, for she was pretty sure to be out, gossiping.

This state of things did not please Mrs. Peckaby. In one point of view the failing of the trade pleased her, because it left her less work to do; but she did not like the failing of their income. Whether the shop had been actually theirs, or whether it had been Roy's, there was no doubt that they had drawn sufficient from it to live comfortably and to find Mrs. Peckaby in smart caps. This source was gone, and all they had now was an ignominious fourteen shillings a week, which Peckaby earned. The prevalent opinion in Clay Lane was that this was quite as much as Peckaby deserved; and that it was a special piece of undeserved good fortune which had taken off the blacksmith's brother and assistant in the nick of time, Joe Chuff, to make room for him. Mrs. Peckaby, however, was in a state of semi-rebellion; the worse, that she did not know upon whom to visit it, or see any remedy. She took to passing her time in groaning and tears, somewhat after the fashion of Dinah Roy, venting her complaints upon anybody that would listen to her.

Lionel had not said to the men, "You shall leave Peckaby's shop." He had not even hinted to them that it might be desirable to leave it. In short, he had not interfered. But, the restraint of Roy being removed from the men, they quitted it of their own accord. "No more Roy; no more Peckaby; no more grinding down—hurrah!" shouted they, and went back to the old shops in the village.

All sorts of improvements had Lionel begun. That is, he had planned them: begun yet, they were not. Building better tenements for the labourers, repairing and draining the old ones, adding whatever might be wanted to make the dwellings healthy: draining, ditching, hedging. "It shall not be said that while I live in a palace, my poor live in pigsties," said Lionel to Mr. Bitterworth one day. "I'll do what I can to drive that periodical ague from the place."

"Have you counted the cost?" was Mr. Bitterworth's rejoinder.

"No," said Lionel. "I don't intend to count it. Whatever the changes may cost, I shall carry them out."

And Lionel, like other new schemers, was red-hot upon them. He drew out plans in his head and with his pencil; he consulted architects, he spent half his days with builders. Lionel was astonished at the mean, petty acts of past tyranny, exercised by Roy, which came to light, far more than he had had any idea of. He blushed for himself and for his uncle, that such a state of things had been allowed to go on; he wondered that it could have gone on; that he had been blind to so much of it, or that the men had not exercised Lynch law upon Roy.

Roy had taken his place in the brick-yard as workman; but Lionel, in the anger of the moment, when these things came out, felt inclined to spurn him from the land. He would have done it but for his promise to the man himself; and for the pale, sad face of Mrs. Roy. In the hour when his anger was at its height, the woman came up to Verner's Pride, stealthily, as it seemed, and craved him to write to Australia, "now he was a grand gentleman," and ask the "folks over there" if they could send back news of her son. "It's going on of a twelvemonth since he writed to us, sir, and we don't know where to write to him, and I'm a'most fretted into my grave."

"My opinion is that he is coming home," said Lionel.

"Heaven sink the ship first!" she involuntarily muttered, and then she burst into a violent flood of tears.

"What do you mean?" exclaimed Lionel. "Don't you want him to come home?"

"No, sir. No."

"But why? Are you fearing"—he jumped to the most probable solution of her words that he could suggest—"are you fearing that he and Roy would not agree?—that there would be unpleasant scenes between them, as there used to be?"

The woman had her face buried in her hands, and she never lifted it as she answered, in a stifled voice, "It's what I'm a-fearing, sir."

Lionel could not quite understand her. He thought her more weak and silly than usual.

"But he is not coming home," she resumed. "No, sir, I don't believe that England will ever see him again; and it's best as it is, for there's nothing but care and sorrow here, in the old country. But I'd like to know what's become of him; whether he is alive or dead, whether he is starving or in comfort. Oh, sir!" she added, with a burst of wailing anguish, "write for me, and ask news of him! They'd answer you. My heart is aching for it."

He did not explain to her then, how very uncertain was the fate of emigrants to that country, how next to impossible it might be to obtain intelligence of an obscure young man like Luke; he contented himself with giving her what he thought would be better comfort.

"Mrs. Frederick Massingbird will be returning in the course of a few months, and I think she may bring news of him. Should she not, I will see what inquiries can be made."

"Will she be coming soon, sir?"

"In two or three months, I should suppose. The Misses West may be able to tell you more definitely, if they have heard from her."

"Thank ye, sir; then I'll wait till she's home. You'll not tell Roy that I have been up here, sir?"

"Not I," said Lionel. "I was debating, when you came in, whether I should not turn Roy off the estate altogether. His past conduct to the men has been disgraceful."

"Ay, it have, sir! But it was my fate to marry him, and I have had to look on in quiet, and see things done, not daring to say as my soul's my own. It's not my fault, sir."

Lionel knew that it was not. He pitied her, rather than blamed.

"Will you go into the servants' hall and eat something after your walk?" he kindly asked.

"No, sir, many thanks. I don't want to see the servants. They might get telling that I have been here."

She stole out from his presence, her pale, sad face, her evidently deep sorrow, whatever might be its source, making a vivid impression upon Lionel. But for that sad face, he might have dealt more harshly with her husband. And so Roy was tolerated still.

It was upon these various past topics that Lionel's mind was running as he walked away from Deerham Court after that afternoon's interview with Lucy, which he had made so significant. He had pleaded an engagement, as an excuse for quitting his mother's drawing-room and her guests. It must have been at home, we must suppose, for ho took his way straight towards Verner's Pride, sauntering through the village as if he had leisure to look about him, his thoughts deep in his projected improvements.

Here, a piece of stagnant water was to be filled in; there was the site of his new tenements; yonder, was the spot for a library and reading-room; on he walked, throwing his glances everywhere. As he neared the shop of Mrs. Duff, a man came suddenly in view, facing him; a little man, in a suit of rusty black, and a white neckcloth, with a pale face and red whiskers, whom Lionel remembered to have seen once before, a day or two previously. As soon as he caught sight of Lionel he turned short off, crossed the street, and darted out of sight down the Belvidere Road.

"That looks as though he wanted to avoid me," thought Lionel. "I wonder who he may be? Do you know who that man is, Mrs. Duff?" asked he aloud; for that lady was taking the air at her shop-door, and had watched the movement.

"I don't know much about him, sir. He have been stopping in the place this day or two. What did I hear his name was, again?" added Mrs. Duff, putting her fingers to her temples in a considering fit. "Jarrum, I think. Yes, that was it. Brother Jarrum, sir."

"Brother Jarrum?" repeated Lionel, uncertain whether the "Brother" might be spoken in a social point of view, or was a name bestowed upon the gentleman in baptism.

"He's a missionary from abroad, or something of that sort, sir. He is come to see what he can do towards converting us."

"Oh, indeed," said Lionel, his lip curling with a smile. The man's face had not taken his fancy. "Honest missionaries do not need to run away to avoid meeting people, Mrs. Duff."

"He have got cross eyes," responded Mrs. Duff. "Perhaps that's a reason he mayn't like to look gentlefolks in the face, sir."

"Where does he come from?"

"Well, now, sir, I did hear," replied Mrs. Duff, putting on her considering cap again, "it were some religious place, sir, that's talked of a good deal in the Bible. Jericho, were it? No. It began with a J, though. Oh, I have got it, sir! It were Jerusalem. He conies all the way from Jerusalem."

"Where is he lodging?" continued Lionel.

"He have been lodging at the George and Dragon, sir. But to-day he have gone and took that spare bedroom as the Peckabys have wanted to let, since their custom fell off."

"He means to make a stay, then?"

"It looks like it, sir. Susan Peckaby, she were in here half an hour ago, a-buying new ribbons for a cap, all agog with it. He's a-going to hold forth in their shop, she says, and see how many of the parish he can turn into saints. I say it won't be a bad 'turn,' if it keeps the men from the beer-houses."

Lionel laughed as he went on. He supposed it was a new movement that would have its brief day and then be over, leaving results neither good nor bad behind it; and he dismissed the man from his memory.

He walked on, in the elasticity of his youth and health. All nature seemed to be smiling around him. Outward things take their hue very much from the inward feelings, and Lionel felt happier than he had done for months and months. Had the image of Lucy Tempest anything to do with this? No—nothing. He had not yet grown to love Lucy in that idolising manner, as to bring her ever present to him. He was thinking of the change in his own fortunes; he cast his eyes around to the right and the left, and they rested on his own domains—domains which had for a time been wrested from him; and as his quick steps rung on the frosty road, his heart went up in thankfulness to the Giver of all good.

Just before he reached Verner's Pride, he overtook Mr. Bitterworth, who was leaning against a roadside gate. He had been attacked by sudden giddiness, he said, and asked Lionel to give him an arm home. Lionel proposed that he should come in and remain for a short while at Verner's Pride; but Mr. Bitterworth preferred to go home.

"It is one of my bilious attacks coming on," he remarked, as he went along. "I have not had a bad one for this four months."

Lionel took him safe home, and remained with him for some time, talking; the chief theme being his own contemplated improvements, and how to go to work upon them; a topic which seemed to bring no satiety to Lionel Verner.

CHAPTER XXXV

BACK AGAIN

It was late when Lionel reached Verner's Pride. Night had set in, and his dinner was waiting.

He ate it hurriedly—he mostly did eat hurriedly when he was alone, as if he were glad to get it over—Tynn waiting on him. Tynn liked to wait upon his young master. Tynn had been in a state of glowing delight since the accession of Lionel. Attached to the old family, Tynn had felt it almost as keenly as Lionel himself, when the estate had lapsed to the Massingbirds. Mrs. Tynn was in a glow of delight also. There was no mistress, and she ruled the household, including Tynn.

The dinner gone away and the wine on the table, Lionel drew his chair in front of the fire, and fell into a train of thought, leaving the wine untouched. Full half an hour had he thus sat, when the entrance of Tynn aroused him. He poured out a glass, and raised it to his lips. Tynn bore a note on his silver waiter.

"Matiss's boy has just brought it. He is waiting to know whether there's any answer."

Lionel opened the note, and was reading it, when a sound of carriage wheels came rattling on to the terrace, passed the windows, and stopped at the hall door. "Who can be paying me a visit to-night, I wonder?" cried he. "Go and see, Tynn."

"It sounded like one of them rattling one-horse flies from the railway station," was Tynn's comment to his master, as he left the room.

Whoever it might be, they appeared pretty long in entering, and Lionel, very greatly to his surprise, heard a sound as of much luggage being deposited in the hall. He was on the point of going out to see, when the door opened, and a lovely vision glided forward—a young, fair face and form, clothed in deep mourning, with a shower of golden curls shading her damask cheeks. For one single moment, Lionel was lost in the beauty of the vision. Then he recognised her, before Tynn's announcement was heard; and his heart leaped as if it would burst its bounds—

"Mrs. Massingbird, sir."

—leaped within him fast and furiously. His pulses throbbed, his blood coursed on, and his face went hot and cold with emotion. Had he been fondly persuading himself, during the past months, that she was forgotten? Truly the present moment rudely undeceived him.

Tynn shut the door, leaving them alone. Lionel was not so agitated as to forget the courtesies of life. He shook hands with her, and, in the impulse of the moment, called her Sibylla; and then bit his tongue for doing it.

She burst into tears. There, as he held her hand. She lifted her lovely face to him with a yearning, pleading look. "Oh, Lionel!—you will give me a home, won't you?"

What was he to say? He could not, in that first instant, abruptly say to her—No, you cannot have a home here. Lionel could not hurt the feelings of any one. "Sit down, Mrs. Massingbird," he gently said, drawing an easy-chair to the fire. "You have taken me quite by surprise. When did you land?"

She threw off her bonnet, shook back those golden curls, and sat down in the chair, a large heavy shawl on her shoulders. "I will not take it off yet," she said in a plaintive voice. "I am very cold."

She shivered slightly. Lionel drew her chair yet nearer the fire, and brought a footstool for her feet, repeating his question as he did so.

"We reached Liverpool late yesterday, and I started for home this morning," she answered, her eyelashes wet still, as she gazed into the fire. "What a miserable journey it has been!" she added, turning to Lionel. "A miserable voyage out; a miserable ending!"

"Are you aware of the changes that have taken place since you left?" he asked. "Your aunt is dead."

"Yes, I know it," she answered. "They told me at the station just now. That lame porter came up and knew me; and his first news to me was that Mrs. Verner was dead. What a greeting! I was coming home here to live with her."

"You could not have received my letter. One which I wrote at the request of Mrs. Verner in answer to yours."

"What news was in it?" she asked. "I received no letter from you."

"It contained remittances. It was sent, I say, in answer to yours, in which you requested money should be forwarded for your home passage. You did not wait for it?"

"I was tired of waiting. I was sick for home. And one day, when I had been crying more than usual, Mrs. Eyre said to me that if I were so anxious to go, there need be no difficulty about the passage-money, that they would advance me any amount I might require. Oh, I was so glad! I came away by the next ship."

"Why did you not write saying that you were coming?"

"I did not think it mattered—and I knew I had this home to come to. If I had had to go to my old home again at papa's, then I should have written. I should have seemed like an intruder arriving at their house, and have deemed it necessary to warn them of it."

"You heard in Australia of Mr. Verner's death, I presume?"

"I heard of that, and that my husband had inherited Verner's Pride. The news came out just before I sailed for home. Of course I thought I had a right to come to this home, though he was dead. I suppose it is yours now?"

"Yes."

"Who lives here?"

"Only myself."

"Have I a right to live here—as Frederick's widow?" she continued, lifting her large blue eyes anxiously at Lionel. "I mean would the law give it me?"

"No," he replied, in a low tone. He felt that the truth must be told to her without disguise. She was placing both him and herself in an embarrassing situation.

"Was there any money left to me?—or to Frederick?"

"None to you. Verner's Pride was left to your husband; but at his demise it came to me."

"Did my aunt leave me nothing?"

"She had nothing to leave, Mrs. Massingbird. The settlement which Mr. Verner executed on her, when they married, was only for her life. It lapsed back to the Verner's Pride revenues when she died."

"Then I am left without a shilling, to the mercy of the world!"

Lionel felt for her—felt for her rather more than was safe. He began planning in his own mind how he could secure to her an income from the Verner's Pride estate, without her knowing whence it came. Frederick Massingbird had been its inheritor for a short three or four months, and Lionel's sense of justice revolted against his widow being thrown on the world, as she expressed it, without a shilling.

"The revenues of the estate during the short time that elapsed between Mr. Verner's death and your husband's are undoubtedly yours, Mrs. Massingbird," he said. "I will see Matiss about it, and they shall be paid over."

"How long will it be first?"

"A few days, possibly. In a note which I received but now from Matiss, he tells me he is starting for London, but will be home the beginning of the week. It shall be arranged on his return."

"Thank you. And, until then, I may stay here?"

Lionel was at a nonplus. It is not a pleasing thing to tell a lady that she must quit your house, in which, like a stray lamb, she has taken refuge. Even though it be, for her own fair sake, expedient that she should go.

"I am here alone," said Lionel, after a pause. "Your temporary home had better be with your sisters."

"No, that it never shall," returned Sibylla, in a hasty tone of fear. "I will never go home to them, now papa's away. Why did he leave Deerham? They told me at the station that he was gone, and Jan was doctor."

"Dr. West is travelling on the Continent, as medical attendant and companion to a nobleman. At least—I think I heard it was a nobleman," continued Lionel. "I am really not sure."

"And you would like me to go home to those two cross, fault-finding sisters!" she resumed. "They might reproach me all day long with coming home to be kept. As if it were my fault that I am left without anything. Oh, Lionel! don't turn me out! Let me stay until I can see what is to be done for myself. I shall not hurt you. It would have been all mine had Frederick lived."

He did not know what to do. Every moment there seemed to grow less chance that she would leave the house. A bright thought darted into his mind. It was, that he would get his mother or Decima to come and stay with him for a time.

"What would you like to take?" he inquired. "Mrs. Tynn will get you anything you wish. I—"

"Nothing yet," she interrupted. "I could not eat; I am too unhappy. I will take some tea presently, but not until I am warmer. I am very cold."

She cowered over the fire again, shivering much. Lionel, saying he had a note to write, sat down to a distant table. He penned a few hasty lines to his mother, telling her that Mrs. Massingbird had arrived, under the impression that she was coming to Mrs. Verner, and that he could not well turn her out again that night, fatigued and poorly as she appeared to him to be. He begged his mother to come to him for a day or two, in the emergency, or to send Decima.

An undercurrent of conviction ran in Lionel's mind during the time of writing it that his mother would not come; he doubted even whether she would allow Decima to come. He drove the thought away from him; but the impression remained. Carrying the note out of the room when written, he despatched it to Deerham Court by a mounted groom. As he was returning to the dining-room he encountered Mrs. Tynn.

"I hear Mrs. Massingbird has arrived, sir," cried she.

"Yes," replied Lionel. "She will like some tea presently. She appears very much fatigued."

"Is the luggage to be taken upstairs, sir?" she continued, pointing to the pile in the hall. "Is she going to stay here?"

Lionel really did not know what answer to make.

"She came expecting to stay," he said, after a pause. "She did not know but your mistress was still here. Should she remain, I dare say Lady Verner, or my sister, will join her. You have beds ready?"

"Plenty of them, sir, at five minutes' notice."

When Lionel entered the room, Sibylla was in the same attitude, shivering over the fire. Unnaturally cold she appeared to be, and yet her cheeks were brilliantly bright, as if with a touch of fever.

"I fear you have caught cold on the journey to-day," he said.

"I don't think so," she answered. "I am cold from nervousness. I went cold at the station when they told me that my aunt was dead, and I have been shivering ever since. Never mind me; it will go off presently."

Lionel drew a chair to the other side of the fire, compassionately regarding her. He could have found in his heart to take her in his arms, and warm her there.

"What was that about a codicil?" she suddenly asked him. "When my aunt wrote to me upon Mr. Verner's death, she said that a codicil had been lost: or that, otherwise, the estate would have been yours."

Lionel explained it to her, concealing nothing.

"Then—if that codicil had been forthcoming, Frederick's share would have been but five hundred pounds?"

"That is all."

"It was very little to leave him," she musingly rejoined.

"And still less to leave me, considering my nearer relationship—my nearer claims. When the codicil could not be found, the will had to be acted upon: and five hundred pounds was all the sum it gave me."

"Has the codicil never been found?"

"Never."

"How very strange! What became of it, do you think?"

"I wish I could think what," replied Lionel. "Although Verner's Pride has come to me without it, it would be satisfactory to solve the mystery."

Sibylla looked round cautiously, and sunk her voice. "Could Tynn or his wife have done anything with it? You say they were present when it was signed."

"Most decidedly they did not. Both of them were anxious that I should succeed."

"It is so strange! To lock a paper up in a desk, and for it to disappear of its own accord! The moths could not have got in and eaten it?"

"Scarcely," smiled Lionel. "The day before your aunt died, she—"

"Don't talk of that," interrupted Mrs. Massingbird. "I will hear about her death to-morrow. I shall be ill if I cry much to-night."

She sank into silence, and Lionel did not interrupt it. It continued, until his quick ears caught the sound of the groom's return. The man rode his horse round to the stables at once. Presently Tynn came in with a note. It was from Lady Verner. A few lines, written hastily with a pencil:—

"I do not understand your request, Lionel, or why you make it. Whatever may be my opinion of Frederick Massingbird's widow, I will not insult her sense of propriety by supposing that she would attempt to remain at Verner's Pride now her aunt is dead. It is absurd of you to ask me to come; neither shall I send Decima. Were I and Decima residing with you, it would not be the place for Sibylla Massingbird. She has her own home to go to."

There was no signature. Lionel knew his mother's handwriting too well to require the addition. It was just the note that he might have expected her to write.

What was he to do? In the midst of his ruminations, Sibylla rose.

"I am warm now," she said. "I should like to go upstairs and take this heavy shawl off."

Lionel rang the bell for Mrs. Tynn. And Sibylla left the room with her.

"I'll get her sisters here!" he suddenly exclaimed, the thought of them darting into his mind. "They will be the proper persons to explain to her the inexpediency of her remaining here. Poor girl! she is unable to think of it in her fatigue and grief."

He did not give it a second thought, but snatched his hat, and went down himself to Dr. West's with strides as long as Jan's. Entering the general sitting-room without ceremony, his eyes fell upon a supper-table and Master Cheese; the latter regaling himself upon apple-puffs to his heart's content.

"Where are the Misses West?" asked Lionel.

"Gone to a party," responded the young gentleman, as soon as he could get his mouth sufficiently empty to speak.

"Where to?"

"To Heartburg, sir. It's a ball at old Thingumtight's, the doctor's. They are gone off in gray gauze, with, branches of white flowers hanging to their curls, and they call that mourning. The fly is to bring them back at two in the morning. They left these apple-puffs for me and Jan. Jan said he should not want any; he'd eat meat; so I have got his share and mine!"

And Master Cheese appeared to be enjoying the shares excessively. Lionel left him to it, and went thoughtfully back to Verner's Pride.

CHAPTER XXXVI

A MOMENT OF DELIRIUM

The dining-room looked a picture of comfort, and Lionel thought so as he entered. A blaze of light and warmth burst upon him. A well-spread tea-table was there, with cold meat, game and else, at one end of it. Standing before the fire, her young, slender form habited in its black robes, was Sibylla. No one, looking at her, would have believed her to be a widow; partly from her youth, partly that she did not wear the widow's dress. Her head was uncovered, and her fair curls fell, shading her brilliant cheeks. It has been mentioned that her chief beauty lay in her complexion: seen by candle-light, flushed as she was now, she was inexpressibly beautiful. A dangerous hour, a perilous situation for the yet unhealed heart of Lionel Verner.

The bright flush was the result of excitement, of some degree of inward fever. Let us allow that it was a trying time for her. She had arrived to find Mrs. Verner dead, her father absent; she had arrived to find that no provision had been made for her by Mr. Verner's will, as the widow of Frederick Massingbird. Frederick's having succeeded to the inheritance debarred her even of the five hundred pounds. It is true there would be the rents, received for the short time it had been his. There was no doubt that Sibylla, throughout the long voyage, had cherished the prospect of finding a home at Verner's Pride. If her husband had lived, it would have been wholly hers; she appeared still to possess a right in it; and she never gave a thought to the possibility that her aunt would not welcome her to it. Whether she cast a reflection to Lionel Verner in the matter, she best knew: had she reflected properly, she might have surmised that Lionel would be living at it, its master. But, the voyage ended, the home gained, what did she find? That Mrs. Verner was no longer at Verner's Pride, to press the kiss of welcome upon her lips; a few feet of earth was all her home now.

It was a terrible disappointment. There could be no doubt of that. And another disappointment was, to find Dr. West away. Sibylla's sisters had been at times over-strict with her, much as they loved her, and the vision of returning to her old home, to them, was one of bitterness. So bitter, in fact, that she would not glance at its possibility.

Fatigued, low-spirited, feverishly perplexed, Sibylla did not know what she could do. She was not in a state that night to give much care to the future. All she hoped was, to stay in that haven until something else could be arranged for her. Let us give her her due. Somewhat careless, naturally, of the punctilios of life, it never occurred to her that it might not be the precise thing for her to remain, young as she was, the sole guest of Lionel Verner. Her voyage out, her residence in that very unconventional place, Melbourne, the waves and storms which had gone over her there in more ways than one, the voyage back again alone, all had tended to give Sibylla Massingbird an independence of thought; a contempt for the rules and regulations, the little points of etiquette obtaining in civilised society. She really thought no more harm of staying at Verner's Pride with Lionel, than she would have thought it had old Mr. Verner been its master. The eyelashes, resting on her hot cheeks, were wet, as she turned round when Lionel entered.

"Have you taken anything, Mrs. Massingbird?"

"No."

"But you should have done so," he remonstrated, his tone one of the most considerate kindness.

"I did not observe that tea waited," she replied, the covered table catching her eye for the first time. "I have been thinking."

He placed a chair for her before the tea-tray, and she sat down. "Am I to preside?" she asked.

"If you will. If you are not too tired."

"Who makes tea for you in general?" she continued.

"They send it in, made."

Sibylla busied herself with the tea, in a languid sort of manner. In vain Lionel pressed her to eat. She could touch nothing. She took a piece of rolled bread-and-butter, but left it.

"You must have dined on the road, Mrs. Massingbird?" he said, with a smile.

"I? I have not taken anything all day. I kept thinking 'I shall get to Verner's Pride in time for my aunt's dinner.' But the train arrived later than I anticipated; and when I got here she was gone."

Sibylla bent her head, as if playing with her teaspoon. Lionel detected the dropping tears.

"Did you wonder where I was going just now, when I went out?"

"I did not know you had been out," replied Sibylla.

"I went to your sisters'. I thought it would be better for them to come here. Unfortunately, I found them gone out; and young Cheese says they will not be home until two in the morning."

"Why, where can they be gone?" cried Sibylla, aroused to interest. It was so unusual for the Misses West to be out late.

"To some gathering at Heartburg. Cheese was eating apple-puffs with unlimited satisfaction."

The connection of apple-puffs with Master Cheese called up a faint smile into Sibylla's face. She pushed her chair away from the table, turning it towards the fire.

"But you surely have not finished, Mrs. Massingbird?"

"Yes, thank you. I have drunk my tea. I cannot eat anything."

Lionel rang, and the things were removed. Sibylla was standing before the mantel-piece when they were left alone, unconsciously looking at herself in the glass. Lionel stood near her.

"I have not got a widow's cap," she exclaimed, turning to him, the thought appearing suddenly to strike her. "I had two or three curious things made, that they called widows' caps in Melbourne, but they were spoiled on the voyage."

"You have seen some trouble since you went out," Lionel observed.

"Yes, I have. It was an ill-starred voyage. It has been ill-starred from the beginning to the end; all of it together."

"The voyage has, you mean?"

"I mean more than the voyage," she replied. But her tone did not invite further question.

"Did you succeed in getting particulars of the fate of John?"

"No. Captain Cannonby promised to make inquiries, but we had not heard from him before I came away. I wish we could have found Luke Roy."

"Did you not find him?"

"We heard of him from the Eyres—the friends I was staying with. It was so singular," she continued, with some animation in her tone. "Luke Roy came to Melbourne after John was killed, and fell in with the Eyres. He told them about John, little thinking that I and Frederick should meet the Eyres afterwards. John died from a shot."

"From a shot!" involuntarily exclaimed Lionel.

"He and Luke were coming down to Melbourne from—where was it?—the Bendigo Diggings, I think; but I heard so much of the different names, that I am apt to confound one with another. John had a great deal of gold on him, in a belt round his waist, and Luke supposes that it got known. John was attacked as they were sleeping by night in the open air, beaten, and shot. It was the shot that killed him."

"Poor fellow!" exclaimed Lionel, his eyes fixed on vacancy, mentally beholding John Massingbird. "And they robbed him!"

"They had robbed him of all. Not a particle of gold was left upon him. And the report sent home by Luke, that the gold and men were taken, proved to be a mistaken one. Luke came on afterwards to Melbourne, and tried to discover the men; but he could not. It was this striving at discovery which brought him in contact with Mr. Eyre. After we reached Melbourne and I became acquainted with the Eyres, they did all they could to find out Luke, but they were unsuccessful."

"What had become of him?"

"They could not think. The last time Mr. Eyre saw him, Luke said he thought he had obtained a clue to the men who killed John. He promised to go back the following day and tell Mr. Eyre more about it. But he did not. And they never saw him afterwards. Mrs. Eyre used to say to me that she sincerely trusted no harm had come to Luke."

"Harm in what way?" asked Lionel.

"She thought—but she would say that it was a foolish thought—if Luke should have found the men, and been imprudent enough to allow them to know that he recognised them, they might have worked him some ill. Perhaps killed him."

Sibylla spoke the last words in a low tone. She was standing very still; her hands lightly resting before her, one upon another. How Lionel's heart was beating as he gazed on her, he alone knew. She was once again the Sibylla of past days. He forgot that she was the widow of another; that she had left him for that other of her own free will. All his past resentment faded in that moment: nothing was present to him but his love; and Sibylla with her fascinating beauty.

"You are thinner than when you left home," he remarked.

"I grew thin with vexation; with grief. He ought not to have taken me."

The concluding sentence was spoken in a strangely resentful tone. It surprised Lionel. "Who ought not to have taken you?—taken you where?" he asked, really not understanding her.

"He. Frederick Massingbird. He might have known what a place that Melbourne was. It was not fit for a lady. We had lodgings in a wooden house, near a spot that had used to be called Canvas Town. The place was crowded with people."

"But surely there are decent hotels at Melbourne?"

"All I know is he did not take me to one. He inquired at one or two, but they were full; and then somebody recommended him to get a lodging. It was not right. He might have gone to it himself, but he had me with him. He lost his desk, you know."

"I heard that he did," replied Lionel.

"And I suppose that frightened him. Everything was in the desk—money and letters of credit. He had a few bank-notes, only, left in his pocket-book. It never was recovered. I owe my passage-money home, and I believe Captain Cannonby supplied him with some funds—which of course ought to be repaid. He took to drinking brandy," she continued.

"I am much surprised to hear it."

"Some fever came on. I don't know whether he caught it, or whether it came to him naturally. It was a sort of intermittent fever. At times he was very low with it, and then it was that he would drink the brandy. Only fancy what my position was!" she added, her face and voice alike full of pain. "He, not always himself; and I, out there in that wretched place, alone. I went down on my knees to him one day, and begged him to send me back to England."

"Sibylla!"

He was unconscious that he called her by the familiar name. He was wishing he could have shielded her from all this. Painful as the retrospect might be to her, the recital was far more painful to him.

"After that, we met Captain Cannonby. I did not much like him, but he was kind to us. He got us to change to an hotel—made them find room for us—and then introduced me to the Eyres. Afterwards, he and Fred started from Melbourne, and I went to stay at the Eyres."

Lionel did not interrupt her. She had made a pause, her eyes fixed on the fire.

"A day or two, and Captain Cannonby came back, and said that my husband was dead. I was not very much surprised. I thought he would not live when he left me: he had death written in his face. And so I am alone in the world."

She raised her large blue eyes, swimming in tears, to Lionel. It completely disarmed him. He forgot all his prudence, all his caution; he forgot things that it was incumbent upon him to remember; and, as many another has done before him, older and wiser than Lionel Verner, he suffered a moment's impassioned impulse to fix the destiny of a life.

"Not alone from henceforth, Sibylla," he murmured, bending towards her in agitation, his lips apart, his breath coming fast and loud, his cheeks scarlet. "Let me be your protector. I love you more fondly than I have ever done."

She was entirely unprepared for the avowal. It may be that she did not know what to make of it—how to understand it. She stepped back, her eyes strained on him inquiringly, her face turning to pallor. Lionel threw his arms around her, drew her to him, and sheltered her on his breast, as if he would ward off ill from her for ever.

"Be my wife," he fondly cried, his voice trembling with its own tenderness. "My darling, let this home be yours! Nothing shall part us more."

She burst into tears, raised herself, and looked at him. "You cannot mean it! After behaving to you as I did, can you love me still?"

"I love you far better than ever," he answered, his voice becoming hoarse with emotion. "I have been striving to forget you ever since that cruel time; and not until to-night did I know how utterly futile has been the strife. You will let me love you! you will help me to blot out its remembrance!"

She drew a long, deep sigh, like one who is relieved from some wearing pain, and laid her head down again as he had placed it. "I can love you better than I loved him," she breathed, in a low whisper.

"Sibylla, why did you leave me? Why did you marry him?"

"Oh, Lionel, don't reproach me!—don't reproach me!" she answered, bursting into tears. "Papa made me. He did, indeed."

"He made you! Dr. West?"

"I liked Frederick a little. Yes, I did; I will not deny it. And oh, how he loved me! All the while, Lionel, that you hovered near me—never speaking, never saying that you loved—he told me of it incessantly."

"Stay, Sibylla. You could not have mistaken me."

"True. Yours was silent love; his was urgent. When it came to the decision, and he asked me to marry him, and to go out to Australia, then papa interfered. He suspected that I cared for you—that you cared for me; and he—he—"

Sibylla stopped and hesitated.

"Must I tell you all?" she asked. "Will you never, never repeat it to papa, or reproach him? Will you let it remain a secret between us?"

"I will, Sibylla. I will never speak upon the point to Dr. West."

"Papa said that I must choose Frederick Massingbird. He told me that Verner's Pride was left to Frederick, and he ordered me to marry him. He did not say how he knew, it—how he heard it; he only said that it was so. He affirmed that you were cut off with nothing, or next to nothing; that you would not be able to take a wife for years—perhaps never. And I weakly yielded."

A strangely stern expression had darkened Lionel's face. Sibylla saw it, and wrung her hands.

"Oh, don't blame me!—don't blame me more than you can help! I know how weak, how wrong it was; but you cannot tell how entirely obedient we have always been to papa."

"Dr. West became accidentally acquainted with the fact that the property was left away from me," returned Lionel, in a tone of scorn he could not entirely suppress. "He made good use, it seems, of his knowledge."

"Do not blame me!" she reiterated. "It was not my fault."

"I do not blame you, my dearest."

"I have been rightly served," she said, the tears streaming down. "I married him, pressed to it by my father, that I might share in Verner's Pride; and, before the news came out that Verner's Pride was ours, he was dead. It had lapsed to you, whom I rejected! Lionel, I never supposed that you would cast another thought to me; but, many a time have I felt that I should like to kneel and ask your forgiveness."

He bent his head, fondly kissing her. "We will forget it together, Sibylla."

A sudden thought appeared to strike her, called forth, no doubt, by this new state of things, and her face turned crimson as she looked at Lionel.

"Ought I to remain here now?"

"You cannot well do anything else, as it is so late," he answered. "Allow Verner's Pride to afford you an asylum for the present, until you can make arrangements to remove to some temporary home. Mrs. Tynn will make you comfortable. I shall be, during the time, my mother's guest."

"What is the time now?" asked Sibylla.

"Nearly ten; and I dare say you are tired. I will not be selfish enough to keep you up," he added, preparing to depart. "Good-night, my dearest."

She burst into fresh tears, and clung to his hand. "I shall be thinking it must be a dream as soon as you leave me. You will be sure to come back and see me to-morrow?"

"Come back—ay!" he said, with a smile; "Verner's Pride never contained the magnet for me that it contains now."

He gave a few brief orders to Mrs. Tynn and to his own servant, and quitted the house. Neither afraid of ghosts nor thieves, he took the field way, the road which led by the Willow Pond. It was a fine, cold night, his mind was unsettled, his blood was heated, and the lonely route appeared to him preferable to the one through the village.

"He caught a glimpse of a figure bending over it."

As he passed the Willow Pond with a quick step, he caught a glimpse of some figure bending over it, as if it were looking for something in the water, or else about to take a leap in. Remembering the fate of Rachel, and not wishing to have a second catastrophe of the same nature happen on his estate, Lionel strode towards the figure and caught it by the arm. The head was flung upwards at the touch, and Lionel recognised Robin Frost.

"Robin! what do you do here?" he questioned, his tone somewhat severe in spite of its kindness.

"No harm," answered the man. "There be times, Mr. Lionel, when I am forced to come. If I am in my bed, and the thought comes over me that I may see her if I only stay long enough upon the brink of this here water, which was her ending, I'm obliged to get up and come here. There be nights, sir, when I have stood here from sunset to sunrise."

"But you never have seen her, Robin?" returned Lionel, humouring his grief.

"No; never. But it's no reason why I never may. Folks say there be some of the dead that comes again, sir—not all."

"And if you did see her, what end would it answer?"

"She'd tell me who the wicked one was that put her into it," returned Robin, in a low whisper; and there was something so wild in the man's tone as to make Lionel doubt his perfect sanity. "Many a time do I hear her voice a-calling to me. It comes at all hours, abroad and at home; in the full sunshine, and in the dark night. 'Robin!' it says, 'Robin!' But it never says nothing more."

Lionel laid his hand on the man's shoulder, and drew him with him. "I am going your way, Robin; let us walk together."

Robin made no resistance; he went along with his head down.

"I heard a word said to-night, sir, as Miss Sibylla had come back," he resumed, more calmly; "Mrs. Massingbird, that is. Somebody said they saw her at the station. Have you seen her, sir?"

"Yes; I have," replied Lionel.

"Does she say anything about John Massingbird?" continued the man, with feverish eagerness. "Is he dead? or is he alive?"

"He is dead, Robin. There has never been a doubt upon the point since the news first came. He died by violence."

"Then he got his deserts," returned Robin, lifting his hand in the air, as he had done once before when speaking upon the same subject. "And Luke Roy, sir? Is he coming? I'm a-waiting for him."

"Of Luke, Mrs. Massingbird knows nothing. For myself, I think he is sure to come home, sooner or later."

"Heaven send him!" aspirated Robin.

Lionel saw the man turn to his home, and very soon afterwards he was at his mother's. Lady Verner had retired for the night. Decima and Lucy were about retiring. They had risen from their seats, and Decima—who was too cautious to trust it to servants—was taking the fire off the grate. They looked inexpressibly surprised at the entrance of Lionel.

"I have come an a visit, Decima," began he, speaking in a gay tone. "Can you take me in?"

She did not understand him, and Lionel saw by the questioning expression of her face that Lady Verner had not made public the contents of his note to her; he saw that they were ignorant of the return of

Sibylla. The fact that they were so seemed to rush over his spirit as a refreshing dew. Why it should do so, he did not seek to analyse; and he was all too self-conscious that he dared not.

"A friend has come unexpectedly on a visit, and taken possession of Verner's Pride," he pursued. "I have lent it for a time."

"Lent it all?" exclaimed the wondering Decima.

"Lent it all. You will make room for me, won't you?"

"To be sure," said Decima, puzzled more than she could express. "But was there no room left for you?"

"No," answered Lionel.

"What very unconscionable people they must be, to invade you in such numbers as that! You can have your old chamber, Lionel. But I will just go and speak to Catherine."

She hastened from the room. Lionel stood before the fire, positively turning his back upon Lucy Tempest. Was his conscience already smiting him? Lucy, who had stood by the table, her bed candle in her hand, stepped forward and held out the other hand to Lionel.

"May I wish you good-night?" she said.

"Good-night," he answered, shaking her hand. "How is your cold?"

"Oh! it is so much better!" she replied, with animation. "All the threatened soreness of the chest is gone. I shall be well by to-morrow. Lady Verner said I ought to have gone to bed early, but I felt too well. I knew Jan's advice would be good."

She left him, and Lionel leaned his elbow on the mantel-piece, his brow contracting as does that of one in unpleasant thought. Was he recalling the mode in which he had taken leave of Lucy earlier in the day?

CHAPTER XXXVII

NEWS FOR LADY VERNER: AND FOR LUCY

If he did not recall it then, he recalled it later, when he was upon his bed, turning and tossing from side to side. His conscience was smiting him—smiting him from more points than one. Carried away by the impulse of the moment, he had spoken words that night, in his hot passion, which might not be redeemed; and now that the leisure for reflection was come, he could not conceal from himself that he had been too hasty. Lionel Verner was one who possessed excessive conscientiousness; even as a boy, had impetuosity led him into a fault—as it often did—his silent, inward repentance would be always keenly real, more so than the case deserved. It was so now. He loved Sibylla—there had been no mistake there; but it is certain that the unexpected delight of meeting her, her presence palpably before him in all its beauty, her manifested sorrow and grief, her lonely, unprotected position, had all worked their effect upon his heart and mind, had imparted to his love a false intensity. However the agitation of the moment may have caused him to fancy it, he did not love Sibylla as he had loved her of old; else why should the image of Lucy Tempest present itself to him surrounded by a halo of regret? The point is as unpleasant for us to touch upon, as it was to Lionel to think of: but the fact was all too palpable, and cannot be suppressed. He did love Sibylla: nevertheless there obtruded the unwelcome reflection that, in asking her to be his wife, he had been hasty; that it had been better had he taken time for consideration. He almost doubted whether Lucy would not have been more acceptable to him; not loved yet so much as Sibylla, but better suited to him in all other ways; worse than this, he doubted whether he had not in honour bound himself tacitly to Lucy that very day.

The fit of repentance was upon him, and he tossed and turned from side to side upon his uneasy bed. But, toss and turn as he would, he could not undo his night's work. There remained nothing for him but to carry it out, and make the best of it; and he strove to deceive his conscience with the hope that Lucy Tempest, in her girlish innocence, had not understood his hinted allusions to her becoming his wife; that she had looked upon his snatched caresses as but trifling pastime, such as he might offer to a child. Most unjustifiable he now felt those hints, those acts to have been, and his brow grew red with shame at their recollection. One thing he did hope, hope sincerely—that Lucy did not care for him. That she liked him very much, and had been on most confidential terms with him, he knew; but he did hope her liking went no deeper. Strange sophistry! how it will deceive the human heart! how prone we are to admit it! Lionel was honest enough in his hope now: but, not many hours before, he had been hugging his heart with the delusion that Lucy did love him.

Towards morning he dropped into an uneasy sleep. He awoke later than his usual hour from a dream of Frederick Massingbird. Dreams play us strange fantasies. Lionel's had taken him to that past evening, prior to Frederick Massingbird's marriage, when he had sought him in his chamber, to offer a word of warning against the union. He seemed to be living the interview over again, and the first words when he awoke, rushing over his brain with minute and unpleasant reality, were those he had himself spoken in reference to Sibylla:—"Were she free as air this moment, were she to come to my feet, and say 'Let me be your wife,' I should tell her that the whole world was before her to choose from, save myself. She can never again be anything to me."

Brave words: fully believed in when they were spoken: but what did Lionel think of them now?

He went down to breakfast. He was rather late, and found they had assembled. Lady Verner, who had just heard for the first time of Lionel's presence in the house, made no secret now of Lionel's note to her. Therefore Decima and Lucy knew that the "invasion" of Verner's Pride had been caused by Mrs. Massingbird.

She—Lady Verner—scarcely gave herself time to greet Lionel before she commenced upon it. She did not conceal, or seek to conceal, her sentiments—either of Sibylla herself, or of the step she had taken. And Lionel had the pleasure of hearing his intended bride alluded to in a manner that was not altogether complimentary.

He could not stop it. He could not take upon himself the defence of Sibylla, and say, "Do you know that you are speaking of my future wife?" No, for Lucy Tempest was there. Not in her presence had he the courage to bring home to himself his own dishonour: to avow that, after wooing her (it was very like it), he had turned round and asked another to marry him. The morning sun shone into the room upon the snowy cloth, upon the silver breakfast service, upon the exquisite cups of painted porcelain, upon those seated round the table. Decima sat opposite to Lady Verner, Lionel and Lucy were face to face on either side. The walls exhibited a few choice paintings; the room and its appurtenances were in excellent taste. Lady Verner liked things that pleased the eye. That silver service had been a recent present of Lionel's, who had delighted in showering elegancies and comforts upon his mother since his accession.

"What could have induced her ever to think of taking up her residence at Verner's Pride on her return?" reiterated Lady Verner to Lionel.

"She believed she was coming to her aunt. It was only at the station, here, that she learned Mrs. Verner was dead."

"She did learn it there?"

"Yes. She learned it there."

"And she could come to Verner's Pride after that? knowing that you, and you alone, were its master?"

Lionel toyed with his coffee-cup. He wished his mother would spare her remarks.

"She was so fatigued, so low-spirited, that I believed she was scarcely conscious where she drove," he returned. "I am certain that the idea of there being any impropriety in it never once crossed her mind."

Lady Verner drew her shawl around her with a peculiar movement. If ever action expressed scorn, that one did—scorn of Sibylla, scorn of her conduct, scorn of Lionel's credulity in believing in her. Lionel read it all. Happening to glance across the table, he caught the eyes of Lucy Tempest fixed upon him with an open expression of wonder. Wonder at what? At his believing in Sibylla? It might be. With all Lucy's straightforward plainness, she would have been one of the last to storm Lionel's abode, and take refuge in it. A retort, defending Sibylla, had been upon Lionel's tongue, but that gaze stopped it.

"How long does she purpose honouring Verner's Pride with her presence, and keeping you out of it?" resumed Lady Verner.

"I do not know what her plans for the present may be," he answered, his cheeks burning at the thought of the avowal he had to make—that her future plans would be contingent upon his. Not the least painful of the results which Lionel's haste had brought in its train, was the knowledge of the shock it would prove to his mother, whom he so loved and reverenced. Why had he not thought of it at the time?

Breakfast over, Lionel went out, a very coward. A coward, in so far as that he had shrunk from making yet the confession. He was aware that it ought to be done. The presence of Decima and Lucy Tempest had been his mental excuse for putting off the unwelcome task.

But a better frame of mind came over him ere he had gone many paces from the door; better, at any rate, as regarded the cowardice.

"A Verner never shrank yet from his duty," was his comment, as he bent his steps back again. "Am I turning renegade?"

He went straight up to Lady Verner, and asked her, in a low tone, to grant him a minute's private interview. They had breakfasted in the room which made the ante-room to the drawing-room; it was their usual morning-room. Lady Verner answered her son by stepping into the drawing-room.

He followed her and closed the door. The fire was but just lighted, scarcely giving out any heat. She slightly shivered, and requested him to stir it. He did so mechanically—wholly absorbed by the revelation he had to impart. He remembered how she had once fainted at nearly the same revelation.

"Mother, I have a communication to make to you," he began with desperate energy, "and I don't know how to do it. It will pain you greatly. Nothing that I can think of, or imagine, would cause you so much pain."

Lady Verner seated herself in her low violet-velvet chair, and looked composedly at Lionel. She did not dread the communication very much. He was secure in Verner's Pride; what could there be that she need fear? She no more cast a glance to the possibility of his marrying the widow of Frederick Massingbird, than she would have done to his marrying that gentleman's wife. Buried in this semi-security, the shock must be all the greater.

"I am about to marry," said Lionel, plunging into the news headlong. "And I fear that you will not approve my choice. Nay, I know you will not."

A foreshadowing of the truth came across her then. She grew deadly pale, and put up her hands, as if to ward off the blow. "Oh, Lionel! don't say it! don't say it!" she implored. "I never can receive her."

"Yes, you will, mother," he whispered, his own face pale too, his tone one of painful entreaty. "You will receive her for my sake."

"Is it—she?"

The aversion with which the name was avoided was unmistakable. Lionel only nodded a grave affirmative.

"Have you engaged yourself to her?"

"I have. Last night."

"Were you mad?" she asked in a whisper.

"Stay, mother. When you were speaking against Sibylla at breakfast, I refrained from interference, for you did not then know that defence of her was my duty. Will you forgive me for reminding you that I cannot permit it to be continued, even by you?"

"But do you forget that it is not a respectable alliance for you?" resumed Lady Verner. "No, not a respectable—"

"I cannot listen to this; I pray you cease!" he broke forth, a blaze of anger lighting his face. "Have you forgotten of whom you are speaking, mother? Not respectable!"

"I say that it is not a respectable alliance for you—Lionel Verner," she persisted. "An obscure surgeon's daughter, he of not too good repute, who has been out to the end of the world, and found her way back alone, a widow, is not a desirable alliance for a Verner. It would not be desirable for Jan; it is terrible for you?"

"We shall not agree upon this," said Lionel, preparing to take his departure. "I have acquainted you, mother, and I have no more to say, except to urge—if I may do so—that you will learn to speak of Sibylla with courtesy, remembering that she will shortly be my wife."

Lady Verner caught his hand as he was retreating.

"Lionel, my son, tell me how you came to do it," she wailed. "You cannot love her! the wife, the widow of another man! It must have been the work of a moment of folly. Perhaps she drew you into it!"

The suggestion, "the work of a moment of folly," was so very close a representation of what it had been, of what Lionel was beginning to see it to have been now, that the rest of the speech was lost to him in the echo of that one sentence. Somehow, he did not care to refute it.

"She will be my wife, respected and honoured," was all he answered, as he quitted the room.

Lady Verner followed him. He went straight out, and she saw him walk hastily across the courtyard, putting on his hat as he traversed it. She wrung her hands, and broke into a storm of wailing despair, ignoring the presence of Decima and Lucy Tempest.

"I had far rather that she had stabbed him!"

The words excited their amazement. They turned to Lady Verner, and were struck with the marks of agitation on her countenance.

"Mamma, what are you speaking of?" asked Decima.

Lady Verner pointed to Lionel, who was then passing through the front gates. "I speak of him," she answered: "my darling; my pride; my much-loved son. That woman has worked his ruin."

Decima verily thought her mother must be wandering in her intellect. Lucy could only gaze at Lady Verner in consternation.

"What woman?" repeated Decima.

"She. She who has been Lionel's bane. She who came and thrust herself into his home last night in her unseemly conduct. What passed between them Heaven knows; but she has contrived to cajole him out of a promise to marry her."

Decima's pale cheek turned to a burning red. She was afraid to ask questions.

"Oh, mamma! it cannot be!" was all she uttered.

"It is, Decima. I told Lionel that he could not love her, who had been the wife of another man; and he did not refute it. I told him she must have drawn him into it; and that he left unanswered. He replied that she would be his wife, and must be honoured as such. Drawn in to marry her! one who is so utterly unworthy of him! whom he does not even love! Oh, Lionel, my son, my son!"

In their own grievous sorrow they noticed not the face of Lucy Tempest, or what they might have read there.

CHAPTER XXXVIII

THE MISSES WEST EN PAPILLOTES

Lionel went direct to the house of Dr. West. It was early; and the Misses West, fatigued with their night's pleasure, had risen in a scuffle, barely getting down at the breakfast hour. Jan was in the country attending on a patient, and, not anticipating the advent of visitors, they had honoured Master Cheese with hair en papillotes. Master Cheese had divided his breakfast hour between eating and staring. The meal had been some time over, and the young gentleman had retired, but the ladies sat over the fire in unusual idleness, discussing the dissipation they had participated in. A scream from the two arose upon the entrance of Lionel, and Miss Amilly flung her pocket-handkerchief over her head.

"Never mind," said Lionel, laughing good-naturedly; "I have seen curl-papers before, in my life. Your sitting here quietly, tells me that you do not know what has occurred."

"What has occurred?" interrupted Deborah, before he could continue. "It—it"—her voice grew suddenly timid—"is nothing bad about papa?"

"No, no. Your sister has arrived from Australia. In this place of gossip, I wonder the news has not travelled to Jan or to Cheese."

They had started up, poor things, their faces flushed, their eyelashes glistening, forgetting the little episode of the mortified vanity, eager to embrace Sibylla.

"Come back from Australia!" uttered Deborah in wild astonishment. "Then where is she, that she is not here, in her own home?"

"She came to mine," replied Lionel. "She supposed Mrs. Verner to be its mistress still. I made my way here last night to ask you to come up, and found you were gone to Heartburg."

"But—she—is not remaining at it?" exclaimed Deborah, speaking with hesitation, in her doubt, the flush on her face deepening.

"I placed it at her disposal until other arrangements could be made," replied Lionel. "I am at present the guest of Lady Verner. You will go to Sibylla, will you not?"

Go to her? Ay! They tore the curl-papers out of their hair, and flung on bonnets and shawls, and hastened to Verner's Pride.

"Say that I will call upon her in the course of the morning, and see how she is after her journey," said Lionel.

In hurrying out, they encountered Jan. Deborah stopped to say a word about his breakfast: it was ready, she said, and she thought he must want it.

"I do," responded Jan. "I shall have to get an assistant, after all, Miss Deb. I find it doesn't answer to go quite without meals and sleep; and that's what I have done lately."

"So you have, Mr. Jan. I say every day to Amilly that it can't go on, for you to be walked off your legs in this way. Have you heard the cheering news, Mr. Jan? Sibylla's come home. We are going to her now, at Verner's Pride?"

"I have heard it," responded Jan. "What took her to Verner's Pride?"

"We have yet to learn all that. You know, Mr. Jan, she never was given to consider a step much, before she took it."

They tripped away, and Jan, in turning from them, met his brother. Jan was one utterly incapable of finesse: if he wanted to say a thing, he said it out plainly. What havoc Jan would have made, enrolled in the corps of diplomatists!

"I say, Lionel," began he, "is it true that you are going to marry Sibylla West?"

Lionel did not like the plain question, so abruptly put. He answered curtly—

"I am going to marry Sibylla Massingbird."

"The old name comes the readiest," said Jan. "How did it come about, Lionel?"

"May I ask whence you derived your information, Jan?" returned Lionel, who was marvelling where Jan could have heard this.

"At Deerham Court. I have been calling in, as I passed it, to see Miss Lucy. The mother is going wild, I think. Lionel, if it is as she says, that Sibylla drew you into it against your will, don't you carry it out. I'd not. Nobody should hook me into anything."

"My mother said that, did she? Be so kind as not to repeat it, Jan. I am marrying Sibylla because I love her; I am marrying her of my own free will. If anybody—save my mother—has aught of objection to make to it, let them make it to me."

"Oh! that's it, is it?" returned Jan. "You need not be up, Lionel, it is no business of mine. I'm sure you are free to marry her for me. I'll be groomsman, if you like."

"Lady Verner has always been prejudiced against Sibylla," observed Lionel. "You might have remembered that, Jan."

"So I did," said Jan; "though I assumed that what she said was sure to be true. You see, I have been on the wrong scent lately. I thought you were getting fond of Lucy Tempest. It has looked like it."

Lionel murmured some unintelligible answer, and turned away, a hot flush dyeing his brow.

Meanwhile Sibylla was already up, but not down. Breakfast she would have carried up to her room, she told Mrs. Tynn. She stood at the window, looking forth; not so much at the extensive prospect that swept the horizon in the distance, as at the fair lands immediately around. "All his," she murmured, "and I shall be his wife at last!"

She turned languidly round at the opening of the door, expecting to see her breakfast. Instead of which, two frantic little bodies burst in and seized upon her. Sibylla shrieked—

"Don't, Deb! don't, Amilly! Are you going to hug me to death?"

Their kisses of welcome over, they went round about her, fondly surveying her from all points with their tearful eyes. She was thinner; but she was more lovely. Amilly expressed an opinion that the bloom on her delicate wax face was even brighter than of yore.

"Of course it is, at the present moment," answered Sibylla, "when you have been kissing me into a fever."

"She is not tanned a bit with her voyage, that I see," cried Deborah, with undisguised admiration. "But Sibylla's skin never did tan. Child," she added, bending towards her, and allowing her voice to become grave, "how could you think of coming to Verner's Pride? It was not right. You should have come home."

"I thought Mrs. Verner was living still."

"And if she had been?—This is Mr. Lionel's house now; not hers. You ought to have come home, my dear. You will come home with us now, will you not?"

"I suppose you'll allow me to have some breakfast first," was Sibylla's answer. Secure in her future position, she was willing to go home to them temporarily now. "Why is papa gone away, Deborah?"

"He will be coming back some time, dear," was Deborah's evasive answer, spoken soothingly. "But tell us a little about yourself, Sibylla. When poor Frederick—"

"Not this morning, Deborah," she interrupted, putting up her hand. "I will tell you all another time. It was an unlucky voyage."

"Have you realised John's money that he left? That he lost, I should rather say."

"I have realised nothing," replied Sibylla—"nothing but ill luck. We never got tidings of John in any way, beyond the details of his death; we never saw a particle of the gold belonging to him, or could hear of it. And my husband lost his desk the day we landed—as I sent you word; and I had no money out there, and I have only a few shillings in my pocket."

This catalogue of ills nearly stunned Deborah and Amilly West. They had none too much of life's great need, gold, for themselves; and the burden of keeping Sibylla would be sensibly felt. A tolerably good table it was indispensable to maintain, on account of Jan, and that choice eater, Master Cheese; but how they had to pinch in the matter of dress, they alone knew. Sibylla also knew, and she read arightly the drooping of their faces.

"Never mind, Deborah; cheer up, Amilly. It is only for a time. Ere very long I shall be leaving you again."

"Surely not for Australia!" returned Deborah, the hint startling her.

"Australia? Well, I am not sure that it will be quite so far," answered Sibylla, in a little spirit of mischief. And, in the bright prospect of the future, she forgot past and present grievances, turned her laughing blue eyes upon her sisters, and, to their great scandal, began to waltz round and round the room.

CHAPTER XXXIX

BROTHER JARRUM

By the light of a single tallow candle which flared aloft on a shelf in Peckaby's shop, consecrated in more prosperous days to wares, but bare now, a large collected assemblage was regarding each other with looks of eager interest. There could not have been less than thirty present, all crammed together in that little space of a few feet square. The first comers had taken their seats on the counters; the others stood as they could. Two or three men, just returned from their day's labour, were there; but the crowd was chiefly composed of the weaker sex.

The attention of these people was concentrated on a little man who faced them, leaning against the wall at the back of the shop, and holding forth in a loud, persuasive tone. If you object to the term "holding forth," you must blame Mrs. Duff; it is borrowed from her. She informed us, you may remember, that the stranger who met, and appeared to avoid, Lionel Verner, was no other than a "missionary from Jerusalem," taken with an anxiety for the souls of Deerham, and about to do what he could to convert them—"Brother Jarrum."

Brother Jarrum had entered upon his work, conjointly with his entry upon Peckaby's spare bedroom. He held nightly meetings in Peckaby's shop, and the news of his fame was spreading. Women of all ages flocked in to hear him—you know how impressionable they have the character of being. A sprinkling of men followed out of curiosity, of idleness, or from propensity to ridicule. Had Brother Jarrum proved to be a real missionary from Jerusalem—though, so far as my knowledge goes, such messengers from that city are not common—genuinely desirous of converting them from wrath to grace, I fear his audience would, after the first night or two, have fallen off considerably. This missionary, however, contrived both to keep his audience and to increase it; his promises partaking more of the mundane nature than do such promises in general. In point of fact, Brother Jarrum was an Elder from a place that he was pleased to term "New Jerusalem"; in other words, from the Salt Lake city.

It has been the fate of certain spots of England, more so than of most other parts of the European world, to be favoured by periodical visits from these gentry. Deerham was now suffering under the infliction, and Brother Jarrum was doing all that lay in his power to convert half its female population into Mormon proselytes. His peculiar doctrines it is of no consequence to transcribe; but some of his promises were so rich that it is a pity you should lose the treat of hearing them. They commenced with—husbands to all. Old or young, married or single, each was safe to be made the wife of one of these favoured prophets the instant she set foot in the new city. This, of course, was a very grand thing for the women—as you may know if you have any experience of them—especially for those who were getting on the shady side of forty, and had not changed their name. They, the women, gathered together and pressed into Peckaby's shop, and stared at Brother Jarrum with eager eyes, and listened with strained ears, only looking off him to cast admiring glances one to another.

"Stars and snakes!" said Brother Jarrum, whose style of oratory was more peculiar than elegant, "what flounders me is, that the whole lot of you Britishers don't migrate of yourselves to the desired city—the promised land—the Zion on the mountains. You stop here to pinch and toil and care, and quarrel one of another, and starve your children through having nothing to give 'em, when you might go out there to ease, to love, to peace, to plenty. It's a charming city; what else should it be called the City of the Saints for? The houses have shady veranders round 'em, with sweet shrubs a-creeping up, and white posts and pillows to lean against. The bigger a household is, the more rooms it have got; not a lady there, if there was a hundred of 'em in family, but what's got her own parlour and bedroom to herself, which no stranger thinks of going in at without knocking for leaf. All round and about these houses is productive gardens, trees and flowers for ornament, and fruits and green stuff to eat. There's trees that they call cotton wood, and firs, and locusts, and balsams, and poplars, and pines, and acacias, some of 'em in blossom. A family may live for nothing upon the produce of their own ground. Vegetables is to be had for the cutting; their own cows gives the milk—such milk and butter as this poor place, Deerham, never saw—but the rich flavour's imparted to 'em from the fine quality of the grass; and fruit you might feed upon till you got a surfeit. Grapes and peaches is all a-hanging in clusters to the hand, only waiting to be plucked! Stars! my mouth's watering now at the thoughts of 'em! I—"

"Please, sir, what did you say the name of the place was again?" interrupted a female voice.

"New Jerusalem," replied Brother Jarrum. "It's in the territory of Utah. On the maps and on the roads, and for them that have not awoke to the new light, it's called the Great Salt Lake City; but for us favoured saints, it's New Jerusalem. It's Zion—it's Paradise—it's anything beautiful you may like to call it. There's a ballroom in it."

This abrupt wind-up rather took some of the audience aback. "A ballroom!"

"A ballroom," gravely repeated Brother Jarrum. "A public ballroom not far from a hundred feet long; and we have got a theatre for the acting of plays; and we go for rides in winter in sleighs. Ah! did you think it was with us, out there, as it is with you in the old country?—one's days to be made up of labour, labour, labour; no interlude to it but starvation and the crying of children as can't get nursed or fed! We like amusement; and we have it; dancing in particular. Our great prophet himself dances; and all the apostles and bishops dance. They dance themselves down."

The assemblage sat with open eyes. New wonders were revealed to them every moment. Some of the younger legs grew restless at the mental vision conjured up.

"It's part of our faith to dance," continued Brother Jarrum. "Why shouldn't we? Didn't David dance? Didn't Jephthah dance? Didn't the prodigal son dance? You'll all dance on to the last if you come to us. Such a thing as old legs is hardly known among us. As the favoured climate makes the women's faces beautiful, so it keeps the limbs from growing old. The ballroom is hung with green branches and flags; you might think it was a scene of trees lit with lamps; and you'd never tire of listening to the music, or of looking at the supper-table. If you could only see the suppers given, in a picture to-night, it 'ud spoil your sleep, and you'd not rest till you had started to partake of 'em. Ducks and turkeys, and oysters, and fowls, and fish, and meats, and custards, and pies, and potatoes, and greens, and jellies, and coffee, and tea, and cake, and drinks, and so many more things that you'd be tired only of hearing me say the names. There's abundance for all."

Some commotion amid Brother Jarrum's hearers, and a sound as of licking of lips. That supper account was a great temptation. Had Brother Jarrum started then, straight off for the Salt Lake, the probability is that three-parts of the room would have formed a tail after him.

"What's the drinks?" inquired Jim Clark, the supper items imparting to his inside a curious feeling of emptiness.

"There's no lack of drinks in the City of the Saints," returned Brother Jarrum. "Whisky's plentiful. Have you heard of mint julep? That is delicious. Mint is one of the few productions not common out there, and we are learning to make the julep with sage instead. You should see the plains of sage! It grows wild."

"And there's ducks, you say?" observed Susan Peckaby. "It's convenient to have sage in plenty where there's ducks," added she to the assembly in general. "What a land it must be!"

"A land that's not to be ekalled! A land flowing with milk and honey!" rapturously echoed Brother Jarrum. "Ducks is in plenty, and sage grows as thick as nettles do here; you can't go out to the open country but you put your foot upon it. Nature's generally in accordance with herself. What should she give all them bushes of wild sage for, unless she gave ducks to match?"

A problem that appeared indisputable to the minds of Brother Jarrum's listeners. They sincerely wished themselves in New Jerusalem.

"Through the streets runs a stream of sparkling water, clear as crystal," continued Brother Jarrum. "You have only got to stoop down with a can on a hot summer's day, and take a drink of it. It runs on both sides the streets for convenience; folks step out of their houses, and draw it up with no trouble. You have not got to toil half a mile to a spring of fresh water there! You'd never forget the silver lake at the base of Antelope Island, once you set eyes on it."

Several haggard eyes were lifted at this. "Do silver grow there, like the sage?"

"I spoke metaphorical," explained Brother Jarrum. "Would I deceive you? No. It's the Great Salt Lake, that shines out like burnished silver, and bursts on the sight of the new pilgrims when they arrive in bands at the holy city—the emigrants from this land."

"Some do arrive then, sir?" timidly questioned Dinah Roy.

"Some!" indignantly responded Brother Jarrum. "They are arriving continual. The very evening before I left, a numerous company arrived. It was just upon sunset. The clouds was all of rose colour, tipped with purple and gold, and there lay the holy city at their feet, in the lovely valley I told you of last night, with the lake of glittering silver in the distance. It is a sight for 'em, I can tell you! The regular-built houses, inclosed in their gardens and buildings, like farm homesteads, and the inhabitants turning out with fiddles, to meet and welcome the travellers. Some of the pilgrims fainted with joy; some shouted; lots danced; and sobs and tears of delight burst from all. If the journey had been a little fatiguing—what of that, with that glorious scene at the end of it?"

"And you see this?" cried a man, Davies, in a somewhat doubtful tone.

"I see it with my two eyes," answered Brother Jarrum. "I often see it. We had had news in the city that a train of new-comers was approaching, mostly English, and we went out to meet 'em. Not one of us saints, hardly, but was expecting some friend by it—a sister, or a father, or a sweetheart, maybe; and away we hurried outside the city. Presently the train came in sight."

"They have railroads there, then?" spoke a man, who was listening with eager interest. It was decent, civil Grind.

"Not yet; we shall have 'em shortly," said Brother Jarrum. "The train consisted of carts, carriages, vehicles of all sorts; and some rode mules, and some were walking on their legs. They were all habited nicely, and singing hymns. A short way afore they arrive at the holy city, it's the custom for the emigrants to make a halt, and wash and dress themselves, so as to enter proper. Such a meeting! the kissing and the greeting drownding the noise of the music, and the old men and the little children dancing. The prophet himself came out, and shook hands with 'em all, his brass band blowing in front of him, and he standing up in his carriage. Where else would you travel to, I'd like to know, and find such a welcome at the end of your journey? Houses, and friends, and plenty, all got ready aforehand; and gentlemen waiting to marry the ladies that may wish to enter the holy state!"

"There is a plenty?" questioned again that unbelieving man, Davies.

"There's such a plenty that the new arrivals are advised to eat, for a week or two, only half their fill," returned Brother Jarrum—"of fruits in partic'lar. Some, that have gone right in at the good things without mercy, have been laid up through it, and had to fine themselves down upon physic for a week after. No; it's best to be a little sparing at the beginning."

"What did he say just now about all the Mormons being beautiful?" questioned a pretty-looking girl of her neighbours. And Brother Jarrum caught the words, although they were spoken in an undertone.

"And so they are," said he. "The climate's of a nature that softens the faces, keeps folks in health, and stops 'em from growing old. If you see two females in the street, one a saint's wife, the t'other a new arrival, you can always tell which is which. The wife's got a slender waist, like a lady, with a delicate colour in her face, and silky hair; the new-comer's tanned, and fat, and freckled, and clumsy. If you don't believe me, you can ask them as have been there. There's something in the dress they wear, too, that sets 'em off. No female goes out without a veil, which hangs down behind. They don't want to hide their pretty faces, not they."

Mary Green, a damsel of twenty, she who had previously spoken, really did possess a pretty face; and a rapturous vision came over her at this juncture, of beholding it shaded and set off by a white lace veil, as she had often seen Miss Decima Verner's.

"Now, I can't explain to you why it is that the women in the city should be fair to the eye, or why the men don't seem to grow old," resumed Brother Jarrum. "It is so, and that's enough. People, learned in such things, might tell the cause; but I'm not learned in 'em. Some says it's the effect of the New Jerusalem climate; some thinks it's the fruits of the happy and plentiful life we lead: my opinion is, it's a mixture of both. A man of sixty hardly looks forty, out there. It's a great favour!"

One of the ill-doing Dawsons, who had pushed his way in at the shop door in time to hear part of the lavished praise on New Jerusalem, interrupted at this juncture.

"I say, master, if this is as you're a-telling us, how is it that folks talk so again' the Mormons? I met a man in Heartburg once, who had been out there, and he couldn't say bad enough of 'em."

"Snakes! but that's a natural question of yours, and I'm glad to answer it," replied Brother Jarrum, with a taking air of candour. "Those evil reports come from our enemies. There's another tribe living in the Great Salt Lake City besides ours; and that's the Gentiles. Gentiles is our name for 'em. It's this set that spreads about uncredible reports, and we'd like to sew their mouths up—"

Brother Jarrum probably intended to say "unaccredited." He continued, somewhat vehemently—

"To sew their mouths up with a needle and thread, and let 'em be sewed up for ever. They are jealous of us; that's what it is. Some of their wives, too, have left 'em to espouse our saints, at which they naggar greatly. The outrageousest things that enemies' tongues can be laid to, they say. Don't you ever believe 'em; it flounders me to think as anybody can. Whoever wants to see my credentials, they are at their beck and call. Call to-morrow morning—in my room upstairs—call any other morning, and my certificates is open to be looked at, with spectacles or without 'em, signed in full, at the Great Salt Lake City, territory of Utah, by our prophet, Mr. Brigham Young, and two of his councillors, testifying that I am Elder Silas Jarrum, and that my mission over here is to preach the light to them as are at present asleep in darkness, and bring 'em to the community of the Latter Day Saints. I'm no impostor, I'm not; and I tell you that the false reports come from them unbelieving Gentiles. Instead of minding their own affairs, they pass their days nagging at the saints."

"Why don't they turn saints theirselves?" cried a voice sensibly.

"Because Satan stops 'em. You have heard of him, you know. He's busy everywhere, as you've been taught by your parsons. I put my head inside of your church door, last Sunday night, while the sermon was going on, and I heard your parson tell you as Satan was the foundation of all the ill that was in you. He was right there; though I'm no friend to parsons in general. Satan is the head and tail of bad things, and he fills up the Gentiles with proud notions, and blinds their eyes against us. No wonder! If every soul in the world turned Latter Day Saint, and come over to us at New Jerusalem, where 'ud Satan's work be? We are striving to get you out of the clutches of Satan, my friends, and you must strive for yourselves also. Where's the use of us elders coming among you to preach and convert, unless you meet us half-way? Where's the good of keeping up that 'Perpetual Emigration Fund Company,' if you don't reap its benefit and make a start to emigrate? These things is being done for you, not for us. The Latter Day Saints have got nothing mean nor selfish about 'em. They are the richest people in the world—in generosity and good works."

"Is servants allowed to dress in veils, out there?" demanded Mary Green, during a pause of Brother Jarrum's, afforded to the audience that they might sufficiently revolve the disinterested generosity of the Latter Day Saint community.

"Veils! Veils, and feathers, too, if they are so minded," was Brother Jarrum's answer; and it fell like a soothing sound on Mary Green's vain ear. "It's not many servants, though, that you'd find in New Jerusalem."

"Ain't servants let go out to New Jerusalem?" quickly returned Mary Green. She was a servant herself, just now out of place, given to spend all her wages upon finery, and coming to grief perpetually with her mistresses upon the score.

"Many of 'em goes out," was the satisfactory reply of Brother Jarrum. "But servants here are not servants there. Who'd be a servant if she could be a missis? Wouldn't a handsome young female prefer to be her master's wife than to be his servant?"

Mary Green giggled; the question had been pointedly put to her.

"If a female servant chooses to remain a servant, in course she can," Brother Jarrum resumed, "and precious long wages she'd get; eighty pound a year—good."

A movement of intense surprise amid the audience. Brother Jarrum went on—

"I can't say I have knowed many as have stopped servants, even at that high rate of pay. My memory won't charge me with one. They have married and settled, and so have secured for themselves paradise."

This might be taken as a delicate hint that the married state, generally, deserved that happy title. Some of the experiences of those present, however, rather tended to accord it a less satisfactory one, and there arose some murmuring. Brother Jarrum explained—

"Women is not married with us for time, but for eternity—as I tried to beat into you last night. Once the wife of a saint, their entrance into paradise is safe and certain. We have not got a old maid among us— not a single old maid!"

The sensation that this information caused, I'll leave you to judge; considering that Deerham was famous for old maids, and that several were present.

"No old maids, and no widders," continued Brother Jarrum, wiping his forehead, which was becoming moist with the heat of argument. "We have respect to our women, we have, and like to make 'em comfortable."

"But if their husbands die off?" suggested a puzzled listener.

"The husband's successor marries his widders," explained Brother Jarrum. "Look at our late head and prophet, Mr. Joe Smith—him that appeared in a vision to our present prophet, and pointed out the spot for the new temple. He died a martyr, Mr. Joe Smith did—a prey to wicked murderers. Were his widders left to grieve and die out after him? No. Mr. Brigham Young, he succeeded to his honours, and he married the widders."

This was received somewhat dubiously; the assemblage not clear whether to approve it or to cavil at it.

"Not so much to be his wives, you know, as to be a kind of ruling matrons in his household," went on Brother Jarrum. "To have their own places apart, their own rooms in the house, and to be as happy as the day's long. They don't—"

"How they must quarrel, a lot of wives together!" interrupted a discontented voice.

Brother Jarrum set himself energetically to disprove this supposition. He succeeded. Belief is easy to willing minds.

"Which is best?" asked he.—"To be one of the wives of a rich saint, where all the wives is happy, and honoured, and well dressed; or to toil and starve, and go next door to naked, as a poor man's solitary wife does here? I know which I should choose if the two chances was offered me. A woman can't put her foot inside the heavenly kingdom, I tell you, unless she has got a husband to lay hold of her hand and draw her in. The wives of a saint are safe; paradise is in store for 'em; and that's why the Gentiles' wives—them folks that's for ever riling at us—leave their husbands to marry the saints."

"Does the saints' wives ever leave 'em to marry them others—the Gentiles?" asked that troublesome Davies.

"Such cases have been heered of," responded Brother Jarrum, shaking his head with a grave solemnity of manner. "They have braved the punishment and done it. But the act has been rare."

"What is the punishment?" inquired somebody's wife.

"When a female belonging to the Latter Day Saints—whether she's married or single—falls off from grace and goes over to them Gentiles, and marries one of 'em, she's condemned to be buffeted by Satan for a thousand years."

A pause of consternation.

"Who condemns her?" a voice, more venturesome than the rest, was heard to ask.

"There's mysteries in our faith which can't be disclosed even to you," was the reply of Brother Jarrum. "Them apostate women are condemned to it; and that's enough. It's not everybody as can see the truth. Ninety-nine may see it, and the hundredth mayn't."

"Very true, very true," was murmured around.

"I think I see the waggins and the other vehicles arriving now!" rapturously exclaimed Brother Jarrum, turning his eyes right up into his head, the better to take in the mental vision. "The travellers, tired with their journey, washed and shaved, and dressed, and the women's hair anointed, all flagrant with oil and frantic with joy—shouting, singing, and dancing to the tune of the advancing fiddles! I think I see the great prophet himself, with his brass-band in front and his body-guard around him, meeting the travellers and shaking their hands individ'ally! I think I see the joy of the women, and the nice young girls, when they are led to the hyminial halter in our temple by the saints that have fixed on 'em, to be inducted into the safety of paradise! Happy those that the prophet chooses for himself! While them other poor mistaken backsliders shall be undergoing their thousand years of buffetings, they'll reign triumphant, the saved saints of the Mil—"

How long Brother Jarrum's harangue might have rung on the wide ears of his delighted listeners, it is not easy to say. But an interruption occurred, to the proceeding's. It was caused by the entrance of Peckaby; and the meeting was terminated somewhat abruptly. While Susan Peckaby sat at the feet of the saint, a willing disciple of his doctrine, her lord and master, however disheartening it may be to record it, could not, by any means, be induced to open his heart and receive the grace. He remained obdurate. Passively obdurate during the day; but rather demonstratively obdurate towards night. Peckaby, a quiet, civil man enough when sober, was just the contrary when ivre; and since he had joined the blacksmith's shop, his evening visits to a noted public-house—the Plough and Harrow—had become frequent. On his return home from these visits, his mind had once or twice been spoken out pretty freely as to the Latter Day Saint doctrine: once he had gone the length of clearing the shop of guests, and marshalling the saint himself to the retirement of his own apartment. However contrite he may have shown himself for this the next morning, nobody desired to have the scene repeated. Consequently, when Peckaby now entered, defiance in his face and unsteadiness in his legs, the guests filed out of their own accord; and Brother Jarrum, taking the flaring candle from the shelf, disappeared with it up the stairs.

This has been a very fair specimen of Brother Jarrum's representations and eloquence. It was only one meeting out of a great many. As I said before, the precise tenets of his religious faith need not be enlarged upon: it is enough to say that they were quite equal to his temporal promises. You will, therefore, scarcely wonder that he made disciples. But the mischief, as yet, had only begun to brew.

CHAPTER XL

A VISIT OF CEREMONY

Whatever may have been Lionel Verner's private sentiments, with regard to his choice of a wife— whether he repented his hasty bargain or whether he did not, no shade of dissatisfaction escaped him. Sibylla took up her abode with her sisters, and Lionel visited her, just as other men visit the young ladies they may be going to marry. The servants at Verner's Pride were informed that a mistress for them was in contemplation, and preparations for the marriage were begun. Not until summer would it take place, when twelve months should have elapsed from the demise of Frederick Massingbird.

Deerham was, of course, free in its comments, differing in no wise on that score from other places. Lionel Verner was pitied, and Sibylla abused. The heir of Verner's Pride, with his good looks, his manifold attractions, his somewhat cold impassibility as to the tempting snares laid out for him in the way of matrimony, had been a beacon for many a young lady to steer towards. Had he married Lucy Tempest, had he married Lady Mary Elmsley, had he married a royal princess, he and she would both have been equally cavilled at. He, for placing himself beyond the pale of competition; she, for securing the prize. It always was so, and it always will be.

His choice of Mrs. Massingbird, however, really did afford some grounds for grumbling. She was not worthy of Lionel Verner. So Deerham thought; so Deerham said. He was throwing himself away; he would live to repent it; she must have been the most crafty of women, so to have secured him! Free words enough, and harshly spoken; but they were as water by the side of those uttered by Lady Verner.

In the first bitter hour of disappointment, Lady Verner gave free speech to harsh things. It was in her love for Lionel that she so grieved. Setting aside the facts that Sibylla had been the wife of another man, that she was, in position, beneath Lionel—which facts, however, Lady Verner could not set aside, for they were ever present to her—her great objection lay in the conviction that Sibylla would prove entirely unsuited to him; that it would turn out an unhappy union. Short and sharp was the storm with Lady Verner; but in a week or two she subsided into quietness, buried her grief and resentment within her, and made no further outward demonstration.

"Mother, you will call upon Sibylla?" Lionel said to her one day that he had gone to Deerham Court. He spoke in a low, deprecating tone, and his face flushed; he anticipated he knew not what torrent of objection.

Lady Verner met the request differently.

"I suppose it will be expected of me, that I should do so," she replied, strangely calm. "How I dislike this artificial state of things! Where the customs of society must be bowed to, by those who live in it; their actions, good or bad, commented upon and judged! You have been expecting that I should call before this, I suppose, Lionel?"

"I have been hoping, from day to day, that you would call."

"I will call—for your sake. Lionel," she passionately added, turning to him, and seizing his hands between hers, "what I do now, I do for your sake. It has been a cruel blow to me; but I will try to make the best of it, for you, my best-loved son."

He bent down to his mother, and kissed her tenderly. It was his mode of showing her his thanks.

"Do not mistake me, Lionel. I will just so far in this matter as may be necessary to avoid open disapproval. If I appear to approve it, that the world may not cavil and you complain, it will be little more than an appearance. I will call upon your intended wife, but the call will be one of etiquette, of formal ceremony: you must not expect me to get into the habit of repeating it. I shall never become intimate with her."

"You do not know what the future may bring forth," returned Lionel, looking at his mother with a smile. "I trust the time will come when you shall have learned to love Sibylla."

"I do not think that time will ever arrive," was the frigid reply of Lady Verner. "Oh, Lionel!" she added, in an impulse of sorrow, "what a barrier this has raised between us—what a severing for the future!"

"The barrier exists in your own mind only, mother," was his answer, spoken sadly. "Sibylla would be a loving daughter to you, if you would allow her so to be."

A slight, haughty shake of the head, suppressed at once, was the reply of Lady Verner. "I had looked for a different daughter," she continued. "I had hoped for Mary Elmsley."

"Upon this point, at any rate, there need be no misunderstanding," returned Lionel. "Believe me once for all, mother: I should never have married Mary Elmsley. Had I and Sibylla remained apart for life, separated as wide as the two poles, it is not Mary Elmsley whom I should have made my wife. It is more than probable that my choice would have pleased you only in a degree more than it does now."

The jealous ears of Lady Verner detected an undercurrent of meaning in the words.

"You speak just as though you had some one in particular in your thoughts!" she uttered.

It recalled Lucy, it recalled the past connected with her, all too plainly to his mind; and he returned an evasive answer. He never willingly recalled her: or it: if they obtruded themselves on his memory—as they very often did—he drove them away, as he was driving them now.

He quitted the house, and Lady Verner proceeded upstairs to Decima's room—that pretty room, with its blue panels and hangings, where Lionel used to be when he was growing convalescent. Decima and Lucy were in it now. "I wish you to go out with me to make a call," she said to them.

"Both of us, mamma?" inquired Decima.

"Both," repeated Lady Verner. "It is a call of etiquette," she added, a sound of irony mixing in the tone, "and, therefore, you must both make it. It is to Lionel's chosen wife."

A hot flush passed into the face of Lucy Tempest; hot words rose to her lips. Hasty, thoughtless, impulsive words, to the effect that she could not pay a visit to the chosen wife of Lionel Verner.

But she checked them ere they were spoken. She turned to the window, which had been opened to the early spring day, and suffered the cool air to blow on her flushed face, and calmed down her impetuous thoughts. Was this the course of conduct that she had marked out for herself? She looked round at Lady Verner and said, in a gentle tone, that she would be ready at any hour named.

"We will go at once," replied Lady Verner. "I have ordered the carriage. The sooner we make it—as we have to make it—the better."

There was no mistake about it. Lucy had grown to love Lionel Verner. How she loved him, esteemed him, venerated him, none, save her own heart, could tell. Her days had been as one long dream of Eden. The very aspect of the world had changed. The blue sky, the soft-breathing wind, the scent of the budding flowers, had spoken a language to her, never before learned: "Rejoice in us, for we are lovely!" It was the strange bliss in her own heart that threw its rose hues over the face of nature, the sweet, mysterious rapture arising from love's first dream; which can never be described by mortal pen; and never, while it lasts, can be spoken of by living tongue. While it lasts. It never does last. It is the one sole ecstatic phase of life, the solitary romance stealing in once, and but once, amidst the world's hard realities; the "fire filched for us from heaven." Has it to arise yet for you—you, who read this? Do not trust it when it comes, for it will be fleeting as a summer cloud. Enjoy it, revel in it while you hold it; it will lift you out of earth's clay and earth's evil with its angel wings; but trust not to its remaining: even while you are saying, "I will make it mine for ever," it is gone. It had gone for Lucy Tempest. And, oh!

better for her, perhaps, that it should go; better, perhaps, for all; for if that sweet glimpse of paradise could take up its abode permanently in the heart, we should never look, or wish, or pray for that better paradise which has to come hereafter.

But who can see this in the sharp flood tide of despair? Not Lucy. In losing Lionel she has lost all; and nothing remained for her but to do battle with her trouble alone. Passionately and truly as Lionel had loved Sibylla; so, in her turn, did Lucy love him.

It is not the fashion now for young ladies to die of broken hearts—as it was in the old days. A little while given to "the grief that kills," and then Lucy strove to arouse herself to better things. She would go upon her way, burying all feelings within her; she would meet him and others with a calm exterior and placid smile; none should see that she suffered; no, though her heart were breaking.

"I will forget him," she murmured to herself ten times in the day. "What a mercy that I did not let him see I loved him! I never should have loved him, but that I thought he—Psha! why do I recall it? I was mistaken; I was stupid—and all that's left to me is to make the best of it."

So she drove her thoughts away, as Lionel did. She set out on her course bravely, with the determination to forget him. She schooled her heart, and schooled her face, and believed she was doing great things. To Lionel she cast no blame—and that was unfortunate for the forgetting scheme. She blamed herself; not Lionel. Remarkably simple and humble-minded, Lucy Tempest was accustomed to think of every one before herself. Who was she, that she should have assumed Lionel Verner was growing to love her? Sometimes she would glance at another phase of the picture: That Lionel had been growing to love her; but that Sibylla Massingbird had, in some weak moment, by some sleight of hand, drawn him to her again, extracted from him a promise that he could not retract. She did not dwell upon this; she drove it from her, as she drove away, or strove to drive away, the other thoughts; although the theory, regarding the night of Sibylla's return, was the favourite theory of Lady Verner. Altogether, I say, circumstances were not very favourable towards Lucy's plan of forgetting him.

Lady Verner's carriage—the most fascinating carriage in all Deerham, with its blue and silver appointments, its fine horses, all the present of Lionel—conveyed them to the house of Dr. West. Lady Verner would not have gone otherwise than in state, for untold gold. Distance allowing her, for she was not a good walker, she would have gone on foot, without attendants, to visit the Countess of Elmsley and Lady Mary; but not Sibylla. You can understand the distinction.

They arrived at an inopportune moment, for Lionel was there. At least, Lionel thought it inopportune. On leaving his mother's house he had gone to Sibylla's. And, however gratified he may have been by the speedy compliance of his mother with his request, he had very much preferred not to be present himself, if the call comprised, as he saw it did comprise, Lucy Tempest.

Sibylla was at home alone; her sisters were out. She had been leaning back in an invalid chair, listening to the words of Lionel, when a servant opened the door and announced Lady Verner. Neither had observed the stopping of the carriage. Carriages often stopped at the house, and visitors entered it; but they were most frequently professional visits, concerning nobody but Jan. Lady Verner swept in. For her very life she could not avoid showing hauteur in that moment. Sibylla sprung from her chair, and stood with a changing face.

Lionel's countenance, too, was changing. It was the first time he had met Lucy face to face in the close proximity necessitated by a room. He had studiously striven not to meet her, and had contrived to succeed. Did he call himself a coward for it? But where was the help?

A few moments given to greeting, to the assuming of seats, and they were settled down. Lady Verner and Decima on a sofa opposite Sibylla; Lucy in a low chair—what she was sure to look out for; Lionel leaning against the mantel-piece—as favourite a position of his, as a low seat was of Lucy's. Sibylla had been startled by their entrance, and her chest was beating. Her brilliant colour went and came, her hand was pressed upon her bosom, as if to still it, and she lay rather back in her chair for support. She had not assumed a widow's cap since her arrival, and her pretty hair fell around her in a shower of gold. In spite of Lady Verner's prejudices, she could not help thinking her very beautiful; but she looked suspiciously delicate.

"It is very kind of you to come to see me," said Sibylla, speaking timidly across to Lady Verner.

Lady Verner slightly bowed. "You do not look strong," she observed to Sibylla, speaking in the moment's impulse. "Are you well?"

"I am pretty well. I am not strong. Since I returned home, a little thing seems to flutter me, as your entrance has done now. Lionel had just told me you would call upon me, he thought. I was so glad to hear it! Somehow I had feared you would not."

Candid, at any rate; and Lady Verner did not disapprove the apparent feeling that prompted it; but how her heart revolted at hearing those lips pronounce "Lionel" familiarly, she alone could tell. Again came the offence.

"Lionel tells me sometimes I am so changed since I went out, that even he would scarcely have known me. I do not think I am so changed as all that. I had a great deal of vexation and trouble, and I grew thin. But I shall soon be well again now."

A pause.

"You ascertained no certain news of John Massingbird, I hear," observed Lady Verner.

"Not any. A gentleman there is endeavouring to trace out more particulars. I heard—did Lionel mention to you—that I heard, strange to say, of Luke Roy, from the family I was visiting—the Eyres? Lionel"— turning to him—"did you repeat it to Lady Verner?"

"I believe not," replied Lionel. He could not say to Sibylla, "My mother would tolerate no conversation on any topic connected with you."

Another flagging pause.

Lionel, to create a divertisement, raised a remarkably, fine specimen of coral from the table, and carried it to his mother.

"It is beautiful," he remarked. "Sibylla brought it home with her."

Lady Verner allowed that it was beautiful.

"Show it to Lucy," she said, when she had examined it with interest. "Lucy, my dear, do you remember what I was telling you the other evening, about the black coral?"

Sibylla rose and approached Lucy with Lionel.

"I am so pleased to make your acquaintance," she said warmly. "You only came to Deerham a short while before I was leaving it, and I saw scarcely anything of you. Lionel has seen a great deal of you, I fancy, though he will not speak of you. I told him one day it looked suspicious; that I should be jealous of you, if he did not mind."

It was a foolish speech—foolish of Sibylla to give utterance to it; but she did so in all singleness of heart, meaning nothing. Lucy was bending over the coral, held by Lionel. She felt her own cheeks flush, and she saw by chance, not by direct look, that Lionel's face had turned a deep scarlet. Jealous of her! She continued to admire the coral some little time longer, and then resigned it to him with a smile.

"Thank you, Mr. Verner. I am fond of these marine curiosities. We had a good many of them at the rectory. Mr. Cust's brother was a sailor."

Lionel could not remember the time when she had called him "Mr. Verner." It was right, however, that she should do so; but in his heart he felt thankful for that sweet smile. It seemed to tell him that she, at any rate, was heart-whole, that she certainly bore him no resentment. He spoke freely now.

"You are not looking well, Lucy—as we have been upon the subject of looks."

"I? Oh, I have had another cold since the one Jan cured. I did not try his remedies in time, and it fastened upon me. I don't know which barked the most—I or Growler."

"Jan says he shall have Growler here," remarked Sibylla.

"No, Sibylla," interposed Lionel; "Jan said he should like to have Growler here, if it were convenient to do so, and my mother would spare him. A medical man's is not the place for a barking dog; he might attack the night applicants."

"Is it Jan's dog?" inquired Lucy.

"Yes," said Lionel. "I thought you knew it. Why, don't you remember, Lucy, the day I—"

Whatever reminiscence Lionel may have been about to recall, he cut it short midway, and subsided into silence. What was his motive? Did Lucy know? She did not ask for the ending, and the rest were then occupied, and had not heard.

More awkward pauses—as in these visits where the parties do not amalgamate is sure to be the case, and then Lady Verner slightly bowed to Lucy, as she might have done on their retiring from table, and rose. Extending the tips of her delicately-gloved fingers to Sibylla, she swept out of the room. Decima shook hands with her more cordially, although she had not spoken half a dozen words during the interview, and Sibylla turned and put her hand into Lucy's.

"I hope we shall be intimate friends," she said. "I hope you will be our frequent guest at Verner's Pride."

"Thank you," replied Lucy. And perhaps the sudden flush on her face might have been less vivid had Lionel not been standing there.

He attended them to the carriage, taking up his hat as he passed through the vestibule; for really the confined space that did duty for hall in Dr. West's house did not deserve the name. Lady Verner sat on one side the carriage, Decima and Lucy on the seat opposite. Lionel stood a moment after handing them in.

"If you can tear yourself away from the house for half an hour, I wish you would take a drive with us," said Lady Verner, her tone of voice no more pleasant than her words. Try as she would, she could not help her jealous resentment against Sibylla from peeping out.

Lionel smiled, and took his seat by his mother, opposite to Lucy. He was resolved to foster no ill-feeling by his own conduct, but to do all that lay in his power to subdue it in Lady Verner. He had not taken leave of Sibylla; and it may have been this, the proof that he was about to return to her, which had excited the ire of my lady. She, his mother, nothing to him; Sibylla all in all. Sibylla stood at the window, and Lionel bent forward, nodded his adieu, and raised his hat.

The footman ascended to his place, and the carriage went on. All in silence for some minutes. A silence which Lady Verner suddenly broke.

"What have you been doing to your cheeks, Lucy? You look as if you had caught a fever."

Lucy laughed. "Do I, Lady Verner? I hope it is not a third cold coming on, or Jan will grumble that I take them on purpose—as he did the last time."

She caught the eyes of Lionel riveted on her with a strangely perplexed expression. It did not tend to subdue the excitement of her cheeks.

Another moment, and Decima's cheeks appeared to have caught the infection. They had suddenly become one glowing crimson; a strange sight on her delicately pale face. What could have caused it? Surely not the quiet riding up to the carriage of a stately old gentleman who was passing, wearing a white frilled shirt and hessian boots. He looked as if he had come out of a picture-frame, as he sat there, his hat off and his white hair flowing, courteously, but not cordially, inquiring after the health of my Lady Verner.

"Pretty well, Sir Rufus. I have had a great deal of vexation to try me lately."

"As we all have, my dear lady. Vexation has formed a large portion of my life. I have been calling at Verner's Pride, Mr. Verner."

"Have you, Sir Rufus? I am sorry I was not at home."

"These fine spring days tempt me out. Miss Tempest, you are looking remarkably well. Good-morning, Lady Verner. Good-morning."

A bow to Lady Verner, a sweeping bow to the rest collectively, and Sir Rufus rode away at a trot, putting on his hat as he went. His groom trotted after him, touching his hat as he passed the carriage.

But not a word had he spoken to Decima Verner, not a look had he given her. The omission was unnoticed by the others; not by Decima. The crimson of her cheeks had faded to an ashy paleness, and she silently let fall her veil to hide it.

What secret understanding could there be between herself and Sir Rufus Hautley?

CHAPTER XLI

A SPECIAL VISION TOUCHING MRS PECKABY

Not until summer, when the days were long and the nights short, did the marriage of Lionel Verner take place. Lady Verner declined to be present at it: Decima and Lucy were. It was a grand ceremony, of course; that is, it would have been grand, but for an ignominious interruption which occurred to mar it. At the very moment they were at the altar, Lionel placing the ring on his bride's finger, and all around wrapt in breathless silence, in a transport of enthusiasm, the bride's-maids uncertain whether they must go off in hysterics or not, there tore into the church Master Dan Duff, in a state of extreme terror and ragged shirt sleeves, fighting his way against those who would have impeded him, and shouting out at the top of his voice: "Mother was took with the cholic, and she'd die right off if Mr. Jan didn't make haste to her." Upon which Jan, who had positively no more sense of what was due to society than Dan Duff himself had, went flying away there and then, muttering something about "those poisonous mushrooms." And so they were made man and wife; Lionel, in his heart of hearts, doubting if he did not best love Lucy Tempest.

A breakfast at Dr. West's: Miss Deborah and Miss Amilly not in the least knowing (as they said afterwards) how they comported themselves at it; and then Lionel and his bride departed. He was taking her to Paris, which Sibylla had never seen.

Leaving them to enjoy its attractions—and Sibylla, at any rate, would not fail to do so—we must give another word to that zealous missionary, Brother Jarrum.

The seed, scattered broadcast by Brother Jarrum, had had time to fructify. He had left the glowing promises of all that awaited them, did they decide to voyage out to New Jerusalem, to take root in the imaginations of his listeners, and absented himself for a time from Deerham. This may have been crafty policy on Brother Jarrum's part; or may have resulted from necessity. It was hardly likely that so talented and enlightened an apostle as Brother Jarrum should confine his labours to the limited sphere of Deerham: in all probability, they had to be put in requisition elsewhere. However it may have been, for several weeks towards the end of spring, Brother Jarrum was away from Deerham. Mr. Bitterworth, and one or two more influential people, of whom Lionel was one, had very strongly objected to Brother Jarrum's presence in it at all; and, again, this may have been the reason of his quitting it. However it was, he did quit it; though not without establishing a secret understanding with the more faithful of his converts. With the exception of these converts, Deerham thought he had left it for good; that it was, as they not at all politely expressed it, "shut of him." In this Deerham was mistaken.

On the very day of Lionel Verner's marriage, Brother Jarrum reappeared in the place. He took up his abode, as before, in Mrs. Peckaby's spare room. Peckaby, this time, held out against it. However welcome the four shillings rent, weekly, was from Brother Jarrum, Peckaby assumed a lordly indifference to it, and protested he'd rather starve, nor have pison like him in the house. Peckaby, however, possessed a wife, who, on occasion, wore, metaphorically speaking, his nether garments, and it was her will and pleasure to countenance the expected guest. Brother Jarrum, therefore, was received and welcomed.

He did not hold forth this time in Peckaby's shop. He did not in public urge the delights of New Jerusalem, or the expediency of departure for it. He kept himself quiet and retired, receiving visits in the privacy of his chamber. After dark, especially, friends would drop in; admitted without noise or bustle by Mrs. Peckaby; parties of ones, of twos, of threes, until there would be quite an assembly collected upstairs; why should not Brother Jarrum hold his levees as well as his betters?

That something unusual was in the wind, was very evident; some scheme, or project, which it appeared expedient to keep a secret. Had Peckaby been a little less fond Of the seductions of the Plough and Harrow, his suspicions must have been aroused. Unfortunately, Peckaby yielded unremittingly to that renowned inn's temptations, and spent every evening there, leaving full sway to his wife and Brother Jarrum.

About a month thus passed on, and Lionel Verner and his wife were expected home, when Deerham woke up one morning to a commotion. A flitting had taken place from it in the night. Brother Jarrum had departed, conveying with him a train of followers.

One of the first to hear of it was Jan Verner; and, curious to say, he heard it from Mrs. Baynton, the lady at Chalk Cottage. Jan, who, let him be called abroad in the night as he would, was always up with the sun, stood one morning in his surgery, between seven and eight o'clock, when he was surprised by the entrance of Mrs. Baynton—a little woman, with a meek, pinched face, and gray hair. Since Dr. West's departure, Jan had attended the sickly daughter, therefore he knew Mrs. Baynton, but he had never seen her abroad in his life. Her bonnet looked ten years old. Her daughters were named—at least, they were called—Flore and Kitty; Kitty being the sickly one. To see Mrs. Baynton arrive thus, Jan jumped to the conclusion that Kitty must be dying.

"Is she ill again?" he hastily asked, with his usual absence of ceremony, giving the lady no time to speak.

"She's gone," gasped Mrs. Baynton.

"Gone—dead?" asked Jan, with wondering eyes.

"She's gone off with the Mormons."

Jan stood upright against the counter, and stared at the old lady. He could not understand. "Who is gone off with the Mormons?" was his rejoinder.

"Kitty is. Oh, Mr. Jan, think of her sufferings! A journey like that before her! All the way to that dreadful place! I have heard that even strong women die on the road of the hardships."

Jan had stood with open mouth. "Is she mad?" he questioned.

"She has not been much better than mad since—since—But I don't wish to go into family troubles. Can you give me Dr. West's address? She might come back for him."

Now Jan had received positive commands from that wandering physician not to give his address to chance applicants, the inmates of Chalk Cottage having come in for a special interdiction. Therefore Jan could only decline.

"He is moving about from one place to another," said Jan. "To-day in Switzerland, to-morrow in France; the next day in the moon, for what we can tell. You can give me a letter, and I'll try and get it conveyed to him somehow."

Mrs. Baynton shook her head.

"It would be too late. I thought if I could telegraph to him, he might have got to Liverpool in time to stop Kitty. There's a large migration of Mormons to take place in a day or two, and they are collecting at Liverpool."

"Go and stop her yourself," said Jan sensibly.

"She'd not come back for me," replied Mrs. Baynton, in a depressed tone. "What with her delicate health, and what with her wilfulness, I have always had trouble with her. Dr. West was the only one— But I can't refer to those matters. Flore is broken-hearted. Poor Flore! she has never given me an hour's grief in her life. Kitty has given me little else. And now to go off with the Mormons!"

"Who has she gone with?"

"With the rest from Deerham. They have gone off in the night. That Brother Jarrum and a company of about five-and-twenty, they say."

Jan could scarcely keep from exploding into laughter. Part of Deerham gone off to join the Mormons! "Is it a fact?" cried he.

"It is a fact that they are gone," replied Mrs. Baynton. "She has been out several times in an evening to hear that Brother Jarrum, and had become infected with the Mormon doctrine. In spite of what I or Flore could say, she would go to listen to the man, and she grew to believe the foolish things he uttered. And you can't give me Dr. West's address?"

"No, I can't," replied Jan. "And I see no good that it would be to you, if I could. He could not get to Liverpool in time, from wherever he may be, if the flight is to take place in a day or two."

"Perhaps not," sighed Mrs. Baynton. "I was unwilling to come, but it seemed like a forlorn hope."

She let down her old crape veil as she went out at the door; and Jan, all curious for particulars, went abroad to pick up anything he could learn.

About fifteen had gone off, exclusive of children. Grind's lot, as it was called, meaning Grind, his wife, and their young ones; Davies had gone, Mary Green had gone, Nancy from Verner's Pride had gone, and sundry others whom it is not necessary to enumerate. It was said that Dinah Roy made preparations to go, but her heart failed her at the last. Some accounts ran that she did start, but was summarily brought up by the appearance of her husband, who went after her. At his sight she turned without a word, and walked home again, meekly submitting to the correction he saw fit to inflict. Jan did not believe this. His private opinion was, that had Dinah Roy started, her husband would have deemed it a red-letter day, and never have sought to bring her back more.

Last, but not least, Mrs. Peckaby had not gone. No: for Brother Jarrum had stolen a march upon her. What his motive in doing this might be was best known to himself. Of all the converts, none had been so eager for the emigration, so fondly anticipative of the promised delights, as Susan Peckaby; and she had made her own private arrangements to steal off secretly, leaving her unbelieving husband to his solitary fate. As it turned out, however, she was herself left; the happy company stole off, and abandoned her.

Brother Jarrum so contrived it, that the night fixed for the exodus was kept secret from Mrs. Peckaby. She did not know that he had even gone out of the house, until she got up in the morning and found him absent. Brother Jarrum's personal luggage was not of an extensive character. It was contained in a blue bag; and this bag was likewise missing. Not, even then, did a shadow of the cruel treachery played her darken the spirit of Mrs. Peckaby. Her faith in Brother Jarrum was of unlimited extent; she would as soon have thought of deceiving her own self, as that he could deceive. The rumour that the migration had taken place, the company off, awoke her from her happy security to a state of raving torture. Peckaby dodged out of her way, afraid. There is no knowing but Peckaby himself may have been the stumbling-block in the mind of Brother Jarrum. A man so dead against the Latter Day Saints as Peckaby had shown himself, would be a difficult customer to deal with. He might be capable of following them and upsetting the minds of all the Deerham converts, did his wife start with them for New Jerusalem.

All this information was gathered by Jan. Jan had heard nothing for many a day that so tickled his fancy. He bent his steps to Peckaby's, and went in. Jan, you know, was troubled neither with pride nor ceremony; nobody less so in all Deerham. Where inclination took him, there went Jan.

Peckaby, all black, with a bar of iron in his hand, a leather apron on, and a broad grin upon his countenance, was coming out of the door as Jan entered. The affair seemed to tickle Peckaby's fancy as much as it tickled Jan's. He touched his hair. "Please, sir, couldn't you give her a dose of jalap, or something comforting o' that sort, to bring her to?" asked he, pointing with his thumb indoors, as he stamped across the road to the forge.

Mrs. Peckaby had calmed down from the rampant state to one of prostration. She sat in her kitchen behind the shop, nursing her knees, and moaning. Mrs. Duff, who, by Jan's help, had survived the threatened death fro "cholic," and was herself again, stood near the sufferer, in company with one or two more cronies. All the particulars, Susan Peckaby's contemplated journey, with the deceitful trick played her, had got wind; and the Deerham ladies were in consequence flocking in.

"You didn't mean going, did you?" began Jan.

"Not mean going!" sobbed Susan Peckaby, rocking herself to and fro. "I did mean going, sir, and I'm not ashamed to own to it. If folks is in the luck to be offered a chance of paradise, I dun know many as ud say they wouldn't catch at it."

"Paradise, was it?" said Jan. "What was it chiefly to consist of?"

"Of everything," moaned Susan Peckaby. "There isn't a thing you could wish for under the sun, but what's to be had in plenty at New Jerusalem. Dinners and teas, and your own cows, and big houses and parlours, and gardens loaded with fruit, and garden stuff as decays for want o' cutting, and veils when you go out, and evening dances, like the grand folks here has, and new caps perpetual! And I have lost it! They be gone and have left me!—oh, o-o-o-h!"

"And husbands, besides; one for everybody!" spoke up a girl. "You forget that, Mrs. Peckaby."

"Husbands besides," acquiesced Susan Peckaby, aroused from her moaning. "Every woman's sure to be chose by a saint as soon as she gets out. There's not such a thing as a old maid there, and there needn't be no widders."

Mrs. Duff turned up bar nose, and turned it wrathfully on the girl who had spoken.

"If they call husbands their paradise, keep me away from 'em, say I. You girls be like young bears—all your troubles have got to come. You just try a husband, Bess Dawson; whether he's a saint, or whether he's a sinner, let him be of a cranky temper, thwarting you at every trick and turn, and you'll see what sort of a paradise marriage is! Don't you think I'm right, sir?"

Jan's mouth was extended from ear to ear, laughing.

"I never tried it," said he. "Were you to have been espoused by Brother Jarrum?" he asked, of Susan Peckaby.

"No, sir, I was not," she answered, in much anger. "I did not favour Brother Jarrum. I'd prefer to pick and choose when I got there. But I had a great amount of respect for Brother Jarrum, sir, which I'm proud to speak to. And I don't believe that he has served me this shameful trick of his own knowledge," she added, with emphasis. "I believe there has been some unfortinate mistake, and that when he finds I'm not among the company, he'll come back for me. I'd go after them, only that Peckaby's on the watch. I never see such a altered man as Peckaby; it had used to be as I could just turn him round my little finger, but he won't be turned now."

She finished up with a storm of sobs. Jan, in an Ecstasy of mirth yet, offered to send her some cordials from the surgery, by way of consolation; not, however, the precise one suggested by Peckaby. But cordials had no charm in that unhappy moment for Mrs. Peckaby's ear.

Jan departed. In quitting the door he encountered a stranger, who inquired if that was Peckaby's shop. Jan fancied the man looked something the cut of Brother Jarrum, and sent him in. His coat and boots were white with dust. Looking round on the assembled women when he reached the kitchen, the stranger asked which was Mrs. Peckaby. Mrs. Peckaby looked up, and signified that she was.

"I have a message from the saint and elder, Brother Jarrum," he mysteriously whispered in her ear. "It must be give to you in private."

Mrs. Peckaby, in a tremble of delight, led the stranger to a small shed in the yard, which she used for washing purposes, and called the back 'us. It was the most private place she could think of, in her fluster. The stranger, propping himself against a broken tub, proceeded, with some circumlocution and not remarkable perspicuity of speech, to deliver the message with which he was charged. It was to the effect that a vision had revealed to Brother Jarrum the startling fact, that Susan Peckaby was not to go out with the crowd at present on the wing. A higher destiny awaited her. She would be sent for in a different manner—in a more important form; sent for special, on a quadruped. That is to say, on a white donkey.[A]

[A] A fact.

"On a white donkey?" echoed the trembling and joyful woman.

"On a white donkey," gravely repeated the brother—for that he was another brother of the community, there could be little doubt. "What the special honour intended for you may be, me and Brother Jarrum don't pertend to guess at. It's above us. May be you are fated to be chose by our great prophet hisself. Any how, it's something at the top of the tree."

"When shall I be sent for, sir?" eagerly asked Mrs. Peckaby.

"That ain't revealed neither. It may be next week—it mayn't be for a year; you must always be on the look-out. One of these days or nights, you'll see a white donkey a-standing at your door. It'll be the messenger for you from New Jerusalem. You mount him without a minute's loss of time, and come off."

But that Mrs. Peckaby's senses were exalted at that moment far above the level of ordinary mortals', it might have occurred to her to inquire whether the donkey would be endowed with the miraculous power of bearing her over the sea. No such common question presented itself. She asked another.

"Why couldn't Brother Jarrum have told me this hisself, sir? I have been a'most mad this morning, ever since I found as they had gone."

The brother—this brother—turned up the whites of his eyes. "When unknown things is revealed to us, and mysterious orders give, they never come to us a minute afore the time," he replied. "Not till Brother Jarrum was fixing the night of departure, did the vision come to him. It was commanded him that it should be kept from you till the rest were off, and then he were to send back a messenger to tell you— and many a mile I've come! Brother Jarrum and me has no doubt that it is meant as a trial of your faith."

Nothing could be more satisfactory to the mind of Mrs. Peckaby than this explanation. Had any mysterious vision appeared to herself, showing her that it was false, commanding her to disbelieve it, it could not have shaken her faith. If the white donkey arrived at her door that very night, she would be sure to mount him.

"Do you think it'll be very long, sir, that I shall have to wait?" she resumed, feverishly listening for the answer.

"My impression is that it'll be very short," was the reply. "And it's Brother Jarrum's also. Any way, you be on the look-out—always prepared. Have a best robe at hand continual, ready to clap on the instant the quadruped appears, and come right away to New Jerusalem."

In the openness of her heart, Mrs. Peckaby offered refreshment to the brother. The best her house afforded: which was not much. Peckaby should be condemned to go foodless for a week, rather than that he should depart fasting. The brother, however, declined: he appeared to be in a hurry to leave Deerham behind him.

"I'd not disclose this to anybody if I was you," was his parting salutation. "Leastways, not for a day or two. Let the ruck of 'em embark first at Liverpool. If it gets wind, some of them may be for turning crusty, because they are not favoured with special animals, too."

Had the brother recommended Susan Peckaby to fill the tub with water, and stand head downwards in it for a day or two, she was in the mood to obey him. Accordingly, when questioned by Mrs. Duff, and the other curious ones, what had been the business of the stranger, she made a great mystery over it, and declined to answer.

"It's good news, by the signs of your face," remarked Mrs. Duff.

"Good news!" rapturously repeated Susan Peckaby, "it's heaven. I say, Mother Duff, I want a new gownd: something of the very best. I'll pay for it by degrees. There ain't no time to be lost, neither; so I'll come down at once and choose it."

"What has happened?" was the wondering rejoinder of Mother Duff.

"Never you mind, just yet. I'll tell you about it afore the week's out."

And, accordingly, before the week was out, all Deerham was regaled with the news; full particulars. And Susan Peckaby, a robe of purple, of the stuff called lustre, laid up in state, to be donned when the occasion came, passed her time, night and day, at her door and windows, looking out for the white donkey that was to bear her in triumph to New Jerusalem.

CHAPTER XLII

A SURPRISE FOR MRS TYNN

In the commodious dressing-room at Verner's Pride, appropriated to its new mistress, Mrs. Verner, stood the housekeeper, Tynn, lifting her hands and her eyes. You once saw the chamber of John Massingbird, in this same house, in a tolerable litter: but that was as nothing compared with the litter in this dressing-room, piles and piles of it, one heap by the side of another. Mary Tynn stood screwed against the wainscoting of the wall: she had got in, but to get out was another matter: there was not a free place where she could put her foot. Strictly speaking, perhaps, it could not be called litter, and Mrs. Verner and her French maid would have been alike indignant at hearing it so classed. Robes of rich and rare texture; silks standing on end with magnificence; dinner attire, than which nothing could be more exquisite; ball dresses in all sorts of gossamer fabrics; under-skirts, glistening with their soft lustre; morning costumes, pure and costly; shawls of Cashmere and other recherché stuffs, enough to stock a shop; mantles of every known make; bonnets that would send an English milliner crazy; veils charming to look upon; laces that might rival Lady Verner's embroideries, their price fabulous; handkerchiefs that surely never were made for use; dozens of delicately-tinted gloves, cased in ornamental boxes, costing as much as they did; every description of expensive chaussure; and trinkets, the drawn cheques for which must have caused Lionel Verner's sober bankers to stare. Tynn might well heave her hands and eyes in dismay. On the chairs, on the tables, on the drawers, on the floor, on every conceivable place and space they lay; a goodly mass of vanity, just unpacked from their cases.

Flitting about amidst them was a damsel of coquettish appearance, with a fair skin, light hair, and her nose a turn-up. Her gray gown was flounced to the waist, her small cap of lace, its pink strings flying, was lodged on the back of her head. It was Mademoiselle Benoite, Mrs. Verner's French maid, one she had picked up in Paris. Whatever other qualities the damsel might lack, she had enough of confidence. Not many hours yet in the house, and she was assuming more authority in it than her mistress did.

Mr. and Mrs. Verner had returned the night before, Mademoiselle Benoite and her packages making part of their train. A whole fourgon could not have been sufficient to convey these packages from the French capital to the frontier. Phoeby, the simple country maid whom Sibylla had taken to Paris with her, found her place a sinecure since the engagement of Mademoiselle Benoite. She stood now on the opposite side of the room to Tynn, humbly waiting Mademoiselle Benoite's imperious commands.

"Where on earth will you stow 'em away?" cried Tynn, in her wonder. "You'll want a length of rooms to do it in."

"Where I stow 'em away!" retorted Mademoiselle Benoite, in her fluent speech, but broken English. "I stow 'em where I please. Note you that, Madame Teen. Par example! The château is grand enough."

"What has its grandeur got to do with it?" was Mary Tynn's answer. She knew but little of French phrases.

"Now, then, what for you stand there, with your eyes staring and your hands idle?" demanded Mademoiselle Benoite sharply, turning her attack on Phoeby.

"If you'll tell me what to do, I'll do it," replied the girl. "I could help to put the things up, if you'd show me where to begin."

"I like to see you dare to put a finger on one of these things!" returned Mademoiselle Benoite. "You can confine your services to sewing, and to waiting upon me; but not you dare to interfere with my lady's toilette. Tiens, I am capable, I hope! I'd give up the best service to-morrow where I had not sole power! Go you down to the office, and order me a cup of chocolate, and wait you and bring it up to me. That maudite drogue, that coffee, this morning, has made me as thirsty as a panthère."

Phoeby, glancing across at Mrs. Tynn, turned somewhat hesitatingly to pick her way out of the room. The housekeeper, though not half understanding, contrived to make out that the morning coffee was not approved of. The French mademoiselle had breakfasted with her, and, in Mrs. Tynn's opinion, the coffee had been perfect, fit for the table of her betters.

"Is it the coffee that you are abusing?" asked she. "What was the matter with it?"

"Ciel! You ask what the matter with it!" returned Mademoiselle Benoite, in her rapid tongue. "It was everything the matter with it. It was all bad. It was drogue, I say; medicine. There!"

"Well, I'm sure!" resentfully returned the housekeeper. "Now, I happened to make that coffee myself this morning—Tynn, he's particular in his coffee, he is—and I put in—"

"I not care if you put in the whole canastre," vehemently interrupted Mademoiselle Benoite. "You English know not to make coffee. All the two years I lived in London with Madame la Duchesse, I never got one cup of coffee that was not enough to choke me. And they used pounds of it in the house, where they might have used ounces. Bah! You can make tea, I not say no; but you cannot make coffee. Now, then! I want a great number sheets of silk-paper."

"Silk-paper?" repeated Tynn, whom the item puzzled. "What's that?"

"You know not what silk-paper is!" angrily returned Mademoiselle Benoite. "Quelle ignorance!" she apostrophised, not caring whether she was understood or not. "Ellé ne connait pas ce que c'est, papier-de-soie! I must have it, and a great deal of it, do you hear? It is as common as anything—silk-paper."

"Things common in France mayn't be common with us," retorted Mrs. Tynn. "What is it for?"

"It is for some of these articles. If I put them by without the paper-silk round them in the cartons, they'll not keep their colour."

"Perhaps you mean silver-paper," said Mary Tynn. "Tissue-paper, I have heard my Lady Verner call it. There's none in the house, Madmisel Bennot."

"Madmisel Bennot" stamped her foot. "A house without silk-paper in it! When you knew my lady was coming home!"

"I didn't know she'd bring—a host of things with her that she has brought," was the answering shaft lanced by Mrs. Tynn.

"Don't you see that I am waiting? Will you send out for some?"

"It's not to be had in Deerham," said Mrs. Tynn. "If it must be had, one of the men must go to Heartburg Why won't the paper do that was over 'em before?"

"There not enough of that. And I choose to have fresh, I do."

"Well, you had better give your own orders about it," said Mary Tynn. "And then, if there's any mistake, it'll be nobody's fault, you know."

Mademoiselle Benoite did not on the instant reply. She had her hands full just then. In reaching over for a particular bonnet, she managed to turn a dozen or two on to the floor. Tynn watched the picking up process, and listened to the various ejaculations that accompanied it, in much grimness.

"What a sight of money those things must have cost!" cried she.

"What that matter?" returned the lady's-maid. "The purse of a milor Anglais can stand anything."

"What did she buy them for?" went on Tynn. "For what purpose?"

"Bon!" ejaculated Mademoiselle. "She buy them to wear. What else you suppose she buy them for?"

"Why! she would never wear out the half of them in all her whole life!" uttered Tynn, speaking the true sentiments of her heart. "She could not."

"Much you know of things, Madame Teen!" was the answer, delivered in undisguised contempt for Tynn's primitive ignorance. "They'll not last her six months."

"Six months!" shrieked Tynn. "She couldn't come to an end of them dresses in six months, if she wore three a day, and never put on a dress a second time!"

"She want to wear more than three different a day sometimes. And it not the mode now to put on a robe more than once," returned Mademoiselle Benoite carelessly.

Tynn could only open her mouth. "If they are to be put on but once, what becomes of 'em afterwards?" questioned she, when she could find breath to speak.

"Oh, they good for jupons—petticoats, you call it. Some may be worn a second time; they can be changed by other trimmings to look like new. And the rest will be good for me: Madame la Duchesse gave me a great deal. 'Tenez, ma fille,' she would say, 'regardez dans ma garde-robe, et prenez autant que vous voudrez.' She always spoke to me in French."

Tynn wished there had been no French invented, so far as her comprehension was concerned. While she stood, undecided what reply to make, wishing very much to express her decided opinion upon the extravagance she saw around her, yet deterred from it by remembering that Mrs. Verner was now her mistress, Phoeby entered with the chocolate. The girl put it down on the mantel-piece—there was no other place—and then made a sign to Mrs. Tynn that she wished to speak with her. They both left the room.

"Am I to be at the beck and call of that French madmizel?" she resentfully asked. "I was not engaged for that, Mrs. Tynn."

"It seems we are all to be at her beck and call, to hear her go on," was Mrs. Tynn's wrathful rejoinder. "Of course it can't be tolerated. We shall see in a day or two. Phoeby, girl, what could possess Mrs. Verner to buy all them cart-loads of finery? She must have spent the money like water."

"So she did," acquiesced Phoeby. "She did nothing all day long but drive about from one place to another and choose pretty things. You should see the china that's coming over!"

"I wonder Mr. Lionel let her," was the thoughtlessly-spoken remark of Tynn. And she tried, when too late, to cough it down.

"He helped her, I think," answered Phoeby. "I know he bought some of that beautiful jewellery for her himself, and brought it home. I saw him kiss her, through the doorway, as he clasped that pink necklace on her neck."

"Oh, well, I don't want to hear about that rubbish," tartly rejoined Tynn. "If you take to peep through doorways, girl, you won't suit Verner's Pride."

Phoeby did not like the rebuff. She turned one way, and Mrs. Tynn went off another.

In the breakfast-room below, in her charming French morning costume, tasty and elegant, sat Sibylla Verner. With French dresses, she seemed to be acquiring French habits. Late as the hour was, the breakfast remained on the table. Sibylla might have sent the things away an hour ago; but she kept a little chocolate in her cup, and toyed with it. She had never tasted chocolate for breakfast in all her life, previous to this visit to Paris: now she protested she could take nothing else. Possibly she may have caught the taste for it from Mademoiselle Benoite. Her husband sat opposite to her, his chair drawn from the table, and turned to face the room. A perfectly satisfied, happy expression pervaded his face; he appeared to be fully contented with his lot and with his bride. Just now he was laughing immoderately.

Perched upon the arm of a sofa, having there come to an anchor, his legs hanging down and swaying about in their favourite fashion, was Jan Verner. Jan had come in to pay them a visit and congratulate them on their return. That is speaking somewhat figuratively, however, for Jan possessed no notion of congratulating anybody. As Lady Verner sometimes resentfully said, Jan had no more social politeness in him than a bear. Upon entering, Sibylla asked him to take some breakfast. Breakfast! echoed Jan, did she call that breakfast? He thought it was their lunch—it was getting on for his dinner-time. Jan was giving Lionel a history of the moonlight flitting, and of Susan Peckaby's expected expedition to New Jerusalem on a white donkey.

"It ought to have been stopped," said Lionel, when his laughter had subsided. "They are going out to misery, and to nothing else, poor deluded creatures!"

"Who was to stop it?" asked Jan.

"Some one might have told them the truth. If this Brother Jarrum represented things in rose-coloured hues, could nobody open to their view the other side of the picture? I should have endeavoured to do it, had I been here. If they chose to risk the venture after that, it would have been their own fault."

"You'd have done no good," said Jan. "Once let 'em get the Mormon fever upon 'em, and it must run its course. It's like the gold fever; nothing will convince folks they are mistaken as to that, except the going out to Australia to the diggings. That will."

A faint tinge of brighter colour rose to Sibylla's cheeks at this allusion, and Lionel knit his brow. He would have avoided for ever any chain of thought that led his memory to Frederick Massingbird: he could not bear to think that his young bride had been another's before she was his. Jan, happily ignorant, continued.

"There's Susan Peckaby. She has got it in her head that she's going straight off to Paradise, once she is in the Salt Lake City. Well, now, Lionel, if you, and all the world to help you, set yourselves on to convince her that she's mistaken, you couldn't do it. They must go out and find the level of things for themselves—there's no help for it."

"Jan, it is not likely that Susan Peckaby really expects a white donkey to be sent for her!" cried Sibylla.

"She as fully expects the white donkey, as I expect that I shall go from here presently, and drop in on Poynton, on my way home," earnestly said Jan. "He has had a kick from a horse on his shin, and a nasty place it is," added Jan in a parenthesis. "Nothing on earth would convince Susan Peckaby that the donkey's a myth, or will be a myth; and she wastes all her time looking out for it. If you were opposite their place now, you'd see her head somewhere; poked out at the door, or peeping from the upstairs window."

"I wish I could get them all back again—those who have gone from here!" warmly spoke Lionel.

"I wish sometimes I had got four legs, that I might get over double ground, when patients are wanting me on all sides," returned Jan. "The one wish is just as possible as the other, Lionel. The lot sailed from Liverpool yesterday, in the ship American Star. And I'll be bound, what with the sea-sickness, and the other discomforts, they are wishing themselves out of it already! I say, Sibylla, what did you think of Paris?"

"Oh, Jan, it's enchanting! And I have brought the most charming things home. You can come upstairs and see them, if you like. Benoite is unpacking them."

"Well, I don't know," mused Jan. "I don't suppose they are what I should care to see. What are the things?"

"Dresses, and bonnets, and mantles, and lace, and coiffures," returned Sibylla. "I can't tell you half the beautiful things. One of my cache-peignes is of filigrane silver-work, with drops falling from it, real diamonds."

"What d'ye call a cache-peigne?" asked Jan.

"Don't you know? An ornament for the hair, that you put on to hide the comb behind. Combs are coming into fashion. Will you come up and see the things, Jan?"

"Not I! What do I care for lace and bonnets?" ungallantly answered Jan. "I didn't know but Lionel might have brought me some anatomical studies over. They'd be in my line."

Sibylla shrieked—a pretty little shriek of affectation. "Lionel, why do you let him say such things to me? He means amputated arms and legs."

"I'm sure I didn't," said Jan. "I meant models. They'd not let the other things pass the customs. Have you brought a dress a-piece for Deb and Amilly?"

"No," said Sibylla, looking up in some consternation. "I never thought about it."

"Won't they be disappointed, then! They have counted upon it, I can tell you. They can't afford to buy themselves much, you know; the doctor keeps them so short," added Jan.

"I would have brought them something, if I had thought of it; I would, indeed!" exclaimed Sibylla, in an accent of contrition. "Is it not a pity, Lionel?"

"I wish you had," replied Lionel. "Can you give them nothing of what you have brought?"

"Well—I—must—consider," hesitated Sibylla, who was essentially selfish. "The things are so beautiful, so expensive; they are scarcely suited to Deborah and Amilly."

"Why not?" questioned Jan.

"You have not a bit of sense, Jan," grumbled Sibylla. "Things chosen to suit me, won't suit them."

"Why not?" repeated Jan obstinately.

"There never was any one like you, Jan, for stupidity," was Sibylla's retort. "I am young and pretty, and a bride; and they are two faded old maids."

"Dress 'em up young, and they'll look young," answered Jan, with composure. "Give 'em a bit of pleasure for once, Sibylla."

"I'll see," impatiently answered Sibylla. "Jan, how came Nancy to go off with the Mormons? Tynn says she packed up her things in secret, and started."

"How came the rest to go?" was Jan's answer. "She caught the fever too, I suppose."

"What Nancy are you talking of?" demanded Lionel. "Not Nancy from here!"

"Oh, Lionel, yes! I forgot to tell you," said Sibylla. "She is gone indeed. Mrs. Tynn is so indignant. She says the girl must be a fool!"

"Little short of it," returned Lionel. "To give up a good home here for the Salt Lake! She will repent it."

"Let 'em all alone for that," nodded Jan, "I'd like to pay an hour's visit to 'em, when they have been a month in the place—if they ever get to it."

"Tynn says she remembers, when that Brother Jarrum was here in the spring, that Nancy made frequent excuses for going to Deerham in the evening," resumed Sibylla.

"She thinks it must have been to frequent those meetings in Peckaby's shop."

"I thought the man, Jarrum, had gone off, leaving the mischief to die away," observed Lionel.

"So did everybody else," said Jan. "He came back the day that you were married. Nancy's betters got lured into Peckaby's, as well as Nancy," he added. "That sickly daughter at Chalk Cottage, she's gone."

Lionel looked very much astonished.

"No!" he uttered.

"Fact!" said Jan. "The mother came to me the morning after the flitting, and said she had been seduced away. She wanted to telegraph to Dr. West—"

Jan stopped dead, remembering that Sibylla was present, as well as Lionel. He leaped off the sofa.

"Ah, we shall see them all back some day, if they can only contrive to elude the vigilance of the Mormons. I'm off, Lionel; old Poynton will think I am not coming to-day. Good-bye, Sibylla."

Jan hastened from the room. Lionel stood at the window, and watched him away. Sibylla glided up to her husband, nestling against him.

"Lionel, tell me. Jan never would, though I nearly teased his life out; and Deborah and Amilly persisted that they knew nothing. You tell me."

"Tell you what, my dearest?"

"After I came home in the winter, there were strange whispers about papa and that Chalk Cottage. People were mysterious over it, and I never could get a word of explanation. Jan was the worst; he was coolly tantalising, and it used to put me in a passion. What was the tale told?"

An involuntary darkening of Lionel's brow. He cleared it instantly, and looked down on his wife with a smile.

"I know of no tale worth telling you, Sibylla."

"But there was a tale told?"

"Jan—who, being in closer proximity to Dr. West than any one, may be supposed to know best of his private affairs—tells a tale of Dr. West's having set a chimney on fire at Chalk Cottage, thereby arousing the ire of its inmates."

"Don't you repeat such nonsense to me, Lionel; you are not Jan," she returned, in a half peevish tone. "I fear papa may have borrowed money from the ladies, and did not repay them," she added, her voice sinking to a whisper. "But I would not say it to any one but you. What do you think?"

"If my wife will allow me to tell her what I think, I should say that it is her duty—and mine now—not to seek to penetrate into any affairs belonging to Dr. West which he may wish to keep to himself. Is it not so, Sibylla mine?"

Sibylla smiled, and held up her face to be kissed. "Yes, you are right, Lionel."

Swayed by impulse, more than by anything else, she thought of her treasures upstairs, in the process of dis-interment from their cases by Benoite, and ran from him to inspect them. Lionel put on his hat, and strolled out of doors.

A thought came over him that he would go and pay a visit to his mother. He knew how exacting of attention from him she was, how jealous, so to speak, of Sibylla's having taken him from her. Lionel hoped by degrees to reduce the breach. Nothing should be wanting on his part to effect it; he trusted that nothing would be wanting on Sibylla's. He really wished to see his mother after his month's absence; and he knew she would be pleased at his going there on this, the first morning of his return. As he turned into the high road, he met the vicar of Deerham, the Reverend James Bourne.

They shook hands, and the conversation turned, not unnaturally, on the Mormon flight. As they were talking of it, Roy, the ex-bailiff, was observed crossing the opposite field.

"My brother tells me the report runs that Mrs. Roy contemplated being of the company, but was overtaken by her husband and brought back," remarked Lionel.

"How it may have been, about his bringing her back, or whether she actually started, I don't know," replied Mr. Bourne, who was a man with a large pale face and iron-gray hair. "That she intended to go, I have reason to believe."

He spoke the last words significantly, lowering his voice. Lionel looked at him.

"She paid me a mysterious visit at the vicarage the night before the start," continued the clergyman. "A very mysterious visit, indeed, taken in conjunction with her words. I was in my study, reading by candle-light, when somebody came tapping at the glass door, and stole in. It was Mrs. Roy. She was in a state of tremor, as I have heard it said she appeared the night the inquiry was held at Verner's Pride, touching the death of Rachel Frost. She spoke to me in ambiguous terms of a journey she was about to take—that she should probably be away for her whole life—and then she proceeded to speak of that night."

"The night of the inquiry?" echoed Lionel.

"The night of the inquiry—that is, the night of the accident," returned Mr. Bourne. "She said she wished to confide a secret to me, which she had not liked to touch upon before, but which she could not leave the place without confiding to some one responsible, who might use it in case of need. The secret she proceeded to tell me was—that it was Frederick Massingbird who had been quarrelling with Rachel that night by the Willow Pool. She could swear it to me, she said, if necessary."

"But—if that were true—why did she not proclaim it at the time?" asked Lionel, after a pause.

"It was all she said. And she would not be questioned. 'In case o' need, sir, in case anybody else should ever be brought up for it, tell 'em that Dinah Roy asserted to you with her last breath in Deerham, that Mr. Fred Massingbird was the one that was with Rachel.' Those were the words she used to me; I dotted them down after she left. As I tell you, she would not be questioned, and glided out again almost immediately."

"Was she wandering in her mind?"

"I think not. She spoke with an air of truth. When I heard of the flight of the converts the next morning, I could only conclude that Mrs. Roy had intended to be amongst them. But now, understand me, Mr. Verner, although I have told you this, I have not mentioned it to another living soul. Neither do I intend to do so. It can do no good to reap up the sad tale; whether Frederick Massingbird was or was not with Rachel that night; whether he was in any way guilty, or was purely innocent, it boots not to inquire now."

"It does not," warmly replied Lionel. "You have done well. Let us bury Mrs. Roy's story between us, and forget it, so far as we can."

They parted. Lionel took his way to Deerham Court, absorbed in thought. His own strong impression had been, that Mr. Fred Massingbird was the black sheep with regard to Rachel.

CHAPTER XLIII

LIONEL'S PRAYER FOR FORGIVENESS

Lady Verner, like many more of us, found that misfortunes do not come singly. Coeval almost with that great misfortune, Lionel's marriage—at any rate, coeval with his return to Verner's Pride with his bride—another vexation befell Lady Verner. Had Lady Verner found real misfortunes to contend with, it is hard to say how she would have borne them. Perhaps Lionel's marriage to Sibylla was a real misfortune; but this second vexation assuredly was not—at any rate to Lady Verner.

Some women—and Lady Verner was one—are fond of scheming and planning. Whether it be the laying out of a flower-bed, or the laying out of a marriage, they must plan and project. Disappointment with regard to her own daughter—for Decima most unqualifyingly disclaimed any match-making on her own score—Lady Verner had turned her hopes in this respect on Lucy Tempest. She deemed that she should be ill-fulfilling the responsibilities of her guardianship, unless when Colonel Tempest returned to England, she could present Lucy to him a wife, or, at least, engaged to be one. Many a time now did she unavailingly wish that Lionel had chosen Lucy, instead of her whom he had chosen. Although—and mark how we estimate things by comparison—when, in the old days, Lady Verner had fancied Lionel was growing to like Lucy, she had told him emphatically it "would not do." Why would it not do? Because, in the estimation of Lady Verner, Lucy Tempest was less desirable in a social point of view than the Earl of Elmsley's daughter, and upon the latter lady had been fixed her hopes for Lionel.

All that was past and gone. Lady Verner had seen the fallacy of sublunary hopes and projects. Lady Mary Elmsley was rejected—Lionel had married in direct defiance of everybody's advice—and Lucy was open to offers. Open to offers, as Lady Verner supposed; but she was destined to find herself unpleasantly disappointed.

One came forward with an offer to her. And that was no other than the Earl of Elmsley's son, Viscount Garle. A pleasant man, of eight-and-twenty years; and he was often at Lady Verner's. He had been intimate there a long while, going in and out as unceremoniously as did Lionel or Jan. Lady Verner and Decima could tell a tale that no one else suspected. How, in the years gone by—some four or five years ago now—he had grown to love Decima with his whole heart; and Decima had rejected him. In spite of his sincere love; of the advantages of the match; of the angry indignation of Lady Verner; Decima had steadfastly rejected him. For some time Lord Garle would not take the rejection; but one day, when my lady was out, Decima spoke with him privately for five minutes, and from that hour Lord Garle had known there was no hope; had been content to begin there and then, and strive to love her only as a sister. The little episode was never known; Decima and Lady Verner had kept counsel, and Lord Garle had not told tales of himself. Next to Lionel, Lady Verner liked Lord Garle better than any one—ten times better than she liked unvarnished Jan; and he was allowed the run of the house as though he had been its son. The first year of Lucy's arrival—the year of Lionel's illness, Lord Garle had been away from the neighbourhood; but somewhere about the time of Sibylla's return, he had come back to it. Seeing a great deal of Lucy, as he necessarily did, being so much at Lady Verner's, he grew to esteem and love her. Not with the same love he had borne for Decima—a love, such as that, never comes twice in a lifetime—but with a love sufficiently warm, notwithstanding. And he asked her to become his wife.

There was triumph for Lady Verner! Next to Decima—and all hope of that was dead for ever—she would like Lord Garle to marry Lucy. A real triumph, the presenting her to Colonel Tempest on his return, my Lady Viscountess Garle! In the delight of her heart she betrayed something of this to Lucy.

"But I am not going to marry him, Lady Verner," objected Lucy.

"You are not going to marry him, Lucy? He confided to me the fact of his intention this morning before he spoke to you. He has spoken to you, has he not?"

"Yes," replied Lucy; "but I cannot accept him."

"You—cannot! What are you talking of?" cried Lady Verner.

"Please not to be angry, Lady Verner! I could not marry Lord Garle."

Lady Verner's lips grew pale. "And pray why can you not?" she demanded.

"I—don't like him," stammered Lucy.

"Not like him!" repeated Lady Verner. "Why, what can there be about Lord Garle that you young ladies do not like?" she wondered; her thoughts cast back to the former rejection by Decima. "He is good-looking, he is sensible; there's not so attractive a man in all the county, Lionel Verner excepted."

Lucy's face turned to a fiery glow. "Had I known he was going to ask me, I would have requested him not to do so beforehand, as my refusal has displeased you," she simply said. "I am sorry you should be vexed with me, Lady Verner."

"It appears to me that nothing but vexation is to be the portion of my life!" uttered Lady Verner. "Thwarted—thwarted always!—on all sides. First the one, then the other—nothing but crosses and vexations! What did you say to Lord Garle?"

"I told Lord Garle that I could not marry him; that I should never like him well enough—for he said, if I did not care for him now, I might later. But I told him no; it was impossible. I like him very well as a friend, but that is all."

"Why don't you like him?" repeated Lady Verner.

"I don't know," whispered Lucy, standing before Lady Verner like a culprit, her eyes cast down, and her eyelashes resting on her hot crimsoned face.

"Do you both mean to make yourselves into old maids, you and Decima?" reiterated the angry Lady Verner. "A pretty pair of you I shall have on my hands! I never was so annoyed in all my life."

Lucy burst into tears. "I wish I could go to papa in India!" she said.

"Do you know what you have rejected?" asked Lady Verner. "You would have been a peeress of England. His father will not live for ever."

"But I should not care to be a peeress," sobbed Lucy. "And I don't like him."

"Mamma, please do not say any more," pleaded Decima. "Lucy is not to blame. If she does not like Lord Garle she could not accept him."

"Of course she is not to blame—according to you, Miss Verner! You were not to blame, were you, when you rejected—some one we knew of? Not the least doubt that you will take her part! Young Bitterworth wished to have proposed to you; you sent him away—as you send all—and refuse to tell me your motive! Very dutiful you are, Decima!"

Decima turned away her pale face. She began to think Lucy would do better without her advocacy than with it.

"I cannot allow it to end thus," resumed Lady Verner to Lucy. "You must reconsider your determination and recall Lord Garle."

The words frightened Lucy.

"I never can—I never can, Lady Verner!" she cried. "Please not to press it; it is of no use."

"I must press it," replied Lady Verner. "I cannot allow you to throw away your future prospects in this childish manner. How should I answer for it to Colonel Tempest?"

She swept out of the room as she concluded, and Lucy, in an uncontrollable fit of emotion, threw herself on the bosom of Decima, and sobbed there. Decima hushed her to her soothingly, stroking her hair from her forehead with a fond gesture.

"What is it that has grieved you lately, Lucy?" she gently asked. "I am sure you have been grieving. I have watched you. Gay as you appear to have been, it is a false gaiety, seen only by fits and starts."

Lucy moved her face from the view of Decima. "Oh, Decima! if I could but go back to papa!" was all she murmured. "If I could but go away, and be with papa!"

This little episode had taken place the day that Lionel Verner and his wife returned. On the following morning Lady Verner renewed the contest with Lucy. And they were deep in it—at least my lady was, for Lucy's chief part was only a deprecatory silence, when Lionel arrived at Deerham Court, to pay that visit to his mother which you have heard of.

"I insist upon it, Lucy, that you recall your unqualified denial," Lady Verner was saying. "If you will not accept Lord Garle immediately, at any rate take time for consideration. I will inform Lord Garle that you do it by my wish."

"I cannot," replied Lucy in a firm, almost a vehement tone. "I—you must not be angry with me, Lady Verner—indeed, I beg your pardon for saying it—but I will not."

"How dare you, Lucy—"

Her ladyship stopped at the sudden opening of the door, turning angrily to see what caused the interruption. Her servant appeared.

"Mr. Verner, my lady."

How handsome he looked as he came forward! Tall, noble, commanding. Never more so; never so much so in Lucy's sight. Poor Lucy's heart was in her mouth, as the saying runs, and her pulses quickened to a pang. She did not know of his return.

He bent to kiss his mother. He turned and shook hands with Lucy. He looked gay, animated, happy. A joyous bridegroom, beyond doubt.

"So you have reached home, Lionel?" said Lady Verner.

"At ten last night. How well you are looking, mother mine!"

"I am flushed just now," was the reply of Lady Verner, her accent a somewhat sharp one from the remembrance of the vexation which had given her the flush. "How is Paris looking? Have you enjoyed yourself?"

"Paris is looking hot and dusty, and we have enjoyed ourselves much," replied Lionel. He answered in the plural, you observe; my lady had put the question in the singular. Where is Decima?"

"Decima is sure to be at some work or other for Jan," was the answer, the asperity of Lady Verner's tone not decreasing. "He turns the house nearly upside down with his wants. Now a pan of broth must be made for some wretched old creature; now a jug of beef tea; now a bran poultice must be got; now some linen cut up for bandages. Jan's excuse is that he can't get anything done at Dr. West's. If he is doctor to the parish, he need not be purveyor; but you may just as well speak to a post as speak to Jan. What do you suppose he did the other day? Those improvident Kellys had their one roomful of things taken from them by their landlord. Jan went there—the woman's ill with a bad breast, or something— and found her lying on the bare boards; nothing to cover her, not a saucepan left to boil a drop of water. Off he comes here at the pace of a steam engine, got an old blanket and pillow from Catherine, and a tea-kettle from the kitchen. Now, Lionel, would you believe what I am going to tell you? No! No one would. He made the pillow and blanket into a bundle, and walked off with it under his arm; the kettle— never so much as a piece of paper wrapped round it—in his other hand! I felt ready to faint with shame when I saw him crossing the road opposite, that spectacle, to get to Clay Lane, the kettle held out a yard before him to keep the black off his clothes. He never could have been meant to be your brother and my son!"

Lucy laughed at the recollection. She had had the pleasure of beholding the spectacle. Lionel laughed now at the description. Their mirth did not please Lady Verner. She was serious in her complaint.

"Lionel, you would not have liked it yourself. Fancy his turning out of Verner's Pride in that guise, and encountering visitors! I don't know how it is, but there's some deficiency in Jan; something wanting. You know he generally chooses to come here by the back door: this day, because he had got the black kettle in his hand like a travelling tinker, he must go out by the front. He did! It saved him a few steps, and he went out without a blush. Out of my house, Lionel! Nobody ever lived, I am certain, who possessed so little innate notion of the decencies of life as Jan. Had he met a carriage full of visitors in the courtyard, he would have swung the kettle back on his arm, and gone up to shake hands with them. I had the nightmare that night, Lionel. I dreamt a tall giant was pursuing me, seeking to throw some great machine at me, made of tea-kettles."

"Jan is an odd fellow," assented Lionel.

"The worst is, you can't bring him to see, himself, what is proper or improper," resumed Lady Verner. "He has no sense of the fitness of things. He would go as unblushingly through the village with that black kettle held out before him, as he would if it were her Majesty's crown, borne on a velvet cushion."

"I am not sure but the crown would embarrass Jan more than the kettle," said Lionel, laughing still.

"Oh, I dare say; it would be just like him. Have you heard of the disgraceful flitting away of some of the inhabitants here to go after the Mormons?" added my lady.

"Jan has been telling me of it. What with one thing and another, Deerham will rise into notoriety. Nancy has gone from Verner's Pride."

"Poor deluded woman!" ejaculated Lady Verner.

"There's a story told in the village about that Peckaby's wife—Decima can tell it best, though. I wonder where she is?"

Lucy rose. "I will go and find her, Lady Verner."

No sooner had she quitted the room, than Lady Verner turned to Lionel, her manner changing. She began to speak rapidly, with some emotion.

"You observed that I looked well, Lionel. I told you I was flushed. The flush was caused by vexation, by anger. Not a week passes but something or other occurs to annoy me. I shall be worried into my grave."

"What has happened?" inquired Lionel.

"It is about Lucy Tempest. Here she is, upon my hands, and of course I am responsible. She has no mother, and I am responsible to Colonel Tempest and to my own conscience for her welfare. She will soon be twenty years of age—though I am sure nobody would believe it, to look at her—and it is time that her settlement in life should, at all events, be thought of. But now, look how things turn out! Lord Garle—than whom a better parti could not be wished—has fallen in love with her. He made her an offer yesterday, and she won't have him."

"Indeed!" replied Lionel, constrained to say something, but wishing Lady Verner would entertain him with any other topic.

"We had quite a scene here yesterday. Indeed, it has been renewed this morning, and your coming in interrupted it. I tell her that she must have him: at any rate, must take time to consider the advantages of the offer. She obstinately protests that she will not. I cannot think what can be her motive for rejection; almost any girl in the county would jump at Lord Garle."

"I suppose so," returned Lionel, pulling at a hole in his glove.

"I must get you to speak to her, Lionel. Ask her why she declines. Show her—"

"I speak to her!" interrupted Lionel in a startled tone. "I cannot speak to her about it, mother. It is no business of mine."

"Good heavens, Lionel! are you going to turn disobedient?—And in so trifling-a matter as this!—trifling so far as you are concerned. Were it of vital importance to you, you might run counter to me; it is only what I should expect."

This was a stab at his marriage. Lionel replied by disclaiming any influence over Miss Tempest. "Where your arguments have failed, mine would not be likely to succeed."

"Then you are mistaken, Lionel. I am certain that you hold a very great influence over Lucy. I observed it first when you were ill, when she and Decima were so much with you. She has betrayed it in a hundred little ways; her opinions are formed upon yours; your tastes unconsciously bias hers. It is only natural. She has no brother, and no doubt has learned to regard you as one."

Lionel hoped in his inmost heart that she did regard him only as a brother. Lady Verner continued—

"A word from you may have great effect upon her; and I desire, Lionel, that you will, in your duty to me, undertake that word. Point out to her the advantages of the match; tell her that you speak to her as her father; urge her to accept Lord Garle; or, as I say, not to summarily reject him without consideration, upon the childish plea that she 'does not like him.' She was terribly agitated last night; nearly went into hysterics, Decima tells me, after I left her; all her burden being that she wished she could go away to India."

"Mother—you know how pleased I should be to obey any wish of yours; but this is really not a proper business for me to interfere with," urged Lionel, a red spot upon his cheek.

"Why is it not?" pointedly asked Lady Verner, looking hard at him and waiting for an answer.

"I do not deem it to be so. Neither would Lucy consider my interference justifiable."

"But, Lionel, you take up wrong notions! I wish you to speak in my place, just as if you were her father; in short, acting for her father. As to what Lucy may consider or not consider in the matter, that is of very little consequence. Lucy is so perfectly unsophisticated, so simple in her ideas, that were I to desire my maid Thérèse to give her a lecture, she would receive it as something proper."

"I should be most unwilling to—"

"Hold your tongue, Lionel. You must do it. Here she is."

"I could not find Decima, Lady Verner," said Lucy, entering. "When I had been all over the house for her, Catherine told me Miss Decima had gone out. She has gone to Clay Lane on some errand for Jan."

"Oh, of course for Jan!" resentfully spoke Lady Verner. "Nothing else, I should think, would take her to Clay Lane. You see, Lionel!"

"There's nothing in Clay Lane that will hurt Decima, mother."

Lady Verner made no reply. She walked to the door, and stood with the handle in her hand, turning round to speak.

"Lucy, I have been acquainting Lionel with this affair between you and Lord Garle. I have requested him to speak to you upon the point; to ascertain your precise grounds of objection, and—so far as he can— to do away with them. Try your best, Lionel."

She quitted the room, leaving them standing opposite each other. Standing like two statues. Lionel's heart smote him. She looked so innocent, so good, in her delicate morning dress, with its gray ribbons and its white lace on the sleeves, open to the small fair arms! Simple as the dress was, it looked, in its exquisite taste, worth ten of Sibylla's elaborate French costumes. Her cheeks were glowing, her hands were trembling, as she stood there in her self-consciousness.

Terribly self-conscious was Lionel. He strove to say something, but in his embarrassment could not get out a single word. The conviction of the grievous fact, that she loved him, went right to his heart in that moment, and seated itself there. Another grievous fact came home to him; that she was more to him than the whole world. However he had pushed the suspicion away from his mind, refused to dwell on it, kept it down, it was all too plain to him now. He had made Sibylla his wife. He stood there, feeling that he loved Lucy above all created things.

He crossed over to her, and laid his hand fondly and gently on her head, as he moved to the door. "May God forgive me, Lucy!" broke from his white and trembling lips. "My own punishment is heavier than yours."

There was no need of further explanation on either side. Each knew that the love of the other was theirs, the punishment keenly bitter, as surely as if a hundred words had told it. Lucy sat down as the door closed behind him, and wondered how she should get through the long dreary life before her.

And Lionel? Lionel went out by Jan's favourite way, the back, and plunged into a dark lane where neither ear nor eye was on him. He uncovered his head, he threw back his coat, he lifted his breath to catch only a gasp of air. The sense of dishonour was stifling him.

CHAPTER XLIV

FARMER BLOW'S WHITE-TAILED PONY

Lionel Verner was just in that frame of mind which struggles to be carried out of itself. No matter whether by pleasure or pain, so that it be not that particular pain from which it would fain escape, the mind seeks yearningly to forget itself, to be lifted out anywhere, or by any means, from its trouble. Conscience was doing heavy work with Lionel. He had destroyed his own happiness—that was nothing; he could battle it out, and nobody be the wiser or the worse, save himself; but he had blighted Lucy's. There was the sting that tortured him. A man of sensitively refined organisation, keenly alive to the feelings of others—full of repentant consciousness when wrong was worked through him, he would have given his whole future life and all its benefits, to undo the work of the last few months. Either that he had never met Lucy, or that he had not married Sibylla. Which of those two events he would have preferred to recall, he did not trust himself to think; whatever may have been his faults, he had, until now, believed himself to be a man of honour. It was too late. Give what he would, strive as he would, repent as he would, the ill could neither be undone nor mitigated; it was one of those unhappy things for which there is no redress; they must be borne, as they best can, in patience and silence.

With these thoughts and feelings full upon him, little wonder was there that Lionel Verner, some two hours after quitting Lucy, should turn into Peckaby's shop. Mrs. Peckaby was seated back from the open door, crying, and moaning, and swaying herself about, apparently in terrible pain, physical or mental. Lionel remembered the story of the white donkey, and he stepped in to question her; anything for a minute's divertisement; anything to drown the care that was racking him. There was a subject on which he wished to speak to Roy, and that took him down Clay Lane.

"What's the matter, Mrs. Peckaby?"

Mrs. Peckaby rose from her chair, curtseyed, and sat down again. But for the state of tribulation she was in, she would have remained standing.

"Oh, sir, I have had a upset," she sobbed. "I see the white tail of a pony a-going by, and I thought it might be some'at else. It did give me a turn!"

"What did you think it might be?"

"I thought it might be the tail of a different sort of animal. I be a-going a far journey, sir, and I thought it was, may be, the quadruple come to fetch me I'm a-going to New Jerusalem on a white donkey."

"So I hear," said Lionel, suppressing a smile, in spite of his heavy heart. "Do you go all the way on the white donkey, Mrs. Peckaby?"

"Sir, that's a matter that's hid from me," answered Mrs. Peckaby. "The gentleman that was sent back to me by Brother Jarrum, hadn't had particulars revealed to him. There's difficulties in the way of a animal on four legs which can't swim, doing it all, that I don't pretend to explain away. I'm content, when the hour comes, sir, to start, and trust. Peckaby, he's awful sinful, sir. Only last evening, when I was saying the quadruple might have mirac'lous parts give to it, like Balum's had in the Bible, Peckaby he jeered, and said he'd like to see Balum's or any other quadruple, set off to swim to America—that he'd find the bottom afore he found the land. I wonder the kitchen ceiling don't drop down upon his head! For myself, sir, I'm rejoiced to trust, as I says; and as soon as the white donkey do come, I shall mount him without fear."

"What do you expect to find at New Jerusalem?" asked Lionel.

"I could sooner tell you, sir, what I don't expect; it 'ud take up less time. There's a'most everything good at New Jerusalem that the world contains—Verner's Pride's a poor place to it, sir—saving your presence for saying so. I could have sat and listened to Brother Jarrum in this here shop for ever, sir, if it hadn't been that the longing was upon me to get there. In this part o' the world we women be poor, cast down, half-famished, miserable slaves; but in New Jerusalem we are the wives of saints, well cared for, and clothed and fed, happy as the day's long, and our own parlours to ourselves, and nobody to interrupt us. Yes, Peckaby, I'm a-telling his honour, Mr. Verner, what's a-waiting for me at New Jerusalem! And the sooner I'm on my road to it, the better."

The conclusion was addressed to Peckaby himself. Peckaby had just come in from the forge, grimed and dirty. He touched his hair to Lionel, an amused expression playing on his face. In point of fact, this New Jerusalem vision was affording the utmost merriment to Peckaby and a few more husbands. Peckaby had come home to his tea, which meal it was the custom of Deerham to enjoy about three o'clock. He saw no signs of its being in readiness; and, but for the presence of Mr. Verner, might probably have expressed his opinion demonstratively upon the point. Peckaby, of late, appeared to have changed his nature and disposition. From being a timid man, living under wife-thraldom, he had come to exercise thraldom over her. How far Mrs. Peckaby's state of low spirits, into which she was generally sunk, may have explained this, nobody knew.

"I have had a turn, Peckaby. I caught sight of a white tail a-going by, and I thought it might be the quadruple a-coming for me. I was shook, I can tell you. 'Twas more nor an hour ago, and I've been able to do nothing since, but sit here and weep; I couldn't redd up after that."

"Warn't it the quadrepid?" asked Peckaby in a mocking tone.

"No, it weren't," she moaned. "It were nothing but that white pony of Farmer Blow's."

"Him, was it," said Peckaby, with affected scorn. "He is in the forge now, he is; a-having his shoes changed, and his tail trimmed."

"I'd give a shilling to anybody as 'ud cut his tail off;" angrily rejoined Mrs. Peckaby. "A-deceiving of me, and turning my inside all of a quake! Oh, I wish it 'ud come! The white donkey as is to bear me to New Jerusalem!"

"Don't you wish her joy of her journey, sir?" cried the man respectfully, a twinkle in his eye, while she rocked herself too and fro. "She have got a bran new gownd laid up in a old apron upstairs, ready for the start. She, and a lot more to help her, set on and made it in a afternoon, for fear the white donkey should arrive immediate. I asks her, sir, how much back the gownd'll have left in him, by the time she have rode from here to New Jerusalem."

"Peckaby, you are a mocker!" interposed his lady, greatly exasperated. "Remember the forty-two as was eat up by bears when they mocked at Elisher!"

"Mrs. Peckaby," said Lionel, keeping his countenance, "don't you think you would have made more sure of the benefits of the New Jerusalem, had you started with the rest, instead of depending upon the arrival of the white donkey?"

"They started without her, sir," cried the man, laughing from ear to ear. "They give her the slip, while she were a-bed and asleep."

"It were revealed to Brother Jarrum so to do, sir," she cried eagerly. "Don't listen to him. Brother Jarrum as much meant me to go, sir, and I as much thought to go, as I mean to go to my bed this night—always supposing the white donkey don't come," she broke off in a different voice.

"Why did you not go, then?" demanded Lionel.

"I'll tell you about it, sir. Me and Brother Jarrum was on the best of terms—which it's a real gentleman he was, and never said a word nor gave a look as could offend me. I didn't know the night fixed for the start; and Brother Jarrum didn't know it; in spite of Peckaby's insinuations. On that last night, which it was Tuesday, not a soul came near the place but that pale lady where Dr. West attended. She stopped a minute or two, and then Brother Jarrum goes out, and says he might be away all the evening. Well, he was; but he came in again; I can be on my oath he did; and I give him his candle and wished him a good-night. After that, sir, I never heard nothing till I got up in the morning. The first thing I see was his door wide open, and the bed not slept in. And the next thing I heard was, that the start had took place; they a-walking to Heartburg, and taking the train there. You might just have knocked me down with a puff of wind."

"Such a howling and screeching followed on, sir," put in Peckaby. "I were at the forge, and it reached all the way to our ears, over there. Chuff, he thought as the place had took fire and the missis was a-burning."

"But it didn't last; it didn't last," repeated Mrs. Peckaby. "Thanks be offered up for it, it didn't last, or I should ha' been in my coffin afore the day were out! A gentleman came to me: a Brother he were, sent express by Brother Jarrum; and had walked afoot all the way from Heartburg. It had been revealed to Brother Jarrum, he said, that they were to start that partic'lar night, and that I was to be left behind special. A higher mission was—What was the word? resigned?—no—reserved—reserved for me, and I was to be conveyed special on a quadruple, which was a white donkey. I be to keep myself in readiness, sir, always a-looking out for the quadruple's coming and stopping afore the door."

Lionel leaned against the counter, and went into a burst of laughter. The woman told it so quaintly, with such perfect good faith in the advent of the white donkey! She did not much like the mirth. As to that infidel Peckaby, he indulged in sundry mocking doubts, which were, to say the least of them, very mortifying to a believer.

"What's your opinion, sir?" she suddenly asked of Lionel.

"Well," said Lionel, "my opinion—as you wish for it—Would incline to the suspicion that your friend, Brother Jarrum, deceived you. That he invented the fable of the white donkey to keep you quiet while he and the rest got clear off."

Mrs. Peckaby went into a storm of shrieking sobs. "It couldn't be! it couldn't be! Oh, sir, you be as cruel as the rest! Why should Brother Jarrum take the others, and not take me?"

"That is Brother Jarrum's affair," replied Lionel. "I only say it looks like it."

"I telled Brother Jarrum, the very day afore the start took place, that if he took off my wife, I'd follor him on and beat every bone to smash as he'd got in his body," interposed Peckaby, glancing at Lionel with a knowing smile. "I did, sir. Her was out"—jerking his black thumb at his wife—"and I caught Brother Jarrum in his own room and shut the door on us both, and there I telled him. He knew I meant it, too, and he didn't like the look of a iron bar I happened to have in my hand. I saw that. Other wives' husbands might do as they liked; but I warn't a-going to have mine deluded off by them Latter Day Saints. Were I wrong, sir?"

"I do not think you were," answered Lionel.

"I'd Latter Day 'em! and saint 'em too, if I had my will!" continued wrathful Peckaby. "Arch-deceiving villuns!"

"Well, good-day, Mrs. Peckaby," said Lionel, moving to the door. "I would not spend too much time were I you, looking out for the white donkey."

"It'll come! it'll come!" retorted Mrs. Peckaby, in an ecstasy of joy, removing her hands from her ears, where she had clapped them during Peckaby's heretical speech. "I am proud, sir, to know as it'll come, in spite of opinions contrairey and Peckaby's wickedness; and I'm proud to be always a-looking out for it."

"This is never it, is it, drawing up to the door now?" cried Lionel, with gravity.

Something undoubtedly was curveting and prancing before the door; something with a white flowing tail. Mrs. Peckaby caught one glimpse, and bounded from her seat, her chest panting, her nostrils working. The signs betrayed how implicit was the woman's belief; how entirely it had taken hold of her.

Alas! for Mrs. Peckaby. Alas! for her disappointment. It was nothing but that deceiving animal again, Farmer Blow's white pony. Apparently the pony had been so comfortable in the forge, that he did not care to leave it. He was dodging about and backing, wholly refusing to go forward, and setting at defiance a boy who was striving to lead him onwards. Mrs. Peckaby sat down and burst into tears.

CHAPTER XLV

STIFLED WITH DISHONOUR

"Now, then," began Peckaby, as Lionel departed, "what's the reason my tea ain't ready for me."

"Be you a man to ask?" demanded she. "Could I redd up and put on kettles, and, see to ord'nary work, with my inside turning?"

Peckaby paused for a minute. "I've a good mind to wallop you!"

"Try it," she aggravatingly answered. "You have not kep' your hands off me yet to be let begin now. Anybody but a brute 'ud comfort a poor woman in her distress. You'll be sorry for it when I'm gone off to New Jerusalem."

"Now, look here, Suke," said he, attempting to reason with her. "It's quite time as you left off this folly; we've had enough on't. What do you suppose you'd do at Salt Lake? What sort of a life 'ud you lead?"

"A joyful life!" she responded, turning her glance sky-ward. "Brother Jarrum thinks as the head saint, the prophet hisself, has a favour to me! Wives is as happy there as the day's long."

Peckaby grinned; the reply amused him much. "You poor ignorant creatur," cried he, "you have got your head up in a mad-house; and that's about it. You know Mary Green?"

"Well?" answered she, looking surprised at this divertissement.

"And you know Nancy from Verner's Pride as is gone off," he continued, "and you know half a dozen more nice young girls about here, which you can just set on and think of. How 'ud you like to see me marry the whole of 'em, and bring 'em home here? Would the house hold the tantrums you'd go into, d'ye think?"

"You hold your senseless tongue, Peckaby! A man 'ud better try and bring home more nor one wife here! The law 'ud be on to him."

"In course it would," returned Peckaby! "And the law knowed what it was about when it made itself into the law. A place with more nor one wife in it 'ud be compairable to nothing but that blazing place you've heerd on as is under our feet, or the Salt Lake City."

"For shame, you wicked man!"

"There ain't no shame, in saying that; it's truth," composedly answered Peckaby. "Brother Jarrum said, didn't he, as the wives had a parlour a-piece. Why do they? 'Cause they be obleeged to be kep' apart, for fear o' damaging each other, a-tearing and biting and scratching, and a-pulling of eyes out. A nice figure you'd cut among 'em! You'd be a-wishing yourself home again afore you'd tried it for a day. Don't you be a fool, Susan Peckaby."

"Don't you!" retorted she. "I wonder you ain't afraid o' some judgment falling on you. Lies is sure to come home to people."

"Just take your thoughts back to the time as we had the shop here, and plenty o' custom in it. One day you saw me just a-kissing of a girl in that there corner—leastways you fancied as you saw me," corrected Peckaby, coughing down his slip. "Well, d'ye recollect the scrimmage? Didn't you go a'most mad, never keeping' your tongue quiet for a week, and the place hardly holding of ye? How 'ud you like to have eight or ten more of 'em, my married wives, like you be, brought in here?"

"You are a fool, Peckaby. The cases is different."

"Where's the difference?" asked Peckaby. "The men be men, out there; and the women be women. I might pertend as I'd had visions and revelations sent to me, and dress myself up in a black coat and a white neck-an-kecher, and suchlike paycock's plumes—I might tar and feather myself if I pleased, if it come to that—and give out as I was a prophit and a Latter Day Saint; but where 'ud be the difference, I want to know? I should just be as good and as bad a man as I be now, only a bit more of a hypocrite. Saints and prophits, indeed! You just come to your senses, Susan Peckaby."

"I haven't lost 'em yet," answered she, looking inclined to beat him.

"You have lost 'em; to suppose as a life, out with them reptiles, could be anything but just what I told you—a hell. It can't be otherways. It's again human female natur. If you went angry mad with jealousy, just at fancying you see a innocent kiss give upon a girl's face, how 'ud you do, I ask, when it come to wives? Tales runs as them 'saints' have got any number a-piece, from four or five, up to seventy. If you don't come to your senses, Mrs. Peckaby, you'll get a walloping, to bring you to 'em; and that's about it. You be the laughing-stock o' the place as it is."

He swung out at the door, and took his way towards the nearest public-house, intending to solace himself with a pint of ale, in lieu of tea, of which he saw no chance. Mrs. Peckaby burst into a flood of tears, and apostrophised the expected white donkey in moving terms: that he would forthwith appear and bear her off from Peckaby and trouble, to the triumphs and delights of New Jerusalem.

Lionel, meanwhile, went to Roy's dwelling. Roy, he found, was not in it. Mrs. Roy was; and, by the appearance of the laid-out tea-table, she was probably expecting Roy to enter. Mrs. Roy sat doing nothing, her arms hung listlessly down, her head also; sunk apparently in that sad state of mind—whatever may have been its cause—which was now habitual to her. By the start with which she sprang from her chair, as Lionel Verner appeared at the open door, it may be inferred that she took him for her husband. Surely nobody else could have put her in such tremor.

"Roy's not in, sir," she said, dropping a curtsey, in answer to Lionel's inquiry. "May be, he'll not be long. It's his time for coming home, but there's no dependence on him."

Lionel glanced round. He saw that the woman was alone, and he deemed it a good opportunity to ask her about what had been mentioned to him, two or three hours previously, by the Vicar of Deerham. Closing the door, and advancing towards her, he began.

"I want to say a word to you, Mrs. Roy. What were your grounds for stating to Mr. Bourne that Mr. Frederick Massingbird was with Rachel Frost at the Willow Pool the evening of her death?"

Mrs. Roy gave a low shriek of terror, and flung her apron over her face. Lionel ungallantly drew it down again. Her countenance was turning livid as death.

"You will have the goodness to answer me, Mrs. Roy."

"It were just a dream sir," she said, the words issuing in unequal jerks from her trembling lips, "I have been pretty nigh crazed lately. What with them Mormons, and the uncertainty of fixing what to do—whether to believe 'em or not—and Roy's crabbed temper, which grows upon him, and other fears and troubles, I've been a-nigh crazed. It were just a dream as I had, and nothing more; and I be vexed to my heart that I should have made such a fool of myself, as to go and say what I did to Mr. Bourne."

One word above all others, caught the attention of Lionel in the answer. It was "fears." He bent towards her, lowering his voice.

"What are these fears that seem to pursue you? You appear to me to have been perpetually under the influence of fear since that night. Terrified you were then; terrified you remain. What is the cause?"

The woman trembled excessively.

"Roy keeps me in fear, sir. He's for ever a-threatening. He'll shake me, or he'll pinch me, or he'll do for me, he says. I'm in fear of him always."

"That is an evasive answer," remarked Lionel. "Why should you fear to confide in me? You have never known me to take an advantage to anybody's injury. The past is past. That unfortunate night's work appears now to belong wholly to the past. Nevertheless, if you can throw any light upon it, it is your duty to do so. I will keep the secret."

"I didn't know a thing, sir, about the night's work. I didn't," she sobbed.

"Hush!" said Lionel. "I felt sure at the time that you did know something, had you chosen to speak. I feel more sure of it now."

"No, I don't, sir; not if you pulled me in pieces for it. I had a horrid dream, and I went straight off, like a fool, to Mr. Bourne and told it, and—and—that was all, sir."

She was flinging her apron up again to hide her countenance, when, with a faint cry, she let it fall, sprung from her seat, and stood before Lionel.

"For the love of heaven, sir, say nothing to him!" she uttered, and disappeared within an inner door. The sight of Roy, entering, explained the enigma; she must have seen him from the window. Roy took off his cap by way of salute.

"I hope I see you well, sir, after your journey."

"Quite well. Roy, some papers have been left at Verner's Pride for my inspection, regarding the dispute in Farmer Hartright's lease. I do not understand them. They bear your signature, not Mrs. Verner's. How is that?"

Roy stopped a while—to collect his thoughts, possibly. "I suppose I signed it for her, sir."

"Then you did what you had no authority to do. You never received power to sign from Mrs. Verner."

"Mrs. Verner must have give me power, sir, if I have signed. I don't recollect signing anything. Sometimes, when she was ill, or unwilling to be disturbed, she'd say, 'Roy, do this,' or, 'Roy, do the other.' She—"

"Mrs. Verner never gave you authority to sign," impressively repeated Lionel. "She is gone, and therefore cannot be referred to; but you know as well as I do, that she never did give you such authority. Come to Verner's Pride to-morrow morning at ten, and see these papers."

Roy signified his obedience, and Lionel departed. He bent his steps towards home, taking the field way; all the bitter experiences of the day rising up within his mind. Ah! try as he would, he could not deceive himself; he could not banish or drown the one ever-present thought. The singular information imparted by Mr. Bourne; the serio-comic tribulation of Mrs. Peckaby, waiting for her white donkey; the mysterious behaviour of Dinah Roy, in which there was undoubtedly more than met the ear; all these could not cover for a moment the one burning fact—Lucy's love, and his own dishonour. In vain Lionel flung off his hat, heedless of any second sun-stroke, and pushed his hair from his heated brow. It was of no use; as he had felt when he went out from the presence of Lucy, so he felt now—stifled with dishonour.

Sibylla was at a table, writing notes, when he reached home. Several were on it, already written, and in their envelopes. She looked up at him.

"Oh, Lionel, what a while you have been out! I thought you were never coming home."

He leaned down and kissed her. Although his conscience had revealed to him, that day, that he loved another better, she should never feel the difference. Nay, the very knowledge that it was so would render him all the more careful to give her marks of love.

"I have been to my mother's, and to one or two more places. What are you so busy over, dear?"

"I am writing invitations," said Sibylla.

"Invitations! Before people have called upon you?"

"They can call all the same. I have been asking Mary Tynn how many beds she can, by dint of screwing, afford. I am going to fill them all. I shall ask them for a month. How grave you look, Lionel!"

"In this first early sojourn together in our own house, Sibylla, I think we shall be happier alone."

"Oh, no, we should not. I love visitors. We shall be together all the same, Lionel."

"My little wife," he said, "if you cared for me as I care for you, you would not feel the want of visitors just now."

And there was no sophistry in this speech. He had come to the conviction that Lucy ought to have been his wife, but he did care for Sibylla very much. The prospect of a house full of guests at the present moment, appeared most displeasing to him, if only as a matter of taste.

"Put it off for a few weeks, Sibylla."

Sibylla pouted. "It is of no use preaching, Lionel. If you are to be a preaching husband, I shall be sorry I married you. Fred was never that."

Lionel's face turned blood-red. Sibylla put up her hand, and drew it carelessly down.

"You must let me have my own way for this once," she coaxingly said. "What's the use of my bringing all those loves of things from Paris, if we are to live in a dungeon, and nobody's to see them? I must invite them, Lionel."

"Very well," he answered, yielding the point. Yielding it the more readily from the consciousness above spoken of.

"There's my dear Lionel! I knew you would never turn tyrant. And now I want something else."

"What's that?" asked Lionel.

"A cheque."

"A cheque? I gave you one this morning, Sibylla."

"Oh! but the one you gave me is for housekeeping—for Mary Tynn, and all that. I want one for myself. I am not going to have my expenses come out of the housekeeping."

Lionel sat down to write one, a good-natured smile on his face. "I'm sure I don't know what you will find to spend it in, after all the finery you bought in Paris," he said, in a joking tone. "How much shall I fill it in for?"

"As much as you will," replied Sibylla, too eagerly. "Couldn't you give it me in blank, and let me fill it in?"

He made no answer. He drew it for £100, and gave it her.

"Will that do, my dear?"

She drew his face down again caressingly. But, in spite of the kisses left upon his lips, Lionel had awoke to the conviction, firm and undoubted, that his wife did not love him.

CHAPTER XLVI

SHADOWED-FORTH EMBARRASSMENT

The September afternoon sun streamed into the study at Verner's Pride, playing with the bright hair of Lionel Verner. His head was bending listlessly over certain letters and papers on his table, and there was a wearied look upon his face. Was it called up by the fatigue of the day? He had been out with some friends in the morning; it was the first day of partridge shooting, and they had bagged well. Now Lionel was home again, had changed his attire, and was sitting down in his study—the old study of Mr. Verner. Or, was the wearied look, were the indented upright lines between the eyes, called forth by inward care?

Those lines were not so conspicuous when you last saw him. Twelve or fourteen months have elapsed since then. A portion of that time only had been spent at Verner's Pride. Mrs. Verner was restless; ever wishing to be on the wing; living but in gaiety. Her extravagance was something frightful, and Lionel did not know how to check it. There were no children; there had been no signs of any; and Mrs. Verner positively made the lack into a sort of reproach, a continual cause for querulousness.

She had filled Verner's Pride with guests after their marriage—as she had coveted to do. From that period until early spring she had kept it filled, one succession of guests, one relay of visitors arriving after the other. Pretty, capricious, fascinating, youthful, Mrs. Verner was of excessive popularity in the country, and a sojourn at Verner's Pride grew to be eagerly sought. The women liked the attractive master; the men bowed to the attractive mistress; and Verner's Pride was never free. On the contrary, it was generally unpleasantly crammed; and Mrs. Tynn, who was a staid, old-fashioned housekeeper, accustomed to nothing beyond the regular, quiet household maintained by the late Mr. Verner, was driven to the verge of desperation.

"It would be far pleasanter if we had only half the number of guests," Lionel had said to his wife in the winter. He no longer remonstrated against any: he had given that up as hopeless. "Pleasanter for them, pleasanter for us, pleasanter for the servants."

"The servants!" slightingly returned Sibylla. "I never knew before that the pleasure of servants was a thing to be studied."

"But their comfort is. At least, I have always considered so, and I hope I always shall. They complain much, Sibylla."

"Do they complain to you?"

"They do. Tynn and his wife say they are nearly worked to death. They hint at leaving. Mrs. Tynn is continually subjected also to what she calls insults from your French maid. That of course I know nothing of; but it might be as well for you to listen to her on the subject."

"I cannot have Benoite crossed. I don't interfere in the household myself, and she does it for me."

"But, my dear, if you would interfere a little more, just so far as to ascertain whether these complaints have grounds, you might apply a remedy."

"Lionel, you are most unreasonable! As if I could be worried with looking into things! What are servants for? You must be a regular old bachelor to think of my doing it."

"Well—to go to our first point," he rejoined. "Let us try half the number of guests, and see how it works. If you do not find it better, more agreeable in all ways, I will say no more about it."

He need not have said anything, then. Sibylla would not listen to it. At any rate, would not act upon it. She conceded so far as to promise that she would not invite so many next time. But, when that next time came, and the new sojourners arrived, they turned out to be more. Beds had to be improvised in all sorts of impossible places; the old servants were turned out of their chambers and huddled into corners; nothing but confusion and extravagance reigned. Against some of the latter, Mrs. Tynn ventured to remonstrate to her mistress. Fruits and vegetables out of season; luxuries in the shape of rare dishes, many of which Verner's Pride had never heard of, and did not know how to cook, and all of the most costly nature, were daily sent down from London purveyors. Against this expense Mary Tynn spoke. Mrs. Verner laughed good-naturedly at her, and told her it was not her pocket that would be troubled to pay the bills. Additional servants were obliged to be had; and, in short, to use an expression that was much in vogue at Deerham about that time, Verner's Pride was going the pace.

This continued until early spring. In February Sibylla fixed her heart upon a visit to London. "Of course," she told Lionel, "he would treat her to a season in town." She had never been to London in her life to stay. For Sibylla to fix her heart upon a thing, was to have it; Lionel was an indulgent husband.

To London they proceeded in February. And there the cost was great. Sibylla was not one to go to work sparingly in any way; neither, in point of fact, was Lionel. Lionel would never have been unduly extravagant; but, on the other hand, he was not accustomed to spare. A furnished house in a good position was taken; servants were imported to it from Verner's Pride; and there Sibylla launched into all the follies of the day. At Easter she "set her heart" upon a visit to Paris, and Lionel acquiesced. They remained there three weeks; Sibylla laying in a second stock of toilettes for Mademoiselle Benoite to rule over; and then they went back to London.

The season was prolonged that year. The House sat until August, and it was not until the latter end of that month that Mr. and Mrs. Verner returned to Verner's Pride. Though scarcely home a week yet, the house was filled again—filled to overflowing; Lionel can hear sounds of talking and laughter from the various rooms, as he bends over his table. He was opening his letters, three or four of which lay in a stack. He had gone out in the morning before the post was in.

Tynn knocked at the door and entered, bringing a note.

"Where's this from?" asked Lionel, taking it from the salver. Another moment, and he had recognised the handwriting of his mother.

"From Deerham Court, sir. My lady's footman brought it. He asks whether there is any answer."

Lionel opened the note, and read as follows:—

"MY DEAR LIONEL,—I am obliged to be a beggar again. My expenses seem to outrun my means in a most extraordinary sort of way. Sometimes I think it must be Decima's fault, and tell her she does not properly look after the household. In spite of my own income, your ample allowance, and the handsome remuneration received for Lucy, I cannot make both ends meet. Will you let me have two or three hundred pounds?

"Ever your affectionate mother,

"LOUISA VERNER."

"I will call on Lady Verner this afternoon, Tynn."

Tynn withdrew with the answer. Lionel leaned his brow upon his hand; the weary expression terribly plain just then.

"My mother shall have it at once—no matter what my own calls may be," was his soliloquy. "Let me never forget that Verner's Pride might have been hers all these years. Looking at it from our own point of view, my father's branch in contradistinction of my uncle's, it ought to have been hers. It might have been her jointure-house now, had my father lived, and so willed it. I am glad to help my mother," he continued, an earnest glow lighting his face. "If I get embarrassed, why, I must get embarrassed; but she shall not suffer."

That embarrassment would inevitably come, if he went on at his present rate of living, he had the satisfaction of knowing beyond all doubt. That was not the worst point upon his conscience. Of the plans and projects that Lionel had so eagerly formed when he came into the estate, some were set afloat, some were not. Those that were most wanted—that were calculated to do the most real good—lay in abeyance; others, that might have waited, were in full work. Costly alterations were making in the stables at Verner's Pride, and the working man's institute at Deerham—reading-room, club, whatever it was to be—was progressing swimmingly. But the draining of the land near the poor dwellings was not begun, and the families, many of them, still herded in consort—father and mother, sons and daughters, sleeping in one room—compelled to it by the wretched accommodation of the tenements. It was on this last score that Lionel was feeling a pricking of conscience. And how to find the money to make these improvements now, he knew not. Between the building in progress and Sibylla, he was drained.

A circumstance had occurred that day to bring the latter neglect forcibly to his mind. Alice Hook—Hook the labourer's eldest daughter—had, as the Deerham phrase ran, got herself into trouble. A pretty child she had grown up amongst them—she was little more than a child now—good-tempered, gay-hearted. Lionel had heard the ill news the previous week on his return from London. When he was out shooting that morning he saw the girl at a distance, and made some observation to his gamekeeper, Broom, to the effect that it had vexed him.

"Ay, sir, it's a sad pity," was Broom's answer; "but what else can be expected of poor folks that's brought up to live as they do—like pigs in a sty?"

Broom had intended no reproach to his master; such an impertinence would not have crossed his mind; but the words carried a sting to Lionel. He knew how many, besides Alice Hook, had had their good conduct undermined through the living "like pigs in a sty." Lionel had, as you know, a lively conscience; and his brow reddened with self-reproach as he sat and thought these things over. He could not help comparing the contrast: Verner's Pride, with its spacious bedrooms, one of which was not deemed sufficient for the purposes of retirement, where two people slept together, but a dressing-closet must be attached; and those poor Hooks, with their growing-up sons and daughters, and but one room, save the kitchen, in their whole dwelling!

"I will put things on a better footing," impulsively exclaimed Lionel. "I care not what the cost may be, or how it may fall upon my comforts, do it I will. I declare, I feel as if the girl's blight lay at my own door!"

Again he and his reflections were interrupted by Tynn.

"Roy has come up, sir, and is asking to see you."

"Roy! Let him come in," replied Lionel. "I want to see him."

It frequently happened, when agreements, leases, and other deeds were examined, that Roy had to be referred to. Things would turn out to have been drawn up, agreements made, in precisely the opposite manner to that expected by Lionel. For some of these Roy might have received sanction; but, for many, Lionel felt sure Roy had acted on his own responsibility. This chiefly applied to the short period of the management of Mrs. Verner; a little, very little, to the latter year of her husband's life. Matiss was Lionel's agent during his absences; when at home, he took all management into his own hands.

Roy came in. The same ill-favoured, hard-looking man as ever. The ostensible business which had brought him up to Verner's Pride, proved to be of a very trivial nature, and was soon settled. It is well to say "ostensible," because a conviction arose in Lionel's mind afterwards that it was but an excuse: that

Roy made it a pretext for the purpose of obtaining an interview. Though why, or wherefore, or what he gained by it, Lionel could not imagine. Roy merely wanted to know if he might be allowed to put a fresh paper on the walls of one of his two upper rooms. He'd get the paper at his own cost, and hang it at his own leisure, if Mr. Verner had no objection.

"Of course I can have no objection to it," replied Lionel. "You need not have lost an afternoon's work, Roy, to come here to inquire that. You might have asked me when I saw you by the brick-field this morning. In fact, there was no necessity to mention it at all."

"So I might, sir. But it didn't come into my mind at the moment to do so. It's poor Luke's room, and the missis, she goes on continual about the state it's in, if he should come home. The paper's all hanging off it in patches, sir, as big as my two hands. It have got damp through not being used."

"If it is in that state, and you like to find the time to hang the paper, you may purchase it at my cost," said Lionel, who was of too just a nature to be a hard landlord.

"Thank ye, sir," replied Roy, ducking his head. "It's well for us, as I often says, that you be our master at last, instead of the Mr. Massingbirds."

"There was a time when you did not think so, Roy, if my memory serves me rightly," was the rebuke of Lionel.

"Ah, sir, there's a old saying, 'Live and learn.' That was in the days when I thought you'd be a over strict master; we have got to know better now, taught from experience. It was a lucky day for the Verner Pride estate when that lost codicil was brought to light! The Mr. Massingbirds be dead, it's true, but there's no knowing what might have happened; the law's full of quips and turns. With the codicil found, you can hold your own again' the world."

"Who told you anything about the codicil being found?" demanded Lionel.

"Why, sir, it was the talk of the place just about the time we heard of Mr. Fred Massingbird's death. Folks said, whether he had died, or whether he had not, you'd have come in all the same. T'other day, too, I was talking of it to Lawyer Matiss, and he said what a good thing it was, that that there codicil was found."

Lionel knew that a report of the turning up of the codicil had travelled to Deerham. It had never been contradicted. But he wondered to hear Roy say that Matiss had spoken of it. Matiss, himself, Tynn, and Mrs. Tynn, were the only persons who could have testified that the supposed codicil was nothing but a glove. From the finding of that, the story had originally got wind.

"I don't know why Matiss should have spoken to you on the subject of the codicil," he remarked to Roy.

"It's not much that Matiss talks, sir," was the man's answer. "All he said was as he had got the codicil in safe keeping under lock and key. Just put to Matiss the simplest question, and he'll turn round and ask what business it is of yours."

"Quite right of him, too," said Lionel. "Have you any news of your son yet, Roy?"

Roy shook his head. "No, sir. I'm a-beginning to wonder now whether there ever will be news of him."

After the man had departed, Lionel looked at his watch. There was just time for a ride to Deerham Court before dinner. He ordered his horse, and mounted it, a cheque for three hundred pounds in his pocket.

He rode quickly, musing upon what Matiss had said about the codicil—as stated by Roy. Could the deed have been found?—and Matiss forgotten to acquaint him with it. He turned his horse down the Belvedere Road, telling his groom to wait at the corner, and stopped before the lawyer's door. The latter came out.

"Matiss, is that codicil found?" demanded Lionel, bending down his head to speak.

"What codicil, Mr. Verner?" returned Matiss, looking surprised.

"The codicil. The one that gave me the estate. Roy was with me just now, and he said you stated to him that the codicil was found—that it was safe under lock and key."

The lawyer's countenance lighted up with a smile. "What a meddler the fellow is! To tell you the truth, sir, it rather pleases me to mislead Roy, and put him on the wrong scent. He comes here, pumping, trying to get what he can out of me: asking this, asking that, fishing out anything there is to fish. I recollect, he did say something about the codicil, and I replied, 'Ay, it was a good thing it was found, and safe under lock and key.' He tries at the wrong handle when he pumps at me."

"What is his motive for pumping at all?" returned Lionel.

"There's no difficulty in guessing at that, sir. Roy would give his two ears to get into place again; he'd like to fill the same post to you that he did to the late Mr. Verner. He thinks if he can hang about here and pick up any little bit of information that may be let drop, and carry it to you, that it might tell in his favour. He would like you to discover how useful he could be. That is the construction I put upon it."

"Then he wastes his time," remarked Lionel, as he turned his horse. "I would not put power of any sort into Roy's hands, if he paid me in diamonds to do it. You can tell him so, if you like, Matiss."

Arrived at Deerham Court, Lionel left his horse with his groom, and entered. The first person to greet his sight in the hall was Lucy Tempest. She was in white silk; a low dress, somewhat richly trimmed with lace, and pearls in her hair. It was the first time that Lionel had seen her since his return from London. He had been at his mother's once or twice, but Lucy did not appear. They met face to face. Lucy's turned crimson, in spite of herself.

"Are you quite well?" asked Lionel, shaking hands, his own pulses beating. "You are going out this evening, I see?"

He made the remark as a question, noticing her dress; and Lucy, gathering her senses about her, and relapsing into her calm composure, looked somewhat surprised.

"We are going to dinner to Verner's Pride; I and Decima. Did you not expect us?"

"I—did not know it," he was obliged to answer. "Mrs. Verner mentioned that some friends would dine with us this evening, but I was not aware that you and Decima were part of them. I am glad to hear it."

Lucy continued her way, wondering what sort of a household it could be where the husband remained in ignorance of his wife's expected guests. Lionel passed on to the drawing-room.

Lady Verner sat in it. Her white gloves on her delicate hands as usual, her essence bottle and laced handkerchief beside her, Lionel offered her his customary fond greeting, and placed the cheque in her hands.

"Will that do, mother mine?"

"Admirably, Lionel. I am so much obliged to you. Things get behind-hand in the most unaccountable manner, and then Decima comes to me with a long face, and says here's this debt and that debt. It is quite a marvel to me how the money goes. Decima would like to put her accounts into my hands that I may look over them. The idea of my taking upon myself to examine accounts! But how it is she gets into such debt, I cannot think."

Poor Decima knew only too well. Lionel knew it also; though, in his fond reverence, he would not hint at such a thing to his mother. Lady Verner's style of living was too expensive, and that was the cause.

"I met Lucy in the hall, dressed. She and Decima are coming to dine at Verner's Pride, she tells me."

"Did you not know it?"

"No. I have been out shooting all day. If Sibylla mentioned it to me, I forgot it."

Sibylla had not mentioned it. But Lionel would rather take any blame to himself than suffer a shade of it to rest upon her.

"Mrs. Verner called yesterday, and invited us. I declined for myself. I should have declined for Decima, but I did not think it right to deprive Lucy of the pleasure, and she could not go alone. Ungrateful child!" apostrophised Lady Verner. "When I told her this morning I had accepted an invitation for her to Verner's Pride, she turned the colour of scarlet, and said she would rather remain at home. I never saw so unsociable a girl; she does not care to go out, as it seems to me. I insisted upon it for this evening."

"Mother, why don't you come?"

Lady Verner half turned from him.

"Lionel, you must not forget our compact. If I visit your wife now and then, just to keep gossiping tongues quiet, from saying that Lady Verner and her son are estranged, I cannot do it often."

"Were there any cause why you should show this disfavour to Sibylla—"

"Our compact, our compact, my son! You are not to urge me upon this point, do you remember? I rarely break my resolutions, Lionel."

"Or your prejudices either, mother."

"Very true," was the equable answer of Lady Verner.

Little more was said. Lionel found the time drawing on, and left. Lady Verner's carriage was already at the door, waiting to convey Decima and Lucy Tempest to the dinner at Verner's Pride. As he was about to mount his horse, Peckaby passed by, rolling a wheel before him. He touched his cap.

"Well," said Lionel, "has the white donkey arrived yet?"

A contraction of anger, not, however, unmixed with mirth, crossed the man's face.

"I wish it would come, sir, and bear her off on't!" was his hearty response. "She's more a fool nor ever over it, a-whining and a-pining all day long, 'cause she ain't at New Jerusalem. She wants to be in Bedlam, sir; that's what she do! it 'ud do her more good nor t'other."

Lionel laughed, and Peckaby struck his wheel with such impetus that it went off at a tangent, and he had to follow it on the run.

CHAPTER XLVII

THE YEW-TREE ON THE LAWN

The rooms were lighted at Verner's Pride; the blaze from the chandeliers fell on gay faces and graceful forms. The dinner was over, its scene "a banquet hall deserted"; and the guests were filling the drawing-rooms.

The centre of an admiring group, its chief attraction, sat Sibylla, her dress some shining material that glimmered in the light, and her hair confined with a band of diamonds. Inexpressibly beautiful by this light she undoubtedly was, but she would have been more charming had she less laid herself out for attraction. Lionel, Lord Garle, Decima, and young Bitterworth—he was generally called young Bitterworth, in contradistinction to his father, who was "old Bitterworth"—formed another group; Sir Rufus Hautley was talking to the Countess of Elmsley; and Lucy Tempest sat apart near the window.

Sir Rufus had but just moved away from Lucy, and for the moment she was alone. She sat within the embrasure of the window, and was looking on the calm scene outside. How different from the garish scene within! See the pure moonlight, side by side with the most brilliant light we earthly inventors can produce, and contrast them! Pure and fair as the moonlight looked Lucy, her white robes falling softly round her, and her girlish face wearing a thoughtful expression. It was a remarkably light night; the terrace, the green slopes beyond it, and the clustering trees far away, all standing out clear and distinct in the moon's rays. Suddenly her eye rested on a particular spot. She possessed a very clear sight, and it appeared to detect something dark there; which dark something had not been there a few moments before.

Lucy strained her eyes, and shaded them, and gazed again. Presently she turned her head, and glanced at Lionel. An expression in her eyes seemed to call him, and he advanced.

"What is it, Lucy? We must have a set of gallant men here to-night, to leave you alone like this!"

The compliment fell unheeded on her ear. Compliments from him! Lionel only so spoke to hide his real feelings.

"Look on the lawn, right before us," said Lucy to him, in a low tone. "Underneath the spreading yew-tree. Do you not fancy the trunk looks remarkably dark and thick?"

"The trunk remarkably dark and thick!" echoed Lionel. "What do you mean, Lucy?" For he judged by her tone that she had some hidden meaning.

"I believe that some man is standing there. He must be watching this room."

Lionel could not see it. His eyes had not been watching so long as Lucy's, consequently objects were less distinct. "I think you must be mistaken, Lucy," he said. "No one would be at the trouble of standing there to watch the room. It is too far off to see much, whatever may be their curiosity."

Lucy held her hands over her eyes, gazing attentively from beneath them. "I feel convinced of it now," she presently said. "There is some one, and it looks like a man, standing behind the trunk, as if hiding himself. His head is pushed out on this side, certainly, as though he were watching these windows. I have seen the head move twice."

Lionel placed his hands in the same position, and took a long gaze. "I do think you are right, Lucy!" he suddenly exclaimed. "I saw something move then. What business has any one to plant himself there?"

He stepped impulsively out as he spoke—the windows opened to the ground—crossed the terrace, descended the steps, and turned on the lawn, to the left hand. A minute, and he was up at the tree.

But he gained no satisfaction. The spreading tree, with its imposing trunk—which trunk was nearly as thick as a man's body—stood all solitary on the smooth grass, no living thing being near it.

"We must have been mistaken, after all," thought Lionel.

Nevertheless, he stood under the tree, and cast his keen glances around. Nothing could he see; nothing but what ought to be there. The wide lawn, the sweet flowers closed to the night, the remoter parts where the trees were thick, all stood cold and still in the white moonlight. But of human disturber there was none.

Lionel went back again, plucking a white geranium blossom and a sprig of sweet verbena on his way. Lucy was sitting alone, as he had left her.

"It was a false alarm," he whispered. "Nothing's there, except the tree."

"It was not a false alarm," she answered. "I saw him move away as you went on to the lawn. He drew back towards the thicket."

"Are you sure?" questioned Lionel, his tone betraying that he doubted whether she was not mistaken.

"Oh, yes, I am sure," said Lucy. "Do you know what my old nurse used to tell me when I was a child?" she asked, lifting her face to his. "She said I had the Indian sight, because I could see so far and so distinctly. Some of the Indians have the gift greatly, you know. I am quite certain that I saw the object—and it looked like the figure of a man—go swiftly away from the tree across the grass. I could not see him to the end of the lawn, but he must have gone into the plantation. I dare say he saw you coming towards him."

Lionel smiled. "I wish I had caught the spy. He should have answered to me for being there. Do you like verbena, Lucy?"

He laid the verbena and geranium on her lap, and she took them up mechanically.

"I do not like spies," she said, in a dreamy tone. "In India they have been known to watch the inmates of a house in the evening, and to bow-string one of those they were watching before the morning. You are laughing! Indeed, my nurse used to tell me tales of it."

"We have no spies in England—in that sense, Lucy. When I used the word spy, it was with no meaning attached to it. It is not impossible but it may be a sweetheart of one of the maid-servants, come up from Deerham for a rendezvous. Be under no apprehension."

At that moment, the voice of his wife came ringing through the room. "Mr. Verner!"

He turned to the call. Waiting to say another word to Lucy, as a thought struck him. "You would prefer not to remain at the window, perhaps. Let me take you to a more sheltered seat."

"Oh, no, thank you," she answered impulsively. "I like being at the window. It is not of myself that I am thinking." And Lionel moved away.

"Is it not true that the fountains at Versailles played expressly for me?" eagerly asked Sibylla, as he approached her. "Sir Rufus won't believe that they did. The first time we were in Paris, you know."

Sir Rufus Hautley was by her side then. He looked at Lionel. "They never play for private individuals, Mr. Verner. At least, if they do, things have changed."

"My wife thought they did," returned Lionel, with a smile. "It was all the same."

"They did, Lionel, you know they did," vehemently asserted Sibylla. "De Coigny told me so; and he held authority in the Government."

"I know that De Coigny told you so, and that you believed him," answered Lionel, still smiling. "I did not believe him."

Sibylla turned her head away petulantly from her husband. "You are saying it to annoy me. I'll never appeal to you again. Sir Rufus, they did play expressly for me."

"It may be bad taste, but I'd rather see the waterworks at St. Cloud than at Versailles," observed a Mr. Gordon, some acquaintance that they had picked up in town, and to whom it had been Sibylla's pleasure to give an invitation. "Cannonby wrote me word last week from Paris—"

"Who?" sharply interrupted Sibylla.

Mr. Gordon looked surprised. Her tone had betrayed something of eager alarm, not to say terror.

"Captain Cannonby, Mrs. Verner. A friend of mine just returned from Australia. Business took him to Paris as soon as he landed."

"Is he from the Melbourne port? Is his Christian name Lawrence?" she reiterated breathlessly.

"Yes—to both questions," replied Mr. Gordon.

Sibylla shrieked, and lifted her handkerchief to her face. They gathered round her in consternation. One offering smelling-salts, one running for water. Lionel gently drew the handkerchief from her face. It was white as death.

"What ails you, my dear?" he whispered.

She seemed to recover her equanimity as suddenly as she had lost it, and the colour began to appear in her cheeks again.

"His name—Cannonby's—puts me in mind of those unhappy days," she said, not in the low tone used by her husband, but aloud—speaking, in fact, to all around her. "I did not know Captain Cannonby had returned. When did he come, Mr. Gordon?"

"About eight or nine days ago."

"Has he made his fortune?"

Mr. Gordon laughed. "I fancy not. Cannonby was always of a roving nature. I expect he got tired of the Australian world before fortune had time to find him out."

Sibylla was soon deep in her flirtations again. It is not erroneous to call them so. But they were innocent flirtations—the result of vanity. Lionel moved away.

Another commotion. Some great long-legged fellow, without ceremony or warning, came striding in at the window close to Lucy Tempest. Lucy's thoughts had been buried—it is hard to say where, and her eyes were strained to the large yew-tree upon the grass. The sudden entrance startled her, albeit she was not of a nervous temperament. With Indian bow-strings in the mind, and fancied moonlight spies before the sight, a scream was inevitable.

Whom should it be but Jan! Jan, of course. What other guest would be likely to enter in that unceremonious fashion? Strictly speaking, Jan was not a guest—at any rate, not an invited one.

"I had got a minute to spare this evening, so thought I'd come up and have a look at you," proclaimed unfashionable Jan to the room, but principally addressing Lionel and Sibylla.

And so Jan had come, and stood there without the least shame, in drab trousers, and a loose, airy coat, shaking hands with Sir Rufus, shaking hands with anybody who would shake hands with him. Sibylla looked daggers at Jan, and Lionel cross. Not from the same cause. Sibylla's displeasure was directed to Jan's style of evening costume; Lionel felt vexed with him for alarming Lucy. But Lionel never very long retained displeasure, and his sweet smile stole over his lips as he spoke.

"Jan, I shall be endorsing Lady Verner's request—that you come into a house like a Christian—if you are to startle ladies in this fashion."

"Whom did I startle?" asked Jan.

"You startled Lucy."

"Nonsense! Did I, Miss Lucy?"

"Yes, you did a little, Jan," she replied.

"What a stupid you must be!" retorted gallant Jan. "I should say you want doctoring, if your nerves are in that state. You take—"

"Oh, Jan, that will do," laughed Lucy. "I am sure I don't want medicine. You know how I dislike it."

They were standing together within the large window, Jan and Lionel, Lucy sitting close to them. She sat with her head a little bent, scenting her verbena.

"The truth is, Jan, I and Lucy have been watching some intruder who had taken up his station on the lawn, underneath the yew-tree," whispered Lionel. "I suppose Lucy thought he was bursting in upon us."

"Yes, I did really think he was," said Lucy, looking up with a smile.

"Who was it?" asked Jan.

"He did not give us the opportunity of ascertaining," replied Lionel. "I am not quite sure, mind, that I did see him; but Lucy is positive upon the point. I went to the tree, but he had disappeared. It is rather strange why he should be watching."

"He was watching this room attentively," said Lucy, "and I saw him move away when Mr. Verner went on the lawn. I am sure he was a spy of some sort."

"I can tell you who it was," said Jan. "It was Roy."

"Roy!" repeated Lionel. "Why do you say this?"

"Well," said Jan, "as I turned in here, I saw Roy cross the road to the opposite gate. I don't know where he could have sprung from, except from these grounds. That he was neither behind me nor before me as I came up the road, I can declare."

"Then it was Roy!" exclaimed Lionel. "He would have had about time to get into the road, from the time we saw him under the tree. That the fellow is prying into my affairs and movements, I was made aware of to-day; but why he should watch my house I cannot imagine. We shall have an account to settle, Mr. Roy!"

Decima came up, asking what private matter they were discussing, and Lionel and Lucy went over the ground again, acquainting her with what had been seen. They stood together in a group, conversing in an undertone. By and by, Mrs. Verner passed, moving from one part of the room to another, on the arm of Sir Rufus Hautley.

"Quite a family conclave," she exclaimed, with a laugh. "Decima, however much you may wish for attention, it is scarcely fair to monopolise that of Mr. Verner in his own house. If he forgets that he has guests present, you should not help him in the forgetfulness."

"It would be well if all wished for attention as little as does Miss Verner," exclaimed Lord Garle. His voice rung out to the ends of the room, and a sudden stillness fell upon it; his words may have been taken as a covert reproof to Mrs. Verner. They were not meant as such. There was no living woman of whom Lord Garle thought so highly as he thought of Decima Verner; and he had spoken in his mind's impulse.

Sibylla believed he had purposely flung a shaft at her. And she flung one again—not at him, but at Decima. She was of a terribly jealous nature, and could bear any reproach to herself, better than that another woman should be praised beside her.

"When young ladies find themselves neglected, their charms wasted on the desert air, they naturally do covet attention, although it be but a brother's."

Perhaps the first truly severe glance that Lionel Verner ever gave his wife he gave her then. Disdaining any defence off his sister, he stood, haughty, impassive, his lips drawn in, his eyes fixed sternly on Sibylla. Decima remained quiet under the insult, save that she flushed scarlet. Lord Garle did not. Lord Garle spoke up again, in the impetuosity of his open, honest nature.

"I can testify that if Miss Verner is neglected, it is her own fault alone. You are mistaken in your premises, Mrs. Verner."

The tone was pointedly significant, the words were unmistakably clear, and the room could not but become enlightened to the fact that Miss Verner might have been Lady Garle. Sibylla laughed a little laugh of disbelief, as she went onwards with Sir Rufus Hautley; and Lionel remained enshrined in his terrible mortification. That his wife should so have forgotten herself!

"I must be going off," cried Jan, good-naturedly interrupting the unpleasant silence.

"You have not long come," said Lucy.

"I didn't leave word where I was coming, and somebody may be going dead while they are scouring the parish for me. Good-night to you all; good-night, Miss Lucy."

With a nod to the room, away went Jan as unceremoniously as he had come; and, not very long afterwards, the first carriage drew up. It was Lady Verner's. Lord Garle hastened to Decima, and Lionel took out Lucy Tempest.

"Will you think me very foolish, if I say a word of warning to you?" asked Lucy, in a low tone to Lionel, as they reached the terrace.

"A word of warning to me, Lucy!" he repeated. "Of what nature?"

"That Roy is not a good man. He was greatly incensed at your putting him out of his place when you succeeded to Verner's Pride, and it is said that he cherishes vengeance. He may have been watching to-night for an opportunity to injure you. Take care of him."

Lionel smiled as he looked at her. Her upturned face looked pale and anxious in the moonlight. Lionel could not receive the fear at all: he would as soon have thought to dread the most improbable thing imaginable, as to dread this sort of violence, whether from Roy, or from any one else.

"There's no fear whatever, Lucy."

"I know you will not see it for yourself, and that is the reason why I am presumptive enough to suggest the idea to you. Pray be cautious! pray take care of yourself!"

He shook his head laughingly as he looked down upon her. "Thank you heartily all the same for your consideration, Lucy," said he, and for the very life of him he could not help pressing her hand warmer than was needful as he placed her in the carriage.

They drove away. Lord Garle returned to the room; Lionel stood against one of the outer pillars, looking forth on the lovely moonlight scene. The part played by Roy—if it was Roy—in the night's doings disturbed him not; but that his wife had shown herself so entirely unlike a lady did disturb him. In bitter contrast to Lucy did she stand out to his mind that night. He turned away, after some minutes, with an impatient movement, as if he would fain throw remembrance and vexation from him, Lionel had himself chosen his companion in life, and none knew better than he that he must abide by it; none could be more firmly resolved to do his full duty by her in love. Sibylla was standing outside the window alone. Lionel approached her, and gently laid his hand upon her shoulder.

"Sibylla, what caused you to show agitation when Cannonby's name was mentioned?"

"I told you," answered Sibylla. "It is dreadful to be reminded of that miserable time. It was Cannonby, you know, who buried my husband."

And before Lionel could say more, she had shaken his hand from her shoulder, and was back amidst her guests.

Jan had said somebody might be going dead while the parish was being scoured for him; and, in point of fact, Jan found, on reaching home, that that undesirable consummation was not unlikely to occur. As you will find also, if you will make an evening call upon Mrs. Duff.

Mrs. Duff stood behind her counter, sorting silks. Not rich piece silks that are made into gowns; Mrs. Duff's shop did not aspire to that luxurious class of goods; but humble skeins of mixed sewing-silks, that were kept tied up in a piece of wash-leather. Mrs. Duff's head and a customer's head were brought together over the bundle, endeavouring to fix upon a skein of a particular shade, by the help of the one gas-burner which flared away overhead.

"Drat the silk!" said Mrs. Duff at length. "One can't tell which is which, by candle-light. The green looks blue, and the blue looks green. Look at them two skeins, Polly; which is the green?"

Miss Polly Dawson, a showy damsel with black hair and a cherry-coloured net at the back of it—one of the family that Roy was pleased to term the ill-doing Dawsons, took the two skeins in her hand.

"Blest if I can tell!" was her answer. "It's for doing up mother's green silk bonnet, so it won't do to take blue. You be more used to it nor me, Mrs. Duff."

"My eyes never was good for sorting silks by this light," responded Mrs. Duff. "I'll tell you what, Polly; you shall take 'em both. Your mother must take the responsibility of fixing on one herself; or let her keep 'em till the morning and choose it then. She should have sent by daylight. You can bring back the skein you don't use to-morrow; but mind you keep it clean."

"Wrap 'em up," curtly returned Miss Polly Dawson.

Mrs. Duff was proceeding to do so, when some tall thin form, bearing a large bundle, entered the shop in a fluster. It was Mrs. Peckaby. She sat herself down on the only stool the shop contained, and let the bundle slip to the floor.

"Give a body leave to rest a bit, Mother Duff! I be turned a'most inside out."

"What's the matter?" asked Mrs. Duff, while Polly Dawson surveyed her with a stare.

"There's a white cow in the pound. I can't tell ye the turn it give me, coming sudden upon it. I thought nothing less, at first glance, but it was the white quadruple."

"What! hasn't that there white donkey come yet?" demanded Polly Dawson; who, in conjunction with sundry others of her age and sex in the village, was not sparing of her free remarks to Mrs. Peckaby on the subject, thereby aggravating that lady considerably.

"You hold your tongue, Polly Dawson, and don't be brazen, if you can help it," rebuked Mrs. Peckaby. "I was so took aback for the minute, that I couldn't neither stir nor speak," she resumed to Mrs. Duff. "But when I found it was nothing but a old strayed wretch of a pounded cow, I a'most dropped with the disappointment. So I thought I'd come back here and take a rest. Where's Dan?"

"Dan's out," answered Mrs. Duff.

"Is he? I thought he might have took this parcel down to Sykes's, and saved me the sight o' that pound again and the deceiver in it. It's just my luck!"

"Dan's gone up to Verner's Pride," continued Mrs. Duff. "That fine French madmizel, as rules there, come down for some trifles this evening, and took him home with her to carry the parcel. It's time he was back, though, and more nor time. 'Twasn't bigger, neither, nor a farthing bun, but 'twas too big for her. Isn't it a-getting the season for you to think of a new gownd, Mrs. Peckaby?" resumed Mother Duff, returning to business. "I have got some beautiful winter stuffs in."

"I hope the only new gownd as I shall want till I gets to New Jerusalem, is the purple one I've got prepared for it," replied Mrs. Peckaby. "I don't think the journey's far off. I had a dream last night as I saw a great crowd o' people dressed in white, a-coming out to meet me. I look upon it as it's a token that I shall soon be there."

"I wouldn't go out to that there New Jerusalem if ten white donkeys come to fetch me!" cried Polly Dawson, tossing her head with scorn. "It is a nice place, by all that I have heard! Them saints—"

A most appalling interruption. Snorting, moaning, sobbing, his breath coming in gasps, his hair standing up on end, his eyes starting, and his face ghastly, there burst in upon them Master Dan Duff. That he was in the very height of terror, there could be no mistaking. To add to the confusion, he flung his arms out as he came in, and his hand caught one of the side panes of glass in the bow window and shattered it, the pieces falling amongst the displayed wares. Dan leaped in, caught hold of his mother with a spasmodic howl, and fell down on some bundles in a corner of the small shop.

Mrs. Duff was dragged down with him. She soon extricated herself, and stared at the boy in very astonishment. However inclined to play tricks out of doors, Mr. Dan never ventured to play them, in. Polly Dawson stared. Susan Peckaby, forgetting New Jerusalem for once, sprang off her stool and stared. But that his terror was genuine, and Mrs. Duff saw that it was, Dan had certainly been treated then to that bugbear of his domestic life—a "basting."

"What has took you now?" sharply demanded Mrs. Duff, partly in curiosity, partly in wrath.

"I see'd a dead man," responded Dan, and he forthwith fell into convulsions.

They shook him, they pulled him, they pinched him. One laid hold of his head, another of his feet; but, make nothing of him, could they. The boy's face was white, his hands and arms were twitching, and froth was gathering on his lips. By this time the shop was full.

"Run across, one of you," cried the mother, turning her face to the crowd, "and see if you can find Mr. Jan Verner."

CHAPTER XLIX

Jan Verner was turning in at his own door—the surgery—at a swinging pace. Jan's natural pace was a deliberate one; but Jan found so much to do, now he was alone in the business, that he had no resource but to move at the rate of a steam engine. Otherwise he would never have got through his day's work. Jan had tried one assistant, who had proved to be more plague than profit, and Jan was better without him. Master Cheese, promoted now to tail-coats and turn-up collars, was coming on, and could attend to trifling cases. Master Cheese wished to be promoted also to "Mister" Cheese; but he remained obstinately excessively short, and people would still call him "Master." He appeared to grow in breadth instead of height, and underwent, in consequence, a perpetual inward mortification. Jan would tell him he should eat less and walk more; but the advice was not taken.

Jan Verner was turning into the surgery at a swinging pace, and came in violent contact with Master Cheese, who was coming out at another sharp pace. Jan rubbed his chest, and Cheese his head.

"I say, Jan," said he, "can't you look where your going?"

"Can't you look?" returned Jan. "Where are you off to?"

"There's something the matter at Duff's. About a dozen came here in a body, wanting you. Bob says Dan Duff was dying."

Jan turned his eyes on Bob, the surgery-boy. Bob answered the look—

"It's what they said, sir. They said as Dan Duff was a-dying and a-frothing at the mouth. It's about five minutes ago, sir."

"Did you go over?" asked Jan of Cheese. "I saw a crowd round Mrs. Duff's door."

"No, I didn't. I am going now. I was indoors, having my supper."

"Then you need not trouble yourself," returned Jan. "Stop where you are, and digest your supper."

He, Jan, was speeding off, when a fresh deputation arrived. Twenty anxious faces at the least, all in a commotion, their tongues going together. "Dan was frothing dreadful, and his legs was twitchin' like one in the epilepsies."

"What has caused it?" asked Jan. "I saw him well enough an hour or two ago."

"He see a dead man, sir; as it's said. We can't come to the bottom of it, 'cause of his not answering no questions. He be too bad, he be."

"He did see a dead man," put in Polly Dawson, who made one of the deputation, and was proud of being able to add her testimony to the asserted fact. "Leastways, he said he did. I was a-buying some silk, sir, in at Mother Duff's shop, and Susan Peckaby was in there too, she was, a-talking rubbish about her white donkey, when Dan flounders in upon us in a state not to be told, a-frightening of us dreadful, and a-smashing in the winder with his arm. And he said he'd seen a dead man."

Jan could not make sense of the tale. There was nobody lying dead in Deerham, that he knew of. He pushed the crowd round the door right and left to get space to enter. The shop was pretty full already, but numbers pushed in after Jan. Dan had been carried into the kitchen at the back of the shop, and was laid upon the floor, a pillow under his head. The kitchen was more crowded than the shop; there was not breathing space; and room could hardly be found for Jan.

The shop was Mrs. Duff's department. If she chose to pack it full of people to the ceiling, it was her affair: but Jan made the kitchen, where the boy lay, his.

"What's the matter with him, sir?" was the eager question to Jan, the moment he had cast his eyes on the invalid.

"I may be able to ascertain as soon as I have elbow room," replied Jan. "Suppose you give it me. Mrs. Duff may stop, but nobody else."

Jan's easy words carried authority in their tone, and the company turned tail and began to file out.

"Couldn't you do with me in, as well as his mother, sir?" asked Susan Peckaby. "I was here when he came in, I was; and I knowed what it was a'most afore he spoke. He have been frightened by that thing in the pound. Only a few minutes afore, it had turned my inside almost out."

"No, I can't," answered Jan. "I must have the room clear. Perhaps I shall send away his mother."

"I should ha' liked to know for sure," meekly observed Susan Peckaby, preparing to resign herself to her fate. "I hope you'll ask him, sir, when he comes to, whether it were not that thing in the pound as frightened him. I took it for some'at else, more's the grief! but it looks, for all the world, like a ghost in the moonlight."

"What is in the pound?" demanded Jan.

"It's a white cow," responded Susan Peckaby. "And it strikes me as it's Farmer Blow's. He have got a white cow, you know, sir, like he have got a white pony, and they be always a-giving me a turn, one or t'other of 'em. I'd like old Blow to be indicted for a pest, I would! a-keeping white animals to upset folks. It's not a week ago that I met that cow in the road at dusk—strayed through a gap in the hedge. Tiresome beast, a-causing my heart to leap into my mouth!"

"If Dan have put himself into this state, and done all this damage, through nothing but seeing of a white cow, won't I baste him!" emphatically rejoined Mrs. Duff.

Jan at length succeeded in getting the kitchen clear. But for some time, in spite of all his skill and attention—and he spared neither—he could make no impression upon the unhappy Dan. His mother's bed was made ready for him—Dan himself sharing the accommodation of a dark closet in an ordinary way, in common with his brothers—and Jan carried him up to it. There he somewhat revived, sufficiently to answer a question or two rationally. It must be confessed that Jan felt some curiosity upon the subject; to suppose the boy had been thrown into that state, simply by seeing a white cow in the pound, was ridiculous.

"What frightened you?" asked Jan.

"I see'd a dead man," answered the boy. "Oh, lor!"

"Well?" said Jan, with composure, "he didn't eat you. What is there in a dead man to be alarmed at? I have seen scores—handled 'em too. What dead man was it?"

The boy pulled the bed-clothes over him, and moaned. Jan pulled them down again.

"Of course you can't tell! There's no dead man in Deerham. Was it in the churchyard?"

"No."

"Was it in the pound?" asked Jan triumphantly, thinking he had got it right this time.

"No."

The answer was an unexpected one.

"Where was it, then?"

"Oh-o-o-o-oh!" moaned the boy, beginning to shake and twitch again.

"Now, Dan Duff, this won't do," said Jan. "Tell me quietly what you saw, and where you saw it."

"I see'd a dead man," reiterated Dan Duff. And it appeared to be all he was capable of saying.

"You saw a white cow on its hind legs," returned Jan. "That's what you saw. I am surprised at you, Dan Duff. I should have thought you more of a man."

Whether the reproof overcame Master Duff's nerves again, or the remembrance of the "dead man," certain it was, that he relapsed into a state which rendered it imprudent, in Jan's opinion, to continue for the present the questioning. One more only he put—for a sudden thought crossed him, which induced it.

"Was it in the copse at Verner's Pride?"

"'Twas at the Willow Pool; he was a-walking round it. Oh-o-o-o-o-oh!"

Jan's momentary fear was dispelled. A night or two back there had been a slight affray between Lionel's gamekeeper and some poachers: and the natural doubts arose whether anything fresh of the same nature had taken place. If so, Dan Duff might have come upon one of them lying, dead or wounded. The words—"walking round the pool"—did away with this. For the present, Jan departed.

But, if Dan's organs of disclosure are for the present in abeyance, there's no reason why we should not find out what we can for ourselves. You may be very sure that Deerham would not fail to do it.

The French madmizel—as Mrs. Duff styled her, meaning, of course, Mademoiselle Benoite—had called in at Mrs. Duff's shop and made a purchase. It consisted—if you are curious to know—of pins and needles, and a staylace. Not a parcel that would have weighed her down, certainly, had she borne it herself; but it pleased her to demand that Dan should carry it for her. This she did, partly to display her own consequence, chiefly that she might have a companion home, for Mademoiselle Benoite did not relish the walk alone by moonlight to Verner's Pride. Of course young Dan was at the beck and call of Mrs. Duff's customers, that being, as mademoiselle herself might have said, his spécialité. Whether a customer bought a parcel that would have filled a van, or one that might have gone inside a penny thimble, Master Dan was equally expected to be in readiness to carry the purchase to its destination at night, if called upon. Master Dan's days being connected now with the brick-fields, where his spécialité appeared to be, to put layers of clay upon his clothes.

Accordingly, Dan started with Mademoiselle Benoite. She had been making' purchases at other places, which she had brought away with her—shoes, stationery, and various things, all of which were handed over to the porter, Dan. They arrived at Verner's Pride in safety, and Dan was ordered to follow her in, and deposit his packages on the table of the apartment that was called the steward's room.

"One, two, three, four," counted Mademoiselle Benoite, with French caution, lest he should have dropped any by the way. "You go outside now, Dan, and I bring you something from my pocket for your trouble."

Dan returned outside accordingly, and stood gazing at the laundry windows, which were lighted up. Mademoiselle dived in her pocket, took something from thence, which she screwed carefully up in a bit of newspaper, and handed it to Dan. Dan had watched the process in a glow of satisfaction, believing it could be nothing less than a silver sixpence. How much more it might prove, Dan's aspirations were afraid to anticipate.

"There!" said Mademoiselle, when she put it into his hand. "Now you can go back to your mother."

She shut the door in his face somewhat inhospitably, and Dan eagerly opened his cadeau. It contained— two lumps of fine white sugar.

"Mean old cat!" burst forth Dan. "If it wasn't that mother 'ud baste me, I'd never bring a parcel for her again, not if she bought up the shop. Wouldn't I like to give all the French a licking?"

Munching his sugar wrathfully, he passed across the yard, and out at the gate. There he hesitated which way home he should take, as he had hesitated that far gone evening, when he had come up upon the errand to poor Rachel Frost. More than four years had elapsed since then, and Dan was now fourteen; but he was a young and childish boy of his age, which might be owing to the fact of his being so kept under by his mother.

"I have a good mind to trick her!" soliloquised he; alluding, it must be owned, to that revered mother. "She wouldn't let me go out to Bill Hook's to-night; though I told her as it wasn't for no nonsense I wanted to see him, but about that there gray ferret. I will, too! I'll go back the field way, and cut down there. She'll be none the wiser."

Now, this was really a brave resolve for Dan Duff. The proposed road would take him past the Willow Pool; and he, in common with other timorous spirits, had been given to eschew that place at night, since the end of Rachel. It must be supposed that the business touching the gray ferret was one of importance, for Dan to lose sight of his usual fears, and turn towards that pool.

Not once, from that time to this, had Dan Duff taken this road alone at night. From that cause probably, no sooner had he now turned into the lane, than he began to think of Rachel. He would have preferred to think of anything else in the world; but he found, as many others are obliged to find, that unpleasant thoughts cannot be driven away at will. It was not so much that the past night of misfortune was present to him, as that he feared to meet the ghost of Rachel.

He went on, glancing furtively on all sides, his face and his hair growing hotter and hotter. There, on his right, was the gate through which he had entered the field to give chase to the supposed cat; there, on the left, was the high hedge; before him lay the length of lane traversed that evening by the tall man, who had remained undiscovered from that hour to this. Dan could see nothing now; no tall man, no cat; even the latter might have proved a welcome intruder. He glanced up at the calm sky, at the bright moon riding overhead. The night was perfectly still; a lovely night, could Dan only have kept the ghosts out of his mind.

Suddenly a horse, in the field on the other side the hedge, set up a loud neigh, right in Dan's ear. Coming thus unexpectedly, it startled Dan above everything. He half resolved to go back, and turned round and looked the way he had come. But he thought of the gray ferret, and plucked up some courage and went on again, intending, the moment he came in sight of the Willow Pool, to make a dash past at his utmost speed.

The intention was not carried out. Clambering over the gate which led to the enclosure, a more ready way to Dan than opening it, he was brought within view of the pool. There it was, down in the dreary lower part, near the trees. The pool itself was distinct enough, lying to the right, and Dan involuntarily looked towards it. Not to have saved his life, could Dan have helped looking.

Susan Peckaby had said to Jan, that her heart leaped into her mouth at the sight of the white cow in the pound. Poor Dan Duff might have said that his heart leaped right out of him, at sight now of the Willow Pool. For there was some shadowy figure moving round it.

Dan stood powerless. But for the gate behind him he would have turned and ran; to scramble back over that, his limbs utterly refused. The delay caused him, in spite of his fear, to discern the very obvious fact, that the shadowy figure was not that of a woman habited in white—as the orthodox ghost of Rachel ought to have been—but a man's, wearing dark clothes. There flashed into Dan's remembrance the frequent nightly visits of Robin Frost to the pond, bringing with it a ray of relief.

Robin had been looked upon as little better than a lunatic since the misfortune; but, to Dan Duff, he appeared in that moment worth his weight in gold. Robin's companionship was as good as anybody's to ward off the ghostly fears, and Dan set off, full speed, towards him. To go right up to the pond would take him a few yards out of his way to Bill Hook's. What of that? To exchange words with a human tongue, Dan, in that moment of superstitious fright, would have gone as many miles.

He had run more than half the intervening distance, when he brought himself to a halt. It had become evident to Dan's sight that it was not Robin Frost. Whoever it might be, he was a head and shoulders taller than Robin; and Dan moved up more quietly, his eyes strained forward in the moonlight. A suspicion came over him that it might be Mr. Verner; Dan could not, at the moment, remember anybody else so tall, unless it was Mr. Jan. The figure stood now with its back to him; apparently gazing into the pool. Dan advanced with slow steps; if it was Mr. Verner, he would not presume to intrude upon him; but when he came nearly close, he saw that it bore no resemblance to the figure of Mr. Verner. Slowly, glidingly, the figure turned round; turned its face right upon Dan, full in the rays of the bright moon; and the most awful yell you ever heard went forth upon the still night air.

It came from Dan Duff. What could have been its meaning? Did he think he saw the ghost, which he had been looking out for the last half-hour—poor Rachel's?—saw it beyond this figure which had turned upon him? Dan alone knew. That he had fallen into the most appalling terror, was certain. His eyes were starting, the drops of perspiration poured off him, and his hair rose up on end. The figure—just as if it had possessed neither sight nor hearing, neither sense nor sympathy for human sound—glided noiselessly away; and Dan went yelling on.

Towards home now. All thought of Bill Hook and the gray ferret was gone. Away he tore, the nearest way, which took him past the pound. He never saw the white cow: had the cow been a veritable ghost, Dan had not seen it then. The yells subsiding into moans, and the perspiration into fever heat, he gained his mother's, and broke the window, as you have heard, in passing in.

Such were the particulars; but as yet they were not known. The first person to elicit them was Roy the bailiff.

After Jan Verner had departed, saying he should be back by and by, and giving Mrs. Duff strict orders to keep the boy quiet, to allow nobody near him but herself, and, above all, no questioning, Mrs. Duff quitted him, "that he might get a bit o' sleep," she said. In point of fact, Mrs. Duff was burning to exercise her gossiping powers with those other gossipers below. To them she descended; and found Susan Peckaby holding forth upon the subject of the white cow.

"You be wrong, Susan Peckaby," said Mrs. Duff, "It warn't the white cow at all; Dan warn't a-nigh the pound. He told Mr. Jan so."

"Then what was it?" returned Susan Peckaby.

One of the present auditors was Roy the bailiff. He had only recently pushed in, and had stood listening in silence, taking note of the various comments and opinions. As silently, he moved behind the group, and was stealing up the stairs. Mrs. Duff placed herself before him.

"Where be you a-going, Mr. Roy? Mr. Jan said as not a soul was to go a-nigh him to disturb him with talk. A nice thing, it 'ud be, for it to settle on his brain!"

"I ain't a-going to disturb him," returned Roy. "I have seen something myself to-night that is not over-kind. I'd like to get a inkling if it's the same that has frightened him."

"Was it in the pound?" eagerly asked Mrs. Peckaby.

"The pound be smoked!" was the polite answer vouchsafed by Roy. "Thee'll go mad with th' white donkey one of these days."

"There can't be any outlet to it, but one," observed Mrs. Chuff, the blacksmith's wife, giving her opinion in a loud key. "He must ha' seen Rachel Frost's ghost."

"Have you been and seen that to-night, Mr. Roy?" cried Susan Peckaby.

"Maybe I have, and maybe I haven't," was Roy's satisfactory reply, "All I say is, I've seen something that I'd rather not have seen; something that 'ud have sent all you women into fits. 'Twarn't unlike Rachel, and 'twere clothed in white. I'll just go and take a look at Dan, Mother Duff. No fear o' my disturbing him."

Mother Duff, absorbed with her visitors, allowed him to go on without further impediment. The first thing Roy did upon getting upstairs, was to shut the chamber door; the next, to arouse and question the suffering Dan. Roy succeeded in getting from him the particulars already related, and a little more; insomuch that Dan mentioned the name which the dead man had borne in life.

Roy sat and stared at him after the revelation, keeping silence. It may have been that he was digesting the wonder; it may have been that he was deliberating upon his answer.

"Look you here, Dan Duff," said he, by and by, holding the shaking boy by the shoulder. "You just breathe that name again to living mortal, and see if you don't get hung up by the neck for it. 'Twas nothing but Rachel's ghost. Them ghosts takes the form of anything that it pleases, 'em to take; whether it's a dead man's, or whether it's a woman's, what do they care? There's no ghost but Rachel's 'ud be a-hovering over that pond. Where be your senses gone, not to know that?"

Poor Dan's senses appeared to be wandering somewhere yet; they certainly were not in him. He shook and moaned, and finally fell into the same sort of stupor as before. Roy could make nothing further of him, and he went down.

"Well," said he to the assemblage, "I've got it out of him. The minute he saw me, he stretched his arm out—'Mr. Roy,' says he, 'I'm sick to unburden myself to somebody'; and he up and told. He's fell off again now, like one senseless, and I question if he'd remember telling me."

"And what was it? And what was it?" questioned the chorus. "Rachel's ghost?"

"It was nothing less, you may be sure," replied Roy, his tone expressive of contempt that they should have thought it could be anything less. "The young idiot must take and go by the pond on this bright night, and in course he saw it. Right again' his face, he says, it appeared; there wasn't no mistaking of it. It was a-walking round and round the pool."

Considerable shivering in the assembly. Polly Dawson, who was on its outskirts, shrieked, and pushed into its midst, as if it were a safer place. The women drew into a closer circle, and glanced round at an imaginary ghost behind their shoulders.

"Was it that as you saw yourself to-night, Mr. Roy?"

"Never mind me," was Roy's answer. "I ain't one to be startled to death at sight of a sperit, like boys and women is. I had my pill in what I saw, I can tell ye. And my advice to ye all is, keep within your own doors after nightfall."

Without further salutation, Roy departed. The women, with one accord, began to make for the staircase. To contemplate one who had just been in actual contact with the ghost—which some infidels had persistently asserted throughout was nothing but a myth—was a sight not to be missed. But they were driven back again. With a succession of yells, the like of which had never been heard, save at the Willow Pond that night, Dan appeared leaping down upon them, his legs naked and his short shirt flying behind him. To be left alone, a prey to ghosts or their remembrances, was more than the boy, with his consciousness upon him, could bear. The women yelled also, and fell back one upon another; not a few being under the impression that it was the ghost itself.

What was to be done with him? Before the question was finally decided, Mrs. Bascroft, the landlady of the Plough and Harrow, who had made one of the company, went off to her bar, whence she hastened back again with an immense hot tumbler, three parts brandy, one part water, the whole of which was poured down the throat of Dan.

"There's nothing like it for restoring folks after a fright," remarked Mrs. Bascroft.

The result of the dose was, that Dan Duff subsided into a state of real stupor, so profound and prolonged that even Jan began to doubt whether he would awake from it.

CHAPTER L

MR AND MRS VERNER

Lionel Verner sat over his morning letters, bending upon one of them a perplexed brow. A claim which he had settled the previous spring—at least, which he believed had been settled—was now forwarded to him again. That there was very little limit to his wife's extravagance, he had begun to know.

In spite of Sibylla's extensive purchases made in Paris at the time of their marriage, she had contrived by the end of the following winter to run up a tolerable bill at her London milliner's. When they had gone to town in the early spring, this bill was presented to Lionel. Four hundred and odd pounds. He gave Sibylla a cheque for its amount, and some gentle, loving words of admonition at the same time—not to spend him out of house and home.

A second account from the same milliner had arrived this morning—been delivered to him with other London letters. Why it should have been sent to him, and not to his wife, he was unable to tell—unless it was meant as a genteel hint that payment would be acceptable. The whole amount was for eleven hundred pounds, but part of this purported to be "To bill delivered"—four hundred and odd pounds—the precise sum which Lionel believed to have been paid. Eleven hundred pounds! and all the other claims upon him! No wonder he sat with a bent brow. If things went on at this rate, Verner's Pride would come to the hammer.

He rose, the account in his hand, and proceeded to his wife's dressing-room. Among other habits, Sibylla was falling into that of indolence, scarcely ever rising to breakfast now. Or, if she rose, she did not come down. Mademoiselle Benoite came whisking out of a side room as he was about to enter.

"Madame's toilette is not made, sir," cried she, in a tart tone, as if she thought he had no right to enter.

"What of that?" returned Lionel. And he went in.

Just as she had got out of bed, save that she had a blue quilted silk dressing-gown thrown on, and her feet were thrust into blue quilted slippers, sat Sibylla, before a good fire. She leaned in an easy-chair, reading; a miniature breakfast service of Sèvres china, containing chocolate, on a low table at her side. Some people like to read a word or two of the Bible, as soon as conveniently may be, after getting up in the morning. Was that good book the study of Sibylla? Not at all. Her study was a French novel. By dint of patience, and the assistance of Mademoiselle Benoite in the hard words and complicated sentences, Mrs. Verner contrived to arrive tolerably well at its sense.

"Good gracious!" she exclaimed, when Lionel appeared, "are you not gone shooting with the rest?"

"I did not go this morning," he answered, closing the door and approaching her.

"Have you taken breakfast?" she asked.

"Breakfast has been over a long while. Were I you, Sibylla, when I had guests staying in the house, I should try and rise to breakfast with them."

"Oh, you crafty Lionel! To save you the trouble of presiding. Thank you," she continued good-humouredly, "I am more comfortable here. What is this story about a ghost? The kitchen's in a regular commotion, Benoite says."

"To what do you allude?" asked Lionel.

"Dan Duff is dying, or dead," returned Sibylla. "Benoite was in Deerham last night, and brought him home to carry her parcels. In going back again, he saw, as he says, Rachel Frost's ghost, and it terrified him out of his senses. Old Roy saw it too, and the news has travelled up here."

Sibylla laughed as she spoke. Lionel looked vexed.

"They are very stupid," he said. "A pity but they kept such stories to themselves. If they were only as quiet as poor Rachel's ghost is, it might be better for some of them."

"Of course you would wish it kept quiet," said Sibylla, in a tone full of significance. "I like to hear of these frights—it is good fun."

He did not fathom in the remotest degree the meaning of her tone. But he had not gone thither to dispute about ghosts.

"Sibylla," he gravely said, putting the open account into her hand, "I have received this bill this morning."

Sibylla ran her eyes over it with indifference; first at the bill's head, to see whence it came, next at its sum total.

"What an old cheat! Eleven hundred pounds! I am sure I have not had the half."

Lionel pointed to the part "bill delivered." "Was that not paid in the spring?"

"How can I recollect?" returned Sibylla, speaking as carelessly as before.

"I think you may recollect if you try. I gave you a cheque for the amount."

"Oh, yes, I do recollect now. It has not been paid."

"But, my dear, I say I gave the cheque for it."

"I cashed the cheque myself. I wanted some money just then. You can't think how fast money goes in London, Lionel."

The avowal proved only what he suspected. Nevertheless it hurt him greatly—grieved him to his heart's core. Not so much the spending of the money, as the keeping the fact from him. What a lack of good feeling, of confidence, it proved.

He bent towards her, speaking gently, kindly. Whatever might be her faults to him, her provocations, he could never behave otherwise to her than as a thorough gentleman, a kind husband.

"It was not right to use that cheque, Sibylla. It was made out in Madame Lebeau's name, and should have been paid to her. But why did you not tell me?"

Sibylla shrugged her shoulders in place of answer. She had picked up many such little national habits of Mademoiselle Benoite's. Very conspicuous just then was the upright line on Lionel's brow.

"The amount altogether is, you perceive, eleven hundred pounds," he continued.

"Yes," said Sibylla. "She's a cheat, that Madame Lebeau. I shall make Benoite write her a French letter, and tell her so."

"It must be paid. But it is a great deal of money. I cannot continue to pay these large sums, Sibylla. I have not the money to do it with."

"Not the money! When you know you are paying heaps for Lady Verner! Before you tell me not to spend, you should cease supplying her."

Lionel's very brow flushed. "My mother has a claim upon me only in a degree less than you have," he gravely said. "Part of the revenues of Verner's Pride ought to have been hers years ago; and they were not."

"If my husband had lived—if he had left me a little child—Verner's Pride would have been his and mine, and never yours at all."

"Hush, Sibylla! You don't know how these allusions hurt me," he interrupted, in a tone of intense pain.

"They are true," said Sibylla.

"But not—forgive me, my dear, for saying it—not the less unseemly."

"Why do you grumble at me, then?"

"I do not grumble," he answered in a kind tone. "Your interests are mine, Sibylla, and mine are yours. I only tell you the fact—and a fact it is—that our income will not stand these heavy calls upon it. Were I to show you how much you have spent in dress since we were married—what with Paris, London, and Heartburg—the sum total would frighten you."

"You should not keep the sum total," resentfully spoke Sibylla. "Why do you add it up?"

"I must keep my accounts correctly. My uncle taught me that."

"I am sure he did not teach you to grumble at me," she rejoined. "I look upon Verner's Pride as mine, more than yours; if it had not been for the death of my husband, you would never have had it."

Inexpressibly vexed—vexed beyond the power to answer, for he would not trust himself to answer—Lionel prepared to quit the room. He began to wish he had not had Verner's Pride, if this was to be its domestic peace. Sibylla petulantly threw the French book from her lap upon the table, and it fell down with its page open.

Lionel's eyes caught its title, and a flush, not less deep than the preceding flush, darkened his brow. He laid his open palm upon the page with an involuntary movement, as if he would guard it from the eyes of his wife. That she should be reading that notorious work!

"Where did you get this?" he cried. "It Is not a fit book for you."

"There's nothing-the matter with the book as far as I have gone."

"Indeed you must not read it! Pray don't, Sibylla! You will be sorry for it afterwards."

"How do you know it is not a fit book?"

"Because I have read it."

"There! You have read it! And you would like to deny the pleasure to me! Don't say you are never selfish."

"Sibylla! What is fit for me to read may be most unfit for you. I read the book when I was a young man; I would not read it now. Is it Benoite's?" he inquired, seeing the name in the first page.

"Yes, it is."

Lionel closed the book. "Promise me, Sibylla, that you will not attempt to read more of it. Give it her back at once, and tell her to send it out of the house, or to keep it under lock and key while it remains within it."

Sibylla hesitated.

"Is it so very hard a promise?" he tenderly asked. "I would do a great deal more for you."

"Yes, Lionel, I will promise," she replied, a better feeling coming over her. "I will give it her back now. Benoite!"

She called loudly. Benoite heard, and came in.

"Mr. Verner says this is not a nice book. You may take it away."

Mademoiselle Benoite advanced with a red face, and took the book.

"Have you any more such books?" inquired Lionel, looking at her.

"No, sir, I not got one other," hardily replied she.

"Have the goodness to put this one away. Had your mistress been aware of the nature of the book, she had not suffered you to produce it."

Mademoiselle went away, her skirts jerking. Lionel bent down to his wife.

"You know that it pains me to find fault, Sibylla," he fondly whispered. "I have ever your welfare and happiness at heart. More anxiously, I think, than you have mine."

CHAPTER LI

COMMOTION IN DEERHAM

Lionel Verner was strolling out later in the day, and met the shooting-party coming home. After congratulating them on their good sport, he was turning home with them, when the gamekeeper intimated that he should be glad to speak a word to him in private. Upon which, Lionel let the gentlemen go on.

"What is it, Broom?" asked he.

"I'm much afeared, sir, if thing's are not altered, that there'll be murder committed some night," answered Broom, without circumlocution.

"I hope not," replied Lionel. "Are you and the poachers again at issue?"

"It's not about the poachers, hang 'em! It's about Robin Frost, sir. What on earth have come to him I can't conceive. This last few nights he have took to prowling out with a gun. He lays himself down in the copse, or a ditch, or the open field—no matter where—and there he stops, on the watch, with his gun always pointed."

"On the watch for what?" asked Lionel.

"He best knows himself, sir. He's going quite cracked, it's my belief; he have been half-way to it this long while. Sometimes he's trailing through the brushwood on all fours, the gun ever pointed; but mostly he's posted on the watch. He'll get shot for a poacher, or some of the poachers will shoot him, as sure as it's a gun that he carries."

"What can be his motive?" mused Lionel.

"I'm inclined to think, sir, though he is Robin Frost, that he's after the birds," boldly returned Broom.

"Then rely upon it that you think wrong, Broom," rebuked Lionel, "Robin Frost would no more go out poaching, than I should go out thieving."

"I saw him trailing along last night in the moonlight, sir. I saw his old father come up and talk to him, urging him to go home, as it seemed to me. But he couldn't get him; and the old man had to hobble back without Robin. Robin stopped in his cold berth on the ground."

"I did not think old Matthew was capable of going out at night."

"He did last night, sir; that's for certain. It was not far; only down away by the brick-kilns. There's a tale going abroad that Dan Duff was sent into mortal fright by seeing something that he took to be Rachel's ghost; my opinion is, that he must have met old Frost in his white smock-frock, and took him for a ghost. The moon did cast an uncommon white shade last night. Though old Frost wasn't a-nigh the Willow Pool, nor Robin neither, and that's where they say Dan Duff got his fright. Formerly, Robin was always round that pool, but lately he has changed his beat. Anyhow, sir, perhaps you'd be so good as drop a warning to Robin of the risk he runs. He may mind you."

"I will," said Lionel.

The gamekeeper touched his hat, and walked away. Lionel considered that he might as well give Robin the warning then; and he turned towards the village. Before fairly entering it, he had met twenty talkative persons, who gave him twenty different versions of the previous night's doings, touching Dan Duff.

Mrs. Duff was at her door when Lionel went by. She generally was at her door, unless she was serving customers. He stopped to accost her.

"What's the truth of this affair, Mrs. Duff?" asked he. "I have heard many reports of it?"

Mrs. Duff gave as succinct an account as it was in her nature to give. Some would have told it in a third of the time: but Lionel had patience; he was in no particular hurry.

"I have been one of them to laugh at the ghost, sir a-saying that it never was Rachel's, and that it never walked," she added. "But I'll never do so again. Roy, he see it, as well as Dan."

"Oh! he saw it, too, did he," responded Lionel, with a good-natured smile of mockery. "Mrs. Duff, you ought to be too old to believe in ghosts," he more seriously resumed. "I am sure Roy is, whatever he may choose to say."

"If it was no ghost, sir, what could have put our Dan into that awful fright? Mr. Jan doesn't know as he'll overget it at all. He's a-lying without a bit of conscientiousness on my bed, his eyes shut, and his breath a-coming hard."

"Something frightened him, no doubt. The belief in poor Rachel's ghost has been so popular, that every night fright is attributed to that. Who was it went into a fainting fit in the road, fancying Rachel's ghost was walking down upon them; and it proved afterwards to have been only the miller's man with a sack of flour on his back?"

"Oh, that!" slightingly returned Mrs. Duff. "It was that stupid Mother Grind, before they went off with the Mormons. She'd drop at her shadder, sir, she would."

"So would some of the rest of you," said Lionel. "I am sorry to hear that Dan is so ill."

"Mr. Jan's in a fine way over him, sir. Mrs. Bascroft gave him just a taste of weak brandy and water, and Mr. Jan, when he come to know it, said we might just as well have give him pison; and he'd not answer for his life or his reason. A pretty thing it'll be for Deerham, if there's more lives to be put in danger, now the ghost have took to walk again! Mr. Bourne called in just now, sir, to learn the rights of it. He went up and see Dan; but nothing could he make of him. Would you be pleased to go up and take a look at him, sir?"

Lionel declined, and wished Mrs. Duff good-day.

He could do the boy no good, and had no especial wish to look at him, although he had been promoted to the notoriety of seeing a ghost. A few steps farther he encountered Jan.

"What is it that's the matter with the boy?" asked Lionel.

"He had a good fright; there's no doubt about that," replied Jan. "Saw a white cow on its hind legs, it's my belief. That wouldn't have been much. The boy would have been all right by now, but the women drenched him with brandy, and made him stupidly drunk. He'll be better this evening. I can't stop, Lionel; I am run off my legs to-day."

The commotion in the village increased as the evening approached. Jan knew that young Dan would be well—save for any little remembrance of the fright which might remain—when the fumes of the brandy had gone off; But he wisely kept his own counsel, and let the public think he was in danger. Otherwise, a second instalment of the brandy might have been administered behind Jan's back. To have a boy dying of fright from seeing a ghost was a treat in the marvellous line, which Deerham had never yet enjoyed. There had been no agitation like unto it, since the day of poor Rachel Frost.

Brave spirits, some of them! They volunteered to go out and meet the apparition. As twilight approached you could not have got into Mrs. Duff's shop, for there was the chief gathering. Arguments were being used to prove that, according to all logic, if a ghost appeared one night, it was safe to appear a second.

"Who'll speak up to go and watch for it?" asked Mrs. Duff. "I can't. I can't leave Dan. Sally Green's a-sitting up by him now; for Mr. Jan says if he's left again, he shall hold me responsible. It don't stand to reason as I can leave Sally Green in charge of the shop, though I can leave her a bit with Dan. Not but what I'd go alone to the pond, and stop there; I haven't got no fear."

It singularly happened that those who were kept at home by domestic or other duties, had no fear; they, to hear them talk, would rather have enjoyed an encounter solus with the ghost, than not. Those who could plead no home engagement professed themselves willing to undertake the expedition in company; but freely avowed they would not go alone for the world.

"Come! who'll volunteer?" asked Mrs. Duff. "It 'ud be a great satisfaction to see the form it appears in, and have that set at rest. Dan, he'll never be able to tell, by the looks of him now."

"I'll go for one," said bold Mrs. Bascroft. "And them as joins me shall each have a good stiff tumbler of some'at hot afore starting, to prime 'em again' the cold."

Whether it was the brave example set, or whether it was the promise accompanying it, certain it was, that there was no lack of volunteers now. A good round dozen started, filling up the Plough and Harrow bar, as Mrs. Bascroft dealt out her treat with no niggard hand.

"What's a-doing now?" asked Bascroft, a stupid-looking man with red hair combed straight down his forehead, and coloured shirt-sleeves, surveying the inroad on his premises with surprise.

"Never you mind," sharply reproved his better half. "These ladies is my visitors, and if I choose to stand treat round, what's that to you? You takes your share o' liquor, Bascroft."

Bascroft was not held in very great estimation by the ladies generally, and they turned their backs upon him.

"We are a-going out to see the ghost, if you must know, Bascroft," said Susan Peckaby, who made one of the volunteers.

Bascroft stared. "What a set of idiots you must be!" grunted he. "Mr. Jan says as Dan Duff see nothing but a white cow; he told me so hisself. Be you a-thinking to meet that there other white animal on your road, Mrs. Peckaby?"

"Perhaps I am," tartly returned Mrs. Peckaby.

"One 'ud think so. You can't want to go out to meet ghostesses; you be a-going out to your saints at New Jerusalem. I'd whack that there donkey for being so slow, when he did come, if I was you."

Hastening away from Bascroft and his aggravating tongue, the expedition, having drained their tumblers, filed out. Down by the pound—relieved now of its caged inmate—went they, on towards the

Willow Pond. The tumblers had made them brave. The night was light, as the preceding one had been; the ground looked white, as if with frost, and the air was cold. The pond in view, they halted, and took a furtive glance, beginning to feel somewhat chill. So far as these half glances allowed them to judge, there appeared to be nothing near to it, nothing upon its brink.

"It's of no good marching right up to it," said Mrs. Jones, the baker's wife. "The ghost mightn't come at all, if it saw all us there. Let's get inside the trees."

Mrs. Jones meant inside the grove of trees. The proposition was most acceptable, and they took up their position, the pond in view, peeping out, and conversing in a whisper. By and by they heard the church clock strike eight.

"I wish it'ud make haste," exclaimed Susan Peckaby, with some impatience. "I don't never like to be away from home long together, for fear of that there blessed white animal arriving."

"He'd wait, wouldn't he?" sarcastically rejoined Polly Dawson. "He'd—"

A prolonged hush—sh—sh! from the rest restored silence. Something was rustling the trees at a distance. They huddled closer together, and caught hold one of another.

Nothing appeared. The alarm went off. And they waited, without result, until the clock struck nine. The artificial strength within them had cooled by that time, their ardour had cooled, and they were feeling chill and tired. Susan Peckaby was upon thorns, she said, and urged their departure.

"You can go if you like," was the answer. "Nobody wants to keep you."

Susan Peckaby measured the distance between the pond and the way she had to go, and came to the determination to risk it.

"I'll make a rush for it, I think," said she. "I sha'n't see nothing. For all I know, that quadruple may be right afore our door now. If he—"

Susan Peckaby stopped, her voice subsiding into a shriek. She, and those with her, became simultaneously aware that some white figure was bearing down upon them. The shrieks grew awful.

It proved to be Roy in his white fustian jacket. Roy had never had the privilege of hearing a dozen women shriek in concert before; at least, like this. His loud derisive laugh was excessively aggravating. What with that, what with the fright his appearance had really put them in, they all tore off, leaving some hard words for him; and never stopped to take breath until they burst into the shop of Mrs. Duff.

It was rather an ignominious way of returning, and Mrs. Duff did not spare her comments. If she had went out to meet the ghost, sh'd ha' stopped till the ghost came, she would! Mrs. Jones rejoined that them watched-for ghosts, as she had heered, never did come—which she had said so afore she went out!

Master Dan, considerably recovered, was downstairs then. Rather pale and shaky, and accommodated with a chair and pillow, in front of the kitchen fire. The expedition pressed into the kitchen, and five hundred questions were lavished upon the boy.

"What was it dressed in, Dan? Did you get a good sight of her face, Dan? Did it look just as Rachel used to look? Speak up, Dan."

"It warn't Rachel at all," replied Dan.

This unexpected assertion brought a pause of discomfiture. "He's head ain't right yet," observed Mrs. Duff apologetically; "and that's why I've not asked him nothing."

"Yes, it is right, mother," said Dan. "I never see Rachel last night. I never said as I did."

Another pause—spent in contemplating Dan. "I knowed a case like this, once afore," observed old Miss Till, who carried round the milk to Deerham. "A boy got a fright, and they couldn't bring him to at all. Epsum salts did it at last. Three pints of 'em they give, I think it was, and that brought his mind round."

"It's a good remedy," acquiesced Mrs. Jones. "There's nothing like plenty of Epsum salts for boys. I'd try 'em on him, Mother Duff."

"Dan, dear," said Susan Peckaby insinuatingly—for she had come in along with the rest, ignoring for the moment what might be waiting at her door—"was it in the pound as you saw Rachel's ghost?"

"'Twarn't Rachel's ghost as I did see," persisted Dan.

"Tell us who it was, then?" asked she, humouring him.

The boy answered. But he answered below his breath; as if he scarcely dared to speak the name aloud. His mother partially caught it.

"Whose?" she exclaimed, in a sharp voice, her tone changing. And Dan spoke a little louder.

"It was Mr. Frederick Massingbird's!"

CHAPTER LII

MATTHEW FROST'S NIGHT ENCOUNTER

Old Matthew Frost sat in his room at the back of the kitchen. It was his bedroom and sitting-room combined. Since he had grown feeble, the bustle of the kitchen and of Robin's family disturbed him, and he sat much in his chamber, they frequently taking his dinner in to him.

A thoroughly comfortable arm-chair had Matthew. It had been the gift of Lionel Verner. At his elbow was a small round table, of very dark wood, rubbed to brightness. On that table Matthew's large Bible might generally be found open, and Matthew's spectacled eyes bending over it. But the Bible was closed to-day. He sat in deep thought. His hands clasped upon his stick, something after the manner of old Mr. Verner; and his eyes fixed through the open window at the September sun, as it played on the gooseberry and currant bushes in the cottage garden.

The door opened, and Robin's wife—her hands and arms white, for she was kneading dough—appeared, showing in Lionel; who had come on after his conversation with Mrs. Duff, as you read of in the last chapter; for it is necessary to go back a few hours. One cannot tell two portions of a history at one and the same time. The old man rose, and stood leaning on his stick.

"Sit down, Matthew," said Lionel, in a kindly tone. "Don't let me disturb you." He made him go into his seat again, and took a chair opposite to him.

"The time's gone, sir, for me to stand afore you. That time must go for us all."

"Ay, that it must, Matthew, if we live. I came in to speak to Robin. His wife says she does not know where he is."

"He's here and there and everywhere," was old Matthew's answer. "One never knows how to take him, sir, or when to see him. My late master's bounty to me, sir, is keeping us in comfort, but I often ask Robin what he'll do when I am gone. It gives me many an hour's care, sir. Robin, he don't earn the half of a living now."

"Be easy, Matthew," was Lionel's answer. "I am not sure that the annuity, or part of it, will not be continued to Robin. My uncle left it in my charge to do as I should see fit. I have never mentioned it, even to you; and I think it might be as well for you not to speak of it to Robin. It is to be hoped that he will get steady and hard-working again; were he to hear that there was a chance of his being kept without work, he might never become so."

"The Lord bless my old master!" aspirated Matthew, lifting his hands. "The Lord bless you, sir! There's not many gentlemen would do for us what him and you have."

Lionel bent his head forward, and lowered his voice to a whisper. "Matthew, what is this that I hear, of Robin's going about the grounds at night with a loaded gun?"

Matthew flung up his hands. Not with the reverence of the past minute, but with a gesture of despair. "Heaven knows what he does it for, sir! I'd keep him in; but it's beyond me."

"I know you would. You went yourself after him last night, Broom tells me."

Matthew's eyes fell. He hesitated much in his answer. "I—yes, sir—I—I couldn't get him home. It's a pity."

"You got as far as the brick-kilns, I hear. I was surprised. I don't think you should be out at night, Matthew."

"No, sir, I am not a-going again."

The words this time were spoken readily enough. But, from some cause or other, the old man was evidently embarrassed. His eyes were not lifted, and his clear face had gone red. Lionel searched his imagination for a reason, and could only connect it with his son.

"Matthew," said he, "I am about to ask you a painful question. I hope you will answer it. Is Robin perfectly sane?"

"Ay, sir, as sane as I am. Unsettled he is, ever dwelling on poor Rachel, ever thinking of revenge; but his senses be as much his as they ever were. I wish his mind could be set at rest."

"At rest in what way?"

"As to who it was that did the harm to Rachel. He has had it in his head for a long while, sir, that it was Mr. John Massingbird; but he can't be certain, and it's the uncertainty that keeps his mind on the worrit."

"Do you know where he picked up the notion that it was Mr. John Massingbird?" inquired Lionel, remembering the conversation on the same point that Robin had once held with him, on that very garden bench, in the face of which he and Matthew were now sitting.

Old Matthew shook his head. "I never could learn, sir. Robin's a dutiful son to me, but he'd never tell me that. I know that Mr. John Massingbird has been like a pill in his throat this many a day. Oftentimes have I felt thankful that he was dead, or Robin would surely have gone out to where he was, and murdered him. Murder wouldn't mend the ill, sir—as I have told him many a time."

"Indeed it would not," replied Lionel. "The very fact of Mr. John Massingbird's being dead, should have the effect of setting Robin's mind at rest—if it was to him that his suspicions were directed. For my part, I think Robin is wrong in suspecting him."

"I think so too, sir. I don't know how it is, but I can't bring my mind to suspect him more than anybody else. I have thought over things in this light, and I have thought 'em over in that light; and I'd rather incline to believe that she got acquainted with some stranger, poor dear! than that it was anybody known to us. Robin is in doubt; he has had some cause given him to suspect Mr. John Massingbird, but he is not sure, and it's that doubt, I say, that worrits him."

"At any rate, doubt or no doubt, there is no cause for him to go about at night with a gun. What does he do it for?"

"I have asked him, sir, and he does not answer. He seems to me to be on the watch."

"On the watch for what?" rejoined Lionel.

"I'm sure I don't know," said old Matthew. "If you'd say a word to him, sir, it might stop it. He got a foolish notion into his mind that poor Rachel's spirit might come again, and he'd used to be about the pond pretty near every moonlight night. That fancy passed off, and he has gone to his bed at night as the rest of us have, up to the last week or so, when he has taken to go out again, and to carry a gun."

"It was a foolish notion," remarked Lionel. "The dead do not come again, Matthew."

Matthew made no reply.

"I must try and come across Robin," said Lionel, rising. "I wish you would tell him to come up to me, Matthew."

"Sir, if you desire that he shall wait upon you at Verner's Pride, he will be sure to do so," said the old man, leaning on his stick as he stood. "He has not got to the length of disobeying an order of yours. I'll tell him."

It happened that Lionel did "come across" Robin Frost. Not to any effect, however, for he could not get to speak to him. Lionel was striking across some fields towards Deerham Court, when he came in view of Roy and Robin Frost leaning over a gate, their heads together in close confab. It looked very much as though they were talking secrets. They looked up and saw him; but when he reached the place, both were gone. Roy was in sight, but the other had entirely disappeared. Lionel lifted his voice.

"Roy, I want you."

Roy could not fain deafness, although there was every appearance that he would like to do it. He turned and approached, putting his hand to his hat in a half surly manner.

"Where's Robin Frost?"

"Robin Frost, sir? He was here a minute or two agone. I met him accidental, and I stopped him to ask what he was about, that he hadn't been at work this three days. He went on his way then, down the gap. Did you want him, sir?"

Lionel Verner's perceptive faculties were tolerably developed. That Roy was endeavouring to blind him, he had no doubt. They had not met "accidental," and the topic of conversation had not been Robin's work—of that he felt sure. Roy and Robin Frost might meet and talk together all day long. It was nothing to him. Why they should strive to deceive him was the only curious part about it. Both had striven to avoid meeting him; and Roy was talking to him now unwillingly. In a general way, Robin Frost was fond of meeting and receiving a word from Mr. Verner.

"I shall see him another time," carelessly remarked Lionel. "Not so fast, Roy"—for the man was turning away—"I have not done with you. Will you be good enough to inform me what you were doing in front of my house last night?"

"I wasn't doing anything, sir. I wasn't there."

"Oh, yes, you were," said Lionel. "Recollect yourself. You were posted under the large yew tree on the lawn, watching my drawing-room windows."

Roy looked up at this, the most intense surprise in his countenance. "I never was on your lawn last night, sir; I wasn't near it. Leastways not nearer than the side field. I happened to be in that, and I got through a gap in the hedge, on to the high road."

"Roy, I believe that you were on the lawn last night, and watching the house," persisted Lionel, looking fixedly at his countenance. For the life of him he could not tell whether the man's surprise was genuine, his denial real. "What business had you there?"

"I declare to goodness, if it was the last word I had to speak, that I was not on your lawn, sir—that I did not watch the house. I did not go near the house. I crossed the side field, cornerwise, and got out into the road; and that's the nearest I was to the house last night."

Roy spoke unusually impressive for him, and Lionel began to believe that, so far, he was telling truth. He did not make any immediate reply, and Roy resumed.

"What cause have you got to accuse me, sir? I shouldn't be likely to watch your house—why should I?"

"Some man was watching it," replied Lionel. "As you were seen in the road shortly afterwards, close to the side field, I came to the conclusion that it was you."

"I can be upon my oath that it wasn't, sir," answered Roy.

"Very well," replied Lionel, "I accept your denial. But allow me to give you a recommendation, Roy—not to trouble yourself with my affairs in any way. They do not concern you; they never will concern you; therefore, don't meddle with them."

He walked away as he spoke. Roy stood and gazed after him, a strange expression on his countenance. Had Lucy Tempest seen it, she might have renewed her warning to Lionel. And yet she would have been puzzled to tell the meaning of the expression, for it did not look like a threatening one.

Had Lionel Verner turned up Clay Lane, upon leaving Matthew Frost's cottage, instead of down it, to take a path across the fields at the back, he would have encountered the Vicar of Deerham. That gentleman was paying parochial visits that day in Deerham, and in due course he came to Matthew Frost's. He and Matthew had long been upon confidential terms; the clergyman respected Matthew, and Matthew revered his pastor.

Mr. Bourne took the seat which Lionel had but recently vacated. He was so accustomed to the old man's habitual countenance that he could detect every change in it; and he saw that something was troubling him.

"I am troubled in more ways than one, sir," was the old man's answer. "Poor Robin, he's giving me trouble again; and last night, sir, I had a sort of fright. A shock, it may be said. I can't overget it."

"What was its nature?" asked Mr. Bourne.

"I don't much like to speak of it, sir; and, beside yourself, there's not a living man that I'd open my lips to. It's an unpleasant thing to have upon the mind. Mr. Verner, he was here but a few minutes a-gone, and I felt before him like a guilty man that has something to conceal. When I have told it to you, sir, you'll be hard of belief."

"Is it connected with Robin?"

"No, sir. But it was my going after Robin that led to it, as may be said. Robin, sir, has took these last few nights to go out with a gun. It has worrited me so, sir, fearing some mischief might ensue, that I couldn't sleep; and last evening, I thought I'd hobble out and see if I couldn't get him home. Chuff, he said as he had seen him go toward the brick-field, and I managed to get down; and, sure enough, I came upon

Robin. He was lying down at the edge of the field, watching, as it seemed to me. I couldn't get him home, sir. I tried hard, but 'twas of no use. He spoke respectful to me, as he always does: 'Father, I have got my work to do, and I must do it. You go back home, and go to sleep in quiet.' It was all I could get from him, sir, and at last I turned to go back—"

"What was Robin doing?" interrupted Mr. Bourne.

"Sir, I suppose it's just some fancy or other that he has got into his head, as he used to get after the poor child died. Mr. Verner has just asked me whether he is sane, but there's nothing of that sort wrong about him. You mind the clump of trees that stands out, sir, between here and the brick-field, by the path that would lead to Verner's Pride?" added old Matthew in an altered tone.

"Yes," said Mr. Bourne.

"I had just got past it, sir, when I saw a figure crossing that bare corner from the other trees. A man's shape, it looked like. Tall and shadowy it was, wearing what looked like a long garment, or a woman's riding-habit, trailing nearly on the ground. The very moment my eyes fell upon it, I felt that it was something strange, and when the figure passed me, turning its face right upon me—I saw the face, sir."

Old Matthew's manner was so peculiar, his pause so impressive, that Mr. Bourne could only gaze at him, and wait in wonder for what was coming.

"Sir, it was the face of one who has been dead these two years past—Mr. Frederick Massingbird."

If the rector had gazed at old Matthew before, he could only stare now. That the calm, sensible old man should fall into so extraordinary a delusion, was incomprehensible. He might have believed it of Deerham in general, but not of Matthew Frost.

"Matthew, you must have been deceived," was his quiet answer.

"No, sir. There never was another face like Mr. Frederick Massingbird's. Other features may have been made like his—it's not for me to say they have not—but whose else would have the black mark upon it? The moonlight was full upon it, and I could see even the little lines shooting out from the cheek, so bright was the night. The face was turned right upon me as it passed, and I am as clear about its being his as I am that it was me looking at it."

"But you know it is a thing absolutely impossible," urged Mr. Bourne. "I think you must have dreamt this, Matthew."

Old Matthew shook his head. "I wouldn't have told you a dream, sir. It turned me all in a maze. I never felt the fatigue of a step all the way home after it. When I got in, I couldn't eat my supper; I couldn't go to bed. I sat up thinking, and the wife, she came in and asked what ailed me that I didn't go to rest. I had got no sleep in my eyes, I told her, which was true; for, when I did get to bed, it was hours afore I could close 'em."

"But, Matthew, I tell you that it is impossible. You must have been mistaken."

"Sir, until last night, had anybody told me such a thing, I should have said it was impossible. You know, sir, I have never been given to such fancies. There's no doubt, sir; there's no doubt that it was the spirit of Mr. Frederick Massingbird."

Matthew's clear, intelligent eye was fixed firmly on Mr. Bourne's—his face, as usual, bending a little forward. Mr. Bourne had never believed in "spirits"; clergymen, as a rule, do not. A half smile crossed his lips.

"Were you frightened?" he asked.

"I was not frightened, sir, in the sense that you, perhaps, put the question. I was surprised, startled. As I might have been surprised and startled at seeing anybody I least expected to see—somebody that I had thought was miles away. Since poor Rachel's death, sir, I have lived, so to say, in communion with spirits. What with Robin's talking of his hope to see hers, and my constantly thinking of her; knowing also that it can't be long, in the course of nature, before I am one myself, I have grown to be, as it were, familiar with the dead in my mind. Thus, sir, in that sense, no fear came upon me last night. I don't think, sir, I should feel fear at meeting or being alone with a spirit, any more than I should at meeting a man. But I was startled and disturbed."

"Matthew," cried Mr. Bourne, in some perplexity, "I had always believed you superior to these foolish things. Ghosts might do well enough for the old days, but the world has grown older and wiser. At any rate, the greater portion of it has."

"If you mean, sir, that I was superior to the belief in ghosts, you are right. I never had a grain of faith in such superstition in my life; and I have tried all means to convince my son what folly it was of him to hover round about the Willow Pond, with any thought that Rachel might 'come again.' No, sir, I have never been given to it."

"And yet you deliberately assure me, Matthew, that you saw a ghost last night!"

"Sir, that it was Mr. Frederick Massingbird, dead or alive, that I saw, I must hold to. We know that he is dead, sir, his wife buried him in that far land; so what am I to believe? The face looked ghastly white, not like a person's living."

Mr. Bourne mused. That Frederick Massingbird was dead and buried, there could not be the slightest doubt. He hardly knew what to make of old Matthew. The latter resumed.

"Had I been flurried or terrified by it, sir, so as to lose my presence of mind, or if I was one of those timid folks that see signs in dreams, or take every white post to be a ghost, that they come to on a dark night, you might laugh at and disbelieve me. But I tell it to you, sir, as you say, deliberately; just as it happened. I can't have much longer time to live, sir; but I'd stake it all on the truth that it was the spirit of Mr. Frederick Massingbird. When you have once known a man, there are a hundred points by which you may recognise him, beyond possibility of being mistaken. They have got a story in the place, sir, to-day— as you may have heard—that my poor child's ghost appeared to Dan Duff last night, and that the boy has been senseless ever since. It has struck me, sir, that perhaps he also saw what I did."

Mr. Bourne paused. "Did you say anything of this to Mr. Verner?"

"Not I, sir. As I tell you, I felt like a guilty man in his presence, one with something to hide. He married Mr. Fred's widow, pretty creature, and it don't seem a nice thing to tell him. If it had been the other gentleman's spirit, Mr. John's, I should have told him at once."

Mr. Bourne rose. To argue with old Matthew in his present frame of mind, appeared to be about as useless a waste of time as to argue with Susan Peckaby on the subject of the white donkey. He told him he would see him again in a day or two, and took his departure.

But he did not dismiss the subject from his thoughts. No, he could not do that. He was puzzled. Such a tale from one like old Matthew—calm, pious, sensible, and verging on the grave, made more impression on Mr. Bourne than all Deerham could have made. Had Deerham come to him with the story, he would have flung it to the winds.

He began to think that some person, from evil design or love of mischief, must be personating Frederick Massingbird. It was a natural conclusion. And Matthew's surmise, that the same thing might have alarmed Dan Duff, was perfectly probable. Mr. Bourne determined to ascertain the latter fact, as soon as Dan should be in a state of sufficient convalescence, bodily and mentally, to give an account. He had already paid one visit to Mrs. Duff's—as that lady informed Lionel.

Two or three more visits he paid there during the day, but not until night did he find Dan revived. In point of fact, the clergyman penetrated to the kitchen just after that startling communication had been made by Dan. The women were standing in consternation when the vicar entered, one of them strongly recommending that the copper furnace should be heated, and Dan plunged into it to "bring him round."

"How is he now?" began Mr. Bourne. "Oh! I see; he is sensible."

"Well, sir, I don't know," said Mrs Duff. "I'm afraid as his head's a-going right off. He persists in saying now that it wasn't the ghost of Rachel at all—but somebody else's."

"If he was put into a good hot furnace, sir, and kep' at a even heat up to biling pint for half an hour—that is, as near biling as his skin could bear it—I know it 'ud do wonders," spoke up Mrs. Chuff. "It's a excellent remedy, where there's a furnace convenient, and water not short."

"Suppose you allow me to be alone with him for a few minutes," suggested Mr. Bourne. "We will try and find out what will cure him; won't we, Dan?"

The women filed out one by one. Mr. Bourne sat down by the boy, and took his hand. In a soothing manner he talked to him, and drew from him by gentle degrees the whole tale, so far as Dan's memory and belief went. The boy shook in every limb as he told it. He could not boast immunity from ghostly fears as did old Matthew Frost.

"But, my boy, you should know that there are no such things as ghosts," urged Mr. Bourne. "When once the dead have left this world, they do not come back to it again."

"I see'd it, sir," was Dan's only argument—an all sufficient one with him. "It was stood over the pool, it was, and it turned round right upon me as I went up. I see the porkypine on his cheek, sir, as plain as anything."

The same account as old Matthew's!

"How was the person dressed?" asked Mr. Bourne. "Did you notice?"

"It had got on some'at long—a coat or a skirt, or some'at. It was as thin as thin, sir."

"Dan, shall I tell you what it was—as I believe? It was somebody dressed up to frighten you and other timid persons."

Dan shook his head. "No, sir, 'twasn't. 'Twas the ghost of Mr. Frederick Massingbird."

CHAPTER LIII

MASTER CHEESE'S FRIGHT—OTHER FRIGHTS

Strange rumours began to be rife in Deerham. The extraordinary news told by Dan Duff would have been ascribed to some peculiar hallucination of that gentleman's brain, and there's no knowing but that the furnace might have been tried as a cure, had not other testimony arisen to corroborate it. Four or five different people, in the course of as many days—or rather nights—saw, or professed to have seen, the apparition of Frederick Massingbird.

One of them was Master Cheese. He was one night coming home from paying a professional visit—in slight, straightforward cases Jan could trust him—when he saw by the roadside what appeared to be a man standing up under the hedge, as if he had taken his station there to look at the passers-by.

"He's up to no good," quoth Master Cheese to himself. "I'll go and dislodge the fellow."

Accordingly Master Cheese turned off the path where he was walking, and crossed the waste bit—only a yard or two in breadth—that ran by the side of the road. Master Cheese, it must be confessed, did not want for bravery; he had a great deal rather face danger of any kind than hard work; and the rumour about Fred Massingbird's ghost had been rare nuts for him to crack. Up he went, having no thought in his head at that moment of ghosts, but rather of poachers.

"I say, you fellow—" he was beginning, and there he stopped dead.

He stopped dead, both in step and tongue. The figure, never moving, never giving the faintest indication that it was alive, stood there like a statue. Master Cheese looked in its face, and saw the face of the late Frederick Massingbird.

It is not pleasant to come across a dead man at moonlight—a man whose body has been safely reposing in the ground ever so long ago. Master Cheese did not howl as Dan Duff had done. He set off down the road—he was too fat to propel himself over or through the hedge, though that was the nearest way—he took to his heels down the road, and arrived in an incredibly short space of time at home, bursting into the surgery and astonishing Jan and the surgery boy.

"I say, Jan, though, haven't I had a fright?"

Jan, at the moment, was searching in the prescription-book. He raised his eyes, and looked over the counter. Master Cheese's face had turned white, and drops of wet were pouring off it—in spite of his bravery.

"What have you been at?" asked Jan.

"I saw the thing they are talking about, Jan. It is Fred Massingbird's."

Jan grinned. That Master Cheese's fright was genuine, there could be no mistaking, and it amused Jan excessively.

"What had you been taking?" asked he, in his incredulity.

"I had taken nothing," retorted Master Cheese, who did not like the ridicule. "I had not had the opportunity of taking anything—unless it was your medicine. Catch me tapping that! Look here, Jan. I was coming by Crow Corner, when I saw a something standing back in the hedge. I thought it was some poaching fellow hiding there, and went up to dislodge him. Didn't I wish myself up in the skies? It was the face of Fred Massingbird."

"The face of your fancy," slightingly returned Jan.

"I swear it was, then! There! There's no mistaking him. The hedgehog on his cheek looked larger and blacker than ever."

Master Cheese did not fail to talk of this abroad; the surgery boy, Bob, who had listened with open ears, did not fail to talk of it, and it spread throughout Deerham; additional testimony to that already accumulated. In a few days' time, the commotion was at its height; nearly the only persons who remained in ignorance of the reported facts being the master and mistress of Verner's Pride, and those connected with them, relatives on either side.

That some great internal storm of superstition was shaking Deerham, Lionel knew. In his happy ignorance, he attributed it to the rumour which had first been circulated, touching Rachel's ghost. He was an ear-witness to an angry colloquy at home. Some indispensable trifle for his wife's toilette was required suddenly from Deerham one evening, and Mademoiselle Benoite ordered that it should be sent for. But not one of the maids would go. The Frenchwoman insisted, and there ensued a stormy war. The girls, one and all, declared they'd rather give up their service, than go abroad after nightfall.

When the fears and the superstitions came palpably in Lionel's way, he made fun of them—as Jan might have done. Once or twice he felt half provoked; and asked the people, in a tone between earnest and jest, whether they were not ashamed of themselves. Little reply made they; not one of them but seemed to shrink from mentioning to Lionel Verner the name that the ghost had borne in life.

On nearly the last evening that it would be light during this moon, Mr. Bourne started from home to pay a visit to Mrs. Hook, the labourer's wife. The woman had been ailing for some time; partly from natural illness, partly from chagrin—for her daughter Alice was the talk of the village—and she had now become seriously ill. On this day Mr. Bourne had accidentally met Jan; and, in conversing upon parish matters, he had inquired after Mrs. Hook.

"Very much worse," was Jan's answer. "Unless a change takes place, she'll not last many days."

The clergyman was shocked; he had not deemed her to be in danger. "I will go and see her to-day," said he. "You can tell her that I am coming."

He was a conscientious man; liking to do his duty, and especially kind to those that were in sickness or trouble. Neither did he willingly break a specific promise. He made no doubt that Jan delivered the message, and therefore he went; though it was late at night when he started, other duties having detained him throughout the day.

His most direct way from the vicarage to Hook's cottage, took him past the Willow Pond. He had no fear of ghosts, and therefore he chose it, in preference to going down Clay Lane, which was farther round. The Willow Pool looked lonely enough as he passed it, its waters gleaming in the moonlight, its willows bending. A little farther on, the clergyman's ears became alive to the sound of sobs, as from a person in distress. There was Alice Hook, seated on a bench underneath some elm-trees, sobbing enough to break her heart.

However the girl might have got herself under the censure of the neighbourhood, it is a clergyman's office to console, rather than to condemn. And he could not help liking pretty Alice; she had been one of the most tractable pupils in his Sunday-school. He addressed her as soothingly, as considerately, as though she were one of the first ladies in his parish; harshness would not mend the matter now. Her heart opened to the kindness.

"I've broke mother's heart, and killed her!" cried she, with a wild burst of sobs. "But for me, she might have got well."

"She may get well still, Alice," replied the vicar. "I am going on to see her now. What are you doing here?"

"I am on my way, sir, to get the fresh physic for her. Mr. Jan, he said this morning as somebody was to go for it; but the rest have been out all day. As I came along, I got thinking of the time, sir, when I could go about by daylight with my head up, like the best of 'em; and it overcame me."

She rose up, dried her eyes with her shawl, and Mr. Bourne proceeded onwards. He had not gone far, when something came rushing past him from the opposite direction. It seemed more like a thing than a man, with its swift pace—and he recognised the face of Frederick Massingbird.

Mr. Bourne's pulses stood still, and then gave a bound onwards. Clergyman though he was, he could not, for his life, have helped the queer feeling which came over him. He had sharply rebuked the superstition in his parishioners; had been inclined to ridicule Matthew Frost; had cherished a firm and unalterable belief that some foolish wight was playing pranks with the public; but all these suppositions and convictions faded in this moment; and the clergyman felt that that which had rustled past was the veritable dead-and-gone Frederick Massingbird, in the spirit or in the flesh.

He shook the feeling off—or strove to shake it. That it was Frederick Massingbird in the flesh he did not give a second supposition to; and that it could be Frederick Massingbird in the spirit, was opposed to every past belief of the clergyman's life. But he had never seen such a likeness; and though the similarity in the features might be accidental, what of the black star?

He strove to shake the feeling off; to say to himself that some one, bearing a similar face, must be in the village; and he went on to his destination. Mrs. Hook was better; but she was lying in the place unattended, all of them out somewhere or other. The clergyman talked to her and read to her; and then waited impatiently for the return of Alice. He did not care to leave the woman alone.

"Where are they all?" he asked, not having inquired before.

They were gone to the wake at Broxley, a small place some two miles distant. Of course! Had Mr. Bourne remembered the wake, he need not have put the question.

An arrival at last. It was Jan. Jan, attentive to poor patients as he was to rich ones, had come striding over, the last thing. They asked him if he had seen anything of Alice in his walk. But Jan had come across from Deerham Court, and that would not be the girl's road. Another minute, and the husband came in. The two gentlemen left together.

"She is considerably better, to-night," remarked Jan. "She'll get about now, if she does not fret too much over Alice."

"It is strange where Alice can have got to," remarked Mr. Bourne. Her prolonged absence, coupled with the low spirits the girl appeared to be in, rather weighed upon his mind. "I met her as I was coming here an hour ago," he continued. "She ought to have been home long before this."

"Perhaps she has encountered the ghost," said Jan, in a joke.

"I saw it to-night, Jan."

"Saw what?" asked Jan, looking at Mr. Bourne.

"The—the party that appears to be personating Frederick Massingbird."

"Nonsense!" uttered Jan.

"I did. And I never saw such a likeness in my life."

"Even to the porcupine," ridiculed Jan.

"Even to the porcupine," gravely replied Mr. Bourne. "Jan, I am not joking. Moreover, I do not consider it a subject for a joke. If any one is playing the trick, it is an infamous thing, most disrespectful to your brother and his wife. And if not—"

"If not—what?" asked Jan.

"In truth, I stopped because I can't continue. Frederick Massingbird's spirit it cannot be—unless all our previous belief in the non-appearance of spirits is to be upset—and it cannot be Frederick Massingbird in life. He died in Australia, and was buried there. I am puzzled, Jan."

Jan was not. Jan only laughed. He believed there must be something in the moonlight that deceived the people, and that Mr. Bourne had caught the infection from the rest.

"Should it prove to be a trick that any one is playing," resumed the clergyman, "I shall—"

"Hollo!" cried Jan. "What's this? Another ghost?"

They had nearly stumbled over something lying on the ground. A woman, dressed in some light material. Jan stooped.

"It's Alice Hook!" he cried.

The spot was that at which Mr. Bourne had seen her sitting. The empty bottle for medicine in her hand told him that she had not gone upon her errand. She was insensible and cold.

"She has fainted," remarked Jan. "Lend a hand, will you, sir?"

Between them they got her on the bench, and the stirring revived her. She sighed once or twice, and opened her eyes.

"Alice, girl, what is it? How were you taken ill?" asked the vicar.

She looked up at him; she looked at Jan. Then she turned her eyes in an opposite direction, glanced fearfully round, as if searching for some sight that she dreaded; shuddered, and relapsed into insensibility.

"We must get her home," observed Jan.

"There are no means of getting her home in her present state, unless she is carried," said Mr. Bourne.

"That's easy enough," returned Jan. And he caught her up in his long arms, apparently having to exert little strength in the action. "Put her petticoats right, will you?" cried he, in his unceremonious fashion.

The clergyman put her things as straight as he could, as they hung over Jan's arm. "You'll never be able to carry her, Jan," said he.

"Not carry her!" returned Jan. "I could carry you, if put to it."

And away he went, bearing his burden as tenderly and easily as though it had been a little child. Mr. Bourne could hardly keep pace with him.

"You go on, and have the door open," said Jan, as they neared the cottage. "We must get her in without the mother hearing, upstairs."

They had the kitchen to themselves. Hook, the father, a little the worse for what he had taken, had gone to bed, leaving the door open for his children. They got her in quietly, found a light, and placed her in a chair. Jan took off her bonnet and shawl—he was handy as a woman; and looked about for something to give her. He could find nothing except water. By and by she got better.

Her first movement, when she fully recovered her senses, was to clutch hold of Jan on the one side, of Mr. Bourne on the other.

"Is it gone?" she gasped, in a voice of the most intense terror.

"Is what gone, child?" asked Mr. Bourne.

"The ghost," she answered. "It came right up, sir, just after you left me. I'd rather die than see it again."

She was shaking from head to foot. There was no mistaking that her terror was intense. To attempt to meet it with confuting arguments would have been simply folly, and both gentlemen knew that it would. Mr Bourne concluded that the same sight, which had so astonished him, had been seen by the girl.

"I sat down again after you went, sir," she resumed, her teeth chattering. "I knew there was no mighty hurry for my being back, as you had gone on to mother, and I sat on ever so long, and it came right up again me, brushing my knees with its things as it passed. At the first moment I thought it might be you coming back, to say something to me, sir, and I looked up. It turned its face upon me, and I never remember nothing after that."

"Whose face?" questioned Jan.

"The ghost's, sir. Mr. Fred Massingbird's."

"Bah!" said Jan. "Faces look alike in the moonlight."

"Twas his face," answered the girl, from between her shaking lips. "I saw its every feature, sir."

"Porcupine and all?" retorted Jan, ironically.

"Porkypine and all, sir. I'm not sure that I should have knowed it at first, but for the porkypine."

What were they to do with the girl? Leave her there, and go? Jan, who was more skilled in ailments than Mr. Bourne, thought it possible that the fright had seriously injured her.

"You must go to bed at once," said he. "I'll just say a word to your father."

Jan was acquainted with the private arrangements of the Hooks' household. He knew that there was but one sleeping apartment for the whole family—the room above, where the sick mother was lying. Father, mother, sons, and daughters all slept there together. The "house" consisted of the kitchen below and the room above it. There were many such on the Verner estate.

Jan, carrying the candle to guide him, went softly up the creaky staircase. The wife was sleeping. Hook was sleeping, too, and snoring heavily. Jan had something to do to awake him; shaking seemed useless.

"Look here," said he in a whisper, when the man was aroused, "Alice has had a fright, and I think she may perhaps be ill through it; if so, mind you come for me without loss of time. Do you understand, Hook?"

Hook signified that he did.

"Very well," replied Jan. "Should—"

"What's that! what's that?"

The alarmed cry came from the mother. She had suddenly awoke.

"It's nothing," said Jan. "I only had a word to say to Hook. You go to sleep again, and sleep quietly."

Somehow Jan's presence carried reassurance with it to most people. Mrs. Hook was contented. "Is Ally not come in yet?" asked she.

"Come in, and downstairs," replied Jan. "Good-night. Now," said he to Alice, when he returned to the kitchen, "you go on to bed and get to sleep; and don't get dreaming of ghosts and goblins."

They were turning out at the door, the clergyman and Jan, when the girl flew to them in a fresh attack of terror.

"I daren't be left alone," she gasped. "Oh, stop a minute! Pray stop, till I be gone upstairs."

"Here," said Jan, making light of it. "I'll marshal you up."

He held the candle, and the girl flew up the stairs as fast as young Cheese had flown from the ghost. Her breath was panting, her bosom throbbing. Jan blew out the candle, and he and Mr. Bourne departed, merely shutting the door. Labourers' cottages have no fear of midnight robbers.

"What do you think now?" asked Mr. Bourne, as they moved along.

Jan looked at him. "You are not thinking, surely, that it is Fred Massingbird's ghost!"

"No. But I should advise Mr. Verner to place a watch, and have the thing cleared up—who it is, and what it is."

"Why, Mr. Verner?"

"Because it is on his land that the disturbance is occurring. This girl has been seriously frightened."

"You may have cause to know that, before many hours are over," answered Jan.

"Why! you don't fear that she will be seriously ill?"

"Time will show," was all the answer given by Jan. "As to the ghost, I'll either believe in him, or disbelieve him, when I come across him. If he were a respectable ghost, he'd confine himself to the churchyard, and not walk in unorthodox places, to frighten folks."

They looked somewhat curiously at the seat near which Alice had fallen; at the Willow Pond, farther on. There was no trace of a ghost about then—at least, that they could see—and they continued their way. In emerging upon the high road, whom should they meet but old Mr. Bitterworth and Lionel, arm in arm. They had been to an evening meeting of the magistrates at Deerham, and were walking home together.

To see the vicar and surgeon of a country village in company by night, imparts the idea that some one of its inhabitants may be in extremity. It did so now to Mr. Bitterworth—

"Where do you come from?" he asked.

"From Hook's," answered Jan. "The mother's better to-night; but I have had another patient there. The girl, Alice, has seen the ghost, or fancied that she saw it, and was terrified, literally, out of her senses."

"How is she going on?" asked Mr. Bitterworth.

"Physically, do you mean, sir?"

"No, I meant morally, Jan. If all accounts are true, the girl has been losing herself."

"Law!" said Jan. "Deerham has known that this many a month past. I'd try and stop it, if I were Lionel."

"Stop what?" asked Lionel.

"I'd build 'em better dwellings," composedly went on Jan. "They might be brought up to decency then."

"It's true that decency can't put its head into such dwellings as that of the Hooks'," observed the vicar. "People have accused me of showing leniency to Alice Hook, since the scandal has been known; but I cannot show harshness to her when I think of the home the girl was reared in."

The words pricked Lionel. None could think worse of the homes than he did. He spoke in a cross tone; we are all apt to do so, when vexed with ourselves. "What possesses Deerham to show itself so absurd just now? Ghosts! They only affect fear, it is my belief."

"Alice Hook did not affect it, for one," said Jan. "She may have been frightened to some purpose. We found her lying on the ground, insensible. They are stupid, though, all the lot of them."

"Stupid is not the name for it," remarked Lionel. "A little superstition, following on Rachel's peculiar death, may have been excusable, considering the ignorance of the people here, and the tendency to superstition inherent in human nature. But why it should have been revived now, I cannot imagine."

Mr. Bitterworth and Jan had walked on. The vicar touched Lionel on the arm, not immediately to follow them.

"Mr. Verner, I do not hold good with the policy which seems to prevail, of keeping this matter from you," he said, in a confidential tone. "I cannot see the expediency of it in any way. It is not Rachel's Frost's ghost that is said to be terrifying people."

"Whose then?" asked Lionel.

"Frederick Massingbird's."

Lionel paused, as if his ears deceived him.

"Whose?" he repeated.

"Frederick Massingbird's."

"How perfectly absurd!" he presently exclaimed.

"True," said Mr. Bourne. "So absurd that, were it not for a circumstance which has happened to-night, I scarcely think I should have brought myself to repeat it. My conviction is, that some person bearing an extraordinary resemblance to Frederick Massingbird is walking about to terrify the neighbourhood."

"I should think there's not another face living, that bears a resemblance to Fred Massingbird's," observed Lionel. "How have you heard this?"

"The first to tell me of it was old Matthew Frost. He saw him plainly, believing it to be Frederick Massingbird's spirit—although he had never believed in spirits before. Dan Duff holds to it that he saw it; and now Alice Hook; besides others. I turned a deaf ear to all, Mr. Verner; but to-night I met one so like Frederick Massingbird that, were Massingbird not dead, I could have sworn it was himself. It was wondrously like him, even to the mark on the cheek."

"I never heard such a tale!" uttered Lionel.

"That is precisely what I said—until to-night. I assure you the resemblance is so great, that if we have all female Deerham in fits, I shall not wonder. It strikes me—it is the only solution I can come to—that some one is personating Frederick Massingbird for the purpose of a mischievous joke—though how they get up the resemblance is another thing. Let me advise you to see into it, Mr. Verner."

Mr. Bitterworth and Jan were turning round in front, waiting; and the vicar hastened on, leaving Lionel glued to the spot where he stood.

CHAPTER LIV

MRS DUFF'S BILL

Peal! peal! peal! came the sound of the night-bell at Jan's window as he lay in bed. For Jan had caused the night-bell to be hung there since he was factotum. "Where's the good of waking up the house?" remarked Jan; and he made the alteration.

Jan got up with the first sound, and put his head out at the window. Upon which, Hook—for he was the applicant—advanced. Jan's window being, as you may remember, nearly on a level with the ground, presented favourable auspices for holding a face to face colloquy with night visitors.

"She's mortal bad, sir," was Hook's salutation.

"Who is?" asked Jan. "Alice, or the missis?"

"Not the missis, sir. The other. But I shouldn't ha' liked to trouble you, if you hadn't ordered me."

"I won't be two minutes," said Jan.

It seemed to Hook that Jan was only one, so speedily did he come out. A belief was popular in Deerham that Mr. Jan slept with his clothes on; no sooner would a night summons be delivered to Jan, than Jan was out with the summoner, ready for the start. Before he had closed the surgery door, through which he had to pass, there came another peal, and a woman ran up to him. Jan recognised her for the cook of a wealthy lady in the Belvedere Road, a Mrs. Ellis.

"Law, sir! what a provident mercy that you are up and ready!" exclaimed she. "My mistress is attacked again."

"Well, you know what to do," returned Jan. "You don't want me."

"But she do want you, sir. I have got orders not to go back without you."

"I suppose she has been eating cucumber again," remarked Jan.

"Only a bit of it, sir. About the half of a small one, she took for her supper. And now the spasms is on her dreadful."

"Of course they are," replied Jan. "She knows how cucumber serves her. Well, I can't come. I'll send Mr. Cheese, if you like. But he can do no more good than you can. Give her the drops and get the hot flannels; that's all."

"You are going out, sir!" cried the woman, in a tone that sounded as if she would like to be impertinent. "You are come for him, I suppose?" turning a sharp tongue upon Hook.

"Yes, I be," humbly replied Hook. "Poor Ally—"

The woman set up a scream. "You'd attend her, that miserable castaway, afore you'd attend my mistress!" burst out she to Jan. "Who's Ally Hook, by the side of folks of standing?"

"If she wants attendance, she must have it," was the composed return of Jan. "She has got a body and a soul to be saved, as other folks have. She is in danger; your mistress is not."

"Danger! What has that got to do with it?" angrily answered the woman. "You'll never get paid there, sir."

"I don't expect it," returned Jan. "If you'd like Cheese, that's his window," pointing to one in the house. "Throw a handful of gravel up, and tell them I said he was to attend."

Jan walked off with Hook. He heard a crash of gravel behind him; so concluded the cook was flinging at Mr. Cheese's window in a temper. As she certainly was, giving Mr. Jan some hard words in the process. Just as Lady Verner had never been able to inculcate suavity on Jan, so Dr. West had found it a hopeless task to endeavour to make Jan understand that, in medical care, the rich should be considered before the poor. Take, for example, that bête noire of Deerham just now, Alice Hook, and put her by the side of a born duchess; Jan would have gone to the one who had most need of him, without reference to which of the two it might be. Evidently there was little hope for Jan.

Jan, with his long legs, outstripped the stooping and hard worked labouring man. In at the door and up the stairs he went, into the sleeping room.

Did you ever pay a visit to a room of this social grade? If not, you will deem the introduction of this one highly coloured. Had Jan been a head and shoulders shorter, he might have been able to stand up in the lean-to attic, without touching the lath and plaster of the roof. On a low bedstead, on a flock mattress, lay the mother and two children, about eight and ten. How they made room for Hook also, was a puzzle. Opposite to it, on a straw mattress, slept three sons, grown up, or nearly so; between these beds was another straw mattress where lay Alice and her sister, a year younger; no curtains, no screens, no anything. All were asleep, with the exception of the mother and Alice; the former could not rise from her bed; Alice appeared too ill to rise from hers. Jan stooped his head and entered.

A few minutes, and he set himself to arouse the sleepers. They might make themselves comfortable in the kitchen, he told them, for the rest of the night: he wanted room in the place to turn himself round, and they must go out of it. And so he bundled them out. Jan was not given to stand upon ceremony. But it is not a pleasant room to linger in, so we will leave Jan to it.

It was pleasanter at Lady Verner's. Enough of air, and light, and accommodation there. But even in that desirable residence it was not all couleur de rose. Vexations intrude into the most luxurious home, whatever may be the superfluity of room, the admirable style of the architecture; and they were just now agitating Deerham Court.

On the morning which rose on the above night—as lovely a morning as ever September gave us—Lady Verner and Lucy Tempest received each a letter from India. Both were from Colonel Tempest. The contents of Lady Verner's annoyed her, and the contents of Lucy's annoyed her.

It appeared that some considerable time back, nearly, if not quite, twelve months, Lucy had privately written to Colonel Tempest, urgently requesting to be allowed to go out to join him. She gave no reason or motive for the request, but urged it strongly. That letter, in consequence of the moving about of Colonel Tempest, had only just reached him; and now had arrived the answer to it. He told Lucy that he should very shortly be returning to Europe; therefore it was useless for her to think of going out.

So far, so good. However Lucy might have been vexed or disappointed at the reply—and she was both; still more at the delay which had taken place—there the matter would have ended. But Colonel Tempest, having no idea that Lady Verner was a stranger to this request; inferring, on the contrary, that she was a party to it, and must, therefore, be growing tired of her charge, had also written to her an elaborate apology for leaving Lucy so long upon her hands, and for being unable to comply with her wish to be relieved of her. This enlightened Lady Verner as to what Lucy had done.

She was very angry. She was worse than angry; she was mortified. And she questioned Lucy a great deal more closely than that young lady liked, as to what her motive could have been, and why she was tired of Deerham Court.

Lucy, all self-conscious of the motive by which she had been really actuated, stood before her like a culprit. "I am not tired of Deerham Court, Lady Verner. But I wished to be with papa."

"Which is equivalent to saying that you wish to be away from me," retorted my lady. "I ask you why?"

"Indeed, Lady Verner, I am pleased to be with you; I like to be with you. It was not to be away from you that I wrote. It is a long while since I saw papa; so long, that I seem to have forgotten what he is like."

"Can you assure me, in all open truth, that the wish to be with Colonel Tempest was your sole reason for writing, unbiassed by any private feeling touching Deerham?" returned Lady Verner, searching her face keenly. "I charge you answer me, Lucy."

Lucy could not answer that it was her sole reason, unless she told an untruth. Her eyes fell under the gaze bent upon her.

"I see," said Lady Verner. "You need not equivocate more. Is it to me that you have taken a dislike? or to any part of my arrangements?"

"Believe me, dear Lady Verner, that it is neither to you nor to your home," she answered, the tears rising to her eyes. "Believe me, I am as happy here as I ever was; on that score I have no wish to change."

It was an unlucky admission of Lucy's, "on that score." Of course, Lady Verner immediately pressed to know on what other score the wish might be founded. Lucy pleaded the desire to be with her father, which Lady Verner did not believe; and she pleaded nothing else. It was not satisfactory to my lady, and she kept Lucy the whole of the morning, harping upon the sore point.

Lionel entered, and interrupted the discussion. Lady Verner put him in possession of the facts. That for some cause which Lucy refused to explain, she wanted to leave Deerham Court; had been writing, twelve months back, to Colonel Tempest, to be allowed to join him in India; and the negative answer had arrived but that morning. Lady Verner would like the motive for her request explained; but Lucy was obstinate, and would not explain it.

Lionel turned his eyes on Lucy. If she had stood self-conscious before Lady Verner, she stood doubly self-conscious now. Her eyelashes were drooping, her cheeks were crimson.

"She says she has no fault to find with me, no fault to find with the arrangements of my house," pursued Lady Verner. "Then I want to know what else it is that should drive her away from Deerham. Look at her, Lionel! That is how she stands—unable to give me an answer."

Lady Verner might equally well have said, Look at Lionel. He stood self-conscious also. Too well he knew the motive—absence from him—which had actuated Lucy. From him, the married man; the man who had played her false; away, anywhere, from witnessing the daily happiness of him and his wife. He read it all, and Lucy saw that he did.

"It were no such strange wish, surely, to be where my dear papa is!" she exclaimed, the crimson of her cheeks turning to scarlet.

"No," murmured Lionel, "no such strange wish. I wish I could go to India, and free the neighbourhood of my presence!"

A curious wish! Lady Verner did not understand it. Lionel gave her no opportunity to inquire its meaning, for he turned to quit the room and the house. She rose and laid her hand upon his arm to detain him.

"I have an engagement," pleaded Lionel.

"A moment yet. Lionel, what is this nonsense that is disturbing the equanimity of Deerham? About a ghost!"

"Ah, what indeed?" returned Lionel, in a careless tone, as if he would make light of it. "You know what Deerham is, mother. Some think Dan Duff saw his own shadow; some, a white cow in the pound. Either is sufficient marvel for Deerham."

"So vulgar a notion!" reiterated Lady Verner, resuming her seat, and taking her essence bottle in her delicately gloved hand. "I wonder you don't stop it, Lionel."

"I!" cried Lionel, opening his eyes in considerable surprise. "How am I to stop it?"

"You are the Lord of Deerham. It is vulgar, I say, to have such a report afloat on your estate."

Lionel smiled. "I don't know how you are to put away vulgarity from stargazers and villagers. Or ghosts either—if they once get ghosts in their heads."

He finally left the Court, and turned towards home. His mother's words about the ghost had brought the subject to his mind; if, indeed, it had required bringing; but the whispered communication of the vicar the previous night had scarcely been out of his thoughts since. It troubled him. In spite of himself, of his good sense and reason, there was an undercurrent of uneasiness at work within him. Why should there be? Lionel could not have explained had he been required to do it. That Frederick Massingbird was dead and buried, there could be no shade of doubt; and ghosts had no place in the creed of Lionel Verner. All true; but the consciousness of uneasiness was there, and he could not ignore it.

In the last few days, the old feeling touching Lucy had been revived with unpleasant force. Since that night which she had spent at his house, when they saw, or fancied they saw, a man hiding himself under the tree, he had thought of her more than was agreeable; more than was right, he would have said, but that he saw not how to avoid it. The little episode of this morning at his mother's house had served to open his eyes most completely, to show him how intense was his love for Lucy Tempest. It must be confessed that his wife did little towards striving to retain his love.

He went along, thinking of these things. He would have put them from him; but he could not. The more he tried, the more unpleasantly vivid they became. "Tush!" said Lionel. "I must be getting nervous! I'll ask Jan to give me a draught."

He was passing Dr. West's as he spoke, and he turned into the surgery. Sitting on the bung of a large stone jar was Master Cheese, his attitude a disconsolate one, his expression of countenance rebellious.

"Is Mr. Jan at home?" asked Lionel.

"No, he's not at home, sir," replied Master Cheese, as if the fact were some personal grievance of his own. "Here's all the patients, all the making up of the physic left in my charge, and I'd like to know how I am to do it? I can't go out to fifty folks at a time?"

"And so you expedite the matter by not going to one! Where is Mr. Jan?"

"He was fetched out in the night to that beautiful Ally Hook," grumbled Master Cheese. "It's a shame, sir, folks are saying, for him to give his time to her. I had to leave my warm bed and march out to that fanciful Mother Ellis, through it, who's always getting the spasms. And I had about forty poor here this morning, and couldn't get a bit of comfortable breakfast for 'em. Miss Deb, she never kept my bacon warm, or anything; and somebody had eaten the meat out of the veal pie when I got back. Jan will have those horrid poor here twice a week, and if I speak against it, he tells me to hold my tongue."

"But is Mr. Jan not back yet from Hook's?"

"No, sir, he's not," was the resentful response. "He has never come back at all since he went, and that was at four o'clock this morning. If he had gone to cut off all the arms in the house, he couldn't have been longer! And I wish him joy of it! He'll get no breakfast. They have got nothing for themselves but bread and water."

Lionel left his draught an open question, and departed. As he turned into the principal street again, he saw Master Dan Duff at the door of his mother's shop. A hasty impulse prompted Lionel to question the boy of what he saw that unlucky night; or believed he saw. He crossed over; but Master Dan retreated inside the shop. Lionel followed him.

"Well, Dan! Have you overcome the fright of the cow yet?"

"'Twarn't a cow, please, sir," replied Dan, timidly. "'Twere a ghost."

"Whose ghost?" returned Lionel.

Dan hesitated. He stood first on one leg, then on the other.

"Please, sir, 'twarn't Rachel's," said he, presently.

"Whose then?" repeated Lionel.

"Please, sir, mother said I warn't to tell you. Roy, he said, if I told it to anybody, I should be took and hanged."

"But I say that you are to tell me," said Lionel. And his pleasant tone, combined, perhaps, with the fact that he was Mr. Verner, effected more with Dan Duff than his mother's sharp tone or Roy's threatening one.

"Please, sir," glancing round to make sure that his mother was not within hearing, "'twere Mr. Fred Massingbird's. They can't talk me out on't, sir. I see'd the porkypine as plain as I see'd him. He were—"

Dan brought his information to a summary standstill. Bustling down the stairs was that revered mother. She came in, curtseying fifty times to Lionel. "What could she have the honour of serving him with?" He was leaning over the counter, and she concluded he had come to patronise the shop.

Lionel laughed. "I am a profitless customer, I believe, Mrs. Duff. I was only talking to Dan."

Dan sidled off to the street door. Once there, he took to his heels, out of harm's way. Mr. Verner might begin telling his mother more particulars, and it was as well to be at a safe distance.

Lionel, however, had no intention to betray trust. He stood chatting a few minutes with Mrs. Duff. He and Mrs. Duff had been great friends when he was an Eton boy; many a time had he ransacked her shop over for flies and gut and other fishing tackle, a supply of which Mrs. Duff professed to keep. She listened to him with a somewhat preoccupied manner; in point of fact, she was debating a question with herself.

"Sir," said she, rubbing her hands nervously one over the other, "I should like to make bold to ask a favour of you. But I don't know how it might be took. I'm fearful it might be took as a cause of offence."

"Not by me. What is it?"

"It's a delicate thing, sir, to have to ask about," resumed she. "And I shouldn't venture, sir, to speak to you, but that I'm so put to it, and that I've got it in my head it's through the fault of the servants."

She spoke with evident reluctance. Lionel, he scarcely knew why, leaped to the conclusion that she was about to say something regarding the subject then agitating Deerham—the ghost of Frederick Massingbird. Unconsciously to himself, the pleasant manner changed to one of constraint.

"Say what you have to say, Mrs. Duff."

"Well, sir—but I'm sure I beg a hundred thousand pardings for mentioning of it—it's about the bill," she answered, lowering her voice. "If I could be paid, sir, it 'ud be the greatest help to me. I don't know hardly how to keep on."

No revelation touching the ghost could have given Lionel the surprise imparted by these ambiguous words. But his constraint was gone.

"I do not understand you, Mrs. Duff. What bill?"

"The bill what's owing to me, sir, from Verner's Pride. It's a large sum for me, sir—thirty-two pound odd. I have to keep up my payments for my goods, sir, whether or not, or I should be a bankrupt to-morrow.

Things is hard upon me just now, sir; though I don't want everybody to know it. There's that big son o' mine, Dick, out o' work. If I could have the bill, or only part of it, it 'ud be like a God-send."

"Who owes you the bill?" asked Lionel.

"It's your good lady, sir, Mrs. Verner."

"Who?" echoed Lionel, his accent quite a sharp one.

"Mrs. Verner, sir."

Lionel stood gazing at the woman. He could not take in the information; he believed there must be some mistake.

"It were for things supplied between the time Mrs. Verner came home after your marriage, sir, and when she went to London in the spring. The French madmizel, sir, came down and ordered some on 'em; and Mrs. Verner herself, sir, ordered others."

Lionel looked around the shop. He did not disbelieve the woman's words, but he was in a maze of astonishment. Perhaps a doubt of the Frenchwoman crossed his mind.

"There's nothing here that Mrs. Verner would wear!" he exclaimed.

"There's many odds and ends of things here, sir, as is useful to a lady's tilette—and you'd be surprised, sir, to find how such things mounts up when they be had continual. But the chief part o' the bill, sir, is for two silk gownds as was had of our traveller. Mrs. Verner, sir, she happened to be here when he called in one day last winter, and she saw his patterns, and she chose two dresses, and said she'd buy 'em of me if I ordered 'em. Which in course I did, sir, and paid for 'em, and sent 'em home. I saw her wear 'em both, sir, after they was made up, and very nice they looked."

Lionel had heard quite enough. "Where is the bill?" he inquired.

"It have been sent in, sir, long ago. When I found Mrs. Verner didn't pay it afore she went away, I made bold to write and ask her. Miss West, she gave me the address in London, and said she wished she could pay me herself. I didn't get an answer, sir, and I made bold to write again, and I never got one then. Twice I have been up to Verner's Pride, sir, since you come home this time, but I can't get to see Mrs. Verner. That French madmizel's one o' the best I ever see at putting folks off. Sir, it goes again the grain to trouble you; and if I could have got to see Mrs. Verner, I never would have said a word. Perhaps if you'd be so good as to tell her, sir, how hard I'm put to it, she'd send me a little."

"I am sure she will," said Lionel. "You shall have your money to-day, Mrs. Duff."

He turned out of the shop, a scarlet spot of emotion on his cheek. Thirty-two pounds owing to poor Mrs. Duff! Was it thoughtlessness on Sibylla's part? He strove to beat down the conviction that it was a less excusable error.

But the Verner pride had been wounded to its very core.

CHAPTER LV

SELF WILL

Gathered before a target on the lawn, in their archery costume gleaming with green and gold, was a fair group, shooting their arrows in the air. Far more went into the air than struck the target. They were the visitors of Verner's Pride; and Sibylla, the hostess, was the gayest, the merriest, the fairest among them.

Lionel came on to the terrace, descended the steps, and crossed the lawn to join them—as courtly, as apparently gay, as if that bill of Mrs. Duff's was not making havoc of his heartstrings. They all ran to surround him. It was not often they had so attractive a host to surround; and attractive men are, and always will be, welcome to women. A few minutes, a quarter of an hour given to them, an unruffled smoothness on his brow, a smile upon his lips, and then he contrived to draw his wife aside.

"Oh, Lionel, I forgot to tell you," she exclaimed. "Poynton has been here. He knows of the most charming pair of gray ponies, he says. And they can be ours if secured at once."

"I don't want gray ponies," replied Lionel.

"But I do," cried Sibylla. "You say I am too timid to drive. It is all nonsense; I should soon get over the timidity. I will learn to drive, Lionel. Mrs. Jocelyn, come here," she called out.

Mrs. Jocelyn, a young and pretty woman, almost as pretty as Sibylla, answered to the summons.

"Tell Mr. Verner what Poynton said about the ponies."

"Oh, you must not miss the opportunity," cried Mrs. Jocelyn to Lionel. "They are perfectly beautiful, the man said. Very dear, of course; but you know nobody looks at money when buying horses for a lady. Mrs. Verner must have them. You might secure them to-day."

"I have no room in my stables for more horses," said Lionel, smiling at Mrs. Jocelyn's eagerness.

"Yes, you have, Lionel," interposed his wife. "Or, if not, room must be made. I have ordered the ponies to be brought."

"I shall send them back," said Lionel, laughing.

"Don't you wish your wife to take to driving, Mr. Verner? Don't you like to see a lady drive? Some do not."

"I think there is no necessity for a lady to drive, while she has a husband at her side to drive for her," was the reply of Lionel.

"Well—if I had such a husband as you to drive for me, I don't know but I might subscribe to that doctrine," candidly avowed Mrs. Jocelyn. "I would not miss these ponies, were I Mrs. Verner. You can drive them, you know. They are calling me. It is my turn, I suppose."

She ran back to the shooting, Sibylla was following her, but Lionel caught her hand and drew her into a covered walk. Placing her hand within his arm, he began to pace it.

"I must go back, too, Lionel."

"Presently. Sibylla, I have been terribly vexed this morning."

"Oh, now Lionel, don't you begin about 'vexing,'" interrupted Sibylla, in the foolish, light, affected manner, which had grown worse of late, more intolerable to Lionel. "I have ordered the ponies. Poynton will send them in; and if there's really not room in the stables, you must see about it, and give orders that room must be made."

"I cannot buy the ponies," he firmly said. "My dear, I have given in to your every wish, to your most trifling whim; but, as I told you a few days ago, these ever-recurring needless expenses I cannot stand. Sibylla"—and his voice grew hoarse—"do you know that I am becoming embarrassed?"

"I don't care if you are," pouted Sibylla. "I must have the ponies."

His heart ached. Was this the loving wife—the intelligent companion for whom he had once yearned?—the friend who should be as his own soul? He had married the Sibylla of his imagination; and he woke to find Sibylla—what she was. The disappointment was heavy upon him always; but there were moments when he could have cried out aloud in its sharp bitterness.

"Sibylla, you know the state in which some of my tenants live; the miserable dwellings they are forced to inhabit. I must change this state of things. I believe it to be a duty for which I am accountable to God. How am I to set about it if you ruin me?"

Sibylla put her fingers to her ears. "I can't stand to listen when you preach, Lionel. It is as bad as a sermon."

Sibylla put her fingers to her ears.

It was ever thus. He could not attempt to reason with her. Anything like sensible conversation she could not, or would not, hold. Lionel, considerate to her as he ever was, felt provoked.

"Do you know that this unfortunate affair of Alice Hook's is laid remotely to me?" he said, with a sternness, which he could not help, in his tone. "People are saying that if I gave them decent dwellings, decent conduct would ensue. It is so. God knows that I feel its truth more keenly than my reproachers."

"The dwellings are good enough for the poor."

"Sibylla! You cannot think it. The laws of God and man alike demand a change. Child," he continued in a softer tone, as he took her hand in his, "let us bring the case home to ourselves. Suppose that you and I had to sleep in a room a few feet square, no chimney, no air, and that others tenanted it with us? Girls and boys growing up—nay, grown up, some of them; men and women as we are, Sibylla. The beds huddled together, no space between them; sickness, fever—"

"I am only shutting my ears," interrupted Sibylla. "You pretend to be so careful of me—you would not even let me go to that masked ball in Paris—and yet you put these horrid pictures into my mind! I think you ought to be ashamed of it, Lionel. People sleeping in the same room with us!"

"If the picture be revolting, what must be the reality?" was his rejoinder. "They have to endure it."

"They are used to it," retorted Sibylla. "They are brought up to nothing better."

"Just so. And therefore their perceptions of right and wrong are deadened. The wonder is, not that Alice Hook has lost herself, but that—"

"I don't want to hear about Alice Hook," interrupted Sibylla. "She is not very good to talk about."

"I have been openly told, Sibylla, that the reproach should lie at my door."

"I believe it is not the first reproach of the kind that has been cast on you," answered Sibylla, with cutting sarcasm.

He did not know what she meant, or in what sense to take the remark; but his mind was too preoccupied to linger on it. "With these things staring me in the face, how can I find money for superfluous vanities? The time has come when I am compelled to make a stand against it. I will, I must, have decent dwellings on my estate, and I shall set about the work without a day's loss of time. For that reason, if for no other, I cannot buy the ponies."

"I have bought them," coolly interrupted Sibylla.

"Then, my dear, you must forgive me if I countermand the purchase. I am resolute, Sibylla," he continued, in a firm tone. "For the first time since our marriage, I must deny your wish. I cannot let you bring me to beggary, because it would also involve you. Another year or two of this extravagance, and I should be on the verge of it."

Sibylla flung his arms from her. "Do you want to keep me as a beggar? I will have the ponies!"

He shook his head. "The subject is settled, Sibylla. If you cannot think for yourself, I must think for you. But it was not to speak of the ponies that I brought you here. What is it that you owe to Mrs. Duff?"

Sibylla's colour heightened. "It is no business of yours, Lionel, what I owe her. There may be some trifle or other down in her book. It will be time enough for you to concern yourself with my little petty debts when you are asked to pay them."

"Then that time is the present one, with regard to Mrs. Duff. She applied to me for the money this morning. At least, she asked if I would speak to you—which is the same thing. She says you owe her thirty-two pounds. Sibylla, I had far rather been stabbed than have heard it."

"A fearful sum, truly, to be doled out of your coffers!" cried Sibylla, sarcastically. "You'll never recover it, I should think!"

"Not that—not that," was the reply of Lionel, his tone one of pain. "Sibylla! have you no sense of the fitness of things? Is it seemly for the mistress of Verner's Pride to keep a poor woman, as Mrs. Duff is, out of her money; a humble shopkeeper who has to pay her way as she goes on?"

"I wish Fred had lived! He would never have taken me to task as you do."

"I wish he had!" was the retort in Lionel's heart; but he bit his lips to silence, exchanging the words, after a few minutes' pause, for others.

"You would have found Frederick Massingbird a less indulgent husband to you than I have been," he firmly said. "But these remarks are profitless, and will add to the comfort of neither you nor me. Sibylla, I shall send, in your name, to pay this bill of Mrs. Duff's. Will you give it me?"

"I dare say Benoite can find it, if you choose to ask her."

"And, my dear, let me beg of you not to contract these paltry debts. There have been others, as you know. I do not like that Mrs. Verner's name should be thus bandied in the village. What you buy in the village, pay for at once."

"How can I pay while you stint me?"

"Stint you!" repeated Lionel, in amazement. "Stint you!"

"It's nothing but stinting—going on at me as you do!" she sullenly answered. "You would like to deprive me of the horses I have set my mind upon! You know you would!"

"The horses you cannot have, Sibylla," he answered, his tone a decisive one. "I have already said it."

It aroused her anger. "If you don't let me have the horses, and all other things I want, I'll go where I can have them."

What did she mean? Lionel's cheek turned white with the taunt the words might be supposed to imply. He held her two hands in his, pressing them nervously.

"You shall not force me to quarrel with you, Sibylla," he continued, with emotion. "I have almost registered a vow that no offensive word or conduct on your part shall make me forget myself for a moment; or render me other than an ever considerate, tender husband. It may be that our marriage was a mistake for both of us; but we shall do well to make the best of it. It is the only course remaining."

He spoke in a strangely earnest tone; one of deep agitation. Sibylla was aroused. She had believed that Lionel blindly loved her. Otherwise she might have been more careful to retain his love—there's no knowing.

"How do you mean that our marriage was a mistake for both of us?" she hastily cried.

"You do your best to remind me continually that it must be so," was his reply.

"Psha!" returned Sibylla. And Lionel, without another word, quitted her and walked away. In these moments, above all others, would the image of Lucy Tempest rise up before his sight. Beat it down as he would, it was ever present to him. A mistake in his marriage! Ay; none save Lionel knew how fatal a one.

He passed on direct to the terrace, avoiding the lawn, traversed it, and went out at the large gates. Thence he made his way to Poynton's, the veterinary surgeon, who also dealt in horses. At least, dealt in them so far as that he would buy and sell when employed to do so.

The man was in his yard, watching a horse go through his paces. He came forward to meet Lionel.

"Mrs. Verner has been talking to you about some ponies, she tells me," began Lionel. "What are they?"

"A very handsome pair, sir. Just the thing for a lady to drive. They are to be sold for a hundred and fifty pounds. It's under their value."

"Spirited?"

"Yes. They have their mettle about them. Good horses always have, you know, sir. Mrs. Verner has given me the commission."

"Which I am come to rescind," replied Lionel, calling up a light smile to his face. "I cannot have my wife's neck risked by her attempting to drive spirited ponies, Poynton. She knows nothing of driving, is constitutionally timid, and—in short, I do not wish the order executed."

"Very well, sir," was the man's reply. "There's no harm done. I was at Verner's Pride with that horse that's ill, and Mrs. Verner spoke to me about some ponies. It was only to-day I heard these were in the market, and I mentioned them to her. But, for all I know, they may be already sold."

Lionel turned to walk out of the yard. "After Mrs. Verner shall have learned to drive, then we shall see; perhaps we may buy a pair," he remarked. "My opinion is that she will not learn. After a trial or two she will give it up."

"All right, sir."

CHAPTER LVI

A LIFE HOVERING IN THE BALANCE

Jan was coming up the road from Deerham with long strides, as Lionel turned out of Poynton's yard. Lionel advanced leisurely to meet him.

"One would think you were walking for a wager, Jan!"

"Ay," said Jan. "This is my first round to-day. Bitterworths have sent for me in desperate haste. Folks always get ill at the wrong time."

"Why don't you ride?" asked Lionel, turning with Jan, and stepping out at the same pace.

"There was no time to get the horse ready. I can walk it nearly as fast. I have had no breakfast yet."

"No breakfast!" echoed Lionel.

"I dived into the kitchen and caught up a piece of bread out of the basket. Half my patients must do without me to-day. I have only just got away from Hook's."

"How is the girl?"

"In great danger," replied Jan.

"She is ill, then?"

"So ill, that I don't think she'll last the day out. The child's dead. I must cut across the fields back there again, after I have seen what's amiss at Bitterworth's."

The words touching Alice Hook caused quite a shock to Lionel. "It will be a sad thing, Jan, if she should die!"

"I don't think I can save her. This comes of the ghost. I wonder how many more folks will get frightened to death."

Lionel paused. "Was it really that alone that frightened the girl, and caused her illness? How very absurd the thing sounds! And yet serious."

"I can't make it out," remarked Jan. "Here's Bourne now, says he saw it. There's only one solution of the riddle that I can come to."

"What's that?" asked Lionel.

"Well," said Jan, "it's not a pleasant one."

"You can tell it me, Jan, pleasant or unpleasant."

"Not pleasant for you, I mean, Lionel. I'll tell you if you like."

Lionel looked at him.

"Speak!"

"I think it must be Fred Massingbird himself."

The answer appeared to take Lionel by surprise. Possibly he had not admitted the doubt.

"Fred Massingbird himself; I don't understand you, Jan."

"Fred himself, in life," repeated Jan. "I fancy it will turn out that he did not die in Australia. He may have been very ill perhaps, and they fancied him dead; and now he is well, and has come over."

Every vestige of colour forsook Lionel's face.

"Jan!" he uttered, partly in terror, partly in anger. "Jan!" he repeated from between his bloodless lips. "Have you thought of the position in which your hint would place my wife?—the reflection it would cast upon her? How dare you?"

"You told me to speak," was Jan's composed answer. "I said you'd not like it. Speaking of it, or keeping silence, won't make it any the better, Lionel."

"What could possess you to think of such a thing?"

"There's nothing else that I can think of. Look here! Is there such a thing as a ghost? Is that probable?"

"Nonsense! No," said Lionel.

"Then what can it be, unless it's Fred himself? Lionel, were I you, I'd look the matter full in the face. It is Fred Massingbird, or it is not. If not, the sooner the mystery is cleared up the better, and the fellow brought to book and punished. It's not to be submitted to that he is to stride about for his own pastime, terrifying people to their injury. Is Alice Hook's life nothing? Were Dan Duff's senses nothing?—and, upon my word, I once thought there was good-bye to them."

Lionel did not answer. Jan continued.

"If it is Fred himself, the fact can't be long concealed. He'll be sure to make himself known. Why he should not do it at once, I can't imagine. Unless—"

"Unless what?" asked Lionel.

"Well, you are so touchy on all points relating to Sibylla, that one hesitates to speak," continued Jan. "I was going to say, unless he fears the shock to Sibylla; and would let her be prepared for it by degrees."

"Jan," gasped Lionel, "it would kill her."

"No, it wouldn't," dissented Jan. "She's not one to be killed by emotion of any sort. Or much stirred by it, as I believe, if you care for my opinion. It would not be pleasant for you or for her, but she'd not die of it."

Lionel wiped the moisture from his face. From the moment Jan had first spoken, a conviction seemed to arise within him that the suggestion would turn out to be only too true a one—that the ghost, in point of fact, was Frederick Massingbird in life.

"This is awful!" he murmured. "I would sacrifice my own life to save Sibylla from pain."

"Where'd be the good of that?" asked practical Jan. "If it is Fred Massingbird in the flesh, she's his wife and not your's; your sacrificing yourself—as you call it, Lionel—would not make her any the less or the more so. I am abroad a good deal at night, especially now, when there's so much sickness about, and I shall perhaps come across the fellow. Won't I pin him if I get the chance."

"Jan," said Lionel, catching hold of his brother's arm to detain him as he was speeding away, for they had reached the gate of Verner's Pride, "be cautious that not a breath of this suspicion escapes you. For my poor wife's sake."

"No fear," answered Jan. "If it gets about, it won't be from me, mind. I am going to believe in the ghost henceforth, you understand. Except to you and Bourne."

"If it gets about," mechanically answered Lionel, repeating the words which made most impression upon his mind. "You think it will get about?"

"Think! It's safe to," answered Jan. "Had old Frost and Dan Duff and Cheese not been great gulls, they'd have taken it for Fred himself; not his ghost. Bourne suspects. From a hint he dropped to me just now at Hook's, I find he takes the same view of the case that I do."

"Since when have you suspected this, Jan?"

"Not for many hours. Don't keep me, Lionel. Bitterworth may be dying, for aught I know, and so may Alice Hook."

Jan went on like a steam-engine. Lionel remained, standing at his entrance-gate, more like a prostrate being than a living man.

Thought after thought crowded upon him. If it was really Frederick Massingbird in life, how was it that he had not made his appearance before? Where had he been all this while? Considerably more than two years had elapsed since the supposed death. To the best of Lionel's recollection, Sibylla had said Captain Cannonby buried her husband; but it was a point into which Lionel had never minutely inquired. Allow that Jan's suggestion was correct—that he did not die—where had he been since? What had prevented him from joining or seeking his wife? What prevented him doing it now? From what motive could he be in concealment in the neighbourhood, stealthily prowling about at night? Why did he not appear openly? Oh, it could not—it could not be Frederick Massingbird!

Which way should he bend his steps? Indoors, or away? Not indoors! He could scarcely bear to see his wife, with this dreadful uncertainty upon him. Restless, anxious, perplexed, miserable, Lionel Verner turned towards Deerham.

There are some natures upon whom a secret, awful as this, tells with appalling force, rendering it next to impossible to keep silence. The imparting it to some friend, the speaking of it, appears to be a matter of dire necessity. It was so in this instance to Lionel Verner.

He was on his way to the vicarage. Jan had mentioned that Mr. Bourne shared the knowledge—if knowledge it could be called; and he was one in whom might be placed entire trust.

He walked onwards, like one in a fever dream, nodding mechanically in answer to salutations; answering he knew not what, if words were spoken to him. The vicarage joined the churchyard, and the vicar was standing in the latter as Lionel came up, watching two men who were digging a grave. He crossed over the mounds to shake hands with Lionel.

Lionel drew him into the vicarage garden, amidst the trees. It was shady there; the outer world shut out from eye and ear.

"I cannot beat about the bush; I cannot dissemble," began Lionel, in deep agitation. "Tell me your true opinion of this business, for the love of Heaven! I have come down to ask it of you."

The vicar paused. "My dear friend, I feel almost afraid to give it to you."

"I have been speaking with Jan. He thinks it may be Frederick Massingbird—not dead, but alive."

"I fear it is," answered the clergyman. "Within the last half-hour I have fully believed that it is."

Lionel leaned his back against a tree, his arms folded. Tolerably calm outwardly; but he could not get the healthy blood back to his face. "Why within the last half-hour more than before?" he asked. "Has anything fresh happened?"

"Yes," said Mr. Bourne. "I went down to Hook's; the girl's not expected to live the day through—but that you may have heard from Jan. In coming away, your gamekeeper met me. He stopped, and began asking my advice in a mysterious manner—whether, if a secret affecting his master had come to his knowledge, he ought, or ought not, to impart it to his master. I felt sure what the man was driving at—that it could be no other thing than this ghost affair—and gave him a hint to speak out to me in confidence; which he did."

"Well?" rejoined Lionel.

"He said," continued Mr. Bourne, lowering his voice, "that he passed a man last night who, he was perfectly certain, was Frederick Massingbird. 'Not Frederick Massingbird's ghost, as foolish people were fancying,' Broom added, 'but Massingbird himself.' He was in doubt whether or not it was his duty to acquaint Mr. Verner; and so he asked me. I bade him not acquaint you," continued the vicar, "but to bury the suspicion within his own breast, breathing a word to none."

Evidence upon evidence! Every moment brought less loop-hole of escape for Lionel. "How can it be?" he gasped. "If he is not dead, where can he have been all this while?"

"I conclude it will turn out to be one of those every-day occurrences that have little marvel at all in them. My thoughts were busy upon it, while standing over the grave yonder. I suppose he must have been to the diggings—possibly laid up there by illness; and letters may have miscarried."

"You feel little doubt upon the fact itself—that it is Frederick Massingbird?"

"I feel none. It is certainly he. Won't you come in and sit down?"

"No, no," said Lionel; and, drawing his hand from the vicar's, he went forth again, he, and his heavy weight. Frederick Massingbird alive!

CHAPTER LVII

The fine September morning had turned to a rainy afternoon. A heavy mist hung upon the trees, the hedges, the ground—something akin to the mist which had fallen upon Lionel Verner's spirit. The day had grown more like a November one; the clouds were leaden-coloured, the rain fell. Even the little birds sought the shelter of their nests.

One there was who walked in it, his head uncovered, his brow bared. He was in the height of his fever dream. It is not an inapt name for his state of mind. His veins coursed as with fever; his thoughts took all the vague uncertainty of a dream. Little heeded he that the weather had become chilly, or that the waters fell upon him!

What must be his course? What ought it to be? The more he dwelt on the revelation of that day, the deeper grew his conviction that Frederick Massingbird was alive, breathing the very air that he breathed. What ought to be his course? If this were so, his wife was—not his wife.

It was obvious that his present, immediate course ought to be to solve the doubt—to set it at rest. But how? It could only be done by unearthing Frederick Massingbird; or he who bore so strange a resemblance to him. And where was he to be looked for? To track the hiding-place of a "ghost" is not an easy matter; and Lionel had no clue where to find the track of this one. If staying in the village, he must be concealed in some house; lying perdu by day. It was very strange that it should be so; that he should not openly show himself.

There was another way by which perhaps the doubt might be solved—as it suddenly occurred to Lionel. And that was through Captain Cannonby. If this gentleman really was with Frederick Massingbird when he died, and saw him buried, it was evident that it could not be Frederick come back to life. In that case, who or what it might be, Lionel did not stay to speculate; his business lay in ascertaining by the most direct means in his power, whether it was, or was not, Frederick Massingbird. How was it possible to do this? how could it be possible to set the question at rest?

By a very simple process, it may be answered—the waiting for time and chance. Ay, but do you know what that waiting involves, in a case like this? Think of the state of mind that Lionel Verner must live under during the suspense!

He made no doubt that the man who had been under the tree on the lawn a few nights before, watching his window, whom they had set down as being Roy, was Frederick Massingbird. And yet, it was scarcely believable. Where now was Lionel to look for him? He could not, for Sibylla's sake, make inquiries in the village in secret or openly; he could not go to the inhabitants and ask—have you seen Frederick Massingbird? or say to each individual, I must send a police officer to search your house, for I suspect Frederick Massingbird is somewhere concealed, and I want to find him. For her sake he could not so much as breathe the name, in connection with his being alive.

Given that it was Frederick Massingbird, what could possibly prevent his making himself known? As he dwelt upon this problem, trying to solve it, the idea taken up by Lucy Tempest—that the man under the tree was watching for an opportunity to harm him—came into his mind. That, surely, could not be the solution! If he had taken Frederick Massingbird's wife to be his wife, he had done it in all innocence. Lionel spurned the notion as a preposterous one; nevertheless, a remembrance crossed him of the old days when the popular belief at Verner's Pride had been, that the younger of the Massingbirds was of a remarkably secretive and also of a revengeful nature. But all that he barely glanced at; the terrible fear touching Sibylla absorbed him.

He was leaning against a tree in the covered walk near Verner's Pride, the walk which led to the Willow Pond, his head bared, his brow bent with the most unmistakable signs of care, when something not unlike a small white balloon came flying down the path. A lady, with her silk dress turned over her shoulders, leaving only the white lining exposed to view. She was face to face with Lionel before she saw him.

"Lucy!" he exclaimed, in extreme surprise.

Lucy Tempest laughed, and let her dress drop into a more dignified position. "I and Decima went to call on Mrs. Bitterworth," she explained, "and Decima is staying there. It began to rain as I came out, so I turned into the back walk and put my dress up to save it. Am I not economical, Mr. Verner?"

She spoke quickly. Lionel thought it was done with a view to hide her agitation. "You cannot go home through this rain, Lucy. Let me take you indoors; we are close to Verner's Pride."

"No, thank you," said Lucy hastily, "I must go back to Lady Verner. She will not be pleased at Decima's staying out, therefore I must return. Poor Mrs. Bitterworth has had an attack of—what did they call it?— spasmodical croup, I think. She is better now, and begged Decima to stay with her the rest of the day; Mr. Bitterworth and the rest of them are out. Jan says it is highly dangerous for the time it lasts."

"She has had something of the same sort before, I remember," observed Lionel. "I wish you would come in, Lucy. If you must go home, I will send you in the carriage; but I think you might stay and dine with us."

A soft colour mantled in Lucy's cheeks. She had never made herself a familiar acquaintance at Lionel Verner's. He had observed it, if no one else had. Sibylla had once said to her that she hoped they should be great friends, that Verner's Pride would see a great deal of her. Lucy had never responded to the wish. A formal visit with Decima or Lady Verner when she could not help herself; but alone, in a social manner, she had never put her foot over the threshold of Verner's Pride.

"You are very kind. I must go home at once. The rain will not hurt me."

Lionel, self-conscious, did not urge it further. "Will you remain here, then, under the trees, while I go home and get an umbrella?"

"Oh, dear, no, I don't want an umbrella; thank you all the same. I have my parasol, you see."

She took her dress up again as she spoke; not high, as it was previously, but turning it a little. "Lady Verner scolds me so if I spoil my things," she said, in a tone of laughing apology. "She buys me very good ones, and orders me to take care of them. Good-bye, Mr. Verner."

Lionel took the hand in his which she held out. But he turned with her, and then loosed it again.

"You are not coming with me, Mr. Verner?"

"I shall see you home."

"But—I had rather you did not. I prefer—not to trouble you."

"Pardon me, Lucy. I cannot suffer you to go alone."

It was a calm reply, quietly spoken. There were no fine phrases of its being "no trouble," that the "trouble was a pleasure," as others might indulge in. Fine phrases from them! from the one to the other! Neither could have spoken them.

Lucy said no more, and they walked on side by side in silence, both unpleasantly self-conscious. Lionel's face had resumed its strange expression of care. Lucy had observed it when she came up to him; she observed it still.

"You look as though you had some great trouble upon you, Mr. Verner," she said, after a while.

"Then I look what is the truth. I have one, Lucy."

"A heavy one?" asked Lucy, struck with his tone.

"A grievously heavy one. One that does not often fall to the lot of man."

"May I know it?" she timidly said.

"No, Lucy. If I could speak it, it would only give you pain; but it is of a private nature. Possibly it may be averted; it is at present a suspected dread, not a confirmed one. Should it become confirmed, you will learn it in common with all the world."

She looked up at him, puzzled; sympathy in her mantling blush, in her soft, dark, earnest eyes. He could not avoid contrasting that truthful face with another's frivolous one; and I can't help it if you blame him. He did his best to shake off the feeling, and looked down at her with a careless smile.

"Don't let it give you concern, Lucy. My troubles must rest upon my own head.".

"Have you seen any more of that man who was watching? Roy."

"No. But I don't believe now that it was Roy. He strongly denies it, and I have had my suspicions diverted to another quarter."

"To one who may be equally wishing to do you harm?"

"I cannot say. If it be the party I—I suspect, he may deem that I have done him harm."

"You!" echoed Lucy. "And have you?"

"Yes. Unwittingly. It seems to be my fate, I think, to work harm upon—upon those whom I would especially shield from it."

Did he allude to her? Lucy thought so, and the flush on her cheeks deepened. At that moment the rain began to pour down heavily. They were then passing the thicket of trees where those adventurous ghost-hunters had taken up their watch a few nights previously, in view of the Willow Pond. Lucy stepped underneath their branches.

"Now," said Lionel, "should you have done well to accept my offer of Verner's Pride as a shelter, or not?"

"It may only be a passing storm," observed Lucy. "The rain then was nothing."

Lionel took her parasol and shook the wet off it. He began to wonder how Lucy would get home. No carriage could be got to that spot, and the rain, coming down now, was not, in his opinion, a passing storm.

"Will you promise to remain here, Lucy, while I get an umbrella?" he presently asked.

"Why! where could you get an umbrella from?"

"From Hook's, if they possess such a thing. If not, I can get one from Broom's."

"But you would get so wet, going for it!"

Lionel laughed as he went off.

"I don't wear a silk dress; to be scolded for it, if it gets spoiled."

Not ten steps had he taken, however, when who should come striding through an opening in the trees, but Jan. Jan was on his way from Hook's cottage, a huge brown cotton umbrella over his head, more useful than elegant.

"What, is that you, Miss Lucy! Well, I should as soon have thought of seeing Mrs. Peckaby's white donkey!"

"I am weather-bound, Jan," said Lucy. "Mr. Verner was about to get me an umbrella."

"To see if I could get one," corrected Lionel. "I question if the Hooks possess such a commodity."

"Not they," cried Jan. "The girl's rather better," added he unceremoniously. "She may get through it now; at least there's a shade of a chance. You can have my umbrella, Miss Lucy."

"Won't you let me go with you, Jan?" she asked.

"Oh, I can't stop to take you to Deerham Court," was Jan's answer, given with his accustomed plainness. "Here, Lionel!"

He handed over the umbrella, and was walking off.

"Jan, Jan, you will get wet," said Lucy.

It amused Jan. "A wetting more or less is nothing to me," he called out, striding on.

"Will you stay under shelter a few minutes yet, and see whether it abates?" asked Lionel.

Lucy looked up at the skies, stretching her head beyond the trees to do so.

"Do you think it will abate?" she rejoined.

"Honestly to confess it, I think it will get worse," said Lionel. "Lucy, you have thin shoes on! I did not see that until now."

"Don't you tell Lady Verner," replied Lucy, with the pretty dependent manner which she had brought from school with her, and which she probably would never lose. "She would scold me for walking out in them."

Lionel smiled, and held the great umbrella—large enough for a carriage—close to the trees, that it might shelter her as she came forth.

"Take my arm, Lucy."

She hesitated for a single moment—a hesitation so temporary that any other than Lionel could not have observed it, and then took his arm. And again they walked on in silence. In passing down Clay Lane—the way Lionel took—Mrs. Peckaby was standing at her door.

"On the look-out for the white donkey, Mrs. Peckaby?" asked Lionel.

The husband inside heard the words, and flew into a tantrum.

"She's never on the look-out for nothing else, sir, asking pardon for saying it to you."

Mrs. Peckaby clasped her hands together.

"It'll come!" she murmured. "Sometimes, sir, when my patience is well nigh exhausted, I has a vision of the New Jerusalem in the night, and is revived. It'll come, sir, the quadruple'll come!"

"I wonder," laughed Lucy, as they walked on, "whether she will go on to the end of her life expecting it?"

"If her husband will allow her," answered Lionel. "But by what I have heard since I came home, his patience is—as she says by her own with reference to the white 'quadruple'—well nigh exhausted."

"He told Decima, the other day, that he was sick of the theme and of her folly, and he wished the New Jerusalem had her and the white donkey together. Here we are!" added Lucy, as they came in front of

Deerham Court. "Lionel, please, let me go in the back way—Jan's way. And then Lady Verner will not see me. She will say I ought not to have come through the rain."

"She'll see the shoes and the silk dress, and she'll say you should have stopped at Verner's Pride, as a well-trained young lady ought," returned Lionel.

He took her safely to the back door, opened it, and sent her in.

"Thank you very much," said she, holding out her hand to him. "I have given you a disagreeable walk, and now I must give you one back again."

"Change your shoes at once, and don't talk foolish things," was Lionel's answer.

CHAPTER LVIII

THE THUNDER-STORM

A wet walk back Lionel certainly had; but, wet or dry, it was all the same in his present distressed frame of mind. Arrived at Verner's Pride, he found his wife dressed for dinner, and the centre of a host of guests gay as she was. No opportunity, then, to question her about Frederick Massingbird's death, and how far Captain Cannonby was cognisant of the particulars.

He had to change his own things. It was barely done by dinner-time; and he sat down to table, the host of many guests. His brow was smooth, his speech was courtly; how could any of them suspect that a terrible dread was gnawing at his heart? Sibylla, in a rustling silk dress and a coronet of diamonds, sat opposite to him, in all her dazzling beauty. Had she suspected what might be in store for her, those smiles would not have chased each other so incessantly on her lips.

Sibylla went up to bed early. She was full of caprices as a wayward child. Of a remarkably chilly nature— as is the case, sometimes, where the constitution is delicate—she would have a fire in her dressing-room night and morning all the year round, even in the heat of summer. It pleased her this evening to desert her guests suddenly; she had the headache, she said.

The weather on this day appeared to be as capricious as Sibylla, as strangely curious as the great fear which had fallen upon Lionel. The fine morning had changed to the rainy, misty, chilly afternoon; the afternoon to a clear, bright evening; and that evening had now become overcast with portentous clouds.

Without much warning the storm burst forth; peals of thunder reverberated through the air, flashes of forked lightning played in the sky. Lionel hastened upstairs; he remembered how these storms terrified his wife.

She had knelt down to bury her head amidst the soft cushions of a chair when Lionel entered her dressing-room. "Sibylla!" he said.

"Sibylla!" he said.

Up she started at the sound of his voice, and flew to him. There lay her protection; and in spite of her ill-temper and her love of aggravation, she felt and recognised it. Lionel held her in his sheltering arms, bending her head down upon his breast, and drawing his coat over it, so that she might see no ray of light—as he had been wont to do in former storms. As a timid child was she at these times, humble, loving, gentle; she felt as if she were on the threshold of the next world, that the next moment might be her last. Others have been known to experience the same dread in a thunder-storm; and, to be thus brought, as it were, face to face with death, takes the spirit out of people.

He stood, patiently holding her. Every time the thunder burst above their heads, he could feel her heart beat against his. One of her arms was round him; the other he held; all wet it was with fear. He did not speak; he only clasped her closer every now and then, that she might be reminded of her shelter.

Twenty minutes or so, and the violence of the storm abated. The lightning grew less frequent, the thunder distant and more distant. At length the sound wholly ceased, and the lightning subsided into that harmless sheet lightning which is so beautiful to look at in the far-off horizon.

"It is over," he whispered.

She lifted her head from its resting place. Her blue eye was bright with excitement, her delicate cheek was crimson, her golden hair fell in a dishevelled mass around. Her gala robes had been removed, with the diamond coronet, and the storm had surprised her writing a note in her dressing-gown. In spite of the sudden terror which overtook her, she did not forget to put the letter—so far as had been written of it—safely away. It was not expedient that her husband's eyes should fall upon it. Sibylla had many answers to write now to importunate creditors.

"Are you sure, Lionel?"

"Quite sure. Come and see how clear it is. You are not alarmed at the sheet lightning."

He put his arm round her, and led her to the window. As he said, the sky was clear again. Nearly all traces of the storm had passed away; there had been no rain with it; and, but for the remembrance of its sound in their ears, they might have believed that it had not taken place. The broad lands of Verner's Pride lay spreading out before them, the lawns and the terrace underneath; the sheet-lightning illumined the heavens incessantly, rendering objects nearly as clear as in the day.

Lionel held her to his side, his arm round her. She trembled still—trembled excessively; her bosom heaved and fell beneath his hand.

"When I die, it will be in a thunder-storm," she whispered.

"You foolish girl!" he said, his tone half a joking one, wholly tender. "What can have given you this excessive fear of thunder, Sibylla?"

"I was always frightened at a thunder-storm. Deborah says mamma was. But I was not so very frightened until a storm I witnessed in Australia. It killed a man!" she added, shivering and nestling nearer to Lionel.

"Ah!"

"It was only a few days before Frederick left me, when he and Captain Cannonby went away together," she continued. "We had hired a carriage, and had gone out of the town ever so far. There was something to be seen there; I forget what now; races perhaps. I know a good many people went; and an awful thunder-storm came on. Some ran under the trees for shelter; some would not; and the lightning killed a man. Oh, Lionel, I shall never forget it! I saw him carried past; I saw his face! Since then I have felt ready to die myself with the fear."

She turned her face, and hid it upon his bosom. Lionel did not attempt to soothe the fear; he knew that for such fear time alone is the only cure. He whispered words of soothing to her; he stroked fondly her golden hair. In these moments, when she was gentle, yielding, clinging to him for protection, three parts of his old love for her would come back again. The lamp, which had been turned on to its full blaze of light, was behind them, so that they might have been visible enough to anybody standing in the nearer portion of the grounds.

"Captain Cannonby went away with Frederick Massingbird," observed Lionel, approaching by degrees to the questions he wished to ask. "Did they start together?"

"Yes. Don't talk about it, Lionel."

"My dear wife, I must talk about it," he gravely answered. "You have always put me off in this manner, so that I know little or nothing of the circumstances. I have a reason for wishing to become cognisant of those past particulars. Surely," he added, a shade of deeper feeling in his tone, "at this distance of time it cannot be so very painful to your feelings to speak of Frederick Massingbird. I am by your side."

"What is the reason that you wish to know?"

"A little matter that regarded him and Cannonby. Was Cannonby with him when he died?"

Sibylla, subdued still, yielded to the wish as she would probably have yielded at no other time.

"Of course he was with him. They were but a day's journey from Melbourne. I forget the name of the place; a sort of small village or settlement, I believe, where the people halted that were going to, or returning from, the diggings. Frederick was taken worse as they got there, and in a few hours he died."

"Cannonby remaining with him?"

"Yes. I am sure I have told you this before, Lionel. I told it to you on the night of my return."

He was aware she had. He could not say: "But I wish to press you upon the points; to ascertain beyond doubt that Frederick Massingbird did really die; that he is not living." "Did Cannonby stay until he was buried?" he asked aloud.

"Yes."

"You are sure of this?"

Sibylla looked at him curiously. She could not think why he was recalling this; why want to know it?

"I am sure of it only so far as that Captain Cannonby told me so," replied Sibylla.

The reservation struck upon him with a chill; it seemed to be a confirmation of his worst fears. Sibylla continued, for he did not speak—

"Of course he stayed with him until he was buried. When Captain Cannonby came back to me at Melbourne, he said he had waited to lay him in the ground. Why should he have said it, if he did not?"

"True," murmured Lionel.

"He said the burial-service had been read over him. I remember that, well. I reproached Captain Cannonby with not having come back to me immediately, or sent for me that I might at least have seen him dead, if not alive. He excused himself by saying that he did not think I should like to see him; and he had waited to bury him before returning."

Lionel fell into a reverie. If this, that Captain Cannonby had stated, was correct, there was no doubt that Frederick Massingbird was safely dead and buried. But he could not be sure that it was correct; Captain Cannonby may not have relished waiting to see a dead man buried; although he had affirmed so much to Sibylla. A thousand pounds would Lionel have given out of his pocket at that moment, for one minute's interview with Captain Cannonby.

"Lionel!"

The call came from Sibylla with sudden intensity, half startling him. She had got one of her fingers pointed to the lawn.

"Who's that—peeping forth from underneath the yew-tree?"

The same place, the same tree which had been pointed to by Lucy Tempest! An impulse, for which Lionel could not have accounted, caused him to turn round and put out the lamp.

"Who can it be?" wondered Sibylla. "He appears to be watching us. How foolish of any of them to go out! I should not feel safe under a tree, although that lightning is only sheet-lightning."

Every perceptive faculty that Lionel Verner possessed was strained upon the spot. He could make out a tall man; a man whose figure bore—unless his eyes and his imagination combined to deceive him—a strong resemblance to Frederick Massingbird's. Had it come to it? Were he and his rival face to face; was she, by his own side now, about to be bandied between them?—belonging, save by the priority of the first marriage ceremony, no more to one than to the other? A stifled cry, suppressed instantly, escaped his lips; his pulses stood still, and then throbbed on with painful violence.

"Can you discern him, Lionel?" she asked. "He is going away—going back amidst the trees. Perhaps because he can't see us any longer, now you have put the light out. Who is it? Why should he have stood there, watching us?"

Lionel snatched her to him with an impulsive gesture. He would have sacrificed his life willingly, to save Sibylla from the terrible misfortune that appeared to be falling upon her.

A merry breakfast-table. Sibylla, for a wonder, up, and present at it. The rain of the preceding day, the storm of the night had entirely passed away, and as fine a morning as could be wished was smiling on the earth.

"Which of you went out before the storm was over, and ventured under the great yew-tree?"

It was Mrs. Verner who spoke. She looked at the different gentlemen present, and they looked at her. They did not know what she meant.

"You were under it, one of you," persisted Sibylla.

All, save one, protested that they had neither been out nor under the tree. That one—it happened to be Mr. Gordon, of whom casual mention has been made—confessed to having been on the lawn, so far as crossing it went; but he did not go near the tree.

"I went out with my cigar," he observed, "and had strolled some distance from the house when the storm came on. I stood in the middle of a field and watched it. It was grandly beautiful."

"I wonder you were not brought home dead!" ejaculated Sibylla.

Mr. Gordon laughed. "If you once witnessed the thunder-storms that we get in the tropics, Mrs. Verner, you would not associate these with danger."

"I have seen dreadful thunder-storms, apart from what we get here, as well as you, Mr. Gordon," returned Sibylla.

"Perhaps you will deny that anybody's ever killed by them in this country. But why did you halt underneath the yew-tree?"

"I did not," he repeated. "I crossed the lawn, straight on to the upper end of the terrace. I did not go near the tree."

"Some one did, if you did not. They were staring right up at my dressing-room window. I was standing at it with Mr. Verner."

Mr. Gordon shook his head. "Not guilty, so far as I am concerned, Mrs. Verner. I met some man, when I was coming home, plunging into the thicket of trees as I emerged from them. It was he, possibly."

"What man?" questioned Sibylla.

"I did not know him. He was a stranger. A tall, dark man with stooping shoulders, and something black upon his cheek."

"Something black upon his cheek;" repeated Sibylla, thinking the words bore an odd sound.

"A large black mark it looked like. His cheek was white—sallow would be the better term—and he wore no whiskers, so it was a conspicuous looking brand. In the moment he passed me, the lightning rendered the atmosphere as light as—"

"Sibylla!" almost shouted Lionel, "we are waiting for more tea in this quarter. Never mind, Gordon."

They looked at him with surprise. He was leaning towards his wife; his face crimson, his tones agitated. Sibylla stared at him, and said, if he called out like that, she would not get up another morning. Lionel replied, talking fast; and just then the letters were brought in. Altogether, the subject of the man with the mark upon his cheek dropped out of the discussion.

Bread fast over, Lionel put his arm within Mr. Gordon's and drew him outside upon the terrace. Not to question him upon the man he had seen—Lionel would have been glad that that encounter should pass out of Mr. Gordon's remembrance, as affording less chance of Sibylla's hearing of it again—but to get information on another topic. He had been rapidly making up his mind during the latter half of breakfast, and had come to a decision.

"Gordon, can you inform me where Captain Cannonby is to be found?"

"Can you inform me where the comet that visited us last year may be met with this?" returned Mr. Gordon. "I'd nearly as soon undertake to find out the locality of the one as of the other. Cannonby did go to Paris; but where he may be now, is quite another affair."

"Was he going there for any length of time?"

"I fancy not. Most likely he is back in London by this time. Had he told me he was coming back, I should have paid no attention to it. He never knows his own mind two hours together."

"I particularly wish to see him," observed Lionel. "Can you give me any address where he may be found in London?—if he has returned?"

"Yes. His brother's in Westminster. I can give you the exact number and address by referring to my notebook. When Cannonby's in London, he makes it his headquarters. If he is away, his brother may know where he is."

"His brother may be out of town also. Few men are in it at this season."

"If they can get out. But Dr. Cannonby can't. He is a physician, and must stop at his post, season or no season."

"I am going up to town to-day," remarked Lionel, "and—"

"You are! For long?"

"Back to-morrow, I hope; perhaps to-night. If you will give me the address, I'll copy it down."

Lionel wrote it down; but Mr. Gordon told him there was no necessity; any little ragged boy in the street could direct him to Dr. Cannonby's. Then he went to make his proposed journey known to Sibylla. She was standing near one of the terrace pillars, looking up at the sky, her eyes shaded with her hand. Lionel drew her inside an unoccupied room.

"Sibylla, a little matter of business is calling me to London," he said. "If I can catch the half-past ten train, I may be home again to-night, late."

"How sudden!" cried Sibylla. "Why didn't you tell me? What weather shall we have to-day, do you think?"

"Fine. But it is of little consequence to me whether it be fine or wet."

"Oh! I was not thinking of you," was the careless reply. "I want it to be fine for our archery."

"Good-bye," he said, stooping to kiss her. "Take care of yourself."

"Lionel, mind, I shall have the ponies," was her answer, given in a pouting, pretty, affected manner.

Lionel smiled, shook his head, took another kiss, and left her. Oh, if he could but shield her from the tribulation that too surely seemed to be ominously looming!

The lightest and fleetest carriage he possessed had been made ready, and was waiting for him at the stables. He got in there, and drove off with his groom, saying farewell to none, and taking nothing with him but an overcoat. As he drove past Mrs. Duff's shop, the remembrance of the bill came over him. He had forwarded the money to her the previous night in his wife's name.

He caught the train; was too soon for it; it was five minutes behind time. If those who saw him depart could but have divined the errand he was bent on, what a commotion would have spread over Deerham! If the handsome lady, seated opposite to him, the only other passenger in that compartment, could but have read the cause which rendered him so self-absorbed, so insensible to her attractions, she would have gazed at him with far more interest.

"Who is that gentleman?" she privately asked of the guard when she got the opportunity.

"Mr. Verner, of Verner's Pride."

He sat back on his seat, heeding nothing. Had all the pretty women of the kingdom been ranged before him, in a row, they had been nothing to Mr. Verner then. Had Lucy Tempest been there, he had been equally regardless of her. If Frederick Massingbird were indeed in life, Verner's Pride was no longer his. But it was not of that he thought; it was of the calamity that would involve his wife. A calamity which, to the refined, sensitive mind of Lionel Verner, was almost worse than death itself.

What would the journey bring forth for him? Should he succeed in seeing Captain Cannonby? He awaited the fiat with feverish heat; and wished the fast express engine would travel faster.

The terminus gained at last, a hansom took him to Dr. Cannonby's. It was half-past two o'clock. He leaped out of the cab and rang, entering the hall when the door was opened.

"Can I see Dr. Cannonby?"

"The doctor's just gone out, sir. He will be home at five."

It was a sort of checkmate, and Lionel stood looking at the servant—as if the man could telegraph some impossible aerial message to his master to bring him back then.

"Is Captain Cannonby staying here?" was his next question.

"No, sir. He was staying here, but he went away this morning."

"He is home from Paris then?"

"He came back two or three days ago, sir," replied the servant.

"Do you know where he is gone?"

"I don't, sir. I fancy it's somewhere in the country."

"Dr. Cannonby would know?"

"I dare say he would, sir. I should think so."

Lionel turned to the door. Where was the use of his lingering? He looked back to ask a question.

"You are sure that Captain Cannonby has gone out of town?"

"Oh, yes, sir."

He descended the steps, and the man closed the door upon him. Where should he go? What should he do with himself for the next two and a half mortal hours? Go to his club? Or to any of the old spots of his London life? Not he; some familiar faces might be in town; and he was in no mood for familiar faces then.

Sauntering hither, sauntering thither, he came to Westminster Bridge. One of the steamers was approaching the pier to take in passengers, on its way down the river. For want of some other mode in which to employ his time, Lionel went down to the embarking place, and stepped on board.

Does anything in this world happen by chance? What secret unknown impulse could have sent Lionel Verner on board that steamer? Had Dr. Cannonby been at home he would not have gone near it; had he turned to the right hand instead of to the left, on leaving Dr. Cannonby's house, the boat would never have seen him.

It was not crowded, as those steamers sometimes are crowded, suggesting visions of the bottom of the river. The day was fine; warm for September, but not too hot; the gliding down the stream delightful. With a heart at ease, Lionel would have found it so; as it was, he could scarcely have told whether he was going down the stream or up, whether it was wet or dry. He could see but one thing—the image of Frederick Massingbird.

As the boat drew up to the Temple Pier, the only person waiting to embark was a woman; a little body in a faded brown silk dress. Whether, seeing his additional freight was to be so trifling, the manager of the steamer did not take the usual care to bring it alongside, certain it is, that in some way the woman fell, in stepping on board; her knees on the boat, her feet hanging down to the water. Lionel, who was sitting near, sprang forward and pulled her out of danger.

"I declare I never ought to come aboard these nasty steamers!" she exclaimed, as he placed her in a seat. "I'm greatly obliged to you, sir; I might have gone in, else; there's no saying. The last time I was aboard one I was in danger of being killed. I fell through the port-hole, sir."

"Indeed!" responded Lionel, who could not be so discourteous as not to answer. "Perhaps your sight is not good?"

"Well, yes it is, sir, as good as most folks, at middle age. I get timid aboard 'em, and it makes me confused and awkward, and I suppose I don't mind where I put my feet. This was in Liverpool, sir, a week or two ago. It was a passenger-ship just in from Australia, and the bustle and confusion aboard was dreadful—they say it's mostly so with them vessels that are coming home. I had gone down to meet my husband, sir; he has been away four years—and it's a pity he ever went, for all the good he has done. But he's back safe himself, so I must not grumble."

"That's something," said Lionel.

"True, sir. It would have been a strange thing if I had lost my life just as he had come home. And I should, but for a gentleman on board. He seized hold of me by the middle, and somehow contrived to drag me up again. A strong man he must have been! I shall always remember him with gratitude, I'm sure; as I shall you, sir. His name, my husband told me afterwards, was Massingbird."

All Lionel's inertness was gone at the sound of the name. "Massingbird?" he repeated.

"Yes, sir. He had come home in the ship from the same port as my husband—Melbourne. Quite a gentleman, my husband said he was, with grand relations in England. He had not been out there over long—hardly as long as my husband, I fancy—and my husband don't think he has made much, any more than himself has."

Lionel had regained all his outward impassiveness. He stood by the talkative woman, his arms folded. "What sort of a looking man was this Mr. Massingbird?" he asked. "I knew a gentleman once of that name, who went to Australia."

The woman glanced up at him, measuring his height. "I should say he was as tall as you, sir, or close upon it, but he was broader made, and had got a stoop in the shoulders. He was dark; had dark eyes and hair, and a pale face. Not the clear paleness of your face, sir, but one of them sallow faces that get darker and yellower with travelling; never red."

Every word was as fresh testimony to the suspicion that it was Frederick Massingbird. "Had he a black mark upon his cheek?" inquired Lionel.

"Likely he might have had, sir, but I couldn't see his cheeks. He wore a sort of fur cap with the ears tied down. My husband saw a good bit of him on the voyage, though he was only a middle-deck passenger, and the gentleman was a cabin. His friends have had a surprise before this," she continued, after a pause. "He told my husband that they all supposed him dead; had thought he had been dead these two years past and more; and he had never sent home to contradict it."

Then it was Frederick Massingbird! Lionel Verner quitted the woman's side, and leaned over the rail of the steamer, apparently watching the water. He could not, by any dint of reasoning or supposition, make out the mystery. How Frederick Massingbird could be alive; or, being alive, why he had not come home before to claim Sibylla—why he had not claimed her before she left Australia—why he did not claim her now he was come. A man without a wife might go roving where he would and as long as he would, letting his friends think him dead if it pleased him; but a man with a wife could not in his sane senses be supposed to act so. It was a strange thing, his meeting with this woman—a singular coincidence; one that he would hardly have believed, if related to him, as happening to another.

It was striking five when he again knocked at Dr. Cannonby's. He wished to see Captain Cannonby still; it would be the crowning confirmation. But he had no doubt whatever that that gentleman's report would be: "I saw Frederick Massingbird die—as I believed—and I quitted him immediately. I conclude that I must have been in error in supposing he was dead."

Dr. Cannonby had returned, the servant said. He desired Lionel to walk in, and threw open the door of the room. Seven or eight people were sitting in it, waiting. The servant had evidently mistaken him for a patient, and placed him there to wait his turn with the rest. He took his card from his pocket, wrote on it a few words, and desired the servant to carry it to his master.

The man came back with an apology. "I beg your pardon, sir. Will you step this way?"

The physician was bowing a lady out as he entered the room—a room lined with books, and containing casts of heads. He came forward to shake hands, a cordial-mannered man. He knew Lionel by reputation, but had never seen him.

"My visit was not to you, but to your brother," explained Lionel. "I was in hopes to have found him here."

"Then he and you have been playing at cross-purposes to-day," remarked the doctor, with a smile. "Lawrence started this morning for Verner's Pride."

"Indeed," exclaimed Lionel. "Cross-purposes indeed!" he muttered to himself.

"He heard some news in Paris which concerned you, I believe, and hastened home to pay you a visit."

"Which concerned me!" repeated Lionel.

"Or rather Mrs. Massingbird—Mrs. Verner, I should say."

A sickly smile crossed Lionel's lips. Mrs. Massingbird! Was it already known? "Why," he asked, "did you call her Mrs. Massingbird?"

"I beg your pardon for my inadvertence, Mr. Verner," was the reply of Dr. Cannonby. "Lawrence knew her as Mrs. Massingbird, and on his return from Australia he frequently spoke of her to me as Mrs. Massingbird, so that I got into the habit of thinking of her as such. It was not until he went to Paris that he heard she had exchanged the name for that of Verner."

A thought crossed Lionel that this was the news which had taken Captain Cannonby down to him. He might know of the existence of Frederick Massingbird, and had gone to break the news to him, Lionel; to tell him that his wife was not his wife.

"You do not know precisely what his business was with me?" he inquired, quite wistfully.

"No, I don't. I don't know that it was much beyond the pleasure of seeing you and Mrs. Verner."

Lionel rose. "If I—"

"But you will stay and dine with me, Mr. Verner?"

"Thank you, I am going back at once. I wished to be home this evening if possible, and there's nothing to hinder it now."

"A letter or two has come for Lawrence since the morning," observed the doctor, as he shook hands. "Will you take charge of them for him?"

"With pleasure."

Dr. Cannonby turned to a letter rack over the mantel-piece, selected three letters from it, and handed them to Lionel.

Back again all the weary way. His strong suspicions were no longer suspicions now, but confirmed certainties. The night grew dark; it was not darker than the cloud which had fallen upon his spirit.

Thought was busy in his brain. How could it be otherwise? Should he get home to find the news public property? Had Captain Cannonby made it known to Sybilla? Most fervently did he hope not. Better that he, Lionel, should be by her side to help her to bear it when the dreadful news came out. Next came another thought. Suppose Frederick Massingbird should have discovered himself? should have gone to Verner's Pride to take possession? his home now; his wife. Lionel might get back to find that he had no longer a place there.

Lionel found his carriage waiting at the station. He had ordered it to be so. Wigham was with it. A very coward now, he scarcely dared ask questions.

"Has Captain Cannonby arrived at the house to-day, do you know, Wigham?"

"Who, sir?"

"A strange gentleman from London. Captain Cannonby."

"I can't rightly say, sir. I have been about in the stables all day. I saw a strange gentleman cross the yard just at dinner-time, one I'd never seen afore. May be it was him."

A feeling came over Lionel that he could not see Captain Cannonby before them all. Better send for him to a private room, and get the communication over. What his after course would be was another matter. Yes; better in all ways.

"Drive round to the yard, Wigham," he said, as the coachman was about to turn on to the terrace. And Wigham obeyed.

He stepped out. He went in at the back door, almost as if he were slinking into the house, stealthily traversed the passages, and gained the lighted hall. At the very moment that he put his feet on its tessellated floor, a sudden commotion was heard up the stairs. A door was flung open, and Sibylla, with cheeks inflamed and breath panting, flew down, her convulsive cries echoing through the house. She saw Lionel, and threw herself into his arms.

"Oh, Lionel, what is this wicked story?" she sobbed. "It is not true! It cannot be true that I am not your wife, that—"

"Tell me that it is not true!"

"Hush, my darling!" he whispered, placing his hand across her mouth. "We are not alone!"

They certainly were not! Out of the drawing-rooms, out of the dining-room, had poured the guests; out of the kitchen came peeping the servants. Deborah West stood on the stair like a statue, her hands clasped; and Mademoiselle Benoite frantically inquired what anybody had been doing to her mistress. All stared in amazement. She, in that terrible state of agitation; Lionel supporting her with his white and haughty face.

"It is nothing," he said, waving them off. "Mrs. Verner is not well. Come with me, Sibylla."

Waving them off still, he drew her into the study, closed the door, and bolted it. She clung to him like one in the extremity of terror, her throat heaving convulsively.

"Oh, Lionel! is it true that he is come back? That he did not die? What will become of me? Tell me that they have been deceiving me; that it is not true!"

He could not tell her so. He wound his arms tenderly round her and held her face to his breast, and laid his own down upon it. "Strive for calmness," he murmured, his heart aching for her. "I will protect you so long as I shall have the power."

CHAPTER LX

Miss Deborah West did not believe in ghosts. Miss Deb, setting aside a few personal weaknesses and vanities, was a strong-minded female, and no more believed in ghosts than she did in Master Cheese's delicate constitution, which required to be supplied with an unlimited quantity of tarts and other dainties to keep up his strength between meals. The commotion respecting Frederick Massingbird, that his ghost had arrived from Australia, and "walked," reached the ears of Miss Deb. It reached them in this way.

Miss Deb and her sister, compelled to economy by the scanty allowance afforded by Dr. West, had no more helpmates in the household department than were absolutely necessary, and the surgery boy, Bob, found himself sometimes pressed into aiding in the domestic service. One evening Miss Deb entered the surgery, and caught Master Cheese revelling in a hatful of walnuts by gaslight. This was the evening of the storm, previously mentioned.

"Where's Bob?" asked she. "I want a message taken to Mrs. Broom's about those pickled mushrooms that she is doing for me."

"Bob's out," responded Master Cheese. "Have a walnut, Miss Deb?"

"I don't mind. Are they ripe?" answered Miss Deb.

Master Cheese, the greediest chap alive, picked out the smallest he could find, politely cracked it with his teeth, and handed it to her.

"You'll not get Bob over to Broom's at this hour," cried he. "Jan can't get him to Mother Hook's with her medicine after dark. Unless it's made up so that he can take it by daylight, they have to send for it."

"What's that for?" asked Miss Deb.

Master Cheese cracked on at his walnuts. "You have not heard the tale that's going about, I suppose, Miss Deb?" he presently said.

"I have not heard any tale," she answered.

"And I don't know that I must tell it you," continued Master Cheese, filling his mouth with five or six quarters at once, unpeeled. "Jan ordered me to hold my tongue indoors."

"It would be more respectful, Master Cheese, if you said Mr. Jan," rebuked Miss Deborah. "I have told you so often."

"Who cares?" returned Master Cheese. "Jan doesn't. The fact is, Miss Deb, that there's a ghost about at night just now."

"Have they got up that folly again? Rachel Frost rests a great deal quieter in her grave than some of you do in your beds."

"Ah, but it's not Rachel's this time," significantly responded Master Cheese. "It's somebody else's."

"Whose is it, then?" asked Miss Deb, struck with his manner.

"I'll tell you if you won't tell Jan. It's—don't start, Miss Deb—it's Fred Massingbird's."

Miss Deb did not start. She looked keenly at Master Cheese, believing he might be playing a joke upon her. But there were no signs of joking in his countenance. It looked, on the contrary, singularly serious, not to say awe-struck, as he leaned forward to bring it nearer Miss Deborah's.

"It is a fact that Fred Massingbird's ghost is walking," he continued. "Lots have seen it. I have seen it. You'd have heard of it, as everybody else has, if you had not been Mrs. Verner's sister. It's an unpleasantly queer thing for her, you know, Miss Deb."

"What utter absurdity!" cried Deborah.

"Wait till you see it, before you say it's absurdity," replied Master Cheese. "If it's not Fred Massingbird's ghost, it is somebody's that's the exact image of him."

Miss Deborah sat down on a stone jar, and got Master Cheese to tell her the whole story. That he should put in a few exaggerations, and so increase the marvel, was only natural. But Deborah West heard sufficient to send her mind into a state of uneasy perplexity.

"You say Mr. Jan knows of this?" she asked.

"There's nobody about that doesn't know of it except you and the folks at Verner's Pride," responded Master Cheese. "I say, don't you go and tell Jan that you made me betray it to you, Miss Deb! You'll get me into a row if you do."

But this was the very thing that Miss Deb resolved to do. Not to get Master Cheese into a "row," but that she saw no other way of allaying her uncertainty. Ghosts were utterly excluded from Deborah West's creed; and why so many people should be suddenly testifying that Frederick Massingbird's was to be seen, she could not understand. That there must be something in it more than the common absurdity of such tales, the state of Alice Hook appeared to testify.

"Can Bob be spared to go over to Broom's in the morning?" she asked, after a long pause of silence, given apparently to the contemplation of Master Cheese's intense enjoyment of his walnuts; in reality, to deep thought.

"Well, I don't know," answered the young gentleman, who never was ready to accord the services of Bob indoors, lest it might involve any little extra amount of exertion for himself. "There's a sight of medicine to be taken out just now. Jan's got a great deal to do, and I am nearly worked off my legs."

"It looks like it," retorted Miss Deborah. "Your legs will never be much the worse for the amount of work you do. Where's Mr. Jan?"

"He went out to go to Hook's," replied Master Cheese, a desperately hard walnut proving nearly too much for his teeth. "He'll take a round, I dare say, before he comes in."

Deborah returned indoors. Though not much inclined to reticence in general, she observed it now, saying nothing to Amilly. The storm came on, and they sat and watched it. Supper time approached, and Master Cheese was punctual. He found some pickled herrings on the table, of which he was uncommonly fond, and ate them as long as Miss West would supply his plate. The meal was over when Jan came in.

"Don't trouble to have anything brought back for me," said he. "I'll eat a bit of bread and cheese." He was not like his assistant; his growing days were over.

Master Cheese went straight up to bed. He liked to do so as soon as supper was over, lest any summons came, and he should have to go out. Easy Jan, no matter how tired he might be, would attend himself, sooner than wake up Master Cheese—a ceremony more easy to attempt than to accomplish. Fortifying himself with about a pound of sweet cake, which he kept in his box, as dessert to the herrings, and to refresh his dreams, Master Cheese put himself into bed.

Jan meanwhile finished his bread and cheese, and rose. "I wonder whether I shall get a whole night of it tonight?" said he, stretching himself. "I didn't have much bed last night."

"Have you to go out again, Mr. Jan?"

"No. I shall look to the books a bit, and then turn in. Good night, Miss Deborah; good-night, Miss Amilly."

"Good-night," they answered.

Amilly drew to the fire. The chilly rain of the afternoon had caused them to have one lighted. She put her feet on the fender, feeling the warmth comfortable. Deborah sent the supper-tray away, and then left the room. Stealing out of the side door quietly, she tripped across the narrow path of wet gravel, and entered the surgery. Jan had got an account-book open on the counter, and was leaning over it, a pen in his hand.

"Don't be frightened, Mr. Jan; it's only me," said Deborah, who did not at all times confine herself to the rules of severe grammar. "I'll shut the door, if you please, for I want to say a word to yourself alone."

"Is it more physic that you want?" asked Jan. "Has the pain in the side come again?"

"It is not about pains or physic," she answered, drawing nearer to the counter. "Mr. Jan"—dropping her voice to a confidential whisper—"would you be so good as to tell me the truth of this story that is going about?"

Jan paused. "What story?" he rejoined.

"This ghost story. They are saying, I understand, that—that—they are saying something about Frederick Massingbird."

"Did Cheese supply you with the information?" cried Jan, imperturbable as ever.

"He did. But I must beg you not to scold him for it—as he thought you might do. It was I who drew the story from him. He said you cautioned him not to speak of it to me or Amilly. I quite appreciate your motives, Mr. Jan, and feel that it was very considerate of you. But now that I have heard it, I want to know particulars from somebody more reliable than Master Cheese."

"I told Lionel I'd say nothing to any soul in the parish," said Jan, open and single-minded as though he had been made of glass. "But he'd not mind my making you an exception—as you have heard it. You are Sibylla's sister."

"You don't believe in its being a ghost?"

Jan grinned. "I!" cried he. "No, I don't."

"Then what do you suppose it is that's frightening people? And why should they be frightened?"

Jan sat himself down on the counter, and whirled his legs over to the other side, clearing the gallipots; so that he faced Miss Deborah. Not to waste time, he took the mortar before him. And there he was at his ease; his legs hanging, and his hands pounding.

"What should you think it is?" inquired he.

"How can I think, Mr. Jan? Until an hour or two ago, I had not heard of the rumour. I suppose it is somebody who walks about at night to frighten people. But it is curious that he should look like Frederick Massingbird. Can you understand it?"

"I am afraid I can," replied Jan, pounding away.

"Will you tell me, please, what you think."

"Can't you guess at it, Miss Deb?"

Miss Deb looked at him, beginning to think his manner as mysterious as Master Cheese's had been.

"I can't guess at it at all," she presently said. "Please to tell me."

"Then don't you go and drop down in a fit when you hear it," was the rejoinder of Jan. "I suppose it is Fred himself."

The words took her utterly by surprise. Not at first did she understand their meaning. She stared at Jan, her eyes and her mouth gradually opening.

"Fred himself?" she mechanically uttered.

"I suppose so. Fred himself. Not his ghost."

"Do you mean that he has come to life again?" she rapidly rejoined.

"Well, you can call it so if you like," said Jan. "I expect that, in point of fact, he has never been dead. The report of his death must have been erroneous; one of those unaccountable mistakes that do sometimes happen to astonish the world."

Deborah West took in the full sense of the words, and sunk down on the big stone jar. She turned all over of a burning heat; she felt her hands beginning to twitch with emotion.

"You mean that he is alive?—that he has never been dead?" she gasped.

Jan nodded.

"Oh, Mr. Jan! Then, what is—what is Sibylla?"

"Ah," said Jan, "that's just it. She's the wife of both of 'em—as you may say."

For any petty surprise or evil, Miss Deborah would have gone off in a succession of screams, of pseudo-faints. This evil was all too real, too terrible. She sat with her trembling hands clasped to pain, looking hopelessly at Jan.

He told her all he knew; all that was said by others.

"Dan Duff's nothing," remarked he; "and Cheese is nothing; and others, who confess to have seen it, are nothing: and old Frost's not much. But I'd back Bourne's calmness and sound sense against the world, and I'd back Broom's."

"And they have both seen it?"

"Both," replied Jan. "Both are sure that it is Frederick Massingbird."

"What will Mr. Verner do?" she asked, looking round with a shudder, and not speaking above her breath.

"Oh, that's his affair," said Jan. "It's hard to guess what he may do; he is one that won't be dictated to. If it were some people's case, they'd say to Sibylla, 'Now you have got two husbands, choose which you'll have, and keep to him.'"

"Good heavens, Mr. Jan!" exclaimed Miss Deb, shocked at the loose sentiments the words appeared to indicate. "And suppose she should choose the second? Have you thought of the sin? The second can't be her husband; it would be as bad as those Mormons."

"Looking at it in a practical point of view, I can't see much difference, which of the two she chooses," returned Jan. "If Fred was her husband once, Lionel's her husband now; practically I say you know, Miss Deb."

Miss Deb thought the question was going rather into metaphysics, a branch of science which she did not understand, and so was content to leave the controversy.

"Any way, it is dreadful for her," she said, with another shiver. "Oh, Mr. Jan, do you think it can really be true?"

"I think that there's not a doubt of it," he answered, stopping in his pounding. "But you need not think so, Miss Deb."

"How am I to help thinking so?" she simply asked.

"You needn't think either way until it is proved. As I suppose it must be, shortly. Let it rest till then."

"No, Mr. Jan, I differ from you. It is a question that ought to be sought out and probed; not left to rest. Does Sibylla know it?"

"Not she. Who'd tell her? Lionel won't, I know. It was for her sake that he bound me to silence."

"She ought to be told, Mr. Jan. She ought to leave her husband—I mean, Mr. Lionel—this very hour, and shut herself up until the doubt is settled."

"Where should she shut herself?" inquired Jan, opening his eyes. "In a convent? Law, Miss Deb! If somebody came and told me I had got two wives, should you say I ought to make a start for the nearest monastery? How would my patients get on?"

Rather metaphysical again. Miss Deb drew Jan back to plain details—to the histories of the various ghostly encounters. Jan talked and pounded; she sat on her hard seat and listened, her brain more perplexed than it could have been with any metaphysics known to science. Eleven o'clock disturbed them, and Miss Deborah started as if she had been shot.

"How could I keep you until this time!" she exclaimed. "And you scarcely in bed for some nights!"

"Never mind, Miss Deb," answered good-natured Jan. "It's all in the day's work."

He opened the door for her, and then bolted himself in for the night. For the night, that is, if Deerham would allow it to him. Hook's daughter was slowly progressing towards recovery, and Jan would not need to go to her.

Amilly was nodding over the fire, or, rather, where the fire had been, for it had gone out. She inquired with wonder what her sister had been doing, and where she had been. Deborah replied that she had been busy; and they went upstairs to bed.

But not to sleep—for one of them. Deborah West lay awake through the live-long night, tossing from side to side in her perplexity and thought. Somewhat strict in her notions, she deemed it a matter of stern necessity, of positive duty, that Sibylla should retire, at any rate for a time, from the scenes of busy life. To enable her to do this, the news must be broken to her. But how?

Ay, how? Deborah West rose in the morning with the difficulty unsolved. She supposed she must do it herself. She believed it was as much a duty laid upon her, the imparting these tidings to Sibylla, as the separating herself from all social ties, the instant it was so imparted, would be the duty of Sibylla herself.

Deborah West went about her occupations that morning, one imperative sentence ever in her thoughts: "It must be done! it must be done!"

She carried it about with her, ever saying it, through the whole day. She shrank, both for Sibylla's sake and her own, from the task she was imposing upon herself; and, as we all do when we have an unpleasant office to perform, she put it off to the last. Early in the morning she had said, I will go to Verner's Pride after breakfast and tell her; breakfast over, she said, I will have my dinner first and go then.

But the afternoon passed on, and she did not go. Every little trivial domestic duty was made an excuse for delaying it. Miss Amilly, finding her sister unusually bad company, went out to drink tea with some friends. The time came for ordering in tea at home, and still Deborah had not gone.

She made the tea and presided at the table. But she could eat nothing—to the inward gratification of Master Cheese. There happened to be shrimps—a dish which that gentleman preferred, if anything, to pickled herrings; and by Miss Deborah's want of appetite he was able to secure her share and his own, including the heads and tails. He would uncommonly have liked to secure Jan's share also; but Miss Deborah filled a plate and put them aside, against Jan came in. Jan's pressure of work caused him of late to be irregular at his meals.

Scarcely was the tea over, and Master Cheese gone, when Mr. Bourne called. Deborah, the one thought uppermost in her mind, closed the door, and spoke out what she had heard. The terrible fear, her own distress, Jan's belief that it was Fred himself, Jan's representation that Mr. Bourne also believed it. Mr. Bourne, leaning forward until his pale face and his iron-gray hair nearly touched hers, whispered in answer that he did not think there was a doubt of it.

Then Deborah did nerve herself to the task. On the departure of the vicar, she started for Verner's Pride and asked to see Sibylla. The servants would have shown her to the drawing-room, but she preferred to go up to Sibylla's chamber. The company were yet in the dining-room.

How long Sibylla kept her waiting there, she scarcely knew. Sibylla was not in the habit of putting herself to inconvenience for her sisters. The message was taken to her—that Miss West waited in her chamber—as she entered the drawing-room. And there Sibylla let her wait. One or two more messages to the same effect were subsequently delivered. They produced no impression, and Deborah began to think she should not get to see her that night.

But Sibylla came up at length, and Deborah entered upon her task. Whether she accomplished it clumsily, or whether Sibylla's ill-disciplined mind was wholly in fault, certain it is that there ensued a loud and unpleasant scene. The scene to which you were a witness. Scarcely giving herself time to take in more than the bare fact hinted at by Deborah—that her first husband was believed to be alive—not waiting to inquire a single particular, she burst out of the room and went shrieking down the stairs, flying into the arms of Lionel, who at that moment had entered.

CHAPTER LXI

MEETING THE NEWS

Lionel Verner could not speak comfort to his wife; or, at the best, comfort of a most negative nature. He held her to him in the study, the door locked against intruders. They were somewhat at cross-purposes. Lionel supposed that the information had been imparted to her by Captain Cannonby; he never doubted but that she had been told Frederick Massingbird had returned and was on the scene; that he might come in any moment—even that very present one as they spoke—to put in his claim to her. Sibylla, on the contrary, did not think (what little she was capable of thinking) that Lionel had had previous information of the matter.

"What am I to do?" she cried, her emotion becoming hysterical. "Oh, Lionel! don't you give me up!"

"I would have got here earlier had there been means," he soothingly said, wisely evading all answer to the last suggestion. "I feared he would be telling you in my I absence; better that you should have heard of it from me."

She lifted her face to look at him. "Then you know it!"

"I have known it this clay or two. My journey to-day—"

She broke out into a most violent fit of emotion, shrieking, trembling, clinging to Lionel, calling out at the top of her voice that she would not leave him. All his efforts were directed to stilling the noise. He implored her to be tranquil, to remember there were listeners around; he pointed out that, until the blow actually fell, there was no necessity for those listeners to be made cognisant of it. All that he could do for her protection and comfort, he would do, he earnestly said. And Sibylla subsided into a softer mood, and cried quietly.

"I'd rather die," she sobbed, "than have this disgrace brought upon me."

Lionel put her into the large arm-chair, which remained in the study still, the old arm-chair of Mr. Verner. He stood by her and held her hands, his pale face grave, sad, loving, bent towards her with the most earnest sympathy. She lifted her eyes to it, whispering—

"Will they say you are not my husband?"

"Hush, Sibylla! There are moments, even yet, when I deceive myself into a fancy that it may be somewhat averted. I cannot understand how he can be alive. Has Cannonby told you whence the error arose?"

She did not answer. She began to shake again; she tossed back her golden hair. Some blue ribbons had been wreathed in it for dinner; she pulled them out and threw them on the ground, her hair partially falling with their departure.

"I wish I could have some wine?"

He moved to the door to get it for her. "Don't you let her in, Lionel," she called out as he unlocked it.

"Who?"

"That Deborah. I hate her now," was the ungenerous remark.

Lionel opened the door, called to Tynn, and desired him to bring wine. "What time did Captain Cannonby get here?" he whispered, as he took it from the butler.

"Who, sir?" asked Tynn.

"Captain Cannonby."

Tynn paused, like one who does not understand. "There's no gentleman here of that name, sir. A Mr. Rushworth called to-day, and my mistress asked him to stay dinner. He is in the drawing-room now. There is no other stranger."

"Has Captain Cannonby not been here at all?" reiterated Lionel. "He left London this morning to come."

Tynn shook his head to express a negative. "He has not arrived, sir."

Lionel went in again, his feelings undergoing a sort of revulsion, for there now peeped out a glimmer of hope. So long as the nearly certain conviction on Lionel's mind was not confirmed by positive testimony—as he expected Captain Cannonby's would be—he could not entirely lose sight of all hope. That he most fervently prayed the blow might not fall, might even now be averted, you will readily believe. Sibylla had not been to him the wife he had fondly hoped for; she provoked him every hour in the day; she appeared to do what she could, wilfully to estrange his affection. He was conscious of all this; he was all too conscious that his inmost love was another's, not hers. But he lost sight of himself in anxiety for her; it was for her sake he prayed and hoped. Whether she was his wife by law or not; whether she was loved or hated, Lionel's course of duty lay plain before him now—to shield her, so far as he might be allowed, in all care and tenderness. He would have shed his last drop of blood to promote her comfort; he would have sacrificed every feeling of his heart for her sake.

The wine in his hand, he turned into the room again. A change had taken place in her aspect. She had left the chair, and was standing against the wall opposite the door, her tears dried, her eyes unnaturally bright, her cheeks burning.

"Lionel," she uttered, a catching of the breath betraying her emotion, "if he is alive, whose is Verner's Pride?"

"His," replied Lionel, in a low tone.

She shrieked out, very much after the manner of a petulant child. "I won't leave it!—I won't leave Verner's Pride! You could not be so cruel as to wish me. Who says he is alive? Lionel, I ask you who it is that says he is alive?"

"Hush, my dear! This excitement will do you a world of harm, and it cannot mend the matter, however it may be. I want to know who told you of this, Sibylla. I supposed it to be Cannonby; but Tynn says Cannonby has not been here."

The question appeared to divert her thoughts into another channel. "Cannonby! What should bring him here? Did you expect him to come?"

"Drink your wine, and then I will tell you," he said, holding the glass towards her.

She pushed the wine from her capriciously. "I don't want wine now. I am hot. I should like some water."

"I will get it for you directly. Tell me, first of all, how you came to know of this?"

"Deborah told me. She sent for me out of the drawing-room where I was so happy, to tell me this horrid tale. Lionel"—sinking her voice again to a whisper—"is—he—here?"

"I cannot tell you—"

"But you must tell me," she passionately interrupted. "I will know. I have a right to know it, Lionel."

"When I say I cannot tell you, Sibylla, I mean that I cannot tell you with any certainty. I will tell you all I do know. Some one is in the neighbourhood who bears a great resemblance to him. He is seen sometimes at night; and—and—I have other testimony that he has returned from Australia."

"What will be done if he comes here?"

Lionel was silent.

"Shall you fight him?"

"Fight him!" echoed Lionel. "No."

"You will give up Verner's Pride without a struggle! You will give up me! Then, are you a coward, Lionel Verner?"

"You know that I would give up neither willingly, Sibylla."

Grievously pained was his tone as he replied to her. She was meeting this as she did most other things—without sense or reason; not as a thinking, rational being. Her manner was loud, her emotion violent; but deep and true her grief was not. Depth of feeling, truth of nature, were qualities that never yet had place in Sibylla Verner. Not once, throughout all their married life, had Lionel been so painfully impressed with the fact as he was now.

"Am I to die for the want of that water?" she resumed. "If you don't get it for me I shall ring for the servants to bring it."

He opened the door again without a word. He knew quite well that she had thrown in that little shaft about ringing for the servants, because it would not be pleasant to him that the servants should intrude upon them then. Outside the door, about to knock at it, was Deborah West.

"I must go home," she whispered. "Mr. Verner, how sadly she is meeting this!"

The very thought that was in Lionel's heart. But not to another would he cast a shade of reflection on his wife.

"It is a terrible thing for any one to meet," he answered. "I could have wished, Miss West, that you had not imparted it to her. Better that I should have done it, when it must have been done."

"I did it from a good motive," was the reply of Deborah, who was looking sadly down-hearted, and had evidently been crying. "She ought to leave you until some certainty shall be arrived at."

"Nonsense! No!" said Lionel. "I beg you—I beg you, Miss West, not to say anything more that can distress or disturb her. If the—the—explosion comes, of course it must come; and we must all meet it as we best may, and see then what is best to be done."

"But it is not right that she should remain with you in this uncertainty," urged Deborah, who could be obstinate when she thought she had cause. "The world will not deem it to be right. You should remember this."

"I do not act to please the world. I am responsible to God and my conscience."

"Responsible to—Good gracious, Mr. Verner!" returned Deborah, every line in her face expressing astonishment. "You call keeping her with you acting as a responsible man ought! If Sibylla's husband is living, you must put her away from your side."

"When the time shall come. Until then, my duty—as I judge it—is to keep her by my side; to shelter her from harm and annoyance, petty as well as great."

"You deem that your duty!"

"I do," he firmly answered. "My duty to her and to God."

Deborah shook her head and her hands. "It ought not to be let go on," she said, moving nearer to the study door. "I shall urge the leaving you upon her."

Lionel calmly laid his hand upon the lock. "Pardon me, Miss West. I cannot allow my wife to be subjected to it."

"But if she is not your wife?"

A streak of red came into his pale face. "It has yet to be proved that she is not. Until that time shall come, Miss West, she is my wife, and I shall protect her as such."

"You will not let me see her?" asked Deborah, for his hand was not lifted from the handle.

"No. Not if your object be the motives you avow. Sleep a night upon it, Miss West, and see if you do not change your mode of thinking and come over to mine. Return here in the morning with words of love and comfort for her, and none will welcome you more sincerely than I."

"Answer me one thing, Mr. Verner. Do you believe in your heart that Frederick Massingbird is alive and has returned?"

"Unfortunately I have no resource but to believe it," he replied.

"Then, to your way of thinking I can never come," returned Deborah in some agitation. "It is just sin, Mr. Verner, in the sight of Heaven."

"I think not," he quietly answered. "I am content to let Heaven judge me, and the motives that actuate me; a judgment more merciful than man's."

Deborah West, in her conscientious, but severe rectitude, turned to the hall door and departed, her hands uplifted still. Lionel ordered Tynn to attend Miss West home. He then procured some water for his wife and carried it in, as he had previously carried in the wine.

A fruitless service. Sibylla rejected it. She wanted neither water nor anything else, were all the thanks Lionel received, querulously spoken. He laid the glass upon the table, and, sitting down by her side in all patience, he set himself to the work of soothing her, gently and lovingly as though she had been what she was showing herself—a wayward child.

CHAPTER LXII

TYNN PUMPED DRY

Miss West and Tynn proceeded on their way. The side path was dirty, and she chose the middle of the road, Tynn walking a step behind her. Deborah was of an affable nature, Tynn a long-attached and valued servant, and she chatted with him familiarly. Deborah, in her simple good heart, could not have been brought to understand why she should not chat with him. Because he was a servant and she a lady, she thought there was only the more reason why she should, that the man might not be unpleasantly reminded of the social distinction between them.

She pressed down, so far as she could, the heavy affliction that was weighing upon her mind. She spoke of the weather, the harvest, of Mrs. Bitterworth's recent dangerous attack, of other trifling topics patent at the moment to Deerham. Tynn chatted in his turn, never losing his respect of words and manner; a servant worth anything never does. Thus they progressed towards the village, utterly unconscious that a pair of eager eyes were following, and an evil tongue was casting anathemas towards them.

The owner of the eyes and tongue was wanting to hold a few words of private colloquy with Tynn. Could Tynn have seen right round the corner of the pillar of the outer gate when he went out, he would have detected the man waiting there in ambush. It was Giles Roy. Roy was aware that Tynn sometimes attended departing visitors to the outer gate. Roy had come up, hoping that he might so attend them on this night. Tynn did appear, with Miss West, and Roy began to hug himself that fortune had so far favoured him; but when he saw that Tynn departed with the lady, instead of only standing politely to watch her off, Roy growled out vengeance against the unconscious offenders.

"He's a-going to see her home belike," snarled Roy in soliloquy, following them with angry eyes and slow footsteps. "I must wait till he comes back—and be shot to both of 'em!"

Tynn left Miss West at her own door, declining the invitation to go in and take a bit of supper with the maids, or a glass of beer. He was trudging back again, his arms behind his back, and wishing himself at home, for Tynn, fat and of short breath, did not like much walking, when, in a lonely part of the road, he came upon a man sitting astride upon a gate.

"Hollo! is that you, Mr. Tynn? Who'd ha' thought of seeing you out to-night?"

For it was Mr. Roy's wish, from private motives of his own, that Tynn should not know he had been looked for, but should believe the encounter to be accidental. Tynn turned off the road, and leaned his elbow upon the gate, rather glad of the opportunity to stand a minute and get his breath. It was somewhat up-hill to Verner's Pride, the whole of the way from Deerham.

"Are you sitting here for pleasure?" asked he of Roy.

"I'm sitting here for grief," returned Roy; and Tynn was not sharp enough to detect the hollow falseness of his tone. "I had to go up the road to-night on a matter of business, and, walking back by Verner's Pride, it so overcame me that I was glad to bring myself to a anchor."

"How should walking by Verner's Pride overcome you?" demanded Tynn.

"Well," said Roy, "it was the thoughts of poor Mr. and Mrs. Verner did it. He didn't behave to me over liberal in turning me from the place I'd held so long under his uncle, but I've overgot that smart; it's past and gone. My heart bleeds for him now, and that's the truth."

For Roy's heart to "bleed" for any fellow-creature was a marvel that even Tynn, unsuspicious as he was, could not take in. Mrs. Tynn repeatedly assured him that he had been born into the world with one sole quality—credulity. Certainly Tynn was unusually inclined to put faith in fair outsides. Not that Roy could boast much of the latter advantage.

"What's the matter with Mr. Verner?" he asked of Roy.

Roy groaned dismally. "It's a thing that is come to my knowledge," said he—"a awful misfortin that is a-going to drop upon him. I'd not say a word to another soul but you, Mr. Tynn; but you be his friend If anybody be, and I feel that I must either speak or bust."

Tynn peered at Roy's face. As much as he could see of it, for the night was not a very clear one.

"It seems quite a providence that I happened to meet you," went on Roy, as if any meeting with the butler had been as far from his thoughts as an encounter with somebody at the North Pole. "Things does turn out lucky sometimes."

"I must be getting home," interposed Tynn. "If you have anything to say to me, Roy, you had better say it. I may be wanted."

Roy—who was standing now, his elbow leaning on the gate—brought his face nearer to Tynn's. Tynn was also leaning on the gate.

"Have you heered of this ghost that's said to be walking about Deerham?" he asked, lowering his voice to a whisper. "Have you heered whose they say it is?"

Now, Tynn had heard. All the retainers, male and female, at Verner's Pride had heard. And Tynn, though not much inclined to give credence to ghosts in a general way, had felt somewhat uneasy at the ale. More on his mistress's account than on any other score; for Tynn had the sense to know that such a report could not be pleasing to Mrs. Verner, should it reach her ears.

"I can't think why they do say it," replied Tynn, answering the man's concluding question. "For my own part, I don't believe there's anything in it. I don't believe in ghosts."

"Neither didn't a good many more, till now that they have got orakelar demonstration of it," returned Roy. "Dan Duff see it, and a'most lost his senses; that girl of Hook's see it, and you know, I suppose, what it did for her; Broom see it; the parson see it; old Frost see it; and lots more. Not one on 'em but 'ud take their Bible oath, if put to it, that it is Fred Massingbird's ghost."

"But it is not," said Tynn. "It can't be. Leastways I'll never believe it till I see it with my own eyes. There'd be no reason in its coming now. If it wanted to come at all, why didn't it come when it was first buried, and not wait till over two years had gone by?"

"That's the point that I stuck at," was Roy's answer. "When my wife came home with the tales, day after day, that Fred Massingbird's spirit was walking—that this person had seen it, and that person had seen it—'Yah! Rubbish!' I says to her. 'If his ghost had been a-coming, it 'ud have come afore now.' And so it would."

"Of course," answered Tynn. "If it had been coming. But I have not lived to these years to believe in ghosts at last."

"Then, what do you think of the parson, Mr. Tynn?" continued Roy, in a strangely significant tone. "And Broom—he have got his senses about him? How d'ye account for their believing it?"

"I have not heard them say that they do believe it," responded Tynn, with a knowing nod. "Folks may go about and say that I believe it, perhaps; but that wouldn't make it any nearer the fact. And what has all this to do with Mr. Verner?"

"I am coming to it," said Roy. He took a step backward, looked carefully up and down the road, lest listeners might be in ambush; stretched his neck forward, and in like manner surveyed the field On either side the hedge. Apparently it satisfied him, and he resumed his close proximity to Tynn and his meaning whisper. "Can't you guess the riddle, Mr. Tynn?"

"I can't in the least guess what you mean, or what you are driving at," was Tynn's response. "I think you must have been having a drop of drink, Roy. I ask what this is to my master, Mr. Verner?"

"Drink be bothered! I've not had a sup inside my mouth since midday," was Roy's retort. "This secret has been enough drink for me, and meat, too. You'll keep counsel, if I tell it you, Mr. Tynn? Not but what it must soon come out."

"Well?" returned Tynn, in some surprise.

"It's Fred Massingbird fast enough. But it's not his ghost."

"What on earth do you mean?" asked Tynn, never for a moment glancing at the fact of what Roy tried to imply.

"He is come back: Frederick Massingbird. He didn't die, over there."

A pause, devoted by Tynn to staring and thinking. When the full sense of the words broke upon him, he staggered a step or two away from the ex-bailiff.

"Heaven help us, if it's true!" he uttered. "Roy! it can't be!"

"It is," said Roy.

They stood looking at each other by starlight. Tynn's face had grown hot and wet, and he wiped it. "It can't be," he mechanically repeated.

"I tell you it is, Mr. Tynn. Now never you mind asking me how I came to the bottom of it," went on Roy in a sort of defiant tone. "I did come to the bottom of it, and I do know it; and Mr. Fred, he knows that I know it. It's as sure that he is back, and in the neighbourhood, as that you and me is here at this gate. He is alive and he is among us—as certain as that you are Mr. Tynn, and I be Giles Roy."

There came flashing over Tynn's thoughts the scene of that very evening. His mistress's shrieks and agitation when she broke from Miss West; the cries and sobs which had penetrated to their ears when she was shut afterwards in the study with her husband. The unusual scene had been productive of gossiping comment among the servants and Tynn had believed something distressing must have occurred. Not this; he had never glanced a suspicion at this. He remembered the lines of pain which shone out at the moment from his master's pale face, in spite of its impassiveness; and somehow that very face brought conviction to Tynn now, that Roy's news was true. Tynn let his arms fall on the gate again with a groan.

"Whatever will become of my poor mistress?" he uttered.

"She!" slightingly returned Roy. "She'll be better off than him."

"Better off than who?"

"Than Mr. Verner. She needn't leave Verner's Pride. He must."

To expect any ideas but coarse ones from Roy, Tynn could not. But his attention was caught by the last suggestion.

"Leave Verner's Pride?" slowly repeated Tynn. "Must he?—good heavens! must my master be turned from Verner's Pride?"

"Where'll be the help for it?" asked Roy, in a confidential tone. "I tell you, Mr. Tynn, my heart's been a-bleeding for him ever since I heard it. I don't see no help for his turning out. I have been a-weighing it over and over in my mind, and I don't see none. Do you?"

Tynn looked very blank. He was feeling so. He made no answer, and Roy continued, blandly confidential still.

"If that there codicil, that was so much talked on, hadn't been lost, he'd have been all right, would Mr. Verner. No come-to-life-again Fred Massingbird needn't have tried at turning him out. Couldn't it be hunted for again, Mr. Tynn?"

Roy turned the tail of his eye on Tynn. Would his pumping take effect? Mrs. Tynn would have told him that her husband might be pumped dry, and never know it. She was not far wrong. Unsuspicious Tynn went headlong into the snare.

"Where would be the good of hunting for it again—when every conceivable place was hunted for it before?" he asked.

"Well, it was a curious thing, that codicil," remarked Roy. "Has it never been heered on?"

Tynn shook his head. "Never at all. What an awful thing this is, if it's true!"

"It is true, I tell ye," said Roy. "You needn't doubt it. There was a report a short while agone that the codicil had been found, and Matiss had got it in safe keeping. As I sat here, afore you come up, I was thinking how well it 'ud have served Mr. Verner's turn just now, if it was true."

"It is not true," said Tynn. "All sorts of reports get about. The codicil has never been found, and never been heard of."

"What a pity!" groaned Roy, with a deep sigh. "I'm glad I've told it you, Mr. Tynn! It's a heavy secret for a man to carry about inside of him. I must be going."

"So must I," said Tynn. "Roy, are you sure there's no mistake?" he added. "It seems a tale next to impossible."

"Well, now," said Roy, "I see you don't half believe me. You must wait a few days, and see what them days 'll bring forth. That Mr. Massingbird's back from Australia, I'll take my oath to. I didn't believe it at first; and when young Duff was a-going on about the porkypine, I shook him, I did, for a little lying rascal. I know better now."

"But how do you know it?" debated Tynn.

"Now, never you mind. It's my business, I say, and nobody else's. You just wait a day or two, that's all, Mr. Tynn. I declare I am as glad to have met with you to-night, and exchanged this intercourse of opinions, as if anybody had counted me out a bag o' gold."

"Well, good-night, Roy," concluded Tynn, turning his steps towards Verner's Pride. "I wish I had been a hundred miles off, I know, before I had heard it."

Roy slipped over the gate; and there, out of sight, he executed a kind of triumphant dance.

"Then there is no codicil!" cried he. "I thought I could wile it out of him! That Tynn's as easy to be run out as is glass when it's hot."

And, putting his best leg forward, he made his way as fast as he could make it towards his home.

Tynn made his way towards Verner's Pride. But not fast. The information he had received filled his mind with the saddest trouble, and reduced his steps to slowness. When any great calamity falls suddenly upon us, or the dread of any great calamity, our first natural thought is, how it may be mitigated or averted. It was the thought that occurred to Tynn. The first shock over, digested, as may be said, Tynn began to deliberate whether he could do anything to help his master in the strait; and he went along, turning all sorts of suggestions over in his mind. Much as Sibylla was disliked by the old servant—and she had contrived to make herself very much disliked by them all—Tynn could not help feeling warmly the blow that was about to burst upon her head. Was there anything earthly he could do to avert it?—to help her or his master?

He did not doubt the information. Roy was not a particularly reliable person; but Tynn could not doubt that this was true. It was the most feasible solution of the ghost story agitating Deerham; the only solution of it, Tynn grew to think. If Frederick Massingbird—

Tynn's reflections came to a halt. Vaulting over a gate on the other side the road—the very gate through which poor Rachel Frost had glided the night of her death, to avoid meeting Frederick Massingbird and Sibylla West—was a tall man. He came, straight across the road, in front of Tynn, and passed through a gap of the hedge, on to the grounds of Verner's Pride.

But what made Tynn stand transfixed, as if he had been changed into a statue? What brought a cold chill to his heart, a heat to his brow? Why, as the man passed him, he turned his face full on Tynn; disclosing the features, the white, whiskerless cheek, with the black mark upon it, of Frederick Massingbird. Recovering himself as best he could, Tynn walked on, and gained the house.

Mrs. Verner had gone to her room. Mr. Verner was mixing with his guests. Some of the gentlemen were on the terrace smoking, and Tynn made his way on to it, hoping he might get a minute's interview with his master. The impression upon Tynn's mind was that Frederick Massingbird was coming there and then, to invade Verner's Pride: it appeared to Tynn to be his duty to impart what he had heard and seen at once to Mr. Verner.

Circumstances favoured him. Lionel had been talking with Mr. Gordon at the far end of the terrace, but the latter was called to from the drawing-room windows and departed in answer to it. Tynn seized the opportunity; his master was alone.

Quite alone. He was leaning over the outer balustrade of the terrace, apparently looking forth in the night obscurity on his own lands, stretched out before him. "Master!" whispered Tynn, forgetting ceremony in the moment's absorbing agitation, in the terrible calamity that was about to fall, "I have had an awful secret made known to me to-night. I must tell it you, sir."

"I know it already, Tynn," was the quiet response of Lionel.

Then Tynn told—told all he had heard, and how he had heard it; told how he had just seen Frederick Massingbird. Lionel started from the balustrade.

"Tynn! You saw him! Now?"

"Not five minutes ago, sir. He came right on to these grounds through the gap in the hedge. Oh, master! what will be done?" and the man's voice rose to a wail in its anguish. "He may be coming on now to put in his claim to Verner's Pride; to—to—to—all that's in it!"

But that Lionel was nerved to self-control, he might have answered with another wail of anguish. His mind filled up the gap of words, that the delicacy of Tynn would not speak. "He may be coming to claim Sibylla."

CHAPTER LXIII

LOOKING OUT FOR THE WORST

The night passed quietly at Verner's Pride. Not, for all its inmates, pleasantly. Faithful Tynn bolted and barred the doors and windows with his own hand, as he might have done on the anticipated invasion of a burglar. He then took up his station to watch the approaches to the house, and never stirred until morning light. There may have run in Tynn's mind some vague fear of violence, should his master and Frederick Massingbird come in contact.

How did Lionel pass it? Wakeful and watchful as Tynn. He went to bed; but sleep, for him, there was none. His wife, by his side, slept all through the night. Better, of course, for her that it should be so; but, that her frame of mind could be sufficiently easy to admit of sleep, was a perfect marvel to Lionel. Had he needed proof to convince him how shallow was her mind, how incapable she was of depth of feeling, of thought, this would have supplied it. She slept throughout the night. Lionel never closed his eyes; his brain was at work, his mind was troubled, his heart was aching. Not for himself. His position was certainly not one to be envied; but, in his great anxiety for his wife, self passed out of sight. To what conflict might she not be about to be exposed! to what unseemly violence of struggle, outwardly and inwardly, might not she expose herself! He knew quite well that, according to the laws of God and man, she was Frederick Massingbird's wife; not his. He should never think—when the time came—of disputing Frederick Massingbird's claim to her. But, what would she do?—how would she act? He believed in his heart, that Sibylla, in spite of her aggravations shown to him, and whatever may have been her preference for Frederick Massingbird in the early days, best cared for him, Lionel, now. He believed that she would not willingly return to Frederick Massingbird. Or, if she did, it would be for the sake of Verner's Pride.

He was right. Heartless, selfish, vain, and ambitious, Verner's Pride possessed far more attraction for Sibylla than did either Lionel or Frederick Massingbird. Allow her to keep quiet possession of that, and she would not cast much thought to either of them. If the conflict actually came, Lionel felt, in his innate refinement, that the proper course for Sibylla to adopt would be to retire from all social ties, partially to retire from the world—as Miss West had suggested she should do now in the uncertainty. Lionel did not wholly agree with Miss West. He deemed that, in the uncertainty, Sibylla's place was by his side, still his wife; but, when once the uncertainty was set at rest by the actual appearance of Frederick Massingbird, then let her retire. It was the only course that he could pursue, were the case his own. His mind was made up upon one point—to withdraw himself out of the way when that time came. To India, to the wilds of Africa—anywhere, far, far away. Never would he remain to be an eye-sore to Sibylla or Frederick Massingbird—inhabiting the land that they inhabited, breathing the air that sustained life in them. Sibylla might rely on one thing—that when Frederick Massingbird did appear beyond doubt or dispute, that very hour he said adieu to Sibylla. The shock soothed—and he would soothe it for her to the very utmost of his power—he should depart. He would be no more capable of retaining Sibylla in the face of her husband, than he could have taken her, knowingly, from that husband in his lifetime.

But where was Frederick Massingbird? Tynn's opinion had been—he had told it to his master—that when he saw Frederick Massingbird steal into the grounds of Verner's Pride the previous evening, he was coming on to the house, there and then. Perhaps Lionel himself had entertained the same conviction. But the night had passed, and no Frederick Massingbird had come. What could be the meaning of it? What could be the meaning of his dodging about Deerham in this manner, frightening the inhabitants?—of his watching the windows of Verner's Pride? Verner's Pride was his; Sibylla was his; why, then, did he not arrive to assume his rights?

Agitated with these and many other conflicting thoughts, Lionel lay on his uneasy bed, and saw in the morning light. He did not rise until his usual hour; he would have risen far earlier but for the fear of disturbing Sibylla. To lie there, a prey to these reflections, to this terrible suspense, was intolerable to him, but he would not risk waking her. The day might prove long enough and bad enough for her, without arousing her to it before her time. He rose, but she slept on still. Lionel did wonder how she could.

Not until he was going out of the room, dressed, did she awake. She awoke with a start. It appeared as if recollection, or partial recollection, of the last night's trouble flashed over her. She pushed aside the curtain, and called to him in a sharp tone of terror.

"Lionel!"

He turned back. He drew the curtain entirely away, and stood by her side. She caught his arm, clasping it convulsively.

"Is it a dreadful dream, or is it true?" she uttered, beginning to tremble. "Oh, Lionel, take care of me! Won't you take care of me?"

"I will take care of you as long as I may," he whispered tenderly.

"You will not let him force me away from you? You will not give up Verner's Pride? If you care for me, you will not."

"I do care for you," he gently said, avoiding a more direct answer. "My whole life is occupied in caring for you, in promoting your happiness and comfort. How I have cared for you, you alone know."

She burst into tears. Lionel bent his lips upon her hot face. "Depend upon my doing all that I can do," he said.

"Are you going to leave me by myself?" she resumed in fear, as he was turning to quit the room. "How do I know but he may be bursting in upon me?"

"Is that all your faith in me, Sibylla? He shall not intrude upon you here; he shall not intrude upon you anywhere without warning. When he does come, I shall be at your side."

Lionel joined his guests at breakfast. His wife did not. With smiling lips and bland brow, he had to cover a mind full of intolerable suspense, an aching heart. A minor puzzle—though nothing compared to the puzzle touching the movements of Frederick Massingbird—was working within him, as to the movements of Captain Cannonby. What could have become of that gentleman? Where could he be halting on his journey? Had his halt anything to do with them, with this grievous business?

To Lionel's great surprise, just as they were concluding breakfast, he saw the close carriage driven to the door, attended by Wigham and Bennet. You may remember the latter name. Master Dan Duff had called him "Calves" to Mr. Verner. If Verner's Pride could not keep its masters, it kept its servants. Lionel knew he had not ordered it; and he supposed his wife to be still in bed. He went out to the men.

"For whom is the carriage ordered, Bennet?"

"For my mistress, I think, sir."

And at that moment Lionel heard the steps of his wife upon the stairs. She was coming down, dressed. He turned in, and met her in the hall. "Are you going out?" he cried, his voice betokening surprise.

"I can't be worried with this uncertainty," was Sibylla's answer, spoken anything but courteously. "I am going to make Deborah tell me all she knows, and where she heard it."

"But—"

"I won't be dictated to, Lionel," she querulously stopped him with. "I will go. What is it to you?"

He turned without a remonstrance, and attended her to the carriage, placing her in it as considerately as though she had met him with a wife's loving words. When she was seated, he leaned towards her. "Would you like me to accompany you, Sibylla?"

"I don't care about it."

He closed the door in silence, his lips compressed. There were times when her fitful moods vexed him above common. This was one. When they knew not but the passing hour might be the last of their union, the last they should ever spend together, it was scarcely seemly to mar its harmony with ill temper. At least, so felt Lionel. Sibylla spoke as he was turning away.

"Of course, I thought you would go with me. I did not expect you would grumble at me for going."

"Get my hat, Bennet," he said. And he stepped in and took his seat beside her.

Courteously, and smiling as though not a shade of care were within ages of him, Lionel bowed to his guests as the carriage passed the breakfast-room windows. He saw that curious faces were directed to him; he felt that wondering comments, as to their early and sudden drive, were being spoken; he knew that the scene of the past evening was affording food for speculation. He could not help it; but these minor annoyances were as nothing, compared to the great trouble that absorbed him. The windows passed, he turned to his wife.

"I have neither grumbled at you for going, Sibylla, nor do I see cause for grumbling. Why should you charge me with it?"

"There! you are going to find fault with me again! Why are you so cross?"

Cross! He cross! Lionel suppressed at once the retort that was rising to his lips; as he had done hundreds of times before.

"Heaven knows, nothing was further from my thoughts than to be 'cross,'" he answered, his tone full of pain. "Were I to be cross to you, Sibylla, in—in—what may be our last hour together, I should reflect upon myself for my whole life afterwards."

"It is not our last hour together!" she vehemently answered. "Who says it is?"

"I trust it is not. But I cannot conceal from myself the fact that it maybe so. Remember," he added, turning to her with a sudden impulse, and clasping both her hands within his in a firm, impressive grasp—"remember that my whole life, since you became mine, has been spent for you; in promoting your happiness; in striving to give you more love than has been given to me. I have never met you with an unkind word; I have never given you a clouded look. You will think of this when we are separated. And, for myself, its remembrance will be to my conscience as a healing balm."

Dropping her hands, he drew back to his corner of the chariot, his head leaning against the fair, white watered silk, as if heavy with weariness. In truth, it was so; heavy with the weariness caused by carking care. He had spoken all too impulsively; the avowal was wrung from him in the moment's bitter strife. A balm upon his conscience that he had done his duty by her in love? Ay. For the love of his inmost heart had been another's—not hers.

Sibylla did not understand the allusion. It was well. In her weak and trifling manner, she was subsiding into tears when the carriage suddenly stopped. Lionel, his thoughts never free, since a day or two, of Frederick Massingbird, looked up with a start, almost expecting to see him.

Lady Verner's groom had been galloping on horseback to Verner's Pride. Seeing Mr. Verner's carriage, and himself inside it, he had made a sign to Wigham, who drew up. The man rode up to the window, a note in his hand.

"Miss Verner charged me to lose no time in delivering it to you, sir. She said it was immediate. I shouldn't else have presumed to stop your carriage."

He backed his horse a step or two, waiting for the answer, should there be any. Lionel ran his eyes over the contents of the note.

"Tell Miss Verner I will call upon her shortly, Philip."

And the man, touching his hat, turned his horse round, and galloped back towards Deerham Court.

"What does she want? What is it?" impatiently asked Sibylla.

"My mother wishes to see me," replied Lionel.

"And what else? I know that's not all," reiterated Sibylla, her tone a resentful one. "You have always secrets at Deerham Court against me."

"Never in my life," he answered. "You can read the note, Sibylla."

She caught it up, devouring its few lines rapidly. Lionel believed it must be the doubt, the uncertainty, that was rendering her so irritable; in his heart he felt inclined to make every allowance for her; more, perhaps, than she deserved. There were but a few lines:—

"Do come to us at once, my dear Lionel! A most strange report has reached us, and mamma is like one bereft of her senses. She wants you here to contradict it; she says she knows it cannot have any foundation.

DECIMA."

Somehow the words seemed to subdue Sibylla's irritation. She returned the note to Lionel, and spoke in a hushed, gentle tone. "Is it this report that she alludes to, do you think, Lionel?"

"I fear so. I do not know what other it can be. I am vexed that it should already have reached the ears of my mother."

"Of course!" resentfully spoke Sibylla. "You would have spared her!"

"I would have spared my mother, had it been in my power. I would have spared my wife," he added, bending his grave, kind face towards her, "that, and all other ill."

She dashed down the front blinds of the carriage, and laid her head upon his bosom, sobbing repentantly.

"You would bear with me, Lionel, if you knew the pain I have here"—touching her chest. "I am sick and ill with fright."

He did not answer that he did bear with her—bear with her most patiently—as he might have done. He only placed his arm round her that she might feel its shelter; and, with his gentle fingers, pushed the golden curls away from her cheeks, for her tears were wetting them.

She went into her sister's house alone. She preferred to do so. The carriage took Lionel on to Deerham Court. He dismissed it when he alighted; ordering Wigham back to Miss West's, to await the pleasure of his mistress.

CHAPTER LXIV

ENDURANCE

Lionel had probably obeyed the summons sooner than was expected by Lady Verner and Decima; sooner, perhaps, than they deemed he could have obeyed it. Neither of them was in the breakfast-room: no one was there but Lucy Tempest.

By the very way in which she looked at him—the flushed cheeks, the eager eyes—he saw that the tidings had reached her. She timidly held out her hand to him, her anxious gaze meeting his. Whatever may have been the depth of feeling entertained for him, Lucy was too single-minded not to express all she felt of sympathy.

"Is it true?" were her first whispered words, offering no other salutation.

"Is what true, Lucy?" he asked. "How am I to know what you mean?"

They stood looking at each other. Lionel waiting for her to speak; she hesitating. Until Lionel was perfectly certain that she alluded to that particular report, he would not speak of it. Lucy moved a few steps from him, and stood nervously playing with the ends of her waist-band, the soft colour rising in her cheeks.

"I do not like to tell you," she said simply. "It would not be a pleasant thing for you to hear, if it be not true."

"And still less pleasant for me, if it be true," he replied, the words bringing him conviction that the rumour they had heard was correct. "I fear it is true, Lucy."

"That—some one—has come back?"

"Some one who was supposed to be dead."

The avowal seemed to take from her all hope. Her hands fell listlessly by her side, and the tears rose to her eyes. "I am so sorry!" she breathed. "I am so sorry for you, and for—for—"

"My wife. Is that what you were going to say?"

"Yes, it is. I did not like much to say it. I am truly grieved. I wish I could have helped it!"

"Ah! you are not a fairy with an all-powerful wand yet, Lucy, as we read of in children's books. It is a terrible blow, for her and for me. Do you know how the rumour reached my mother?"

"I think it was through the servants. Some of them heard it, and old Catherine told her. Lady Verner has been like any one wild; but for Decima, she would have started—"

Lucy's voice died away. Gliding in at the door, with a white face and drawn-back lips, was Lady Verner. She caught hold of Lionel, her eyes searching his countenance for the confirmation of her fears, or their contradiction. Lionel took her hands in his.

"It is true, mother. Be brave, for my sake."

With a wailing cry she sat down on the sofa, drawing him beside her. Decima entered and stood before them, her hands clasped in pain. Lady Verner made him tell her all the particulars; all he knew, all he feared.

"How does Sibylla meet it?" was her first question when she had listened to the end.

"Not very well," he answered, after a momentary hesitation. "Who could meet it well?" "Lionel, it is a judgment upon her. She—"

Lionel started up, his brow flushing.

"I beg your pardon, mother. You forget that you are speaking of my wife. She is my wife," he more calmly added, "until she shall have been proved not to be."

No. Whatever may have been Sibylla's conduct to him personally, neither before her face nor behind her back, would Lionel forget one jot of the respect due to her. Or suffer another to forget it; although that other should be his mother.

"What shall you do with her, Lionel?"

"Do with her?" he repeated, not understanding how to take the question.

"When the man makes himself known?"

"I am content to leave that to the time," replied Lionel, in a tone that debarred further discussion.

"I knew no good would come of it," resumed Lady Verner, persistent in expressing her opinion. "But for the wiles of that girl you might have married happily, might have married Mary Elmsley."

"Mother, there is trouble enough upon us just now without introducing old vexations," rejoined Lionel. "I have told you before that had I never set eyes upon Sibylla after she married Frederick Massingbird, Mary Elmsley would not have been my wife."

"If he comes back, he comes back to Verner's Pride?" pursued Lady Verner in a low tone, breaking the pause which had ensued.

"Yes. Verner's Pride is his."

"And what shall you do? Turned, like a beggar, out on the face of the earth?"

Like a beggar? Ay, far more like a beggar than Lady Verner, in her worst apprehension, could picture.

"I must make my way on the earth as I best can," he replied in answer, "I shall leave Europe—probably for India. I may find some means, through my late father's friends, of getting my bread there."

Lady Verner appeared to appreciate the motive which no doubt dictated the suggested course. She did not attempt to controvert it; she only wrung her hands in passionate wailing.

"Oh, that you had not married her! that you had not subjected yourself to this dreadful blight!"

Lionel rose. There were limits of endurance even for his aching heart. Reproaches in a moment of trouble are as cold iron entering the soul.

"I will come in another time when you are more yourself, mother," was all he said. "I could have borne sympathy from you this morning, better than complaint."

He shook hands with her. He laid his hand in silence on Decima's shoulder with a fond pressure as he passed her; her face was turned from him, the tears silently streaming down it. He nodded to Lucy, who stood at the other end of the room, and went out. But, ere he was half-way across the ante-room, he heard hasty footsteps behind him. He turned to behold Lucy Tempest, her hands extended, her face streaming down with tears.

"Oh, Lionel, please not to go away thinking nobody sympathises with you! I am so grieved; I am so sorry! If I can do anything for you, or for Sibylla, to lighten the distress, I will do it."

He took the pretty, pleading hands in his, bending his face until it was nearly on a level with hers. But that emotion nearly over-mastered him in the moment's anguish, the very consciousness that he might be free from married obligations, would have rendered his manner cold to Lucy Tempest. Whether Frederick Massingbird was alive or not, he must be a man isolated from other wedded ties, so long as Sibylla remained on the earth. The kind young face, held up to him in its grief, disarmed his reserve. He spoke out to Lucy as freely as he had done in that long-ago illness, when she was his full confidante. Nay, whether from her looks, or from some lately untouched chord in his memory reawakened, that old time was before him now, rather than the present, as his next words proved.

"Lucy, with one thing and another, my heart is half broken. I wish I had died in that illness. Better for me! Better—perhaps—for you."

"Not for me," said she, through her tears. "Do not think of me. I wish I could help you in this great sorrow!"

"Help from you of any sort, Lucy, I forfeited in my blind wilfulness," he hoarsely whispered. "God bless you!" he added, wringing her hands to pain. "God bless you for ever!"

She did not loose them. He was about to draw his hands away, but she held them still, her tears and sobs nearly choking her.

"You spoke of India. Should it be that land that you choose for your exile, go to papa. He may be able to do great things for you. And, if in his power, he would do them, for Sir Lionel Verner's sake. Papa longs to know you. He always says so much about you in his letters to me."

"You have never told me so, Lucy."

"I thought it better not to talk to you too much," she simply said. "And you have not been always at Deerham."

Lionel looked at her, holding her hands still. She knew how futile it was to affect ignorance of truths in that moment of unreserve; she knew that her mind and its feelings were as clear to Lionel as though she had been made of glass, and she spoke freely in her open simplicity. She knew, probably, that his deepest love and esteem were given to her. Lionel knew it, if she did not; knew it to his very heart's core. He could only reiterate his prayer, as he finally turned from her—"God bless you, Lucy, for ever, and for ever!"

CHAPTER LXV

CAPTAIN CANNONBY

Deerham abounded in inns. How they all contrived to get a living, nobody could imagine. That they did jog along somehow, was evident; but they appeared to be generally as void of bustle as were their lazy sign-boards, basking in the sun on a summer's day. The best in the place, one with rather more pretension to superiority than the rest, was the Golden Fleece. It was situated at the entrance to Deerham, not far from the railway station; not far either from Deerham Court; in fact, between Deerham Court and the village.

As Lionel approached it, he saw the landlord standing at its entrance—John Cox. A rubicund man, with a bald head, who evidently did justice to his own good cheer, if visitors did not. Shading his eyes with one hand, he had the other extended in the direction of the village, pointing out the way to a strange gentleman who stood beside him.

"Go as straight as you can go, sir, through the village, and for a goodish distance beyond it," he was saying, as Lionel drew within hearing. "It will bring you to Verner's Pride. You can't mistake it; it's the only mansion thereabouts."

The words caused Lionel to cast a rapid glance at the stranger. He saw a man of some five-and-thirty or forty years, fair of complexion once, but bronzed now by travel, or other causes. The landlord's eyes fell on Lionel.

"Here is Mr. Verner!" he hastily exclaimed. "Sir"—saluting Lionel—"this gentleman was going up to you at Verner's Pride."

The stranger turned, holding out his hand in a free and pleasant manner to Lionel. "My name is Cannonby."

"I could have known it by the likeness to your brother," said Lionel, shaking him by the hand. "I saw him yesterday. I was in town, and he told me you were coming. But why were you not with us last night?"

"I turned aside on my journey to see an old military friend—whom, by the way, I found to be out—and did not get to Deerham until past ten," explained Captain Cannonby. "I thought it too late to invade you, so put up here until this morning."

Lionel linked his arm within Captain Cannonby's, and drew him onwards. The moment of confirmation was come. His mind was in too sad a state to allow of his beating about the bush; his suspense had been too sharp and urgent for him to prolong it now. He plunged into the matter at once.

"You have come to bring me some unpleasant news, Captain Cannonby. Unhappily, it will be news no longer. But you will give me the confirming particulars."

Captain Cannonby looked as if he did not understand. "Unpleasant news?" he repeated.

"I speak"—and Lionel lowered his voice—"of Frederick Massingbird. You know, probably, what I would ask. How long have you been cognisant of these unhappy facts?"

"I declare, Mr. Verner, I don't know what you mean," was Captain Cannonby's answer, given in a hearty tone. "To what do you allude?"

Lionel paused. Was it possible that he—Captain Cannonby—was in ignorance? "Tell me one thing," he said. "Your brother mentioned that you had heard, as he believed, some news connected with me and—and my wife, in Paris, which had caused you to hurry home, and come down to Verner's Pride. What was that news?"

"The news I heard was, that Mrs. Massingbird had become Mrs. Verner. I had intended to find her out when I got to Europe, if only to apologise for my negligence in not giving her news of John Massingbird or his property—which news I could never gather for myself—but I did not know precisely where she might be. I heard in Paris that she had married you, and was living at Verner's Pride."

Lionel drew a long breath. "And that was all?"

"That was all."

Then he was in ignorance of it! But, to keep him in ignorance was impossible. Lionel must ask confirmation or non-confirmation of the death. With low voice and rapid speech he mentioned the fears and the facts. Captain Cannonby gathered them in, withdrew his arm from Lionel's, and stood staring at him.

"Fred Massingbird alive, and come back to England!" he uttered, in bewildered wonder.

"We cannot think otherwise," replied Lionel.

"Then, Mr. Verner, I tell you that it cannot be. It cannot be, you understand. I saw him die. I saw him laid in the grave."

They had not walked on. They stood there, looking at each other, absorbed in themselves, oblivious to the attention that might be fixed on them from any stray passers-by. At that moment there were no passers-by to fix it; the bustle of Deerham only began with the houses, and those they had not yet reached.

"I would give all my future life to believe you," earnestly spoke Lionel; "to believe that there can be no mistake—for my wife's sake."

"There is no mistake," reiterated Captain Cannonby. "I saw him dead; I saw him buried. A parson, in the company halting there, read the burial service over him."

"You may have buried him, fancying he was dead," suggested Lionel, giving utterance to some of the wild thoughts of his imaginings. "And—forgive me for bringing forward such pictures—the mistake may have been discovered in time—and—"

"It could not be," interrupted Captain Cannonby. "I am quite certain he was dead. Let us allow, if you will, for argument's sake, that he was not dead when he was put into the ground. Five minutes' lying there, with the weight of earth upon him, would have effectually destroyed life; had any been left in him to destroy. There was no coffin, you must remember."

"No?"

"Parties to the gold-fields don't carry a supply of coffins with them. If death occurs en route, it has to be provided for in the simplest and most practical form. At least, I can answer that such was the case with regard to Fred Massingbird. He was buried in the clothes he wore when he died."

Lionel was lost in abstraction.

"He died at early dawn, just as the sun burst out to illumine the heavens, and at midday he was buried," continued Captain Cannonby. "I saw him buried. I saw the earth shovelled in upon him; nay, I helped to shovel it. I left him there; we all left him, covered over; at rest for good in this world. Mr. Verner, dismiss this great fear; rely upon it that he was, and is, dead."

"I wish I could rely upon it!" spoke Lionel. "The fear, I may say the certainty, has been so unequivocally impressed upon my belief, that a doubt must remain until it is explained who walks about, bearing his outward appearance. He was a very remarkable-looking man, you know. The black mark on his cheek alone would render him so."

"And that black mark is visible upon the cheek of the person who is seen at night?"

"Conspicuously so. This ghost—as it is taken for—has nearly frightened one or two lives away. It is very strange."

"Can it be anybody got up to personate Fred Massingbird?"

"Unless it be himself, that is the most feasible interpretation," observed Lionel. "But it does not alter the mystery. It is not only in the face and the black mark that the likeness is discernible, but in the figure also. In fact, in all points this man bears the greatest resemblance to Frederick Massingbird—at least, if the eyes of those who have seen him may be trusted. My own butler saw him last night; the man passed close before him, turning his face to him in the moment of passing. He says there can be no doubt that it is Frederick Massingbird."

Captain Cannonby felt a little staggered. "If it should turn out to be Frederick Massingbird, all I can say is that I shall never believe anybody's dead again. It will be like an incident in a drama. I should next expect my old father to come to life, who has lain these twelve years past at Kensal Green Cemetery. Does Mrs. Verner know of this?"

"She does, unfortunately. She was told of it during my absence yesterday. I could have wished it kept from her, until we were at some certainty."

"Oh, come, Mr. Verner, take heart!" impulsively cried Captain Cannonby, all the improbabilities of the case striking forcibly upon him. "The thing is not possible; it is not indeed."

"At any rate, your testimony will be so much comfort for my wife," returned Lionel gladly. "It has comforted me. If my fears are not entirely dispelled, there's something done towards it."

Arrived at the Belvedere Road, Lionel looked about for his carriage. He could not see it. At that moment Jan turned out of the surgery. Lionel asked him if he had seen Sibylla.

"She is gone home," replied Jan. "She and Miss Deb split upon some rock, and Sibylla got into her carriage, and went off in anger."

He was walking away with his usual rapid strides, on his way to some patient, when Lionel caught hold of him. "Jan, this is Captain Cannonby. The friend who was with Frederick Massingbird when he died. He assures me that he is dead. Dead and buried. My brother, Captain Cannonby."

"There cannot be a doubt of it," said Captain Cannonby, alluding to the death. "I saw him die; I helped to bury him."

"Then who is it that walks about, dressed up as his ghost?" debated Jan.

"I cannot tell," said Lionel, a severe expression arising to his lips. "I begin to think with Captain Cannonby; that there can be no doubt that Frederick Massingbird is dead; therefore, he, it is not. But that it would be undesirable, for my wife's sake, to make this doubt public, I would have every house in the place searched. Whoever it may be, he is concealed in one of them."

"Little doubt of that," nodded Jan. "I'll pounce upon him, if I get the chance."

Lionel and Captain Cannonby continued their way to Verner's Pride. The revived hope in Lionel's mind strengthened with every step they took. It did seem impossible, looking at it from a practical, matter-of-fact point of view, that a man buried deep in the earth, and supposed to be dead before he was placed there, could come to life again.

"What a relief for Sibylla!" he involuntarily cried, drawing a long, relieved breath on his own score. "This must be just one of those cases, Captain Cannonby, when good Catholics, in the old days, made a vow to the Virgin of so many valuable offerings, should the dread be removed and turn out to have been no legitimate dread at all."

"Ay. I should like to be in at the upshot."

"I hope you will be. You must not run away from us immediately. Where's your luggage?"

Captain Cannonby laughed. "Talk to a returned gold-digger of his 'luggage'! Mine consists of a hand portmanteau, and that is at the Golden Fleece. I can order it up here if you'd like me to stay with you a few days. I should enjoy some shooting beyond everything."

"That is settled, then," said Lionel. "I will see that you have your portmanteau. Did you get rich at the diggings?"

The captain shook his head. "I might have made something, had I stuck at it. But I grew sick of it altogether. My brother, the doctor, makes a sight of money, and I can get what I want from him," was the candid confession.

Lionel smiled. "These rich brothers in reserve are a terrible drag upon self-exertion. Here we are!" he added, as they turned in at the gates. "This is Verner's Pride."

"What a fine place!" exclaimed Captain Cannonby, bringing his steps to a halt as he gazed at it.

"Yes, it is. Not a pleasant prospect, was it, to contemplate the being turned out of it by a dead man."

"A dead—You do not mean to say that Frederick Massingbird—if in life—would be the owner of Verner's Pride?"

"Yes, he would be. I was its rightful heir, and why my uncle willed it away from me, to one who was no blood relation, has remained a mystery to this day. Frederick Massingbird succeeded, to my exclusion. I only came into it at his death."

Captain Cannonby appeared completely thunderstruck at the revelation. "Why, then," he cried, after a pause, "this may supply the very motive-power that is wanting, for one to personate Fred Massingbird."

"Scarcely," replied Lionel. "No ghost, or seeming ghost, walking about in secret at night, could get Verner's Pride resigned to him. He must come forward in the broad face of day, and establish his identity by indisputable proof."

"True, true. Well, it is a curious tale! I should like, as I say, to witness the winding-up."

Lionel looked about for his wife. He could not find her. But few of their guests were in the rooms; they had dispersed somewhere or other. He went up to Sibylla's dressing-room, but she was not there. Mademoiselle Benoite was coming along the corridor as he left it again.

"Do you know where your mistress is?" he asked.

"Mais certainement," responded mademoiselle. "Monsieur will find madam at the archerie."

He bent his steps to the targets. On the lawn, flitting amidst the other fair archers, in her dress of green and gold, was Sibylla. All traces of care had vanished from her face, her voice was of the merriest, her step of the fleetest, her laugh of the lightest. Truly, Lionel marvelled. There flashed into his mind the grieving face of another, whom he had not long ago parted from; grieving for their woes. Better for his mind's peace that these contrasts had not been forced so continually upon him.

Could she, in some unaccountable manner, have heard the consoling news that Cannonby brought? In the first moment, he thought it must be so: in the next, he knew it to be impossible. Smothering down a sigh, he went forward, and drew her apart from the rest; choosing that covered walk where he had spoken to her a day or two previously, regarding Mrs. Duff's bill. Taking her hands in his, he stood before her, looking with a reassuring smile into her face.

"What will you give me for some good news, Sibylla?"

"What about?" she rejoined.

"Need you ask? There is only one point upon which news could greatly interest either of us, just now. I have seen Cannonby. He is here, and—"

"Here! At Verner's Pride?" she interrupted. "Oh, I shall like to see Cannonby; to talk over old Australian times with him."

Who was to account for her capricious moods? Lionel remembered the evening, during the very moon not yet dark to the earth, when Sibylla had made a scene in the drawing-room, saying she could not bear to hear the name of Cannonby, or to be reminded of the past days in Melbourne. She was turning to fly to the house, but Lionel caught her.

"Wait, wait, Sibylla! Will you not hear the good tidings I have for you? Cannonby says there cannot be a doubt that Frederick Massingbird is dead. He left him dead and buried, as he told you in Melbourne. We have been terrified and pained—I trust—for nothing."

"Lionel, look here," said she, receiving the assurance in the same equable manner that she might have heard him assert it was a fine day, or a wet one, "I have been making up my mind not to let this bother worry me. That wretched old maid Deborah went on to me with such rubbish this morning about leaving you, about leaving Verner's Pride, that she vexed me to anger. I came home and cried; and Benoite found me lying upon the sofa; and when I told her what it was, she said the best plan was, not to mind, to meet it with a laugh, instead of tears—"

"Sibylla!" he interposed in a tone of pain. "You surely did not make a confidante of Benoite!"

"Of course I did," she answered, looking as if surprised at his question, his tone. "Why not? Benoite cheered me up, I can tell you, better than you do. 'What matter to cry?' she asked. 'If he does come back, you will still be the mistress of Verner's Pride.' And so I shall."

Lionel let go her hands. She sped off to the house, eager to find Captain Cannonby. He—her husband—leaned against the trunk of a tree, bitter mortification in his face, bitter humiliation in his heart. Was this the wife to whom he had bound himself for ever? Well could he echo in that moment Lady Verner's reiterated assertion, that she was not worthy of him. With a stifled sigh that was more like a groan, he turned to follow her.

"Be still, be still!" he murmured, beating his hand upon his bosom, that he might still its pain. "Let me bear on, doing my duty by her always in love!"

That pretty Mrs. Jocelyn ran up to Lionel, and intercepted his path. Mrs. Jocelyn would have liked to intercept it more frequently than she did, if she had but received a little encouragement. She tried hard for it, but it never came. One habit, at any rate, Lionel Verner had not acquired, amid the many strange examples of an artificial age—that of not paying considerate respect, both in semblance and reality, to other men's wives.

"Oh, Mr. Verner, what a truant you are! You never come to pick up our arrows."

"Don't I?" said Lionel, with his courteous smile. "I will come presently if I can. I am in search of Mrs. Verner. She is gone in to welcome a friend who has arrived."

And Mrs. Jocelyn had to go back to the targets alone.

CHAPTER LXVI

"DON'T THROTTLE ME, JAN!"

There was a good deal of sickness at present in Deerham: there generally was in the autumn season. Many a time did Jan wish he could be master of Verner's Pride just for twelve months, or of any other "Pride" whose revenues were sufficient to remedy the evils existing in the poor dwellings: the ill accommodation, inside; the ill draining, out. Jan, had that desirable consummation arrived, would not have wasted time in thinking over it; he would have commenced the work in the same hour with his own hands. However, Jan, like most of us, had not to do with things as they might be, but with things as they were. The sickness was great, and Jan, in spite of his horse's help, was, as he often said, nearly worked off his legs.

He had been hastening to a patient when encountered by Lionel and Captain Cannonby. From that patient he had to hasten to others, in a succession of relays, as it were, all day long; sometimes his own legs in requisition, sometimes the horse's. About seven o'clock he got home to tea, at which Miss Deborah made him comfortable. Truth to say, Miss Deborah felt rather inclined to pet Jan as a son. He had gone there a boy, and Miss Deb, though the years since had stolen on and on, and had changed Jan into a man, had not allowed her ideas to keep pace with them. So do we cheat ourselves! There were times when a qualm of conscience came over Miss Deb. Remembering how hard Jan worked, and that her father took more than the lion's share of the profits, it appeared to her scarcely fair. Not that she could alter it, poor thing! All she could do was to be as economical as possible, and to study Jan's comforts. Now and again she had been compelled to go to Jan for money, over and above the stipulated sum paid to her. Jan gave it as freely and readily as he would have filled Miss Amilly's glass pot with castor oil. But Deborah West knew that it came out of Jan's own pocket; and, to ask for it, went terribly against her feelings and her sense of justice.

The tea was over. But she took care of Jan's—some nice tea, and toasted tea-cakes, and a plate of ham. Jan sat down by the fire, and, as Miss Deb said, took it in comfort. Truth to say, had Jan found only the remains of the teapot, and stale bread-and-butter, he might have thought it comfortable enough for him; he would not have grumbled had he found nothing.

"Any fresh messages in, do you know, Miss Deb?" he inquired.

"Now, do pray get your tea in peace, Mr. Jan, and don't worry yourself over 'fresh messages,'" responded Miss Deb. "Master Cheese was called out to the surgery at tea-time, but I suppose it was nothing particular, for he was back again directly."

"Of course!" cried Jan. "He'd not lose his tea without a fight for it."

Jan finished his tea and departed to the surgery, catching sight of the coat-tails of Mr. Bitterworth's servant leaving it. Master Cheese was seated with the leech basin before him. It was filled with Orleans plums, of which he was eating with uncommon satisfaction. Liking variations of flavour in fruit, he occasionally diversified the plums with a sour codlin apple, a dozen or so of which he had stowed away in his trousers' pockets. Bob stood at a respectful distance, his eyes wandering to the tempting collation, and his mouth watering. Amongst the apples Master Cheese had come upon one three parts eaten away by the grubs, and this he benevolently threw to Bob. Bob had disposed of it, and was now vainly longing for more.

"What did Bitterworth's man want?" inquired Jan of Master Cheese.

"The missis is took bad again, he says," responded that gentleman, as distinctly as he could speak for the apples and the plums: "croup, or something. Not as violent as it was before. Can wait."

"You had better go up at once," was Jan's reply.

Master Cheese was taken aback. "I go up!" he repeated, pulling a face as long as his arm. "All that way! I had to go to Baker's and to Flint's between dinner and tea."

"And to how many Bakers and Flints do I have to go between dinner and tea?" retorted Jan. "You know what to give Mrs. Bitterworth. So start."

Master Cheese felt aggrieved beyond everything. For one thing, it might be dangerous to leave those cherished plums in the leech basin, Bob being within arm's length of them; for another, Master Cheese liked his ease better than walking. He cast some imploring glances at Jan, but they produced no effect, so he had to get his hat. Vacillating between the toll that might be taken of the plums if he left them, and the damage to his hair if he took them, he finally decided on the latter course. Emptying the plums into his hat, he put it on his head. Jan was looking over what they termed the call-book.

"Miss Deb says you were called out at tea-time," observed Jan, as Master Cheese was departing. "Who was it?"

"Nobody but old Hook. The girl was worse."

"What! Alice? Why have you not got it down here?" pointing to the book.

"Oh, they are nobody," grumbled Master Cheese. "I wonder the paupers are not ashamed to come here to our faces, asking for attendance and physic! I They know they'll never pay."

"That's my business," said Jan, "Did he say she was very ill?"

"'Took dangerous,' he said," returned Master Cheese. "Thought she'd not live the night out."

Indefatigable Jan put on his hat, and went out with Master Cheese. Master Cheese turned leisurely towards Mr. Bitterworth's; Jan cut across the road at a strapping pace, and took the nearest way to Hook's cottage. It led him past the retired spot where he and the Reverend Mr. Bourne had found Alice lying that former night.

Barely had Jan gained it when some tall, dark form came pushing through the trees at right angles, and was striding off to the distance. One single moment's indecision—for Jan was not sure at first in the uncertain light—and then he put his long legs to their utmost speed, bore down, and pinned the intruder.

"Now, then!" said Jan, "ghost or no ghost, who are you?"

He was answered by a laugh, and some joking words—

"Don't throttle me quite, Jan. Even a ghost can't stand that."

The tone of the laugh, the tone of the voice, fell upon Jan Verner's ears with the most intense astonishment. He peered into the speaker's face with his keen eyes, and gave vent to an exclamation. In spite of the whiskerless cheeks, the elaborate black mark, in spite of the strange likeness to his brother, Jan recognised the features, not of Frederick, but of John Massingbird.

CHAPTER LXVII

DRESSING UP FOR A GHOST

And so the mystery was out. And the ghost proved to be no ghost at all—to be no husband of Sibylla—come to disturb the peace of her and of Lionel; but John Massingbird in real flesh and blood.

There was so much explanation to ask and to be given, that Jan was somewhat hindered on his way to Hook's.

"I can't stop," said he, in the midst of a long sentence of John's. "Alice Hook may be dying. Will you remain here until I come back?"

"If you are not long," responded John Massingbird. "I intend this to be the last night of my concealment, and I want to go about, terrifying the natives. The fun it has been!"

"Fun, you call it?" remarked Jan. "If Hook's girl does die, it will lie at your door."

"She won't die," lightly answered John. "I'll send her a ten-pound note to make amends. Make you haste, Jan, if I am to wait."

Jan sped off to Hook's. He found the girl very ill, but not so much so as Cheese had intimated. Some unseemly quarrel had taken place in the cottage, which had agitated her.

"There's no danger," mentally soliloquised Jan, "but it has thrown her back a good two days."

He found John Massingbird—restless John!—restless as ever!—pacing before the trees with hasty strides, and bursting into explosions of laughter.

"Some woman was coming along from one of the cottages by Broom's and I appeared to her, and sent her on, howling," he explained to Jan. "I think it was Mother Sykes. The sport this ghost affair has been!"

He sat down on a bench, held his sides, and let his laughter have vent. Laughter is contagious, and Jan laughed with him, but in a quieter way.

"Whatever put it into your head to personate Frederick?" inquired Jan. "Was it done to frighten the people?"

"Not at first," answered John Massingbird.

"Because, if to frighten had been your motive, you need only have appeared in your own person," continued Jan. "You were thought to be dead, you know, as much as Fred was. Fred is dead, I suppose?"

"Fred is dead, poor fellow, safe enough. I was supposed to be dead, but I came to life again."

"Did you catch Fred's star when he died?" asked Jan, pointing to the cheek.

"No," replied John Massingbird, with another burst of laughter, "I get that up with Indian-ink."

Bit by bit, Jan came into possession of the details. At least, of as much of them as John Massingbird deemed it expedient to furnish. It appeared that his being attacked and robbed and left for dead, when travelling down to Melbourne, was perfectly correct. Luke Roy quitted him, believing he was dead. Luke would not have quitted him so hastily, but that he wished to be on the track of the thieves, and he hastened to Melbourne. After Luke's departure, John Massingbird came, as he phrased it, to life again. He revived from the suspended animation, or swoon, which, prolonged over some hours, had been mistaken for death. The bullet was extracted from his side, and he progressed pretty rapidly towards recovery.

Luke meanwhile had reached Melbourne; and had come in contact with a family of the name of Eyre. Luke—if you have not forgotten—had said to Mr. Eyre that he had obtained a clue to the men who robbed his master; such, at least, was the information given by that gentleman to Sibylla Massingbird, on her subsequent sojourn at his house. He, Mr. Eyre, had said that Luke had promised to return the following day and inform him how he sped in the search, but that Luke never did return; that he had never seen him afterwards. All true. Luke found the clue, which he thought he had gained, to be no clue at all; but he heard news that pleased him better than fifty clues would have done—that his master, Mr. Massingbird, was alive. One who had travelled down to Melbourne from where John was lying, gave him the information. Without waiting to break bread or draw water, without giving another thought to Mr. Eyre, Luke started off there and then, to retrace his steps to John Massingbird. John was nearly well then, and they returned at once to the diggings. In his careless way, he said the loss must be given up for a bad job; they should never find the fellows, and the best plan was to pick up more gold to replace that gone. Luke informed him he had written home to announce his death. John went into a fit of laughter, forbade Luke to contradict it, and anticipated the fun he should have in surprising them, when he went home on the accumulation of his fortune. Thus he stopped at the diggings, remaining in complete ignorance of the changes which had taken place; the voyage of Frederick and his wife to Melbourne, the death of Mr. Verner, the subsequent death of Frederick; and above all—for that would have told most on John—of the strange will left by Mr. Verner, which had constituted him the inheritor of Verner's Pride.

But fortune did not come in the rapid manner fondly expected by John. The nuggets seemed shy. He obtained enough to rub along with, and that was all. The life did not ill suit him. To such a man as Lionel Verner, of innate refinement, just and conscientious, the life would have been intolerable, almost worse than death. John was not overburdened with any one of those qualities, and he rather liked the life than not. One thing was against him: he had no patience. Roving about from place to place, he was satisfied nowhere long. It was not only that he perpetually changed the spot, or bed, of work, but he changed from one settlement to another. This was the reason probably that Captain Cannonby had never met with him; it was more than probable that it was the cause of his non-success. Luke Roy was not so fond of roving. He found a place likely to answer his expectations, and he remained at it; so that the two parted early, and did not again meet afterwards.

Suddenly John Massingbird heard that he had been left heir to Verner's Pride. He had gone down to Melbourne; and some new arrival from England—from the county in which Verner's Pride was situated—mentioned this in his hearing. The stranger was telling the tale of the unaccountable will of Mr. Verner, of the death of John and Frederick Massingbird, and of the consequent accession of Lionel Verner; telling it as a curious bit of home gossip, unconscious that one of his listeners was the first-named heir—the veritable John Massingbird.

Too much given to act upon impulse, allowing himself no time to ascertain or to inquire whether the story might be correct or not, John Massingbird took a berth in the first ship advertised for home. He possessed very little more money than would pay for his passage; he gave himself no concern how he was to get back to Australia, or how exist in England, should the news prove incorrect, but started away off-hand. Providing for the future had never been made a trouble by John Massingbird.

He sailed, and he arrived safely. But, once in England, it was necessary to proceed rather cautiously; and John, careless and reckless though he was, could not ignore the expediency of so acting. There were certain reasons why it would not be altogether prudent to show himself in the neighbourhood of Verner's Pride, unless his pocket were weighty enough to satisfy sundry claims which would inevitably flock in upon him. Were he sure that he was the legitimate master of Verner's Pride, he would have driven up in a coach-and-six, with flying flags and streamers to the horses' heads, and so have announced his arrival in triumph. Not being sure, he preferred to feel his way, and this could not be done by arriving openly.

There was one place where he knew he could count upon being sheltered, while the way was "felt;" and this was Giles Roy's. Roy would be true to him; would conceal him if need were; and help him off again, did Verner's Pride, for him, prove a myth. This thought John Massingbird put in practice, arriving one dark night at Roy's, and startling Mrs. Roy nearly to death. Whatever fanciful ghosts the woman may have seen before, she never doubted that she saw a real ghost now.

His first question, naturally, was about the will. Roy told him it was perfectly true that a will had been made in his favour; but the will had been superseded by a codicil. And he related the circumstance of that codicil's mysterious loss. Was it found? John eagerly asked. Ah! there Roy could not answer him; he was at a nonplus; he was unable to say whether the codicil had been found or not. A rumour had gone about Deerham, some time subsequently to the loss, that it had been found, but Roy had never come to the rights of it. John Massingbird stared as he heard him say this. Then, couldn't he tell whether he was the heir or not? whether Lionel Verner held it by established right or by wrong? he asked. And Roy shook his head—he could not.

Under these uncertainties, Mr. John Massingbird did not see his way particularly clear. Either to stop, or to go. If he stopped, and showed himself, he might be unpleasantly assured that the true heir of Verner's Pride inhabited Verner's Pride; if he went back to Australia, the no less mortifying fact might come out afterwards, that he was the heir to Verner's Pride, and had run away from his own.

What was to be done? Roy suggested perhaps the best plan that could be thought of—that Mr. Massingbird should remain in his cottage in concealment, while he, Roy, endeavoured to ascertain the truth regarding the codicil. And John Massingbird was fain to adopt it. He took up his abode in the upper bedroom, which had been Luke's, and Mrs. Roy, locking her front door, carried his meals up to him by day, Roy setting himself to ferret out—as you may recollect—all he could learn about the codicil. The "all" was not much. Ordinary gossipers knew no more than Roy, whether the codicil had been found or not; and Roy tried to pump Matiss, by whom he was baffled—he even tried to pump Mr. Verner. He went up to Verner's Pride, ostensibly to ask whether he might paper Luke's old room at his own cost. In point of fact, the paper was in a dilapidated state, and he did wish to put it decent for John Massingbird; but he could have done it without speaking to Mr. Verner. It was a great point with Roy to find favour in the sight of Mr. Massingbird, his possible future master. Lionel partially saw through the man; he believed that he had some covert motive in seeking the interview with him, and that Roy was trying to pry into his affairs. But Roy found himself baffled also by Mr. Verner, as he had been by Matiss, in so far as that he could learn nothing certain of the existence or non-existence of the codicil.

Two days of the condemned confinement were sufficient to tire out John Massingbird. To a man of active, restless temperament, who had lived almost day and night under the open skies, the being shut up in a small, close room was well-nigh unbearable. He could not stamp on its floor (there was no space to walk on it), lest any intrusive neighbour below, who might have popped in, unwanted, should say, "Who have ye got up aloft?" He could not open the window and put his head out, to catch a breath of fresh air, lest prying eyes might be cast upon him.

"I can't stand this," he said to Roy. "A week of it would kill me. I shall go out at night."

Roy opposed the resolve so far as he dared—having an eye always to the not displeasing his future master. He represented to John Massingbird that he would inevitably be seen; and that he might just as well be seen by day as by night. John would not listen to reason. That very night, as soon as dark came on, he went out, and was seen. Seen by Robin Frost.

Robin Frost, whatever superstitions or fond feelings he may have cherished regarding the hoped-for reappearance of Rachel's spirit, was no believer in ghosts in a general point of view. In fact, that it was

John Massingbird's ghost never once entered Robin's mind. He came at once to the more sensible conclusion that some error had occurred with regard to his reported death, and that it was John Massingbird himself.

His deadly enemy. The only one, of all the human beings upon earth, with whom Robin was at issue. For he believed that it was John Massingbird who had worked the ill to Rachel. Robin, in his blind vengeance, took to lying in wait with a gun: and Roy became cognisant of this.

"You must not go out again, sir," he said to John Massingbird; "he may shoot you dead."

Curious, perhaps, to say, John Massingbird had himself come to the same conclusion—that he must not go out again. He had very narrowly escaped meeting one who would as surely have known him, in the full moonlight, as did Robin Frost; one whom it would have been nearly as inconvenient to meet, as it was Robin. And yet, stop in perpetual confinement by day and by night, he could not; he persisted that he should be dead—almost better go back, unsatisfied, to Australia.

A bright idea occurred to John Massingbird. He would personate his brother. Frederick, so far as he knew, had neither creditors nor enemies round Deerham; and the likeness between them was so great, both in face and form, that there would be little difficulty in it. When they were at home together, John had been the stouter of the two: but his wanderings had fined him down, and his figure now looked exactly as Frederick's did formerly. He shaved off his whiskers—Frederick had never worn any; or, for the matter of that, had had any to wear—and painted an imitation star on his cheek with Indian-ink. His hair, too, had grown long on the voyage, and had not yet been cut; just as Frederick used to wear his. John had favoured a short crop of hair; Frederick a long one.

These little toilette mysteries accomplished, so exactly did he look like his brother Frederick, that Roy started when he saw him; and Mrs. Roy went into a prolonged scream that might have been heard at the brick-fields. John attired himself in a long, loose dark coat which had seen service at the diggings, and sallied out; the coat which had been mistaken for a riding habit.

He enjoyed himself to his heart's content, receiving more fun than he had bargained for. It had not occurred to him to personate Frederick's ghost; he had only thought of personating Frederick himself; but to his unbounded satisfaction, he found the former climax arrived at. He met old Matthew Frost; he frightened Dan Duff into fits; he frightened Master Cheese; he startled the parson; he solaced himself by taking up his station under the yew-tree on the lawn at Verner's Pride, to contemplate that desirable structure, which perhaps was his, and the gaiety going on in it. He had distinctly seen Lionel Verner leave the lighted rooms and approach him; upon which he retreated. Afterwards, it was rather a favourite night-pastime of his, the standing under the yew-tree at Verner's Pride. He was there again the night of the storm.

All this, the terrifying people into the belief that he was Frederick's veritable ghost, had been the choicest sport to John Massingbird. The trick might not have availed with Robin Frost, but they had found a different method of silencing him. Of an easy, good-tempered nature, the thought of any real damage from consequences had been completely passed over by John. If Dan Duff did go into fits, he'd recover from them; if Alice Hook was startled into something worse, she was not dead. It was all sport to free-and-easy John; and, but for circumstances, there's no knowing how long he might have carried this game on. These circumstances touched upon a point that influences us all, more or less—pecuniary consideration. John was minus funds, and it was necessary that something should be done; he could not continue to live upon Roy.

It was Roy himself who at length hit upon the plan that brought forth the certainty about the codicil. Roy found rumours were gaining ground abroad that it was not Frederick Massingbird's ghost, but Frederick himself; and he knew that the explanation must soon come. He determined to waylay Tynn and make an apparent confidant of him; by these means he should, in all probability, arrive at the desired information. Roy did so; and found that there was no codicil. He carried his news to John Massingbird, advising that gentleman to go at once and put in his claim to Verner's Pride. John, elated with the news, protested he'd have one more night's fun first.

Such were the facts. John Massingbird told them to Jan, suppressing any little bit that he chose, here and there. The doubt about the codicil, for instance, and its moving motive in the affair, he did not mention.

"It has been the best fun I ever had in my life," he remarked. "I never shall forget the parson's amazed stare, the first time I passed him. Or old Tynn's, either, last night. Jan, you should have heard Dan Duff howl!"

"I have," said Jan. "I have had the pleasure of attending him. My only wonder is that he did not put himself into the pool, in his fright: as Rachel Frost did, time back."

John Massingbird caught the words up hastily, "How, do you know that Rachel put herself in? She may have been put in."

"For all I know, she may. Taking circumstances into consideration, however, I should say it was the other way."

"I say, Jan," interrupted John Massingbird, with another explosion, "didn't your Achates, Cheese, arrive at home in a mortal fright one night?"

Jan nodded.

"I shall never forget him, never. He was marching up, all bravely, till he saw my face. Didn't he turn tail! There has been one person above all others, Jan, that I have wanted to meet, and have not—your brother Lionel."

"He'd have pinned you," said Jan.

"Not he. You would not have done it to-night, but that I let you do it. No chance of anybody catching me, unless I chose. I was on the look-out for all I met, for all to whom I chose to show myself: they met me unawares. Unprepared for the encounter, while they were recovering their astonishment, I was beyond reach. Last night I had been watching over the gate ever so long, when I darted out in front of Tynn, to astonish him. Jan"—lowering his voice—"has it put Sibylla in a fright?"

"I think it has put Lionel in a worse," responded Jan.

"For fear of losing her?" laughed John Massingbird. "Wouldn't it have been a charming prospect for some husbands, who are tired of their wives! Is Lionel tired of his?"

"Can't say," replied Jan. "There's no appearance of it."

"I should be, if Sibylla had been my wife for two years," candidly avowed John Massingbird. "Sibylla and I never hit it off well as cousins. I'd not own her as wife, if she were dowered with all the gold mines in Australia. What Fred saw in her was always a puzzle to me. I knew what was going on between them, though nobody else did. But, Jan, I'll tell you what astonished me more than everything else when I learned it—that Lionel should have married her subsequently. I never could have imagined Lionel Verner taking up with another man's wife."

"She was his widow," cried literal Jan.

"All the same. 'Twas another man's leavings. And there's something about Lionel Verner, with his sensitive refinement, that does not seem to accord with the notion. Is she healthy?"

"Who? Sibylla? I don't fancy she has much of a constitution."

"No, that she has not! There are no children, I hear. Jan, though, you need not have pinched so hard when you pounced upon me," he continued, rubbing his arm. "I was not going to run away."

"How did I know that?" said Jan.

"It's my last night of fun, and when I saw you I said to myself, 'I'll be caught.' How are old Deb and Amilly?"

"Much as usual. Deb's in a fever just now. She has heard that Fred Massingbird's back, and thinks Sibylla ought to leave Lionel on the strength of it."

John laughed again. "It must have put others in a fever, I know, besides poor old Deb. Jan, I can't stop talking to you all night, I should get no more fun. I wish I could appear to all Deerham collectively, and send it into fits after Dan Duff! To-morrow, as soon as I genteelly can after breakfast, I go up to Verner's Pride and show myself. One can't go at six in the morning."

He went off in the direction of Clay Lane as he spoke, and Jan turned to make the best of his way to Verner's Pride.

CHAPTER LXVIII

A THREAT TO JAN

They had dined unusually late at Verner's Pride that evening, and Lionel Verner was with his guests, making merry with the best heart he had. Now, he would rely upon the information given by Captain Cannonby; the next moment he was feeling that the combined testimony of so many eye-witnesses must be believed, and that it could be no other than Frederick Massingbird. Tynn had been with the man face to face only the previous night; Roy had distinctly asserted that he was back, in life, from Australia. Whatever his anxiety may have been, his wife seemed at rest. Full of smiles and gaiety, she sat opposite to him, glittering gems in her golden hair, shining forth from her costly robes.

"Not out from dinner!" cried Jan, in his astonishment, when he arrived, and Tynn denied him to Lionel. "Why, it's my supper-time! I must see him, whether he's at dinner or not. Go and say so, Tynn. Something important, tell him."

The message brought Lionel out. Thankful, probably, to get out. The playing the host with a mind ill at ease, how it jars upon the troubled and fainting spirit! Jan, disdaining the invitation to the drawing-room, had hoisted himself on the top of an old carved ebony cabinet that stood in the hall, containing curiosities, and sat there with his legs dangling. He jumped off when Lionel appeared, wound his arm within his, and drew him out on the terrace.

"I have come to the bottom of it, Lionel," said he, without further circumlocution. "I dropped upon the ghost just now and pinned him. It is not Fred Massingbird."

Lionel paused, and then drew a deep breath; like one who has been relieved from some great care.

"Cannonby said it was not!" he exclaimed. "Cannonby is here, Jan, and he assures me Frederick Massingbird is dead and buried. Who is it, then? Have you found it out?"

"I pinned him, I say," said Jan. "I was going down to Hook's, and he crossed my path. He—"

"It is somebody who has been doing it for a trick?" interrupted Lionel.

"Well—yes—in one sense. It is not Fred Massingbird, Lionel; he is dead, safe enough; but it is somebody from a distance; one who will cause you little less trouble. Not any less, in fact, putting Sibylla out of the question."

Lionel stopped in his walk—they were pacing the terrace—and looked at Jan with some surprise; a smile, in his new security, lightening his face.

"There is nobody in the world, Jan, dead or alive, who could bring trouble to me, save Frederick Massingbird. Anybody else may come, so long as he does not."

"Ah! You are thinking only of Sibylla."

"Of whom else should I think?"

"Yourself," replied Jan.

Lionel laughed in his gladness. How thankful he was for his wife's sake ONE alone knew. "I am nobody, Jan. Any trouble coming to me I can battle with."

"Well, Lionel, the returned man is John Massingbird."

"John—Mass—ingbird!"

Of all the birds in the air and the fishes in the sea—as the children say—he was the very last to whom Lionel Verner had cast a thought. That it was John who had returned, had not entered his imagination. He had never cast a doubt on the fact of his death. Bringing the name out slowly, he stared at Jan in very astonishment.

"Well," said he presently, "John is not Frederick."

"No," assented Jan. "He can put in no claim to your wife. But he can to Verner's Pride."

The words caused Lionel's heart to go on with a bound. A great evil for him; there was no doubt of it; but still slight, compared to the one he had dreaded for Sibylla.

"There is no mistake, I suppose, Jan?"

"There's no mistake," replied Jan. "I have been talking to him this half-hour. He is hiding at Roy's."

"Why should he be in hiding at all?" inquired Lionel.

"He had two or three motives he said;" and Jan proceeded to give Lionel a summary of what he had heard. "He was not very explicit to me," concluded Jan. "Perhaps he will be more so to you. He says he is coming to Verner's Pride to-morrow morning at the earliest genteel hour after breakfast."

"And what does he say to the fright he has caused?" resumed Lionel.

"Does nothing but laugh over it. Says it's the primest fun he ever had in his life. He has come back very poor, Lionel."

"Poor? Then, were Verner's Pride and its revenues not his, I could have understood why he should not like to show himself openly. Well! well! compared to what I feared, it is a mercy. Sibylla is free; and I—I must make the best of it. He will be a more generous master of Verner's Pride—as I believe—than Frederick would ever have been."

"Yes," nodded Jan. "In spite of his faults. And John Massingbird used to have plenty."

"I don't know who amongst us is without them, Jan. Unless—upon my word, old fellow, I mean it!—unless it is you."

Jan opened his great eyes with a wondering stare. It never occurred to humble-minded Jan that there was anything in him approaching to goodness. He supposed Lionel had spoken in joke.

"What's that?" cried he.

Jan alluded to a sudden burst of laughter, to a sound of many voices, to fair forms that were flitting before the windows. The ladies had gone into the drawing-room. "What a relief it will be for Sibylla!" involuntarily uttered Lionel.

"She'll make a face at losing Verner's Pride," was the less poetical remark of Jan.

"Will he turn us out at once, Jan?"

"He said nothing to me on that score, nor I to him," was the answer of Jan. "Look here, Lionel. Old West's a screw, between ourselves; but what I do earn is my own; so don't get breaking your rest, thinking you'll not have a pound or two to turn to. If John Massingbird does send you out, I can manage things for you, if you don't mind living quietly."

Honest Jan! His notions of "living quietly" would have comprised a couple of modest rooms, cotton umbrellas like his own, and a mutton chop a day. And Jan would have gone without the chop himself, to give it to Lionel. To Sibylla, also. Not that he had any great love for that lady, in the abstract; but, for Jan to eat chops, while anybody, no matter how remotely connected with him, wanted them, would have been completely out of Jan's nature.

A lump was rising in Lionel's throat. He loved Jan, and knew his worth, if nobody else did. While he was swallowing it down, Jan went on, quite eagerly.

"Something else might be thought of, Lionel. I don't see why you and Sibylla should not come to old West's. The house is large enough; and Deb and Amilly couldn't object to it for their sister. In point of right, half the house is mine: West said so when I became his partner; and I paid my share for the furniture. He asked if I'd not like to marry, and said there was the half of the house; but I told him I'd rather be excused. I might get a wife, you know, Lionel, who'd be for grumbling at me all day, as my mother does. Now, if you and Sibylla would come there, the matter as to your future would be at rest. I'd divide what I get between you and Miss Deb. Half to her for the extra cost you'd be to the housekeeping; the other half for pocket-money for you and Sibylla. I think you might make it do, Lionel: my share is quite two hundred a year. My own share I mean; besides what I hand over to Miss Deb, and transmit to the doctor, and other expenses. Could you manage with it?"

"Jan!" said Lionel, from between his quivering lips. "Dear Jan, there's—"

They were interrupted. Bounding out at the drawing-room window, the very window at which Lucy Tempest had sat that night and watched the yew-tree, came Sibylla, fretfulness in the lines of her countenance, complaint in the tones of her voice.

"Mr. Jan Verner, I'd like to know what right you have to send for Lionel from the room when he is at dinner? If he is your brother, you have no business to forget yourself in that way. He can't help your being his brother, I suppose; but you ought to know better than to presume upon it."

"Sibylla!—"

"Be quiet, Lionel. I shall tell him of it. Never was such a thing heard of, as for a gentleman to be called out for nothing, from his table's head! You do it again, Jan, and I shall order Tynn to shut the doors to you of Verner's Pride."

Jan received the lecture with the utmost equanimity, with imperturbable good nature. Lionel wound his arms about his wife, gravely and gently; whatever may have been the pain caused by her words, he suppressed it.

"Jan came here to tell me news that quite justified his sending for me, wherever I might be, or however occupied, Sibylla. He has succeeded in solving to-night the mystery which has hung over us; he has discovered who it is that we have been taking for Frederick Massingbird."

"It is not Frederick Massingbird," cried Sibylla, speaking sharply. "Captain Cannonby says that it cannot be."

"No, it is not Frederick Massingbird—God be thanked!" said Lionel. "With that knowledge, we can afford to hear who it is bravely; can we not, Sibylla?"

"But why don't you tell me who it is?" she retorted, in an impatient, fretful tone, not having the discernment to see that he wished to prepare her for what was coming. "Can't you speak, Jan, if he won't? People have no right to come, dressed up in other people's clothes and faces, to frighten us to death. He ought to be transported! Who is it?"

"You will be startled, Sibylla," said Lionel. "It is one whom we have believed to be dead; though it is not Frederick Massingbird."

"I wish you'd tell—beating about the bush like that! You need not stare so, Jan. I don't believe you know."

"It is your cousin, Sibylla; John Massingbird."

A moment's pause. And then, clutching at the hand of Lionel—

"Who?" she shrieked.

"Hush, my dear. It is John Massingbird."

"Not dead! Did he not die?"

"No. He recovered, when left, as was supposed, for dead. He is coming here to-morrow morning, Jan says."

Sibylla let fall her hands. She staggered back to a pillar and leaned against it, her upturned face white in the starlight.

"Is—is—is Verner's Pride yours or his?" she gasped in a low tone.

"It is his."

"His! Neither yours nor mine?"

"It is only his, Sibylla."

She raised her hands again; she began fighting with the air, as if she would beat off an imaginary John Massingbird. Another minute, and her laughter and her cries came forth together, shriek upon shriek.

She was in strong hysterics. Lionel supported her, while Jan ran for water; and the gay company came flocking out of the lighted rooms to see.

CHAPTER LXIX

NO HOME

People talk of a nine days' wonder. But no nine days' wonder has ever been heard or known, equal to that which fell on Deerham; which went booming to the very extremity of the county's boundaries. Lionel Verner, the legitimate heir—it may so be said—the possessor of Verner's Pride, was turned out of it to make room for an alien, resuscitated from the supposed dead.

Sailors tell us that the rats desert a sinking ship. Pseudo friends desert a falling house. You may revel in these friends in prosperity, but when adversity sets in, how they fall away! On the very day that John Massingbird arrived at Verner's Pride, and it became known that not he, but Mrs. and Mr. Verner must leave it, the gay company gathered there dispersed. Dispersed with polite phrases, which went for nothing. They were so very sorry for the calamity, for Mr. and Mrs. Verner; if they could do anything to serve them they had only to be commanded. And then they left; never perhaps to meet again, even as acquaintances. It may be asked, what could they do? They could not invite them to a permanent home; saddle themselves with a charge of that sort; neither would such an invitation stand a chance of acceptance. It did not appear they could do anything; but their combined flight from the house, one after the other, did strike with a chill of mortification upon the nerves of Lionel Verner and his wife.

His wife! Ah, poor Lionel had enough upon his hands, looking on one side and another. She was the heaviest weight. Lionel had thanked God in his true heart that they had been spared the return of Frederick Massingbird; but there was little doubt that the return of Frederick would have been regarded by her as a light calamity, in comparison with this. She made no secret of it. Ten times a day had Lionel to curb his outraged feelings, and compress his lips to stop the retort that would rise bubbling up within them. She would openly lament that it was not Frederick who had returned, in which case she might have remained at Verner's Pride!

"You'll not turn them out, Massingbird?" cried Jan, in his straightforward way, drawing the gentleman into the fruit-garden to a private conference. "I wouldn't."

John Massingbird laughed good-humouredly. He had been in the sunniest humour throughout; had made his first appearance at Verner's Pride in bursts of laughter, heartily grasping the hands of Lionel, of Sibylla, and boasting of the "fun" he had had in playing the ghost. Captain Cannonby, the only one of the guests who remained, grew charmed with John, and stated his private opinion in the ear of Lionel Verner that he was worth a hundred such as Frederick.

"How can I help turning them out?" answered he. "I didn't make the will—it was old Daddy Verner."

"You need not act upon the will," said Jan. "There was a codicil, you know, superseding it, though it can't be found. Sibylla's your cousin—it would be a cruel thing to turn her from her home."

"Two masters never answered in a house yet," nodded John. "I'm not going to try it."

"Let them stop in Verner's Pride, and you go elsewhere," suggested Jan.

John Massingbird laughed for five minutes. "How uncommon young you are, Jan!" said he. "Has Lionel been putting you up to try this on?"

Jan swung himself on a tolerably strong branch of the mulberry-tree, regardless of any damage the ripe fruit might inflict on his nether garments, as he answered—

"Knowing Lionel, you needn't ask it, Massingbird. There'd be a difficulty in getting him to stop in Verner's Pride now, but he might be coaxed to do it for the sake of his wife. She'll have a fit of illness if she has to go out of it. Lionel is one to stand by his own to the last; while Verner's Pride was his, he'd have fought to retain its possession, inch by inch; but let ever so paltry a quibble of the law take it from him, and he'd not lift up his finger to keep it. But, I say, I think he might be got to do it for Sibylla."

"I'll tell you a secret, Jan," cried John Massingbird. "I'd not have Sibylla stop in Verner's Pride if she paid me ten thousand a year for the favour. There! And as to resigning Verner's Pride the minute I come into it, nobody but a child or Jan Verner could ever have started so absurd an idea. If anything makes me feel cross, it is the thought of my having been knocking about yonder, when I might have been living in clover here. I'd get up an Ever-perpetual Philanthropic Benefit-my-fellow-creature Society, if I were you, Jan, and hold meetings at Exeter Hall!"

"Not in my line," said Jan, swaying himself about on the bough.

"Isn't it! I should say it was. Why don't you invite Sibylla to your house, if you are so fond of her?"

"She won't come," said Jan.

"Perhaps you have not asked her!"

"I was beginning to ask her, but she flew at me and ordered me to hold my tongue. No, I see it," Jan added, in self-soliloquy, "she'll never come there. I thought she might: and I got Miss Deb to think so. She'll—she'll—"

"She'll what?" asked John Massingbird.

"She'll be a thorn in Lionel's side, I'm afraid."

"Nothing more likely," acquiesced easy John. "Roses and thorns go together. If gentlemen will marry the one, they must expect to get their share of the other."

Jan jumped off his bough. His projects all appeared to be failing. The more he had dwelt upon his suddenly-thought-of scheme, that Dr. West's house might afford an asylum for Lionel and his wife, the more he had become impressed with its desirability. Jan Verner, though the most unselfish, perhaps it may be said the most improvident of mortals, with regard to himself, had a considerable amount of forethought for the rest of the world. It had struck him, even before it struck Lionel, that, if turned out of Verner's Pride, Lionel would want a home; want it in the broadest acceptation of the word. It would have been Jan's delight to give him one. He, Jan, went home, told Miss Deb the news that it was John Massingbird who had returned, not Frederick, and imparted his views of future arrangements.

Miss Deb was dubious. For Mr. Verner of Verner's Pride to become an inmate of their home, dependent on her housekeeping, looked a formidable affair. But Jan pointed out that, Verner's Pride gone, it appeared to be but a choice of cheap lodgings; their house would be an improvement upon that. And Miss Deb acquiesced; and grew to contemplate the addition to her family, in conjunction with the addition Jan proposed to add to her income, with great satisfaction.

That failed. Failed upon Jan's first hint of it to Mrs. Verner. She—to use his own expression—flew out at him, at the bare hint; and Sibylla Verner could fly out in an unseemly manner when she chose.

Jan's next venture had been with John Massingbird. That was failure the second. "Where are they to go?" thought Jan.

It was a question that Lionel Verner may also have been asking in his inmost heart. As yet he could not look his situation fully in the face. Not from any want of moral courage, but because of the inextricable confusion that his affairs seemed to be in. And, let his moral courage be what it would, the aspect they bore might have caused a more hardy heart than Lionel's to shrink. How much he owed he could not tell; nothing but debt stared him in the face. He had looked to the autumn rents of Verner's Pride to extricate him from a portion of his difficulties; and now those rents would be received by John Massingbird. The furniture in the house, the plate, the linen, none of it was his; it had been left by the will with Verner's Pride. The five hundred pounds, all that he had inherited by that will, had been received at the time—and was gone. One general sinking fund seemed to have swallowed up everything; that, and all else; leaving a string of debts a yard long in its place.

Reproaches now would be useless; whether self-reproach, or reproach to his wife. The latter Lionel would never have given. And yet, when he looked back, and thought how free from debt he might have been, nothing but reproach, however vaguely directed, reproach of the past generally, seemed to fill his heart. To turn out in the world, a free man, though penniless, would have been widely different from turning out, plunged over head and ears in difficulties.

In what quarter did he not owe money? He could not say. He had not been very provident, and Sibylla had not been provident at all. But this much might be said for Lionel: that he had not wasted money on useless things, or self-indulgence. The improvements he had begun on the estate had been the chief drain, so far as he went; and the money they took had caused him to get backward with the general expenses. He had also been over liberal to his mother. Money was owing on all sides; for large things and for small; how much, Lionel did not yet know. He did not know—he was afraid to guess—what private debts might have been contracted by his wife. There had been times lately, when, in contemplating the embarrassment growing so hopelessly upon him, Lionel had felt inclined to wish that some climax would come and end it; but he had never dreamt of such a climax as this. A hot flush dyed his cheeks as he remembered there was nearly a twelvemonth's wages owing to most of his servants; and he had not the means now of paying them.

"Stop on a bit if you like," said John Massingbird, in a hearty tone; "stop a month, if you will. You are welcome. It will be only changing your place from master to guest."

From master to guest! That same day John Massingbird assumed his own place, unasked, at the head of the dinner-table. Lionel went to the side with a flushed face. John Massingbird had never been remarkable for delicacy, but Lionel could not help thinking that he might have waited until he was gone, before assuming the full mastership. Captain Cannonby made the third at the dinner, and he, by John Massingbird's request, took the foot of the table. It was not the being put out of his place that hurt Lionel so much, as the feeling of annoyance that John Massingbird could behave so unlike a gentleman. He felt ashamed for him. Dinner over, Lionel went up to his wife, who was keeping her room, partly from temper, partly from illness.

"Sibylla, I'll not stop here another day," he said. "I see that John Massingbird wants us to go. Now, what shall I do? Take lodgings?"

Sibylla looked up from the sofa, her eyes red with crying, her cheeks inflamed.

"Anybody but you, Lionel, would never allow him to turn you out. Why don't you dispute the right with him? Turn him out, and defy him!"

He did not tell Sibylla that she was talking like a child. He only said that John Massingbird's claim to Verner's Pride was indisputable—that it had been his all along; that, in point of fact, he himself had been the usurper.

"Then you mean," she said, "to give him up quiet possession?"

"I have no other resource, Sibylla. To attempt any sort of resistance would be foolish as well as wrong."

"I shan't give it up. I shall stay here in spite of him. You may do as you like, but he is not going to get me out of my own home."

"Sibylla, will you try and be rational for once? If ever a time called for it, it is the present. I ask you whether I shall seek after lodgings."

"And I wonder that you are not ashamed to ask me," retorted Sibylla, bursting into tears. "Lodgings, after Verner's Pride! No. I'd rather die than go into lodgings. I dare say I shall die soon, with all this affliction."

"I do not see what else there is for us but lodgings," resumed Lionel, after a pause. "You will not hear of Jan's proposition."

"Go back to my old home!" she shrieked. "Like—as poor Fred used to say—bad money returned. No! that I never will. You are wrapt up in Jan; if he proposed to give me poison, you'd say yes. I wish Fred had not died!"

"Will you be so good as tell me what you think ought to be done?" inquired Lionel.

"How can I think? Where's the good of asking me? I think the least you can do in this wretchedness, is to take as much worry off me as you can, Lionel."

"It is what I wish to do," he gently said. "But I can see only one plan for us, Sibylla—lodgings. Here we cannot stay; it is out of the question. To take a house is equally so. We have no furniture—no money, in short, to set up a house, or to keep it on. Jan's plan, until I can turn myself round and see what's to be done, would be the best. You would be going to your own sisters, who would take care of you, should I find it necessary to be away."

"Away! Where?" she quickly asked.

"I must go somewhere and do something. I cannot lead an idle life, living upon other people's charity, or let you live upon it. I must find some way of earning a livelihood: in London, perhaps. While I am looking out, you would be with your sisters."

"Then, Lionel, hear me!" she cried, her throat working, her blue eyes flashing with a strange light. "I will never go home to my sisters! I will never, so long as I live, enter that house again, to reside! You are no better than a bear to wish me to do it."

What was he to do? She was his wife, and he must provide for her; but she would go neither into lodgings, nor to the proposed home. Lionel set his wits to work.

"I wonder—whether—my mother—would invite us there, for a short while?" The words were spoken slowly, reluctantly, as if there were an undercurrent of strong doubt in his mind. "Would you go to Deerham Court for a time, Sibylla, if Lady Verner were agreeable?"

"Yes," said Sibylla, after a minute's consideration. "I'd go there."

Deeming it well that something should be decided, Lionel went downstairs, caught up his hat, and proceeded to Deerham Court. He did not say a word about his wife's caprice; or that two plans, proposed to her, had been rejected. He simply asked his mother whether she would temporarily receive him and his wife, until he could look round and decide on the future.

To his great surprise, Lady Verner answered that she would; and answered readily. Lionel, knowing the light in which she regarded his wife, had anticipated he knew not what of objection, if not of positive refusal.

"I wish you to come here, Lionel; I intended to send for you and tell you so," was the reply of Lady Verner. "You have no home to turn to, and I could not have it said that my son in his strait was at fault for one. I never thought to receive your wife inside my doors, but for your sake I will do so. No servants, you understand, Lionel."

"Certainly not," he answered. "I cannot afford servants now as a matter of luxury."

"I can neither afford them for you, nor is there room in my house to accommodate them. This applies to that French maid of yours," Lady Verner pointedly added. "I do not like the woman; nothing would induce me to admit her here, even were circumstances convenient. Any attendance that your wife may require, she shall have."

Lionel smiled a sad smile. "Be easy, mother. The time for my wife to keep a French maid has gone by. I thank you very sincerely."

And so Lionel Verner was once more to be turned from Verner's Pride, to take up his abode with his wife in his mother's home. When were his wanderings to be at rest?

CHAPTER LXX

TURNING OUT

The battle that there was with Mrs. Verner! She cried, she sobbed, she protested, she stormed, she raved. Willing enough, was she, to go to Lady Verner's; indeed the proposed visit appeared to be exceedingly palatable to her; but she was not willing to go without Mademoiselle Benoite. She was used to Benoite; Benoite dressed her, and waited on her, and read to her, and took charge of her things; Benoite was in her confidence, kept her purse; she could not do without Benoite, and it was barbarous of Lionel to wish it. How could she manage without a maid?

Lionel gravely laid his hand upon her shoulder. Some husbands might have reminded her that until she married him she had never known the services of a personal attendant; that she had gone all the way to Melbourne, had—as John Massingbird had expressed it with regard to himself—been knocking about there, and had come back home again alone, all without so much as thinking of one. Not so Lionel. He laid his hand upon her shoulder in his grave kindness.

"Sibylla, do you forget that we have no longer the means to keep ourselves? I must find a way to do that, before I can afford you a lady's maid. My dear, I am very sorry; you know I am; for that, and all the other discomforts that you are meeting with; but there is no help for it. I trust that some time or other I shall be able to remedy it."

"We should not have to keep her," argued Sibylla. "She'd live with Lady Verner's servants."

Neither did he remind her that Lady Verner would have sufficient tax, keeping himself and her. One would have thought her own delicacy of feeling might have suggested it.

"It cannot be, Sibylla. Lady Verner has no accommodation for Benoite."

"She must make accommodation. When people used to come here to visit us, they brought their servants with them."

"Oh, Sibylla! can you not see the difference? But—what do you owe Benoite?" he added in a different tone.

"I don't owe her anything," replied Sibylla eagerly, quite mistaking the motive of the question. "I have always paid her every month. She'd never let it go on."

"Then there will be the less trouble," thought Lionel.

He called Benoite to him, then packing up Sibylla's things for Deerham Court, inquired into the state of her accounts, and found Sibylla had told him correctly. He gave Benoite a month's wages and a month's board wages, and informed her that as soon as her mistress had left the house, she would be at liberty to leave it. A scene ensued with Sibylla, but for once Lionel was firm.

"You will have every attendance provided for you, Sibylla, my mother said. But I cannot take Benoite; neither would Lady Verner admit her."

John Massingbird had agreed to keep on most of the old servants. The superfluous ones, those who had been engaged when Verner's Pride grew gay, Lionel found the means of discharging; paying them as he had paid Benoite.

Heavy work for him, that day! the breaking up of his home, the turning forth to the world. And, as if his heart were not sufficiently heavy, he had the trouble of Sibylla. The arrangements had been three or four days in process. It had taken that time to pack and settle things, since he first spoke to Lady Verner. There were various personal trifles of his and Sibylla's to be singled out and separated from what was now John Massingbird's. But all was done at last, and they were ready to depart. Lionel went to John Massingbird.

"You will allow me to order the carriage for Sibylla? She will like it better than a hired one."

"Certainly," replied John, with much graciousness. "But what's the good of leaving before dinner?"

"My mother is expecting us," simply answered Lionel.

Just the same innate refinement of feeling which had characterised him in the old days. It so happened that Lionel had never bought a carriage since he came into Verner's Pride. Stephen Verner had been prodigal in his number of carriages, although the carriages had a sinecure of it, and Lionel had found no occasion to purchase. Of course they belonged to John Massingbird; everything else belonged to him. He, for the last time, ordered the close carriage for his wife. His carriage, it might surely be said, more than John Massingbird's. Lionel did not deem it so, and asked permission ere he gave the order.

Sibylla had never seen her husband quietly resolute in opposing her whims, as he had been with regard to Benoite. She scarcely knew what to make of it; but she had deemed it well to dry her tears, and withdraw her opposition. She came down dressed at the time of departure, and looked about for John Massingbird. That gentleman was in the study. Its large desk, a whole mass of papers crowded above it and underneath it, pushed into the remotest corner. Lionel had left things connected with the estate as straight as he could. He wished to explain affairs to John Massingbird, and hand over documents and all else in due form, but he was not allowed. Business and John had never agreed. John was sitting now before the window, his elbows on the sill, a rough cap on his head, and a short clay pipe in his mouth. Lionel glanced with dismay at the confusion reigning amid the papers.

"Fare you well, John Massingbird," said Sibylla.

"Going?" said John, coolly turning round. "Good-day."

"And let me tell you, John Massingbird," continued Sibylla, "that if ever you had got turned out of your home as you have turned us, you would know what it was."

"Bless you! I've never had anything of my own to be turned out of, except a tent," said John, with a laugh.

"It is to be hoped that you may, then, some time, and that you will be turned out of it! That's my best wish for you, John Massingbird."

"I'd recommend you to be polite, young lady," returned John good-humouredly. "If I sue your husband for back rents, you'd not be quite so independent, I calculate."

"Back rents!" repeated she.

"Back rents," assented John. "But we'll leave that discussion to another time. Don't you be saucy, Sibylla."

"John," said Lionel, pointing to the papers, "are you aware that some valuable leases and other agreements are amongst those papers? You might get into inextricable confusion with your tenants, were you to mislay, or lose them."

"They are safe enough," said careless John, taking his pipe from his mouth to speak.

"I wish you had allowed me to put things in order for you. You will be wanting me to do it later."

"Not a bit of it," said John Massingbird. "I am not going to upset my equanimity with leases, and bothers of that sort. Good-bye, old fellow. Lionel!"

Lionel turned round. He had been going out.

"We part friends, don't we?"

"I can answer for myself," said Lionel, a frank smile rising to his lips. "It would be unjust to blame you for taking what you have a right to take."

"All right. Then, Lionel, you'll come and see me here?"

"Sometimes. Yes."

They went out to the carriage, Lionel conducting his wife, and John in attendance, smoking his short pipe. The handsome carriage, with its coat of ultra-marine, its rich white lining, its silver mountings, and its arms on the panels. The Verner arms. Would John paint them out? Likely not. One badge on the panels of his carriages was as good to John Massingbird as another. He must have gone to the Herald's College had he wanted to set up arms on his own account.

And that's how Lionel and his wife went out of Verner's Pride. It seemed as if Deerham pavement and Deerham windows were lined on purpose to watch the exodus. The time of their departure had got wind.

"I have done a job that goes again the grain, sir," said Wigham to his late master, when the carriage had deposited its freight at Deerham Court, and was about to go back again. "I never thought, sir, to drive you out of Verner's Pride for the last time."

"I suppose not, Wigham. I thought it as little as you."

"You'll not forget, sir, that I should be glad to serve you, should you ever have room for me. I'd rather live with you, sir, than with anybody else in the world."

"Thank you, Wigham. I fear that time will be very far off."

"Or, if my lady should be changing her coachman, sir, perhaps she'd think of me. It don't seem nateral to me, sir, to drive anybody but a Verner. Next to yourself, sir, I'd be proud to serve her ladyship."

Lionel, in his private opinion, believed that Lady Verner would soon be compelled to part with her own coachman, to lay down her carriage. Failing the income she had derived from his revenues, in addition to her own, he did not see how she was to keep up many of her present expenses. He said farewell to Wigham and entered the Court.

Decima had hastened forward to welcome Sibylla. Decima was one who, in her quiet way, was always trying to make the best of surrounding circumstances—not for herself, but for others. Let things be ever so dark, she would contrive to extract out of them some little ray of brightness. Opposite as they were in person, in disposition she and Jan were true brother and sister. She came forward to the door, a glad smile upon her face, and dressed rather more than usual. It was one of her ways, the unwonted dress, of showing welcome and consideration to Sibylla.

"You are late, Mrs. Verner," she said, taking her cordially by the hand. "We have been expecting you some time. Catherine! Thérèse, see to these packages."

Lady Verner had actually come out also. She was too essentially the lady to show anything but strict courtesy to Sibylla, now that she was about to become an inmate under her roof. What the effort cost her, she best knew. It was no light one; and Lionel felt that it was not. She stood in the hall, just outside the door of the ante-room, and took Sibylla's hand as she approached.

"I am happy to see you, Mrs. Verner," she said, with stately courtesy. "I hope you will make yourself at home."

They all went together into the drawing-room, in a crowd, as it were. Lucy was there, dressed also. She came up with a smile on her young and charming face, and welcomed Sibylla.

"It is nearly dinner-time," said Decima to Sibylla. "Will you come with me upstairs, and I will show you the arrangements for your rooms. Lionel, will you come?"

She led the way upstairs to the pretty sitting-room with its blue-and-white furniture, hitherto called "Miss Decima's room"; the one that Lionel had sat in when he was growing convalescent.

"Mamma thought you would like a private sitting-room to retire to when you felt disposed," said Decima. "We are only sorry it is not larger. This will be exclusively yours."

"It is small," was the not very gracious reply of Sibylla.

"And it is turning you out of it, Decima!" added Lionel.

"I did not use it much," she answered, proceeding to another room on the same floor. "This is your bedroom, and this the dressing-room," she added, entering a spacious apartment and throwing open the door of a smaller one which led out of it. "We hope that you will find everything comfortable. And the luggage that you don't require to use can be carried upstairs."

Lionel had been looking round, somewhat puzzled. "Decima! was not this Lucy's room?"

"Lucy proposed to give it up to you," said Decima. "It is the largest room we have; the only one that has a dressing-room opening from it, except mamma's. Lucy has gone to the small room at the end of the corridor."

"But it is not right for us to turn out Lucy," debated Lionel. "I do not like the idea of it."

"It was Lucy herself who first thought of it, Lionel. I am sure she is glad to do anything she can to render you and Mrs. Verner comfortable. She has been quite anxious to make it look nice, and moved nearly all the things herself."

"It does look comfortable," acquiesced Lionel as he stood before the blaze of the fire, feeling grateful to Decima, to his mother, to Lucy, to all of them. "Sibylla, this is one of your fires; yea like a blaze."

"And Catherine will wait upon you, Mrs. Verner," continued Decima. "She understands it. She waited on mamma for two years before Thérèse came. Should you require your hair done, Thérèse will do that; mamma thinks Catherine would not make any hand at it."

She quitted the room as she spoke, and closed the door, saying that she would send up Catherine then. Lionel had his eyes fixed on the room and its furniture; it was really an excellent room—spacious, lofty, and fitted up with every regard to comfort as well as to appearance. In the old days it was Jan's room, and Lionel scarcely remembered to have been inside it since; but it looked very superior now to what it used to look then. Lady Verner had never troubled herself to improvise superfluous decorations for Jan. Lionel's chief attention was riveted on the bed, an Arabian, handsomely carved, mahogany bed, with white muslin hangings, lined with pink, matching with the window-curtains. The hangings were new; but he felt certain that the bed was the one hitherto used by his mother.

He stepped into the dressing-room, feeling more than he could have expressed, feeling that he could never repay all the kindness they seemed to be receiving. Equally inviting looked the dressing-room. The first thing that caught Lionel's eye were some delicate paintings on the walls, done by Decima.

His gaze and his ruminations were interrupted. Violent sobs had struck on his ear from the bed-chamber; he hastened back, and found Sibylla extended at full length on the sofa, crying.

"It is such a dreadful change after Verner's Pride!" she querulously complained. "It's not half as nice as it was there! Just this old bedroom and a mess of a dressing-room, and nothing else! And only that stupid Catherine to wait upon me!"

It was ungrateful. Lionel's heart, in its impulse, resented it as such. But, ever considerate for his wife, ever wishing, in the line of conduct he had laid down for himself, to find excuses for her, he reflected the next moment that it was a grievous thing to be turned from a home as she had been. He leaned over her; not answering as he might have answered, that the rooms were all that could be wished, and far superior they, and all other arrangements made for them, to anything enjoyed by Sibylla until she had entered upon Verner's Pride; but he took her hand in his, and smoothed the hair from her brow, and softly whispered—

"Make the best of it, Sibylla, for my sake."

"There's no 'best' to be made," she replied, with a shower of tears, as she pushed his hand and his face away.

Catherine knocked at the door. Miss Decima had sent her and bade her say that dinner was on the point of being served. Sibylla sprang up from the sofa, and dried her tears.

"I wonder whether I can get at my gold combs?" cried she, all her grief flying away.

Lionel turned to Catherine; an active little woman with a high colour and a sensible countenance, looking much younger than her real age. That was not far off fifty; but in movement and lissomeness, she was young as she had been at twenty. Nothing vexed Catherine so much as for Lady Verner to allude to her "age." Not from any notions of vanity, but lest she might be thought growing incapable of her work.

"Catherine, is not that my mother's bed?"

"To think that you should have found it out, Mr. Lionel!" echoed Catherine, with a broad smile. "Well, sir, it is, and that's the truth. We have been making all sorts of changes. Miss Lucy's bed has gone in for my lady, and my lady's has been brought here. See, what a big, wide bed it is!" she exclaimed, putting her arm on the counterpane. "Miss Lucy's was a good-sized bed, but my lady thought it would be hardly big enough for two; so she said hers should come in here."

"And what's Miss Lucy sleeping on?" asked Lionel, amused. "The boards?"

Catherine laughed. "Miss Lucy has got a small bed now, sir. Not, upon my word, that I think she'd mind if we did put her on the boards. She is the sweetest young lady to have to do with, Mr. Lionel! I don't believe there ever was one like her. She's as easy satisfied as ever Mr. Jan was."

"Lionel! I can't find my gold combs!" exclaimed Sibylla, coming from the dressing-room, with a face of consternation. "They are not in the dressing-case. How am I to know which box Benoite has put them in?"

"Never mind looking for the combs now," he answered. "You will have time to search for things to-morrow. Your hair looks nice without combs. I think nicer than with them."

"But I wanted to wear them," she fractiously answered. "It is all your fault! You should not have forced me to discharge Benoite."

Did she wish him to look for the gold combs? Lionel did not take the hint. Leaving her in the hands of Catherine, he quitted the room.

CHAPTER LXXI

Lucy was in the drawing-room alone when Lionel entered it. "Lady Verner," she said to him, "has stepped out to speak to Jan."

"Lucy, I find that our coming here has turned you out of your room," he gravely said. "I should earnestly have protested against it, had I known what was going to be done."

"Should you?" said she, shaking her head quite saucily. "We should not have listened to you."

"We! Whom does the 'we' include?"

"Myself and Decima. We planned everything. I like the room I have now, quite as much as that. It is the room at the end, opposite the one Mrs. Verner is to have for her sitting-room."

"The sitting-room again! What shall you and Decima do without it?" exclaimed Lionel, looking as he felt—vexed.

"If we never have anything worse to put up with than the loss of a sitting-room that was nearly superfluous, we shall not grieve," answered Lucy, with a smile. "How did we do without it before—when you were getting better from that long illness? We had to do without it then."

"I think not, Lucy. So far as my memory serves me, you were sitting in it a great portion of your time—cheering me. I have not forgotten it, if you have."

Neither had she—by her heightened colour.

"I mean that we had to do without it for our own purposes, our drawings and our work. It is but a little matter, after all. I wish we could do more for you and Mrs. Verner. I wish," she added, her voice betraying her emotion, "that we could have prevented your being turned from Verner's Pride."

"Ay," he said, speaking with affected carelessness, and turning about an ornament in his fingers, which he had taken from the mantel-piece, "it is not an every-day calamity."

"What shall you do?" asked Lucy, going a little nearer to him, and dropping her voice to a tone of confidence.

"Do? In what way, Lucy?"

"Shall you be content to live on here with Lady Verner? Not seeking to retrieve your—your position in any way?"

"My living on here, Lucy, will be out of the question. That would never do, for more reasons than one."

Did Lucy Tempest divine what one of these reasons might be? She did not intend to look at him, but she caught his eyes in the pier-glass. Lionel smiled.

"I am thinking what a trouble you must find me—you and Decima."

She did not speak at first. Then she went quite close to him, her earnest, sympathising eyes cast up to his.

"If you please, you need not pretend to make light of it to me," she whispered. "I don't like you to think that I do not know all you must feel, and what a blow it is. I think I feel it quite as much as you can do—for your sake and for Mrs. Verner's. I lie awake at night, thinking of it; but I do not say so to Decima and Lady Verner. I make light of it to them, as you are making light of it to me."

"I know, I know!" he uttered in a tone that would have been a passionate one, but for its wailing despair. "My whole life, for a long while, has been one long scene of acting—to you. I dare not make it otherwise. There's no remedy for it."

She had not anticipated the outburst; she had simply wished to express her true feeling of sympathy for their great misfortunes, as she might have expressed it to any other gentleman who had been turned from his home with his wife. She could not bear for Lionel not to know that he had her deepest, her kindliest, her truest sympathy, and this had nothing to do with any secret feeling she might, or might not, entertain for him. Indeed, but for the unpleasant, latent consciousness of that very feeling, Lucy would have made her sympathy more demonstrative. The outbreak seemed to check her; to throw her friendship back upon herself; and she stood irresolute; but she was too single-minded, too full of nature's truth, to be angry with what had been a genuine outpouring of his inmost heart, drawn from him in a moment of irrepressible sorrow. Lionel let the ornament fall back on the mantel-piece, and turned to her, his manner changing. He took her hands, clasping them in one of his; he laid his other hand lightly on her fair young head, reverently as any old grandfather might have done.

"Lucy!—my dear friend!—you must not mistake me. There are times when some of the bitterness within me is drawn forth, and I say more than I ought: what I never should say, in a calmer moment. I wish I could talk to you; I wish I could give you the full confidence of all my sorrows, as I gave it you on another subject once before. I wish I could draw you to my side, as though you were my sister, or one of my dearest friends, and tell you of the great trouble at my heart. But it cannot be, I thank you, I thank you for your sympathy. I know that you would give me your friendship in all single-heartedness, as Decima might give it me; and it would be to me a green spot of brightness in life's arid desert. But the green spot might for me grow too bright, Lucy; and my only plan is to be wise in time, and to forego it."

"I did but mean to express my sorrow for you and Mrs. Verner," she timidly answered; "my sense of the calamity which has fallen upon you."

"Child, I know it; and I dare not say how I feel it; I dare not thank you as I ought. In truth it is a terrible calamity. All its consequences I cannot yet anticipate; but they may be worse than anybody suspects, or than I like to glance at. It is a deep and apparently an irremediable misfortune. I cannot but feel it keenly; and I feel it for my wife more than for myself. Now and then, something like a glimpse of consolation shows itself—that it has not been brought on by any fault of mine; and that, humanly speaking, I have done nothing to deserve it."

"Mr. Cust used to tell us that however dark a misfortune might be, however hopeless even, there was sure to be a way of looking at it, by which we might see that it might have been darker," observed Lucy. "This would have been darker for you, had it proved to be Frederick Massingbird, instead of John; very sadly darker for Mrs. Verner."

"Ay; so far I cannot be too thankful," replied Lionel. The remembrance flashed over him of his wife's words that day—in her temper—she wished it had been Frederick. It appeared to be a wish that she had already thrown out frequently; not so much that she did wish it, as to annoy him.

"Mr. Cust used to tell us another thing," resumed Lucy, breaking the silence: "that these apparently hopeless misfortunes sometimes turn out to be great benefits in the end. Who knows but in a short time, through some magic or other, you and Mrs. Verner may be back at Verner's Pride? Would not that be happiness?"

"I don't know about happiness, Lucy; sometimes I feel tired of everything," he wearily answered. "As if I should like to run away for ever, and be at rest. My life at Verner's Pride was not a bed of rose-leaves."

He heard his mother's voice in the ante-room, and went forward to open the door for her. Lady Verner came in, followed by Jan. Jan was going to dine there; and Jan was actually in orthodox dinner costume. Decima had invited him, and Decima had told him to be sure to dress himself; that she wanted to make a little festival of the evening to welcome Lionel and his wife. So Jan remembered, and appeared in black. But the gloss of the whole was taken off by Jan having his shirt fastened down the front with pins, where the buttons ought to be. Brassy-looking, ugly, bent pins, as big as skewers, stuck in horizontally.

"Is that a new fashion coming in, Jan?" asked Lady Verner, pointing with some asperity to the pins.

"It's to be hoped not," replied Jan. "It took me five minutes to stick them in, and there's one of the pins running into my wrist now. It's a new shirt of mine come home, and they have forgotten the buttons. Miss Deb caught sight of it, when I went in to tell her I was coming here, and ran after me to the gate with a needle and thread, wanting to sew them on."

"Could you not have fastened it better than that, Jan?" asked Decima, smiling as she looked at the shirt.

"I don't see how," replied Jan. "Pins were the readiest to hand."

Sibylla had been keeping them waiting dinner. She came in now, radiant in smiles and in her gold combs. None, to look at her, would suppose she had that day lost a home. A servant appeared and announced dinner.

Lionel went up to Lady Verner. Whenever he dined there, unless there were other guests besides himself, he had been in the habit of taking her in to dinner. Lady Verner drew back.

"No, Lionel. I consider that you and I are both at home now. Take Miss Tempest."

He could only obey. He held out his arm to Lucy, and they went forward.

"Am I to take anybody?" inquired Jan.

That was just like Jan! Lady Verner pointed to Sibylla, and Jan marched off with her. Lady Verner and Decima followed.

"Not there, not there, Lucy," said Lady Verner, for Lucy was taking the place she was accustomed to, by Lady Verner. "Lionel, you will take the foot of the table now, and Lucy will sit by you."

Lady Verner was rather a stickler for etiquette, and at last they fell into their appointed places. Herself and Lionel opposite each other, Lucy and Decima on one side the table, Jan and Sibylla on the other.

"If I am to have you under my wing as a rule, Miss Lucy, take care that you behave yourself," nodded Lionel.

Lucy laughed, and the dinner proceeded. But there was very probably an undercurrent of consciousness in the heart of both—at any rate, there was in his—that it might have been more expedient, all things considered, that Lucy Tempest's place at dinner had not been fixed by the side of Lionel Verner.

Dinner was half over when Sibylla suddenly laid down her knife and fork, and burst into tears. They looked at her in consternation. Lionel rose.

"That horrid John Massingbird!" escaped her lips. "I always disliked him."

"Goodness!" uttered Jan, "I thought you were taken ill, Sibylla. What's the good of thinking about it?"

"According to you, there's no good in thinking of anything," tartly responded Sibylla. "You told me yesterday not to think about Fred, when I said I wished he had come back instead of John—if one must have come back."

"At any rate, don't think about unpleasant things now," was Jan's answer. "Eat your dinner."

CHAPTER LXXII

JAN'S SAVINGS

Lionel Verner looked his situation full in the face. It was not a desirable one. When he had been turned out of Verner's Pride before, it is probable he had thought that about the extremity of all human calamity; but that, looking back upon it, appeared a position to be coveted, as compared with this. In point of fact it was. He was free then from pecuniary liabilities; he did not owe a shilling in the world; he had five hundred pounds in his pocket; nobody but himself to look to; and—he was a younger man. In the matter of years he was not so very much older now; but Lionel Verner, since his marriage, had bought some experience in human disappointment, and nothing ages a man's inward feelings like it.

He was now, with his wife, a burden upon his mother; a burden she could ill afford. Lady Verner was somewhat embarrassed in her own means, and she was preparing to reduce her establishment to the size that it used to be in her grumbling days. If Lionel had but been free! free from debt and difficulty! he would have gone out into the world and put his shoulder to the wheel.

Claims had poured in upon him without end. Besides the obligations he already knew of, not a day passed but the post brought him from London outstanding accounts, for debts contracted by his wife, with demands for their speedy settlement. Mr. Verner of Verner's Pride might not have been troubled with these accounts for years, had his wife so managed: but Mr. Verner, turned from Verner's Pride, a— it is an ugly word, but expressive of the truth—a pauper, found the demands come pouring thick and threefold upon his head. It was of no use to reproach Sibylla; of no use even to speak, save to ask "Is such-and-such a bill a just claim?" Any approach to such topics was the signal for an unseemly burst of passion on her part; or for a fit of hysterics, in which fashionable affectation Sibylla had lately become an adept. She tried Lionel terribly—worse than tongue can tell or pen can write. There was no social confidential intercourse. Lionel could not go to her for sympathy, for counsel, or for comfort. If he attempted to talk over any plans for the future, for the immediate future; what they could do, what they could not; what might be best, what worst; she met him with the frivolousness of a child, or with a sullen reproach that he "did nothing but worry her." For any purposes of companionship, his wife was a nonentity; far better that he had been without one. She made his whole life a penance; she betrayed the frivolous folly of her nature ten times a day; she betrayed her pettish temper, her want of self-control, dyeing Lionel's face of a blood-red. He felt ashamed for her; he felt doubly ashamed for himself—that his mother, that Lucy Tempest should at last become aware what sort of a wife he had taken to his bosom, what description of wedded life was his.

What was he to do for a living? The only thing that appeared to be open to him was to endeavour to get some sort of a situation, where, by means of the hands or the head, he might earn a competence. And yet, to do this, it was necessary to be free from the danger of arrest. He went about in dread of it. Were he to show himself in London he felt sure that not an hour would pass, but he would be sued and taken. If his country creditors accorded him forbearance, his town ones would not. Any fond hope that he had formerly entertained of studying for the Bar, was not available now. He had neither the means nor the time to give to it—the time for study ere remuneration should come. Occasionally a thought would cross him that some friend or other of his prosperity might procure for him a government situation. A consulship, or vice-consulship abroad, for instance. Any thing abroad. Not to avoid the payment of his creditors, for whether abroad or at home, Lionel would be sure to pay them, if by dint of pinching himself he could find the means; but that he might run away from home and mortification, take his wife and make the best of her. But consulships and other government appointments are more easily talked of than obtained; as any body who has tried for them under difficulties knows. Moreover, although Lionel had never taken a prominent part in politics, the Verner interest had always been given against the government party, then in power. He did not see his way at all clear before him; and he found that it was to be still further obstructed on another score.

After thinking and planning and plotting till his brain was nearly bewildered, he at length made up his mind to go to London, and see whether anything could be done. With regard to his creditors there, he must lay the state of the case frankly before them, and say: "Will you leave me my liberty, and wait? You will get nothing by putting me in prison, for I have no money of my own, and no friend to come forward and advance it to clear me. Give me time, accord me my liberty, and I will endeavour to pay you off by degrees." It was, at any rate, a straightforward mode of going to work, and Lionel determined to adopt it. Before mentioning it to his wife, he spoke to Lady Verner.

And then occurred the obstruction. Lady Verner, though she did not oppose the plan, declined to take charge of Sibylla, or to retain her in her house during Lionel's absence.

"I could not take her with me," said Lionel. "There would be more objections to it than one. In the first place, I have not the means; in the second—"

He came to an abrupt pause, and turned the words off. He had been about incautiously to say, "She would most likely, once in London, run me into deeper debt." But Lionel had kept the fact of her having run him into debt at all, a secret in his own breast. Whatever may have been his wife's faults and failings, he did not make it his business to proclaim them to the world. She proclaimed enough herself, to his grievous chagrin, without his helping to do it.

"Listen, Lionel," said Lady Verner. "You know what my feeling always was with regard to your wife. A closer intercourse has not tended to change that feeling, or to lessen my dislike of her. Now you must forgive my saying this; it is but a passing allusion. Stay on with me as long as you like; stay on for ever, if you will, and she shall stay; but if you leave, she must leave. I should be sorry to have her here, even for a week, without you. In fact, I would not."

"It would be quite impossible for me to take her to London," deliberated Lionel. "I can be there alone at a very trifling cost; but a lady involves so much expense. There must be lodgings, which are dear; and living, which is dear; and attendance; and—and—many other sources of outlay."

"And pray, what should you do, allowing that you went alone, without lodgings and living and attendance, and all the rest of it?" asked Lady Verner. "Take a room at one of their model lodging-houses, at half a crown a week, and live upon the London air?"

"Not very healthy air for fastidious lungs," observed Lionel, with a smile. "I don't quite know how I should manage for myself, mother; except that I should take care to condense my expenses into the very narrowest compass that man ever condensed them yet."

"Not you, Lionel. You were never taught that sort of close economy."

"True," he answered. "But the most efficient of all instructors has come to me now—necessity. I wish you would increase my gratitude and my obligation to you by allowing Sibylla to remain here. In a little time, if I have luck, I may make a home for her in London."

"Lionel, it cannot be," was the reply of Lady Verner. And he knew when she spoke in that quiet tone of emphasis, that it could not be. "Why should you go to London?" she resumed. "My opinion is that you will do no good by going; that it is a wild-goose scheme altogether which you have got in your head. I think I could tell you a better."

"What is yours?"

"Remain contentedly here with me until the return of Colonel Tempest. He may even now be on his road. He will no doubt be able to get you some civil appointment in one of the Presidencies; he has influence here with the people that have to do with India. That will be the best plan, Lionel. You are always wishing you could go abroad. Stay here quietly until he comes; I should like you to stay, and I will put up with your wife."

Some allusion, or allusions, in the words brought the flush to Lionel's cheeks. "I cannot reconcile it to my conscience, mother, to remain on here, a burden, upon your small income."

"But it is not a burden, Lionel," she said. "It is rather a help."

"How can that be?" he asked.

"So long as Jan pays."

"So long as Jan pays!" echoed Lionel, in astonishment. "Does Jan—pay?"

"Yes he does. I thought you knew it? Jan came here the day you arrived—don't you remember it, when he had the pins in his shirt? Decima had invited him to dinner, and he came in ten minutes before it, and called me out of the room here, where I was with Lucy. The first thing he did was to tumble into my lap a roll of bank-notes, which he had been to Heartburg to get. A hundred and forty pounds, it was; the result of his savings since he joined Dr. West in partnership. The next thing he said was that all his own share of the profits of the practice, he should bring to me to make up for the cost of you and Sibylla. Jan said he had proposed that you should go to him; but Sibylla would not consent to it."

Lionel's blood coursed on with a glow. Jan slaving and working for him!

"I never knew this," he cried.

"I am sure I thought you did," said Lady Verner. "I supposed it to have been a prearranged thing between you and Jan. Lionel," looking up into his face with an expression of care, and lowering her voice, "but for that hundred and forty pounds, I don't see how I could have gone on. You had been very liberal to me, but somehow debt upon debt seemed to come in, and I was growing quite embarrassed. Jan's money set me partially straight. My dear—as you see you are no 'burden,' as you call it, you will give up this London scheme, will you not, and remain on?"

"I suppose I must," mechanically answered Lionel, who seemed buried in thought.

He did suppose he must. He was literally without money, and his intention had been to ask the loan of a twenty-pound note from generous Jan, to carry him to London, and keep him there while he turned himself about, and saw what could be done. How could he ask Jan now? There was little doubt that Jan had left himself as void of ready cash as he, Lionel, was. Dr. West's was not a business where patients went and paid their guinea fee, two or three dozen patients a day. Dr. West (or Jan for him) had to doctor his patients for a year, and send in his modest bill at the end of it, very often waiting for another year before the bill was paid. Sibylla on his hands, and no money, he did not see how he was to get to London.

"But just think of it," resumed Lady Verner. "Jan's savings for nearly three years of practice to amount only to a hundred and forty pounds! I questioned him pretty sharply, asking him what on earth he could have done with his money, and he acknowledged that he had given a good deal away. He said Miss West had borrowed some, the doctor kept her so short; then Jan, it seems, forgot to put down the expenses of the horse to the general account, and that had to come out of his pocket. Another thing he acknowledged having done. When he finds the poor can't conveniently pay their bills, he crosses it off in the book, and furnishes the money himself. He has not common-sense, you know, Lionel; and never had."

Lionel caught up his hat, and went out in the moment's impulse, seeking Jan. Jan was in the surgery alone, making up pills, packing up medicines, answering callers; doing, in fact, Master Cheese's work. Master Cheese had a headache, and was groaning dismally in consequence in an arm-chair, in front of Miss Deb's sitting-room fire, and sipping some hot elder wine, with sippets of toast in it, which he had assured Miss Deb was a sovereign specific, though it might not be generally known, to keep off the sickness.

"Jan," said Lionel, going straight up, and grasping him by the hand; "what am I to say to you? I did not know, until ten minutes ago, what it is that you are doing for me."

Jan put down a pill-box he held, and looked at Lionel. "What am I doing for you?" he asked.

"I speak of this money that I find you have handed to my mother. Of the money you have undertaken to hand to her."

"Law, is that all?" said Jan, taking up the pill-box again, and biting one of the pills in two to test its quality. "I thought you were going to tell me I had sent you poison, or something; coming in like that."

"Jan, I can never repay you. The money I may, some time; I hope I shall: the debt of gratitude, never."

"There's nothing to repay," returned Jan, with composure. "As long as I have meat and drink and clothes, what do I want with extra money? You are heartily welcome to it, Lionel."

"You are working your days away, Jan, and for no benefit to yourself. I am reaping it."

"A man can but work," responded Jan. "I like work, for my part; I wouldn't be without it. If old West came home and said he'd take all the patients for a week, and give me a holiday, I should only set on and pound. Look here," pointing to the array on the counter, "I have done more work in two hours than Cheese gets through in a week."

Lionel could not help smiling. Jan went on—

"I don't work for the sake of accumulating money, but because work is life's business, and I like work for its own sake. If I got no money by it, I should work. Don't think about the money, Lionel. While it lay in that bank where was the use of it? Better for my mother to have it, than for me to be hoarding it."

"Jan, did it never strike you that it might be well to make some provision for contingencies? Old age, say; or sudden deprivation of strength, through accident or other cause? If you give away all you might save for yourself, what should you do were the evil day to come?"

Jan looked at his arms. "I am tolerably strong," said he; "feel me. My head's all right, and my limbs are all right. If I should be deprived of strength before my time, I dare say, God, in taking it, would find some means just to keep me from want."

The answer was delivered in the most straightforward simplicity. Lionel looked at him until his eyes grew moist.

"A pretty fellow I should be, to hoard up money while anybody else wanted it!" continued Jan. "You and Sibylla make yourselves comfortable, Lionel, that's all."

They were interrupted by the entrance of John Massingbird and his pipe. John appeared to find his time hang rather heavily on his hands: he could not say that work was the business of his life. He might be seen lounging about Deerham at all hours of the day and night, smoking and gossiping. Jan was often honoured with a visit. Mr. Massingbird of Verner's Pride was not a whit altered from Mr. Massingbird of nowhere: John favoured the tap-rooms as much as he had used to favour them.

"The very man I wanted to see!" cried he, giving Lionel a hearty slap on the shoulder. "I want to talk to you a bit on a matter of business. Will you come up to Verner's Pride?"

"When?" asked Lionel.

"This evening, if you will. Come to dinner: only our two selves."

"Very well," replied Lionel. And he went out of the surgery, leaving John Massingbird talking to his brother.

"On business," John Massingbird had said. Was it to ask him about the mesne profits?—when he could refund them?—to tell him he would be sued, unless he did refund them? Lionel did not know; but he had been expecting John Massingbird to take some such steps.

In going back home, choosing the near cross-field way, as Jan often did, Lionel suddenly came upon Mrs. Peckaby, seated on the stump of a tree, in a very disconsolate fashion. To witness her thus, off the watch for the white animal that might be arriving before her door, surprised Lionel.

"I'm a'most sick of it, sir," she said. "I'm sick to the heart with looking and watching. My brain gets weary and my eyes gets tired. The white quadruple don't come, and Peckaby, he's a-rowing at me everlastin'. I'm come out here for a bit o' peace."

"Don't you think it would be better to give the white donkey up for a bad job, Mrs. Peckaby?"

"Give it up!" she uttered, aghast. "Give up going to New Jerusalem on a white donkey! No, sir, that would be a misfortin' in life!"

Lionel smiled sadly as he left her.

"There are worse misfortunes in life, Mrs. Peckaby, than not going to New Jerusalem on a white donkey."

CHAPTER LXXIII

A PROPOSAL

Lionel Verner was seated in the dining-room at Verner's Pride. Not its master. Its master, John Massingbird, was there, opposite to Lionel. They had just dined, and John was filling his short pipe as an accompaniment to his wine. During dinner, he had been regaling Lionel with choice anecdotes of his Australian life, laughing ever; but not a syllable had he broached yet about the "business" he had put forth as the plea for the invitation to Lionel to come. The anecdotes did not raise the social features of that far-off colony in Mr. Verner's estimation. But he laughed with John; laughed as merrily as his heavy heart would allow him.

It was quite a wintry day, telling of the passing autumn. The skies were leaden-gray; the dead leaves rustled on the paths; and the sighing wind swept through the trees with a mournful sound. Void of brightness, of hope, it all looked, as did Lionel Verner's fortunes. But a few short weeks ago he had been in John Massingbird's place, in the very chair that he now sat in, never thinking to be removed from it during life. And now!—what a change!

"Why don't you smoke, Lionel?" asked John, setting light to his pipe by the readiest way—that of thrusting it between the bars of the grate. "You did not care to smoke in the old days, I remember."

"I never cared for it," replied Lionel.

"I can tell you that you would have cared for it, had you been knocked about as I have. Tobacco's meat and drink to a fellow at the diggings; as it is to a sailor and a soldier."

"Not to all soldiers," observed Lionel. "My father never smoked an ounce of tobacco in his life. I have heard them say so. And he saw some service."

"Every man to his liking," returned John Massingbird. "Folks preach about tobacco being an acquired taste! It's all bosh. Babies come into the world with a liking for it, I know. Talking about your father, would you like to have that portrait of him that hangs in the large drawing-room? You can if you like. I'm sure you have more right to it than I."

"Thank you," replied Lionel. "I should very much like it, if you will give it me."

"What a fastidious chap you are, Lionel!" cried John Massingbird, pulling vigorously; for the pipe was turning refractory, and would not keep alight. "There are lots of things you have left behind you here, that I, in your place, should have marched off without asking."

"The things are yours. That portrait of my father belonged to my Uncle Stephen, and he made no exception in its favour when he willed Verner's Pride, and all it contained, away from me. In point of legal right, I was at liberty to touch nothing, beyond my personal effects."

"Liberty be hanged!" responded John. "You are over fastidious; always were. Your father was the same, I know; can see it in his likeness. I should say, by the look of that, he was too much of a gentleman for a soldier."

Lionel smiled. "Some of our soldiers are the most refined gentlemen in the world."

"I can't tell how they retain their refinement, then, amid the rough and ready of camp life. I know I lost all I had at the diggings."

Lionel laughed outright at the notion of John Massingbird's losing his refinement at the diggings. He never had any to lose. John joined in the laugh.

"Lionel, old boy, do you know I always liked you, with all your refinement; and it's a quality that never found great favour with me. I liked you better than I liked poor Fred; and that's the truth."

Lionel made no reply, and John Massingbird smoked for a few minutes in silence. Presently he began again.

"I say, what made you go and marry Sibylla?"

Lionel lifted his eyes. But John Massingbird resumed, before he had time to speak.

"She's not worth a button. Now you need not fly out, old chap. I am not passing my opinion on your wife; wouldn't presume to do such a thing; but on my cousin. Surely I may find fault with my cousin, if I like! Why did you marry her?"

"Why does anybody else marry?" returned Lionel.

"But why did you marry her? A sickly, fractious thing! I saw enough of her in the old days. There! be quiet! I have done. If it hadn't been for her, I'd have asked you to come here to your old home; you and I should jog along together first-rate. But Sibylla bars it. She may be a model of a wife; I don't insinuate to the contrary, take you note, Mr. Verner; but she's not exactly a model of temper, and Verner's Pride wouldn't be big enough to hold her and me. Would you have taken up your abode with me, had you been a free man?"

"I cannot tell," replied Lionel. "It is a question that cannot arise now."

"No. Sibylla stops it. What are you going to do with yourself?"

"That I cannot tell. I should like an appointment abroad, if I could get one. I did think of going to London, and looking about me a bit; but I am not sure that I shall do so just yet."

"I say, Lionel," resumed John Massingbird, sinking his voice, but speaking in a joking sort of way, "how do you mean to pay your debts? I hear you have a few."

"I have a good many, one way or another."

"Wipe them off," said John.

"I wish I could wipe them off."

"There's nothing more easy," returned John in his free manner. "Get the whitewash brush to work. The insolvent court has its friendly doors ever open."

The colour came into the face of Lionel. A Verner there! He quietly shook his head. "I dare say I shall find a way of paying some time, if the people will only wait."

"Sibylla helped you to a good part of the score, didn't she? People are saying so. Just like her!"

"When I complain of my wife, it will be quite time enough for other people to begin," said Lionel. "When I married Sibylla, I took her with her virtues and her faults; and I am quite ready to defend both."

"All right. I'd rather you had the right of defending them than I," said incorrigible John. "Look here, Lionel, I got you up here to-day to talk about the estate. Will you take the management of it?"

"Of this estate?" replied Lionel, scarcely understanding.

"Deuce a bit of any other could I offer you. Things are all at sixes and sevens already. They are chaos; they are purgatory. That's our word out yonder, Lionel, to express the ultimatum of badness. Matiss comes and bothers; the tenants, one and another, come and bother; Roy comes and bothers. What with it all, I'm fit to bar the outer doors. Roy, you know, thought I should put him into power again! No, no, Mr. Roy; Fred might have done it, but I never will. I have paid him well for the services he rendered me; but put him into power—no. Altogether, things are getting into inextricable confusion; I can't look to them, and I want a manager. Will you take it, Lionel? I'll give you five hundred a year."

The mention of the sum quite startled Lionel. It was far more than he should have supposed John Massingbird would offer to any manager. Matiss would do it for a fourth. Should he take it?

He sat, twirling his wine-glass in his fingers. There was a soreness of spirit to get over, and it could not be done all in a moment. To become a servant (indeed it was no better) on the land that had once been his; that ought to be his now, by the law of right—a servant to John Massingbird! Could he bend to it? John smoked, and sat watching him.

He thought of the position of his wife; he thought of the encumbrance on his mother: he thought of his brother Jan, and what he had done; he thought of his own very unsatisfactory prospects. Was this putting his shoulder to the wheel, as he had resolved to do, thus to hesitate on a quibble of pride? Down, down with his rebellious spirit! Let him be a man in the sight of Heaven!

He turned to John Massingbird, his brow clear, his eye serene. "I will take it, and thank you," he said in a steady, cheerful tone.

"Then let's have some grog on the strength of it," was that gentleman's answer. "Tynn says the worry nearly took my mother's life out of her during the time she managed the estate; and it would take it out of mine. If I kept it in my own hands, it would go to the dogs in a twelvemonth. And you'd not thank me for that, Lionel. You are the next heir."

"You may take a wife yet."

"A wife for me!" he shouted. "No, thank you. I know the value of 'em too well for that. Give me my liberty, and you may have the wives. Lionel, the office had better be in the study as it used to be: you can come up here of a day. I'll turn the drawing-room into my smoke-shop. If there are any leases or other deeds missing, you must get them drawn out again. I'm glad it's settled."

Lionel declined the grog; but he remained on, talking things over. John Massingbird sat in a cloud of smoke, drinking Lionel's share as well as his own, and listening to the rain, which had begun to patter against the window-panes.

CHAPTER LXXIV

GOING TO NEW JERUSALEM ON A WHITE DONKEY

And now we must pay a visit to Mrs. Peckaby; for great events were happening to her on that night.

When Lionel met her in the day, seated on the stump, all disconsolate, she had thrown out a hint that Mr. Peckaby was not habitually in quite so social a mood as he might be. The fact was, Peckaby's patience had run out; and little wonder, either. The man's meals made ready for him in any careless way, often not made ready at all, and his wife spending her time in sighing, and moaning, and looking out for the white donkey! You, my readers, may deem this a rather far-fetched episode in the story; you may deem it next to impossible that any woman should be so ridiculously foolish, or could be so imposed upon; but I am only relating to you the strict truth. The facts occurred precisely as they are being narrated, and not long ago. I have neither added to the story nor taken from it.

Mrs. Peckaby finished out her sitting on the stump under the gray skies. The skies were grayer when she rose to go home. She found on her arrival that Peckaby had been in to his tea, that is, he had been in, hoping to partake of that social meal; but finding no preparation made for it, he had a little relieved his mind by pouring a pail of water over the kitchen fire, thereby putting the fire out and causing considerable damage to the fire-irons and appurtenances generally, which would cause Mrs. Peckaby some little work to remedy.

"The brute!" she ejaculated, putting her foot into the slop on the floor, and taking a general view of things. "Oh, if I was but off!"

"My patience, what a mess!" exclaimed Polly Dawson, who happened to be going by, and turned in for a gossip. "Whatever have done it?"

"Whatever have done it? why that wretch Peckaby," retorted the aggrieved wife. "Don't you never get married, Polly Dawson, if you want to keep on the right side of the men. They be the worst animals in all creation. Many a poor woman's life has been aggrivated out of her."

"If I do get married, I shan't begin the aggrivation by wanting to be off to them saints at New Jerusalem," impudently returned Polly Dawson.

Mrs. Peckaby received it meekly. What with the long-continued disappointment, the perpetual "aggrivations" of Peckaby, and the prospect of work before her, arising from the gratuitous pail of water, she was feeling unusually cowed down.

"I wish I was a hundred mile off," she cried. "Nobody's fate was never so hard as mine."

"It'll take you a good two hours to redd up," observed Polly Dawson. "I'd rather you had to do it nor me."

"I'd see it further—afore it should take me two hours—and Peckaby with it," retorted Mrs. Peckaby, reviving to a touch of temper. "I shall but give it a lick and a promise; just mop up the wet, and dry the grate, and get a bit of fire alight. T'other things may go."

Polly Dawson departed, and Mrs. Peckaby set to her work. By dint of some trouble, she contrived to obtain a cup of tea for herself after awhile, and then she sat on disconsolately as before. Night came on, and she had ample time to indulge her ruminations.

Peckaby had not been in. Mrs. Peckaby concluded he was solacing himself at that social rendezvous, the Plough and Harrow, and would come home in a state of beer. Between nine and ten he entered—hours were early in Deerham—and to Mrs. Peckaby's surprise, he was not only sober, but social.

"It have turned out a pouring wet night," cried he. And the mood was so unwonted, especially after the episode of the wet grate, that Mrs. Peckaby was astonished into answering pleasantly.

"Will ye have some bread and cheese?" asked she.

"I don't mind if I do. Chuff, he gave me a piece of his bread and bacon at eight o'clock, so I ain't over hungry."

Mrs. Peckaby brought forth the loaf and the cheese, and Peckaby cut himself some and ate it. Then he went upstairs. She stayed to put the eatables away, raked out the fire, and followed. Peckaby was already in bed. To get into it was not a very ceremonious proceeding with him, as it is not with many others. There was no superfluous attire to throw off, there was no hindering time with ablutions, there were no prayers. Mrs. Peckaby favoured the same convenient mode, and she had just put the candle out, when some noise struck upon her ear.

It came from the road outside. They slept back, the front room having been the one let to Brother Jarrum; but in those small houses, at that quiet hour noises in the road were heard as distinctly back as front. There was a sound of talking, and then came a modest knock at Peckaby's door.

Mrs. Peckaby went to the front room, opened the casement, and looked out. To say that her heart leaped into her mouth would be a most imperfect figure of speech to describe the state of feeling that rushed over her. In the rainy obscurity of the night she could discern something white drawn up to the door, and the figures of two men standing by it. The only wonder was that she did not leap out; she might have done it, had the window been large enough.

"Do Susan Peckaby live here?" inquired a gruff voice, that seemed as if it were muffled.

"Oh, dear good gentlemen, yes!" she responded, in a tremble of excitement. "Please what is it?"

"The white donkey's come to take her to New Jerusalem."

With a shrieking cry of joy that might have been heard all the way up Clay Lane, Mrs. Peckaby tore back to her chamber.

"Peckaby," she cried, "Peckaby, the thing's come at last! The blessed animal that's to bear me off. I always said it would."

Peckaby—probably from drowsiness—made no immediate response. Mrs. Peckaby stooped down to the low bed, and shook him well by the shoulder.

"It's the white quadruple, Peckaby, come at last!"

Peckaby growled out something that she was in a state of too great excitement to hear. She lighted the candle; she flung on some of the things she had taken off; she ran back to the front before they were fastened, lest the messengers, brute and human, should have departed, and put her head out at the casement again, all in the utmost fever of agitation.

"A minute or two yet, good gentlemen, please! I'm a'most ready. I'm a-waiting to get out my purple gownd."

"All right, missus," was the muffled answer.

The "purple gownd" was kept in this very ex-room of Brother Jarrum's hid in a safe place between some sheets of newspaper. Had Mrs. Peckaby kept it open to the view of Peckaby, there's no saying what grief the robe might not have come to, ere this. Peckaby, in his tantrums, would not have been likely to spare it. She put it on, and hooked it down the front, her trembling fingers scarcely able to accomplish it. That it was full loose for her she was prepared to find; she had grown thin with fretting. Then she put on a shawl; next, her bonnet; last some green leather gloves. The shawl was black, with worked coloured corners—a thin small shawl that hardly covered her shoulders; and the bonnet was a straw, trimmed with pink ribbons—the toilette which had long been prepared.

"Good-bye, Peckaby," said she, going in when she was ready, "You've said many a time as you wished I was off, and now you have got your wish. But I don't want to part nothing but friends."

"Good-bye," returned Peckaby, in a hearty tone, as he turned himself round on his bed. "Give my love to the saints."

To find him in this accommodating humour was more than she had bargained for. A doubt had crossed her sometimes, whether, when the white donkey did come, there might not arise a battle with Peckaby, ere she should get off. This apparently civil feeling on his part awoke a more social one on hers; and a qualm of conscience darted across her, suggesting that she might have made him a better wife had she been so disposed. "He might have shook hands with me," was her parting thought, as she unlocked the street door.

The donkey was waiting outside with all the patience for which donkeys are renowned. It had been drawn up under a sheltering ledge at a door or two's distance, to be out of the rain. Its two conductors were muffled up, as befitted the inclemency of the night, something like their voices appeared to have been. Mrs. Peckaby was not in her sober senses sufficiently to ask whether they were brothers from the New Jerusalem, or whether the style of costume they favoured might be the prevailing mode in that fashionable city; if so, it was decidedly more useful than elegant, consisting apparently of hop sacks, doubled over the head and over the back.

"Ready, missus?"

"I be quite ready," she answered, in a tremble of delight. "There ain't no saddle!" she called out, as the donkey was trotted forward.

"You won't want a saddle; these New Jerusalem animals bain't like the ord'nary uns. Jump on him, missus."

Mrs. Peckaby was so exceedingly tall, that she had not far to jump. She took her seat sideways, settled her gown, and laid hold of the bridle, which one of the men put into her hands. He turned the donkey round, and set it going with a smack; the other helped by crying "Gee-ho!"

Up Clay Lane she proceeded in triumph. The skies were dark, and the rain came soaking down; but Mrs. Peckaby's heart was too warm to dwell on any temporary inconvenience. If a thought crossed her mind that the beauty of the pink ribbons might be marred by the storm, so as somewhat to dim the glory of her entrance into the city and introduction to the saints, she drove it away again. Trouble had no admission in her present frame of mind. The gentlemen in the hop sacks continued to attend her; the one leading the donkey, the other walking behind and cheering the animal on with periodical gee-ho's.

"I suppose as it's a long way, sir?" asked Mrs. Peckaby, breaking the silence, and addressing the conductor.

"Middlin'," replied he.

"And how do we get over the sea, please, sir?" asked she again.

"The woyage is pervided for, missus," was the short and satisfactory response. "Brother Jarrum took care of that when he sent us."

Her heart went into a glow at the name. And them envious disbelievers in Deerham had cast all sorts of disparaging accusations to the brother, openly expressing their opinion that he had gone off purposely without her, and that she'd never hear of him again!

Arrived at the top of Clay Lane, the road was crossed, and the donkey was led down a turning towards the lands of Sir Rufus Hautley. It may have occurred to Mrs. Peckaby to wonder that the highway was not taken, instead of an unfrequented bye-path, that only led to fields and a wood; but, if so, she said nothing. Had the white donkey taken her to a gravel-pit, and pitched headlong in with her, she would have deemed, in her blind faith, that it was the right road to New Jerusalem.

A long way it was, over those wet fields. If the brothers and the donkey partook of the saintly nature of the inhabitants of Salt Lake City, possibly they did not find it a weary one. Mrs. Peckaby certainly did not. She was rapt in a glowing vision of the honours and delights that would welcome her at her journey's end;—so rapt, that she and the donkey had been for some little time in one of the narrow paths of the wood before she missed her two conductors.

It caused Mrs. Peckaby to pull the bridle, and cry "Wo-ho!" to the donkey. She had an idea that they might have struck into the wrong path, for this one appeared to be getting narrower and narrower. The wood was intersected with paths, but only a few of them led right through it. She pulled up, and turned her head the way she had come, but was unable to distinguish anything, save that she was in the heart of the wood.

"Be you behind, gentlemen?" she called out.

There was no reply. Mrs. Peckaby waited a bit, thinking they might have lagged unwittingly, and then called out again, with the like result.

"It's very curious!" thought Mrs. Peckaby.

She was certainly in a dilemma. Without her conductors, she knew no more how to get to New Jerusalem than she did how to get to the new moon. She might find her way through the wood, by one path or another; but, once on the other side, she had no idea which road to turn the donkey to—north, south, east, or west. She thought she would go back and look after them.

But there was some difficulty in doing this. The path had grown so narrow that the donkey could not easily be turned. She slipped off him, tied the bridle to a tree, and ran back as fast as the obscurity of the path allowed her, calling out to the gentlemen.

The more she ran and the more she called, the less did there appear to be anybody to respond to it. Utterly at a nonplus, she at length returned to the donkey—that is, to the spot, so far as she could judge, where she had left it. But the donkey was gone.

Was Mrs. Peckaby awake or asleep? Was the past blissful dream—when she was being borne in triumph to New Jerusalem—only an imaginary one? Was her present predicament real! Which was imagination and which was real? For the last hour she had been enjoying the realisation of all her hopes; now she seemed no nearer their fruition than she had been a year ago. The white donkey was gone, the conducting brothers were gone, and she was alone in the middle of a wood, two miles from home, on a wet night. Mrs. Peckaby had heard of enchantments, and began to think she must have been subjected to something of the sort.

She rubbed her eyes; she pinched her arms. Was she in her senses or not? Sure never was such a situation heard of! The cup of hope presented palpably to her lips, only to vanish again—she could not tell how—and leave no sign. A very disagreeable doubt—not yet a suspicion—began to dawn over Mrs. Peckaby. Had she been made the subject of a practical joke?

She might have flung the doubt from her, but for a distant sound that came faintly on her ears—the sound of covert laughter. Her doubt turned to conviction. Her face became hot; her heart, but for the anger at it, would have grown sick with the disappointment. Her conductors and the donkey were retreating, having played their joke out! Two certainties forced themselves upon her mind. One, that Peckaby and his friends had planned it; she felt sure now that the biggest of the "brothers" had been nobody but Chuff, the blacksmith: the other certainty was, that she should never be sent for to New Jerusalem in any way. Why it should have been, Mrs. Peckaby could not have told, then or afterwards; but the positive conviction that Brother Jarrum had been false, that the story of sending for her on a white donkey had only been invented to keep her quiet, fixed itself in her mind in that moment in the lonely wood. She sunk down amidst the trees and sobbed bitterly.

But all the tears combined that the world ever shed could not bring her nearer to New Jerusalem, or make her present situation better. After awhile she had the sense to remember that. She rose from the ground, turned her gown up over her shoulders, found her way out of the wood, and set off on her walk back again in a very humble frame of mind, arriving home as the clock was striking two.

She could make nobody hear. She knocked at the door, she knocked at the window, gently at first, then louder; she called and called, but there came no answer. Some of the neighbours, aroused by the unwonted disturbance, came peeping at their windows. At length Peckaby opened his; thrusting his head out at the very casement from which Mrs. Peckaby had beheld the deceitful vision earlier in the night.

"Who's there?" called out Peckaby.

"It's me, Peckaby," was the answer, delivered in a forlorn tone. "Come down and open the door."

"Who's 'me'?" asked Peckaby.

"It's me," repeated Mrs. Peckaby, looking up.

And what with her height and the low casement, their faces were really not many inches apart; but yet Peckaby appeared not to know her.

"You be off, will you!" retorted he. "A pretty thing if tramps be to come to decent folks' doors and knock 'em up like this. Who's door did you take it for?"

"It's me!" screamed Mrs. Peckaby. "Don't you know me? Come and undo the door, and let me come in. I be sopping."

"Know you! How should I know you? Who be you?"

"Good heavens, Peckaby! you must know me. Ain't I your wife?"

"My wife! Not a bit on't. You needn't come here with that gammon, missis, whoever you be. My wife's gone off to New Jerusalem on a white donkey."

He slammed to the casement. Mrs. Peckaby, what with the rain and what with the disappointment, burst into tears. In the same moment, sundry other casements opened, and all the heads in the vicinity—including the blacksmith Chuffs, and Mrs. Chuff's—were thrust out to condole with their neighbour, Mrs. Peckaby.

"Had she been and come back a'ready?" "Did she get tired of the saints so soon as this—or did they get tired of her?" "What sort of a city, was it?" "Which was most plentiful—geese or sage?" "How many wives, besides herself, had the gentleman that she chose?" "Who took care of the babies?" "Did they have many public dances?" "Was veils for the bonnets all the go?" "Was it a paradise or warn't it?" "And how was Brother Jarrum?"

Amongst the many questions asked, those came prominently, tingling on the ears of the unhappy Mrs. Peckaby. Too completely prostrate with events to retort, she suddenly let drop her gown, that she had kept so carefully turned, and clapped both her hands upon her face. Then came a real, genuine question from the next door casement—Mrs. Green's.

"Ain't that your plum-coloured gownd? What's come to it?"

Mrs. Peckaby, somewhat aroused, looked at the gown in haste. What had come to it? Patches of dead-white, looking not unlike paint, covered it about on all sides, especially behind. The shawl had caught some white, too, and the green leather gloves looked, inside, as though they had had a coat of whitewash put on them. Her beautiful gownd! laid by so long!—what on earth had ruined it like that?

Chuff, the blacksmith, gave a great grin from his window. "Sure that there donkey never was painted down white!" quoth he.

That it had been painted down white and with exceedingly wet paint too, there could be little doubt. Some poor donkey humble in his coat of gray, converted into a fine white animal for the occasion, by Peckaby and Chuff and their cronies. Mrs. Peckaby shrieked and sobbed with mortification, and drummed frantically on her house door. A chorus of laughter echoed from all sides, and Peckaby's casement flew open again.

"Will you stop that there knocking, then?" roared Peckaby, "Disturbing a man's night's rest."

"I will come in then, Peckaby," she stormed, plucking up a little spirit in her desperation. "I be your wife, you know I be, and I will come in."

"My good woman, what's took you?" cried Peckaby, in a tone of compassionating suavity. "You ain't no wife of mine. My wife's miles on her road by this time. She's off to New Jerusalem on a white donkey."

A new actor came up to the scene—no other than Jan Verner. Jan had been sitting up with some poor patient, and was now going home. To describe his surprise when he saw the windows alive with nightcapped heads, and Mrs. Peckaby in her dripping discomfort, in her paint, in her state altogether, outward and inward, would be a long task. Peckaby himself undertook the explanation, in which he was aided by Chuff; and Jan sat himself down on the public pump, and laughed till he was hoarse.

"Come, Peckaby, you'll let her in," cried he, before he went away.

"Let her in!" echoed Peckaby, "That would be a go, that would! What 'ud the saints say? They'd be for prosecuting of her for bigamy. If she's gone over to them, sir, she can't belong legal to me."

Jan laughed so that he had to hold his sides, and Mrs. Peckaby shrieked and sobbed. Chuff began calling out that the best remedy for white paint was turpentine.

"Coma along, Peckaby, and open the door," said Jan, rising. "She'll catch an illness if she stops here in her wet clothes, and I shall have a month's work, attending on her. Come!"

"Well, sir, to oblige you, I will," returned the man. "But let me ever catch her snivelling after them saints again, that's all! They should have her if they liked; I'd not."

"You hear, Mrs. Peckaby," said Jan in her ear. "I'd let the saints alone for the future, if I were you."

"I mean to, sir," she meekly answered, between her sobs.

Peckaby in his shirt and nightcap, opened the door, and she bounded in. The casements closed to the chorus of subsiding laughter, and the echoes of Jan's footsteps died away in the distance.

CHAPTER LXXV

AN EXPLOSION OF SIBYLLA'S

Sibylla Verner sat at the window of her sitting-room in the twilight—a cold evening in early winter. Sibylla was in an explosive temper. It was nothing unusual for her to be in an explosive temper now; but she was in a worse than customary this evening. Sibylla felt the difference between Verner's Pride and Deerham Court. She lived but in excitement; she cared but for gaiety. In removing to Deerham Court she had gone readily, believing that she should there find a large portion of the gaiety she had been accustomed to at Verner's Pride; that she should, at any rate, be living with the appliances of wealth about her, and should go out a great deal with Lady Verner. She had not bargained for Lady Verner's establishment being reduced to simplicity and quietness, for her laying down her carriage and discharging her men-servants and selling her horses, and living again the life of a retired gentlewoman. Yet all these changes had come to pass, and Sibylla's inward spirit turned restive. She had everything that any reasonable mind could possibly desire, every comfort; but quiet comfort and Sibylla's taste did not accord. Her husband was out a great deal at Verner's Pride and on the estate. As he had resolved to do over John Massingbird's dinner-table, so he was doing—putting his shoulder to the wheel. He had never looked after things as he was looking now. To be the master of Verner's Pride was one thing, to be the hired manager of Verner's Pride was another; and Lionel found every hour of his time occupied. His was no eye-service; his conscience was engaged in his work and he did it efficiently.

Sibylla still sat at the window, looking out into the twilight. Decima stood near the fire in a thoughtful mood. Lucy was downstairs in the drawing-room at the piano. They could hear the faint echo of her soft playing as they sat there in silence. Sibylla was in no humour to talk: she had repulsed Decima rudely— or it may rather be said fractiously—when the latter had ventured on conversation. Lady Verner had gone out to dinner. The Countess of Elmsley had been there that day, and she had asked Lady Verner to go over in the evening and take a friendly dinner with her. "Bring any of them that you like with you," had been her careless words in parting. But Lady Verner had not chosen to take "any of them." She had dressed and driven off in the hired fly alone; and this it was that was exciting the anger of Sibylla. She thought Lady Verner might have taken her.

Lucy came in and knelt down on the rug before the fire, half shivering. "I am so cold!" she said. "Do you know what I did, Decima? I let the fire go out. Some time after Lady Verner went up to dress, I turned round and found the fire was out. My hands are quite numbed."

"You have gone on playing there without a fire!" cried Decima.

"I shall be warm again directly," said Lucy cheerily. "As I passed through the hall, the reflection of the blaze came out of the dining-room. We shall get warm there. Is your head still aching, Mrs. Verner?"

"It is always aching," snapped Sibylla.

Lucy, kind and gentle in spirit, unretorting, ever considerate for the misfortunes which had come upon Mrs. Verner, went to her side. "Shall I get you a little of your aromatic vinegar?" she asked.

"You need not trouble to get anything for me," was the ungracious answer.

Lucy, thus repulsed, stood in silence at the window. The window on this side of the house overlooked the road which led to Sir Rufus Hautley's. A carriage, apparently closely shut up, so far as she could see in the dusk, its coachman and footman attending it, was bowling rapidly down towards the village.

"There's Sir Rufus Hautley's carriage," said Lucy. "I suppose he is going out to dinner."

Decima drew to the window and looked out. The carriage came sweeping round the point, and turned on its road to the village, as they supposed. In the still silence of the room, they could hear its wheels on the frosty road, after they lost sight of it; could hear it bowl before their house and—pull up at the gates.

"It has stopped here!" exclaimed Lucy.

Decima moved quietly back to the fire and sat down. A fancy arose to Lucy that she, Decima, had turned unusually pale. Was it so?—or was it fancy? If it was fancy, why should the fancy have arisen? Ghastly pale her face certainly looked, as the blaze played upon it.

A few minutes, and one of the servants came in, handing a note to Decima.

"Bring lights," said Decima, in a low tone.

The lights were brought; and then Decima's agitation was apparent. Her hands shook as she broke the seal of the letter. Lucy gazed in surprise; Sibylla, somewhat aroused from her own grievances, in curiosity.

"Desire the carriage to wait," said Decima.

"It is waiting, Miss Decima. The servants said they had orders."

Decima crushed the note into her pocket as well as her shaking fingers would allow her, and left the room. What could have occurred, thus to agitate calm and stately Decima? Before Lucy and Mrs. Verner had recovered their surprise she was back again, dressed to go out.

"I am sorry to leave you so abruptly, as mamma is not here," she said. "I dare say Lionel will be in to dinner. If not, you must for once entertain each other."

"But where are you going?" cried Mrs. Verner.

"To Sir Rufus Hautley's. He wishes to see me."

"What does he want with you?" continued Sibylla.

"I do not know," replied Decima.

She quitted the room and went down to the carriage, which had waited for her. Mrs. Verner and Lucy heard it drive away again as quickly as it had driven up. As it turned the corner and pursued its way up the road, past the window they were looking from, but at some distance from it, they fancied they saw the form of Decima inside, looking out at them.

"Sir Rufus is taken ill," said old Catherine to them, by way of news. "The servants say that it's feared he won't live through the night. Mr. Jan is there, and Dr. Hayes."

"But what can he want with Miss Verner?" reiterated Sibylla.

Catherine shook her head. She had not the remotest idea.

Lionel Verner did not come in for dinner, and they descended to it without him. His non-appearance was no improvement to the temper of his wife. It had occurred lately that Lionel did not always get home to dinner.

Sometimes, when detained at Verner's Pride, he would take it with John Massingbird; if out on the estate, and unable to reach home in time, he would eat something when he came in. Her fractious state of mind did not tend to soothe the headache she had complained of earlier in the day. Every half-hour that passed without her husband's entrance, made her worse in all ways, head and temper; and about nine o'clock she went up to her sitting-room and lay down on the sofa, saying that her temples were splitting.

Lucy followed her. Lucy thought she must really be ill. She could not understand that any one should be so fractious, except from wearing pain. "I will bathe your temples," she gently said.

Sibylla did not appear to care whether her temples were bathed or not. Lucy got some water in a basin and two thin handkerchiefs, wringing out one and placing it on Mrs. Verner's head and forehead, kneeling to her task. That her temples were throbbing and her head hot, there was no question; the handkerchief was no sooner on, than it was warm, and Lucy had to exchange it for the other.

"It is Lionel's fault," suddenly burst forth Sibylla.

"His fault?" returned Lucy. "How can it be his fault?"

"What business has he to stop out?"

"But if he cannot help it?" returned Lucy. "The other evening, don't you remember, Mr. Verner said when he came in, that he could not help being late sometimes now?"

"You need not defend him," said Sibylla. "It seems to me that you are all ready to take his part against me."

Lucy made no reply. An assertion more unfounded could not have been spoken. At that moment the step of Lionel was heard on the stairs. He came in, looking jaded and tired.

"Up here this evening!" he exclaimed, laying down a paper or parchment which he had in his hand. "Catherine says my mother and Decima are out. Why, Sibylla, what is the matter?"

Sibylla dashed the handkerchief off her brow as he advanced to her, and rose up, speaking vehemently. The sight of her husband appeared to have brought the climax to her temper.

"Where have you been? Why were you not in to dinner?"

"I could not get home in time. I have been detained."

"It is false," she retorted, her blue eyes flashing fire. "Business, business! it is always your excuse now! You stay out for no good purpose."

The outbreak startled Lucy. She backed a few paces, looking scared.

"Sibylla!" was all the amazed reply returned by Lionel.

"You leave me here, hour after hour, to solitude and tears, while you are out, taking your pleasure! I have all the endurance of our position, and you the enjoyment."

He battled for a moment with his rising feelings; battled for calmness, for forbearance, for strength to bear. There were moments when he was tempted to answer her in her own spirit.

"Pleasure and I have not been very close friends of late, Sibylla," he gravely said. "None can know that better than you. My horse fell lame, and I have been leading him these last two hours. I have now to go to Verner's Pride. Something has arisen on which I must see Mr. Massingbird."

"It is false, it is false," reiterated Sibylla. "You are not going to Verner's Pride; you are not going to see Mr. Massingbird. You know best where you are going; but it is not there. It is the old story of Rachel Frost over again."

The words confounded Lionel; both that they were inexplicable and spoken in passion so vehement.

"What do you say about Rachel Frost?" he asked.

"You know what I say, and what I mean. When Deerham looked far and near for the man who did the injury to Rachel, they little thought they might have found him in Lionel Verner. Lucy Tempest, it is true. He—"

But Lionel had turned imperatively to Lucy, drawing her to the door, which he opened. It was no place for her, a discussion such as this.

"Will you be so kind as to go down and make me a cup of tea, Lucy?" he said, in a wonderfully calm tone, considering the provocation he was receiving. Then he closed the door on Lucy, and turned to his wife.

"Sibylla, allow me to request, nay, to insist, that when you have fault to find, or reproach to cast to me, you choose a moment when we are alone. If you have no care for what may be due to me and to yourself, you will do well to bear in mind that something is due to others. Now, then, tell me what you mean about Rachel Frost."

"I won't," said Sibylla. "You are killing me," and she burst into tears.

Oh, it was weary work!—weary work for him. Such a wife as this!

"In what way am I killing you?"

"Why do you leave me so much alone?"

"I have undertaken work, and I must do it. But, as to leaving you alone, when I am with you, you scarcely ever give me a civil word."

"You are leaving me now—you are wanting to go to Verner's Pride to-night," she reiterated with strange inconsistency, considering that she had just insinuated he did not want to go there.

"I must go there, Sibylla. I have told you why; and I have told you truth. Again I ask you what you meant about Rachel Frost."

Sibylla flung up her hands petulantly. "I won't tell you, I say. And you can't make me. I wish, I wish Fred had not died."

She turned round on the sofa and buried her face in the cushions. Lionel, true to the line of conduct he had carved out for himself, to give her all possible token of respect and affection ever, whatever might be her provocation—and all the more true to it from the very consciousness that the love of his inmost heart grew less hers, more another's, day by day, bent over her and spoke kindly. She flung back her hand in a repelling manner towards him, and maintained an obstinate silence. Lionel, sick and weary, at length withdrew, taking up the parchment.

How sick and weary, none, save himself, could know. Lucy Tempest had the tea before her, apparently ready, when he looked into the drawing-room.

"I am going on now to Verner's Pride, Lucy. You can tell my mother so, should she ask after me when she returns. I may be late."

"But you will take some tea, first?" cried Lucy, in a hasty tone. "You asked me to make it for you."

He knew he had—asked her as an excuse to get her from the room.

"I don't care for it," he wearily answered.

"I am sure you are tired," said Lucy. "When did you dine?"

"I have not dined. I have taken nothing since I left home this morning."

"Oh!" She was hastening to the bell. Lionel stopped her, laying his hand upon her arm.

"I could not eat it, Lucy. Just one cup of tea, if you will."

She, returned to the table, poured out the cup of tea, and he drank it standing.

"Shall I take Mrs. Verner up a cup?" asked Lucy. "Will she drink it, do you think?"

"Thank you, Lucy. It may do her head good. I think it aches much to-night."

He turned, and departed. Lucy noticed that he had left the parchment behind him, and ran after him with it, catching him as he was about to close the hall door. She knew that all such business-looking papers went up to Verner's Pride.

"Did you mean to leave it? Or have you forgotten it?"

He had forgotten it. He took it from her, retaining her hand for a moment. "Lucy, you will not misjudge me?" he said, in a strange tone of pain.

Lucy looked up at him with a bright smile and a very emphatic shake of the head. She knew by instinct that he alluded to the accusation of his wife, touching Rachel Frost. Lucy misjudge him!

"You should have waited to eat some dinner," she gaily said. "Take care you don't faint by the way, as that sick patient of Jan's did the other morning."

Lionel went on. At any rate there was peace outside, if not within; the peace of outward calm. He lifted his hat; he bared his brow, aching with its weight of trouble, to the clear night air; he wondered whether he should have this to bear his whole life long. At the moment of passing the outer gates, the carriage of Sir Rufus Hautley drew up, bearing Decima.

Lionel waited to receive her. He helped her out, and gave her his arm to the hall door. Decima walked with her head down.

"You are silent, Decima. Are you sad?"

"Yes," she answered. "Sir Rufus is dead."

"Dead!" echoed Lionel, in very astonishment, for he had heard nothing of the sudden illness.

"It is so," she replied, breaking into sobs. "Spasms at the heart, they say. Jan and Dr. Hayes were there, but they could not save him."

CHAPTER LXXVI

AN UNEXPECTED ARRIVAL

Deborah and Amilly West were sitting over the fire In the growing dusk of a February evening. Their sewing lay on the table; some home dresses they were making for themselves, for they had never too much superfluous cash for dressmakers, with fashionable patterns and fashionable prices. It had grown too dark to work, and they had turned to the fire for a chat, before the tea came in, and the gas was lighted.

"I tell you, Amilly, it is of no use playing at concealment, or trying to suppress the truth," Deborah was saying. "She is as surely going as that the other two went; as sure as sure can be. I have always felt that she would go. Mr. Lionel was talking to me only yesterday. He was not satisfied with his brother; at least, he thought it as well to act as though he were not satisfied with him; and he was about to ask Dr. Hayes—"

Her voice died away. Master Cheese had come in with a doleful face.

"Miss Deb, I'm sent up to Deerham Hall. There's a bothering note come from Miss Hautley to Jan, about one of the servants, and he says I am to go up and see what it is."

"Well?" returned Miss Deb, wondering why Master Cheese should come in to give the information to her. "You couldn't expect Mr. Jan to go up, after being out all day, as he has."

"Folks are sure to go and fall ill at the most untoward hour of the twenty-four," grumbled Master Cheese. "I was just looking for a good tea. I feel as empty as possible, after my short dinner. I wish—"

"Short dinner!" echoed Miss Deb, in amazement; at least, it would have been in amazement, but that she was accustomed to these little episodes from the young gentleman. "We had a beautiful piece of roast beef; and I'm sure you ate as much as you chose!"

"There was no pudding or pie," resentfully retorted Master Cheese. "I have felt all the afternoon just as if I should sink; and I couldn't get out to buy anything for myself, because Jan never came in, and the boy stopped out. I wish, Miss Deb, you'd give me a thick piece of bread-and-jam, as I have to go off without my tea."

"The fact is, Master Cheese, you have the jam so often, in one way or another, that there's very little left. It will not last the season out."

"The green gooseberries'll be coming on, Miss Deb," was Master Cheese's insinuating reply. "And there's always apples, you know. With plenty of lemon and a clove or two, apples make as good a pudding as anything else."

Miss Deb, always good-natured, went to get him what he had asked for, and Master Cheese took his seat in front of the fire, and toasted his toes.

"There was a great mistake made when you were put to a surgeon," said Miss Amilly, laughing. "You should have gone apprentice to a pastry-cook."

"She's a regular fidgety old woman, that Miss Hautley," broke out Master Cheese with temper, passing over Miss Amilly's remark. "It's not two months yet that she has been at the Hall, and she has had one or the other of us up six times at least. I wonder what business she had to come to it? The Hall wouldn't have run away before Sir Edmund could get home."

Miss Deb came back with the bread-and-jam; a good thick slice, as the gentleman had requested. To look at him eating, one would think he had had nothing for a week. It disappeared in no time, and Master Cheese went out sucking his fingers and his lips. Deborah West folded up the work, and put things straight generally in the room. Then she sat down again, drawing her chair to the side of the fire.

"I do think that Cheese has got a wolf inside him," cried Amilly, with a laugh.

"He is a great gourmand. He said this morning—" began Miss Deb, and then she stopped.

Finding what she was about to say thus brought to an abrupt conclusion, Amilly West looked at her sister. Miss Deb's attention was riveted on the room door. Her mouth was open, her eyes seemed starting from her head with a fixed stare, and her countenance was growing white. Amilly turned her eyes hastily to the same direction, and saw a dark, obscure form filling up the doorway.

Not obscure for long. Amilly, more impulsive than her sister, rose up with a shriek, and darted forward with outstretched arms of welcome; Deborah followed, stretching out hers.

"My dear father!"

It was no other than Dr. West. He gave them each a cool kiss, walked to the fire and sat down, bidding them not smother him. For some little while they could not get over their surprise or believe their senses. They knew nothing of his intention to return, and had deemed him hundreds of miles away. Question after question they showered down upon him, the result of their amazement. He answered just as much as he chose. He had only come home for a day or so, he said, and did not care that it should be known he was there, to be tormented with a shoal of callers.

"Where's Mr. Jan?" asked he.

"In the surgery," said Deborah.

"Is he by himself?"

"Yes, dear papa. Master Cheese has just gone up to Deerham Hall, and the boy is out."

Dr. West rose, and made his way to the surgery. The surgery was empty. But the light of a fire from the half-opened door, led him to Jan's bedroom. It was a room that would persist in remaining obstinately damp, and Jan, albeit not over careful of himself, judged it well to have an occasional fire lighted. The room, seen by this light, looked comfortable. The small, low, iron bed stood in the far corner; in the opposite corner the bureau, as in Dr. West's time, the door opening to the garden (never used now) between them, at the end of the room. The window was on the side opposite the fire, a table in the middle. Jan was then occupied in stirring the fire into a blaze, and its cheerful light flickered on every part of the room.

"Good-evening, Mr. Jan."

Jan turned round, poker in hand, and stared amiably. "Law!" cried he. "Who'd have thought it?"

The old word; the word he had learned at school—law. It was Jan's favourite mode of expressing surprise still, and Lady Verner never could break him of it. He shook hands cordially with Dr. West.

The doctor shut the door, slipping the bolt, and sat down to the fire. Jan cleared a space on the table, which was covered with jars and glass vases, cylinders, and other apparatus, seemingly for chemical purposes, and took his seat there.

The doctor had taken a run home, "making a morning call, as it might be metaphorically observed," he said to Jan. Just to have a sight of home faces, and hear a little home news. Would Mr. Jan recite to him somewhat of the latter?

Jan did so; touching upon all he could recollect. From John Massingbird's return to Verner's Pride, and the consequent turning out of Mr. Verner and his wife, down to the death of Sir Rufus Hautley; not forgetting the pranks played by the "ghost," and the foiled expedition of Mrs. Peckaby to New Jerusalem. Some of these items of intelligence the doctor had heard before, for Jan periodically wrote to him. The doctor looked taller, and stouter, and redder than ever, and as he leaned thoughtfully forward, and the crimson blaze played upon his face, Jan thought how like he was growing to his sister, the late Mrs. Verner.

"Mr. Jan," said the doctor, "it is not right that my nephew, John Massingbird, should enjoy Verner's Pride."

"Of course it's not," answered Jan. "Only things don't go by rights always, you know. It's but seldom they do."

"He ought to give it up to Mr. Verner."

"So I told him," said Jan. "I should, in his place."

"What did he say?"

"Say? Laughed at me, and called me green."

Dr. West sat thoughtfully pulling his great dark whiskers. Dark as they were, they had yet a tinge of red in the fire-light. "It was a curious thing; a very curious thing, that both brothers should die, as was supposed, in Australia," said he. "Better—as things have turned out—that Fred should have turned up afterwards, than John."

"I don't know that," spoke Jan with his accustomed truth-telling freedom. "The pair were not good for much, but John was the best of them."

"I was thinking of Sibylla," candidly admitted the doctor. "It would have been better for her."

Jan opened his eyes considerably.

"Better for her!—for it to turn out that she had two husbands living? That's logic, that is."

"Dear me, to be sure!" cried the doctor. "I was not thinking of that phase of the affair, Mr. Jan. Is she in spirits?"

"Who? Sibylla? She's fretting herself into her grave."

Dr. West turned his head with a start. "What at? The loss of Verner's Pride?"

"Well, I don't know," said Jan, ever plain-spoken. "She puzzles me. When she was at Verner's Pride, she never seemed satisfied. She was perpetually hankering after excitement—didn't seem to care for Lionel, or for anybody else, and kept the house full of people from top to bottom. She has a restless, dissatisfied temper, and it keeps her on the worry. Folks with such tempers know no peace, and let nobody else know any that's about them. A nice life she leads Lionel! Not that he'd drop a hint of it. He'd cut out his tongue before he'd speak a word against his wife; he'd rather make her out to be an angel."

"Are they pretty comfortably off for money?" inquired Dr. West, after a pause. "I suppose Mr. Verner must have managed to feather his nest a little, before leaving?"

"Not a bit of it," returned Jan. "He was over head and ears in debt. Sibylla helped him to a good portion of it. She went the pace. John Massingbird waives the question of the mesne profits, or Lionel would be in worse embarrassment than he is."

Dr. West looked crestfallen. "What do they live on?" he asked. "Does Lady Verner keep them? She can't have too much for herself now."

"Oh! it's managed somehow," said Jan.

Dr. West sat for some time in ruminating silence; pulling his whiskers as before, running his hands through his hair, the large clear blue sapphire ring, which he always wore on his finger, conspicuous. Jan swayed his legs about, and waited to afford any further information. Presently the doctor turned to him, a charming expression of open confidence on his countenance.

"Mr. Jan, I am in great hopes that you will do me a little favour. I have temporary need of a trifle of pecuniary aid—some slight debts which have grown upon me abroad," he added carelessly, with a short cough—"and, knowing your good heart, I have resolved to apply to you. If you can oblige me with a couple of hundred pounds or so, I'll give you my acknowledgment, and return it punctually as soon as I am able."

"I'd let you have it with all the pleasure in life, if I had got it," heartily replied Jan; "but I have not."

"My dear Mr. Jan! Not got it! You must have quite a nice little nest of savings laid by in the bank! I know you never spend a shilling on yourself."

"All I had in the bank, and what I have drawn since, has been handed to my mother. I wanted Lionel and Sibylla to come here: I and Miss Deb arranged it all; and in that case I should have given the money to

Miss Deb. But Sibylla refused; she would not come here, she would not go anywhere but to Lady Verner's. So I handed the money to my mother."

The confession appeared to put the doctor out considerably. "How very imprudent, Mr. Jan! To give away all you possessed, leaving nothing for yourself! I never heard of such a thing!"

"Lionel and his wife were turned out of everything, and had nobody to look to. I don't see that I could have put the money to better use," stoutly returned Jan. "It was not much, there's such a lot of the Clay Lane folks always wanting things when they are ill. And Miss Deb, she had had something. You keep her so short, doctor."

"But you pay her the sum that was agreed upon for housekeeping?" said Dr. West.

"What should hinder me?" returned Jan. "Of course I do. But she cannot make both ends meet, she says, and then she has to come to me. I'm willing: only I can't give money away and put it by, you see."

Dr. West probably did see it. He saw beyond doubt, that all hope of ready money from easy Jan was gone—from the simple fact that Jan's coffers were just now empty. The fact did not afford him satisfaction.

"I'll tell you what, Mr. Jan," said he, brightening up, "you shall give me your signature to a little bill—a bill at two months, let us say. It will be the same as money."

"Can't," said Jan.

"You can't!" replied Dr. West.

"No!" said Jan resolutely. "I'd give away all I had in hand to give, and welcome; but I'd never sign bills. A doctor has no business with 'em. Don't you remember what they did for Jones at Bartholomew's?"

"I don't remember Jones at Bartholomew's," frigidly returned the doctor.

"No! Why, what's gone with your memory?" innocently asked Jan. "If you think a bit, you'll recollect about him, and what his end was. Bills did it; the signing of bills to oblige some friend. I'll never sign a bill, doctor. I wouldn't do it for my own mother."

Thus the doctor's expectations were put a final end to, so far as Jan went—and very certain expectations they had, no doubt, been. As to Jan, a thought may have crossed him that the doctor and his daughter Sibylla appeared to have the same propensity for getting out of money. Dr. West recovered his equanimity, and magnanimously waived the affair as a trifle not worth dwelling on.

"How does Cheese get on?" he asked.

"First rate—in the eating line," replied Jan.

"Have you got him out of his idleness yet?"

"It would take a more clever man than I to do that, doctor. It's constitutional. When he goes up to London, in the autumn, I shall take an assistant: unless you should be coming home yourself."

"I have no intention of it at present, Mr. Jan. Am I to understand you that Sibylla has serious symptoms of disease?"

"There's no doubt of it," said Jan. "You always prophesied it for her, you know. When she was at Verner's Pride she was continually ailing: not a week passed but I was called in to attend her. She was so imprudent too—she would be. Going out and getting her feet wet; sitting up half the night. We tried to bring her to reason; but it was of no use. She defied Lionel; she would not listen to me—as well speak to a post."

"Why should she defy her husband? Are they on bad terms?"

"They are on as good terms as any man and wife could be, Sibylla being the wife," was Jan's rejoinder. "You know something of her temper and disposition, doctor—it is of no use to mince matters—you remember how it had used to be with her here at home. Lionel's a husband in a thousand. How he can possibly put up with her, and be always patient and kind, puzzles me more than any problem ever did in Euclid. If Fred had lived—why, he'd have broken her spirit or her heart long before this."

Dr. West rose and stretched himself. The failings of Sibylla were not a pleasant topic, thus openly mentioned by Jan; but none knew better than the doctor how true were the grounds on which he spoke. None knew better, either, that disease for her was to be feared.

"Her sisters went off about this age, or a little later," he said musingly. "I could not save them."

"And Sibylla's as surely going after them, doctor, as that I am here," returned Jan. "Lionel intends to call in Dr. Hayes to her."

"Since when has she been so ill?"

"Not since any time in particular. There appears to be no real illness yet—only symptoms. She coughs, and gets as thin as a skeleton. Sometimes I think, if she could call up a cheerful temper, she'd keep well. You will see what you think of her."

The doctor walked towards the bureau at the far corner. "Have you ever opened it, Mr. Jan?"

"It's not likely," said Jan. "Didn't you tell me not to open it? Your own papers are in it, and you hold the key."

"It's not inconvenient to your room, my retaining it I hope?" asked the doctor. "I don't know where else I should put my papers."

"Not a bit of it," said Jan. "Have another in here as well, if you like. It's safe here."

"Do you know, Mr. Jan, I feel as if I'd rather sleep in your little bed to-night than indoors," said the doctor looking at Jan's bed. "The room seems like an old friend to me: I feel at home in it."

"Sleep in it, if you like," returned Jan, in his easy good nature. "Miss Deb can put me into some room or other. I say, doctor, it's past tea-time. Wouldn't you like some refreshment?"

"I had a good dinner on my road," replied Dr. West; which Jan might have guessed, for Dr. West was quite sure to take care of himself. "We will go in, if you like; Deb and Amilly will wonder what has become of me. How old they begin to look!"

"I don't suppose any of us look younger," answered Jan.

They went into the house. Deborah and Amilly were in a flutter of hospitality, lading the tea-table with good things that it would have gladdened Master Cheese's heart to see. They had been upstairs to smooth out their curls, to put on clean white sleeves and collars, a gold chain, and suchlike little additions, setting themselves off as they were now setting off the tea-table, all in their affectionate welcome to their father. And Dr. West, who liked eating as well as ever did Master Cheese, surveyed the table with complacency as he sat down to it, ignoring the dinner he had spoken of to Jan. Amilly sat by him, heaping his plate with what he liked best, and Deborah made the tea.

"I have been observing to Mr. Jan that you are beginning to look very old, Deb," remarked the doctor; "Amilly also."

It was a cruel shaft. A bitter return for their loving welcome. Perhaps they were looking older, but he need not have said it so point blank, and before Jan. They turned crimson, poor ladies, and bent to sip their tea, and tried to turn the words off with a laugh, and did not know where to look. In true innate delicacy of feeling, Dr. West and his daughter, Sibylla, rivalled each other.

The meal over, the doctor proposed to pay a visit to Deerham Court, and did so, Jan walking with him, first of all mentioning to Deborah the wish expressed by Dr. West as to occupying Jan's room for the night, that she might see the arrangement carried out.

Which she did. And Jan, at the retiring hour—though this is a little anticipating, for the evening is not yet over—escorted the doctor to the door of the room, and wished him a good night's rest, never imagining but that he enjoyed one. But had fire, or any other accident, burst open the room to public gaze in the lone night hours, Dr. West would have been seen at work, instead of asleep. Every drawer of the bureau was out, every paper it contained was misplaced. The doctor was evidently searching for something, as sedulously as he had once searched for that lost prescription, which at the time appeared so much to disturb his peace.

CHAPTER LXXVII

AN EVENING AT LADY VERNER'S

In the well-lighted drawing-room at Deerham Court was its mistress, Lady Verner. Seated with her on the same sofa was her son, Lionel. Decima, at a little distance, was standing talking to Lord Garle. Lucy Tempest sat at the table cutting the leaves of a new book; and Sibylla was bending over the fire in a shivering attitude, as if she could not get enough of its heat. Lord Garle had been dining with them.

The door opened and Jan entered. "I have brought you a visitor, Sibylla," said he, in his unceremonious fashion, without any sort of greeting to anybody. "Come in, doctor."

It caused quite a confusion, the entrance of Dr. West. All were surprised. Lionel rose, Lucy rose; Lord Garle and Decima came forward, and Sibylla sprang towards him with a cry. Lady Verner was the only one who retained entire calmness.

"Papa! it cannot be you! When did you come?"

Dr. West kissed her, and turned to Lady Verner with some courtly words. Dr. West was an adept at such. Not the courtly words that spring genuinely from a kindly and refined nature; but those that are put on to hide a false one. All people, true-hearted ones, too, cannot distinguish between them; the false and the real. Next, the doctor grasped the hand of Lionel.

"My son-in-law!" he exclaimed in a very demonstrative manner. "The last time you and I had the pleasure of meeting, Mr. Verner, we little anticipated that such a relationship would ensue. I rejoice to welcome you in it, my dear sir."

"True," said Lionel, with a quiet smile. "Coming events do not always cast their shadows before."

With Decima, with Lord Garle, with Lucy Tempest, the doctor severally shook hands; he had a phrase of suavity for them all.

"I should not have known you," he said to the latter.

"No!" returned Lucy. "Why?"

"You have grown, Miss Tempest. Grown much."

"Then I must have been very short before," said Lucy. "I am not tall now."

"You have grown into remarkable beauty," added the doctor.

Whether Lucy had grown into beauty, or not, she did not like being told of it. And she did not like Dr. West. She had not been in love with him ever, as you may recollect; but she seemed to like him now, as he stood before her, less and less. Drawing away from him when she could do so civilly, she went up and talked to Jan.

A little while, and they had become more settled, dispersing into groups. The doctor, his daughter, and Lionel were sitting on a couch apart, conversing in an undertone; the rest disposed themselves as they would. Dr. West had accepted a cup of coffee. He kept it in his hand, sipping it now and then, and slowly ate a biscuit.

"Mr. Jan tells me Sibylla is not very strong," he observed, addressing both of them, but more particularly Lionel.

"Not very," replied Lionel. "The cold weather of this winter has tried her; has given her a cough. She will be better, I hope, when it comes in warm."

"How do you feel, my dear?" inquired the doctor, apparently looking at his coffee-cup instead of Sibylla. "Weak here?"—touching his chest.

"Not more weak than I had used to be," she answered in a cross tone, as if the confession that she did feel weak was not pleasant to her. "There's nothing the matter with me, papa; only Lionel makes a fuss."

"Nay, Sibylla," interposed Lionel good-humouredly, "I leave that to you and Jan."

"You would like to make papa believe you don't make a fuss!" she cried, in a most resentful tone; "when you know, not two days ago, you wanted to prevent my going to the party at Mrs. Bitterworth's!"

"I plead guilty to that," said Lionel. "It was a most inclement night, a cold, raw fog that penetrated everywhere, carriages and all else, and I wished you not to venture out in it. The doing so increased your cough."

"Mr. Verner was right," said Dr. West. "Night fogs are pernicious to a degree, where the chest and lungs are delicate. You should not stir out of the house, Sibylla, after sunset. Now don't interrupt, my dear. Let the carriage be ever so closely shut, it makes no difference. There is the change of atmosphere from the warm room to the cold carriage; there are the draughts of air in passing to it. You must not do it, Sibylla."

"Do you mean to say, papa, that I am to live like a hermit?—never to go out?" she returned, her bosom heaving with vexation. "It is not much visiting that I have had, goodness knows, since quitting Verner's Pride: if I am to give it all up, you may as well put me out of the world. As good be dead!"

"Sibylla," said the doctor, more impressively than he often spoke, "I know your constitution, and I know pretty well what you can and what you can not bear. Don't attempt to stir out after sunset again. Should you get stronger it will be a different matter. At present it must not be. Will you remember this, Mr. Verner?"

"If my wife will allow me to remember it," he said, bending to Sibylla with a kindly tone. "My will was good to keep her in, all this winter; but she would not be kept."

"What has Jan been telling you about me, papa? It is a shame of him! I am not ill."

"Mr. Jan has told me very little indeed of your ailments," replied Dr. West. "He says you are not strong; he says you are fretful, irritable. My dear, this arises from your state of health."

"I have thought so, too," said Lionel, speaking impulsively. Many and many a time, latterly, when she had nearly tired out his heart and his patience, had he been willing to find an excuse for her still—that her illness of body caused in her the irritation of mind. Or, at any rate, greatly increased it.

An eye, far less experienced than that of Dr. West—who, whatever may have been his other shortcomings, was clever in his profession—could have seen at a glance how weak Sibylla was. She wore an evening dress of white muslin, its body very low and its sleeves very short; her chest was painfully thin, and every breath she took lifted it ominously: she seemed to be breathing outside as well as in. The doctor touched the muslin.

"This is not a fit dress for you, Sibylla—"

"Lionel has been putting you up to say it, papa!" she burst forth.

Dr. West looked at her. He surmised, what was indeed the case, that her husband had remonstrated against the unsuitableness of the attire, to one in her condition.

"You have heard every word Mr. Verner has spoken to me, Sibylla. You should be wrapped up warmly always. To be exposed as you are now, is enough to—to"—give you your death, he was about to say, but changed the words—"make you very ill."

"Decima and Lucy Tempest dress so," she returned in a tone that threatened tears.

Dr. West lifted his eyes to where Decima and Lucy were standing with Lord Garle. Decima wore a silk dress, Lucy a white one; each made evening fashion.

"They are both healthy," he said, "and may wear what they please. Look at their necks, compared to yours, Sibylla. I shall ask Mr. Verner to put all these thin dresses, these low bodies, behind the fire."

"He would only have the pleasure of paying for others to replace them," was the undutiful rejoinder. "Papa, I have enough trouble, without your turning against me."

Turning against her! Dr. West did not point out how purposeless were her words. His intention was to come in in the morning, and talk to her seriously of her state of health, and the precautions it was necessary to observe. He took a sip of his coffee, and turned to Lionel.

"I was about to ask you a superfluous question, Mr. Verner—whether that lost codicil has been heard of. But your leaving Verner's Pride is an answer."

"It has never been heard of," replied Lionel. "When John Massingbird returned and put in his claim— when he took possession, I may say, for the one was coeval with the other—the wanting of the codicil was indeed a grievance; far more than it had appeared at the time of its loss."

"You must regret it very much."

"I regret it always," he answered. "I regret it bitterly for Sibylla's sake."

"Papa," she cried, in deep emotion, her cheeks becoming crimson, her blue eyes flashing with an unnatural light, "if that codicil could be found it would save my life. Jan, in his rough, stupid way, tells me I am fretting myself into my grave. Perhaps I am. I want to go back to Verner's Pride."

It was not a pleasant subject to converse on; it was a subject utterly hopeless—and Dr. West sought one more genial. Ranging his eyes over the room, they fell upon Lord Garle, who was still talking with Decima and Lucy.

"Which of the two young ladies makes the viscount's attraction, Mr. Verner?"

Lionel smiled. "They do not take me into their confidence, sir; any one of the three."

"I am sure it is not Decima, papa," spoke up Sibylla. "She's as cold as a stone. I won't answer for its not being Lucy Tempest. Lord Garle comes here a good deal, and he and Lucy seem great friends. I often think he comes for Lucy."

"Then there's little doubt upon the point," observed the doctor, coming to a more rapid conclusion than the words really warranted. "Time was, Mr. Verner, when I thought that young lady would have been your wife."

"Who?" asked Lionel. But that he only asked the question in his confusion, without need, was evident; the tell-tale flush betrayed it. His pale face had turned red; red to the very roots of his hair.

"In those old days when you were ill, lying here, and Miss Tempest was so much with you, I fancied I saw the signs of a mutual attachment," continued the doctor. "I conclude I must have been mistaken."

"Little doubt of that, doctor," lightly answered Lionel, recovering his equanimity, though he could not yet recover his disturbed complexion, and laughing as he spoke.

Sibylla's greedy ears had drunk up the words, her sharp eyes had caught the conscious flush, and her jealous heart was making the most of it. At that unfortunate moment, as ill-luck had it, Lucy brought up the basket of cakes and held it out to Dr. West. Lionel rose to take it from her.

"I was taking your name in vain, Miss Tempest," said the complacent doctor. "Did you hear me?"

"No," replied Lucy, smiling. "What about?"

"I was telling Mr. Verner that in the old days I had deemed his choice was falling upon another, rather than my daughter. Do you remember, young lady?—in that long illness of his?"

Lucy did remember. And the remembrance, thus called suddenly before her, the words themselves, the presence of Lionel, all brought to her far more emotion than had arisen to him. Her throat heaved as with a spasm, and the startled colour dyed her face. Lionel saw it. Sibylla saw it.

"It proves to us how we may be mistaken, Miss Tempest," observed the doctor, who, from that habit of his, already hinted at, of never looking people in the face when he spoke to them, had failed to observe anything. "I hear there is a probability of this fair hand being appropriated by another. One who can enhance his value by coupling it with a coronet."

"Don't take the trouble, Lucy. I am holding it."

It was Lionel who spoke. In her confusion she had not loosed hold of the cake-basket, although he had taken it. Quietly, impassively, in the most unruffled manner spoke he, smiling carelessly. Only for a moment had his self-control been shaken. "Will you take a biscuit, Dr. West?" he asked; and the doctor chose one.

"Lucy, my dear, will you step here to me?"

The request came from the other end of the room, from Lady Verner. Lionel, who was about to place the cake-basket on the table, stopped and held out his arm to Lucy, to conduct her to his mother. They went forward, utterly unconscious that Sibylla was casting angry and jealous glances at them; conscious only that those sacred feelings in either heart, so well hid from the world, had been stirred to their very depths.

The door opened, and one of the servants entered. "Mr. Jan is wanted."

"Who's been taken ill now, I wonder?" cried Jan, descending from the arm of his mother's sofa, where he had been perched.

In the ante-room was Master Cheese, looking rueful.

"There's a message come from Squire Pidcock's," cried he in a most resentful tone. "Somebody's to attend immediately. Am I to go?"

"I suppose you'd faint at having to go, after being up to Miss Hautley's," returned Jan. "You'd never survive the two, should you?"

"Well, you know, Jan, it's a good mile and a half to Pidcock's, and I had to go to the other place without my tea," remonstrated Master Cheese.

"I dare say Miss Deb has given you your tea since you came home."

"But it's not like having it at the usual hour. And I couldn't finish it in comfort, when this message came."

"Be off back and finish it now, then," said Jan. And the young gentleman departed with alacrity, while Jan made the best of his way to Squire Pidcock's.

CHAPTER LXXVIII

AN APPEAL TO JOHN MASSINGBIRD

Lionel Verner walked home with Dr. West, later in the evening. "What do you think of Sibylla?" was his first question, before they had well quitted the gates.

"My opinion is not a favourable one, so far as I can judge at present," replied Dr. West. "She must not be crossed, Mr. Verner."

"Heaven is my witness that she is not crossed by me, Dr. West," was the reply of Lionel, given more earnestly than the occasion seemed to call for. "From the hour I married her, my whole life has been spent in the endeavour to shield her from crosses, so far as lies in the power of man; to cherish her in all care and tenderness. There are few husbands would bear with her—her peculiarities—as I have borne; as I will still bear. I say this to you, her father; I would say it to no one else. My chief regret, at the wrenching from me of Verner's Pride, is for Sibylla's sake."

"My dear sir, I honestly believe you. I know what Sibylla was at home, fretful, wayward, and restless; and those tendencies are not likely to be lessened, now disease has shown itself. I always feared it was in her constitution; that, in spite of all our care, she would follow her sisters. They fell off and died, you may remember, when they seemed most blooming. People talked freely—as I understood at the time—about my allowing her so suddenly to marry Frederick Massingbird; but my course was dictated by one sole motive—that it would give her the benefit of a sea voyage, which might prove invaluable to her constitution."

Lionel believed just as much of this as he liked. Dr. West was his wife's father, and, as such, he deferred to him. He remembered what had been told him by Sibylla; and he remembered the promise he had given her.

"It's a shocking pity that you are turned from Verner's Pride!" resumed the doctor.

"It is. But there's no help for it."

"Does Sibylla grieve after it very much? Has it any real effect, think you, upon her health?—as she seemed to intimate."

"She grieves, no doubt. She keeps up the grief, if you can understand it, Dr. West. Not a day passes, but she breaks into lamentations over the loss, complaining loudly and bitterly. Whether her health would not equally have failed at Verner's Pride, I am unable to say. I think it would."

"John Massingbird, under the circumstances, ought to give it up to you. It is rightfully yours. Sibylla's life—and she is his own cousin—may depend upon it: he ought not to keep it. But for the loss of the codicil, he would never have come to it."

"Of course he could not," assented Lionel. "It is that loss which has upset everything."

Dr. West fell into silence, and continued in it until his house was in view. Then he spoke again.

"What will you undertake to give me, Mr. Verner, if I can bring John Massingbird to hear reason, and re-establish you at Verner's Pride?"

"Not anything," answered Lionel. "Verner's Pride is John Massingbird's according to the law; therefore it cannot be mine. Neither would he resign it."

"I wonder whether it could be done by stratagem?" mused Dr. West. "Could we persuade him that the codicil has turned up?—or something of that? It would be very desirable for Sibylla."

"If I go back to Verner's Pride at all, sir, I go back by right; neither by purchase nor by stratagem," was the reply of Lionel. "Rely upon it, things set about in an underhand manner never prosper."

"I might get John Massingbird to give it up to you," continued the doctor, nodding his head thoughtfully, as if he had some scheme afloat in it. "I might get him to resign it to you, rents and residence and all, and betake himself off. You would give me a per centage?"

"Were John Massingbird to offer such to me to-morrow, of his own free will, I should decline it," decisively returned Lionel. "I have suffered too much from Verner's Pride ever to take possession of it again, except by indisputable right—a right in which I cannot be disturbed. Twice have I been turned from it, as you know. And the turning out has cost me more than the world deemed."

"But surely you would go back to it if you could, for Sibylla's sake?"

"Were I a rich man, able to rent Verner's Pride from John Massingbird, I might ask him to let it me, if it would gratify Sibylla. But, to return there as its master, on sufferance, liable to be expelled again at any moment—never! John Massingbird holds the right to Verner's Pride, and he will exercise it, for me."

"Then you will not accept my offer—to try and get you back again; and to make me a substantial honorarium if I do it?"

"I do not understand you, Dr. West. The question cannot arise."

"If I make it arise; and carry it out?"

"I beg your pardon—No."

It was an emphatic denial, and Dr. West may have felt himself foiled; as he had been foiled by Jan's confession of empty pockets, earlier in the evening.

"Nevertheless," observed he equably, as he shook hands with Lionel, before entering his own house, "I shall see John Massingbird to-morrow, and urge the hardship of the case upon him."

It was probably with that view that Dr. West proceeded early on the following morning to Verner's Pride, after his night of search, instead of sleep, astonishing John Massingbird not a little. That gentleman was enjoying himself in a comfortable sort of way in his bedroom. A substantial breakfast was laid out on a table by the bedside, while he, not risen, smoked a pipe as he lay, by way of whetting his appetite. Dr. West entered without ceremony.

"My stars!" uttered John, when he could believe his eyes. "It's never you, Uncle West! Did you drop from a balloon?"

Dr. West explained. That he had come over for a few hours' sojourn. The state of his dear daughter Sibylla was giving him considerable uneasiness, and he had put himself to the expense and inconvenience of a journey to see her, and judge of her state himself.

That there were a few trifling inaccuracies in this statement, inasmuch as that his daughter's state had had nothing to do with the doctor's journey, was of little consequence. It was all one to John Massingbird. He made a hasty toilette, and invited the doctor to take some breakfast.

Dr. West was nothing loth. He had breakfasted at home; but a breakfast more or less was nothing to Dr. West. He sat down to the table, and took a choice morsel of boned chicken on his plate.

"John, I have come up to talk to you about Verner's Pride."

"What about it?" asked John, speaking with his mouth full of devilled kidneys.

"The place is Lionel Verner's."

"How d'ye make out that?" asked John.

"That codicil revoked the will which left the estate to you. It gave it to him."

"But the codicil vanished," answered John.

"True. I was present at the consternation it excited. It disappeared in some unaccountably mysterious way; but there's no doubt that Mr. Verner died, believing the estate would go in its direct line—to Lionel. In fact, I know he did. Therefore you ought to act as though the codicil were in existence, and resign the estate to Lionel Verner."

The recommendation excessively tickled the fancy of John Massingbird. It set him laughing for five minutes.

"In short, you never ought to have attempted to enter upon it," continued Dr. West. "Will you resign it to him?"

"Uncle West, you'll kill me with laughter, if you joke like that," was the reply.

"I have little doubt that the codicil is still in existence," urged Dr. West. "I remember my impression at the time was that it was only mislaid, temporarily lost. If that codicil turned up, you would be obliged to quit."

"So I should," said John, with equanimity. "Let Lionel Verner produce it, and I'll vacate the next hour. That will never turn up: don't you fret yourself, Uncle West."

"Will you not resign it to him?"

"No, that I won't. Verner's Pride is mine by law. I should be a simpleton to give it up."

"Sibylla's pining for it," resumed the doctor, trying what a little pathetic pleading would do. "She will as surely die, unless she can come back to Verner's Pride, as that you and I are at breakfast here."

"If you ask my opinion, Uncle West, I should say that she'd die, any way. She looks like it. She's fading away just as the other two did. But she won't die a day sooner for being away from Verner's Pride; and she would not have lived an hour longer had she remained in it. That's my belief."

"Verner's Pride never was intended for you, John," cried the doctor. "Some freak caused Mr. Verner to will it away from Lionel; but he came to his senses before he died, and repaired the injury."

"Then I am so much the more obliged to the freak," was the good-humoured but uncompromising rejoinder of John Massingbird.

And more than that Dr. West could not make of him. John was evidently determined to stand by Verner's Pride. The doctor then changed his tactics, and tried a little business on his own account—that of borrowing from John Massingbird as much money as that gentleman would lend.

It was not much. John, in his laughing way, protested he was always "cleaned out." Nobody knew but himself—but he did not mind hinting it to Uncle West—the heaps of money he had been obliged to "shell out" before he could repose in tranquillity at Verner's Pride. There were back entanglements and present expenses, not to speak of sums spent in benevolence.

"Benevolence?" the doctor exclaimed.

"Yes, benevolence," John replied with a semi-grave face; he "had had to give away an unlimited number of bank-notes to the neighbourhood, as a recompense for having terrified it into fits." There were times when he thought he should have to come upon Lionel Verner for the mesne profits, he observed. A procedure which he was unwilling to resort to for two reasons: the reason was that Lionel possessed nothing to pay them with; the other, that he, John, never liked to be hard.

So the doctor had to content himself with a very trifling loan, compared with the sum he had fondly anticipated. He dropped some obscure hints that the evidence he could give, if he chose, with reference to the codicil, or rather what he knew to have been Mr. Verner's intentions, might go far to deprive his nephew John of the estate. But his nephew only laughed at him, and could not by any manner of means be induced to treat the hints as serious. A will was a will, he said, and Verner's Pride was indisputably his.

Altogether, taking one thing with another, Dr. West's visit to Deerham had not been quite so satisfactory as he had anticipated it might be made. After quitting John Massingbird, he went to Deerham Court and remained a few hours with Sibylla. The rest of the day he divided between his daughters in their sitting-room, and Jan in the surgery, taking his departure again from Deerham by the night train.

And Deborah and Amilly, drowned in tears, said his visit could be compared only to the flash of a comet's tail; no sooner seen than gone again.

CHAPTER LXXIX

A SIN AND A SHAME

As the spring advanced, sickness began to prevail in Deerham. The previous autumn, the season when the enemy chiefly loved to show itself, had been comparatively free, but he appeared to be about taking his revenge now. In every third house people were down with ague and fever. Men who ought to be strong for their daily toil, women whose services were wanted for their households and their families, children whose young frames were unfitted to battle with it, were indiscriminately attacked. It was capricious as a summer's wind. In some dwellings it would be the strongest and bravest that were singled out; in some the weakest and most delicate. Jan was worked off his legs. Those necessary appendages to active Jan generally were exercised pretty well; but Jan could not remember the time when they had been worked as they were now. Jan grew cross. Not at the amount of work: it may be questioned whether Jan did not rather prefer that, than the contrary; but at the prevailing state of things. "It's a sin and a shame that precautions are not taken against this periodical sickness," said Jan, speaking out more forcibly than was his wont. "If the place were drained and the dwellings improved, the ague would run away to more congenial quarters. I'd not own Verner's Pride, unless I could show myself fit to be its owner."

The shaft may have been levelled at John Massingbird, but Lionel Verner took it to himself. How full of self-reproach he was, he alone knew. He had had the power in his own hands to make these improvements, and in some manner or other he had let the time slip by: now, the power was wrested from him. It is ever so. Golden opportunities come into our hands, and we look at them complacently, and—do not use them. Bitter regrets, sometimes remorse, take their places when they have flitted away for ever; but neither the regret nor the remorse can recall the opportunity lost.

Lionel pressed the necessity upon John Massingbird. It was all he could do now. John received it with complacent good-humour, and laughed at Lionel for making the request. But that was all.

"Set about draining Clay Lane, and build up new tenements in place of the old?" cried he. "What next, Lionel?"

"Look at the sickness the present state of things brings," returned Lionel. "It is what ought to have been altered years ago."

"Ah!" said John. "Why didn't you alter it, then, when you had Verner's Pride?"

"You may well ask! It was my first thought when I came into the estate. I would set about that; I would set about other improvements. Some I did carry out, as you know; but these, the most needful, I left in abeyance. It lies on my conscience now."

They were in the study. Lionel was at the desk, some papers before him; John Massingbird had lounged in for a chat—as he was fond of doing, to the interruption of Lionel. He was leaning against the door-post; his attire not precisely such that a gentleman might choose, who wished to send his photograph to make a morning call. His pantaloons were hitched up by a belt; braces, John said, were not fashionable at the diggings, and he had learned the comfort of doing without them; a loose sort of round drab coat without tails; no waistcoat; a round brown hat, much bent, and a pair of slippers. Such was John Massingbird's favourite costume, and he might be seen in it at all hours of the day. When he wanted to go abroad, his toilette was made, as the French say, by the exchanging of the slippers for boots, and the taking in his hand a club stick. John's whiskers were growing again, and promised to be as fine a pair as he had worn before going out to Australia; and now he was letting his beard grow, but it looked very grim and stubbly. Truth to say, a stranger passing through the village and casting his eyes on Mr. John Massingbird, would have taken him to be a stable helper, rather than the master of that fine place, Verner's Pride. Just now he had a clay pipe in his mouth, its stem little more than an inch long.

"Do you mean to assert that you'd set about these improvements, as you call them, were you to come again into Verner's Pride?" asked he of Lionel.

"I believe I should. I would say unhesitatingly that I should, save for past experience," continued Lionel. "Before my uncle died, I knew how necessary it was that they should be made, and I as much believed that I should set about them the instant I came into the estate, as that I believe I am now talking to you. But you see I did not begin them. It has taught me to be chary of making assertions beforehand."

"I suppose you think you'd do it?"

"If I know anything of my own resolution I should do it. Were Verner's Pride to lapse to me to-morrow, I believe I should set about it the next day. But," Lionel added after a short pause, "there's no probability of its lapsing to me. Therefore I want you to set about it in my place."

"I can't afford it," replied John Massingbird.

"Nonsense! I wish I could afford things a quarter as well as you."

"I tell you I can't," reiterated John, taking his pipe from his mouth to make a spittoon of the carpet— another convenience he had learned at the diggings. "I'm sure I don't know how on earth my money goes; I never did know all my life how money went; but, go it does. When Fred and I were little chaps, some benevolent old soul tipped us half a crown apiece. Mine was gone by middle-day, and I could not account for more than ninepence of it—never could to this day. Fred, at the end of a twelvemonth's time, had got his half-crown still snug in his pocket. Had Fred come into Verner's Pride, he'd have lived in style on a thousand of his income yearly, and put by the rest."

He never would, Sibylla being his wife, thought Lionel. But he did not say it to John Massingbird.

"An estate, such as this, brings its duties with it, John," said he. "Remember those poor people down with sickness."

"Bother duty," returned John. "Look here, Lionel; you waste your breath and your words. I have not got the money to spend upon it; how do you know, old fellow, what my private expenses may be? And if I had the money, I should not do it," he continued. "The present state of the property was deemed good enough by Mr. Verner; it was so deemed (if we may judge by facts) by Mr. Lionel Verner; and it is deemed good enough by John Massingbird. It is not he who's going to have the cost thrown upon him. So let it drop."

There was no resource but to let it drop; for that he was in full earnest, Lionel saw. John continued—

"You can save up the alterations for yourself, to be commenced when you come into the property. A nice bonne bouche of outlay for you to contemplate."

"I don't look to come into it," replied Lionel.

"The probabilities are that you will come into it," returned John Massingbird, more seriously than he often spoke. "Barring getting shot, or run over by a railway train, you'll make old bones, you will. You have never played with your constitution; I have, in more ways than one: and in bare years I have considerably the advantage of you. Psha! when I am a skeleton in my coffin, you'll still be a young man. You can make your cherished alterations then."

"You may well say in more ways than one," returned Lionel, half joking, half serious. "There's smoking among the catalogue. How many pipes do you smoke in a day? Fifty?"

"Why didn't you say day and night? Tynn lives in perpetual torment lest my bed should ignite some night, and burn up him, as well as Verner's Pride. I go to sleep sometimes with my pipe in my mouth as we do at the diggings. Now and then I feel half inclined to make a rush back there. It suited me better than this."

Lionel bent over some papers that were before him—a hint that he had business to do. Mr. Massingbird did not take it. He began filling his pipe again, scattering the tobacco on the ground wholesale in the process, and talking at the same time.

"I say, Lionel, why did old Verner leave the place away from you? Have you ever wondered?"

Lionel glanced up at him in surprise.

"Have I ever ceased wondering, you might have said. I don't know why he did."

"Did he never give you a reason—or an explanation?"

"Nothing of the sort. Except—yes, except a trifle. Some time after his death, Mrs. Tynn discovered a formidable-looking packet in one of his drawers, sealed and directed to me. She thought it was the missing codicil; so did I, until I opened it. It proved to contain nothing but a glove; one of my old gloves, and a few lines from my uncle. They were to the effect that when I received the glove I should know why he disinherited me."

"And did you know?" asked John Massingbird, applying a light to his pipe.

"Not in the least. It left the affair more obscure, if possible, than it had been before. I suppose I never shall know now."

"Never's a long day," cried John Massingbird. "But you told me about this glove affair before."

"Did I? Oh, I remember. When you first returned. That is all the explanation I have ever had."

"It was not much," said John. "Dickens take this pipe! It won't draw. Where's my knife?"

Not finding his knife about him, he went off to look for it, dragging his slippers along the hall in his usual lazy fashion. Lionel, glad of the respite, applied himself to his work.

CHAPTER LXXX

RECOLLECTIONS OF A NIGHT GONE BY

One was dying in Deerham, but not of ague, and that was old Matthew Frost. Matthew was dying of old age, to which we must all succumb, if we live long enough.

April was in, and the fever and ague were getting better. News was brought to Lionel one morning that old Matthew was not expected to last through the day. Jan entered the breakfast-room at Deerham

Court and told him so. Lionel had been starting to Verner's Pride; but he changed his course towards Clay Lane.

"Jan," said he, as he was turning away, "I wish you'd go up and see Sibylla. I am sure she is very ill."

"I'll go if you like," said Jan. "But there's no use in it. She won't listen to a word I say, or attend to a single direction that I give. Hayes told me, when he came over last week, that it was the same with him. She persists to him, as she does to me, that she has no need of medicine or care; that she is quite well."

"I am aware she persists in it," replied Lionel, "but I feel sure she is very ill."

"I know she is," said Jan, "She's worse than folks think for. Perhaps you amongst them, Lionel. I'll go up to her." He turned back to the house as he spoke, and Lionel went on to Clay Lane.

Old Matthew was lying on his bed, very peaceful—peaceful as to his inward and his outward state. Though exceedingly weak, gradually sinking, he retained both speech and intellect: he was passing away without pain, and with his faculties about him. What a happy death-bed, when all is peace within! His dim eyes lighted up with pleasure when he saw Mr. Verner.

"Have you come to see the last of me, sir?" he asked, as Lionel took his hand.

"Not quite the last yet, I hope, Matthew."

"Don't hope it, sir; nor wish it, neither," returned the old man, lifting his hand with a deprecatory movement. "I'm on the threshold of a better world, sir, and I'd not turn back to this, if God was to give me the choice of it. I'm going to my rest, sir. Like as my bed has waited for me and been welcome to me after a hard day's toil, so is my rest now at hand after my life's toil. It is as surely waiting for me as ever was my bed; and I am longing to get to it."

Lionel looked down at the calm, serene face, fair and smooth yet. The skin was drawn tight over it, especially over the well-formed nose, and the white locks fell on the pillow behind. It may be wrong to say there was a holy expression pervading the face; but it certainly gave that impression to Lionel Verner.

"I wish all the world—when their time comes—could die as you are dying, Matthew!" he exclaimed, in the impulse of his heart.

"Sir, all might, if they'd only live for it. It's many a year ago now, Mr. Lionel, that I learned to make a friend of God: He has stood me in good need. And those that do learn to make a friend of Him, sir, don't fear to go to Him."

Lionel drew forward a chair and sat down in it. The old man continued—

"Things seemed to have been smoothed for me in a wonderful manner, sir. My great trouble, of late years, has been Robin. I feared how it might be with him when I went away and left him here alone; for you know the queer way he has been in, sir, since that great misfortune; and I have been a bit of a check on him, keeping him, as may be said, within bounds. Well, that trouble is done away for me, sir; Robin he has got his mind at rest, and he won't break out again. In a short while I am in hopes he'll be quite what he used to be."

"Matthew, it was my firm intention to continue your annuity to Robin," spoke Lionel. "I am sorry the power to do so has been taken from me. You know that it will not rest with me now, but with Mr. Massingbird. I fear he is not likely to continue it."

"Don't regret it, sir. Robin, I say, is growing to be an industrious man again, and he can get a living well. If he had stopped a half-dazed-do-nothing, he might have wanted that, or some other help; but it isn't so. His trouble's at rest, and his old energies are coming back to him. It seems to have left my mind at leisure, sir; and I can go away, praying for the souls of my poor daughter and of Frederick Massingbird."

The name—his—aroused the attention of Lionel; more, perhaps, than he would have cared to confess. But his voice and manner retained their quiet calmness.

"What did you say, Matthew?"

"It was him, sir; Mr. Frederick Massingbird. It was nobody else."

Down deep in Lionel Verner's heart there had lain a conviction, almost ever since that fatal night, that the man had been no other than the one now spoken of, the younger Massingbird. Why the impression should have come to him he could not have told at the time; something, perhaps, in Frederick's manner had given rise to it. On the night before John Massingbird's departure for Australia, after the long interview he had held with Mr. Verner in the study, which was broken in upon by Lionel on the part of Robin Frost, the three young men—the Massingbirds and Lionel—had subsequently remained together, discussing the tragedy. In that interview it was that a sudden doubt of Frederick Massingbird entered the mind of Lionel. It was impossible for him to tell why. He only knew that the impression—nay, it were more correct to say the conviction, seized hold upon him, never to be eradicated. Perhaps something strange in Frederick's manner awoke it. Lionel surmised not how far his guilt might have extended; but that he was the guilty one, he fully believed. It was not his business to proclaim this; had it been a certainty, instead of a fancy, Lionel would not have made it his business. But when Frederick Massingbird was on the point of marrying Sibylla, then Lionel partially broke through his reserve, and asked him whether he had nothing on his conscience that ought to prevent his making her his wife. Frederick answered freely and frankly, to all appearance, and for the moment Lionel's doubts were dissipated: only, however, to return afterwards with increased force. Consequently he was not surprised to hear this said, though surprised at Matthew Frost's knowing it.

"How did you hear it, Matthew?" he asked.

"Robin got at it, sir. Poor Robin, he was altogether on the wrong scent for a long while, thinking it was Mr. John; but it's set right now, and Robin, he's at ease. May Heaven have mercy upon Frederick Massingbird!"

Successful rival though he had proved to him, guilty man that he had been, Lionel heartily echoed the prayer. He asked no more questions of the old man upon the subject, but afterwards, when he was going out, he met Robin and stopped him.

"Robin, what is this that your father has been telling me about Frederick Massingbird?"

"Only to think of it!" was Robin's response, growing somewhat excited. "To think how our ways get balked! I had swore to be revenged—as you know, sir—and now the power of revenge is took from me! He's gone where my revenge can't reach him. It's of no good—I see it—for us to plan. Our plans'll never be carried out, if they don't please God."

"And it was Frederick Massingbird?"

"It was Frederick Massingbird," assented Robin, his breath coming thick and fast with agitation. "We had got but one little ewe lamb, and he must leave the world that was open to him, and pick her up, and destroy her! I ain't calm yet to talk of it, sir."

"But how did you ascertain this? Your suspicions, you know, were directed to Mr. John Massingbird: wrongly, as I believed; as I told you."

"Yes, they were wrong," said Robin. "I was put upon the wrong scent: but not wilfully. You might remember a dairy wench that lived at Verner's Pride in them days, sir—Dolly, her name was; she that went and got married after to Joe Stubbs, Mr. Bitterworth's wagoner. It was she told me, sir. I used to be up there a good bit with Stubbs, and one day when I was sick and ill there, the wife told me she had seen one of the gentlemen come from the Willow Pool that past night. I pressed her to tell me which of them, and at first she said she couldn't, and then she said it was Mr. John. I never thought but she told me right, but it seems—as she confesses now—that she only fixed on him to satisfy me, and because she thought he was dead, over in Australia, and it wouldn't matter if she did say it. I worried her life out over it, she says; and it's like I did. She says now, if she was put upon her Bible oath, she couldn't say which of the gentlemen it was, more nor the other; but she did see one of 'em."

"But this is not telling me how you know it to have been Mr. Frederick, Robin."

"I learned it from Mr. John," was the reply. "When he come back I saw him; I knew it was him; and I got a gun and watched for him. I meant to take my revenge, sir. Roy, he found me out; and in a night or two, he brought me face to face with Mr. John, and Mr. John he told me the truth. But he'd only tell it me upon my giving him my promise not to expose his brother. So I'm balked even of that revenge. I had always counted on the exposing of the man," added Robin in a dreamy tone, as if he were looking back into the past; "when I thought it was Mr. John, I only waited for Luke Roy to come home, that I might expose him. I judged that Luke, being so much with him in Australia, might have heard a slip word drop as would confirm it. Somehow, though I thought Dolly Stubbs spoke truth, I didn't feel so sure of her as to noise it abroad."

"You say it was Mr. John Massingbird who told you it was his brother?"

"He told me, sir. He told me at Roy's, when he was a-hiding there. When the folks here was going mad about the ghost, I knowed who the ghost was, and had my laugh at 'em. It seemed that I could laugh then," added Robin, looking at Mr. Verner, as if he deemed an apology for the words necessary. "My mind was set at rest."

Did a thought cross Lionel Verner that John Massingbird, finding his own life in peril from Robin's violence, had thrown the blame upon his brother falsely? It might have done so, but for his own deeply-rooted suspicions. That John would not be scrupulously regardful of truth, he believed, where his own turn was to be served. Lionel, at any rate, felt that he should like, for his own satisfaction, to have the matter set at rest, and he took his way to Verner's Pride.

John Massingbird, his costume not improved in elegance, or his clay pipe in length, was lounging at his ease on one of the amber damask satin couches of the drawing-room, his feet on the back of a proximate chair, and his slippers fallen off on the carpet. A copious tumbler of rum-and-water—his favourite beverage since his return—was on a table, handy; and there he lay enjoying his ease.

"Hollo, old fellow! How are you?" was his greeting to Lionel, given without changing his position in the least.

"Massingbird, I want to speak to you," rejoined Lionel. "I have been to see old Matthew Frost, and he has said something which surprises me—"

"The old man's about to make a start of it, I hear," was the interruption of Mr. Massingbird.

"He cannot last long. He has been speaking—naturally—of that unhappy business of his daughter's. He lays it to the door of Frederick; and Robin tells me he had the information from you."

"I was obliged to give it him, in self-defence," said John Massingbird. "The fellow had got it into his head, in some unaccountable manner, that I was the black sheep, and was prowling about with a gun, ready capped and loaded, to put a bullet into me. I don't set so much store by my life as some fidgets do, but it's not pleasant to be shot off in that summary fashion. So I sent for Mr. Robin and satisfied him that he was making the same blunder that Deerham just then was making—mistaking one brother for the other."

"Was it Frederick?"

"It was."

"Did you know it at the time?"

"No. Never suspected him at all."

"Then how did you learn it afterwards?"

John Massingbird took his legs from the chair. He rose, and brought himself to an anchor on a seat facing Lionel, puffing still at his incessant pipe.

"I don't mind trusting you, old chap, being one of us, and I couldn't help trusting Robin Frost. Roy, he knew it before—at least, his wife did; which amounts to something of the same; and she spoke of it to me. I have ordered them to keep a close tongue, under pain of unheard-of penalties—which I should never inflict; but it's as well to let poor Fred's memory rest in quiet and good odour. I believe honestly it's the only scrape of the sort he ever got into. He was cold and cautious."

"But how did you learn it?" reiterated Lionel.

"I'll tell you. I learned it from Luke Roy."

"From Luke Roy!" repeated Lionel, more at sea than before.

"Do you remember that I had sent Luke on to London a few days before this happened? He was to get things forward for our voyage. He was fou—as the French say—after Rachel; and what did he do but come back again in secret, to get a last look at her, perhaps a word. It happened to be this very night, and Luke was a partial witness to the scene at the Willow Pond. He saw and heard her meeting with Frederick; heard quite enough to know that there was no chance for him; and he was stealing away, leaving Fred and Rachel at the termination of their quarrel, when he met his mother. She knew him, it seems, and to that encounter we are indebted for her display when before Mr. Verner, and her lame account of the 'ghost.' You must recollect it. She got up the ghost tale to excuse her own terror; to throw the scent off Luke. The woman says her life, since, has been that of a martyr, ever fearing that suspicion might fall upon her son. She recognised him beyond doubt; and nearly died with the consternation. He glided off, never speaking to her, but the fear and consternation remained. She recognised, too, she says, the voice of Frederick as the one that was quarrelling; but she did not dare confess it. For one thing, she knew not how far Luke might be implicated."

Lionel leaned his brow on his hand, deep in thought. "How far was Frederick implicated?" he asked in a low tone. "Did he—did he put her into the pond?"

"No!" burst forth John Massingbird, with a vehemence that sent the ashes of his pipe flying. "Fred would not be guilty of such a crime as that, any more than you or I would. He had—he had made vows to the girl, and broken them; and that was the extent of it. No such great sin, after all, or it wouldn't be so fashionable a one," carelessly added John Massingbird.

Lionel waited in silence.

"By what Luke could gather," went on John, "it appeared that Rachel had seen Fred that night with his cousin Sibylla—your wife now. What she had seen or heard, goodness knows; but enough to prove to her that Fred's real love was given to Sibylla, that she was his contemplated wife. It drove Rachel mad: Fred had probably filled her up with the idea that the honour was destined for herself. Men are deceivers ever, and women soft, you know, Lionel."

"And they quarrelled over it?"

"They quarrelled over it. Rachel, awakened out of her credulity, met him with bitter reproaches. Luke could not hear what was said towards its close. The meeting—no doubt a concerted one—had been in that grove in view of the Willow Pond, the very spot that Master Luke had chosen for his own hiding-place. They left it and walked towards Verner's Pride, disputing vehemently; Roy made off the other way, and the last he saw of them, when they were nearly out of sight, was a final explosion, in which they parted. Fred set off to run towards Verner's Pride, and Rachel came flying back towards the pond. There's not a shadow of doubt that in her passion, her unhappy state of feeling, she flung herself in; and if Luke had only waited two minutes longer, he might have been in at the death—as we say by the foxes. That's the solution of what has puzzled Deerham for years, Lionel."

"Could Luke not have saved her?"

"He never knew she was in the pond. Whether the unexpected sight of his mother scared his senses away, he has often wondered; but he heard neither the splash in the water nor the shriek. He made off, pretty quick, he says, for fear his mother should attempt to stop him, or proclaim his presence aloud—an inconvenient procedure, since he was supposed to be in London. Luke never knew of her death until we were on the voyage. I got to London only in time to go on board the ship in the docks, and we had been out for days at sea before he learned that Rachel was dead, or I that Luke had been down, on the sly, to Deerham. I had to get over that precious sea-sickness before entering upon that, or any other talk, I can tell you. It's a shame it should attack men!"

"I suspected Fred at the time," said Lionel.

"You did! Well, I did not. My suspicions had turned to a very different quarter."

"Upon whom?"

"Oh, bother! where's the good of ripping it up, now it's over and done with?" retorted John Massingbird. "There's the paper of baccy by your elbow, chum. Chuck it here."

CHAPTER LXXXI

A CRISIS IN SIBYLLA'S LIFE

Sibylla Verner improved neither in health nor in temper. Body and mind were alike diseased. As the spring had advanced, her weakness appeared to increase; the symptoms of consumption became more palpable. She would not allow that she was ill; she, no doubt, thought that there was nothing serious the matter with her; nothing, as she told everybody, but the vexing after Verner's Pride.

Dr. West had expressed an opinion that her irritability, which she could neither conceal nor check, was the result of her state of health. He was very likely right. One thing was certain; that since she grew weaker and worse, this unhappy frame of mind had greatly increased. The whole business of her life appeared to be to grumble, to be cross, snappish, fretful. If her body was diseased, most decidedly her temper was also. The great grievance of quitting Verner's Pride she made a plea for the indulgence of every complaint under the sun. She could no longer gather a gay crowd of visitors around her; she had lost the opportunity with Verner's Pride; she could no longer indulge in unlimited orders for new dresses and bonnets, and other charming adjuncts to the toilette, without reference to how they were to be paid for; she had not a dozen servants at her beck and call; and if she wanted to pay a visit, there was no elegant equipage, the admiration of all beholders, to convey her. She had lost all with Verner's Pride. Not a day—scarcely an hour—passed, but one or other, or all of these vexations, were made the subject of fretful, open repining. Not to Lady Verner—Sibylla would not have dared to annoy her; not to Decima or to Lucy; but to her husband. How weary his ear was, how weary his spirit, no tongue could tell. She tried him in every way—she did nothing but find fault with him. When he stayed out, she grumbled at him for staying, meeting him with reproaches on his entrance; when he remained in, she grumbled at him. In her sad frame of mind it was essential—there are frames of mind in which it is essential, as the medical men will tell you, where the sufferer cannot help it—that she should have some object on whom to vent her irritability. Not being in her own house, there was but her husband. He was the only one sufficiently nearly connected with her to whom the courtesies of life could be dispensed with; and therefore he came in for it all. At Verner's Pride there would have been her servants to share it with him; at Dr. West's there would have been her sisters; at Lady Verner's there was her husband alone. Times upon times Lionel felt inclined to run away; as the disobedient boys run to sea.

The little hint, dropped by Dr. West, touching the past, had not been without its fruits in Sibylla's mind. It lay and smouldered there. Had Lionel been attached to Lucy?—had there been love-scenes, love-making between them? Sibylla asked herself the questions ten times in a day. Now and then she let drop a sharp, acrid bit of venom to him—his "old love, Lucy." Lionel would receive it with impassibility, never answering.

On the day spoken of in the last chapter, when Matthew Frost was dying, she was more ill at ease, more intensely irritable, than usual. Lady Verner had gone with some friends to Heartburg, and was not expected home until night; Decima and Lucy walked out in the afternoon, and Sibylla was alone. Lionel had not been home since he went out in the morning to see Matthew Frost. The fact was Lionel had had a busy day of it: what with old Matthew and what with his conversation with John Massingbird afterwards, certain work which ought to have been done in the morning he had left till the afternoon. It was nothing unusual for him to be out all day; but Sibylla was choosing to make his being out on this day an unusual grievance. As the hours of the afternoon passed on and on, and it grew late, and nobody appeared, she could scarcely suppress her temper, her restlessness. She was a bad one to be alone; had never liked to be alone for five minutes in her life; and thence perhaps the secret of her having made so much of a companion of her maid, Benoite. In point of fact, Sibylla Verner had no resources within herself; and she made up for the want by indulging in her naturally bad temper.

Where were they? Where was Decima? Where was Lucy? Above all, where was Lionel? Sibylla, not being able to answer the questions, suddenly began to get up a pretty little plot of imagination—that Lucy and Lionel were somewhere together. Had Sibylla possessed one of Sam Weller's patent self-acting microscopes, able to afford a view through space and stairs and deal doors, she might have seen Lionel seated alone in the study at Verner's Pride, amidst his leases and papers; and Lucy in Clay Lane, paying visits with Decima from cottage to cottage. Not possessing one of those admirable instruments—if somebody at the West End would but set up a stock of them for sale, what a lot of customers he'd have!—Sibylla was content to cherish the mental view she had conjured up, and to improve upon it. All the afternoon she kept improving upon it, until she worked herself up to that agreeable pitch of distorted excitement when the mind does not know what is real, and what fancy. It was a regular April day; one of sunshine and storm; now the sun shining out bright and clear; now, the rain pattering against the panes; and Sibylla wandered from room to room, upstairs and down, as stormy as the weather.

Had her dreams been types of fact? Upon glancing from the window, during a sharper shower than any they had yet had, she saw her husband coming in at the large gates, Lucy Tempest on his arm, over whom he was holding an umbrella. They were walking slowly; conversing, as it seemed, confidentially. It was quite enough for Mrs. Verner.

But it was a very innocent, accidental meeting, and the confidential conversation was only about the state of poor old Matthew Frost. Lionel had taken Clay Lane on his road home for the purpose of inquiring after old Matthew. There, standing in the kitchen, he found Lucy. Decima was with the old man, and it was uncertain how long she would stay with him; and Lucy, who had no umbrella, was waiting for the shower to be over to get back to Deerham Court. Lionel offered her the shelter of his. As they advanced through the courtyard, Lucy saw Sibylla at the small drawing-room window—the ante-room, as it was called—and nodded a smiling greeting to her. She did not return it, and Lionel saw that his wife looked black as night.

They came in, Lucy untying her bonnet-strings, and addressing Sibylla in a pleasant tone—

"What a sharp storm!" she said. "And I think it means to last, for there seems no sign of its clearing up. I don't know how I should have come, but for Mr. Verner's umbrella."

No reply from Mrs. Verner.

"Decima is with old Matthew Frost," continued Lucy, passing into the drawing-room; "she desired that we would not wait dinner for her."

Then began Sibylla. She turned upon Lionel in a state of perfect fury, her temper, like a torrent, bearing down all before it—all decency, all consideration.

"Where have you been? You and she?"

"Do you allude to Lucy?" he asked, pausing before he replied, and looking at her with surprise. "We have been nowhere. I saw her at old Frost's as I came by, and brought her home."

"It is a falsehood!" raved Sibylla. "You are carrying on a secret intimacy with each other. I have been blind long enough, but—"

Lionel caught her arm, pointing in stern silence to the drawing-room door, which was not closed, his white face betraying his inward agitation.

"She is there!" he whispered. "She can hear you."

But Sibylla's passion was terrible—not to be controlled. All the courtesies of life were lost sight of—its social usages were as nothing. She flung Lionel's hand away from her.

"I hope she can hear me!" broke like a torrent from her trembling lips. "It is time she heard, and others also! I have been blind, I say, long enough. But for papa, I might have gone on in my blindness to the end."

How was he to stop it? That Lucy must hear every word as plainly as he did, he knew; words that fell upon his ear, and blistered them. There was no egress for her—no other door—she was there in a cage, as may be said. He did what was the best to be done under the circumstances; he walked into the presence of Lucy, leaving Sibylla to herself.

At least it might have been the best in some cases. It was not in this. Sibylla, lost in that moment to all sense of the respect due to herself, to her husband, to Lucy, allowed her wild fancies, her passion, to over-master everything; and she followed him in. Her eyes blazing, her cheeks aflame, she planted herself in front of Lucy.

"Are you not ashamed of yourself, Lucy Tempest, to wile my husband from me?"

Lucy looked perfectly aghast. That she thought Mrs. Verner had suddenly gone mad, may be excused to her. A movement of fear escaped her, and she drew involuntary nearer to Lionel, as if for protection.

"No! you shan't go to him! There has been enough of it. You shall not side with him against me! He is my husband! How dare you forget it! You are killing me amongst you."

"I—don't—know—what—you—mean, Mrs. Verner," gasped Lucy, the words coming in jerks from her bloodless lips.

"Can you deny that he cares for you more than he does for me? That you care for him in return? Can not you—"!

"Be silent, Sibylla!" burst forth Lionel. "Do you know that you are speaking to Miss Tempest?"

"I won't be silent!" she reiterated, her voice rising to a scream. "Who is Lucy Tempest that you should care for her? You know you do! and you know that you meant to marry her once! Is it—"

Pushing his wife on a chair, though gently, with one arm, Lionel caught the hand of Lucy, and placed it within the other, his chest heaving with emotion. He led her out of the room and through the ante-room, in silence to the door, halting there. She was shaking all over, and the tears were coursing down her cheeks. He took both her hands in his, his action one of deprecating entreaty, his words falling in the tenderest accents from between his bloodless lips.

"Will you bear for my sake, Lucy? She is my wife. Heaven knows, upon any other I would retort the insult."

How Lucy's heart was wrung!—wrung for him. The insult to herself she could afford to ignore; being innocent, it fell with very slender force; but she felt keenly for his broken peace. Had it been to save her life, she could not help returning the pressure of his hand as she looked up to him her affirmative answer; and she saw no wrong or harm in the pressure. Lionel closed the door upon her, and returned to his wife.

A change had come over Sibylla. She had thrown herself at full length on a sofa, and was beginning to sob. He went up to her, and spoke gravely, not unkindly, his arms folded before him.

"Sibylla, when is this line of conduct to cease? I am nearly wearied out—nearly," he repeated, putting his hand to his brow, "wearied out. If I could bear the exposure for myself, I cannot bear it for my wife."

She rose up and sat down on the sofa facing him. The hectic of her cheeks had turned to scarlet.

"You do love her! You care for her more than you care for me. Can you deny it?"

"What part of my conduct has ever told you so?"

"I don't care for conduct," she fractiously retorted, "I remember what papa said, and that's enough. He said he saw how it was in the old days—that you loved her. What business had you to love her?"

"Stay, Sibylla! Carry your reflections back, and answer yourself. In those old days, when both of you were before me to choose—at any rate, to ask—I chose you, leaving her. Is it not a sufficient answer?"

Sibylla threw back her head on the sofa-frame, and began to cry.

"From the hour that I made you my wife, I have striven to do my duty by you, tenderly as husband can do it. Why do you force me to reiterate this declaration, which I have made before?" he added, his face working with emotion. "Neither by word nor action have I been false to you. I have never, for the briefest moment, been guilty behind your back of that which I would not be guilty of in your presence. No! my allegiance of duty has never swerved from you. So help me Heaven!"

"You can't swear to me that you don't love her?" was Sibylla's retort.

It appeared that he did not intend to swear it. He went and stood against the mantel-piece, in his old favourite attitude, leaning his elbow on it and his face upon his hand—a face that betrayed his inward pain. Sibylla began again: to tantalise him seemed a necessity of her life.

"I might have expected trouble when I consented to marry you. Rachel Frost's fate might have taught me the lesson."

"Stay," said Lionel, lifting his head. "It is not the first hint of the sort that you have given me. Tell me honestly what it is you mean."

"You need not ask; you know already. Rachel owed her disgrace to you."

Lionel paused a moment before he rejoined. When he did, it was in a quiet tone.

"Do you speak from your own opinion?"

"No, I don't. The secret was intrusted to me."

"By whom? You must tell me, Sibylla."

"I don't know why I should not," she slowly said, as if in deliberation. "My husband trusted me with it."

"Do you allude to Frederick Massingbird?" asked Lionel, in a tone whose coldness he could not help.

"Yes, I do. He was my husband," she resentfully added. "One day, on the voyage to Australia, he dropped a word that made me think he knew something about that business of Rachel's, and I teased him to tell me who it was who had played the rogue. He said it was Lionel Verner."

A pause. But for Lionel's admirable disposition, how terribly he might have retorted upon her, knowing what he had learned that day.

"Did he tell you I had completed the roguery by pushing her into the pond?" he inquired.

"I don't know. I don't remember. Perhaps he did."

"And—doubting it—you could marry me!" quietly remarked Lionel.

She made no answer.

"Let me set you right on that point once for all, then," he continued. "I was innocent as you. I had nothing to do with it. Rachel and her father were held in too great respect by my uncle—nay, by me, I may add—for me to offer her anything but respect. You were misinformed, Sibylla."

She laughed scornfully. "It is easy to say so."

"As it was for Frederick Massingbird to say to you what he did."

"If it came to the choice," she retorted, "I'd rather believe him than you."

Bitter aggravation lay in her tone, bitter aggravation in her gesture. Was Lionel tempted to forget himself?—to set her right? If so, he beat the temptation down. All men would not have been so forbearing.

"Sibylla, I have told you truth," he simply said.

"Which is as much as to say that Fred told—" she was vehemently beginning when the words were stopped by the entrance of John Massingbird. John, caught in the shower near Deerham Court, made no scruple of running to it for shelter, and was in time to witness Sibylla's angry tones and inflamed face.

What precisely happened Lionel could never afterwards recall. He remembered John's free and easy salutation, "What's the row?"—he remembered Sibylla's torrent of words in answer. As little given to reticence or delicacy in the presence of her cousin, as she had been in that of Lucy Tempest, she renewed her accusation of her husband with regard to Rachel: she called on him—John—to bear testimony that Fred was truthful. And Lionel remembered little more until he saw Sibylla lying back gasping, the blood pouring from her mouth.

John Massingbird—perhaps in his eagerness to contradict her as much as in his regard to make known the truth—had answered her all too effectually before Lionel could stop him. Words that burned into the brain of Sibylla Verner, and turned the current of her life's pulses.

It was her husband of that voyage, Frederick Massingbird, who had brought the evil upon Rachel, who had been with her by the pond that night.

As the words left John Massingbird's lips, she rose up, and stood staring at him. Presently she essayed to speak, but not a sound issued from her drawn lips. Whether passion impeded her utterance, or startled dismay, or whether it may have been any physical impediment, it was evident that she could not get the words out.

Fighting her hands on the empty air, fighting for breath or for speech, so she remained for a passing space; and then the blood began to trickle from her mouth. The excitement had caused her to burst a blood-vessel.

Lionel crossed over to her: her best support. He held her in his arms, tenderly and considerately, as though she had never given him an unwifely word. Stretching out his other hand to the bell, he rang it loudly. And then he looked at Mr. Massingbird.

"Run for your life," he whispered. "Get Jan here."

CHAPTER LXXXII

TRYING ON WREATHS

The months went on, and Deerham was in a commotion: not the Clay Lane part of it, of whom I think you have mostly heard, but that more refined if less useful portion, represented by Lady Verner, the Elmsleys, the Bitterworths, and other of the aristocracy congregating in its environs.

Summer had long come in, and was now on the wane; and Sir Edmund Hautley, the only son and heir of Sir Rufus, was expected home. He had quitted the service, had made the overland route, and was now halting in Paris; but the day of his arrival at Deerham Hall was fixed. And this caused the commotion: for it had pleased Miss Hautley to determine to welcome him with a fête and ball, the like of which for splendour had never been heard of in the county.

Miss Hautley was a little given to have an opinion of her own, and to hold to it. Sir Rufus had been the same. Their friends called it firmness; their enemies obstinacy. The only sister of Sir Rufus, not cordial with him during his life, she had invaded the Hall as soon as the life had left him, quitting her own comfortable and substantial residence to do it, and persisted in taking up her abode there until Sir Edmund should return; as she was persisting now in giving this fête in honour of it. In vain those who deemed themselves privileged to speak, pointed out to Miss Hautley that a fête might be considered out of place, given before Sir Rufus had been dead a twelvemonth, and that Sir Edmund might deem it so; furthermore, that Sir Edmund might prefer to find quietness on his arrival instead of a crowd.

They might as well have talked to the wind, for all the impression it made upon Miss Hautley. The preparations for the gathering went on quickly, the invitations had gone out, and Deerham's head was turned. Those who did not get invitations were ready to swallow up those who did. Miss Hautley was as exclusive as ever proud old Sir Rufus had been, and many were left out who thought they might have been invited. Amongst others, the Misses West thought so, especially as one card had gone to their house—for Mr. Jan Verner.

Two cards had been left at Deerham Court. For Lady and Miss Verner: for Mr. and Mrs. Verner. By some strange oversight, Miss Tempest was omitted. That it was a simple oversight there was no doubt; and so it turned out to be; for, after the fête was over, reserved old Miss Hautley condescended to explain that it was, and to apologise; but this is dating forward. It was not known to be an oversight when the cards arrived, and Lady Verner felt inclined to resent it. She hesitated whether to treat it resentfully and stay away herself; or to take no notice of it, further than by conveying Lucy to the Hall in place of Decima.

Lucy laughed. She did not seem to care at all for the omission; but as to going without the invitation, or in anybody's place, she would not hear of it.

"Decima will not mind staying at home," said Lady Verner. "She never cares to go out. You will not care to go, will you, Decima?"

An unwonted flush of crimson rose to Decima's usually calm face. "I should like to go to this, mamma, as Miss Hautley has invited me."

"Like to go to it!" repeated Lady Verner. "Are you growing capricious, Decima? You generally profess to 'like' to stay at home."

"I would rather go this time, if you have no objection," was the quiet answer of Decima.

"Dear Lady Verner, if Decima remained at home ever so, I should not go," interposed Lucy. "Only fancy my intruding there without an invitation! Miss Hautley might order me out again."

"It is well to make a joke of it, Lucy, when I am vexed," said Lady Verner. "I dare say it is only a mistake; but I don't like such mistakes."

"I dare say it is nothing else," replied Lucy, laughing. "But as to making my appearance there under the circumstances, I could not really do it to oblige even you, Lady Verner. And I would just as soon be at home."

Lady Verner resigned herself to the decision, but she did not look pleased.

"It is to be I and Decima, then. Lionel," glancing across the table at him—"you will accompany me. I cannot go without you."

It was at the luncheon table they were discussing this; a meal of which Lionel rarely partook; in fact, he was rarely at home to partake of it; but he happened to be there to-day. Sibylla was present. Recovered from the accident—if it may be so called—of the breaking of the blood-vessel; she had appeared to grow stronger and better with the summer weather. Jan knew the improvement was all deceit, and told them so; told her so; that the very greatest caution was necessary, if she would avert a second similar attack; in fact, half the time of Jan's visits at Deerham Court was spent in enjoining perfect tranquillity on Sibylla.

But she was so obstinate! She would not keep herself quiet; she would go out; she would wear those thin summer dresses, low, in the evening. She is wearing a delicate muslin now, as she sits by Lady Verner, and her blue eyes are suspiciously bright, and her cheeks are suspiciously hectic, and the old laboured breath can be seen through the muslin moving her chest up and down, as it used to be seen—a lovely vision still, with her golden hair clustering about her; but her hands are hot and trembling, and her frame is painfully thin. Certainly she does not look fit to enter upon evening gaiety, and Lady Verner in addressing her son, "You will go with me, Lionel," proved that she never so much as cast a thought to the improbability that Sibylla would venture thither.

"If—you—particularly wish it, mother," was Lionel's reply, spoken with hesitation.

"Do you not wish to go?" rejoined Lady Verner.

"I would very much prefer not," he replied.

"Nonsense, Lionel! I don't think you have gone out once since you left Verner's Pride. Staying at home won't mend matters. I wish you to go with me; I shall make a point of it."

Lady Verner spoke with some irritation, and Lionel said no more. He supposed he must acquiesce.

It was no long-timed invitation of weeks. The cards arrived on the Monday, and the fête was for the following Thursday. Lionel thought no more about it; he was not as the ladies, whose toilettes would take all of that time to prepare. On the Wednesday, Decima took him aside.

"Lionel, do you know that Mrs. Verner intends to go to-morrow evening?"

Lionel paused; paused from surprise.

"You must be mistaken, Decima. She sent a refusal."

"I fancy that she did not send a refusal. And I feel sure she is thinking of going. You will not judge that I am unwarrantably interfering," Decima added in a tone of deprecation. "I would not do such a thing. But I thought it was right to apprise you of this. She is not well enough to go out."

With a pressure of the hand on his sister's shoulder, and a few muttered words of dismay, which she did not catch, Lionel sought his wife. No need of questioning, to confirm the truth of what Decima had said. Sibylla was figuring off before the glass, after the manner of her girlish days, with a wreath of white flowers on her head. It was her own sitting-room, the pretty room of the blue and white panels; and the tables and chairs were laden with other wreaths, with various head ornaments. She was trying their different effects, when, on turning round her head as the door opened, she saw it was her husband. His presence did not appear to discompose her, and she continued to place the wreath to her satisfaction, pulling it here and there with her thin and trembling hands.

"What are you doing?" asked Lionel.

"Trying on wreaths," she replied.

"So I perceive. But why?"

"To see which suits me best. This looks too white for me, does it not?" she added, turning her countenance towards him.

If to be the same hue as the complexion was "too white," it certainly did look so. The dead white of the roses was not more utterly colourless than Sibylla's face. She was like a ghost; she often looked so now.

"Sibylla," he said, without answering her question, "you are surely not thinking of going to Sir Edmund's to-morrow night?"

"Yes, I am."

"You said you would write a refusal!"

"I know I said it. I saw how cross-grained you were going to be over it, and that's why I said it to you. I accepted the invitation."

"But, my dear, you must not go!"

Sibylla was flinging off the white wreath, and taking up a pink one, which she began to fix in her hair. She did not answer.

"After all," deliberated she, "I have a great mind to wear pearls. Not a wreath at all."

"Sibylla! I say you must not go."

"Now, Lionel, it is of no use your talking. I have made up my mind to go; I did at first; and go I shall. Don't you remember," she continued, turning her face from the glass towards him, her careless tone changing for one of sharpness, "that papa said I must not be crossed?"

"But you are not in a state to go out," remonstrated Lionel. "Jan forbids it utterly."

"Jan? Jan's in your pay. He says what you tell him to say."

"Child, how can you give utterance to such things?" he asked in a tone of emotion. "When Jan interdicts your going out he has only your welfare at heart. And you know that I have it. Evening air and scenes of excitement are equally pernicious for you."

"I shall go," returned Sibylla. "You are going, you know," she resentfully said. "I wonder you don't propose that I shall be locked up at home in a dark closet, while you are there, dancing."

A moment's deliberation in his mind, and a rapid resolution. "I shall not go, Sibylla," he rejoined. "I shall stay at home with you."

"Who says you are going to stay at home?"

"I say it myself. I intend to do so. I shall do so."

"Oh! Since when, pray, have you come to that decision?"

Had she not the penetration to see that he had come to it then—then, as he talked to her; that he had come to it for her sake? That she should not have it to say he went out while she was at home. Perhaps she did see it; but it was nearly impossible to Sibylla not to indulge in bitter, aggravating retorts.

"I understand!" she continued, throwing up her head with an air of supreme scorn. "Thank you, don't trouble. I am not too ill to stoop, ill as you wish to make me out to be."

In displacing the wreath on her head to a different position, she had let it fall. Lionel's stooping to pick it up had called forth the last remark. As he handed it to her he took her hand.

"Sibylla, promise me to think no more of this. Do give it up."

"I won't give it up," she vehemently answered. "I shall go. And, what's more, I shall dance."

Lionel quitted her and sought his mother. Lady Verner was not very well that afternoon, and was keeping her room. He found her in an invalid chair.

"Mother, I have come to tell you that I cannot accompany you to-morrow evening," he said. "You must please excuse me."

"Why so?" asked Lady Verner.

"I would so very much rather not go," he answered. "Besides, I do not care to leave Sibylla."

Lady Verner made no observation for a few moments. A carious smile, almost a pitying smile, was hovering on her lips.

"Lionel, you are a model husband. Your father was not a bad one, as husbands go; but—he would not have bent his neck to such treatment from me, as you take from Mrs. Verner."

"No?" returned Lionel, with good humour.

"It is not right of you, Lionel, to leave me to go alone, with only Decima."

"Let Jan accompany you, mother."

"Jan!" uttered Lady Verner, in the very extreme of astonishment. "I should be surprised to see Jan attempt to enter such a scene. Jan! I don't suppose he possesses a fit coat and waistcoat."

Lionel smiled, quitted his mother, and bent his steps towards Jan Verner's.

Not to solicit Jan's attendance upon Lady Verner to the festival scene, or to make close inquiries as to the state of Jan's wardrobe. No; Lionel had a more serious motive for his visit.

He found Jan and Master Cheese enjoying a sort of battle. The surgery looked as if it had been turned upside down, so much confusion reigned. White earthenware vessels of every shape and form, glass jars, huge cylinders, brass pots, metal pans, were scattered about in inextricable confusion. Master Cheese had recently got up a taste for chemical experiments, in which it appeared necessary to call into requisition an unlimited quantity of accessories in the apparatus line. He had been entering upon an experiment that afternoon, when Jan came unexpectedly in, and caught him.

Not for the litter and confusion was Jan displeased, but because he found that Master Cheese had so bungled chemical properties in his head, so confounded one dangerous substance with another, that, five minutes later, the result would probably have been the blowing off of the surgery roof, and Master Cheese and his vessels with it. Jan was giving him a sharp and decisive word, not to attempt anything of the sort again, until he could bring more correct knowledge to bear upon it, when Lionel interrupted them.

"I want to speak to you, Jan," he said.

"Here, you be off, and wash the powder from your hands," cried Jan to Master Cheese, who was looking ruefully cross. "I'll put the things straight."

The young gentleman departed. Lionel sat down on the only chair he could see—one probably kept for the accommodation of patients who might want a few teeth drawn. Jan was rapidly reducing the place to order.

"What is it, Lionel?" he asked, when it was pretty clear.

"Jan, you must see Sibylla. She wants to go to Deerham Hall to-morrow night."

"She can't go," replied Jan. "Nonsense."

"But she says she will go."

Jan leaned his long body over the counter, and brought his face nearly on a level with Lionel's, speaking slowly and impressively—

"If she goes, Lionel, it will kill her."

Lionel rose to depart. He was on his way to Verner's Pride. "I called in to tell you this, Jan, and to ask you to step up and remonstrate with her."

"Very well," said Jan. "Mark me, Lionel, she must not go. And if there's no other way of keeping her away, you, her husband, must forbid it. A little more excitement than usual, and there'll be another vessel of the lungs ruptured. If that happens, nothing can save her life. Keep her at home, by force, if necessary: any way, keep her."

"And what of the excitement that that will cause?" questioned Lionel. "It may be as fatal as the other."

"I don't know," returned Jan, speaking for once in his life testily, in the vexation the difficulty brought him. "My belief is that Sibylla's mad. She'd never be so stupid, were she sane."

"Go to her, and see what you can do," concluded Lionel, as he turned away.

Jan proceeded to Deerham Court, and had an interview with Mrs. Verner. It was not of a very agreeable nature, neither did much satisfaction ensue from it. After a few recriminating retorts to Jan's arguments, which he received as equably as though they had been compliments, Sibylla subsided into sullen silence. And when Jan left, he could not tell whether she still persisted in her project, or whether she gave it up.

CHAPTER LXXXIII

WELL-NIGH WEARIED OUT

Lionel returned late in the evening; he had been detained at Verner's Pride. Sibylla appeared sullen still. She was in her own sitting-room, upstairs, and Lucy was bearing her company. Decima was in Lady Verner's chamber.

"Have you had any dinner?" inquired Lucy. She did not ask. She would not have asked had he been starving.

"I took a bit with John Massingbird," he replied. "Is my mother better, do you know?"

"Not much, I think," said Lucy. "Decima is sitting with her."

Lionel stood in his old attitude, his elbow on the mantel-piece by his wife's side, looking down at her. Her eyes were suspiciously bright, her cheeks now shone with their most crimson hectic. It was often the case at this, the twilight hour of the evening. She wore a low dress, and the gold chain on her neck rose and fell with every breath. Lucy's neck was uncovered, too: a fair, pretty neck; one that did not give you the shudders when looked at as poor Sibylla's did. Sibylla leaned back on the cushions of her chair, toying with a fragile hand-screen of feathers; Lucy, sitting on the opposite side, had been reading; but she laid the book down when Lionel entered.

"John Massingbird desired me to ask you, Sibylla, if he should send you the first plate of grapes they cut."

"I'd rather have the first bag of walnuts they shake," answered Sibylla. "I never cared for grapes."

"He can send you both," said Lionel; but an uncomfortable, dim recollection came over him, of Jan's having told her she must not eat walnuts. For Jan to tell her not to do a thing, however—or, in fact, for anybody else—was the sure signal for Sibylla to do it.

"Does John Massingbird intend to go to-morrow evening?" inquired Sibylla.

"To Deerham Hall, do you mean? John Massingbird has not received an invitation."

"What's that for?" quickly asked Sibylla.

"Some whim of Miss Hautley's, I suppose. The cards have been issued very partially. John says it is just as well he did not get one, for he should either not have responded to it, or else made his appearance there with his clay pipe."

Lucy laughed.

"He is glad to be left out," continued Lionel. "It saves him the trouble of a refusal. I don't think any ball would get John Massingbird to it; unless he could be received in what he calls his diggings' toggery."

"I'd not have gone with him; I don't like him well enough," resentfully spoke Sibylla; "but as he is not going, he can let me have the loan of my own carriage—at least, the carriage that was my own. I dislike those old, hired things."

The words struck on Lionel like a knell. He foresaw trouble. "Sibylla," he gravely said, "I have been speaking to Jan. He—"

"Yes, you have!" she vehemently interrupted, her pent-up anger bursting forth. "You went to him, and sent him here, and told him what to say—all on purpose to cross me. It is wicked of you to be so jealous of my having a little pleasure."

"Jealous of—I don't understand you, Sibylla."

"You won't understand me, you mean. Never mind, never mind!"

"Sibylla," he said, bending his head slightly towards her, and speaking in low, persuasive accents, "I cannot let you go to-morrow night. If I cared for you less, I might suffer you to risk it. I have given up going, and—"

"You never meant to go," she interrupted.

"Yes, I did; to please my mother. But that is of no consequence—"

"I tell you, you never meant to go, Lionel Verner!" she passionately burst forth, her cheeks flaming. "You are stopping at home on purpose to be with Lucy Tempest—an arranged plan between you and her. Her society is more to you than any you'd find at Deerham Hall."

Lucy looked up with a start—a sort of shiver—her sweet, brown eyes open with innocent wonder. Then the full sense of the words appeared to penetrate to her, and her face grew hot with a glowing, scarlet flush. She said nothing. She rose quietly, not hurriedly, took up the book she had put on the table, and quietly left the room.

Lionel's face was glowing, too—glowing with the red blood of indignation. He bit his lips for calmness, leaving the mark there for hours. He strove manfully with his angry spirit: it was rising up to open rebellion. A minute, and the composure of self-control came to him. He stood before his wife, his arms folded.

"You are my wife," he said. "I am bound to defend, to excuse you so far as I may; but these insults to Lucy Tempest I cannot excuse. She is the daughter of my dead father's dearest friend; she is living here under the protection of my mother, and it is incumbent upon me to put a stop to these scenes, so far as she is concerned. If I cannot do it in one way, I must in another."

"You know she and you would like to stay at home together—and get the rest of us out."

"Be silent!" he said in a sterner tone than he had ever used to her. "You cannot reflect upon what you are saying. Accuse me as you please; I will bear it patiently, if I can; but Miss Tempest must be spared. You know how utterly unfounded are such thoughts; you know that she is refined, gentle, single-hearted; that all her thoughts to you, as my wife, are those of friendship and kindness. What would my mother think were she to hear this?"

Sibylla made no reply.

"You have never seen a look or heard a word pass between me and Lucy Tempest that was not of the most open nature, entirely compatible with her position, that of a modest and refined gentlewoman, and of mine, as your husband. I think you must be mad, Sibylla."

The words Jan had used. If such temperaments do not deserve the name of madness, they are near akin to it. Lionel spoke with emotion: it all but over-mastered him, and he went back to his place by the mantel-piece, his chest heaving.

"I shall leave this residence as speedily as maybe," he said, "giving some trivial excuse to my mother for the step. I see no other way to put an end to this."

Sibylla, her mood changing, burst into tears. "I don't want to leave it," she said quite in a humble tone.

He was not inclined for argument. He had rapidly made his mind up, believing it was the only course open to him. He must go away with his wife, and so leave the house in peace. Saying something to that effect, he quitted the room, leaving Sibylla sobbing; fractiously on the pillow of the chair.

He went down to the drawing-room. He did not care where he went, or what became of him. It is an unhappy thing when affairs grow to that miserable pitch, that the mind has neither ease nor comfort anywhere. At the first moment of entering, he thought the room was empty, but as his eyes grew accustomed to the dusk, he discerned the form of some one standing at the distant window. It was Lucy Tempest. Lionel went straight up to her. He felt that some apology or notice from him was due. She was crying bitterly, and turned to him before he could speak.

"Mr. Verner, I feel my position keenly. I would not remain here to make things unpleasant to your wife for the whole world. But I cannot help myself. I have nowhere to go until papa shall return to Europe."

"Lucy, let me say a word to you," he whispered, his tones impeded, his breath coming thick and fast from his hot and crimsoned lips. "There are moments in a man's lifetime when he must be true; when the artificial gloss thrown on social intercourse fades out of sight. This is one."

Her tears fell more quietly. "I am so very sorry!" she continued to murmur.

"Were you other than what you are I might meet you with some of this artifice; I might pretend not to know aught of what has been said; I might attempt some elaborate apology. It would be worse than folly from me to you. Let me tell you that could I have shielded you from this insult with my life, I would have done it."

"Yes, yes," she hurriedly answered.

"You will not mistake me. As the daughter of my father's dearest friend, as my mother's honoured guest, I speak to you. I speak to you as one whom I am bound to protect from harm and insult, only in a less degree than I would protect my wife. You will do me the justice to believe it."

"I know it. Indeed I do not blame you."

"Lucy, I would have prevented this, had it been in my power. But it was not. I could not help it. All I can do is to take steps that it shall not occur again in the future. I scarcely know what I am saying to you. My life, what with one thing and another, is well-nigh wearied out."

Lucy had long seen that. But she did not say so.

"It will not be long now before papa is at home," she answered, "and then I shall leave Deerham Court free. Thank you for speaking to me," she simply said, as she was turning to leave the room.

He took both her hands in his; he drew her nearer to him, his head was bent down to hers, his whole frame shook with emotion. Was he tempted to take a caress from her sweet face, as he had taken it years ago? Perhaps he was. But Lionel Verner was not one to lose his self-control where there was real necessity for his retaining it. His position was different now from what it had been then; and, if the temptation was strong, it was kept in check, and Lucy never knew it had been there.

"You will forget it for my sake, Lucy? You will not resent it upon her? She is very ill."

"It is what I wish to do," she gently said. "I do not know what foolish things I might not say, were I suffering like Mrs. Verner."

"God bless you for ever, Lucy!" he murmured. "May your future life be more fortunate than mine is."

Relinquishing her hands, he watched her disappear through the darkness of the room. She was dearer to him than his own life; he loved her better than all earthly things. That the knowledge was all too palpable then, he was bitterly feeling, and he could not suppress it. He could neither suppress the knowledge, nor the fact; it had been very present with him for long and long. He could not help it, as he said. He believed, in his honest heart, that he had not encouraged the passion; that it had taken root and spread unconsciously to himself. He would have driven it away, had it been in his power; he would drive it away now, could he do it by any amount of energy or will. But it could not be. And Lionel Verner leaned in the dark there against the window-frame, resolving to do as he had done before—had done all along. To suppress it ever; to ignore it so far as might be; and to do his duty as honestly and lovingly by his wife, as though the love were not there.

He had been enabled to do this hitherto, and he would still; God helping him.

CHAPTER LXXXIV

GOING TO THE BALL

It was the day of the fête at Deerham Hall. Sibylla awoke in an amiable mood, unusually so for her; and Lionel, as he dressed, talked to her gravely and kindly, urging upon her the necessity of relinquishing her determination to be present. It appeared that she was also reasonable that morning, as well as amiable, for she listened to him, and at length voluntarily said she would think no more about it.

"But you must afford me some treat in place of it," she immediately added. "Will you promise to take me for a whole day next week to Heartburg?"

"Willingly," replied Lionel. "There is to be a morning concert at Heartburg next Tuesday. If you feel well enough, we can attend that."

He did not think morning concerts, and the fatigue they sometimes entail, particularly desirable things for his wife; but, compared with hot ballrooms and the night air, they seemed innocuous. Sibylla liked morning concerts uncommonly, nearly as much as Master Cheese liked tarts; she liked anything that afforded an apology for dress and display.

"Mind, Lionel, you promise to take me," she reiterated.

"Yes. Provided you feel equal to going."

Sibylla took breakfast in her own room, according to custom. Formerly, she had done so through idleness: now, she was really not well enough to rise early. Lionel, when he joined the family breakfast table, announced the news; announced it in his own characteristic manner.

"Sibylla thinks, after all, that she will be better at home this evening," he said. "I am glad she has so decided it."

"Her senses have come to her, have they?" remarked Lady Verner.

He made no reply. He never did make a reply to any shaft lanced by Lady Verner at his wife. My lady was sparing of her shafts in a general way since they had resided with her, but she did throw one out now and then.

"You will go with me then, Lionel?"

He shook his head, telling his mother she must excuse him: it was not his intention to be present.

Sibylla continued in a remarkably quiet, not to say affable, temper all day. Lionel was out, but returned home to dinner. By and by Lady Verner and Decima retired to dress. Lucy went up with Decima, and Lionel remained with his wife.

When they came down, Sibylla was asleep on the sofa. Lady Verner wore some of the magnificent and yet quiet attire that had pertained to her gayer days; Decima was in white. Lionel put on his hat, and went out to hand them into the carriage that waited. As he did so, the aspect of his sister's face struck him.

"What is the matter, Decima?" he exclaimed. "You are looking perfectly white."

She only smiled in answer; a forced, unnatural smile, as it appeared to Lionel. But he said no more; he thought the white hue might be only the shade cast by the moonlight. Lady Verner looked from the carriage to ask a question.

"Is Jan really going, do you know, Lionel? Lucy says she thinks he is. I do hope and trust that he will be attired like a Christian, if he is absurd enough to appear."

"I think I'll go and see," answered Lionel, a smile crossing his face. "Take care, Catherine!"

Old Catherine, who had come out with shawls, was dangerously near the wheels—and the horses were on the point of starting. She stepped back, and the carriage drove on.

The bustle had aroused Sibylla. She rose to look from the window; saw the carriage depart, saw Catherine come in, saw Lionel walk away towards Deerham. It was all clear in the moonlight. Lucy Tempest was looking from the other window.

"What a lovely night it is!" Lucy exclaimed. "I should not mind a drive of ten miles, such a night as this."

"And yet they choose to say that going out would hurt me!" spoke Sibylla in a resentful tone. "They do it on purpose to vex me."

Lucy chose to ignore the subject; it was not her business to enter into it one way or the other. She felt that Mrs. Verner had done perfectly right in remaining at home; that her strength would have been found unequal to support the heat and excitement of a ballroom, following on the night air of the transit to it. Lovely as the night was, it was cold: for some few evenings past the gardeners had complained of frost.

Lucy drew from the window with a half sigh; it seemed almost a pity to shut out that pleasant moonlight: turned and stirred the fire into a blaze. Sibylla's chilly nature caused them to enter upon evening fires before other people thought of them.

"Shall I ring for lights, Mrs. Verner?"

"I suppose it's time, and past time," was Sibylla's answer. "I must have been asleep ever so long."

Catherine brought them in. The man-servant had gone in attendance on his mistress. The moderate household of Lady Verner consisted now but of four domestics; Thérèse, Catherine, the cook, and the man.

"Shall I bring tea in, Miss Lucy?" asked Catherine.

Lucy turned her eyes on Sibylla. "Would you like tea now, Mrs. Verner?"

"No," answered Sibylla. "Not yet."

She left the room as she spoke. Catherine, who had been lowering the curtains, followed next. Lucy drew a chair to the fire, sat down and fell into a reverie.

She was aroused by the door opening again. It proved to be Catherine with the tea-things. "I thought I'd bring them in, and then they'll be ready," remarked she. "You can please to ring, miss, when you want the urn."

Lucy simply nodded, and Catherine returned to the kitchen, to enjoy a social tête-à-tête supper with the cook. Mademoiselle Thérèse, taking advantage of her mistress's absence, had gone out for the rest of the evening. The two servants sat on and chatted together: so long, that Catherine openly wondered at the urn's not being called for.

"They must both have gone to sleep, I should think," quoth she. "Miss Lucy over the fire in the sitting-room, and Mr. Lionel's wife over hers, upstairs. I have not heard her come down—"

Catherine stopped. The cook had started up, her eyes fixed on the doorway. Catherine, whose back was towards it, hastily turned; and an involuntary exclamation broke from her lips.

Standing there was Mrs. Verner, looking like—like a bedecked skeleton. She was in fairy attire. A gossamer robe of white with shining ornaments, and a wreath that seemed to sparkle with glittering dewdrops on her head. But her arms were thin, wasted; and the bones of her poor neck seemed to rattle as they heaved painfully under the gems clasped round it: and her face had not so much as the faintest tinge of hectic, but was utterly colourless—worse, it was wan, ghastly. A distressing sight to look upon, was she, as she stood there; she and the festal attire were so completely at variance. She came forward, before the servants could recover from their astonishment.

"Where's Richard?" she asked, speaking in a low, subdued tone, as if fearing to be heard—though there was nobody in the house to hear her, save Lucy Tempest. And probably it was from her wish to avoid all attention to her proceeding, that caused her to come down stealthily to the servants, instead of ringing for them.

"Richard is not come back, ma'am," answered Catherine. "We have just been saying that he'll most likely stop up there with the Hall servants until my lady returns."

"Not back!" echoed Sibylla. "Cook, you must go out for me," she imperiously added, after a moment's pause. "Go to Dean's and order one of their flys here directly. Wait, and come back with it."

The cook, a simple sort of young woman, save in her own special department, did not demur, or appear to question in the least the expediency of the order. Catherine questioned it very much indeed; but while she hesitated what to do, whether to stop the cook, or to venture on a remonstrance to Mrs. Verner, or to appeal to Miss Tempest to do it, the cook was gone. Servants are not particular in country places, and the girl went straight out as she was, not staying to put anything on.

Sibylla appeared to be shivering. She took up her place right in front of the fire, holding out her hands to the blaze. Her teeth chattered, her whole frame trembled.

"The fire in my dressing-room went out," she remarked. "Take care that you make up a large one by the time I return."

"You'll never go, ma'am!" cried old Catherine, breaking through her reserve. "You are not strong enough."

"Mind your own business," sharply retorted Sibylla. "Do you think I don't know my own feelings, whether I am strong, or whether I am not? I am as strong as you."

Catherine dared no more. Sibylla cowered over the fire, her head turned sideways as she glanced on the table.

"What's that?" she suddenly cried, pointing to the contents of a jug.

"It's beer, ma'am," answered Catherine. "That stupid girl drew as much as if Richard and Thérèse had been at home. Maybe Thérèse will be in yet for supper."

"Give me a glass of it. I am thirsty."

Again old Catherine hesitated. Malt liquor had been expressly forbidden to Mrs. Verner. It made her cough frightfully.

"You know, ma'am, the doctors have said—"

"Will you hold your tongue? And give me what I require? You are as bad as Mr. Verner."

Catherine reached a tumbler, poured it half full, and handed it. Mrs. Verner did not take it.

"Fill it," she said.

So old Catherine, much against her will, had to fill it, and Sibylla drained the glass to the very bottom. In truth, she was continually thirsty; she seemed to have a perpetual inward fever upon her. Her shoulders were shivering as she set down the glass.

"Go and find my opera cloak, Catherine. It must have dropped on the stairs, I know I put it on as I left my room."

Catherine quitted the kitchen on the errand. She would have liked to close the door after her; but it happened to be pushed quite back with a chair against it; and the pointedly shutting it might have been noticed by Sibylla. She found the opera cloak lying on the landing, near Sibylla's bedroom door. Catching it up, she slipped off her shoes at the same moment, stole down noiselessly, and went into the presence of Miss Tempest.

Lucy looked astonished. She sat at the table reading, waiting with all patience the entrance of Sibylla, ere she made tea. To see Catherine steal in covertly with her finger to her lips, excited her wonder.

"Miss Lucy, she's going to the ball," was the old servant's salutation, as she approached close to Lucy, and spoke in the faintest whisper. "She is shivering over the kitchen fire, with hardly a bit of gown to her back, so far as warmth goes. Here's her opera cloak: she dropped it coming down. Cook's gone out for a fly."

Lucy felt startled. "Do you mean Mrs. Verner?"

"Why, of course I do," answered Catherine. "She has been upstairs all this while, and has dressed herself alone. She must not go, Miss Lucy. She's looking like a ghost. What will Mr. Verner say to us if we let her! It may just be her death."

Lucy clasped her hands in her consternation. "Catherine, what can we do? We have no influence over her. She would not listen to us for a moment. If we could but find Mr. Verner!"

"He was going round to Mr. Jan's when my lady drove off. I heard him say it. Miss Lucy, I can't go after him; she'd find me out; I can't leave her, or leave the house. But he ought to be got here."

Did the woman's words point to the suggestion that Lucy should go? Lucy may have thought it; or, perhaps, she entered on the suggestion of her own accord.

"I will go, Catherine," she whispered. "I don't mind it. It is nearly as light as day outside, and I shall soon be at Mr. Jan's. You go back to Mrs. Verner."

Feeling that there was not a moment to be lost; feeling that Mrs. Verner ought to be stopped at all hazards for her own sake, Lucy caught up a shawl and a green sun-bonnet of Lady Verner's that happened to be in the hall, and, thus hastily attired, went out. Speeding swiftly along the moonlit road, she soon gained Deerham, and turned to the house of Dr. West. A light in the surgery guided her at once to that room.

But the light was there alone. Nobody was present to reap its benefit or to answer intruders. Lucy knocked pretty loudly on the counter without bringing forth any result. Apparently she was not heard; perhaps from the fact that the sound was drowned in the noise of some fizzing and popping which seemed to be going on in the next room—Jan's bedroom. Her consideration for Mrs. Verner put ceremony out of the question; in fact, Lucy was not given at the best of times to stand much upon that; and she stepped round the counter, and knocked briskly at the door. Possibly Lionel might be in there with Jan.

Lionel was not there; nor Jan either. The door was gingerly opened about two inches by Master Cheese, who was enveloped in a great white apron and white oversleeves. His face looked red and confused as it peeped out, as does that of one who is caught at some forbidden mischief; and Lucy obtained sight of a perfect mass of vessels, brass, earthenware, glass, and other things, with which the room was strewed. In point of fact, Master Cheese, believing he was safe from Jan's superintendence for some hours, had seized upon the occasion to plunge into his forbidden chemical researches again, and had taken French leave to use Jan's bedroom for the purpose, the surgery being limited for space.

"What do you want?" cried he roughly, staring at Lucy.

"Is Mr. Verner here?" she asked.

Then Master Cheese knew the voice, and condescended a sort of apology for his abruptness.

"I didn't know you, Miss Tempest, in that fright of a bonnet," said he, walking forth and closing the bedroom door behind him. "Mr. Verner's not here."

"Do you happen to know where he is?" asked Lucy. "He said he was coming here, an hour ago."

"So he did come here; and saw Jan. Jan's gone to the ball. And Miss Deb and Miss Amilly are gone to a party at Heartburg."

"Is he?" returned Lucy, referring to Jan, and surprised to hear the news; balls not being in Jan's line.

"I can't make it out," remarked Master Cheese. "He and Sir Edmund used to be cronies, I think; so I suppose that has taken him. But I am glad they are all off: it gives me a whole evening to myself. He and Mr. Verner went away together."

"I wish very much to find Mr. Verner," said Lucy. "It is of great consequence that I should see him. I suppose—you—could not—go and look for him, Master Cheese?" she added pleadingly.

"Couldn't do it," responded Master Cheese, thinking of his forbidden chemicals. "When Jan's away I am chief, you know, Miss Tempest. Some cases of broken legs may be brought in, for anything I can tell."

Lucy wished him good-night and turned away. She hesitated at the corner of the street, gazing up and down. To start on a search for Lionel appeared to be as hopeful a project as that search renowned in proverb—the looking for a needle in a bottle of hay. The custom in Deerham was not to light the lamps on a moonlight night, so the street, as Lucy glanced on either side, lay white and quiet; no glare to disturb its peace, save for some shops, not yet closed. Mrs. Duff's, opposite, was among the latter catalogue: and her son, Mr. Dan, appeared to be taking a little tumbling recreation on the flags before the bay-window. Lucy crossed over to him.

"Dan," said she, "do you happen to have seen Mr. Verner pass lately?"

Dan, just then on his head, turned himself upside down, and alighted on his feet, humble and subdued, "Please, miss, I see'd him awhile agone along of Mr. Jan," was the answer, pulling his hair by way of salutation. "They went that way. Mr. Jan was all in black, he was."

The boy pointed towards Deerham Court, towards Deerham Hall. There was little doubt that Jan was then on his way to the latter. But the question for Lucy was—where had Lionel gone?

She could not tell; the very speculation upon it was unprofitable, since it could lead to no certainty. Lucy turned homewards, walking quickly.

She had got past the houses, when she discerned before her in the distance, a form which instinct—perhaps some dearer feeling told her was that of him of whom she was in search. He was walking with a slow, leisurely step towards his home. Lucy's heart gave a bound—that it did so still at his sight, as it had done in the earlier days, was no fault of hers: Heaven knew that she had striven and prayed against it. When she caught him up she was out of breath, so swiftly had she sped.

"Lucy!" he exclaimed. "Lucy! What do you do here?"

"I came out to look for you," she simply said; "there was nobody else at home to come. I went to Jan's, thinking you might be there. Mrs. Verner has dressed herself to go to Sir Edmund's. You may be in time to stop her, if you make haste."

With a half-uttered exclamation, Lionel was speeding off, when he appeared to remember Lucy. He turned to take her with him.

"No," said Lucy, stopping. "I could not go as quickly as you; and a minute, more or less, may make all the difference. There is nothing to hurt me. You make the best of your way. It is for your wife's sake."

There was good sense in all she said, and Lionel started off with a fleet foot. Before Lucy had quite gained the Court she saw him coming back to meet her. He drew her hand within his arm in silence, and kept his own upon it for an instant's grateful pressure.

"Thank you, Lucy, for what you have done. Thank you now and ever. I was too late."

"Is Mrs. Verner gone?"

"She has been gone these ten minutes past, Catherine says. A fly was found immediately."

They turned into the house; into the sitting-room. Lucy threw off the large shawl and the shapeless green bonnet: at any other moment she would have laughed at the figure she must have looked in them. The tea-things still waited on the table.

"Shall I make you some tea?" she asked.

Lionel shook his head. "I must go up and dress. I shall go after Sibylla."

CHAPTER LXXXV

DECIMA'S ROMANCE

If the fair forms crowding to the fête at Deerham Hall had but known how near that fête was to being shorn of its master's presence, they had gone less hopefully. Scarcely one of the dowagers and chaperones bidden to it, but cast a longing eye to the heir, for their daughters' sakes; scarcely a daughter but experienced a fluttering of the heart, as the fond fancy presented itself that she might be singled out for the chosen partner of Sir Edmund Hautley—for the night, at any rate; and—perhaps—for the long night of the future. But when the clock struck six that evening, Sir Edmund Hautley had not arrived.

Miss Hautley was in a fever—as nearly in one as it is in the nature of a cold, single lady of fifty-eight to go, when some overwhelming disappointment falls abruptly. According to arranged plans, Sir Edmund was to have been at home by middle day, crossing by the night boat from the continent. Middle day came and went; afternoon came and went; evening came—and he had not come. Miss Hautley would have set the telegraph to work, had she known where to set it to.

But good luck was in store for her. A train, arriving between six and seven, brought him; and his carriage—the carriage of his late father, which had been waiting at the station since eleven o'clock in the morning—conveyed him home.

Very considerably astonished was Sir Edmund to find the programme which had been carved out for the night's amusement. He did not like it; it jarred upon his sense of propriety; and he spoke a hint of this to Miss Hautley. It was the death of his father which had called him home; a father with whom he had lived for the last few years of his life upon terms of estrangement—at any rate, upon one point; was it seemly that his inauguration should be one of gaiety? Yes, Miss Hautley decisively answered. Their friends were not meeting to bewail Sir Rufus's death; that took place months ago; but to welcome his, Sir Edmund's, return, and his entrance on his inheritance.

Sir Edmund—a sunny-tempered, yielding man, the very opposite in spirit to his dead father, to his live aunt—conceded the point; doing it with all the better grace, perhaps, that there was now no help for it. In an hour's time the guests would be arriving. Miss Hautley inquired curiously as to the point upon which he and Sir Rufus had been at issue; she had never been able to learn it from Sir Rufus. Neither did it now appear that she was likely to learn it from Sir Edmund. It was a private matter, he said, a smile crossing his lips as he spoke; one entirely between himself and his father, and he could not speak of it. It had driven him abroad she believed, Miss Hautley remarked, vexed that she was still to remain in the dark. Yes, acquiesced Sir Edmund; it had driven him abroad and kept him there.

He was ready, and stood in his place to receive his guests; a tall man, of some five-and-thirty years, with a handsome face and pleasant smile upon it. He greeted his old friends cordially, those with whom he had been intimate, and was laughing and talking with the Countess of Elmsley when the announcement "Lady and Miss Verner" caught his ear.

It caused him to turn abruptly. Breaking off in the midst of a sentence, he quitted the countess and went to meet those who had entered. Lady Verner's greeting was a somewhat elaborate one, and he looked round impatiently for Decima.

She stood in the shade behind her mother. Decima? Was that Decima? What had she done to her cheeks? They wore the crimson hectic which were all too characteristic of Sibylla's. Sir Edmund took her hand.

"I trust you are well?"

"Quite well, thank you," was her murmured answer, drawing away the hand which had barely touched his.

Nothing could be more quiet than the meeting, nothing more simple than the words spoken; nothing, it may be said, more commonplace. But that Decima was suffering from some intense agitation, there could be no doubt; and the next moment her face had turned of that same ghastly hue which had startled her brother Lionel when he was handing her into the carriage. Sir Edmund continued speaking with them a few minutes, and then was called off to receive other guests.

"Have you forgotten how to dance, Edmund?"

The question came from Miss Hautley, disturbing him as he made the centre of a group to whom he was speaking of his Indian life.

"I don't suppose I have," he said, turning to her. "Why?"

"People are thinking so," said Miss Hautley. "The music has been bursting out into fresh attempts this last half-hour, and impatience is getting irrepressible. They cannot begin, Edmund, without you. Your partner is waiting."

"My partner?" reiterated Sir Edmund. "I have asked nobody yet."

"But I have, for you. At least, I have as good as done it. Lady Constance—"

"Oh, my dear aunt, you are very kind," he hastily interrupted, "but when I do dance—which is of rare occurrence—I like to choose my own partner. I must do so now."

"Well, take care, then," was the answer of Miss Hautley, not deeming it necessary to drop her voice in the least. "The room is anxious to see upon whom your choice will be fixed; it may be a type, they are saying, of what another choice of yours may be."

Sir Edmund laughed good-humouredly, making a joke of the allusion. "Then I must walk round deliberately and look out for myself—as it is said some of our royal reigning potentates have done. Thank you for the hint."

But, instead of walking round deliberately, Sir Edmund Hautley proceeded direct to one point of the room, halting before Lady Verner and Decima. He bent to the former, speaking a few words in a joking tone.

"I am bidden to fix upon a partner, Lady Verner. May it be your daughter?"

Lady Verner looked at Decima. "She so seldom dances. I do not think you will persuade her."

"I think I can," he softly said, bending to Decima and holding out his arm. And Decima rose and put hers into it without a word.

"How capricious she is!" remarked Lady Verner to the Countess of Elmsley, who was sitting next her. "If I had pressed her, she would probably have said no—as she has done so many times."

He took his place at the head of the room, Decima by his side in her white silk robes. Decima, with her wondrous beauty, and the hectic on her cheeks again. Many an envious pair of eyes was cast to her. "That dreadful old maid, Decima Verner!" was amongst the compliments launched at her. "She to usurp him! How had my Lady Verner contrived to manoeuvre for it?"

But Sir Edmund did not appear dissatisfied with his partner, if the room was. He paid a vast deal more attention to her than he did to the dance; the latter he put out more than once, his head and eyes being bent, whispering to Decima. Before the dance was over, the hectic on her cheeks had grown deeper.

"Are you afraid of the night air?" he asked, leading her through the conservatory to the door at its other end.

"No. It never hurts me."

He proceeded along the gravel path round to the other side of the house; there he opened the glass doors of a room and entered. It led into another, bright with fire.

"It is my own sitting-room," he observed. "Nobody will intrude upon us here."

Taking up the poker, he stirred the fire into a blaze. Then he put it down and turned to her, as she stood on the hearth-rug.

"Decima!"

It was only a simple name; but Sir Edmund's whole frame was quivering with emotion as he spoke it. He clasped her to him with a strangely fond gesture, and bent his face on hers.

"I left my farewell on your lips when I quitted you, Decima. I must take my welcome from them now."

She burst into tears as she clung to him. "Sir Rufus sent for me when he was dying," she whispered. "Edmund, he said he was sorry to have opposed you; he said he would not if the time could come over again."

"I know it," he answered. "I have his full consent; nay, his blessing. They are but a few words, but they were the last he ever wrote. You shall see them, Decima: he calls you my future wife, Lady Hautley. Oh, my darling! what a long, cruel separation it has been!"

Ay! far more long, more cruel for Decima than for him. She was feeling it bitterly now, as the tears poured down her face. Sir Edmund placed her in a chair. He hung over her scarcely less agitated than she was, soothing her with all the fondness of his true heart, with the sweet words she had once known so well. He turned to the door when she grew calmer.

"I am going to bring Lady Verner. It is time she knew it."

Not through the garden this time, but through the open passages of the house, lined with servants, went Sir Edmund. Lady Verner was in the seat where they left her. He made his way to her, and held his arm out that she might take it.

"Will you allow me to monopolise you for a few minutes?" he said. "I have a tale to tell in which you may feel interested."

"About India?" she asked, as she rose. "I suppose you used to meet some of my old friends there?"

"Not about India," he answered, leading her from the room. "India can wait. About some one nearer and dearer to us than any now in India. Lady Verner, when I asked you just now to permit me to fix upon your daughter as a partner, I could have added for life. Will you give me Decima?"

Had Sir Edmund Hautley asked for herself, Lady Verner could scarcely have been more astonished. He poured into her ear the explanation, the whole tale of their old love, the inveterate opposition to it of Sir Rufus—which had driven him abroad. It had never been made known to Lady Verner.

"It was that caused you to exile yourself!" she reiterated in her amazement.

"It was, Lady Verner. Marry in opposition to my father, I would not—and had I been willing to brave him, Decima never would. So I left my home; I left Decima my father perfectly understanding that our engagement existed still, that it only lay in abeyance until happier times. When he was dying, he repented of his harshness and recalled his interdict: by letter to me, personally to Decima. He died with a blessing for us both on his lips. Jan can tell you so."

"What has Jan to do with it?" exclaimed Lady Verner.

"Sir Rufus made a confidant of Jan, and charged him with the message to me. It was Jan who inclosed to me the few words my father was able to trace."

"I think Jan might have imparted the secret to me," resentfully spoke Lady Verner. "It is just like ungrateful Jan."

"Jan ungrateful?—never!" spoke Sir Edmund warmly. "There's not a truer heart breathing than Jan's. It was not his secret, and I expect he did not consider himself at liberty to tell even you. Decima would have imparted it to you years ago, when I went away, but for one thing."

"What may that have been?" asked Lady Verner.

"Because we feared, she and I, that your pride would be so wounded, and not unjustly, at my father's unreasonable opposition; that you might, in retaliation, forbid the alliance, then and always. You see I am candid, Lady Verner. I can afford to be so, can I not?"

"Decima ought to have told me," was all the reply given by Lady Verner.

"And Decima would have told you, at all hazards, but for my urgent entreaties. The blame is wholly mine, Lady Verner. You must forgive me."

"In what lay the objection of Sir Rufus?" she asked.

"I honestly believe that it arose entirely from that dogged self-will—may I be forgiven for speaking thus irreverently of my dead father!—which was his great characteristic through life. It was I who chose Decima, not he; and therefore my father opposed it. To Decima and to Decima's family he could not have any possible objection—in fact, he had not. But he liked to oppose his will to mine. I—if I know anything of myself—am the very reverse of self-willed, and I had always yielded to him. No question, until this, had ever arisen that was of vital importance to my life and its happiness."

"Sir Rufus may have resented her want of fortune," remarked Lady Verner.

"I think not. He was not a covetous or a selfish man; and our revenues are such that I can make ample settlements on my wife. No, it was the self-will. But it is all over, and I can openly claim her. You will give her to me, Lady Verner?"

"I suppose I must," was the reply of my lady. "But people have been calling her an old maid."

Sir Edmund laughed. "How they will be disappointed! Some of their eyes may be opened to-night. I shall not deem it necessary to make a secret of our engagement now."

"You must permit me to ask one question, Sir Edmund. Have you and Decima corresponded?"

"No. We separated for the time entirely. The engagement existing in our own hearts alone."

"I am glad to hear it. I did not think Decima would have carried on a correspondence unknown to me."

"I am certain that she would not. And for that reason I never asked her to do so. Until I met Decima to-night, Lady Verner, we have had no communication with each other since I left. But I am quite sure that neither of us has doubted the other for a single moment."

"It has been a long while to wait," mused Lady Verner, as they entered the presence of Decima, who started up to receive them.

CHAPTER LXXXVI

WAS IT A SPECTRE?

When they returned to the rooms, Sir Edmund with Decima, Lady Verner by her daughter's side, the first object that met their view was Jan. Jan at a ball! Lady Verner lifted her eyebrows; she had never believed that Jan would really show himself where he must be so entirely out of place. But there Jan was; in decent dress, too—black clothes, and a white neckcloth and gloves. It's true the bow of his neckcloth was tied upside down, and the gloves had their thumbs nearly out. Jan's great hands laid hold of both Sir Edmund's.

"I'm uncommon glad you are back!" cried he—which was his polite phrase for expressing satisfaction.

"So am I, Jan," heartily answered Sir Edmund. "I have never had a real friend, Jan, since I left you."

"We can be friends still," said plain Jan.

"Ay," said Sir Edmund meaningly, "and brothers." But the last word was spoken in Jan's ear alone, for they were in a crowd now.

"To see you here very much surprises me, Jan," remarked Lady Verner, asperity in her tone. "I hope you will contrive to behave properly."

Lady Mary Elmsley, then standing with them, laughed. "What are you afraid he should do, Lady Verner?"

"He was not made for society," said Lady Verner, with asperity.

"Nor society for me," returned Jan good-humouredly. "I'd rather be watching a case of fever."

"Oh, Jan!" cried Lady Mary, laughing still.

"So I would," repeated Jan. "At somebody's bedside, in my easy coat, I feel at home. And I feel that I am doing good; that's more. This is nothing but waste of time."

"You hear?" appealed Lady Verner to them, as if Jan's avowal were a passing proof of her assertion—that he and society were antagonistic to each other, "I wonder you took the thought to attire yourself passably," she added, her face retaining its strong vexation. "Had anybody asked me, I should have given it as my opinion, that you had not things fit to appear in."

"I had got these," returned Jan, looking down at his clothes. "Won't they do? It's my funeral suit."

The unconscious, matter-of-fact style of Jan's avowal was beyond everything. Lady Verner was struck dumb, Sir Edmund smiled, and Mary Elmsley laughed outright.

"Oh, Jan!" said she, "you'll be a child all your days. What do you mean by your 'funeral suit'?"

"Anybody might know that," was Jan's answer to Lady Mary. "It's the suit I keep for funerals. A doctor is always being asked to attend them; and if he does not go he offends the people."

"You might have kept the information to yourself," rebuked Lady Verner.

"It doesn't matter, does it?" asked Jan. "Aren't they good enough to come in?"

He turned his head round, to get a glance at the said suit behind. Sir Edmund laid his hand affectionately on his shoulder. Young as Jan had been before Edmund Hautley went out, they had lived close friends.

"The clothes are all right, Jan. And if you had come without a coat at all, you would have been equally welcome to me."

"I should not have gone to this sort of thing anywhere else, you know; it is not in my line, as my mother says. I came to see you."

"And I would rather see you, Jan, than anybody else in the room—with one exception," was the reply of Sir Edmund. "I am sorry not to see Lionel."

"He couldn't come," answered Jan. "His wife turned crusty, and said she'd come if he did—something of that—and so he stayed at home. She is very ill, and she wants to ignore it, and go out all the same. It is not fit she should."

"Pray do you mean to dance, Jan?" inquired Lady Verner, the question being put ironically.

"I?" returned Jan. "Who'd dance with me?"

"I'll dance with you, Jan," said Lady Mary.

Jan shook his head. "I might get my feet entangled in the petticoats."

"Not you, Jan," said Sir Edmund, laughing. "I should risk that, if a lady asked me."

"She'd not care to dance with me," returned Jan, looking at Mary Elmsley. "She only says it out of good-nature."

"No, Jan, I don't think I do," frankly avowed Lady Mary. "I should like to dance with you."

"I'd stand up with you, if I stood up with anybody," replied Jan. "But where's the good of it? I don't know the figures, and should only put you out, as well as everybody else."

So, what with his ignorance of the figures, and his dreaded awkwardness amidst the trains, Jan was allowed to rest in peace. Mary Elmsley told him that if he would come over sometimes to their house in an evening, she and her young sisters would practise the figures with him, so that he might learn them. It was Jan's turn to laugh now. The notion of his practising dancing, or having evenings to waste on it, amused him considerably.

"Go to your house to learn dancing!" echoed he. "Folks would be for putting me into a lunatic asylum. If I do find an hour to myself any odd evening, I have to get to my dissection. I went shares the other day in a beautiful subject—"

"I don't think you need tell me of that, Jan," interrupted Lady Mary, keeping her countenance.

"I wonder you talk to him, Mary," observed Lady Verner, feeling thoroughly ashamed of Jan, and believing that everybody else did. "You hear how he repays you. He means it for good breeding, perhaps."

"I don't mean it for rudeness, at any rate," returned Jan. "Lady Mary knows that. Don't you?" he added, turning to her.

A strangely thrilling expression in her eyes as she looked at him was her only answer. "I would rather have that sort of rudeness from you, Jan," said she, "than the world's hollow politeness. There is so much of false—"

Mary Elmsley's sentence was never concluded. What was it that had broken in upon them? What object was that, gliding into the room like a ghost, on whom all eyes were strained with a terrible fascination? Was it a ghost? It appeared ghastly enough for one. Was it one of Jan's "subjects" come after him to the ball? Was it a corpse? It looked more like that than anything else. A corpse bedizened with jewels.

"She's mad!" exclaimed Jan, who was the first to recover his speech.

"What is it?" ejaculated Sir Edmund, gazing with something very like fear, as the spectre bore down towards him.

"It is my brother's wife," explained Jan. "You may see how fit she is to come."

There was no time for more. Sibylla had her hand held out to Sir Edmund, a wan smile on her ghastly face. His hesitation, his evident discomposure, as he took it, were not lost upon her.

"You have forgotten me, Sir Edmund; but I should have known you anywhere. Your face is bronzed, and it is the only change. Am I so much changed?"

"Yes, you are; greatly changed," was his involuntary acknowledgment in his surprise. "I should not have recognised you for the Sibylla West of those old days."

"I was at an age to change," she said. "I—"

The words were stopped by a fit of coughing. Not the ordinary cough, more or less violent, that we hear in every-day intercourse; but the dreadful cough that tells its tale of the hopeless state within. She had discarded her opera-cloak, and stood there, her shoulders, back, neck, all bare and naked; très décolletée, as the French would say; shivering palpably; imparting the idea of a skeleton with rattling bones. Sir Edmund Hautley, quitting Decima, took her hand compassionately and led her to a seat.

Mrs. Verner did not like the attention. Pity, compassion was in every line of his face—in every gesture of his gentle hand; and she resented it.

"I am not ill," she declared to Sir Edmund between the paroxysms of her distressing cough. "The wind seemed to take my throat as I got out of the fly, and it is making me cough a little, but I am not ill. Has Jan been telling you that I am?"

She turned round fiercely on Jan as she spoke. Jan had followed her to her chair, and stood near her; he may have deemed that so evident an invalid should possess a doctor at hand. A good thing that Jan was of equable disposition, of easy temperament; otherwise there might have been perpetual open war between him and Sibylla. She did not spare to him her sarcasms and her insults; but never, in all Jan's intercourse with her, had he resented them.

"No one has told me anything about you in particular, Mrs. Verner," was the reply of Sir Edmund. "I see that you look delicate."

"I am not delicate," she sharply said. "It is nothing. I should be very well, if it were not for Jan."

"That's good," returned Jan. "What do I do?"

"You worry me," she answered curtly. "You say I must not go out; I must not do this, or do the other. You know you do. Presently you will be saying I must not dance. But I will."

"Does Lionel know you have come?" inquired Jan, leaving other questions in abeyance.

"I don't know. It's nothing to him. He was not going to stop me. You should pay attention to your own appearance, Jan, instead of to mine; look at your gloves!"

"They split as I was drawing them on," said Jan.

Sibylla turned from him with a gesture of contempt. "I am enchanted that you have come home, Sir Edmund," she said to the baronet.

"I am pleased myself, Mrs. Verner. Home has more charms for me than the world knows of."

"You will give us some nice entertainments, I hope," she continued, her cough beginning to subside. "Sir Rufus lived like a hermit."

That she would not live to partake of any entertainments he might give, Sir Edmund Hautley felt as sure as though he had then seen her in her grave-clothes. No, not even could he be deceived, or entertain the faintest false hope, though the cough became stilled, and the brilliant hectic of reaction shone on her cheeks. Very beautiful would she then have looked, save for her attenuate frame, with that bright crimson flush and her gleaming golden hair.

Quite sufficiently beautiful to attract partners, and one came up and requested her to dance. She rose in acquiescence, turning her back right upon Jan, who would have interposed.

"Go away," said she. "I don't want any lecturing from you."

But Jan did not go away. He laid his hand impressively upon her shoulder. "You must not do it, Sibylla. There's a pond outside; it's just as good you went and threw yourself into that. It would do you no more harm."

She jerked her shoulder away from him; laughing a little, scornful laugh, and saying a few contemptuous words to her partner, directed to Jan. Jan propped his back against the wall, and watched her, giving her a few words in his turn.

"As good try to turn a mule, as turn her."

He watched her through the quadrille. He watched the gradually increasing excitement of her temperament. Nothing could be more pernicious for her; nothing more dangerous; as Jan knew. Presently he watched her plunge into a waltz; and just at that moment his eyes fell on Lionel.

He had just entered; he was shaking hands with Sir Edmund Hautley. Jan made his way to them.

"Have you seen Sibylla, Jan?" was the first question of Lionel to his brother. "I hear she has come."

For answer, Jan pointed towards a couple amidst the waltzers, and Lionel's dismayed gaze fell on his wife, whirling round at a mad speed, her eyes glistening, her cheeks burning, her bosom heaving. With the violence of the exertion, her poor breath seemed to rise in loud gasps, shaking her to pieces, and the sweat-drops poured off her brow.

One dismayed exclamation, and Lionel took a step forward. Jan caught him back.

"It is of no use, Lionel. I have tried. It would only make a scene, and be productive of no end. I am not sure either, whether opposition at the present moment would not do as much harm as is being done."

"Jan!" cried Sir Edmund in an undertone, "is—she—dying?"

"She is not far off it," was Jan's answer.

Lionel had yielded to Jan's remonstrance, and stood back against the wall, as Jan had previously been doing. The waltz came to an end. In the dispersion Lionel lost sight of his wife. A few moments, and strange sounds of noise and confusion were echoing from an adjoining room. Jan went away at his own rate of speed, Lionel in his wake. They had caught the reiterated words, spoken in every phase of terrified tones, "Mrs. Verner! Mrs. Verner!"

Ah, poor Mrs. Verner! That had been her last dance on earth. The terrible exertion had induced a fit of coughing of unnatural violence, and in the straining a blood-vessel had once more broken.

CHAPTER LXXXVII

THE LAMP BURNS OUT AT LAST

From the roof of the house to the floor of the cellar, ominous silence reigned in Deerham Court. Mrs. Verner lay in it—dying. She had been conveyed home from the Hall on the morning following the catastrophe. Miss Hautley and Sir Edmund urged her remaining longer, offering every possible hospitality; but poor Sibylla seemed to have taken a caprice against it. Caprices she would have, up to her last breath. All her words were "Home! home!" Jan said she might be moved with safety; and she was taken there.

She seemed none the worse for the removal—she was none the worse for it. She was dying, but the transit had not increased her danger or her pain. Dr. Hayes had been over in the course of the night, and was now expected again.

"It's all waste of time, his coming; he can't do anything; but it is satisfaction for Lionel," observed Jan to his mother.

Lady Verner felt inclined to blame those of her household who had been left at home, for Sibylla's escapade: all of them—Lionel, Lucy Tempest, and the servants. They ought to have prevented it, she said; have kept her in by force, had need been. But she blamed them wrongly. Lionel might have done so had he been present; there was no knowing whether he would so far have exerted his authority, but the scene that would inevitably have ensued might not have been less fatal in its consequences to Sibylla. Lucy answered, and with truth, that any remonstrance of hers to Sibylla would never have been listened to; and the servants excused themselves—it was not their place to presume to oppose Mr. Verner's wife.

She lay on the sofa in her dressing-room, propped up by pillows; her face wan, her breathing laboured. Decima with her, calm and still; Catherine hovered near, to be useful, if necessary; Lady Verner was in her room within call; Lucy Tempest sat on the stairs. Lucy, remembering certain curious explosions, feared that her presence might not be acceptable to the invalid; but Lucy partook of the general restlessness, and sat down in her simple fashion on the stairs, listening for news from the sick-chamber. Neither she nor any one else in the house could have divested themselves of the prevailing excitement that day, or settled to calmness in the remotest degree. Lucy wished from her very heart that she could do anything to alleviate the sufferings of Mrs. Verner, or to soothe the general discomfort.

By and by, Jan entered, and came straight up the stairs. "Am I to walk over you, Miss Lucy?"

"There's plenty of room to go by, Jan," she answered, pulling her dress aside.

"Are you doing penance?" he asked, as he strode past her.

"It is so dull remaining in the drawing-room by myself," answered Lucy apologetically. "Everybody is upstairs."

Jan went into the sick-room, and Lucy sat on in silence; her head bent down on her knees, as before. Presently Jan returned.

"Is she any better, Jan?"

"She's no worse," was Jan's answer. "That's something, when it comes to this stage. Where's Lionel?"

"I do not know," replied Lucy. "I think he went out. Jan," she added, dropping her voice, "will she get well?"

"Get well!" echoed Jan in his plainness. "It's not likely. She won't be here four-and-twenty hours longer."

"Oh, Jan!" uttered Lucy, painfully startled and distressed. "What a dreadful thing! And all because of her going out last night!"

"Not altogether," answered Jan. "It has hastened it, no doubt; but the ending was not far off in any case."

"If I could but save her!" murmured Lucy in her unselfish sympathy. "I shall always be thinking that perhaps if I had spoken to her last night, instead of going out to find Mr. Verner, she might not have gone."

"Look here," said Jan. "You are not an angel yet, are you, Miss Lucy?"

"Not at all like one, I fear, Jan," was her sad answer.

"Well, then, I can tell you for your satisfaction that an angel, coming down from heaven and endued with angel's powers, wouldn't have stopped her last night. She'd have gone in spite of it; in spite of you all. Her mind was made up to it; and her telling Lionel in the morning that she'd give up going, provided he would promise to take her for a day's pleasure to Heartburg, was only a ruse to throw the house off its guard."

Jan passed down; Lucy sat on. As Jan was crossing the courtyard—for he actually went out at the front door for once in his life, as he had done the day he carried the blanket and the black tea-kettle—he encountered John Massingbird. Mr. John wore his usual free-and-easy costume, and had his short pipe in his mouth.

"I say," began he, "what's this tale about Mrs. Lionel? Folks are saying that she went off to Hautley's last night, and danced herself to death."

"That's near enough," replied Jan. "She would go; and she did; and she danced; and she finished it up by breaking a blood-vessel. And now she is dying."

"What was Lionel about, to let her go?"

"Lionel knew nothing of it. She slipped off while he was out. Nobody was in the house but Lucy Tempest and one or two of the servants. She dressed herself on the quiet, sent for a fly, and went."

"And danced!"

"And danced," assented Jan. "Her back and shoulders looked like a bag of bones. You might nearly have heard them rattle."

"I always said there were moments when Sibylla's mind was not right," composedly observed John Massingbird. "Is there any hope?"

"None. There has not been hope, in point of fact, for a long while," continued Jan, "as anybody might have seen, except Sibylla. She has been obstinately blind to it. Although her father warned her, when he was here, that she could not live."

John Massingbird smoked for some moments in silence. "She was always sickly," he presently said; "sickly in constitution; sickly in temper."

Jan nodded. But what he might further have said was stopped by the entrance of Lionel. He came in at the gate, looking jaded and tired. His mind was ill at ease, and he had not been to bed.

"I have been searching for you, Jan. Dr. West ought to be telegraphed to. Can you tell where he is?"

"No, I can't," replied Jan. "He was at Biarritz when he last wrote; but they were about to leave. I expect to hear from him daily. If we did know where he is, Lionel, telegraphing would be of no use. He could not get here."

"I should like him telegraphed to, if possible," was Lionel's answer.

"I'll telegraph to Biarritz, if you like," said Jan. "He is sure to have left it, though."

"Do so," returned Lionel. "Will you come in?" he added to John Massingbird.

"No, thank you," replied John Massingbird. "They'd not like my pipe. Tell Sibylla I hope she'll get over it. I'll come again by and by, and hear how she is."

Lionel went indoors and passed upstairs with a heavy footstep. Lucy started from her place, but not before he had seen her in it.

"Why do you sit there, Lucy?"

"I don't know," she answered, blushing that he should have caught her there, though she had not cared for Jan's doing so. "It is lonely downstairs to-day; here I can ask everybody who comes out of the room how she is. I wish I could cure her! I wish I could do anything for her!"

He laid his hand lightly on her head as he passed. "Thank you for all, my dear child!" and there was a strange tone of pain in his low voice as he spoke it.

Only Decima was in the room then, and she quitted it as Lionel entered. Treading softly across the carpet, he took his seat in a chair opposite Sibylla's couch. She slept—for a great wonder—or appeared to sleep. The whole morning long—nay, the whole night long, her bright, restless eyes had been wide open; sleep as far from her as it could well be. It had seemed that her fractious temper kept the sleep away. But her eyes were closed now, and two dark, purple rims inclosed them, terribly dark on the wan, white face. Suddenly the eyes unclosed with a start, as if her doze had been abruptly disturbed, though Lionel had been perfectly still. She looked at him for a minute or two in silence, and he, knowing it would be well that she should doze again, neither spoke nor moved.

"Lionel, am I dying?"

Quietly as the words were spoken, they struck on his ear with startling intensity. He rose then and pushed her hair from her damp brow with a fond hand, murmuring some general inquiry as to how she felt.

"Am I dying?" came again from the panting lips.

What was he to answer her? To say that she was dying might send her into a paroxysm of terror; to deceive her in that awful hour by telling her she was not, went against every feeling of his heart.

"But I don't want to die," she urged, in some excitement, interpreting his silence to mean the worst. "Can't Jan do anything for me? Can't Dr. Hayes?"

"Dr. Hayes will be here soon," observed Lionel soothingly, if somewhat evasively. "He will come by the next train."

She took his hand, held it between hers, and looked beseechingly up to his face. "I don't want to leave you," she whispered. "Oh, Lionel! keep me here if you can! You know you are always kind to me. Sometimes I have reproached you that you were not, but it was not true. You have been ever kind, have you not?"

"I have ever striven to be so," he answered, the tears glistening on his eyelashes.

"I don't want to die. I want to get well and go about again, as I used to do when at Verner's Pride. Now Sir Edmund Hautley is come home, that will be a good place to visit at. Lionel, I don't want to die! Can't you keep me in life?"

"If by sacrificing my own life, I could save yours, Heaven knows how willingly I would do it," he tenderly answered.

"Why should I die? Why should I die more than others? I don't think I am dying, Lionel," she added, after a pause. "I shall get well yet."

She stretched out her hand for some cooling drink that was near, and Lionel gave her a teaspoonful. He was giving her another, but she jerked her head away and spilled it.

"It's not nice," she said. So he put it down.

"I want to see Deborah," she resumed.

"My dear, they are at Heartburg. I told you so this morning. They will be home, no doubt, by the next train. Jan has sent to them."

"What should they do at Heartburg?" she fractiously asked.

"They went over yesterday to remain until to-day, I hear."

Subsiding into silence, she lay quite still, save for her panting breath, holding Lionel's hand as he bent over her. Some noise in the corridor outside attracted her attention, and she signed to him to open the door.

"Perhaps it is Dr. Hayes," she murmured. "He is better than Jan."

Better than Jan, insomuch as that he was rather given to assure his patients they would soon be strong enough to enjoy the al fresco delights of a gipsy party, even though he knew that they had not an hour's prolonged life left in them. Not so Jan. Never did a more cheering doctor enter a sick-room than Jan, so long as there was the faintest shade of hope. But, when the closing scene was actually come, the spirit all but upon the wing, then Jan whispered of hope no more. He could not do it in his pure sincerity. Jan could be silent; but Jan could not tell a man, whose soul was hovering on the threshold of the next world, that he might yet recreate himself dancing hornpipes in this. Dr. Hayes would; it was in his creed to do so; and in that respect Dr. Hayes was different from Jan.

It was not Dr. Hayes. As Lionel opened the door, Lucy was passing it, and Thérèse was at the end of the corridor talking to Lady Verner. Lucy stopped to make her kind inquiries, her tone a low one, of how the invalid was then.

"Whose voice is that?" called out Mrs. Verner, her words scarcely reaching her husband's ears.

"It is Lucy Tempest's," he said, closing the door, and returning to her. "She was asking after you."

"Tell her to come in."

Lionel opened the door again, and beckoned to Lucy. "Mrs. Verner is asking if you will come in and see her," he said, as she approached.

All the old grievances, the insults of Sibylla, blotted out from her gentle and forgiving mind, lost sight of in this great crisis, Lucy went up to the couch, and stood by the side of Sibylla. Lionel leaned over its back.

"I trust you are not feeling very ill, Mrs. Verner," she said in a low, sweet tone as she bent towards her and touched her hand. Touched it only; let her own fall lightly upon it; as if she did not feel sufficiently sure of Sibylla's humour to presume to take it.

"No, I don't think I'm better. I am so weak here."

She touched her chest as she spoke. Lucy, perhaps somewhat at a loss what to say, stood in silence.

"I have been very cross to you sometimes, Lucy," she resumed. "I meant nothing. I used to feel vexed with everybody, and said foolish things without meaning it. It was so cruel to be turned from Verner's Pride, and it made me unhappy."

"Indeed I do not think anything about it," replied Lucy, the tears rising to her eyes in her forgiving tenderness. "I know how ill you must have felt. I used to feel that I should like to help you to bear the pain and the sorrow."

Sibylla lay panting. Lucy remained as she was; Lionel also. Presently she, Sibylla, glanced at Lucy.

"I wish you'd kiss me."

Lucy, unnerved by the words, bent closer to her, a shower of tears falling from her eyes on Sibylla's face.

"If I could but save her life for you!" she murmured to Lionel, glancing up at him through her tears as she rose from the embrace. And she saw that Lionel's eyes were as wet as hers.

And now there was a commotion outside. Sounds, as of talking and wailing and crying, were heard. Little need to tell Lionel that they came from the Misses West; he recognised the voices; and Lucy glided forward to open the door.

Poor ladies! They were wont to say ever after that their absence had happened on purpose. Mortified at being ignored in Miss Hautley's invitations, they had made a little plan to get out of Deerham. An old friend in Heartburg had repeatedly pressed them to dine there and remain for the night, and they determined to avail themselves of the invitation this very day of the fête at Deerham Hall. It would be pleasant to have to say to inquisitive friends, "We could not attend it; we were engaged to Heartburg." Many a lady, of more account in the world than Deborah or Amilly West, has resorted to a less innocent ruse to conceal an offered slight. Jan had despatched Master Cheese by the new railway that morning with the information of Sibylla's illness; and here they were back again, full of grief, of consternation, and ready to show it in their demonstrative way.

Lionel hastened out to them, a Hush—sh! upon his tongue. He caught hold of them as they were hastening in.

"Yes; but not like this. Be still, for her sake."

Deborah looked at his pale face, reading it aright. "Is she so ill as tha'?" she gasped. "Is there no hope?"

He only shook his head. "Whatever you do, preserve a calm demeanour before her. We must keep her in tranquillity."

"Master Cheese says she went to the ball—and danced," said Deborah. "Mr. Verner, how could you allow it?"

"She did go," he answered. "It was no fault of mine."

Heavier footsteps up the stairs now. They were those of the physician, who had come by the train which had brought the Misses West. He, Dr. Hayes, entered the room, and they stole in after him; Lionel followed; Jan came bursting in, and made another; and Lucy remained outside.

Lady Verner saw Dr. Hayes when he was going away.

"There was no change," he said, in answer to her inquiries. "Mrs. Verner was certainly in a very weak, sick state, and—there was no change."

The Misses West removed their travelling garments, and took up their stations in the sick-room—not to leave it again, until the life should have departed from Sibylla. Lionel remained in it. Decima and Catherine went in and out, and Jan made frequent visits to the house.

"Tell papa it is the leaving Verner's Pride that has killed me," said Sibylla to Amilly with nearly her latest breath.

There was no bed for any of them that night, any more than there had been the previous one. A life was hovering in the balance. Lucy sat with Lady Verner, and the rest went in to them occasionally, taking news. Dawn was breaking when one went in for the last time.

It was Jan. He had come to break the tidings to his mother, and he sat himself down on the arm of the sofa—Jan fashion—while he did it.

The flickering lamp of life had burned out at last.

CHAPTER LXXXVIII

ACHING HEARTS

If there be one day in the whole year more gladdening to the heart than all others, it is surely the first day of early spring. It may come and give us a glimpse almost in mid-winter; it may not come until winter ought to have been long past: but, appear when it will, it brings rejoicing with it. How many a heart, sinking under its bitter burden of care, is reawakened to hope by that first spring day of brightness! It seems to promise that there shall be yet a change in the dreary lot; it whispers that trouble may not last: that sickness may be superseded by health; that this dark wintry world will be followed by heaven.

Such a day was smiling over Deerham. And they were only in the first days of February. The sun was warm, the fields were green, the sky was blue; all Nature seemed to have put on her brightness. As Mrs. Duff stood at her door and exchanged greetings with sundry gossips passing by—an unusual number of whom were abroad—she gave it as her opinion that the charming weather had been vouchsafed as a special favour to Miss Decima Verner; for it was the wedding-day of that young lady and Sir Edmund Hautley.

Sir Edmund would fain have been married immediately after his return. Perhaps Decima would also. But Lady Verner, always given to study the proprieties of life, considered that it would be more seemly to allow first a few months to roll on after the death of her son's wife. So the autumn and part of the winter were allowed to go by; and in this, the first week of February, they were united; being favoured with weather that might have cheated them into a belief that it was May-day.

How anxious Deerham was to get a sight of her, as the carriages conveying the party to church drove to and fro! Lionel gave her away, and her bride's-maids were Lady Mary Elmsley and Lucy Tempest. The story of the long engagement between her and Edmund Hautley had electrified Deerham; and some began to wish that they had not called her an old maid quite so prematurely. Should it unfortunately have reached her ears, it might tend to place them in the black books of the future Lady Hautley. Lady Verner was rather against Jan's going to church. Lady Verner's private opinion was—indeed it may be said her proclaimed opinion as well as her private one—that Jan would be no ornament to a wedding party. But Decima had already got Jan's promise to be present, which Jan had given conditionally—that no patients required him at the time. But Jan's patients proved themselves considerate that day; and Jan appeared not only at the church, but at the breakfast.

At the dinner, also, in the evening. Sir Edmund and Lady Hautley had left then; but those who remained of course wanted some dinner; and had it. It was a small party, more social than formal: Mr. and Mrs. Bitterworth, Lord Garle and his sister, Miss Hautley and John Massingbird. Miss Hautley was again staying temporarily at Deerham Hall, but she would leave it on the following day. John Massingbird was invited at the special request of Lionel. Perhaps John was less of an ornament to a social party than even Jan, but Lionel had been anxious that no slight should be placed upon him. It would have been a slight for the owner of Verner's Pride to be left out at Decima Verner's wedding. Lady Verner held out a little while; she did not like John Massingbird: never had liked any of the Massingbirds; but Lionel carried his point. John Massingbird showed himself presentable that day, and had left his pipe at home.

In one point Mr. Massingbird proved himself as little given to ceremony as Jan could be. The dinner hour, he had been told, was seven o'clock; and he arrived shortly after six. Lucy Tempest and Mary Elmsley were in the drawing-room. Fair, graceful girls, both of them, in their floating white bride's-maid's robes, which they would wear for the day; Lucy always serene and quiet; Mary, merry-hearted, gay-natured. Mary was to stay with them for some days. They looked somewhat scared at the early entrance of John Massingbird. Curious tales had gone about Deerham of John's wild habits at Verner's Pride, and, it may be, they felt half afraid of him. Lucy whispered to the servant to find Mr. Verner and tell him. Lady Verner had gone to her room to make ready for dinner.

"I say, young ladies, is it six or seven o'clock that we are to dine?" he began. "I could not remember."

"Seven," replied Lucy.

"I am too soon by an hour, then," returned he, sitting down in front of the fire. "How are you by this time, Lionel?"

Lionel shook hands with him as he came in. "Never mind; we are glad to see you," he said in answer to a half apology from John Massingbird about the arriving early. "I can show you those calculations now, if you like."

"Calculations be hanged!" returned John. "When a fellow comes out to dinner, he does not want to be met with 'calculations.' What else, Lionel?"

Lionel Verner laughed. They were certain calculations drawn out by himself, connected with unavoidable work to be commenced on the Verner's Pride estate. For the last month he had been vainly seeking an opportunity of going over them with John Massingbird; that gentleman, who hated details as much as Master Cheese hated work, continually contrived to put it off.

"Have you given yourself the pleasure of making them out in duplicate, that you propose to show them here?" asked he, some irony in his tone. "I thought they were in the study at Verner's Pride."

"I brought them home a day or two ago," replied Lionel. "Some alteration was required, and I thought I would do it quietly here."

"You are a rare—I suppose if I say 'steward' I shall offend your pride, Lionel? 'Bailiff' would be worse. If real stewards were as faithful and indefatigable as you, landlords might get on better than they do. You can't think how he plagues me with his business details, Miss Tempest."

"I can," said Lady Mary freely. "I think he is terribly conscientious."

"All the more so, that he is not going to be a steward long," answered Lionel in a tone through which ran a serious meaning, light as it was. "The time is approaching when I shall render up an account of my stewardship, so far as Verner's Pride is concerned."

"What do you mean by that?" cried John Massingbird.

"I'll tell you to-morrow," answered Lionel.

"I'd like to know now, if it's all the same to you, sir," was John's answer. "You are not going to give up the management of Verner's Pride?"

"Yes, I am," replied Lionel. "I should have resigned it when my wife died, but that—that—Decima wished me to remain in Deerham until her marriage," he concluded after some perceptible hesitation.

"What has Deerham done to you that you want to quit it?" asked John Massingbird.

"I would have left Deerham years ago, had it been practicable," was the remark of Lionel.

"I ask you why?"

"Why? Do you think Deerham and its reminiscences can be so pleasant to me that I should care to stop in it, unless compelled?"

"Bother reminiscences!" rejoined Mr. Massingbird. "I conclude you make believe to allude to the ups and downs you have had in regard to Verner's Pride. That's not the cause, Lionel Verner—if you do want to go away. You have had time to get over that. Perhaps some lady is in the way? Some cross-grained disappointment in that line? Have you been refusing to marry him, Lady Mary?"

Lady Mary threw her laughing blue eyes full in the face of the questioner. "He never asked me, Mr. Massingbird."

"No!" said John.

"No," said she, the lips laughing now, as well as the eyes. "In the old days—I declare I don't mind letting out the secret—in the old days before he was married at all, mamma and Lady Verner contrived to let me know, by indirect hints, that Lionel Verner might be expected to—to—solicit the honour of my becoming his wife. How I laughed behind their backs! It would have been time enough to turn rebellious when the offer came—which I was quite sure never would come—to make them and him a low curtsy, and say, 'You are very kind, but I must decline the honour.' Did you get any teasings on your side, Lionel?" asked she frankly.

A half smile flitted over Lionel's lips. He did not speak.

"No," added Lady Mary, her joking tone turning to seriousness, her blue eyes to earnestness, "I and Lionel have ever been good friends, fond of each other, I believe, in a sober kind of way: but—any closer relationship, we should both have run apart from, as wide as the two poles. I can answer for myself; and I think I can for him."

"I see," said John Massingbird. "To be husband and wife would go against the grain: you'd rather be brother and sister."

What there could be in the remark to disturb the perfect equanimity of Mary Elmsley, she best knew. Certain it was that her face turned of a fiery red, and it seemed that she did not know where to look. She spoke rapid words, as if to cover her confusion.

"So you perceive, Mr. Massingbird, that I have nothing to do with Mr. Verner's plans and projects; with his stopping at Deerham or going away from it. I should not think any lady has. You are not going, are you?" she asked turning to Lionel.

"Yes, I shall go, Mary," he answered. "As soon as Mr. Massingbird can find somebody to replace me—"

"Mr. Massingbird's not going to find anybody to replace you," burst forth John. "I declare, Lionel, if you do go, I'll take on Roy, just to spite you and your old tenants. By the way, though, talking of Roy, who do you think has come back to Deerham?" he broke off, rather less vehemently.

"How can I guess?" asked Lionel. "Some of the Mormons, perhaps."

"No. Luke Roy. He has arrived this afternoon."

"Has he indeed?" replied Lionel, a shade of sadness in his tone, more than surprise, for somehow the name of Luke, coupled with his return, brought back all too vividly the recollection of his departure, and the tragic end of Rachel Frost which had followed so close upon it.

"I have not seen him," rejoined Mr. Massingbird. "I met Mrs. Roy as I came on here, and she told me. She was scuttering along with some muffins in her hand—to regale him on, I suppose."

"How glad she must be!" exclaimed Lucy.

"Rather sorry, I thought," returned John. "She looked very quaky and shivery. I tell you what, Lionel," he continued, turning to him, "your dinner will not be ready this three-quarters of an hour yet. I'll just go as far as old Roy's, and have a word with Luke. I have got a top-coat in the hall."

He went out without ceremony. Lionel walked with him to the door. It was a fine, starlight evening. When he, Lionel, returned, Lucy was alone. Mary Elmsley had left the room.

Lucy had quitted the chair of state she had been sitting in, and was in her favourite place on a low stool on the hearth-rug. She was more kneeling than sitting. The fire-light played on her sweet face, so young and girlish still in its outlines, on her pretty hands clasped on her knees, on her arms which glittered with pearls, on the pearls that rested on her neck. Lionel stood on the other side of the hearth-rug, leaning, as usual, on the mantel-piece.

At least five minutes passed in silence. And then Lucy raised her eyes to his.

"Was it a joke, what you said to John Massingbird—about leaving Deerham?"

"It was sober earnest, Lucy. I shall go as soon as I possibly can now."

"But why?" she presently asked.

"I should have left, as you heard me say, after Mrs. Verner's death, but for one or two considerations. Decima very much wished me to remain until her marriage; and—I did not see my way particularly clear to embark in a new course of life. I do not see it yet."

"Why should you go?" asked Lucy.

"Because I—because it is expedient that I should, for many reasons," he answered.

"You do not like to remain subservient to John Massingbird?"

"It is not that. I have got over that. My prospects have been so utterly blighted, Lucy, that I think some of the old pride of the Verner race has gone out of me. I do not see a chance of getting anything to do half as good as this stewardship—as he but now called it—under John Massingbird. But I shall try at it."

"What shall you try, do you think?"

"I cannot tell. I should like to get something abroad; I should like to go to India. I do not suppose I have any real chance of getting an appointment there; but stopping in Deerham will certainly not bring it to me: that, or anything else."

Lucy's lips had parted. "You will not think of going to India now!" she breathlessly exclaimed.

"Indeed I do think of it, Lucy."

"So far off as that!"

The words were uttered with a strange sound of pain. Lionel passed his hand over his brow, the action betokening pain quite as great as Lucy's tone. Lucy rose from her seat and stood near him, her thoughtful face upturned.

"What is left for me in England?" he resumed. "What am I here? A man without home, fortune, hope. I have worse than no prospects. The ceremony at which we have been assisting this day seems to have brought the bare facts more palpably before me in all their naked truth. Other men can have a home, can form social ties to bless it. I cannot."

"But why?" asked Lucy, her lips trembling.

"Why! Can you ask it, Lucy? There are moments—and they are all too frequent—when a fond vision comes over me of what my future might be; of the new ties I might form, and find the happiness in, that—that I did not find in the last. The vision, I say, comes all too frequently for my peace of mind, when I realise the fact that it can never be realised."

Lucy stood, her hands tightly clasped before her, a world of sadness in her fair, young face. One less entirely single-hearted, less true than Lucy Tempest, might have professed to ignore the drift of his words. Had Lucy, since Mrs. Verner's death, cast a thought to the possibility of certain happy relations arising between her and Lionel—those social ties he now spoke of? No, not intentionally. If any such dreams did lurk in her heart unbidden, there she let them lie, in entire abeyance. Lionel Verner had never spoken a word to her, or dropped a hint that he contemplated such; his intercourse with her had been free and open, just as it was with Decima. She was quite content; to be with him, to see him daily, was enough of happiness for her, without looking to the future.

"The farther I get away from England the better," he resumed. "India, from old associations, naturally suggests itself, but I care not whither I go. You threw out a suggestion once, Lucy, that Colonel Tempest might be able to help me to something there, by which I may get a living. Should I have found no success in London by the time he arrives, it is my intention to ask him the favour. He will be home in a few weeks now."

"And you talk of leaving Deerham immediately!" cried Lucy. "Where's the necessity? You should wait until he comes."

"I have waited too long, as it is. Deerham will be glad to get rid of me. It may hold a jubilee the day it hears I have shipped myself off for India. I wonder if I shall ever come back? Probably not. I and old friends may never meet again on this side heaven."

He had been affecting to speak lightly, jokingly, toying at the same time with some trifle on the mantel-piece. But as he turned his eyes on Lucy at the conclusion of his sentence, he saw that the tears were falling on her cheeks. The words, the ideas they conjured up, had jarred painfully on every fibre of her heart. Lionel's light mood was gone.

"Lucy," he whispered, bending to her, his tone changing to one of passionate earnestness, "I dare not stay here longer. There are moments when I am tempted to forget my position, to forget honour, and speak words that—that—I ought not to speak. Even now, as I look down upon you, my heart is throbbing, my veins are tingling; but I must not touch you with my finger, or tell you of my impassioned love. All I can do is to carry it away with me, and battle with it alone."

Her face had grown white with emotion. She raised her wet eyes yearningly to his; but she still spoke the simple truth, unvarnished, the great agony that was lying at her heart.

"How shall I live on, with you away? It will be more lonely than I can bear."

"Don't, child!" he said in a wailing tone of entreaty. "The temptation from my own heart is all too present to me. Don't you tempt me. Strong man though I am, there are things that I cannot bear."

He leaned on the mantel-piece, shading his face with his hand. Lucy stood in silence, striving to suppress her emotion from breaking forth.

"In the old days—very long ago, they seem now, to look back upon—I had the opportunity of assuring my life's happiness," he continued in a low, steady tone. "I did not do it; I let it slip from me, foolishly, wilfully; of my now free act. But, Lucy—believe me or not as you like—I loved the one I rejected, more than the one I took. Before the sound of my marriage bells had yet rung out on my ears, the terrible conviction was within me that I loved that other better than all created things. You may judge, then, what my punishment has been."

She raised her eyes to his face, but he did not see them, did not look at her. He continued—

"It was the one great mistake of my life; made by myself alone. I cannot plead the excuse which so many are able to plead for life's mistakes—that I was drawn into it. I made it deliberately, as may be said; of my own will. It is but just, therefore, that I should expiate it. How I have suffered in the expiation, Heaven alone knows. It is true that I bound myself in a moment of delirium, of passion; giving myself no time for thought. But I have never looked upon that fact as an excuse; for a man who has come to the years I had should hold his feelings under his own control. Yes; I missed that opportunity, and the chance went by for life."

"For life?" repeated Lucy, with streaming eyes. It was too terribly real a moment for any attempt at concealment. A little reticence, in her maiden modesty; but of concealment, none.

"I am a poor man now, Lucy," he explained; "worse than without prospects, if you knew all. And I do not know why you should not know all," he added after a pause: "I am in debt. Such a man cannot marry."

The words were spoken quietly, temperately; their tone proving how hopeless could be any appeal against them, whether from him, from her, or from without. It was perfectly true: Lionel Verner's position placed him beyond the reach of social ties.

Little more was said. It was a topic which Lucy could not urge or gainsay; and Lionel did not see fit to continue it. He may have felt that it was dangerous ground, even for the man of honour that he strove to be. He held out his hand to Lucy.

"Will you forgive me?" he softly whispered.

Her sobs choked her. She strove to speak, as she crept closer to him, and put out her hands in answer; but the words would not come. She lifted her face to glance at his.

"Not a night passes but I pray God to forgive me," he whispered, his voice trembling with emotion, as he pressed her hands between his, "to forgive the sorrow I have brought upon you. Oh, Lucy! forgive—forgive me!"

"Yes, yes," was all her answer, her sobs impeding her utterance, her tears blinding her. Lionel kept the hands strained to him; he looked down on the upturned face, and read its love there; he kept his own bent, with its mingled expression of tenderness and pain; but he did not take from it a single caress. What right had he? Verily, if he had not shown control over himself once in his life, he was showing it now.

He released one of his hands and laid it gently upon her head for a minute, his lips moving silently. Then he let her go. It was over.

She sat down on the low stool again on the opposite side the hearth, and buried her face and her anguish. Lionel buried his face, his elbow on the mantel-piece, his hand uplifted. He never looked at her again, or spoke; she never raised her head; and when the company began to arrive, and came in, the silence was still unbroken.

And, as they talked and laughed that night, fulfilling the usages of society amidst the guests, how little did any one present suspect the scene which had taken place but a short while before! How many of the smiling faces we meet in society cover aching hearts!

CHAPTER LXXXIX

MASTER CHEESE BLOWN UP

There were other houses in Deerham that night, not quite so full of sociability as was Lady Verner's. For one, may be instanced that of the Misses West. They sat at the table in the general sitting-room, hard at work, a lamp between them, for the gas-burners above were high for sewing, and their eyes were no longer so keen as they had been. Miss Deborah was "turning" a table-cloth; Miss Amilly was darning sundry holes in a pillow-case. Their stock of household linen was in great need of being replaced by new; but, not having the requisite money to spare, they were doing their best to renovate the old.

A slight—they could not help feeling it as such—had been put upon them that day, in not having been invited to Decima Verner's wedding. The sisters-in-law of Lionel Verner, connected closely with Jan, they had expected the invitation. But it had not come. Lionel had pressed his mother to give it; Jan, in his straightforward way, when he had found it was not forthcoming, said, "Why don't you invite them! They'd do nobody any harm." Lady Verner, however had positively declined: the Wests had never been acquaintances of hers, she said. They felt the slight, poor ladies, but they felt it quite humbly and meekly; not complaining; not venturing even to say to each other that they might have been asked. They only sat a little more silent than usual over their work that evening, doing more, and talking less.

The servant came in with the supper-tray, and laid it on the table. "Is the cold pork to come in?" asked she. "I have not brought it. I thought, perhaps, you'd not care to have it in to-night, ma'am, as Mr. Jan's out."

Miss Deborah cast her eyes on the tray. There was a handsome piece of cheese, and a large glass of fresh celery. A rapid calculation passed through her mind that the cold pork, if not cut for supper, would make a dinner the following day, with an apple or a jam pudding.

"No, Martha, this will do for to-night," she answered. "Call Master Cheese, and then draw the ale."

"It's a wonder he waits to be called," was Martha's comment, as she went out. "He is generally in afore the tray, whatever the meals may be, he is."

She went out at the side door, and entered the surgery. Nobody was in it except the surgery-boy. The boy was asleep, with his head and arms on the counter, and the gas flared away over him. A hissing and fizzing from Jan's room, similar to the sounds Lucy Tempest heard when she invaded the surgery the night of the ball at Deerham Hall, saluted Martha's ears. She went round the counter, tried the door, found it fastened, and shook the handle.

"Who's there?" called out Master Cheese from the other side.

"It's me," said Martha "Supper's ready."

"Very well. I'll be in directly," responded Master Cheese.

"I say!" called out Martha wrathfully, rattling the handle again, "if you are making a mess of that room, as you do sometimes, I won't have it. I'll complain to Mr. Jan. There! Messing the floor and places with your powder and stuff! It would take two servants to clear up after you."

"You go to Bath," was the satisfactory recommendation of Master Cheese.

Martha called out another wrathful warning, and withdrew. Master Cheese came forth, locked the door, took out the key, went indoors, and sat down to supper.

Sat down in angry consternation. He threw his eager glances to every point of the table, and could not see upon it what he was longing to see—what he had been expecting all the evening to see—for the terrible event of its not being there had never so much as crossed his imagination. The dinner had consisted of a loin of pork with the crackling on, and apple sauce—a dish so beloved by Master Cheese, that he never thought of it without a watering of the mouth. It had been nothing like half eaten at dinner, neither the pork nor the sauce. Jan was at the wedding-breakfast, and the Misses West, in Master Cheese's estimation, ate like two sparrows: of course he had looked to be regaled with it at supper. Miss West cut him a large piece of cheese, and Miss Amilly handed him the glass of celery.

Now Master Cheese had no great liking for that vulgar edible which bore his name, and which used to form the staple of so many good, old-fashioned suppers. To cheese, in the abstract, he could certainly have borne no forcible objection, since he was wont to steal into the larder, between breakfast and dinner, and help himself—as Martha would grumblingly complain—to "pounds" of it. The state of the case was just this: the young gentleman liked cheese well enough when he could get nothing better. Cheese, however, as a substitute for cold loin of pork, with "crackling" and apple sauce, was hardly to be borne, and Master Cheese sat in dumbfounded dismay, heaving great sighs and casting his eyes upon his plate.

"I feel quite faint," said he.

"What makes you feel faint?" asked Miss Deb.

"Well, I suppose it is for want of my supper," he returned. "Is—is there no meat to-night, Miss Deb?"

"Not any," she answered decisively. She had the pleasure of knowing Master Cheese well.

Master Cheese paused. "There was nearly the whole joint left at dinner," said he in a tone of remonstrance.

"There was a good deal of it left, and that's the reason it's not coming in," replied Miss Deb. "It will be sufficient for to-morrow's dinner with a pudding, I'm sure it will not hurt you to sup upon cheese for one night."

With all his propensity for bonne chère, Master Cheese was really of a modest nature, and would not go the length of demanding luxuries, if denied them by Miss Deb. He was fain to content himself with the cheese and celery, eating so much of it that it may be a question whether the withholding of the cold pork had been a gain in point of economy.

Laying down his knife at length, he put back his chair to return to the surgery. Generally he was not in so much haste; he liked to wait until the things were removed, even to the cloth, lest by a speedy departure he might miss some nice little dainty or other, coming in at the tail of the repast. It is true such impromptu arrivals were not common at Miss West's table, but Master Cheese liked to be on the sure side.

"You are in a hurry," remarked Miss Amilly, surprised at the unwonted withdrawal.

"Jan's out," returned Master Cheese. "Folks may be coming in to the surgery."

"I wonder if Mr. Jan will be late to-night?" cried Miss Deb.

"Of course he will," confidently replied Master Cheese. "Who ever heard of a wedding-party breaking up before morning?"

For this reason, probably, Master Cheese returned to the surgery, prepared to "make a night of it"—not altogether in the general acceptation of that term, but at his chemical experiments. It was most rare that he could make sure of Jan's absence for any length of time. When abroad in pursuance of his professional duties, Jan might be returning at any period; in five minutes or in five hours; there was no knowing; and Master Cheese dared not get his chemical apparatus about, in the uncertainty, Jan having so positively forbidden his recreations in the science. For this night, however, he thought he was safe. Master Cheese's ideas of a wedding festival consisted of unlimited feasting. He could not have left such a board, if bidden to one, until morning light, and he judged others by himself.

Jan's bedroom was strewed with vessels of various sorts and sizes from one end of it to the other. In the old days, Dr. West had been a considerable dabbler in experimental chemistry himself. Jan also understood something of it. Master Cheese did not see why he should not. A roaring fire burned in Jan's grate, and the young gentleman stood before it for a few minutes, previous to resuming his researches, giving his back a roast, and indulging bitter reminiscences touching his deficient supper.

"She's getting downright mean, is that old Deb!" grumbled he; "especially if Jan happens to be out. Wasn't it different in West's time! He knew what was good, he did. Catch her daring to put bread and cheese on the table for supper then. I shall be quite exhausted before the night's over. Bob!"

Bob, his head still on the counter, partially woke up at the call—sufficiently so to return a half sound by way of response.

"Bob!" roared Master Cheese again. "Can't you hear?"

Bob, his eyes blinking and winking, came in, in answer: that is, as far as he could get in, for the litter lying about.

"Bring in the jar of tamarinds."

"The jar of tamarinds!" repeated Bob. "In here?"

"Yes, in here," said Master Cheese. "Now, you needn't stare. All you have got to do is to obey orders."

Bob disappeared, and presently returned, lugging in a big porcelain jar. He was ordered to "take out the bung, and leave it open." He did so, setting it in a convenient place on the floor, near Master Cheese, and giving his opinion gratuitously of the condition of the room. "Won't there be a row when Mr. Jan comes in and finds it like this!"

"Won't there be a row!"

"The things will be put away long before he comes," responded Master Cheese. "Mind your own business. And, look here! if anybody comes bothering, Mr. Jan's out, and Mr. Cheese is out, and they can't be seen till the morning—unless it's some desperate case," added Master Cheese, somewhat qualifying the instructions—"a fellow dying, or anything of that."

Bob withdrew, to fall asleep in the surgery as before, his head and arms on the counter; and Master Cheese recommenced his studies. Solacing himself first of all with a few mouthfuls of tamarinds, as he intended to do at intervals throughout his labours, he plunged his hands into a mass of incongruous substances—nitre, chlorate of potass, and sulphur being amongst them.

The Misses West, meanwhile, had resumed their work after supper, and they sewed until the clock struck ten. Then they put it away, and drew round the fire for a chat, their feet on the fender. A very short while, and they were surprised by the entrance of Jan.

"My goodness!" exclaimed Miss Amilly. "It's never you yet, Mr. Jan!"

"Why shouldn't it be?" returned Jan, drawing forward a chair, and sitting down by them. "Did you fancy I was going to sleep there?"

"Master Cheese thought you would keep it up until morning."

"Oh! did he? Is he gone to bed?"

"He is in the surgery," replied Miss Amilly. "Mr. Jan, you have told us nothing yet about the wedding in the morning."

"It went off," answered Jan.

"But the details? How did the ladies look?"

"They looked as usual, for all I saw," replied Jan.

"What did they wear?"

"Wear? Gowns, I suppose."

"Oh, Mr. Jan! Surely you saw better than that! Can't you tell what sort of gowns?"

Jan really could not. It may be questioned whether he could have told a petticoat from a gown. Miss Amilly was waiting with breathless interest, her lips apart.

"Some were in white, and some were in colours, I think," hazarded Jan, trying to be correct in his good nature. "Decima was in a veil."

"Of course she was," acquiesced Miss Amilly with emphasis. "Did the bridemaids—"

What pertinent question relating to the bridemaids Miss Amilly was about to put, never was known. A fearful sound interrupted it. A sound nearly impossible to describe. Was it a crash of thunder? Had an engine from the distant railway taken up its station outside their house, and gone off with a bang? Or had the surgery blown up? The room they were in shook, the windows rattled, the Misses West screamed with real terror, and Jan started from his seat.

"It can't be an explosion of gas!" he muttered.

Bursting out of the room, he nearly knocked down Martha, who was bursting into it. Instinct, or perhaps sound, took Jan to the surgery, and they all followed in his wake. Bob, the image of terrified consternation, stood in the midst of a débris of glass, his mouth open, and his hair standing-upright. The glass bottles and jars of the establishment had flown from their shelves, causing the unhappy Bob to believe that the world had come to an end.

But what was the débris there, compared to the débris in the next room, Jan's! The window was out, the furniture was split, the various chemical apparatus had been shivered into a hundred pieces, the tamarind jar was in two, and Master Cheese was extended on the floor on his back, his hands scorched, his eyebrows singed off, his face black, and the end of his nose burning.

"Oh! that's it, is it?" said Jan, when his eyes took in the state of things. "I knew it would come to it."

"He have been and blowed hisself up," remarked Bob, who had stolen in after them.

"Is it the gas?" sobbed Miss Amilly, hardly able to speak for terror.

"No, it's not the gas," returned Jan, examining the débris more closely. "It's one of that gentleman's chemical experiments."

Deborah West was bending over the prostrate form in alarm. "He surely can't be dead!" she shivered.

"Not he," said Jan. "Come, get up," he added, taking Master Cheese by the arm to assist him.

He was placed in a chair, and there he sat, coming to, and emitting dismal groans.

"I told you what you'd bring it to, if you persisted in attempting experiments that you know nothing about," was Jan's reprimand, delivered in a sharp tone. "A pretty state of things this is!"

Master Cheese groaned again.

"Are you much hurt?" asked Miss Deb in a sympathising accent.

"Oh-o-o-o-o-o-h!" moaned Master Cheese.

"Is there anything we can get for you?" resumed Miss Deb.

"Oh-o-o-o-o-o-h!" repeated Master Cheese. "A glass of wine might revive me."

"Get up," said Jan, "and let's see if you can walk. He's not hurt, Miss Deb."

Master Cheese, yielding to the peremptory movement of Jan's arm, had no resource but to show them that he could walk. He had taken a step or two as dolefully as it was possible for him to take it, keeping his eyes shut, and stretching out his hands before him, after the manner of the blind, when an interruption came from Miss Amilly.

"What can this be, lying here?"

She was bending her head near the old bureau, which had been rent in the explosion, her eyes fixed upon some large letter or paper on the floor. They crowded round at the words. Jan picked it up, and found it to be a folded parchment bearing a great seal.

"Hollo!" exclaimed Jan.

On the outside was written "Codicil to the will of Stephen Verner."

"What is it?" exclaimed Miss Deborah, and even Master Cheese contrived to get his eyes open to look.

"It is the lost codicil," replied Jan. "It must have been in that bureau. How did it get there?"

How indeed? There ensued a pause.

"It must have been placed there"—Jan was beginning, and then he stopped himself. He would not, before those ladies, say—"by Dr. West."

But to Jan it was now perfectly clear. That old hunting for the "prescription," which had puzzled him at the time, was explained now. There was the "prescription"—the codicil! Dr. West had had it in his hand when disturbed in that room by a stranger: he had flung it back in the bureau in his hurry; pushed it back: and by some unexplainable means, he must have pushed it too far out of sight. And there it had lain until now, intact and undiscovered.

The hearts of the Misses West were turning to sickness, their countenances to pallor. That it could be no other than their father who had stolen the codicil from Stephen Verner's dying chamber, was present to their conviction. His motive could only have been to prevent Verner's Pride passing to Lionel, over his daughter and her husband. What did he think of his work when the news came of Frederick's death? What did he think of it when John Massingbird returned in person? What did he think of it when he read Sibylla's dying message, written to him by Amilly—"Tell papa it is the leaving Verner's Pride that has killed me?"

"I shall take possession of this," said Jan Verner. Master Cheese was conveyed to the house and consigned to bed, where his burnings were dressed by Jan, and restoratives administered to him, including the glass of wine.

The first thing on the following morning the codicil was handed over to Mr. Matiss. He immediately recognised it by its appearance. But it would be opened officially later, in the presence of John Massingbird. Jan betook himself to Verner's Pride to carry the news, and found Mr. Massingbird astride on a pillar of the terrace steps, smoking away with gusto. The day was warm and sunshiny as the previous one had been.

"What, is it you?" cried he, when Jan came in sight. "You are up here betimes. Anybody dying, this way?"

"Not this morning," replied Jan. "I say, Massingbird, there's ill news in the wind for you."

"What's that?" composedly asked John, tilting some ashes out of his pipe.

"That codicil has come to light."

John puffed on vigorously, staring at Jan, but never speaking.

"The thief must have been old West," went on Jan. "Only think! it has been hidden all this while in that bureau of his, in my bedroom."

"What has unhidden it?" demanded Mr. Massingbird in a half-satirical tone, as if he doubted the truth of the information.

"An explosion did that. Cheese got meddling with dangerous substances, and there was a blow-up. The bureau was thrown down and broken, and the codicil was dislodged. To talk of it, it sounds like an old stage trick."

"Did Cheese blow himself up?" asked John Massingbird.

"Yes. But he came down again. He is in bed with burned hands and a scorched face. If I had told him once to let that dangerous play alone—dangerous in his hands—I had told him ten times."

"Where's the codicil?" inquired Mr. Massingbird, smoking away.

"In Matiss's charge. You'd like to be present, I suppose, at the time of its being opened?"

"I can take your word," returned John Massingbird. "This does not surprise me. I have always had an impression that the codicil would turn up."

"It is more than I have had," dissented Jan.

As if by common consent, they spoke no further on the subject of the abstraction and its guilty instrument. It was a pleasant theme to neither. John Massingbird, little refinement of feeling that he possessed, could not forget that Dr. West was his mother's brother; or Jan, that he was his late master, his present partner—that he was connected with him in the eyes of Deerham. Before they had spoken much longer, they were joined by Lionel.

"I shall give you no trouble, old fellow," was John Massingbird's salutation. "You gave me none."

"Thank you," answered Lionel. Though what precise trouble it lay in John Massingbird's power to give him, he did not see, considering that things were now so plain.

"You'll accord me house-room for a bit longer, though, won't you?"

"I will accord it you as long as you like," replied Lionel, in the warmth of his heart.

"You know I would have had you stop on here all along," remarked Mr. Massingbird; "but the bar to it was Sibylla. I am not sorry the thing's found. I am growing tired of my life here. It has come into my mind at times lately to think whether I should not give up to you, Lionel, and be off over the seas again. It's tame work, this, to one who has roughed it at the diggings."

"You'd not have done it," observed Jan, alluding to the giving up.

"Perhaps not," said John Massingbird; "but I have owed a debt to Lionel for a long while. I say, old chap, didn't you think I clapped on a good sum for your trouble when I offered you the management of Verner's Pride?"

"I did," answered Lionel.

"Ay! I was in your debt; am in it still. Careless as I am, I thought of it now and then."

"I do not understand you," said Lionel. "In what way are you in my debt?"

"Let it go for now," returned John. "I may tell you some time, perhaps. When shall you take up your abode here?"

Lionel smiled. "I will not invade you without warning. You and I will take counsel together, John, and discuss plans and expediencies."

"I suppose you'll be for setting about your improvements now?"

"Yes," answered Lionel, his tone changing to one of deep seriousness, not to say reverence. "Without loss of time."

"I told you they could wait until you came into the estate. It has not been long first, you see."

"No; but I never looked for it," said Lionel.

"Ah! Things turn up that we don't look for," concluded John Massingbird, smoking on as serenely as though he had come into an estate, instead of having lost one. "There'll be bonfires all over the place to-night, Lionel—left-handed compliment to me. Here comes Luke Roy. I told him to be here this morning. What nuts this will be for old Roy to crack! He has been fit to stick me, ever since I refused him the management of Verner's Pride."

CHAPTER XC

LIGHT THROWN ON OBSCURITY

And so, the trouble and the uncertainty, the ups and the downs, the turnings out and changes were at an end, and Lionel Verner was at rest—at rest so far as rest can be, in this lower world. He was reinstalled at Verner's Pride, its undisputed master; never again to be sent forth from it during life.

He had not done as John Massingbird did—gone right in, the first day, and taken up his place, sans cérémonie, without word and without apology, at the table's head, leaving John to take his at the side or the foot, or where he could. Quite the contrary. Lionel's refinement of mind, his almost sensitive consideration for the feelings of others, clung to him now, as it always had done, as it always would do, and he was chary of disturbing John Massingbird too early in his sway of the internal economy of Verner's Pride. It had to be done, however; and John Massingbird remained on with him, his guest.

All that had passed; and the spring of the year was growing late. The codicil had been proved; the neighbourhood had tendered their congratulations to the new master, come into his own at last; the improvements, in which Lionel's conscience held so deep a score, were begun and in good progress; and John Massingbird's return to Australia was decided upon, and the day of his departure fixed. People surmised that Lionel would be glad to get rid of him, if only for the sake of his drawing-rooms. John Massingbird still lounged at full length on the amber satin couches, in dropping-off slippers or in dirty boots, as the case might be, still filled them with clouds of tobacco-smoke, so that you could not see across them. Mrs. Tynn declared, to as many people as she dared, that she prayed every night on her bended knees for Mr. Massingbird's departure, before the furniture should be quite ruined, or they burned in their beds.

Mr. Massingbird was not going alone. Luke Roy was returning with him. Luke's intention always had been to return to Australia; he had but come home for a short visit to the old place and to see his mother. Luke had been doing well at the gold-fields. He did not dig; but he sold liquor to those who did dig; at which he was making money rapidly. He had a "chum," he said, who managed the store while he was away. So glowing was his account of his prospects, that old Roy had decided upon going also, and trying his fortune there. Mrs. Roy looked aghast at the projected plans; she was too old for it, she urged. But she could not turn her husband. He had never studied her wishes too much, and he was not likely to begin to do so now. So Mrs. Roy, with incessantly-dropping tears, and continued prognostications that the sea-sickness would kill her, was forced to make her preparations for the voyage. Perhaps one motive, more than all else, influenced Roy's decision—the getting out of Deerham. Since his hopes of having something to do with the Verner's Pride estate—as he had in Stephen Verner's time—had been at an end, Roy had gone about in a perpetual state of inward mortification. This emigration would put an end to it; and what with the anticipation of making a fortune at the diggings, and what with his satisfaction at saying adieu to Deerham, and what with the thwarting of his wife, Roy was in a state of complacency.

The time went on to the evening previous to the departure. Lionel and John Massingbird had dined alone, and now sat together at the open window, in the soft May twilight. A small table was at John's elbow; a bottle of rum, and a jar of tobacco, water and a glass being on it, ready to his hand. He had done his best to infect Lionel with a taste for rum-and-water—as a convenient beverage to be taken at any hour from seven o'clock in the morning onwards—but Lionel had been proof against it. John had the rum-drinking to himself, as he had the smoking. Lionel had behaved to him liberally. It was not in Lionel Verner's nature to behave otherwise, no matter to whom. From the moment the codicil was found, John Massingbird had no further right to a single sixpence of the revenues of the estate. He was in the position of one who has nothing. It was Lionel who had found means for all—for his expenses, his voyage; for a purse when he should get to Australia. John Massingbird was thinking of this as he sat now, smoking and taking draughts of the rum-and-water.

"If ever I turn to work with a will and become a hundred-thousand-pound man, old fellow," he suddenly broke out, "I'll pay you back. This, and also what I got rid of while the estate was in my hands."

Lionel, who had been looking from the window in a reverie, turned round and laughed. To imagine John Massingbird becoming a hundred-thousand-pound man through his own industry, was a stretch of fancy marvellously comprehensive.

"I have to make a clean breast of it to-night," resumed John Massingbird, after puffing away for some minutes in silence. "Do you remember my saying to you, the day we heard news of the codicil's being found, that I was in your debt?"

"I remember your saying it," replied Lionel. "I did not understand what you meant. You were not in my debt."

"Yes, I was. I had a score to pay off as big as the moon. It's as big still; for it's one that never can be paid off; never will be."

Lionel looked at him in surprise; his manner was so unusually serious.

"Fifty times, since I came back from Australia, have I been on the point of clearing myself of the secret. But, you see, there was Verner's Pride in the way. You would naturally have said upon hearing it, 'Give the place up to me; you can have no moral right to it.' And I was not prepared to give it up; it seemed too comfortable a nest, just at first, after the knocking about over yonder. Don't you perceive?"

"I don't perceive, and I don't understand," replied Lionel. "You are speaking in an unknown language."

"I'll speak in a known one, then. It was through me that old Ste Verner left Verner's Pride away from you."

"What!" uttered Lionel.

"True," nodded John, with composure. "I told him a—a bit of scandal of you. And the strait-laced old simpleton took and altered his will on the strength of it. I did not know of that until afterwards."

"And the scandal?" asked Lionel quietly. "What may it have been?"

"False scandal," carelessly answered John Massingbird. "But I thought it was true when I spoke it. I told your uncle that it was you who had played false with Rachel Frost."

"Massingbird!"

"Don't fancy I went to him open-mouthed, and said, 'Lionel Verner's the man.' A fellow who could do such a sneaking trick would be only fit for hanging. The avowal to him was surprised from me in an unguarded moment; it slipped out in self-defence. I'd better tell you the tale."

"I think you had," said Lionel.

"You remember the bother there was, the commotion, the night Rachel was drowned. I came home and found Mr. Verner sitting at the inquiry. It never struck me, then, to suspect that it could be any one of us three who had been in the quarrel with Rachel. I knew that I had had no finger in the pie; I had no cause to think that you had; and, as to Fred, I'd as soon have suspected staid old Verner himself; besides, I believed Fred to have eyes only for Sibylla West. Not but that the affair appeared to me unaccountably strange; for, beyond Verner's Pride, I did not think Rachel possessed an acquaintance."

He stopped to take a few whiffs at his pipe, and then resumed, Lionel listening in silence.

"On the following morning by daylight I went down to the pond, the scene of the previous night. A few stragglers were already there. As we were looking about and talking, I saw on the very brink of the pond, partially hidden in the grass—in fact trodden into it, as it seemed to me—a glove. I picked it up, and was on the point of calling out that I had found a glove, when it struck me that the glove was yours. The others had seen me stoop, and one of them asked if I had found anything. I said 'No.' I had crushed the glove in my hand, and presently I transferred it to my pocket."

"Your motive being good-nature to me?" interrupted Lionel.

"To be sure it was. To have shown that as Lionel Verner's glove, would have fixed the affair on your shoulders at once. Why should I tell? I had been in scrapes myself. And I kept it, saying nothing to anybody. I examined the glove privately, saw it was really yours, and, of course, I drew my own conclusions—that it was you who had been in the quarrel, though what cause of dispute you could have with Rachel, I was at a loss to divine. Next came the inquest, and the medical men's revelation at it: and that cleared up the mystery, 'Ho, ho,' I said to myself, 'so Master Lionel can do a bit of courting on his own account, steady as he seems.' I—"

"Did you assume I threw her into the pond?" again interposed Lionel.

"Not a bit of it. What next, Lionel? The ignoring of some of the Commandments comes natural enough to the conscience; but the sixth—one does not ignore that. I believed that you and Rachel might have come to loggerheads, and that she, in a passion, flung herself in. I held the glove still in my pocket; it seemed to be the safest place for it; and I intended, before I left, to hand it over to you, and to give you my word I'd keep counsel. On the night of the inquest, you were closeted in the study with Mr. Verner. I chafed at it, for I wished to be closeted with him myself. Unless I could get off from Verner's Pride the next day, there would be no chance of my sailing in the projected ship—where our passages had been already secured by Luke Roy. By and by you came into the dining-room—do you remember it?—and told me Mr. Verner wanted me in the study. It was just what I wanted; and I went in. I shan't forget my surprise to the last hour of my life. His greeting was an accusation of me—of me! that it was I who had played false with Rachel. He had proof, he said. One of the house-girls had seen one of us three young men coming from the scene that night—and he, Stephen Verner, knew it could only be me. Fred was too cautious, he said; Lionel he could depend upon; and he bitterly declared that he would not give me a penny piece of the promised money, to take me on my way. A pretty state of things, was it not, Lionel, to have one's projects put an end to in that manner? In my dismay and anger, I blurted out the truth; that one of us might have been seen coming from the scene, but it was not myself; it was Lionel; and I took the glove out of my pocket and showed it to him."

John Massingbird paused to take a draught of the rum-and-water, and then resumed.

"I never saw any man so agitated as Mr. Verner. Upon my word, had I foreseen the effect the news would have had upon him, I hardly think I should have told it. His face turned ghastly; he lay back in his chair, uttering groans of despair; in short, it had completely prostrated him. I never knew how deeply he was attached to you, Lionel, until that night."

"He believed the story?" said Lionel.

"Of course he believed it," assented John Massingbird. "I told it him as a certainty, as a thing about which there was no admission for the slightest doubt: I assumed it, myself, to be a certainty. When he was a little recovered, he took possession of the glove, and bound me to secrecy. You would never have forgotten it, Lionel, had you seen his shaking hands, his imploring eyes, heard his voice of despair; all lifted to beseech secrecy for you—for the sake of his dead brother—for the name of Verner—for his own sake. I heartily promised it; and he handed me over a more liberal sum than even I had expected, enjoined me to depart with the morrow's dawn, and bade me Godspeed. I believe he was glad that I was going, lest I might drop some chance word during the present excitement of Deerham, and by that means direct suspicion to you. He need not have feared. I was already abusing myself mentally for having told him, although it had gained me my ends: 'Live and let live' had been my motto hitherto. The interview was nearly over when you came to interrupt it, asking if Mr. Verner would see Robin Frost. Mr. Verner answered that he might come in. He came; you and Fred with him. Do you recollect old Verner's excitement?—his vehement words in answer to Robin's request that a reward should be posted up? 'He'll never be found, Robin; the villain will never be found, so long as you and I and the world shall last.' I recollect them, you see, word for word, to this hour; but none, save myself, knew what caused Mr.

Verner's excitement, or that the word 'villain' was applied to you. Upon my word and honour, old boy, I felt as if I had the deeper right to it! and I felt angry with old Verner for looking at the affair in so strong a light. But there was no help for it. I went away the next morning—"

"Stay!" interrupted Lionel. "A single word to me would have set the misapprehension straight. Why did you not speak it?"

"I wish I had, now. But—it wasn't done. There! The knowledge that turns up in the future we can't call to aid in the present. If I had had a doubt that it was you, I should have spoken. We were some days out at sea on our voyage to Australia when I and Luke got comparing notes; and I found, to my everlasting astonishment, that it was not you, after all, who had been with Rachel, but Fred."

"You should have written home, to do me justice with Mr. Verner. You ought not to have delayed one instant, when the knowledge came to you."

"And how was I to send the letter? Chuck it into the sea in the ship's wake, and give it orders to swim back to port?"

"You might have posted it at the first place you touched at."

"Look here, Lionel. I never regarded it in that grave light. How was I to suppose that old Verner would disinherit you for that trumpery escapade? I never knew why he had disinherited you, until I came home and heard from yourself the story of the inclosed glove, which he left you as a legacy. It's since then that I have been wanting to make a clean breast of it. I say, only fancy Fred's deepness! We should never have thought it of him. The quarrel between him and Rachel that night appeared to arise from the fact of her having seen him with Sibylla; having overheard that there was more between them than was pleasant to her: at least, so far as Luke could gather it. Lionel, what should have brought your glove lying by the pond?"

"I am unable to say. I had not been there, to drop it. The most feasible solution that I can come to is that Rachel may have had it about her for the purpose of mending, and let it drop herself, when she jumped in."

"Ay. That's the most likely. There was a hole in it, I remember; and it was Rachel who attended to such things in the household. It must have been so."

Lionel fell into a reverie. How—but for this mistake of John Massingbird's, this revelation to his uncle—the whole course of his life's events might have been changed! Verner's Pride bequeathed to him, never bequeathed at all to the Massingbirds, it was scarcely likely that Sibylla, in returning home, would have driven to Verner's Pride. Had she not driven to it that night, he might never have been so surprised by his old feelings as to have proposed to her. He might have married Lucy Tempest; have lived, sheltered with her in Verner's Pride from the storms of life; he might—

"Will you forgive me, old chap?"

It was John Massingbird who spoke, interrupting his day dreams. Lionel shook them off, and took the offered hand stretched out.

"Yes," he heartily said. "You did not do me the injury intentionally. It was the result of a mistake, brought about by circumstances."

"No, that I did not, by Jove!" answered John Massingbird. "I don't think I ever did a fellow an intentional injury in my life. You would have been the last I should single out for it. I have had many ups and downs, Lionel, but somehow I have hitherto always managed to alight on my legs; and I believe it's because I let other folks get along—tit for tat, you see. A fellow who is for ever putting his hindering spoke in the wheel of others, is safe to get hindering spokes put into his. I am not a pattern model," comically added John Massingbird; "but I have never done wilful injury to others, and my worst enemy (if I possess one) can't charge it upon me."

True enough. With all Mr. John Massingbird's failings, his heart was not a bad one. In the old days his escapades had been numerous; his brother Frederick's, none (so far as the world knew); but the one was liked a thousand times better than the other.

"We part friends, old fellow!" he said to Lionel the following morning, when all was ready, and the final moment of departure had come.

"To be sure we do," answered Lionel. "Should England ever see you again, you will not forget Verner's Pride."

"I don't think it will ever see me again. Thanks, old chap, all the same. If I should be done up some unlucky day for the want of a twenty-pound note, you won't refuse to let me have it, for old times' sake?"

"Very well," laughed Lionel.

And so they parted. And Verner's Pride was quit of Mr. John Massingbird, and Deerham of its long-looked-upon bête noir, old Grip Roy. Luke had gone forward to make arrangements for the sailing, as he had done once before; and Mrs. Roy took her seat with her husband in a third-class carriage, crying enough tears to float the train.

CHAPTER XCI

MEDICAL ATTENDANCE GRATIS, INCLUDING PHYSIC

As a matter of course, the discovery of the codicil, and the grave charge it served to establish against Dr. West, could not be hid under a bushel. Deerham was remarkably free in its comments, and was pleased to rake up various unpleasant reports, which, from time to time, in the former days had arisen, touching that gentleman. Deerham might say what it liked, and nobody be much the worse; but a more serious question arose with Jan. Easy as Jan was, little given to think ill, even he could not look over this. Jan, if he would maintain his respectability as a medical man and a gentleman, if he would retain his higher class of patients, he must give up his association with Dr. West.

The finding of the codicil had been communicated to Dr. West by Matiss, the lawyer, who officially demanded at the same time an explanation of its having been placed where it was found. The doctor replied to the communication, but conveniently ignored the question. He was "charmed" to hear that the long-missing deed was found, which restored Verner's Pride to the rightful owner, Lionel Verner; but he appeared not to have read, or else not to have understood the very broad hint implicating himself, for not a word was returned to that part, in answer. The silence was not less a conclusive proof than the admission of guilt would have been; and it was so regarded by those concerned.

Jan was the next to write. A characteristic letter. He said not a word of reproach to the doctor; he appeared, indeed, to ignore the facts as completely as the doctor himself had done in answer to Matiss; he simply said that he would prefer to "get along" now alone. The practice had much increased, and there was room for them both. He would remove to another residence—a lodging would do, he said—and run his chance of patients coming to him. It was not his intention to take one from Dr. West by solicitation. The doctor could either come back and resume practice in person, or take a partner in place of him, Jan.

To this a bland answer was received. Dr. West was agreeable to the dissolution of partnership; but he had no intention of resuming practice in Deerham. He and his noble charge (who was decidedly benefiting by his care, skill, and companionship, he elaborately wrote), were upon the best of terms; his engagement with him was likely to be a long one (for the poor youth would require a personal guide up to his fortieth year, nay, to his eightieth, if he lived so long); and therefore (not to be fettered) he, Dr. West, was anxious to sever his ties with Deerham. He should never return to it. If Mr. Jan would undertake to pay him a trifling sum, say five hundred pounds, or so he could have the entire business; and the purchase-money, if more convenient, might be paid by instalments. Mr. Jan, of course, would become sole proprietor of the house (the rent of which had hitherto been paid out of the joint concern), but perhaps he would not object to allow those "two poor old things, Deborah and Amilly, a corner in it." He should, of course, undertake to provide for them, remitting them a liberal annual sum.

In writing this—fair, nay liberal, as the offered terms appeared to the sight of single-hearted Jan—Dr. West had probably possessed as great an eye as ever to his own interest. He had a shrewd suspicion that, the house divided, his, Dr. West's, would stand but a poor chance against Jan Verner's. That Jan would be entirely true and honourable in not soliciting the old patients to come to him, he knew; but he equally knew that the patients would flock to Jan unsolicited. Dr. West had not lived in ignorance of what was going on in Deerham; he had one or two private correspondents there; besides the open ones, his daughters and Jan; and he had learned how popular Jan had grown with all classes. Yes, it was decidedly politic on Dr. West's part to offer Jan terms of purchase. And Jan closed with them.

"I couldn't have done it six months ago, you know, Lionel," he said to his brother. "But now that you have come in again to Verner's Pride, you won't care to have my earnings any longer."

"What I shall care for now, Jan, will be to repay you so far as I can. The money can be repaid: the kindness never."

"Law!" cried Jan, "that's nothing. Wouldn't you have done as much for me? To go back to old West: I shall be able to complete the purchase in little more than a year, taking it out of the profits. The expenses will be something considerable. There'll be the house, and the horses, for I must have two, and I shall take a qualified assistant as soon as Cheese leaves, which will be in autumn; but there'll be a margin of six or seven hundred a year profit left me then. And the business is increasing. Yes, I shall be able to pay him out in a year, or thereabouts. In offering me these easy terms, I think he is behaving liberally. Don't you, Lionel?"

"That may be a matter of opinion, Jan," was Lionel's answer. "He has stood to me in the relation of father-in-law, and I don't care to express mine too definitely. He is wise enough to know that when you leave him, his chance of practice is gone. But I don't advise you to cavil with the terms. I should say, accept them."

"I have done it," answered Jan. "I wrote this morning. I must get a new brass plate for the door. 'Jan Verner, Surgeon, etc.,' in place of the present one, 'West and Verner.'"

"I think I should put Janus Verner, instead of Jan," suggested Lionel, with a half smile.

"Law!" repeated Jan. "Nobody would know it was meant for me if I put Janus. Shall I have 'Mr.' tacked on to it, Lionel?—'Mr. Jan Verner.'"

"Of course you will," answered Lionel. "What is going to be done about Deborah and Amilly West?"

"In what way?"

"As to their residence."

"You saw what Dr. West says in his letter. They can stop."

"It is not a desirable arrangement, Jan, their remaining in the house."

"They won't hurt me," responded Jan. "They are welcome."

"I think, Jan, your connection with the West family should be entirely closed. The opportunity offers now: and, if not embraced, you don't know when another may arise. Suppose, a short while hence, you were to marry? It might be painful to your feelings, then, to have to say to Deborah and Amilly—'You must leave my house: there's no further place for you in it.' Now, in this dissolution of partnership, the change can take place as in the natural course of events."

Jan had opened his great eyes wonderingly at the words. "I marry!" uttered he. "What should bring me marrying?"

"You may be marrying some time, Jan."

"Not I," answered Jan. "Nobody would have me. They can stop on in the house, Lionel. What does it matter? I don't see how I and Cheese should get on without them. Who'd make the pies? Cheese would die of chagrin, if he didn't get one every day."

"I see a great deal of inconvenience in the way," persisted Lionel. "The house will be yours then. Upon what terms would they remain? As visitors, as lodgers—as what?"

Jan opened his eyes wider. "Visitors! lodgers!" cried he. "I don't know what you mean, Lionel. They'd stop on as they always have done—as though the house were theirs. They'd be welcome, for me."

"You must do as you like, Jan; but I do not think the arrangement a desirable one. It would be establishing a claim which Dr. West may be presuming upon later. With his daughters in the house, as of right, he may be for coming back some time and taking up his abode in it. It would be better for you and the Misses West to separate; to have your establishments apart."

"I shall never turn them out," said Jan. "They'd break their hearts. Look at the buttons, too! Who'd sew them on? Cheese bursts off two a day, good."

"As you please, Jan. My motive in speaking was not ill-nature towards the Misses West; but regard for you. As the sisters of my late wife, I shall take care that they do not want—should their resources from Dr. West fail. He speaks of allowing them a liberal sum annually; but I fear they must not make sure that the promise will be carried out. Should it not be, they will have no one to look to, I expect, but myself."

"They won't want much," said Jan; "just a trifle for their bonnets and shoes, and suchlike. I shall pay the house-bills, you know. In fact, I'd as soon give them enough for their clothes, as not. I dare say I should have it, even the first year, after paying expenses and old West's five hundred."

It was hopeless to contend with Jan upon the subject of money, especially when it was his money. Lionel said no more. But he had not the slightest doubt it would end in Jan's house being saddled with the Misses West; and that help for them from Dr. West would never come.

Miss West herself was thinking the same—that help from her father never would come.

This conversation between Jan and Lionel had taken place at Verner's Pride, in the afternoon subsequent to the arrival of Dr. West's letter. Deborah West had also received one from her father. She learned by it that he was about to retire from the partnership, and that Mr. Jan Verner would carry on the practice alone. The doctor intimated that she and Amilly would continue to live on in the house with Mr. Jan's permission, whom he had asked to afford them house-room; and he more loudly promised to transmit them one hundred pounds per annum, in stated payments, as might be convenient to him.

The letter was read three times over by both sisters. Amilly did not like it, but upon Deborah it made a painfully deep impression. Poor ladies! Since the discovery of the codicil they had gone about Deerham with veils over their faces and their heads down, inclined to think that lots in this world were dealt out all too unequally.

At the very time that Jan was at Verner's Pride that afternoon, Deborah sat alone in the dining-room, pondering over the future. Since the finding of the codicil, neither of the sisters had cared to seat themselves in state in the drawing-room, ready to receive visitors, should they call. They had no heart for it. They chose, rather, to sit in plain attire, and hide themselves in the humblest and most retired apartment. They took no pride now in anointing their scanty curls with castor oil, in contriving for their dress, in setting off their persons. Vanity seemed to have gone out for Deborah and Amilly West.

Deborah sat there in the dining-room, her hair looking grievously thin, her morning dress of black print with white spots upon it not changed for the old turned black silk of the afternoon. Her elbow rested on the faded and not very clean table-cover, and her fingers were running unconsciously through that scanty hair. The prospect before her looked, to her mind, as hopelessly forlorn as she looked.

But it was necessary that she should gaze at the future steadily; should not turn aside from it in carelessness or in apathy; should face it, and make the best of it. If Jan Verner and her father were about to dissolve partnership, and the practice henceforth was to be Jan's, what was to become of her and Amilly? Taught by past experience, she knew how much dependence was to be placed upon her father's promise to pay to them an income. Very little reliance indeed could be placed on Dr. West in any way; this very letter in her hand and the tidings it contained, might be true, or might be—pretty little cullings from Dr. West's imagination. The proposed dissolution of partnership she believed in: she had expected Jan to take the step ever since that night which restored the codicil.

"I had better ask Mr. Jan about it," she murmured. "It is of no use to remain in this uncertainty."

Rising from her seat, she proceeded to the side-door, opened it, and glanced cautiously out through the rain, not caring to be seen by strangers in her present attire. There was nobody about, and she crossed the little path and entered the surgery. Master Cheese, with somewhat of a scorchy look in the eyebrows, but full of strength and appetite as ever, turned round at her entrance.

"Is Mr. Jan in?" she asked.

"No, he is not," responded Master Cheese, speaking indistinctly, for he had just filled his mouth with Spanish liquorice. "Did you want him, Miss Deb?"

"I wanted to speak to him," she replied. "Will he be long?"

"He didn't announce the hour of his return," replied Master Cheese. "I wish he would come back! If a message came for one of us, I don't care to go out in this rain: Jan doesn't mind it. It's sure to be my luck! The other day, when it was pouring cats and dogs, a summons came from Lady Hautley's. Jan was out, and I had to go, and got dripping wet. After all, it was only my lady's maid, with a rubbishing whitlow on her finger."

"Be so kind as tell Mr. Jan, when he does come in, that I should be glad to speak a word to him, if he can find time to step into the parlour."

Miss Deb turned back as she spoke, ran across through the rain, and sat down in the parlour, as before. She knew that she ought to go up and dress, but she had not spirits for it.

She sat there until Jan entered. Full an hour, it must have been, and she had turned over all points in her mind, what could and what could not be done. It did not appear much that could be. Jan came in, rather wet. On his road from Verner's Pride he had overtaken one of his poor patients, who was in delicate health, and had lent the woman his huge cotton umbrella, hastening on, himself, without one.

"Cheese says you wish to see me, Miss Deb."

Miss Deb turned round from her listless attitude, and asked Mr. Jan to take a chair. Mr. Jan responded by partially sitting down on the arm of one.

"What is it?" asked he, rather wondering.

"I have had a letter from Prussia this morning, Mr. Jan, from my father. He says you and he are about to dissolve partnership; that the practice will be carried on by you alone, on your own account; and that—but you had better read it," she broke off, taking the letter from her pocket, and handing it to Jan.

He ran his eyes over it. Dr. West's was not a plain handwriting, but Jan was accustomed to it. The letter was soon read.

"It's true, Miss Deb. The doctor thinks he shall not be returning to Deerham, and so I am going to take to the whole of the practice," continued Jan, who possessed too much innate good feeling to hint to Miss Deb of any other cause.

"Yes. But—it will place me and Amilly in a very embarrassing position, Mr. Jan," added the poor lady, her thin cheeks flushing painfully. "I—we shall have no right to remain in this house then."

"You are welcome to remain," said Jan.

Miss Deb shook her head. She felt, as she said, that they should have no "right."

"I'd rather you did," pursued Jan, in his good-nature. "What do I and Cheese want with all this big house to ourselves? Besides, if you and Amilly go, who'd see to our shirts and the puddings?"

"When papa went away at first, was there not some arrangement made by which the furniture became yours?"

"No," stoutly answered Jan. "I paid something to him to give me, as he called it, a half-share in it with himself. It was a stupid sort of arrangement, and one that I should never care to act upon, Miss Deb. The furniture is yours; not mine."

"Mr. Jan, you would give up your right in everything, I believe. You will never get rich."

"I shall get as rich as I want to, I dare say," was Jan's answer. "Things can go on just the same as usual, you know, Miss Deb, and I can pay the housekeeping bills. Your stopping here will be a saving," good-naturedly added Jan. "With nobody in the house to manage, except servants, only think the waste there'd be! Cheese would be for getting two dinners a day served, fish, and fowls, and tarts at each."

The tears were struggling in Deborah West's eyes. She did her best to repress them: but it could not be, and she gave way with a burst.

"I beg your pardon, Mr. Jan," she said. "Sometimes I feel as if there was no longer any place in the world for me and Amilly. You may be sure I would not mention it, but that you know it as well as I do—that there is, I fear, no dependence to be placed on this promise of papa's, to allow us an income. I have been thinking—"

"Don't let that trouble you, Miss Deb," interrupted Jan, tilting himself backwards over the arm of the chair in a very ungraceful fashion, and leaving his legs dangling. "Others will, if he wo—if he can't. Lionel has just been saying that as Sibylla's sisters, he shall see that you don't want."

"You and he are very kind," she answered, the tears dropping faster than she could wipe them away. "But it seems to me the time is come when we ought to try and do something for ourselves. I have been thinking, Mr. Jan, that we might get a few pupils, I and Amilly. There's not a single good school in Deerham, as you know; I think we might establish one."

"So you might," said Jan, "if you'd like it."

"We should both like it. And perhaps you'd not mind our staying on in this house while we were getting a few together; establishing it, as it were. They would not put you out, I hope, Mr. Jan."

"Not they," answered Jan. "I shouldn't eat them. Look here, Miss Deb, I'd doctor them for nothing. Couldn't you put that in the prospectus? It might prove an attraction."

It was a novel feature in a school prospectus, and Miss Deb had to take some minutes to consider it. She came to the conclusion that it would look remarkably well in print. "Medical attendance gratis."

"Including physic," put in Jan.

"Medical attendance gratis, including physic," repeated Miss Deb. "Mr. Jan, it would be sure to take with the parents. I am so much obliged to you. But I hope," she added, moderating her tone of satisfaction, "that they'd not think it meant Master Cheese. People would not have much faith in him, I fear."

"Tell them to the contrary," answered Jan. "And Cheese will be leaving shortly, you know."

"True," said Miss Deb. "Mr. Jan," she added, a strange eagerness in her tone, in her meek, blue eyes, "if we, I and Amilly, can only get into the way of doing something for ourselves, by which we may be a little independent, and look forward to be kept out of the workhouse in our old age, we shall feel as if removed from a dreadful nightmare. Circumstances have been preying upon us, Mr. Jan: the care is making us begin to look old before we might have looked it."

Jan answered with a laugh. That notion of the workhouse was so good, he said. As well set on and think that he should come to the penitentiary! It had been no laughing matter, though, to the hearts of the two sisters, and Miss Deb sat on, crying silently.

How many of these silent tears must be shed in the path through life! It would appear that the lot of some is only made to shed them, and to bear.

CHAPTER XCII

AT LAST!

Meanwhile the spring was going on to summer—and in the strict order of precedence that conversation of Miss Deb's with Jan ought to have been related before the departure of John Massingbird and the Roys from Deerham. But it does not signify. The Misses West made their arrangements and sent out their prospectuses, and the others left: it all happened in the spring-time. That time was giving place to summer when the father of Lucy Tempest, now Colonel Sir Henry Tempest, landed in England.

In some degree his arrival was sudden. He had been looked for so long, that Lucy had almost given over looking for him. She did believe he was on his road home, by the sea passage, but precisely when he might be expected, she did not know.

Since the marriage of Decima, Lucy had lived on alone with Lady Verner. Alone, and very quietly; quite uneventfully. She and Lionel met occasionally, but nothing further had passed between them. Lionel was silent; possibly he deemed it too soon after his wife's death to speak of love to another, although the speaking of it would have been news to neither. Lucy was a great deal at Lady Hautley's. Decima would have had her there permanently; but Lady Verner negatived it.

They were sitting at breakfast one morning, Lady Verner and Lucy, when the letter arrived. It was the only one by the post that morning. Catherine laid it by Lady Verner's side, to whom it was addressed; but the quick eyes of Lucy caught the superscription.

"Lady Verner! It is papa's handwriting."

Lady Verner turned her head to look at it. "It is not an Indian letter," she remarked.

"No. Papa must have landed."

Opening the letter, they found it to be so. Sir Henry had arrived at Southampton, Lucy turned pale with agitation. It seemed a formidable thing, now it had come so close, to meet her father, whom she had not seen for so many years.

"When is he coming here?" she breathlessly asked.

"To-morrow," replied Lady Verner; not speaking until she had glanced over the whole contents of the letter. "He purposes to remain a day and a night with us, and then he will take you with him to London."

"But a day and a night! Go away then to London! Shall I never come back?" reiterated Lucy, more breathlessly than before.

Lady Verner looked at her with calm surprise. "One would think, child, you wanted to remain in Deerham. Were I a young lady, I should be glad to get away from it. The London season is at its height."

Lucy laughed and blushed somewhat consciously. She thought she should not care about the London season; but she did not say so to Lady Verner. Lady Verner resumed.

"Sir Henry wishes me to accompany you, Lucy. I suppose I must do so. What a vast deal we shall have to think of to-day! We shall be able to do nothing to-morrow when Sir Henry is here."

Lucy toyed with her tea-spoon, toyed with her breakfast; but the capability of eating more had left her. The suddenness of the announcement had taken away her appetite, and a hundred doubts were tormenting her. Should she never again return to Deerham?—never again see Li—

"We must make a call or two to-day, Lucy."

The interruption, breaking in upon her busy thoughts, caused her to start. Lady Verner resumed.

"This morning must be devoted to business; to the giving directions as to clothes, packing, and such like. I can tell you, Lucy, that you will have a great deal of it to do yourself; Catherine's so incapable since she got that rheumatism in her hand. Thérèse will have enough to see to with my things."

"I can do it all," answered Lucy. "I can—"

"What next, my dear? You pack! Though Catherine's hand is painful, she can do something."

"Oh, yes, we shall manage very well," cheerfully answered Lucy. "Did you say we should have to go out, Lady Verner?"

"This afternoon. For one place, we must go to the Bitterworths. You cannot go away without seeing them, and Mrs. Bitterworth is too ill just now to call upon you. I wonder whether Lionel will be here to-day?"

It was a "wonder" which had been crossing Lucy's own heart. She went to her room after breakfast, and soon became deep in her preparations with old Catherine; Lucy doing the chief part of the work, in spite of Catherine's remonstrances. But her thoughts were not with her hands; they remained buried in that speculation of Lady Verner's—would Lionel be there that day?

The time went on to the afternoon, and he had not come. They stepped into the carriage (for Lady Verner could indulge in the luxury of horses again now) to make their calls, and he had not come. Lucy's heart palpitated strangely at the doubt of whether she should really depart without seeing him. A very improbable doubt, considering the contemplated arrival at Deerham Court of Sir Henry Tempest.

As they passed Dr. West's old house, Lady Verner ordered the carriage to turn the corner and stop at the door. "Mr. Jan Verner" was on the plate now, where "West and Verner" used to be. Master Cheese unwillingly disturbed himself to come out, for he was seated over a washhand-basin of gooseberry fool, which he had got surreptitiously made for him in the kitchen. Mr. Jan was out, he said.

So Lady Verner ordered the carriage on, leaving a message for Jan that she wanted some more "drops" made up.

They paid the visit to Mrs. Bitterworth. Mr. Bitterworth was not at home. He had gone to see Mr. Verner. A sudden beating of the heart, a rising flush in the cheeks, a mist for a moment before her eyes, and Lucy was being whirled to Verner's Pride. Lady Verner had ordered the carriage thither, as they left Mrs. Bitterworth's.

They found them both in the drawing-room. Mr. Bitterworth had just risen to leave, and was shaking hands with Lionel. Lady Verner interrupted them with the news of Lucy's departure; of her own.

"Sir Henry will be here to-morrow," she said to Lionel. "He takes Lucy to London with him the following day, and I accompany them."

Lionel, startled, looked round at Lucy. She was not looking at him. Her eyes were averted—her face was flushed.

"But you are not going for good, Miss Lucy!" cried Mr. Bitterworth.

"She is," replied Lady Verner. "And glad enough, I am sure, she must be, to get away from stupid Deerham. She little thought, when she came to it, that her sojourn in it would be so long as this. I have seen the rebellion, at her having to stop in it, rising often."

Mr. Bitterworth went out on the terrace. Lady Verner, talking to him, went also. Lionel, his face pale, his breath coming in gasps, turned to Lucy.

"Need you go for good, Lucy?"

She raised her eyes to him with a shy glance, and Lionel, with a half-uttered exclamation of emotion, caught her to his breast, and took his first long silent kiss of love from her lips. It was not like those snatched kisses of years ago.

"My darling! my darling! God alone knows what my love for you has been."

Another shy glance at him through her raining tears. Her heart was beating against his. Did the glance seem to ask why, then, had he not spoken? His next words would imply that he understood it so.

"I am still a poor man, Lucy. I was waiting for Sir Henry's return, to lay the case before him. He may refuse you to me!"

"If he should—I will tell him—that I shall never have further interest in life," was her agitated answer.

And Lionel's own face was working with emotion, as he kissed those tears away.

At last! at last!

CHAPTER XCIII

LADY VERNER'S "FEAR"

The afternoon express-train was steaming into Deerham station, just as Jan Verner was leaping his long legs over rails and stones and shafts, and other obstacles apt to collect round the outside of a halting-place for trains, to get to it. Jan did not want to get to the train; he had no business with it. He only wished to say a word to one of the railway-porters, whose wife he was attending. By the time he had reached the platform the train was puffing on again, and the few passengers who had descended were about to disperse.

"Can you tell me my way to Lady Verner's?"

The words were spoken close to Jan's ear. He turned and looked at the speaker. An oldish man with a bronzed countenance and upright carriage, bearing about him that indescribable military air which bespeaks the soldier of long service, in plain clothes though he may be.

"Sir Henry Tempest?" involuntarily spoke Jan, before the official addressed had time to answer the question. "I heard that my mother was expecting you."

Sir Henry Tempest ran his eyes over Jan's face and figure: an honest face, but an ungainly figure; loose clothes that would have been all the better for a brush, and the edges of his high shirt-collar jagged out.

"Mr. Verner?" responded Sir Henry doubtingly.

"Not Mr. Verner. I'm only Jan. You must have forgotten me long ago, Sir Henry."

Sir Henry Tempest held out his hand, "I have not forgotten what you were as a boy; but I should not have known you as a man. And yet—it is the same face."

"Of course it is," said Jan, "Ugly faces, such as mine, don't alter. I will walk with you to my mother's: it is close by. Have you any luggage?"

"Only a portmanteau. My servant is looking after it. Here he is."

A very dark man came up—an Indian—nearly as old as his master. Jan recognised him.

"I remember you!" he exclaimed "It is Batsha."

The man laughed, hiding his dark eyes, but showing his white teeth. "Massa Jan!" he said, "used to call me Bat."

Without the least ceremony, Jan shook him by the hand. He had more pleasant reminiscences of him than of his master. In fact, Jan could only remember Colonel Tempest by name. He, the colonel, had despised and shunned the awkward and unprepossessing boy; but the boy and Bat used to be great friends.

"Do you recollect carrying me on your shoulder, Bat? You have paid for many a ride in a palanquin for me. Riding on shoulders or in palanquins, in those days, used to be my choice recreation. The shoulders and the funds both ran short at times."

Batsha remembered it all. Next to his master, he had never liked anybody so well as the boy Jan.

"Stop where you are a minute or two," said unceremonious Jan to Sir Henry. "I must find one of the porters, and then I'll walk with you."

Looking about in various directions, in holes and corners and sheds, inside carriages and behind trucks, Jan at length came upon a short, surly-looking man, wearing the official uniform. It was the one of whom he was in search.

"I say, Parkes, what is this I hear about your forcing your wife to get up, when I have given orders that she should lie in bed? I went in just now, and there I found her dragging herself about the damp brewhouse. I had desired that she should not get out of her bed."

"Too much bed don't do nobody much good, sir," returned the man in a semi-resentful tone. "There's the work to do—the washing. If she don't do it, who will?"

"Too much bed wouldn't do you good; or me, either; but it is necessary for your wife in her present state of illness. I have ordered her to bed again. Don't let me hear of your interfering a second time, and forcing her up. She is going to have a blister on now."

"I didn't force her, sir," answered Parkes. "I only asked her what was to become of the work, and how I should get a clean shirt to put on."

"If I had got a sick wife, I'd wash out my shirt myself, before I'd drag her out of bed to do it," retorted Jan. "I can tell you one thing, Parkes; that she is worse than you think for. I am not sure that she will be long with you; and you won't get such a wife again in a hurry, once you lose her. Give her a chance to get well. I'll see that she gets up fast enough, when she is fit for it."

Parkes touched his peaked cap as Jan turned away. It was very rare that Jan came out with a lecture; and when he did, the sufferers did not like it. A sharp word from Jan Verner seemed to tell home.

Jan returned to Sir Henry Tempest, and they walked a way in the direction of Deerham Court.

"I conclude all is well at Lady Verner's," remarked Sir Henry.

"Well enough," returned Jan. "I thought I heard you were not coming until to-morrow. They'll be surprised."

"I wrote word I should be with them to-morrow," replied Sir Henry. "But I got impatient to see my child. Since I left India and have been fairly on my way to her, the time of separation has seemed longer to me than it did in all the previous years."

"She's a nice girl," returned Jan. "The nicest girl in Deerham."

"Is she pretty?" asked Sir Henry.

The question a little puzzled Jan. "Well, I think so," answered he. "Girls are much alike for that, as far as I see. I like Miss Lucy's look, though; and that's the chief thing in faces."

"How is your brother, Janus?"

Jan burst out laughing. "Don't call me Janus, Sir Henry. I am not known by that name. They wanted me to have Janus on my door-plate; but nobody would have thought it meant me, and the practice might have gone off."

"You are Jan, as you used to be, then? I remember Lucy has called you so in her letters to me."

"I shall never be anything but Jan. What does it matter? One name's as good as another. You were asking after Lionel. He has got Verner's Pride again: all in safety now."

"What a very extraordinary course of events seems to have taken place, with regard to Verner's Pride!" remarked Sir Henry. "Now your brother's, now not his, then his again, then not his! I cannot make it out."

"It was extraordinary," assented Jan. "But the uncertain tenure is at an end, and Lionel is installed there for life. There ought never to have been any question of his right to it."

"He has had the misfortune to lose his wife," observed Sir Henry.

"It was not much of a misfortune," returned Jan, always plain. "She was too sickly ever to enjoy life; and I know she must have worried Lionel nearly out of his patience."

Jan had said at the station that Deerham Court was "close by." His active legs may have found it so; but Sir Henry began to think it rather far than close. As they reached the gates Sir Henry spoke.

"I suppose there is an inn near, where I can send my servant to lodge. There may not be accommodation for him at Lady Verner's?"

"There's accommodation enough for that," said Jan. "They have plenty of room, and old Catherine can make him up a bed."

Lady Verner and Lucy were out. They had not returned from the call on Mrs. Bitterworth—for it was the afternoon spoken of in the last chapter. Jan showed Sir Henry in; told him to ring for any refreshment he wanted; and then left.

"I can't stay," he remarked. "My day's rounds are not over yet."

But scarcely had Jan reached the outside of the gate when he met the carriage. He put up his hand, and the coachman stopped. Jan advanced to the window, a broad smile upon his face.

"What will you give me for some news, Miss Lucy?"

Lucy's thoughts were running upon certain other news; news known but to herself and to one more. A strangely happy light shone in her soft, brown eyes, as she turned them on Jan; a rich damask flush on the cheeks where his lips had so lately been.

"Does it concern me, Jan?"

"It doesn't much concern anybody else.—Guess."

"I never can guess anything; you know I can't, Jan," she answered, smiling. "You must please tell me."

"Well," said Jan, "there's an arrival. Come by the train."

"Oh, Jan! Not papa?"

Jan nodded.

"You will find him indoors. Old Bat's come with him."

Lucy never could quite remember the details of the meeting. She knew that her father held her to him fondly, and then put her from him to look at her; the tears blinding her eyes and his.

"You are pretty, Lucy," he said, "very pretty. I asked Jan whether you were not, but he could not tell me."

"Jan!" slightingly spoke Lady Verner, while Lucy laughed in spite of her tears. "It is of no use asking Jan anything of that sort, Sir Henry, I don't believe Jan knows one young lady's face from another."

It seemed to be all confusion for some time; all bustle; nothing but questions and answers. But when they had assembled in the drawing-room again, after making ready for dinner, things wore a calmer aspect.

"You must have thought I never was coming home!" remarked Sir Henry to Lady Verner. "I have contemplated it so long."

"I suppose your delays were unavoidable," she answered.

"Yes—in a measure. I should not have come now, but for the relieving you of Lucy. Your letters, for some time past, have appeared to imply that you were vexed with her, or tired of her; and, in truth, I have taxed your patience and good nature unwarrantably. I do not know how I shall repay your kindness, Lady Verner."

"I have been repaid throughout, Sir Henry," was the quiet reply of Lady Verner. "The society of Lucy has been a requital in full. I rarely form an attachment, and when I do form one it is never demonstrative; but I have learned to love Lucy as I love my own daughter, and it will be a real grief to part with her. Not but that she has given me great vexation."

"Ah! In what way?"

"The years have gone on and on since she came to me; and I was in hopes of returning her to you with some prospect in view of the great end of a young lady's life—marriage. I was placed here as her mother; and I felt more responsibility in regard to her establishment in life than I did to Decima's. We have been at issue upon the point, Sir Henry; Lucy and I."

Sir Henry turned his eyes on his daughter: if that is not speaking figuratively, considering that he had scarcely taken his eyes off her. A fair picture she was, sitting there in her white evening dress and her pearl ornaments. Young, lovely, girlish, she looked, as she did the first day she came to Lady Verner's and took up her modest seat on the hearth-rug. Sir Henry Tempest had not seen many such faces as that; he had not met with many natures so innocent and charming. Lucy was made to be admired as well as loved.

"If there is one parti more desirable than another in the whole county, it is Lord Garle," resumed Lady Verner. "The eldest son of the Earl of Elmsley, his position naturally renders him so; but had he neither rank nor wealth, he would not be much less desirable. His looks are prepossessing; his qualities of head and heart are admirable; he enjoys the respect of all. Not a young lady for miles round but—I will use a vulgar phrase, Sir Henry, but it is expressive of the facts—would jump at him. Lucy refused him."

"Indeed," replied Sir Henry, gazing at Lucy's glowing face, at the smile that hovered round her lips.

Lady Verner resumed—

"She refused him in the most decidedly positive manner that you can imagine. She has refused also one or two others. They were not so desirable in position as Lord Garle; but they were very well. And her motive I never have been able to get at. It has vexed me much. I have pointed out to her that when ever you returned home, you might think I had been neglectful of her interests."

"No, no," replied Sir Henry, "I could not fancy coming home to find Lucy married. I should not have liked it. She would have seemed to be gone from me."

"But she must marry some time, and the years are going on," returned Lady Verner.

"Yes, I suppose she must."

"At least, I should say she would, were it anybody but Lucy," rejoined Lady Verner, qualifying her words. "After the refusal of Lord Garle, one does not know what to think. You will see him and judge for yourself."

"What was the motive of the refusal, Lucy?" inquired Sir Henry.

He spoke with a smile, in a gay, careless tone; but Lucy appeared to take the question in a serious light. Her eyelids drooped, her whole face became scarlet, her demeanour almost agitated.

"I did not care to marry, papa," she answered in a low tone. "I did not care for Lord Garle."

"One grievous fear has been upon me ever since, haunting my rest at night, disturbing my peace by day," resumed Lady Verner. "I must speak of it to you, Sir Henry. Absurd as the notion really is, and as at times it appears to me that it must be, still it does intrude, and I should scarcely be acting an honourable part by you to conceal it, sad as the calamity would be."

Lucy looked up in surprise. Sir Henry in a sort of puzzled wonder.

"When she refused Lord Garle, whom she acknowledged she liked, and forbade him to entertain any future hope whatever, I naturally began to look about me for the cause. I could only come to one conclusion, I am sorry to say—that she cared too much for another."

Lucy sat in an agony; the scarlet of her face changing to whiteness.

"I arrived at the conclusion, I say," continued Lady Verner, "and I began to consider whom the object could be. I called over in my mind all the gentlemen she was in the habit of seeing; and unfortunately there was only one—only one upon whom my suspicions could fix. I recalled phrases of affection openly lavished upon him by Lucy; I remembered that there was no society she seemed to enjoy and be so much at ease with as his. I have done what I could since to keep him at arm's length; and I shall never forgive myself for having been so blind. But, you see, I no more thought she, or any other girl, could fall in love with him, than that she could with one of my serving men."

"Lady Verner, you should not say it!" burst forth Lucy, with vehemence, as she turned her white face, her trembling lips, to Lady Verner. "Surely I might refuse to marry Lord Garle without caring unduly for another!"

Lady Verner looked quite aghast at the outburst. "My dear, does not this prove that I am right?"

"But who is it?" interrupted Sir Henry Tempest.

"Alas!—Who! I could almost faint in telling it to you," groaned Lady Verner. "My unfortunate son, Jan."

The relief was so great to Lucy; the revulsion of feeling so sudden; the idea called up altogether so comical, that she clasped her hands one within the other, and laughed out in glee.

"Oh, Lady Verner! Poor Jan! I never thought you meant him. Papa," she said, turning eagerly to Sir Henry, "Jan is downright worthy and good, but I should not like to marry him."

"Jan may be worthy; but he is not handsome," gravely remarked Sir Henry.

"He is better than handsome," returned Lucy. "I shall love Jan all my life, papa; but not in that way."

Her perfect openness, her ease of manner, gave an earnest of the truth with which she spoke; and Lady Verner was summarily relieved of the fear which had haunted her rest.

"Why could you not have told me this before, Lucy?"

"Dear Lady Verner, how could I tell it you? How was I to know anything about it?"

"True," said Lady Verner. "I was simple; to suppose any young lady could ever give a thought to that unfortunate Jan! You saw him, Sir Henry. Only fancy his being my son and his father's!"

"He is certainly not like either of you," was Sir Henry's reply. "Your other son was like both. Very like his father."

"Ah! he is a son!" spoke Lady Verner, in her enthusiasm. "A son worth having; a son that his father would be proud of, were he alive. Handsome, good, noble;—there are few like Lionel Verner. I spoke in praise of Lord Garle, but he is not as Lionel. A good husband, a good son, a good man. His conduct under his misfortunes was admirable."

"His misfortunes have been like a romance," remarked Sir Henry.

"More like that than reality. You will see him presently. I asked him to dine with me, and expect him in momentarily. Ah, he has had trouble in all ways. His wife brought him nothing else."

"Jan dropped a hint of that," said Sir Henry. "I should think he would not be in a hurry to marry again!

"I should think not, indeed. He—Lucy, where are you going?"

Lucy turned round with her crimsoned face. "Nowhere, Lady Verner."

"I thought I heard a carriage stop, my dear. See if it is Lionel."

Lucy walked to the window in the other room. Sir Henry followed her. The blue and silver carriage of Verner's Pride was at the Court gates, Lionel stepping from it. He came in, looking curiously at the gray head next to Lucy's.

"A noble form, a noble face!" murmured Sir Henry Tempest.

He wore still the mourning for his wife. A handsome man never looks so well in other attire. There was no doubt that he divined now who the stranger was, and a glad smile of welcome parted his lips. Sir Henry met him on the threshold, and grasped both his hands.

"I should have known you, Lionel, anywhere, from your likeness to your father."

CHAPTER XCIV

IT MIGHT HAVE BEEN JAN!

Lionel could not let the evening go over without speaking of the great secret. When he and Sir Henry were left together in the dining-room, he sought the opportunity. It was afforded by a remark of Sir Henry's.

"After our sojourn in London shall be over, I must look out for a residence, and settle down. Perhaps I shall purchase one. But I must first of all ascertain what locality would be agreeable to Lucy."

"Sir Henry," said Lionel in a low tone, "Lucy's future residence is fixed upon—if you will accord your permission."

Sir Henry Tempest, who was in the act of raising his wine-glass to his lips, set it down again and looked at Lionel.

"I want her at Verner's Pride."

It appeared that Sir Henry could not understand—did not take in the meaning of the words.

"What did you say?" he asked.

"I have loved her for years," answered Lionel, the, scarlet spot of emotion rising to his cheeks. "We—we have known each other's sentiments a long while. But I did not intend to speak more openly to Lucy until I had seen you. To-day, however, in the sudden excitement of hearing of her contemplated departure, I betrayed myself. Will you give her to me, Sir Henry?"

Sir Henry Tempest looked grave. "It cannot have been so very long an attachment," he observed. "The time since your wife's death can only be counted by months."

"True. But the time since I loved Lucy can be counted by years. I loved her before I married," he added in a low tone.

"Why, then, have married another?" demanded Sir Henry, after a pause.

"You may well ask it, Sir Henry," he replied, the upright line in his brow showing out just then all too deep and plain. "I engaged myself to my first wife in an unguarded moment; as soon as the word was spoken I became aware that she was less dear to me than Lucy. I might have retracted; but the retractation would have left a stain on my honour that could never be effaced. I am, not the first man who has paid by years of penitence for a word spoken in the heat of passion."

True enough! Sir Henry simply nodded his head in answer.

"Yes, I loved Lucy; I married another, loving her; I never ceased loving her all throughout my married life. And I had to force down my feelings; to suppress and hide them in the best manner that I could."

"And Lucy?" involuntarily uttered Sir Henry.

"Lucy—may I dare to say it to you?—loved me," he answered, his breath coming fast. "I believe, from my very heart, that she loved me in that early time, deeply perhaps as I loved her. I have never exchanged a word with her upon the point; but I cannot conceal from myself that it was the unhappy fact."

"Did you know it at the time?"

"No!" he answered, raising his hand to his brow, on which the drops were gathering, "I did not suspect it until it was too late; until I was married. She was so child-like."

Sir Henry Tempest sat in silence, probably revolving the information.

"If you had known it—what then?"

"Do not ask me," replied Lionel, his bewailing tone strangely full of pain. "I cannot tell what I should have done. It would have been Lucy—love—versus honour. And a Verner never sacrificed honour yet. And yet—it seems to me that I sacrificed honour in the course I took. Let the question drop, Sir Henry. It is a time I cannot bear to recur to."

Neither spoke for some minutes. Lionel's face was shaded by his hand. Presently he looked up.

"Do not part us, Sir Henry!" he implored, his voice quite hoarse with its emotion, its earnestness. "We could neither of us bear it. I have waited for her long."

"I will deal candidly with you," said Sir Henry. "In the old days it was a favourite project of mine and your father's that our families should become connected by the union of our children—you and Lucy. We only spoke of it to each other; saying nothing to our wives: they might have set to work, women fashion, and urged it on by plotting and planning: we were content to let events take their course, and to welcome the fruition, should it come. Nearly the last words Sir Lionel said to me, when he was dying of his wound, were, that he should not live to see the marriage; but he hoped I might. Years afterwards, when Lucy was placed with Lady Verner—I knew, no other friend in Europe to whom I would entrust her—her letters to me were filled with Lionel Verner. 'Lionel was so kind to her!'—'Everybody liked Lionel!' In one shape or other you were sure to be the theme. I heard how you lost the estate; of your coming to stay at Lady Verner's; of a long illness you had there; of your regaining the estate through the death of the Massingbirds; and—next—of your marriage to Frederick Massingbird's widow. From that time Lucy said less: in fact, her letters were nearly silent as to you: and, for myself, I never gave another thought to the subject. Your present communication has taken me entirely by surprise."

"But you will give her to me?"

"I had rather—forgive me if I speak candidly—that she married one who had not called another woman wife."

"I heartily wish I never had called another woman wife," was the response of Lionel. "But I cannot alter the past. I shall not make Lucy the less happy; and, for moving her—I tell you that my love for her, throughout, has been so great, as to have put it almost beyond the power of suppression."

A servant entered, and said my lady was waiting tea. Lionel waved his hand towards the man with an impatient movement, and they were left at peace again.

"You tell me that her heart is engaged in this, as well as yours?" resumed Sir Henry.

A half-smile flitted for a moment over Lionel's face; he was recalling Lucy's whispered words to him that very afternoon.

"Yes," he answered, "her heart is bound up in me: I may almost say her life. If ever love served out its apprenticeship, Sir Henry, ours has. It is stronger than time and change."

"Well, I suppose you must have her," conceded Sir Henry. "But for your own marriage, I should have looked on this as a natural result. What about the revenues of Verner's Pride?"

"I am in debt," freely acknowledged Lionel. "In my wife's time we spent too much, and outran our means. Part of my income for three or four years must be set apart to pay it off."

He might have said, "In my wife's time she spent too much;" said it with truth. But, as he spared her feelings, living, so he spared her memory, dead.

"Whoever takes Lucy, takes thirty thousand pounds on her wedding-day," quietly remarked Sir Henry Tempest.

The words quite startled Lionel. "Thirty thousand pounds!" he repeated mechanically.

"Thirty thousand pounds. Did you think I should waste all my best years in India, Lionel, and save up nothing for my only child?"

"I never thought about it," was Lionel's answer. "Or if I ever did think, I suppose I judged by my father. He saved no money."

"He had not the opportunity that I have had; and he died early. The appointment I held, out there, has been a lucrative one. That will be the amount of Lucy's present fortune."

"I am glad I did not know it!" heartily affirmed Lionel.

"It might have made the winning her more difficult, I suppose you think?"

"Not the winning her," was Lionel's answer, the self-conscious smile again on his lips. "The winning your consent, Sir Henry."

"It has not been so hard a task, either," quaintly remarked Sir Henry, as he rose. "I am giving her to you, understand, for your father's sake; in the trust that you are the same honourably good man, standing well before the world and Heaven, that he was. Unless your looks belie you, you are not degenerate."

Lionel stood before him, almost too agitated to speak. Sir Henry stopped him, laying his hand upon his shoulder.

"No thanks, Lionel. Gratitude? You can pay all that to Lucy after she shall be your wife."

They went together into the drawing-room, arm-in-arm. Sir Henry advanced straight to his daughter.

"What am I to say to you, Lucy? He has been talking secrets."

She looked up, like a startled fawn. But a glimpse at Lionel's face reassured her, bringing the roses into her cheeks. Lady Verner, wondering, gazed at them in amazement, and Lucy hid her hot cheeks on her father's breast.

"Am I to scold you? Falling in love without my permission!"

The tone, the loving arm wound round her, brought to her confidence. She could almost afford to be saucy.

"Don't be angry, papa!" were her whispered words. "It might have been worse."

"Worse!" returned Sir Henry, trying to get a look at her face. "You independent child! How could it have been worse?"

"It might have been Jan, you know, papa."

And Sir Henry Tempest burst into an irrepressible laugh as he sat down.

CHAPTER XCV

We have had many fine days in this history, but never a finer one gladdened Deerham than the last that has to be recorded, ere its scene in these pages shall close. It was one of those rarely lovely days that now and then do come to us in autumn. The air was clear, the sky bright, the sun hot as in summer, the grass green almost as in spring. It was evidently a day of rejoicing. Deerham, since the afternoon, seemed to be taking holiday, and as the sun began to get lower in the heavens, groups in their best attire were wending their way towards Verner's Pride.

There was the centre of attraction. A fête—or whatever you might please to call it, where a great deal of feasting is going on—was about to be held on no mean scale. Innumerable tables, some large, some small, were set out in different parts of the grounds, their white cloths intimating that they were to be laden with good cheer. Tynn and his satellites bustled about, and believed they had never had such a day of work before.

A day of pleasure also, unexampled in their lives; for their master, Lionel Verner, was about to bring home his bride.

Everybody was flocking to the spot; old and young, gentle and simple. The Elmsleys and the half-starved Hooks; the Hautleys and those ill-doing Dawsons; the Misses West and their pupils; Lady Verner and the Frosts; Mr. Bitterworth in a hand-chair, his gouty foot swathed up in linen; Mrs. Duff, who had shut up her shop to come; Dan, in some new clothes; Mr. Peckaby and lady; Chuff the blacksmith, with rather a rolling gait; and Master Cheese and Jan. In short, all Deerham and its neighbourhood had turned out.

This was to be Master Cheese's last appearance on any scene—so far as Deerham was concerned. The following day he would quit Jan for good; and that gentleman's new assistant, a qualified practitioner, had arrived, and was present. Somewhat different arrangements from what had been originally contemplated were about to be entered on, as regarded Jan. The Misses West had found their school prosper so well during the half-year it had been established that they were desirous of taking the house entirely on their own hands. They commanded the good will and respect of Deerham, if their father did not. Possibly it was because he did not, and that their position was sympathised with and commiserated, that their scheme of doing something to place themselves independent of him, obtained so large a share of patronage. They wished to take the whole house on their own hands. Easy Jan acquiesced; Lionel thought it the best thing in all ways; and Jan began to look out for another home. But Jan seemed to waver in the fixing upon one. First, he had thought of lodgings; next he went to see a small, pretty new house that had just been built close to the Misses West. "It is too small for you, Mr. Jan," had observed Miss Deborah.

"It will hold me and my assistant, and the boy, and a cook, and the surgery," answered Jan. "And that's all I want."

Neither the lodgings, however, nor the small house had been taken; and now it was rumoured than Jan's plans were changed again. The report ran that the surgery was to remain where it was, and that the assistant, a gentleman of rather mature age, would remain with it; occupying Jan's bedroom (which had been renovated after the explosion of Master Cheese), and taking his meals with the Misses West: Jan meanwhile being about that tasty mansion called Belvedere House, which was situated midway between his old residence and Deerham Court. Deerham's curiosity was uncommonly excited on the point. What, in the name of improbability, could plain Jan Verner want with a fine place like that? He'd have to keep five or six servants, if he went there. The most feasible surmise that could be arrived at was, that Jan was about to establish a mad-house—as Deerham was in the habit of phrasing a receptacle for insane patients—of the private, genteel order. Deerham felt very curious; and Jan, being a person whom they felt at ease to question without ceremony, was besieged upon the subject. Jan's answer (all they could get from him this time) was—that he was thinking of taking Belvedere House, but had no intention yet of setting up a mad-house. And affairs were in this stage at the present time.

Lionel and his bride were expected momentarily, and the company of all grades formed themselves into groups as they awaited them. They had been married in London some ten days ago, where Sir Henry Tempest had remained, after quitting Deerham with Lucy. The twelvemonth had been allowed to go by consequent to the death of Sibylla. Lionel liked that all things should be done decorously and in order. Sir Henry was now on a visit to Sir Edmund Hautley and Decima: he was looking out for a suitable residence in the neighbourhood, where he meant to settle. This gathering at Verner's Pride to welcome Lionel, had been a thought of Sir Henry's and old Mr. Bitterworth's. "Why not give the poor an afternoon's holiday for once?" cried Sir Henry. "I will repay them the wages they must lose in taking it." And so—here was the gathering, and Tynn had carried out his orders for the supply of plenty to eat and drink.

They formed in groups, listening for the return of the carriage, which had gone in state to the railway station to receive them. All, save Master Cheese. He walked about somewhat disconsolately, thinking the proceedings rather slow. In his wandering he came upon Tynn, placing good things upon one of the tables, which was laid in an alcove.

"When's the feasting going to begin?" asked he.

"Not until Mr. Verner shall have come," replied Tynn. "The people will be wanting to cheer him; and they can't do that well, if they are busy round the tables, eating."

"Who's the feast intended for?" resumed Master Cheese.

"It's chiefly intended for those who don't get feasts at home," returned Tynn. "But anybody can partake of it that pleases."

"I should like just a snack," said Master Cheese. "I had such a short dinner to-day. Now that all those girls are stuck down at the dining-table, Miss Deb sometimes forgets to ask one a third time to meat," he added in a grumbling tone. "And there was nothing but a rubbishing rice pudding after it to-day! So I'd like to take a little, Tynn. I feel quite empty."

"You can take as much as you choose," said Tynn, who had known Master Cheese's appetite before to-day. "Begin at once, if you like, without waiting for the others. Some of the tables are spread."

"I think I will," said Master Cheese, looking lovingly at a pie on the table over which they were standing. "What's inside this pie, Tynn?"

Tynn bent his head to look closely. "I think that's partridge," said he. "There are plenty of other sorts: and there's a vast quantity of cold meats; beef and ham, and that. Sir Henry Tempest said I was not to stint 'em."

"I like partridge pie," said Master Cheese, as he seated himself before it, his mouth watering. "I have not tasted one this season. Do you happen to have a drop of bottled ale, Tynn?"

"I'll fetch a bottle," answered Tynn. "Is there anything else you'd like, sir?"

"What else is there?" asked Master Cheese. "Anything in the sweets line?"

"There's about a hundred baked plum puddings. My wife has got some custards, too, in her larder. The custards are not intended for out here, but you can have one."

Master Cheese wiped his damp face; he had gone all over into a glow of delight. "Bring a pudding and a custard or two, Tynn," said he. "There's nothing in the world half so nice as a plate of plum pudding swimming in custard."

Tynn was in the act of supplying his wants, when a movement and a noise in the distance came floating on the air. Tynn dashed the dish of custards on to the table, and ran like the rest. Everybody ran—except Master Cheese.

It was turning slowly into the grounds—the blue and silver carriage of the Verners, its four horses prancing under their studded harness. Lionel and his wife of a few days descended from it, when they found themselves in the midst of this unexpected crowd. They had cause, those serfs, to shout out a welcome to their lord; for never again would they live in a degrading position, if he could help it. The various improvements for their welfare, which he had so persistently and hopefully planned, were not only begun, but nearly ended.

Sir Henry clasped Lucy's sweet face to his own bronzed one, pushing back her white bonnet to take his kiss from it. Then followed Lady Verner, then Decima, then Mary Elmsley. Lucy shook herself free, and laughed.

"I don't like so many kisses all at once," said she.

Lionel was everywhere. Shaking hands with old Mr. Bitterworth, with the Misses West, with Sir Edmund Hautley, with Lord Garle, with the Countess of Elmsley, with all that came in his way. Next he looked round upon a poorer class; and the first hand taken in his was Robin Frost's. By and by he encountered Jan.

"Well, Jan, old fellow!" said he, his affection shining out in his earnest, dark-blue eyes, "I am glad to be with you again. Is Cheese here?"

"He came," replied Jan. "But where he has disappeared to, I can't tell."

"Please, sir, I see'd him just now in an alcove," interposed Dan Duff, addressing Lionel.

"And how are you, Dan?" asked Lionel, with his kindly smile. "Saw Mr. Cheese in an alcove, did you?"

"It was that there one," responded Dan, extending his finger in the direction of a spot not far distant. "He was tucking in at a pie. I see'd him, please sir."

"I must go to him," said Lionel, winding his arm within Jan's, and proceeding in the direction of the alcove. Master Cheese, his hands full of cold pudding and his mouth covered with custard, started up when surprised at his feast.

"It's only a little bit I'm tasting," said he apologetically, "against it's time to begin. I hope you have come back well, sir."

"Taste away, Cheese," replied Lionel, with a laugh, as he cast his eyes on some remaining fragments. "Partridge pie! do you like it?"

"Like it!" returned Master Cheese, the tears coming into his eyes with eagerness, "I wish I could be where I should have nothing else for a whole week."

"The first week's holiday you get at Bartholomew's, you must come and pay Verner's Pride a visit, and we will keep you supplied. Mrs. Verner will be glad to see you."

Master Cheese gave a great gasp. The words seemed too good to be real.

"Do you mean it, sir?" he asked.

"Of course I mean it," replied Lionel. "I owe you a debt, you know. But for your having blown yourself and the room up, I might not now be in possession of Verner's Pride. You come and spend a week with us when you can."

"That's glorious, and I'm much obliged to you, sir," said Master Cheese, in an ecstasy. "I think I'll have just another custard on the strength of it."

Jan was imperturbable—he had seen too much of Master Cheese for any display to affect him—but Lionel laughed heartily as they left the gentleman and the alcove. How well he looked—Lionel! The indented line of pain had gone from his brow: he was as a man at rest within.

"Jan, I feel truly glad at the news sent to us a day or two ago!" he exclaimed, pressing his brother's arm. "I always feared you would not marry. I never thought you would marry one so desirable as Mary Elmsley."

"I don't think I'd have had anybody else," answered Jan. "I like her; always did like her; and if she has taken a fancy to me, and doesn't mind putting up with a husband that's called out at all hours, why—it's all right."

"You will not give up your profession, Jan?"

"Give up my profession?" echoed Jan, in surprise, staring with all his eyes at Lionel. "What should I do that for?"

"When Mary shall be Lady Mary Verner, she may be for wishing it."

"No, she won't," answered Jan. "She knows her wishing it would be of no use. She marries my profession as much as she marries me. It is all settled. Lord Elmsley makes it a point that I take my degree, and I don't mind doing that to please him. I shall be a hard-working doctor always, and Mary knows it."

"Have you taken Belvedere House?"

"I intend to take it. Mary likes it, and I can afford it, with her income joined to mine. If she is a lady, she's not a fine one," added Jan, "and I shall be just as quiet and comfortable as I have been in the old place. She says she'll see to the housekeeping and to my shirts, and—"

Jan stopped. They had come up with Lady Verner, and Mary Elmsley. Lionel spoke laughingly.

"So Jan is appreciated at last!"

Lady Verner lifted her hands with a deprecatory movement. "It took me three whole days before I would believe it," she gravely said. "Even now, there are times when I think Mary must be playing with him."

Lady Mary shook her head with a blush and a smile. Lionel took her on his arm, and walked away with her.

"You cannot think how happy it has made me and Lucy. We never thought Jan was, or could be, appreciated."

"He was by me. He is worth—shall I tell it you, Lionel?—more than all the rest of Deerham put together. Yourself included."

"I will indorse the assertion," answered Lionel. "I am glad you are going to have him."

"I would have had him, had he asked me, years ago," candidly avowed Lady Mary.

"I was inquiring of Jan, whether you would not wish him to give up his profession. He was half offended with me for suggesting it."

"If Jan could ever be the one to lead an idle, useless life, I think half my love for him would die out," was her warm answer. "It was Jan's practical industry, his way of always doing the right in straightforward simplicity, that I believe first won me to like him. This world was made to work in; the next for rest—as I look upon it, Lionel. I shall be prouder of being wife to the surgeon Jan Verner, than I should be had I married a duke's eldest son."

"He is to take his degree, he says."

"I believe so: but he will practise generally all the same—just as he does now. Not that I care that he should become Dr. Verner; it is papa."

"If he—Why, who can they be?"

Lionel Verner's interrupted sentence and question of surprise were caused by the appearance of some singular-looking forms who were stalking into the grounds. Poor, stooping, miserable, travel-soiled objects, looking fit for nothing but the tramp-house. A murmer of astonishment burst from all present when they were recognised. It was Grind's lot. Grind and his family, who had gone off with the Mormons, returning now in humility, like dogs with burnt tails.

"Why, Grind, can it be you?" exclaimed Lionel, gazing with pity at the man's despairing aspect.

He, poor meek Grind, not less meek and civil than of yore, sat down upon a bench and burst into tears. They gathered round him in crowds, while he told his tale. How they had, after innumerable hardships on the road, too long to recite then, after losing some of their party by death, two of his children being amongst them—how they had at length reached the Salt Lake city, so gloriously depicted by Brother Jarrum. And what did they find? Instead of an abode of peace and plenty, of luxury, of immunity from work, they found misery and discomfort. Things were strange to them, and they were strange in turn. He'd describe it all another time, he said; but it was quite enough to tell them what it was, by saying that he resolved to come away if possible, and face again the hardships of the way, though it was only to die in the old land, than he'd stop in it. Brother Jarrum was a awful impostor, so to have led 'em away!

"Wasn't there no saints?" breathlessly asked Susan Peckaby, who had elbowed herself to the front.

"Saints!" echoed Grind. "Yes, they be saints! A iniketous, bad-doing, sensitive lot. I'd starve on a crust here, sooner nor I'd stop among 'em. Villains!"

Poor Grind probably substituted the word "sensitive" for another, in his narrow acquaintance with the English language. Susan Peckaby seemed to resent this new view of things. She was habited in the very plum-coloured gown which had been prepared for the start, the white paint having been got out of it by some mysterious process, perhaps by the turpentine suggested by Chuff. It looked tumbled and crinkled, the beauty altogether gone out of it. Her husband, Peckaby, stood behind, grinning.

"Villains, them saints was, was they?" said he.

"They was villains," emphatically answered Grind.

"And the saintesses?" continued Peckaby—"What of them?"

"The less said about 'em the better, them saintesses," responded Grind. "We should give 'em another name over here, we should. I had to leave my eldest girl behind me," he added, lifting his face in a pitying appeal to Mr. Verner's. "She warn't but fifteen, and one of them men took her, and she's his thirteenth wife."

"I say, Grind," put in the sharp voice of Mrs. Duff, "what's become of Nancy, as lived up here?"

"She died on the road," he answered. "She married Brother Jarrum in New York—"

"Married Brother Jarrum in New York!" interrupted Polly Dawson tartly. "You are asleep, Grind. It was Mary Green as married him. Leastways, news, that she did, come back to us here."

"He married 'em both," answered Grind. "The consekence of which was, that the two took to quarrelling perpetual. It was nothing but snarling and fighting everlasting. Nancy again Mary, and Mary again her. We hadn't nothing else with 'em all the way to the Salt Lake city, and Nancy, she got ill. Some said 'twas pining; some said 'twas a in'ard complaint as took her; some said 'twas the hardships killed her—the cold, and the fatigue, and the bad food, and the starvation. Anyhow, Nancy died."

"And what became of Mary?" rather more meekly inquired Mrs. Peckaby.

"She's Jarrum's wife still. He have got about six of 'em, he have. They be saints, they be!"

"They bain't as bad off as the saintesses," interrupted Mrs. Grind. "They has their own way, the saints, and the saintesses don't. Regular cowed down the saintesses be; they daredn't say as their right hand's their own. That poor sick lady as went with us, Miss Kitty Baynton—and none on us thought she'd live to get there, but she did, and one of the saints chose her. She come to us just afore we got away, and she said she wanted to write a letter to her mother to tell her how unhappy she was, fit to die with it. But she knowed the letter could never be got to her in England, cause letters ain't allowed to leave the city, and she must stop in misery for her life, she said; for she couldn't never undertake the journey back again; even if she could get clear away; it would kill her. But she'd like her mother to know how them Mormons deceived with their tales, and what sort of a place New Jerusalem was."

Grind turned again to Lionel.

"It is just blasphemy, sir, for them to say what they do; calling it the holy city, and the New Jerusalem. Couldn't they be stopped at it, and from deluding poor ignorant people here with their tales?"

"The only way of stopping it is for people to take their tales for what they are worth," said Lionel.

Grind gave a groan. "People is credilous, sir, when they think they are going to better theirselves. Sir," he added, with a yearning, pleading look, "could I have a bit of work again upon the old estate, just to keep us from starving? I shan't hanker after much now; to live here upon the soil will be enough, after having been at that Salt Lake city. It's a day's wonder, and 'ud take a day to tell, the way we stole away from it, and how we at last got home."

"You shall have work, Grind, as much as you can do," quietly answered Lionel. "Work, and a home, and, I hope, plenty. If you will go there,"—pointing to the tables—"with your wife and children, you will find something to eat and drink."

Grind clasped his hands together in an attitude of thankfulness, tears streaming down his face. They had walked from Liverpool.

"What about the ducks, Grind?" called out one of the Dawsons. "Did you get 'em in abundance?"

Grind turned his haggard face round.

"I never see a single duck the whole time I stopped there. If ducks was there, we didn't see 'em."

"And what about the white donkeys, Grind?" added Peckaby. "Be they in plenty?"

Grind was ignorant of the white donkey story, and took the question literally. "I never see none," he repeated. "There's nothing white there but the great Salt Lake, which strikes the eyes with blindness—"

"Won't I treat you to a basting!"

The emphatic remark, coming from Mrs. Duff, caused a divertisement, especially agreeable to Susan Peckaby. The unhappy Dan, by some unexplainable cause, had torn the sleeve of his new jacket to ribbons. He sheltered himself from wrath behind Chuff the blacksmith, and the company began to pour in a stream towards the tables.

The sun had sunk in the west when Verner's Pride was left in quiet; the gratified feasters, Master Cheese included, having wended their way home. Lionel was with his wife at the window of her dressing-room, where he had formerly stood with Sibylla. The rosy hue of the sky played upon Lucy's face. Lionel watched it as he stood with his arm round her. Lifting her eyes suddenly, she saw how grave his looked, as they were bent upon her.

"What are you thinking of, Lionel?"

"Of you, my darling. Standing with you here in our own home, feeling that you are mine at last; that nothing, save the hand of Death, can part us, I can scarcely yet believe in my great happiness."

Lucy raised her hand, and drew his face down to hers. "I can," she whispered. "It is very real."

"Ay, yes! it is real," he said, his tone one of almost painful intensity. "God be thanked! But we waited. Lucy, how we waited for it!"

MRS HENRY WOOD (aka ELLEN WOOD) – A CONCISE BIBLIOGRAPHY

Danesbury House (1860)
East Lynne (1861)
The Elchester College Boys (1861)
A Life's Secret (1862)
Mrs. Halliburton's Troubles (1862)
The Channings (1862)
The Foggy Night at Offord: A Christmas Gift for the Lancashire Fund (1863)
The Shadow of Ashlydyat (1863)
Verner's Pride (1863)
Lord Oakburn's Daughters (1864)
Oswald Cray (1864)
Trevlyn Hold; or, Squire Trevlyn's Heir (1864)
William Allair; or, Running away to Sea (1864)
Mildred Arkell: A Novel (1865)
The Argosy (1865)
Elster's Folly: A Novel (1866)
St. Martin's Eve: A Novel (1866)
Lady Adelaide's Oath (1867)
Orville College: A Story (1867)
The Ghost of the Hollow Field (1867)
Anne Hereford: A Novel (1868)

Castle Wafer; or, The Plain Gold Ring (1868)
The Red Court Farm: A Novel (1868)
Roland Yorke: A Novel (1869)
Bessy Rane: A Novel (1870)
George Canterbury's Will (1870)
Dene Hollow (1871)
Within the Maze: A Novel (1872)
The Master of Greylands (1872)
Johnny Ludlow (1874)
Bessy Wells (1875)
Told in the Twilight: Containing 'Parkwater' and nine short stories (1875)
Adam Grainger: A Tale (1876)
Edina (1876)
Our Children (1876)
Parkwater: With four other tales (1876)
Pomeroy Abbey (1878)
Lady Adelaide (1879)
Johnny Ludlow, Second Series (1880)
A Tale of Sin and Other Tales (1881)
Court Netherleigh: A Novel (1881)
About Ourselves (1883)
Johnny Ludlow. Third Series (1885)
Lady Grace and Other Stories (1887)
The Story of Charles Strange (1888)
Featherston's Story. A Tale by Johnny Ludlow (1889)
The Unholy Wish and Other Stories (1890)
The House of Halliwell. A Novel (1890)
Ashley and Other Stories (1897)
Victor Serenus (1898)
Johnny Ludlow. Fifth series (1899)
Johnny Ludlow. Sixth series (1899)

Translations
Les Channing. Traduit de l'Anglais par Mme Abric-Encontre (1864)
Les Filles de Lord Oakburn: Roman traduit de l'anglais par L. Bochet (1876)
La Gloire des Verner: Roman traduit de l'anglais par L. de L'Estrive (1878)
Le Serment de Lady Adelaïde: Roman traduit de l'anglais par Léon Bochet (1878)

www.ingramcontent.com/pod-product-compliance
Lightning Source LLC
Chambersburg PA
CBHW022235020726

47496CB00004B/910